STEEL DEMONS MC

BOOKS 1-3

USA TODAY BESTSELLING AUTHOR
CRYSTAL ASH

Cover Art by MoorBooks Design

Published by Voluspa Press

SDMC SERIES PLAYLIST

All American Nightmare - Hinder
Notorious - Adelitas Way
Hail to the King - Avenged Sevenfold
O Death - Ashley H
Joan of Arc - In This Moment
Radioactive - Imagine Dragons
Bad Company - Five Finger Death Punch
Love Me to Death - No Resolve
(Don't Fear) The Reaper - HIM
David - Noah Gunderson
Apocalyptic - Halestorm
Blue on Black - Five Finger Death Punch
Machine Gun Blues - Social Distortion
Wanted Dead or Alive - Chris Daughtry
I Get Off - Halestorm
You Shook Me All Night Long - AC/DC
Nobody Praying for Me - Seether
Loyal to No One - Dropkick Murpheys
Crazy in Love - Daniel De Bourg
Be Free - King Dude & Chelsea Wolfe
Raise Hell - Dorothy
Coming Home - Skylar Grey

Listen on Spotify at:
crystalashbooks.com/sdmc-playlist

Content Warnings

This series is set in a dystopian world and contains graphically violent scenes throughout.

Please note the following content warnings for each book in this set:

Lawless:
kidnapping, sexual assault of a side character (off-page), injured animal, fighting ring, gun violence, amateur surgery in an unsterile environment

Powerless:
Gun violence, dubious consent with a future love interest

Fearless:
Torture/mutilation until death, kidnapping, threat of sexual assault, sexual assault of a man, mentions of sex trafficking

LAWLESS

STEEL DEMONS MC BOOK ONE

Prologue

MARIPOSA

Have you ever been to a graduation that felt like a funeral?

That was exactly how mine felt. Somber. Tense. Everyone, graduates and faculty alike, kept their true feelings under a neutral mask. No one wanted to say it, but we all knew.

Instead of celebrating our bright new future, we were already mourning the death of it.

The Collapse happened during my freshman year at Northwestern Medical College. We were still bright-eyed and hopeful then, so confident we'd be the ones to restore order and justice to the world upon graduation.

The United States of America ceased to exist and every state became its own independent faction with its own laws and regulations. Some slid right back into the dark ages, stripping away the rights of women and minorities as their people cheered.

Others went in the complete opposite direction, welcoming *all* people and practices with open arms. This led to violent internal conflicts as ideas and opinions clashed.

Still, we remained hopeful.

Then the wars broke out, too many to count or name. Some dragged on for years, others mere skirmishes that lasted less than a day.

Every morning, news spread of another self-appointed governor being assassinated, or the invasion of one territory into another. Borders were redrawn and new capitals erected, always by some power-hungry maniac who seized the opportunity when it suited him best. Until the next one assassinated him and started the process all over again.

Those who weren't killed or kidnapped, and could afford to do so, fled the country. Many took the dangerous trek to Canada, others fled to Latin America, although the situation wasn't much better down there. And the ultra-rich, the ones who could still afford plane passage after half of the international airports were bombed, flew across the oceans to greener pastures in Europe and Africa.

Most African countries succeeded in overthrowing their tyrannical dictators in the last century. America had apparently forgotten how to do it. The home of the brave became a land of lawlessness.

And we, the graduating class of 2100, would be the ones inheriting that land.

Congratulations to us.

So, can you blame us for having such a grim graduation ceremony? Not even anyone's parents cracked a smile.

Dr. Brooks, the dean of the Gonzalez Nursing School, stepped up to the podium like he was about to deliver a eulogy.

"I prepared a speech for today that was full of hope and optimism," he began, his jaw tense as he took in the faces of the graduates. "But then I heard the news this morning and realized what a disservice it would be to the young people at this ceremony if I were to sugarcoat the truth."

Aside from paper programs and graduation robes fluttering in the warm breeze, no one made a sound. Early this morning, the battle that had been waging for weeks sixty miles south of here, had ceased. Because the last of those defending our last little shred of independence had been gunned down by armed rebels. As of nine o'clock this morning, Warsaw County, Texas had been annexed into the Republic of Texahoma.

Dr. Brooks looked out grimly over all of the graduates, as if he were sentencing us to death himself.

"The world you have inherited is cruel," he said. "It's unjust. It's lawless and unfair. Your generation will be the one to pay for our shortcomings. Our sorrys are too little, too late."

In the silence between his words, the wind carried sounds of gunfire, explosions, and screams from the distant battleground. Although at this point, it was nothing more than a massacre.

No one reacted. We had all gotten used to those sounds.

The faculty in attendance wore harrowed expressions throughout the speech, their eyes staring blankly forward. It was clear that no one disagreed with him.

"There is only one piece of advice I can give to you all," his voice cracked as he went on. "Be better than what we've become. Bring compassion and heart back to this violent world."

"You've gotta be kidding me."

I rolled my eyes toward the clock on the wall. It had been nearly an hour since I was put on hold and the looping music made me want to blow my brains out.

And get lost in all the other brain matter scattered across the street? I don't think so, sister.

"Sorry to keep you waiting. What can I do for you?"

Finally.

"Yeah, hi. I'm trying to get my nursing license registered."

A pause stretched on for just a few moments too long.

"What's your name?"

"Mariposa Wilder."

Another pause.

"I'm sorry. I can't. There's nothing I can do."

"What?" I pulled the phone back from my ear and looked at it like something wasn't working. "What do you mean? I graduated from Northwestern Medical College this morning. I *need* this license to be able to work." Why I had to explain this to someone whose job it was to process licenses was beyond me.

"I'm sorry," the person on the other line repeated, their voice cracking with emotion. "I can't. They'll shoot me if I do."

My heart squeezed in my chest like a cruel fist had wrapped around it.

"They've already gotten to the capital?" I squeaked, my voice lost in disbelief.

"They decreed it not even a half hour ago," the voice answered, seconds away from sobbing. "In the Republic of Texahoma, women are forbidden from holding any kind of medical license."

Chapter 1

MARIPOSA

Three Years Later

The van lurched to a stop. I grabbed my pack like it would slip away from me before sliding my arms through the straps. The driver's eyes in the rearview mirror told me enough. He wouldn't be driving any further west.

I waited for the half dozen other people hitching a ride to get off before rising from the back seat. As I approached him, I pulled a small baggie from my pocket and held it out to him.

"For your trouble," I muttered.

He just scowled as he snatched the single tablet of valium from me. "You're a fool to come out this far west. The biker gangs eat girls like you alive."

"I'll survive." Those words have been a mantra I've repeated for years. So far, it proved to be true so I wasn't about to doubt it yet.

"After they get their hands on ya," he shook his head, "you might be wishin' for death." With that, he shooed me off his vehicle and drove off in a cloud of dust and exhaust.

I took a moment to observe my surroundings. The first thing I noticed was the fucking heat. This used to be Phoenix, Arizona. Now, like everywhere else, its name and borders changed depending on who was in charge. The latest I heard it being referred to was Old Phoenix.

Creative, these tyrants.

Miles of dry, dusty desert surrounded me in all directions, with the occasional saguaro cactus standing tall like soldiers. A mountain range stood off in the distance, the only not-flat part of the landscape. It would have been pretty and majestic, if anybody could bring themselves to feel good about anything these days.

The van driver dropped his passengers off in front of a service station, which had once been a hotel. Now, these places provided everything from temporary shelter, food, cheap hookers referred to as service girls, and if they were lucky, medical services. Which was what I hoped to provide.

Gripping the edges of my bag straps, I headed for the building that had seen better days. Weeds grew tall, choking off the once charming landscaping. Dust and mud caked the exterior walls and the glass front door, which was also scarred with a few bullet holes.

But I had to count my blessings. There were no motorcycles parked outside. At least not yet.

The smell of must greeted me as I stepped inside. No one bothered to clean anymore, not when gangs and deviants tore through homes and places like these to ransack goods. Even in the twenty-second century, humans still got the urge to pillage and loot.

With the lobby completely empty, I bypassed the front desk and headed straight for the kitchen. Not that I was hoping to run into a biker gang, but the quietness of this place unnerved me. People usually flocked to places like this once their homes were no longer theirs.

Crossing the dining area, I pushed open a swinging door to find a remarkably clean, stainless steel kitchen. And three people cooking.

"Hello," the girl of about sixteen greeted me first while the two adults watched me with suspicious eyes.

"Hi," I said. "Um, I'm a nur—a medic. Are you in need of medical services at this station?" *Please say yes.*

Even after three years of being strictly forbidden to call myself a nurse, it was still a habit.

The man, balding with curly grey hair, wiped his hands on his apron, still looking at me warily.

"You got supplies?" he asked.

I nodded sharply. "Pain medication, a wide range of antibiotics and antivirals, sterile tools for minor surgeries, general first aid gear. I also have some pregnancy tests and different forms of birth control."

His eyebrows shot up at that. In a place full of prostitutes and limited amounts of food, no one wanted extra mouths to feed.

"What'll ya have in return?" he asked.

Since the US Dollar became essentially worthless during the Collapse, bartering became the main currency. Some factions tried establishing their own but they then ran into the problem of no other territory accepting that currency.

"Room and board for roughly two weeks," I said. "And food." My eyes fell to their cutting boards, where potatoes, onions, and carrots sat waiting to finish being chopped.

The older woman spoke up next, her bun unable to contain her wild, frizzy grey hair.

"Can you cook and serve up some food to guests?" *Or are you too good for that?* I heard the hidden question in her voice loud and clear.

"I can do basic cooking and yes, I'll do whatever other tasks you would like. Cleaning and such, too." *But I won't sell my body.*

The couple exchanged a look and a quick nod before the man addressed me.

"We have a deal. But you stay no more than two weeks."

"That's fine," I nodded eagerly, ready for even a dirty, bug-infested bed over sleeping on rest stop benches.

"Gretchen will show you to your room, where you can drop your things." The man picked up his knife and resumed his potato chopping. "Then you come straight back here and help us prepare for tonight."

"What's tonight?" I asked, suddenly aware of the piles and piles of food strewn across the steel counter. It looked as though a large group of people were about to eat like kings.

"The Steel Demons MC will be riding through and staying," the man answered, steadfast in his chopping. "They have massive appetites, and not just for food."

THE TEENAGE GIRL, GRETCHEN, INFORMED ME ALL ABOUT the Steel Demons while we chopped through an endless sea of potatoes, carrots, and celery.

"They ride through here twice a month," she told me. "Reaper, their president, worked out some kind of deal with the owners, Tom and Liza. The whole club stops here on the way to their destination and on the way back. Their club house is way up in Old Flagstaff somewhere. The Doomsdayers say that place is the mouth of Hell itself. Nothing but sin and violence."

I absorbed her words as my stainless blade went *chop-chop-chop* through the vegetables.

"Why is their president called Reaper?" I asked.

"Because," Gretchen lowered her voice, despite the two of us being the only ones in the kitchen, "seeing his club is a death omen. The minute you hear their bikes in the distance, someone's time is up."

"So the rumors are true." I heard whispers of the notorious biker gang all the way in East Texas. One of my patients, a guy hopped up on painkillers from a broken arm, swore they were actual demons, complete with a pack of hellhounds running alongside their bikes.

Gretchen nodded. "The Steel Demons control the southwestern desert from the San Diego Gulf to the Sandia Mountains, and they didn't do that by asking nicely. Wherever they go, hell follows."

She put on a bright smile, her demeanor changing from spooky story teller back to bubbly sixteen-year-old. "They're not so bad when they stop here, though. We're one of the few service centers that still have cured meat and cheese, and they pay well for it."

"They've never hurt you?" I was genuinely surprised. "Or your parents?"

"Oh, Tom and Liza aren't my parents. They just took me in after I was dumped here on their doorstep. And no. The club pretty much eats our food, drinks our ale, stays a few nights to rest, and then they leave. Sure, they're messy and sometimes they fight and break stuff, which is annoying. And it sounds like they're rough with the service girls sometimes, but no one has died since I've been here."

Oh. Well, at least there's that.

"How long have you been here?" I dumped two handfuls of chopped potatoes into a bowl, then emptied the bowl into the awaiting pot of boiling water on the stove.

"About three months." Gretchen hacked off the end of a carrot and brought it to her mouth, biting down with a loud crunch.

"And how's that been? Okay?" I helped myself to a carrot snack as well.

She chewed thoughtfully before answering. "I'm still alive. That's the best you can hope for in a world like this, right?"

With so many dying senselessly in the skirmishes over territory, and plenty more dying from treatable conditions due to the lack of medical care, I felt inclined to agree with her.

But I could still remember a time when people wanted so much more out of life. They wanted stable jobs, degrees from universities, families and friends who loved them, maybe even the occasional luxury like a vacation or a pet.

Then the Collapse happened and the world turned to shit. Humanity couldn't afford to focus on luxury and comfort if we wanted to survive. Mild-mannered family men, like my father, turned into ruthless killers out of necessity. Mom and I cried daily for months when Dad came home from the border skirmishes drenched in blood.

I wondered if the Steel Demons had always been fearsome bikers or if they had been normal citizens at one point, too. The Collapse seemed to bring out the worst in everyone. Self-preservation became the only goal at the forefront of everyone's mind, which ironically, only led to more widespread suffering.

For those that preyed on the weak and sought control in the most sadistic ways, the Collapse was an answered prayer. I heard horror stories of women being treated like cattle, rounded up in corrals and used for breeding. Others said slavery had returned in the territories that was once the South. No one could verify what was true or not, but those whispers made me grateful that being forbidden from receiving my nursing license was the worst that happened in East Texas.

"What brought you out this way?" Gretchen asked, dumping her bowl of chopped carrots into a separate pot of boiling water.

"I was hoping to find women's groups out west, or just a place I could be a medic without the risk of going to jail," I told her. "I got my nursing degree the same day East Texas got annexed. Women were outlawed from holding any kind of medical license within hours of me graduating."

"At least you got a degree," Gretchen mumbled. "I was pulled out of school at fourteen and sent to a girls' camp. They said we didn't need to know how to read, write, or do math. Being a good, Godly wife was all that mattered and that's what they would teach us."

"Ugh." I shook my head, still disgusted by this jarring, new reality although I was no longer surprised. Girls' camps were popping up all over the place, turning girls and young women into docile, obedient wives for men to purchase.

"How did you get out of there?" I put down my knife and stretched out my hand, my fingers cramping up from all the chopping.

She gave a sly smirk. "My ex-husband bought me, but pushed me out of a moving car right in front of this place when I almost bit his dick off."

"Holy shit! On the highway? It's amazing that you survived!"

"I knew to roll," she shrugged. "Just got a bit of road rash and a sprained wrist. And I've been here ever since."

I considered asking her if she wanted to go with me after I left in two weeks. We could keep heading north toward Canada. Women's rights groups were supposedly all along the border, taking in refugees. Gretchen could finish her education and with luck, I might be able to call myself a nurse again.

But I held my tongue and kept chopping. I just met this girl and wasn't sure if I wanted a travel companion for the next few thousand miles. The loneliness sucked, but it was better than waking up to having half of my supplies stolen. Lesson learned—I could only trust myself in this lawless world.

After a few moments of chopping and cooking, a sound like continuous thunder drowned out everything else. My stomach flipped over on itself, knowing it could only be a crew of motorcycles descending on the inn like a pack of wild dogs coming in for the kill.

"They're here!" Gretchen wiped her hands on her apron and ran to the large walk-in refrigerator. She returned holding two frosted glass pitchers. "Help me fill these up with ale? They like it cold and ready to drink first thing when they arrive."

I took one and followed her to the kegerator, noticing the tremor in her hand as she pulled the tap handle to let the beer flow. For as non-murderous as the Steel Demons were to this place, they apparently still scared the shit out of her.

And if she really did nearly bite the dick off the abusive man who owned her, seeing her tremble at the sound of growling bikes made me especially uneasy.

The Texas and Texahoma territories had their fair share of biker gangs, too, but none had a reputation as notorious as the Steel Demons. As I filled up my pitcher and followed Gretchen out to the lobby, I wondered if not dying by their hands was really the better option.

The front doors burst open with a bang just as we set the pitchers on the coffee tables in front of the couches. Raucous laughter followed booted footsteps as six tall, leather-clad figures entered the lobby, their mere presence commanding respect and fear.

The man leading them leveled his gaze at me. Gretchen and I had dropped off the pitchers and were scurrying back to the kitchen for more, but those catlike green eyes seemed to nail my feet to the floor.

Dark brown hair fell across his forehead as if tousled by a helmet. A straight nose sat above full lips that scowled cruelly at me. Dark stubble peppered an angular jaw and olive, sun-kissed skin.

It stunned me how handsome and young he was. Bikers didn't look like *this*. They were old and grizzled with long hair and beards. Like scary, monstrous versions of Santa Claus.

With the way this man looked at me, though, I had no doubt he was capable of monstrous things.

My eyes fell to his leather cut, where the word PRESIDENT was embroidered on the left side. A curving scythe patch hung ominously over the word, leaving no question as to who this man was.

Reaper. The man who rode with the wrath of Hell at his back.

A growling sound brought my eyes lower, to the massive Doberman Pinscher at his side. I'd never seen such a huge dog, nor one that looked so ready to rip out my throat with a single command from its owner. The dog's black coat had a glossy, healthy sheen, but nothing shone as brightly as those white teeth it bared at me.

"Come, Hades." Reaper's voice was softer than I imagined for someone with such a reputation behind him.

I blinked like a spell had been broken as Reaper's eyes shifted away from me, heading toward the furthest couch with a beer pitcher in front of it. Hades trotted obediently at his side.

His men filed in after him, throwing their booted feet on the coffee tables as they drank directly from the pitchers. Some drank half the containers in a single gulp. No wonder we needed so many.

Reaper wasn't the only one with a pet. A man with a falcon on his shoulder sat at the second couch. He had golden hair falling down to his shoulders in soft waves. Women used to kill for hair like that, when looking nice was once important to us.

His eyes were blue as a bright summer sky and his mouth formed a wide smile, the complete opposite of Reaper's hard scowl. The blonde man caught my eye as he raised a pitcher to his mouth and winked at me over the rim.

Shit, I forgot there were service girls here. Now these men probably thought I was one.

I turned on my heel and headed back to the kitchen, where Gretchen had two more full pitchers waiting and was in the middle of filling a third. Taking a deep breath to steel myself before going back out there, I wrapped my fingers around the handles and let the breath out.

It didn't matter what these men looked like. They were murderers, thieves, and probably rapists. They reached their godlike level of fame with violence and brutality. I couldn't let my guard down for a single minute.

I was a mouse in a pit of snakes, and I *had* to survive.

Chapter 2
REAPER

Not even the service girl crawling into my lap could distract me from the new kitchen server. With hazel eyes intent and focused, red lips tight, and rich brown hair cascaded down her back in a loose ponytail, she served food and drinks to my club along with the blonde teenager we'd seen here before.

"I missed you," a raspy voice whispered in my ear while a pair of stretchmarked, used-up tits shoved themselves into my face. "The way you fucked me last time, mmm! It was all I could think about."

"Look, can I get a minute to breathe?" I leaned away from the whore rubbing on me like a cat in heat. I couldn't remember this one's name, but she was blocking my view from the pretty little new girl.

"Sure, honey. Just let me know when you want me." She gave me a wink and squeezed my dick through my pants before rising up to offer her services to my men. Sure enough, she hopped on Brick's cock right when he was in the middle of a conversation with Big G.

The sound of over-exaggerated moans and slapping flesh faded in the background as I popped a fat cheese cube in my mouth. I washed it down with the last of the ale on the table, hoping the new girl would hurry her ass out to refill it.

Jandro took a seat next to me, leaning back on the couch with a sigh. "I cannot fucking wait to sleep in an actual bed tonight. Think I'll grab two girls while I'm at it."

"How are the steeds?" I asked.

"Fine. Just had to clear a bunch of dust from Shadow's bike. Yours is getting low on oil, but should be fine until we make it back to Sheol."

My vice president was not only my second in command, but the most accomplished motorcycle mechanic I'd ever seen. He'd know exactly what was wrong with someone's ride just from the sound she made.

"Damn," Jandro breathed softly, looking across the lounge to the kitchen. The door had been propped open with how much running the girls had to go back and forth.

I followed his gaze to the new girl, fast on her feet as she replaced empty beer pitchers with full ones.

"Yeah," I agreed, leaning forward to scratch Hades' ears. "She wasn't here last time."

"Nope. I'd remember an ass like that, no matter how fucked up I was." He grinned. "She looks Latina, too. You know how long it's been since I had a woman of my own culture?"

"I dunno, two weeks?" I scoffed.

"Exactly. Too long."

His eyes followed her as she came to our table, although hers remained low and focused on her tasks at hand.

"Excuse me." Jandro reached out to catch her wrist, making her flinch but she didn't pull away. Smart girl.

"*Como se llama?*" he asked for her name in his mother tongue.

She lifted her hazel eyes to him, her gaze flickering to me for a moment before answering his question.

"Mariposa," she answered.

Jandro grinned broadly, his fingers sliding from her wrist to the inside of her palm. I suppressed an eyeroll. The man was far too flirtatious than necessary. Any one of us in the Steel Demons could bed a woman without much effort, but my Latin VP treated it like an art form.

"Mariposa," he repeated, tasting her name in his mouth. "And what's a pretty little butterfly like you doing in a place like this?"

"I'm actually a medic," she answered, straightening her spine. "I'm just passing through, helping out while I stay here."

"Medic?" I repeated, not bothering to hide my surprise. "A *female* medic?"

"That's right," she returned her gaze to me. "I was educated before the law passed."

My eyebrows lifted. Even years before the Collapse, women being educated was a rarity. As their rights were gradually stripped away, girls of high school age and even younger were kidnapped and never seen again. The few who escaped and tried to press charges got laughed out of the courtrooms. Then it became illegal in most jurisdictions for a woman to file a criminal case without a reliable male witness.

Frightened parents started keeping their daughters locked away at home. While temporarily safer this way, it didn't exactly provide them with tools to survive a post-Collapse society. Once the border wars broke out, every home, car, and business was a pillaging free-for-all. Safety simply didn't exist anymore.

Survival was no longer a right. It was a privilege to be earned, as I and the men of my club knew all too well.

"Now, Mariposa," Jandro leaned back, still holding her hand and causing her to lean over the table. "We've had a long, exhausting ride. What'll you take for a full body examination with those skilled hands of yours?"

Her expression morphed from apprehensive to hardened determination within a second. She snatched her hand from Jandro's grip and straightened up.

"I don't deal in sex. There's plenty of girls here who provide that."

Jandro smirked. "It wasn't a yes or no question. Everyone has a price. Just name yours."

"The answer is still no." She grabbed our empty pitchers and charcuterie board. "I'll bring you more food and drink."

Jandro chuckled to himself as she beelined back toward the kitchen. "She has no idea who she's saying no to. Good thing I like a challenge."

"Have fun with that," I muttered, rolling my neck around on my shoulders.

For the last fifty miles or so, I'd been looking forward to getting off the bike and burying my cock in a woman. But now that I was here, a night of long, uninterrupted sleep sounded much better. Although Jandro's proposition of a full-body rub down didn't sound bad. Unfortunately, I too preferred it from Mariposa the pretty medic. As President, I had every right to claim her for myself but I wasn't petty enough do that to my VP.

Even so, the thought turned over in my head as I watched her slicing cheese and meats through the open kitchen doors. She'd taken off her windbreaker and her bare shoulders looked small enough for me to wrap my whole hands around. Her neck was long and graceful, a few shades lighter than Jandro's tan.

"You ready for me, Reaper baby?"

My view was blocked yet again by yet another unwelcome service girl crawling into my lap. Jandro hid his laugh by swiping some of Gunner's beer from the next table. Gun's falcon, Horus, screeched and flapped his wings in annoyance, to which Jandro promptly flipped him the bird.

Hades growled with irritation at my feet, echoing my feelings exactly as the girl turned to face me, straddling my thighs as she ground herself against my very unexcited dick.

"Let's go up to my room," she mewled, bouncing in my lap. "You can lay back and just let me ride you. I won't make ya work, baby."

And that was exactly what made me stay soft. I didn't chase skirt like Jandro did, but desperation was always a turn-off. Especially from a whore.

"I haven't eaten a damn meal yet," I growled, shoving her off just hard enough to get my point across. "Your pussy is not the fucking holy grail."

She quickly composed herself, smoothing out her flimsy dress and lowering her eyes demurely.

"Jandro?" she inquired almost shyly.

"Sorry, babe. I have different tastes tonight. Here's an idea, though." He pointed down the length of the couches to the man closest to the door. "Why don't you give Shadow some love? He hasn't gotten any in a while."

The girl wrinkled her nose with displeasure. "The big, scarred one? He's scary."

"You ought to be a lot more scared of us," I warned her. Jandro nodded in agreement.

She looked back and forth between us and Shadow a few times, chewing her lip. "He's just not as handsome as you two and Gunner, though. And Gunner says I'm not his type," she whined.

"You fuck men for smokes and liquor," I snapped at her. "Before the Collapse, you would have fucked for money. If you're gonna beg, don't be a chooser."

She shrank back as I raised my voice at her, and finally scurried away. Jandro shook his head at me as he laughed quietly. I reached down to pet Hades again, only to find my dog was no longer at my side.

"What the—? Hades!" I looked around, no sign of my four-legged beast anywhere. He never left my side unless I gave him a command. If one of these service bitches actually fucking did something to him...

Next to me, Jandro just chuckled. "Looks like we're not the only ones who want to sniff out Miss Mariposa." He nodded toward the kitchen and I followed his gaze.

As the leader of the most notorious MC in the Southwest, I saw a lot of weird shit before, during, and after the Collapse. But I never saw anything like what played out before my eyes that very moment.

Hades had walked right up next to Mariposa as she chopped cheese cubes and salami. He stared at her intently while she appeared to be talking to him in a low voice. Then he sat.

My dog fucking *sat* for another human being. To add insult to injury, he tilted his head and licked his greedy lips as she held a cheese cube a few inches in front of his nose. The morsel of food grew closer and closer to him until he scarfed it off of her fingers.

And if that wasn't enough, he licked her hand and allowed her to scratch his head. No one, not even men in my own club, had been permitted to touch him that way.

I raised that dog since finding him in a pile of rubble next to an abandoned house. We were cleaning up and scavenging after a border battle, and heard something like a baby screaming bloody murder. He could fit in the palm of my hand and those little puppy lungs wouldn't shut the hell up. Not until after we raided a vet clinic down the road and I got my hands on some puppy formula.

I'd never cared for an animal in my life, so I wasn't sure what brought me to hold onto the little mutt rather than put him out of his misery. All I knew was Hades and I developed a bond closer to friendship between people, rather than animal and owner. Gunner told me he felt similarly when he found Horus as a chick.

I found Hades a few months after losing Daren, so I chalked it up to filling the void that my little brother left behind. That was a year ago, and Hades had been loyal and protective only to me since the beginning. He even guarded me while I slept and saved our asses from being ambushed several times. So imagine my shock when he just wandered off to get a piece of cheese from some girl we'd never seen before.

"Hades!" I bellowed loud enough for the whole place to hear me.

The damn dog finally turned to look at me, still licking his chops from his treat like he did nothing wrong.

"Get your ass over here, mutt."

As he trotted back to my side, my eyes lifted to catch Mariposa's once again, before she turned her back to continue her work.

Chapter 3

MARIPOSA

Tom wasn't kidding about these bikers having voracious appetites. They drank the beer and ate all the meat and cheese we put out faster than we could refill them. When the service girls came down from their rooms in their high heels and flimsy dresses that left little to the imagination, the Steel Demons consumed them with their eyes just as greedily. Some of them, anyway.

Reaper didn't seem interested in the girl practically humping his leg, nor did the Hispanic man who sat next to him. But I felt their eyes on me far more than was comfortable, and it made my skin crawl.

You're new here. They're curious and are probably going to test how much shit you'll take. Just do your job and roll with it.

I slammed the tap handle back with more force than necessary just before the beer sloshed dangerously close to the pitcher's rim. This was actually *not* my job. This was why I went into debt for a top-tier nursing degree—so I wouldn't become a walking piece of meat for men to ogle. Tension and conflict had been brimming for years before the Collapse. Everyone knew war was coming, and I wanted to help in a way that was meaningful.

A high-pitched squeal and the sound of flesh slapping pulled my attention away from my painstaking care not to spill any beer as I walked. Next to the blonde man with the falcon on his shoulder, a woman was already riding the cock of a fellow biker. She bounced on him with gusto, putting in the work while the man she rode all but ignored her, talking to the blonde man next to him as if this was a completely normal occurrence.

The man sitting on the other side of the sex rodeo polished off his beer pitcher and scooted closer to the cowgirl. He smacked her ass once to get her attention, which had been on the blonde man. When she turned her head to look at who spanked her, he said something and put a hand over his crotch. She leaned over, yanked down his zipper, and proceeded to suck him loudly while still bouncing on the first guy. It was like a trainwreck I couldn't stop myself from watching.

"Get in on this, Gunner! Her asshole's free," laughed the guy getting his dick sucked, stretching his arms wide along the back of the couch.

The blonde man shook his head with an amused chuckle and said something I couldn't hear, the falcon on his shoulder ruffling its feathers as its sharp eyes darted all over the room.

Someone poked me in the back, startling me out of watching the debauchery happening before my eyes.

"Don't watch like that," Gretchen muttered. "They'll think you want to join in."

Ugh, no thanks. It had been over a year since I'd gotten laid, but being used by rough, manhandling outlaws did not sound like fun. I put a birth control implant in my arm just a few months ago, so I was cleared on that front. But the nurse in me was all too aware of the rise of STIs and physical injuries from widespread rape and using sex as currency since the Collapse. At least a third of my patients had some sort of infection or physical trauma related to sex. I could only imagine what the emotional and mental impact did to them.

As I fought to ignore the public threesome and keep my feet moving, I couldn't help but notice the four best-looking members of the club were the only ones not participating in the debauchery. I pushed the thought away just as quickly as it came. Those men were probably just holding out for more attractive, expensive whores.

Not even the guy sitting closest to the door, a huge, powerfully-built man with black hair to his collar, had a woman draping off of him. Some of the hair hung over his face to cover his right eye, and I thought I got a glimpse of some scarring on his forehead. He didn't touch the beer in front of him or talk to anyone. The service girls almost seemed to purposely avoiding him, not that he appeared to care. He just ate salami, cheese, and olives with slow, methodical precision, popping each morsel into his mouth and chewing slowly. The muscles in his jaw moved under a dense, but trimmed black beard dusted with a few grey hairs. His chocolate brown, uncovered eye swept across the entire lobby in silent observation.

I caught myself staring once again—he had that ultra-rugged handsome thing going on that I was a total sucker for—and bumped my shin into the coffee table in front of him.

"Oh shit, I'm sorry!"

I pulled a dish rag from my back pocket and quickly wiped up the beer that sloshed onto the table. My heart crashed against my sternum as I kept my eyes glued to the mess I made. I had no idea if these guys liked to torture or kill their service people for making mistakes, and hoped I didn't just make my first day here my last.

Once the spill was quickly absorbed by my rag, the large man in front of me said nothing. I dared to look up at him and wished I hadn't. His scowl made Reaper's look like a joyful grin.

"Sorry about that," I repeated, praying I wasn't digging myself into a deeper hole. My eyes flickered back down to the nearly full beer pitcher in front of him. "I can take that and get you something else if you prefer?" It would save me a trip from filling up yet another empty pitcher.

He didn't answer—not with words, in any case. His lip curled with disgust, like I was a piece of dog shit on his boot, then flung his hand out toward me as if to say, *get out of my sight and take this shit away.*

I grabbed the pitcher's handle and made off for the next table, where another one of these animals might appreciate it more. Keeping my eyes focused on my work and *not* on the threesome still happening on the next couch, I swapped the full pitcher for an empty one when a hand snapped out and grabbed my wrist.

"Como se llama?" a warm voice asked me.

I looked up. Big mistake. Now I couldn't look away from the hazel eyes so similar to mine. His fingers on my wrist were strong and calloused, but the skin along his muscular arm was smooth and the color of caramel. The smile he wore was far too charming. I had no doubt this man was not only good at breaking hearts, but treated it like a sport. In the bedroom, he probably recited takeout menus in Spanish, making women think he uttered proclamations of love and romance while in the throes of passion.

That smile and the confidence to touch me showed all the signs of a man who wanted to play with more than just a woman's body. Giving him my name like he asked would already be too much. Men didn't care about asking for names or getting to know someone anymore, not when they could just take what they wanted.

And he knew that. He touched on a pre-Collapse custom, knowing such a small gesture would make me feel a little bit like a human again. It was all part of his game, and yet I couldn't resist giving it to him.

"Mariposa," I answered.

His eyes flashed with recognition at the word as his smile grew brighter. It was a look I saw often whenever introducing myself to Spanish speakers. My name meant butterfly, but I unfortunately never got a good grasp of the language. Dad was never around enough to teach me.

"Mariposa," the biker repeated, clearly pleased. His cut read VICE PRESIDENT. "And what's a pretty little butterfly like you doing in a place like this?"

"I'm actually a medic," I said, hoping to squash any nefarious ideas he might be having. "I'm just passing through, helping out while I stay here."

"Medic?"

My eyes slid over to see Reaper's intense green gaze leveled on me again. Jesus, these men had zero qualms about unabashedly staring.

"A *female* medic?" he repeated, eyes sliding over me like trying to figure out how a dude could crossdress so well.

I bristled at his skepticism. It wasn't *that* long ago that women were outlawed from medical jobs in over 80% of post-Collapse territories.

"That's right," I answered, lifting my chin slightly. "I was educated before the laws passed."

"Now, Mariposa." The vice president leaned back into the couch, pulling me forward across the coffee table like he fully expected me to tumble into his lap. He smelled like motor oil and smoke, though not entirely unappealing. "What'll you take for a full-body examination with those skilled hands of yours?"

So much for deterring him. There was a girl getting fucked on the next couch over, why would he bother with me? I snatched my hand away and was surprised at how easily he let go.

"I don't deal in sex," I hissed. "There's plenty of girls here who provide that."

"It wasn't a yes or no question," he remarked, eyes flashing playfully. "Everyone has a price. Just name yours."

Fuck you and the bike you rode in on. I am not playing your game, pig.

"The answer is still no." I grabbed the empty beer pitcher and food plate, fighting every instinct to throw them right at his smug, grinning face. "I'll bring you more food and drink."

My hands shook so hard, I nearly dropped the dishes on the counter when I made it back to the kitchen. My heart beat erratically and my feet were already sore from the constant running around. The likelihood of making it through the next two weeks seemed abysmally low. There was no avoiding these men, so I could only hope they'd be gone in the next day or two and grow bored of me during that time.

With a shaky breath, I picked up a knife and began cutting into a cheese block. I just had to make it through tonight. Then the next night. Then the one after that. *You'll survive. You'll survive.*

I became so entranced in my cheese-cubing, I nearly jumped out of my skin when something cold and wet nudged my arm.

"Ah! What?" I blinked down at a face with two round dark eyes, pointed ears, and a smiling toothy mouth with a pink tongue lolling out.

"What are you doing here?" I demanded Reaper's dog like he could answer. Hades, I think he called him.

Up close, the animal was even bigger than I initially thought. His shoulder came up to my waist. Sleek muscles across his chest and a glossy coat showed he was well taken care of, neither thin nor overweight. That, at least, was a relief. I'd seen companion animals in far worse conditions since the Collapse. When most people could barely feed themselves or their children, animals always suffered the worst.

"Go away." I made a shooing motion but the dog only stepped closer, nudging my arm out of the way to reach his prize on the counter —cheese.

"Damn it, dog." I covered the food with my hand, looking over my shoulder to see his owner preoccupied with a service girl in his lap.

Hades licked his lips and tilted his head at me as if to say, *See? He'll never know. Just one little piece? Pwease?*

"This is all you get," I said, holding up a cheese cube between my thumb and forefinger. "But you better not get me in trouble with your human, okay?"

Hades' eyes brightened as he lowered his haunches to the floor like a good boy. I stood stunned for a moment. This dog looked like he would have ripped my throat out the moment he walked in next to his owner. Now he was working the puppy dog eyes and begging for treats like he grew up with a sweet old lady.

"Please don't bite my fingers off," I muttered as I slowly held the cheese out to him.

To my relief, only his tongue touched my hand as he scarfed down the cube in two big, chomping bites. It brought a smile to my face for the first time in weeks. He looked like such a sweet puppy for a moment. I forgot about who he came with and what those big eyes must have witnessed his owner do. In that one innocent moment, I allowed myself to reach out and tentatively scratch one of his ears.

"Hades!" The yell came from across the room and made me flinch. "Get your ass over here, mutt."

The dog trotted back to lay at his owner's feet, Reaper's unforgiving gaze holding me rooted to my spot. Fuck. He must have seen me feed him and pet him. The sick, churning feeling in my stomach told me the Steel Demons president wouldn't take kindly to someone touching his pet.

Turning back to my chopping, I struggled to calm the fearful, ragged breaths in and out of my chest as Reaper's eyes felt like daggers in my back.

Chapter 4

MARIPOSA

I woke up the next morning to a line of prostitutes outside my door. Not for anything fun, considering I don't swing that way.

Nope, they heard what I offered and came to receive my services. I got a cup of stale coffee from the kitchen, tied my hair back, opened my pack, and got down to work.

Most of them wanted birth control, as expected. Thankfully I stocked up from the pharmacy I stayed at before coming here. I had pills, patches, rings, implants, and IUDs up the wazoo.

The majority of them preferred the implant like the one I had in my arm. It lasted for three years and was relatively easy to insert and remove. Pills were too easy to lose, forget, or be tampered with. IUDs were invasive and more painful to insert, plus I was not the best at putting them in. While in school, my dream was to be a labor and delivery nurse. I wanted to catch babies as they came out, not shove things back in.

But at this point in my post-Collapse medic career, most of my skills came from straight-up winging it. I'd never implanted a birth control device before until I put my first one in my arm. I never performed any kind of surgery myself until I had to dig shrapnel out of a kid's thigh at the old Texas-New Mexico border.

Sometimes I was lucky enough to learn from other medics on the road. Former doctors, nurse practitioners, and physician's assistants all gave me tricks of the trade I never would have learned in a pre-Collapse job. They made me realize how vital it was to share skills in a world like this. One day I could be pulling a dead tooth from a guy's mouth and the next day, giving methadone to a drug addict. To be truly useful, we had to adapt to everything.

In between birth control implants and morning-after pills, some of the girls talked to me about physical symptoms they were feeling. A few were embarrassed, understandably so, but I heard it all before. I handed out antibiotics and could only hope their infections weren't the kind that resisted medication. With no reliable labs around, I couldn't do blood or urine tests to verify anything.

My line finally started to go down around mid-morning, and my stomach cramped from hunger. I knew there was some leftover stew from the Steel Demons' dinner last night. I yearned for flavorful broth and hearty potatoes by the time the last woman sat down on my bed.

"My stomach's been hurting," she whined, holding her forearm low against her abdomen. I recognized her as the girl having sex on the couch with the two bikers yesterday.

"Okay, for how long?" I asked, snapping on a fresh pair of gloves.

"I dunno, three days?"

I stared at her. "You've been in pain like this for *three days* and still offered your services to those men last night?"

"Save the judgment, bitch," she hissed, teeth grinding in pain. "Last night guaranteed food and clothes for my daughter for another two weeks. Besides," her eyes flashed with hard determination, "if I stayed up in my room, one of them would have come up and found me. And those men aren't the kind you can say no to."

"I'm sorry, I wasn't trying to judge," I sighed with a small shake of my head. When did humanity become such a shithole? "May I touch you?"

She allowed me to press gently on her stomach while I asked all the routine questions. I had my suspicions but after just a few minutes of examining her, I was all but certain.

"What's your name?" I pulled my hands away from her and sat up.

"Kitty," she answered, fear creeping into her eyes. "What's wrong with me?"

"Kitty, your stomach's fine. But my suspicion is you have an ovarian cyst. With your permission, I'd like to perform a pelvic exam to make sure."

Her eyes widened. "What the hell is that?"

"An ovarian cyst is a growth on one of your ovaries that can cause pain and cramping. They're usually benign, meaning not cancerous, but carry a risk of rupturing, which can cause internal bleeding and severe pain. Sexual intercourse, especially if it's rough, can increase the risk of a rupture."

"And you want to do what?"

"A pelvic exam," I replied clinically. "I'll need to insert two fingers in your vagina and put pressure around your lower abdomen for a few seconds to examine your uterus, fallopian tubes, and ovaries."

Kitty scooted away from me, a grimace of disgust on her face. "I don't do chicks."

"Neither do I. There's nothing sexual about this," I told her. "It's purely medical. But it's also your body. I won't do anything without your permission."

She hesitated, nearly doubled over with pain. "And if it is that thing you said? Then what?"

"Considering how much pain you're in," I chewed my lip, always hating this part, "I think removal of the cyst would be the best option."

"Removal?! How?"

"With surgery," I said as gently as I could. "It's a relatively minor surgery, although that depends on the size and where exactly the cyst is located. And I need to do the pelvic exam to find that out."

Kitty's face paled as she scrambled off on my bed, heading for the door as she clutched her stomach. "Fuck no! You are *not* touching my pussy and you sure as fuck are *not* cutting me open!"

I nodded, completely unsurprised at her reaction. “Let me know if you change your mind, Kitty." I began cleaning up my supplies. "I'll be here for two more weeks. I just want to help."

She left my room, muttering to herself about fucking dykes while I threw all my used gloves and wrappers into a plastic bag and tied it off. Years ago, she would have offended me. I remembered the helpless feeling of trying to make a fellow woman understand that examining her was part of my job. The more I tried to explain it to her, the more she freaked out. I almost *did* feel like some kind of predator, even though I only wanted to help.

An OB/GYN consoled me after that, reminding me that consent and respect for our patients' autonomy was paramount in today's world. Above all else, people needed to feel like they could trust us, and that meant backing off when they said no. Even if their lives were at risk.

I cleaned everything off my bed and began tidying up before heading down to eat, when a small voice came from my open doorway.

"Mari?"

I whirled around. "Gretchen!" I gasped, stunned at the girl's face.

She had two black eyes and a split lip caked in dried blood. Bruises covered her neck, arms, and probably more places I couldn't see. It took all my self-control to quell the rage within me. Choosing the life of a prostitute was one thing, but she was just a kid, for fuck's sake.

"Come here, sweetie." I sat on the bed and patted the spot next to me. "Who did this?"

"It doesn't matter," she rasped, allowing me to feel gently around her face. No broken bones as far as I could tell.

"Did those fucking bikers attack you?" I got up to rummage through my pack for pain relievers.

"Don't worry about me, Mari. I'm used to it," she gave a weak smile that broke my heart. "But do you have any, ah, morning-after pills left?"

Of course, I knew before she said it. But for some reason, her saying those words hit me like a sledgehammer to the chest. I'd treated dozens of sexual assault victims before. Why her asking me that affected me so much, I had no idea. Maybe because she was young with so much potential, or that she'd just escaped the exact same abuse months before. Or it could have been the way she smiled through the pain in her face, as if trying to encourage *me* to chin up and get through the day.

"Gretchen..." I didn't know what to say. My chest felt so heavy. So I just pulled the sealed package of pills from my pack. "Take these right away. Both at the same time. You might feel some side effects—"

"Thanks, Mari. I'll pay you back in some way. I don't have much to trade but I can clean your room or—"

"Don't, please. You don't owe me anything." I sat next to her on the bed, taking her small hands between mine. "Do you want to come with me when I leave?" The question tumbled out faster than I could think about it. All I could focus on was keeping this girl safe and far away from the brutal men probably sleeping in the rooms right next to ours.

Her eyes brightened with hope. "Really? Can I?"

It was too late to go back on my word now, so I nodded. "We'll be safer together. I can teach you basic medic skills, too."

"That would be amazing, Mari!" She glanced nervously toward my open door as sounds from the other rooms floated down the hallway. It was nearly noon and sounded like the Steel Demons were just rising.

"We shouldn't say anything to Tom and Liza," she whispered. "I told them I'd be staying a lot longer and...they wouldn't understand."

"My lips are sealed," I told her, making a zipping motion over my mouth. "And hey, if any of those bikers try to mess with you, yell for me. I'm pretty handy with a scalpel."

"I will," she nodded. "But they probably want nothing to do with me now, looking like this."

"Let's hope they leave both of us alone, but still," I gave her shoulder a gentle squeeze. "Just be careful."

GRETCHEN WANTED TO GO DOWN TO THE KITCHEN WITH ME, but I insisted she rest in her room until at least it was time to cook dinner.

"Doctor's orders," I told her sternly, fluffing her pillows up behind her head.

"You're not a doctor," she teased back with a smile. How she could still bring herself to joke around was beyond me.

"Medic's orders, then," I tapped her nose. "I'll bring you some lunch."

"Fine," she sighed, relaxing back at last.

Perhaps it was naive of me to think the Steel Demons wouldn't be milling about the place like they owned it, but the last thing I expected to see was one of them reading a book in the lobby.

And not just any book. The Bible.

The blonde one with hair to his collarbone, his falcon perched on his shoulder as it preened its feathers, studied the thin pages in front of him like the surrounding world didn't exist.

His long legs stretched out in front of him, leather boots propped up on the coffee table as his blue eyes moved, entranced by ancient prophecies transcribed hundreds if not thousands of times.

Like with the big scarred guy last night, I was so fixed on staring at him that my clumsy ass walked right into the kitchen doors with a hard *thunk* to my forehead.

"Fuck!" I slapped my palms to my head, knowing getting through unnoticed was impossible now.

"Take it easy," the blonde biker grinned at me. "There are better ways to cure a hangover."

"Not hungover," I grumbled, pushing my way through the door. My cheeks burned and I wanted to forget what had just happened. So when Blonde Biker and his falcon followed me into the kitchen, I wished to sink into the floor from embarrassment and fear.

"Can I help you?" I asked apprehensively, moving to put the counter between me and him.

"Coffee would be great. There's none in my room and not a soul down here 'til you headbutted the door." He shot me a cocky grin.

"Uh, okay." I turned slowly toward the cabinets, keeping my eyes on him. "I'll make some."

"Thanks, *Marrriposa.*" He said my name with an exaggerated rolling r and Spanish accent. "My boy Jandro couldn't stop saying your name last night. I'm Gunner, by the way. This is Horus." He pointed to the bird on his shoulder.

I couldn't think of what to say. *Pleased to meet you* would have been an obvious lie. *Your hair is pretty* would give him the wrong idea. So I opted for an awkward joke.

"Does Horus want coffee, too?" I started cringing before the words ever left my mouth.

Gunner threw his head back and laughed, clutching his flat stomach like it was the funniest thing he heard all day. A smile peeked at the corner of my mouth before I could stop myself.

"Nah, he's a fancy bastard and likes his tea," Gunner winked when he could breathe. "But seriously, he caught a big breakfast this morning. A nice fat gopher, didn't you, boy?"

He scratched the bird under its wickedly curved beak and my smile grew. How long had it been since I just had a silly conversation with a cute guy? Gunner almost seemed normal, if even nice. He looked just like a guy at my college campus I would flirt with, pre-Collapse. I'd even let him buy me a drink.

Then my eyes fell to his leather cut and reality slapped the smile right off my face. The patch on the left side depicted two crossed assault rifles with "2A" beneath them. I didn't know much about MC life, but I knew 2A referred to the Second Amendment of the United States, a law that no longer existed in this gigantic land mass which didn't even have a name anymore.

2A became an emblem for those that thrived on the new violent, chaotic nature of modern society. Those who wore it lived for the bloodlust of the border wars, the power of taking someone's life with a handheld machine. They lived and breathed death and violence.

Because the Second Amendment, once central to American culture, was the right to bear arms.

If that wasn't enough, a long bandolier of ammunition stretched from Gunner's shoulder to his hip. I don't know how I missed it before, but the kitchen lights made the bullets gleam like endless rows of small, golden missiles.

A black handgun sat in a holster on his opposite hip, and there was no telling how many other weapons he had on him. This easy-smiling, angelic-looking man absolutely *loved* violence.

"How about that coffee, Mari?" he teased, resting a hand on the weapon at his hip. "Can I call you Mari? Not that *Marrriposa* isn't pretty. It's just a hell of a mouthful."

"Uh, sure." I turned uneasily toward the coffee pot, fumbling for cups with shaking hands. "Call me whatever you like."

"In that case, I might call you Maripos-*ass*, 'cause *damn*, mami."

In two steps, he was right behind me. I froze at the heat of his breath on my neck. My eyes squeezed shut, bracing myself for his hands on me, and then the gun or knife that would surely follow.

"Relax," his lips brushed my ear as fingertips trailed across my waist. "You're shaking like a leaf. I'll make it good for you, baby girl."

His thick erection pressing against my ass stole a gasp from my mouth. Gunner let out a groan in reply, his lips falling to my neck as he held my waist in place. My core roared like an inferno, my touch-starved body leaning into his heat and hardness as if of it's own will, but that didn't stop the frantic thoughts.

At least he's not doing this to Gretchen. At least she's safe upstairs. I'll survive this.

"Screeeeech!"

Horus, still on Gunner's shoulder, suddenly began flapping his wings and screaming bloody murder. Temporary relief flooded me as Gunner pulled away.

"Go away, Horus. I'm busy," he chastised the bird with a swat of his hand, but the falcon would not let up. His talons curled into the worn leather at Gunner's shoulder, holding on and screeching in his human's face.

"...Mari?"

"Gretchen!" Hot shame filled me as her swollen, bruised eyes widened with fear, peeking through the gap in the swinging kitchen door.

She took in Gunner standing so close to me and seemed to understand exactly what was about to happen.

"I told you to rest," I blurted out, my heart pounding wildly. In truth, I could have kissed her with gratitude for showing up right then.

"I came down to grab some water." Her eyes darted nervously toward Gunner, who stared back at her intensely.

"I'll bring you some," I said quickly. "And some food. Go on back up. I'll be right there."

She nodded and retreated back, letting the door close softly.

"Holy shit," Gunner turned back to me, bewilderment on his face. "What the fuck happened to her?"

I glared at him, unable to help myself. "Like you don't know."

His eyes widened in shock before narrowing venomously at me in return. "Look. I know what I look like, but I do *not* fucking beat up little girls. No one in the SDMC does that shit."

"Okay, Gunner," I said placidly. "If you don't mind, I'd like to make coffee and lunch unmolested. Thank you."

I turned back to the coffee machine without waiting for an answer, although still fully expecting a gun or knife in my back.

Instead, I heard the ruffling of feathers as Horus finally calmed down, then Gunner's booted feet walking away and out the kitchen doors.

CHAPTER 5

JANDRO

I drummed my fingers on the long conference table stretched out in front of me. Reaper sat to my left, hands folded calmly in his lap, and Hades lying at his feet like usual. Tom, the owner of this service station, sat across from us, visibly nervous and sweating.

Any man with two brain cells to rub together would have seen this meeting coming, but Tom chose to play dumb. That might have worked with some little wannabe MC, but not with us.

"When we made our protection agreement, I assumed your club would be around to, you know, protect me," Tom whined. "*And* my assets! Just last week, a bunch of masked thugs on dirt bikes rode up and took three of my girls. Expensive ones, too! And where the hell were you guys?"

My fingers closed into a fist as I opened my mouth to retort but Reaper raised a hand, asking me for silence. I closed my trap, fighting my temper to jump to my President and best friend's defense.

"We're not responsible for the consequences of your provocations," Reaper answered him. "You brought this on yourself, Tom. Our agreement was for *protection*, not babysitting and cleaning up your messes."

Tom's face twisted into a well-practiced look of shock. If Hollywood didn't get swallowed by the ocean fifty years ago, he would have been nominated for an Oscar.

"Provocations? I have no idea what you're talking about! I run an honest business! I'm--"

"Shut the fuck up, old man," I snapped. "Don't talk to us like we're fucking idiots. We keep our ears to the ground and word spreads. We know. And everyone in the Southwest is going to learn how honest your business really is."

"What?!"

"I'm sure you can recall our agreement also included discretion. If you forgot, I have the original signed copy right here," Reaper tapped the left side of his cut. "So if you're as honest as you say, why would the bartender at the Shady Lady say you were bragging all night long about having the Steel Demons in your back pocket?"

A flash of panic passed through Tom's watery eyes. "Because she's a lying whore!"

"Or you're a lying sack of shit," I suggested. "You start making claims like that, people are going to test to see if they're true. You're basically the kid on the playground goading everyone with, 'my dad can beat up your dad.'"

"Okay, I might have told a couple of close friends after I had a few but it wasn't like that! It doesn't mean I deserve to have punks ransacking my business!"

"Actually, that's exactly what it means." Reaper rose to his feet, Hades loyally glued to his side, and I followed. "You agreed to discretion in exchange for reasonable protection. You've broken that agreement so the deal is off."

He started for the door and I fell in after him, leaving Tom to scramble desperately after us from the other side of the room.

"Wait! I haven't broken anything! I kept my side of the bargain! You have garages for your bikes, all the food you can eat, women to fuck, all because of me!"

I whipped around and thrust my palm in the center of Tom's chest, making him stumble back with fear in his eyes.

"You accuse my president of lying again and you're a dead man," I threatened in a low voice. "You're lucky to still be breathing right now after breaking a deal with us."

As Tom shivered like a chihuahua, Reaper turned slowly to face him again.

"Everything you provide, we can easily find somewhere else. But you'll never have the protection of an MC again, because they'll all know you can't be trusted."

Tom's mouth flopped open like a fish, glub-glubbing uselessly. I felt no sympathy for the bastard. He of all people should have known that in this world, where everything could be taken in an instant, a man's word was the most valuable thing he had.

I slapped him on the shoulder and gave him a shit-eating grin. "We leave before dawn tomorrow. And if it wasn't obvious, we won't be returning next month."

Reaper, Hades, and I left the room, already halfway down the hall and pulling out our cloves to smoke when Tom came tearing down after us.

"Wait!" He nearly tripped over his own feet to reach us. "Please rethink this! You're making a mistake."

"Tom, I don't know if you realized this," Reaper glared, his patience thinning as the black cigarette bobbed between his lips, "But you need us a lot more than we need you. It's not our fault you fucked it up."

"I know, I know. If you could just, maybe," he rubbed his shiny forehead, grasping at straws, "accept a parting gift! As my deepest apology, you can have Kitty. She's one of my best."

"No thanks," I scoffed, flicking open my Zippo to light up right in the hallway. "We aren't lacking in pussy. And even if we were, we prefer a higher quality."

"The kitchen girl, then!" Tom spoke quickly, reeking of desperation. "Gretchen. She's a good cook and young enough that she hasn't been fully broken in yet."

"No," Reaper barked with an air of disgust. "We don't deal in brainwashed children."

"My new girl then." Tom refused to let this go. "She served you last night. She's a medic, although I don't know about her bedroom skills."

"Mariposa," I exhaled her name in a thick cloud of smoke, making Tom cough pathetically.

Reaper said nothing right away. His expression was pensive as he lit up his own cigarette and took a long drag, almost as though he was actually considering it. Tom looked hopeful for a moment, a grin starting to spread across his face. That was until Reaper's hand shot out, catching the old man by the throat and shoving him against the wall so hard, the back of his head bounced. Hades pinned his ears back, lowering his head and growling with his teeth inches away from Tom's dick.

"No parting gifts. No more deal," Reaper said, low and menacing next to Tom's face. "SDMC is washing our hands of you."

He released Tom's throat and headed for the exit, not looking back as the old man sank to the floor, clutching his throat as he struggled to regain his breath.

Hades and I followed Reaper outside. I leaned against the railing next to him while his dog sat on his haunches. We were on some balcony overlooking a dirty crater in the ground that had once been a pool. Years ago we would smoke just like this and then skateboard in empty pools, hoping to impress girls with our skills. Pre-Collapse life had been so much simpler.

"You almost said yes to the medic," I observed, flicking my ash over the railing. "Why didn't you?"

"Because," he exhaled, "accepting any parting gift would just be a string that keeps us tied to him. If we accept something from him, we'll still owe something in return. Better to cut the strings altogether."

That wasn't the question I asked, and he knew that. Still, I humored him and tried again in another way.

"All of that is true. But we could just steal her."

Reaper hissed in a sharp breath as he dragged on his clove. "No."

"Why not?" I was genuinely surprised by his refusal. "I thought you wanted a medic for the club after Daren--"

"I do. Just not her."

"Bro," I laughed in disbelief. "I dunno if you noticed, but medics aren't exactly growing on trees. She might be the last one we see in a while."

"I'm fine with that. You jerkoffs just need to not die on me in the meantime."

"Okay," I mused. "Humor me, then. Why *not* her? Because she's female?"

"Yes."

"Reaper, my man!" A laugh barked out of me so loud and sudden, it made Hades look at me with his ears pinned back. "Come on, now. We were both adults pre-Collapse, so I know you don't believe that horseshit. Not even twenty years ago, the US had plenty of female doctors, lawyers—"

"I'm sure she can do the job," Reaper snapped, stroking Hades' forehead. "But have you thought about what an educated woman in the club will mean? We might as well paint targets on our backs."

"We already do, essentially," I pointed out. Half the clubs in the Southwest wanted to join us, the other half wanted us wiped off the map. We bled for every square inch of territory we took and earned every whisper of our reputation. That kind of fame made us heroes to some and an obstacle to others.

"It's not just making us a target," Reaper leaned closer to me. "Educated women get ideas. They're dangerous because they want to change things. We need a man who can fall in line with club politics and not be a constant thorn up my ass."

"I hear you, bro," I nodded, tossing my cigarette butt into the empty pool. "I understand. I just know how hard it was for you to lose Daren—"

"I swear to God, Jandro, get the fuck off my nutsack."

"I am, man, for real. I'm just saying the whole club lost a brother, not just you. I figured finding any medic, male or female, would give you some peace of mind that we won't lose someone like that again."

"I am at peace. It happened. There's nothing we can do about it." He flung his cigarette into the pool, the stiffness in his arm showing he

was all but at peace with his little brother's death. But I didn't mention it again. That was his own demon to wrestle with.

"*Nothing* like that is going to happen again," he said. "Having a medic would just be an insurance policy. Whoever we find needs to fit in with the club, first and foremost. They need to be trustworthy above all."

"And you don't think a woman can be trusted?"

"Fuck no," he barked. "If the Collapse fucked us over as badly as it fucked them, I wouldn't trust my own goddamn shadow."

"You make a good point," I chuckled, pulling out another slim black cigarette.

Reaper and I barely lit up our second smokes when Hades rose stiffly from his sitting position. His ears pricked forward as he pointed through the balcony railing to the pool deck below.

"Easy, boy," Reaper assured him gently.

Within seconds, Gunner and Horus came into view. Our blonde arms dealer and captain of the guard usually had a sunny disposition about him, but his face was pinched into a frown as he walked hurriedly toward us alongside the pool.

"Been looking all over for you fucks," he yelled up irritably.

Horus released his shoulder with a screech, flying the short distance toward us until he grabbed the balcony railing in his talons. Hades, now relaxed at the sight of his feathered friend, placed his front paws on either side of the falcon to stand on his hind legs. I swore that dog never stopped growing. At this height, he was almost taller than me and Reaper.

"What's the matter, Gun?" Reaper reached around to scratch his Doberman's belly.

Gunner huffed out a sigh and looked up at us grimly. "I gotta talk to you guys about something."

CHAPTER 6

MARIPOSA

"You really should be resting," I grumbled, watching Gretchen carry a twenty-pound bag of rice across the kitchen.

"And leave you to do everything yourself? No way, Jose!" She cut open the bag and began dumping its contents into a large pot. "I'll just work back here while you serve drinks and stuff if you don't mind. They prefer a pretty face to look at, or at least not a fucked up one."

I simmered in my anger as I sliced through cheese and salami for the Steel Demons' appetizers. We had no ice for the swelling on Gretchen's face, although cool towels and Tylenol helped somewhat. She was obviously still in pain by the way she worked. I had no idea why she insisted on waiting hand and foot on the men who did this to her, rather than rest and wait it out until they were gone.

"Why don't Tom and Liza ever help out?" I asked. "This is their place, after all."

"Tom would never do women's work," Gretchen muttered, now dumping water over the rice. "And Liza's lost too many brain cells to do anything. She's probably high out of her mind on fentanyl right now."

"Perfect," I muttered, arranging the cheese and meat on a board. "What would they even do without us?"

"Find other girls. We're replaceable like machines, after all."

No, we're not. We're fucking people. But I kept my mouth shut as I headed out to the lobby—food board in one hand, pitcher of beer in the other.

Being the only one running food and drinks out, I had to hustle extra fast. Sweat collected on my brow and my feet never stopped moving. The bikers were just as voracious eaters and drinkers as the first night, although this time felt different.

The men were quieter, talking to each other in low voices and all but ignoring the service girls. Tension hung in the air like the first moments before a fight. Even Reaper's dog seemed more vigilant than normal.

I looked for Kitty among the bored and rejected service girls, but she was nowhere to be seen. Chewing my lip in concern, I hoped I'd be able to check on her if I ever got a break tonight.

My rounds took me back to the large man all dressed in black, with his long hair covering one eye. Again he sat by the door, not touching his beer, nor talking to anyone.

"You know, if you don't drink," I paused, balancing my empty tray on my hip, "you could say something and I won't waste a trip putting a beer pitcher in front of you."

His uncovered brown eye lifted to me, widening slightly as though surprised. Then just as quickly, his gaze snapped back down to the table, fists clenching on his knees. I couldn't help but look at him with curiosity. *Is he* able *to talk? And if not, what made him that way?*

Someone else's hand clapped down on the big man's shoulder, and a charming smile made my pulse quicken.

"Shadow prefers hard liquor." The handsome vice president took a seat next to his silent comrade. "Beer takes too long for this guy to feel anything, and he just ends up pissing like a racehorse the whole night." His bright hazel eyes drank me in seductively. "I don't think I introduced myself. I'm Jandro, Reaper's right hand man."

"Jandro?" I repeated. "So your real name is Alejandro, I take it? Why not just go by that, or Alex, like a normal person?"

It probably wasn't smart of me to get snippy with these guys, but my irritation was at an all-time high. They assaulted a teenage girl, who just wanted to sweep it under the rug, treated women like fuck toys in general, and consumed their collective weight in food and beer for what, exactly? And I was just expected to smile, look pretty, and give whatever they asked? Fuck that.

Jandro's grin just spread wider at my dig about his name. "Because I'm not a normal guy, *Marrriposa*. None of us in the SDMC are. Isn't that right, Shadow?"

The large man just grunted as he popped a cheese cube in his mouth and chewed.

"Let me guess," I mused. "You're Shadow because you're tall, dark, and silent?"

He didn't answer, as expected, but I was kind of hoping he would look up at me again. Something about this large, silent man piqued my curiosity.

"You're not far off," Jandro answered instead. "He's also our last line of defense. Shadow rides in the rear, watching our backs because nothing gets past him."

"Well, if it makes you any happier, Shadow," I shifted my trays to my opposite hip. "I think we have some whiskey in the back."

That did it. He looked at me again, just for a brief moment before jerking his gaze back down.

Jandro chuckled, nudging his friend's arm. "*Tu eres un angel, Mariposa*."

My chest fluttering more than it should, I just nodded and turned back to the kitchen. As I walked away, I swore I overheard Jandro saying something like, "See? Not all women are..."

Once again, I dropped off empties in the kitchen and returned with stocked platters and full drinks, including a fifth of whiskey for Shadow. My feet and arms screamed at me but I was doing the work of at least two people and couldn't afford to stop. I only did so when trying to breeze by Reaper and Gunner's table, and the Steel Demons president shot out like a snake to grab my forearm.

"Where's Tom tonight?" he asked, green eyes heavy and intense.

"I don't know," my teeth clenched against his unforgiving grip on my arm. "He owns the place, he could be anywhere."

"I need to see him."

"You're welcome to find him yourself. I'm kind of busy."

"Fine."

He released me so suddenly, I stumbled backwards and nearly fell on my ass. Despite recovering quickly and continuing my rounds to the tables, I felt his gaze on me as heavily as though his hands rested on my shoulders.

Ignoring him as best I could while I worked my tail off, he and his men finally reached a point where they slowed down on their eating and drinking. I took the opportunity to run upstairs to check on Kitty. Something inside had been nagging at me to check on her ever since she came to me this morning. If I focused on nothing else, I swore I could feel a stabbing pain on the lower left side of my abdomen, where my ovary was. I couldn't begin to explain how I knew, but my gut told me that sensation had to do with her.

I didn't know which room was hers, so I walked down the first hallway of doors slowly, listening through the thin wood for any sounds of someone in pain. Muffled moans and groans came through some of them, most likely sex sounds. Then a sharp cry at the end of the hall had me stopping in my tracks.

When I heard it again, I ran to the nearest door and pressed my ear to the wood. My pulse shot up at the sounds of agony on the other side.

"Kitty? It's me, the medic. Can I come in?"

A wail of pain answered me, and I opened the door to see a woman writhing on the bed, clutching her stomach. At her bedside, a girl of about seven years old sat with her knees up to her chin and tears streaming down her face. They both looked up at me with desperation in their eyes as I approached the bed.

"It hurts so bad," Kitty whimpered, her face screwed up in a mask of pain. "God, make it stop..."

"Kitty," I placed a hand on her cheek to make her look at me. "I can help you. Will you let me?"

"Yes, please! Fuck!"

I turned to the girl, who I suspected was her daughter, and gave her my best reassuring smile. "Hi, sweetie. I'm going to make your mom feel better, but I need my pack. Can you grab it for me? It's down the hall, fourth door on the left."

The girl nodded and took off, then I tried my best to examine Kitty despite her wriggling around.

"I don't care if you cut it out of me," the woman sobbed. "Just make it stop hurting."

"You're not going to feel a thing in just a minute," I promised.

Her daughter returned with my pack seconds later and I got started on Kitty's pain management. Morphine was too damn expensive and I was far from a qualified anesthesiologist. So I pulled out the box of small, metal canisters to give her the next best thing—nitrous oxide.

Within seconds of inhaling, Kitty's body relaxed and she stopped crying out in pain.

"You fixed her!" the little girl shrieked with relief. "Mommy, you're better!"

Kitty's head rolled toward the sound of her daughter's voice, a smile spreading across her lips. "Hi, baby..."

"She's not all better yet," I muttered, working quickly to clean and prep where I felt the cyst. The laughing gas wouldn't last long and Kitty would still be conscious so I couldn't afford to dally.

"This is going to look messy," I warned them. "Don't look down here. And I need you to hold still, Kitty."

"Okay..."

I made a small, surface-level incision and paused, waiting for a reaction from Kitty. When it was clear she didn't feel any pain, I continued, making the best of the poor lighting and less-than-sterile conditions in the room. The cyst was nearly twice the size of her ovary and I let out a huge sigh of relief as I cut that fucker off.

"You're going to be okay, Kitty. Hold still for me." I gave her another dose of nitrous before preparing my surgical thread. "This won't bother you anymore."

"Thank you," she breathed dreamily, high as a kite. "I should have listened to you...this morning..."

"Don't worry about it." I was a master at surgical sutures now and stitched her up quickly, only glancing once out the window.

The bikers came down for dinner around dusk and now it was pitch black outside. I worked on Kitty as quickly as I could, but still lost complete track of time. Poor Gretchen had to be struggling downstairs.

Just as I cleaned the incision and taped a bandage over it, a piercing scream floated down the hallway.

Fuck, Gretchen! It only occurred to me right then how dangerous it was to leave her alone with men who had already abused her.

I grabbed the hand of Kitty's daughter. "I'll be right back but in case I don't, make sure this stays covered and dry for two days, okay?"

"Um, okay." Fear returned to her once-calm face. "But promise you won't leave us?"

"I can't. I'm sorry."

In the next moment, I flew down the hall back toward the lobby. I realized in hindsight I should have grabbed a scalpel, but all I could think about was reaching Gretchen in time.

An unarmed woman against six members of the most dangerous motorcycle club members in the Southwest? My odds weren't good but I'd give them hell like they'd never seen before.

At least I was able to help Kitty.

The scene laid out before me when I reached the lobby was the last thing I expected to see.

A pool of blood spread slowly across the tiled floor, coming from the lifeless body of Liza. Her eyes and mouth were wide open in horror, fingers still curled and stained red. Where her throat had once been was now a gaping, shredded hole.

My eyes followed the red paw prints that led away from her body to the terrified women huddled together against the wall. Gretchen and the two service girls trembled and cried as Hades, lips pulled back and stained red teeth on display, snarled inches from their faces like he wanted to kill them next.

"Call your fucking dog off!" I ordered, my mouth going faster than my brain. "Don't hurt them!"

"Take it easy, baby girl." The request came from Gunner, a short-barreled shotgun in one hand. "He's not gonna hurt them. Hades is making sure they stay out of harm's way."

"Bullshit! Look what he did!" I cried, thrusting a hand out toward Liza.

I never got a chance to know her, but even if she was a useless junkie like Gretchen said, she didn't deserve to have her throat ripped out by a dog.

"Hades' work was a kindness. She deserved much worse." Reaper's words floated down another hallway as he approached, dragging something, no, *someone*, behind him. "As do you, Tom."

"No!" My voice squeaked out with shock. Tom was bleeding from the head but alive, wheezing with labored breaths. His legs dragged uselessly behind him at odd angles.

With cool indifference, Reaper grabbed a chunk of Tom's white hair, pulling his head back to bare his throat. In his other hand, he brandished a dagger and pressed it to Tom's neck.

"Stop!" I cried, my voice returning to me. "Why the fuck are you doing this? Just, please stop!"

Reaper looked up, his bright green eyes full of curiosity. "You want me to spare his life?"

"Yes," I breathed, my whole body vibrating with adrenaline. "Please, don't kill any more people."

A cruel smirk pulled at his lips. It didn't matter how attractive he was. In that moment, he was the living embodiment of evil.

He leaned down close to Tom's ear, but I still heard every word.

"Say hello to the devil for me."

Then he pulled the blade across the old man's neck, creating a thin red line that soon began weeping.

"No!"

I ran toward him, not knowing what else to do. My instinct was to heal, to save lives. Death was all around me but I refused to let life slip away without a fight.

Something hard hit me from the side, knocking the wind out of me and sending me tumbling to the floor. My eyes met Tom's, also lying on the floor as he choked on his own blood. Still dizzy and out of breath, I began pulling myself toward him. Four paws clicked across the tile to stand in my way, a menacing growl rumbling right above my head.

Hades, ears pinned back and teeth bared, lowered his head and barked once in my face.

"Fuck you, son of a bitch," I hissed back. The fucking dog must have been the one to run into me, too.

I kept pulling myself forward, fighting to get my legs underneath me. It was probably too late to save Tom, but what kind of medic would I be if I didn't try?

It was no use, though. Teeth grabbed my pant leg and began pulling me backward.

"Let go of me, fucking dog!" I flailed my legs wildly, hoping to kick him in the face, when a human hand wrapped around my arm and yanked me up.

"Let's move." Reaper's hold transferred from my arm to around my waist, pinning me to his side as he dragged me toward the front door. "Jandro, we good?"

"All bikes are good, boss."

The realization hitting me was like a swinging door crashing right into my face.

"What the fuck?" I tried to squirm against Reaper's side but he was too strong and solidly built. "I'm not coming with you! No, you're not taking me! Let me go!"

"Shadow, tie her up, then hand her back to me." He passed me off to the large silent man who already had a length of rope ready.

"Shadow, please," I begged, my whole body trembling as he bound my wrists and forearms. "Don't do this. Please look at me. I—" my throat tightened into a dry knot but I forced the words out anyway. "I like it when you look at me."

He paused, his dark pupil dilated in the dim light coming from inside the building. Bikes turned on and revved up, chasing away the quiet night with their roaring. I knew my time was limited, so I spilled every last plea that I had.

"I'll do whatever you want but I have to stay here. I'm a medic and I have patients at this center that need me. You can come see me any time but please, don't make me go. I can't go. Please make Reaper understand—"

"Shadow?"

With a grunt, the large man shoved me toward the cold-blooded murderer he called President. I stumbled without the use of my arms and Reaper caught me, holding me for a moment against his chest like we were lovers embracing.

The way he looked at me was anything but loving, though, and knowing what those hands did made me want to scrub his touch off of me for hours.

He dragged me toward his bike, his surrounding men already seated on theirs and waiting for their leader. When I dug my feet into the ground, he picked me up and placed me in his bitch seat.

"I'm going to fall off if I can't hold onto anything!" I cried out as he seated himself in front of me.

"Really now?" he looked at me over his shoulder with feigned interest. "You wouldn't prefer that over riding with us?"

I bit back a sob, looking down sullenly at my bound arms in front of me. I would rather do anything than go with them, but dying or getting run over didn't sound appealing either.

"Scoot forward."

When I looked up, Reaper had pulled another length of rope from inside his cut. I did as he instructed, scooting an inch closer to him.

"Closer."

I kept moving forward in the seat as he barked out commands until my thighs were touching his. He then wrapped the rope around both of our torsos, tying it secure at his chest.

"You're welcome to try throwing us both off," he said coolly just as the thought came to me. "But I wouldn't recommend it."

My hope sank like a stone as he reached for the handlebars and took his feet off the ground. The bike lurched forward, picking up speed. Fuck, this was really happening. I'd never reach the Canadian border. I'd never see Gretchen again or give her the chance at her own life.

As Reaper took off, he let out a loud, high-pitched whistle. Seconds later, a dark form ran alongside us. Of course it was Hades, but my fear-stricken brain couldn't comprehend the impossibility of it. A dog running leisurely, lips smiling and tongue lolling out with joy, alongside a motorcycle?

No, all I could do was stare at the Steel Demons' skull emblem, grinning mockingly at me from the back of Reaper's cut, as we rode off into the night.

CHAPTER 7

MARIPOSA

I thought of throwing myself and Reaper off that bike no less than a dozen times. But every time I glanced in one of his mirrors and saw the army of bikes behind us, I chickened out.

Hours crawled by and my body protested every passing minute. I was exhausted but too in pain and desperate to survive to sleep. My ass and thighs cried out from soreness. My arms, still bound in front of me, tingled from numbness, and my back and shoulders killed me. The dry air and sand turned my lips, throat, and eyes to sandpaper.

I'd never ridden on a motorcycle in my life, but it seemed innate to these men. Reaper barely moved in his seat, despite my shifting and wiggling from all the aches and pains.

A dark shape and white teeth grinned at me from the darkness alongside us. Hades? He was *still* running next to his master? Some part of my brain knew that wasn't possible for a normal dog, but it wasn't the main thought plaguing me. My main concern was getting the hell off this bike and escaping whatever the Steel Demons had in store for me.

Some time after the darkness of night began lifting, structures popped up on the horizon to break up the endless landscape of desert.

The houses, all abandoned or taken over by squatters, were some of the largest I'd ever seen. All at least two stories and relatively new, complete with solar panels that became standard about twenty years ago. The rusted, broken sign of the Ferrari dealership in the distance makes it clear that this was once a wealthy neighborhood.

A sudden flapping of wings near my head jolted me upright. Despite all the noise, pain, and fear, it seemed I did manage to doze off for a second. With my face against the back of Reaper's shoulder no less.

Blinking, my dry eyes made out Gunner's falcon flying ahead of the bikes, the blonde demon himself pulling up next to Reaper.

Helmetless, his hair flew out around his face like a halo as he shot a winning grin at his president.

"Woohoo!" he yelled over the roaring engines, raising a hand in the air. My eyes followed the length of his arm to the assault rifle he waved like a flag. "Morning, boys! Welcome home, Demons!"

He sped up ahead to lead the pack of bikers, his falcon keeping pace with him just as Hades was with Reaper. A long, horizontal black line materialized a quarter mile in front of us. As we rode closer my exhausted, dry eyes watched as the line took on the form of a tall, wrought-iron gate, complete with armed guards. Once the guards spotted Gunner waving his weapon, the gates began to open slowly.

Mounted to one of the gate posts, a black flag with the grinning skull of the Steel Demons' emblem waved like from the mast of a pirate ship. It looked to be laughing at me as Reaper's bike passed underneath it and through the gates.

The houses we passed by earlier looked like rundown shacks compared to the ones inside these gates. This was a small community but every single home was a sprawling mansion. When it came to taking up residence somewhere, apparently the Steel Demons had a taste for the finer things.

Motorcycles, pickup trucks, and a few RV campers filled the massive driveways where Ferraris and Porsches once sat. But aside from the stark contrast between homes and vehicles, the lots looked otherwise well-maintained. Lawns were still manicured, front porches were swept and tastefully decorated, and there was no graffiti on the garage doors or other signs of careless squatting.

Reaper turned off of the main road to a cul-de-sac where a single McMansion overtook more than its fair share of the landscape. He stopped his bike in front of the monstrous house, turning to address the convoy of bikers behind him.

"Church at noon," he yelled over the rumbling engines. "Get a few hours of sleep, but don't be fuckin' late."

The others broke away, assumedly riding off to their own million-dollar homes, if dollars were still worth anything.

Reaper pulled up to the driveway and cut the engine before loosening the rope that tied us together. Sore, stiff, and numb, my limbs cried out in protest at this new allocation of movement. Fire shot up my legs and I was suddenly going down, the pavement coming up fast to slap me.

Strong hands grabbed me at the last moment, righting me up as Reaper began dragging me to the front door.

"Please, no," I rasped through cracked lips, my legs buckling underneath me. "Please just let me go."

"Yeah? Be my guest."

Reaper released me suddenly and I fell hard on my ass. He loomed over me, scowling like a fed up father disciplining his child as he thrust a hand out toward the street.

"Go ahead. See how far you make it on foot in the desert. You'll even get to enjoy the sunrise."

I should have moved. I should have scooted, crawled, or even rolled down his damn driveway, but I remained sitting on the pavement. Because I didn't know which scared me more, him or being out there with no resources. I didn't even have my medic pack.

"I didn't think so," he remarked, pulling me to my feet as he shoved the door open. "Noelle!" His voice echoed off the marble tiled floor and high vaulted ceilings as he dragged me inside. "Noelle! Get your ass up!"

I couldn't even appreciate the finery of his house with him yelling like that. My eyes bounced around the elegant fixtures and furniture only in search of a place to hide.

"What the fuck are you yelling so goddamned early for?" a woman's voice called from the top of an elegant, winding staircase.

"Just get down here," Reaper huffed in reply.

A woman with shocking red hair, clearly dyed, floated down the staircase, her silk robe fluttering around her. Colorful tattoos decorated from her wrists up her forearms and disappearing under her robe sleeves. When she reached the bottom step and approached us with a piercing stare, her eyes looked to be the same green as Reaper's.

"Noelle, put her up in one of the guest suites for now," Reaper sighed, his voice heavy with exhaustion. "I need to sleep before holding church in a few hours."

"Okay, sure. By the way, hi, big brother. Nice to see you, too." She folded her arms across her chest, staring at him crossly. "Thanks for bringing home *another* stray before the ass-crack of dawn."

Hades, who had been silent at this point, approached the woman with a high-pitched whine.

"Yeah, mutt. I'm talking about you," she grumbled, stroking the dog's face.

"I've been riding all fuckin' night, I don't have time for this." Reaper was already crossing the room, pulling off his cut and then his T-shirt before disappearing down a hallway. Hades quickly trotted after him, nails clicking over the pristine tiles.

"Well," Noelle placed her hands on her hips, examining me from head to toe. "I'd prefer sleep, too, but guess you're my problem now. Come on up." She began ascending the staircase, throwing me a look over her shoulder when I remained rooted to my spot. "Or just stay there, it makes no difference to me. I assume you want a bath, though. Plus some food and water. Maybe a bed?"

My dry tongue darted out to lick my equally parched lips. I was still too tired, too scared, too fucking confused to make sense of whether I was a guest or a prisoner. My hands were still tied, which had to mean something. But a bath sounded so damn good.

I took small, shuffling steps toward the staircase. It was all I could do as every muscle in my body screamed.

Noelle's face softened as I approached. "That's it. What's your name, hun?"

"Mariposa," I said in a harsh whisper.

"Okay. I know you're skittish but don't be scared, okay?"

She withdrew a knife from the sleeve of her robe, then proceeded to cut the rope binding my wrists and forearms.

"Reaper, you forgetful prick," she muttered, tossing the rope over the railing. "Men are so inconsiderate, aren't they?"

She gave me a smile, but staring back dumbly was the extent of my reaction. Inconsiderate didn't begin to cover murderer, rapist, and abuser.

"Come with me. I'll run you a bath and we'll get some food in you."

I hesitated, wondering if I could make a break for it with my hands now free, but the cramps in my thighs told me I'd end up with a broken neck if I tried going down these stairs by myself. So I followed Noelle up on shaky, excruciating steps.

"I take it you're a virgin?" She flicked a light to reveal a bathroom twice the size of my room back at the service center.

"Huh?" My eyes immediately fell to the mini-fridge stocked with bottles of water and containers of sliced fruit.

"To riding motorcycles." Noelle followed my gaze and opened the fridge, holding out a water and a covered bowl of pineapple chunks. "You're walking like you've never had one of those things between your legs before."

I was too busy tearing open the bottle to respond, dumping the sweet, delicious source of life down my throat until I choked on it.

"Easy," Noelle chuckled, turning two handles on a gigantic porcelain tub. "You'll feel sick."

I emptied the bottle and helped myself to a second one, shoving down pineapple slices in between sips.

"Feeling better?" Noelle looked amused, maybe a little annoyed, but nowhere near as downright murderous as Reaper.

I nodded, my body no longer feeling as thrashed with some food and hydration.

"The water's perfect," Noelle skimmed her hand over the surface of the bathtub. "I turned the jets on, too. They'll help with the soreness you'll feel tomorrow."

"I already feel like roadkill," I muttered, running a hand through my hair. Sand and dirt felt like it caked every inch of my skin and hair. That bath water was going to turn brown the moment I stepped in.

"Ah, she speaks." Noelle smirked. "Well, get on in. I'd give you some privacy but I'm still salty about being woken up, plus the simple fact is you're a stranger in my house. So you're just going to have to deal with me."

Nudity was nothing to me, so I didn't care if she stayed. I'd seen hundreds of different bodies in all kinds of unflattering positions. I just shrugged and stripped out of my well-loved scrubs, eager to wash away the dirt and grime of the desert.

Noelle watched me passively, perched on the edge of the tub as I shed my clothing and sank into the warm water. A soft gasp escaped my mouth at the gentle, kneading pressure of the jets on my exhausted muscles. I closed my eyes and leaned my head back to rest it on the cool, porcelain tile. For the first time in hours, I allowed myself to relax. I might still get killed, but at least I got this bath first.

"So why did my brother bring you home?" Noelle's tone was curious over the soft rumbling of the jets.

"I have no idea," I kept my eyes closed as I answered her, not yet willing to face the reality of where I was. "We've barely spoken a word to each other."

"Where did he find you?"

"At a service center in Old Phoenix."

"Did he fuck you?"

"No." I lifted my head and opened my eyes to look at her. "I don't deal in sex. I'm a trained medic. I had just gotten to that center myself and was helping in the kitchen, too. That's how I had the pleasure of meeting him." I couldn't keep the disdain out of my voice.

Noelle's tattooed eyebrows lifted as she leaned back, her face softening like my admission made perfect sense.

"I see. That explains a lot," she mused.

"I'm glad it does to you. Why not explain it to me since I'm still in the fucking dark?"

She chewed her lips slowly, now taking apparent care to watch what she said.

"Reaper and I lost someone very dear to us," she said softly. "The whole club did, really. That person would still be alive if they had gotten medical attention in time."

"So, what? I'm the new walking, talking first aid kit?" I demanded. "I can refuse to treat people, you know. You can't force me to perform my services."

"Yeah? " Noelle arched a brow with an amused smile. "You'd let people with treatable conditions just get worse and die? Somehow I doubt that, miss medic."

"He could have just asked me!" My anger was returning along with my strength. "He didn't have to kill two people, tie me up, and throw me on the back of a bike like a fucking pirate!"

"But we *are* pirates," Noelle grinned. "We don't ask, we take. It's our way of life."

"I'm a person. You can't just force me to do something against my will."

"Here's where you're forgetting something, Mariposa." Noelle leaned over the tub, bringing her face closer to mine. "There was a little event that happened six years ago called the Collapse."

"I know—“

"No, you really don't," she cut me off. "You were lucky. You were privileged enough to get your fancy medic training, but most of us weren't. So let me spell this out for you."

She grabbed my chin, forcing me to look at her.

"No one has rights anymore. Not to their body, their skills, nothing. If you want to be treated like a person, you have to fight for that. If you don't want to be forced into something, you gotta be stronger than the ones forcing you. Do you understand? Most of the time, it's easier just to go along without a fight. If you value your life, that's what I suggest you do."

She pulled back, pinning me with a green-eyed stare. "If I'm being honest, you're lucky you got picked up by my brother's crew over someone else's."

"What makes you say that?"

"Because in times like these," she rose to her feet, "things can't get much better. But they can always be much, much worse."

Chapter 8

GUNNER

I drained the rest of my coffee and brought the cup down heavily on the table. Six hours of sleep after riding all night was nowhere near enough. Jandro yawned next to me in agreement. The others around the table looked just as worse for wear, but they knew better than to skip official SDMC meetings, otherwise known as church.

Only Reaper and Shadow looked bright-eyed and bushy-tailed, as far as those two scowling bastards could anyway.

"If you're all done nodding off at my table," Reaper growled. "We can begin the meeting." He struck his gavel down on the block and brought up the first and most pressing order of business.

"We will no longer be utilizing the service center outside of Old Phoenix, due to the owner being unable to keep his fucking mouth shut. We'll need a new place to stop for R&R on our eastbound ride. Any ideas?"

"How about that place that used to be a casino?" Brick suggested, scratching his crotch. I told him not to fuck that girl or he'd catch something. "It's a bit north but not too far out of the way."

"Too big," Reaper shook his head. "With so many drifters congregating in one place, it'd be easy for someone to sneak up and gank one of us."

"You saying we need somewhere more intimate?" Jandro asked with a lazy smile. "Some place cozy and comfortable, with some home cookin'?"

Reaper rolled his eyes at his VP's choice of words, but nodded. "It was unfortunate Tom had to break our agreement, but that place was damn near perfect for our needs. Good food, space for the bikes, comfortable beds, and right on our main route. It'll be hard to replace."

"Pussy was top-notch, too," added Big G with a sad shake of his head.

Jandro shifted uncomfortably in his seat, illustrating how we all felt. Big G's wife was heavily pregnant with their third child. None of us ordinarily cared how others conducted their personal lives—we all came from different backgrounds after all. Being married with side chicks was just how some men lived their lives. But Tess was a good, loyal woman. One of the few who would never even look at another man. The least he could do was be more discreet about messing around on her.

I cleared my throat to break up the awkwardness. "Maybe we ought to look at some maps and scout some places out first. We got two weeks until our next drop, so that should give us time."

Reaper nodded. "You, me, and Jandro will discuss it this evening at my house, if nobody else has any bright ideas."

Reaper's eyes swept across the faces at the table. When no one responded, he leaned back in his leather chair and lifted his chin at me.

"Gunner, what's the latest on this drop?"

"Smooth sailing as usual, boys," I announced, unfolding my inventory sheet with a smile to my brothers. "General Tash's resistance has the weapons they need to maintain control of the border. In exchange for ten handguns, twenty-four hunting rifles, six assault rifles, four cases of grenades, plus accessories like extended mags, scopes, and speedloaders, we have received one full pallet of the finest motor oil, already processed, half a pallet of fresh steaks, none of that dried meat, boys!"

I paused in my report to let everyone moan and salivate, rubbing their bellies at the thought of a freshly grilled hunk of meat fit for a king. Salami and jerky could only whet a man's appetite so much.

"God, I can't wait to fire up the grill tonight," Jandro licked his lips.

"We also received," I continued, "two kilos of solid copper, one kilo of high-grade steel, and one pound of dried chilis." I set my paper down. "To season our meat with, I'm assuming."

That got a light chuckle out of some people, but Reaper's voice barked out from across the table. "What's General Tash renaming the New Mexico territory again?"

"New Ireland," I scoffed with an eye roll. "Because dried chilis and Southwestern desert is exactly what one pictures when you think of Ireland."

"So what's in store for the next drop?" Hades' black nose peered over the edge of the table next to his master, earning an affectionate ear stroke.

"Mostly ammo for the guns," I answered. "I already contacted our supplier to put that together. General Tash also asked me," I rubbed my chin, the five o'clock shadow itching my usually clean-shaven face, "about getting a few drones, which I haven't dealt with before. I'm putting some feelers out there to see what I can find but no major bites yet."

"Drones," Jandro scoffed. "Good for dropping off packages, pretty useless for actual warfare, unless anyone can break into the old Pentagon."

"Not to mention, they're easy to shoot," Reaper added. "Probably expensive and not really worth it."

"If they have cameras, the video can be saved immediately," I pointed out. "Even if the drone is lost, they're good for gathering intel. I made no promises, except to look into it."

Reaper spread his hands and shrugged. "I'm open to it, as long as the cost is low and we exchange for resources valuable to us."

"Oh, you know me, Mr. President," I winked across the table. "I'll find the best deal I can and nothing else."

"Great. So does anyone else have club business they need to address?"

Nothing but silence around the table, to which Reaper nodded. "Good. Church will resume on Sunday next week, usual time." He lifted the gavel, but before he could strike it down, Jandro raised a hand.

"Hold up, boss. You're not gonna say a word about *Marrriposa?*"

Reaper's hard scowl across the table at his VP could make a man shit himself. It only made Jandro smile smugly in return.

"We took a girl from the Old Phoenix center," Reaper voiced reluctantly. "She's currently in one of my guest rooms, and may or may not fit in to club life. That has yet to be seen."

"Pres, I've never seen you take a girl for yourself before. Why's this one special?" Big G shot him a toothy smile. "And are ya up for sharing?"

"You'll keep your cock zipped up, G," Reaper snarled at him. "The truth is, she's a medic, but that means nothing at this point. Like I said, we'll see if she fits in."

"And if she doesn't?"

Reaper lifted his eerily bright green eyes to me. "Then we'll return her to where we found her."

Chapter 9

MARIPOSA

I had no idea how long I slept. All I knew was this bed was *damn* comfortable.

With a groan, I flopped over, pressing my face into the pillow that perfectly supported my sore neck and shoulders all night. Or all day, rather.

Sunlight peeked through thick curtains and the room was quiet. It even felt peaceful. I couldn't remember the last time I slept that deeply. Traveling on my own kept me on edge. Peace and comfort felt strange and unfamiliar.

I sat up and looked around the simply furnished room. There wasn't much to it besides the bed, a desk, dresser, and an armchair in the corner. Compared to the service station, though, it was downright luxurious.

A set of folded clothes, which I assumed to be Noelle's, sat on top of the dresser. I climbed out of bed and went to get dressed, the strangeness of this room and everything that happened crawling over me like fingers on my skin.

Why was she lending me clothes? Why was this room so nice? This was some kind of biker gang compound. Why wasn't I chained up in a dark, dingy basement?

The questions continued racing through my brain as I pulled on the breezy harem pants and form-fitting tank top. Typical desert dweller clothes, nothing that would suggest I was a prisoner.

Tiptoeing to the bedroom door, I pushed it open with painstaking care to not make a sound. Male voices floated up to my ears from somewhere downstairs. I looked both ways down the hall and saw no sign of Noelle.

I crept toward the balcony overlooking the first floor. A quick peek down showed no one near the stairs, so I began my slow descent down.

The voices grew louder and more clear as I reached the bottom, coming from somewhere near the kitchen.

"...the Sandia Mountains? It's too far out of the way, it'll be murder on the bikes..." That sounded like Jandro.

I glued myself to the wall like a gecko as I made my way closer. If they were planning a ride, maybe I could overhear when and make my escape.

"Horus can scout for us from those high vantage points. Isn't that right, boy?"

A screech echoing off the wall announced Gunner's presence with his falcon. The skin on my neck shivered at the memory of the blonde man's lips touching me, but I couldn't place if the reaction was out of disgust or enjoyment.

He associates with a murderer, I reminded myself. *And as a 2A advocate, he's very likely a murderer himself.*

"We've got to stay out of Razor Wire territory." The gruffest voice in the room could only be Reaper. "The mountains can give us shelter if we pack accordingly."

"It's a risk, man." Jandro seemed to be the only one hesitant about the idea. "It's a longer ride, big elevation climbs, plus we're going to be carrying heavier loads. Some of the older bikes might not be able to handle it."

"I'm leaving it up to you to ensure the bikes are in the best possible shape. Even if that means scrapping the old ones and putting together new ones."

"Man, you know how attached these guys are to their babies. I can't just—"

"You will."

"So, what, this is a done deal already? Don't we need to vote on this at church?"

I couldn't hear Reaper's answer over the clicking of claws on the tiled floor, growing louder with every second. When a long snout and shiny black eyes came around the corner to greet me, I panicked.

"Shoo!" I whispered at Hades, flinging my hands at him. "Go away!"

The large dog smiled at me instead, wagging his stubby tail as he lifted his front paws to my shoulders to greet me.

"Hades, no!" I groaned under his weight as I tried to shove him off. The damn dog had to weigh at least a hundred pounds and was built out of dense, solid muscle. It was like trying to shove off a person-sized brick that fell on me.

"Hades!" Reaper's voice barked from inside the dining room, followed by a high-pitched whistle.

With a soft, whining growl, the Doberman brought all four paws back to the floor but it was too late then. Heavy footsteps stomped across the floor until I was looking at three distinct but ridiculously handsome faces.

"*Marrriposa*," Jandro grinned, saying my name in that stupidly hot accent of his. "You look well-rested. And if I may say, *well*." His eyes lowered deliberately from my face to the deep V in my tank top. I felt the red flush creeping up my neck immediately.

"What were you doing out here?" Reaper was clearly not amused like his VP, but he asked the question with a simmering calm. "Eavesdropping?"

"What else am I supposed to do?" I shot back. "I'm here against my will, I have this whole house to roam, and no fucking clue why I'm here."

It was probably unwise to talk back to a killer, but not knowing a damn thing was eating away at me. I was also banking on the idea that if I was a guest in his house, my head was probably not on the chopping block. Plus his dog liked me, so that had to be something, right?

"Mm." Gunner sucked his bottom lip between his teeth, blue eyes shimmering with mischief. "She's a feisty one, Reap. Whatever you plan with her, hope you keep her around."

"Get the fuck out of here," his surly president replied. "Both of you. Get shit set up for the barbecue. I'll catch you there later."

Jandro and Gunner left while snickering to each other, which made my stomach drop.

"Hades," Reaper breathed softly. "Kennel, boy."

The dog trotted off obediently back toward the study. Then it was just the Steel Demons' president staring me down in his decked-out luxury home. He had all the power here and we both knew it. I was well and truly fucked.

"What were you hoping to gain by listening to my conversation?" He started toward me, prompting me to back away.

"What do you want from me?" I stammered in return—my mind, body, and soul now in complete fight or flight mode.

Something hit my back—the bannister to the stairs. Reaper's hands shot out to grab it on either side of me, caging me in with no escape.

"Answer my question." He leaned in so close, the intensity of his eyes burning into mine. When I lowered my gaze, I got an eyeful of those full lips and the dimple in his chin I hadn't noticed before. He had shaved since coming home.

"To find out when you'd be going on another ride," I confessed. "So I could escape."

"Escape?" he barked out a laugh in my face and pulled one hand off of the railing, gesturing to the front door. "I told you this morning. You're welcome to leave whenever you'd like."

"I don't believe you," I seethed, willing my voice not to shake. "You're a murderer. You'll leave me to die."

He rolled his eyes as if dealing with a petulant teenager. "I'm not responsible for you if you leave this place. If you die out there, it's your own fucking problem."

I noticed he made no denial to me calling him a murderer, which just scared me even more. The way his eyes started roaming over my bare shoulders and chest made me fucking paralyzed.

"I don't see you running," he mocked. "Still too sore from the ride?"

His fingers closed around my shoulders and I gasped—partially from the fear of him touching me, but also at the pressure he put on a certain point right between my shoulder and my back.

It felt...*good*.

His fingers worked in a circle, driving deep into the knot behind my shoulder. I gasped again, the massage toeing the line between pleasure and pain. A smug grin crossed his face at my reaction.

"Turn around," he instructed.

"No."

"Turn. Around."

"I don't want to—" my lip wobbled, images of Gretchen, Kitty, and all the girls standing in my line at the service center. I didn't want to join them as one of the sea of faces used by men.

"It'll feel better if I can reach your sore spots easier," Reaper said.

"You expect me to believe that's *all* you want to do?" I hissed through gritted teeth.

He merely looked annoyed. "I don't fuck women against their will, so you can relax. It does nothing for me."

The admission was surprising but I was not about to let my guard down. "You say that like you've tried it a few times before."

"I haven't." He withdrew his hands from my shoulders, shoving them in his jeans pockets. "The thought of it doesn't even get me hard."

"Oh, how noble of you," I sneered. "You don't rape women but you still kill people. What a stand-up guy you are."

"Can you name three men who haven't killed someone since the Collapse?" he shot back. "Of course, I kill when it's necessary. But preying on women, who are naturally smaller and weaker than men?

Only cowards and weaklings do that, and I have no room for them in my club."

I stared at him, genuinely surprised to hear this coming from the leader of a ruthless road crew. So many men these days believed they were entitled to everything, including a woman's body. It was the main reason our rights were stripped away in so many areas, so we couldn't fight back with the law, our education, anything.

"So you didn't kidnap me to...have your way with me?"

A lazy grin pulled at the corners of Reaper's lips. "Do you know why SDMC has the reputation that it does?" When I shook my head, he explained, "Because I gathered a crew of *real* men. Men of strength and integrity. We're strong because we push our limits. We seek fights that challenge us. A dog doesn't get stronger by chasing prey that's already limping."

He rubbed his palms together, tilting his head in an almost dog-like way. I could see Hades doing the exact same thing. "And as a result of that," he concluded. "Women flock to us of their own free will."

My stomach tightened with a feeling I couldn't place. He, Jandro, Gunner, and even Shadow, were gorgeous specimens. Of course they had plenty of women to choose from.

"None of that explains what you want with me," I reminded him. "Noelle said you—"

His arms shot out again, muscles flexing as he gripped the bannister on both sides of me.

"Turn around and I might tell you." His voice carried a hint of teasing, a far cry from his snapping president voice.

This time I did as he ordered, my heart crashing so hard against my ribs, I was certain he'd feel it.

After a moment of nothing, the weight of his hands came down on my shoulders with more gentleness than I expected. The moment his thumbs pressed into the aching knots in my back, another gasp escaped my mouth. This time followed by a small moan.

He didn't react to the noise, the pressure of his thumbs steadily digging into my flesh. I clamped my mouth shut in an effort to not let out any more embarrassing noises, but I couldn't help allowing my eyelids to flutter closed.

It hurt so fucking good.

When those muscles turned to jelly, he moved onto my arms without a word, rubbing into my triceps with painful, releasing bliss.

"Why are you doing this?" I asked as the minutes stretched on, and his skilled hands moved to the center of my back.

"Because I want to and you're letting me."

"What's the *real* answer?"

"You know," he mused, fingertips skimming across my waist. "You'd enjoy this a lot more without clothes in the way."

"Not happening," I snapped.

"Just thought I'd try," he chuckled.

Any retort I had went out the window as his hands continued working magic on my back. He stayed completely focused on the muscles and didn't try to sneak a feel anywhere else. I stayed tense and alert, just waiting for him to try something but it never came.

Just as I was about to fully let go and completely melt under his touch, the pressure of his hands lifted away.

"Have you eaten today?"

I turned to face him, still a bit on edge despite being far more relaxed than before. He stood a respectful distance away, hands shoved back in his pockets with an expectant look.

"No, I guess I haven't."

"Come to the barbecue tonight." The way he said it made it clear it was an order, not a suggestion. "Have a small taste of our life, and a plate of ribeye while you're at it."

My eyes widened. "Ribeye like the steak?" Fresh meat, especially red meat, was incredibly expensive and hard to come by.

"No, like the ribs with eyes," he teased. "Of course the steak."

"Who'd you have to kill for that?"

"No one. This time." His green eyes danced with humor, but those words slapped me with cold, hard reality.

He was a killer. And unlike men conscripted for the border wars like my father, he was comfortable joking about killing people. It didn't haunt him like it did normal men.

If nothing else, Reaper did live up to his name.

"Get cleaned up. Noelle will loan you a hairbrush, I'm sure. We'll see you there."

Ah yes, now was the perfect time to remember I just rolled out of bed and looked like a hot mess while being sensually massaged by a murderer's hands.

"We?" I repeated. "The, uh, whole club will be there?"

"Yes." His green gaze slid away from me as he turned and began a slow walk back to his study. "But so will Noelle and the old ladies of my men. The women will make you feel safe and welcome."

I watched his back retreat and he disappeared without another word.

Chapter 10

MARIPOSA

I stared at myself in Noelle's vanity mirror as she ran a brush through my hair, which nearly hit my waist at this point.

"You lucky bitch, I'm so jealous," Noelle mused. "I wish I had hair like yours. Mine always starts breaking off when it hits a certain length. I can't let it grow past my tits for the life of me."

"Seriously?" I looked up at her reflection. "At least your color is way more fun than mine." There was nothing special about my hair, as far as I could tell. It was just a plain, normal brown.

"Oh, please," Noelle huffed. "This shit's from a box. My natural color is a dishwater dirty blonde. At least yours has some richness to it."

"Really? I figured your hair would be dark like Reaper's."

"Nah." She sprayed some kind of fruity-smelling mist over my hair before continuing with her brushing. "Aside from our eye color, no one would know we're related. We're actually half siblings. Same mom, different dads, not that it mattered to us. Daren had a different dad, too—"

She stopped talking abruptly, her face hardening as she brushed through the last of my bedhead tangles.

"Had?" I pressed gently. "Is he the one you guys lost?"

"I shouldn't talk about it," she muttered, tidying up her products on the vanity. "Reaper gets pissed if I so much as think about him. You ready?"

Deciding not to press anymore, I returned my gaze to myself in the mirror. Noelle turned my tangled, dried-out rat's nest into soft waves cascading over my shoulders. The brown locks framing my face, I looked more like my Latino dad's side of the family. The Southwestern sun had darkened my skin to a medium-olive, and my now-moisturized lips were redder thanks to Noelle's tinted lip balm. Only my hazel, not quite brown, eyes alluded to something else in my ancestry.

"Yeah. Thanks, Noelle." I allowed a tiny smile at my reflection. "I look like a different person."

"I knew there was a cutie-patootie hiding under there," she grinned. "Let's go. I'm dying for a steak dinner."

Following her lead down the ridiculous staircase, which no longer made my thighs scream as badly, we went out the front door and walked across the cul-de-sac to a small path through the neighborhood.

"Where is the barbecue?" I asked her, hoping my nervousness didn't show. "At someone else's house?"

"Nah, you'll see," she answered. "There's a central clubhouse where they hold church and any kind of parties or meetings for the whole 'hood. Did I tell you what this place is called, by the way?"

"No, what?"

She smiled at me over her shoulder. “Sheol.”

“What’s it mean?”

“It’s an old Biblical term for the grave, or Hell. Gunner thought of it. Fitting, huh?”

“Yeah...” My enthusiasm was nowhere near the same level as hers.

I smelled the food cooking before we saw it, and my stomach rippled with a growl of hunger. Voices began floating up in the warm, early evening air, accompanied by what sounded like water splashing.

We came to a flat-roofed single-story building a few minutes later, clearly the HOA clubhouse for this ritzy community before the SDMC moved in. Noelle led me around to the back side of the building. Sure enough, there was a glittering blue pool, illuminated by lights both inside and outside of the water. People were swimming, splashing, talking, and drinking.

Noelle opened the wrought-iron gate of the surrounding fence and led me inside. Only then did I get a true sense of how many people lived here.

Two men laughing over beers tended to thick, juicy steaks sizzling on a grate over a rectangular fire pit. More people, men and women, checked over the four smaller barbecue pits near the perimeter of the patio area. A large awning from the main building hung over the grills and patio furniture scattered around, while still a safe distance from the pool. Long tables stretched in front of the couches and smaller, bistro tables were placed by lounge chairs.

At least thirty people gathered here, drinking and eating together like family. What shocked me the most was seeing that there were *actual* families. I recognized one of Reaper's men holding a toddler against his waist, his arm around a woman's shoulders as he talked to another guy. I stared openly as he kissed the woman's temple, and she beamed at him with pure love in her eyes.

I felt like my brain was broken. I found it impossible to reconcile that these men—road pirates, thieves, and murderers—had children and loved ones waiting for them at home.

"Let's sit with Tessa." Noelle broke into my thoughts and pulled me toward a heavily pregnant woman sitting on one of the couches.

"Nellie!" The woman squealed and began pushing herself but Noelle put a stop to that immediately.

"Nope! None of that, old lady! You stay right where you are."

Tessa relented, relaxing back as she held her arms out to hug Noelle. "Oh, I miss you, hun," she cooed against Noelle's bright red hair. "These kids don't give me a free minute, I tell you."

"Honey, I told you I can help with them," Noelle chastised gently before looking over at me. "Tessie, this is Mariposa. Reaper brought her from a service center on the last ride."

"Ohh welcome, sweetie! Nice to meet you!" Tessa smiled glowingly up at me. "It's so nice to see Reaper's found someone—"

"Oh no, there's nothing between us," I interrupted her. "No offense, but I didn't exactly come here willingly."

Tessa's smile didn't falter. "Well, he must've seen something special in you, to have rescued you from your situation."

I couldn't believe my ears. Was she brainwashed by these people?

"He did *not* rescue me. He kinda—"

"Hey, let's grab a drink!" Noelle cut me off with a tense smile before pulling me over to a large tub of ice with various cans and bottles stuck inside. "Can you just cool it for a damn minute?" she hissed under her breath. "I get why you're upset, but don't take it out on my pregnant, hormonal friend."

Shit, I definitely should've known better. Picking my battles was not my strong suit.

"Sorry," I sighed, leaning over the ice tub. "What's good to drink?" Maybe a few alcoholic beverages would take the edge off. *Although another massage from Reaper wouldn't hurt.*

I shook the thought from my head just as Noelle began pointing out drinks. "The hard lemonade's pretty good. The dark bottles are malt liquor some of the guys made. Drink that at your own risk."

"Hard lemonade it is." I pulled a bottle out and twisted off the cap as we made our way back to Tessa.

"Sorry about that earlier," I forced a smile at her as I sank down next to her on the couch. "I just...didn't expect to end up here and I don't know anything about MC life."

"Aww, that's all right, sweetie," she clasped one of my hands and returned my smile. "It's a different way of life, for sure. Takes some getting used to. Life after the Collapse either swallowed men up whole, or it made them stronger. These men," she nodded out toward the barbecue pits and the pool, "they're the strong ones. But carrying all that weight on their shoulders has its consequences, too. That's why they need good women around," she added with a pat to my hand.

I drank from my bottle as I listened to her. "So, I take it you're someone's old lady?"

"Mm-hmm. That one's mine right there, with the two rugrats," she pointed to the other side of the pool, where a large, burly man held the hands of two children. "You can't have him," she added with a playful smack to my thigh.

I forced a chuckle, then swallowed my response with another pull of my lemonade. That was the guy getting his dick sucked by Kitty out in the lobby. With how dreamily Tessa looked at him with their children, I couldn't imagine she had any idea.

"What about you, Noelle?" I looked down the couch to her. "Are you with anyone?"

"Hah," she scoffed. "Even if I was, Reaper would have him dead and buried within a week. The bastard's so overprotective, he's more like a father than a brother sometimes."

"Well, that's understandable, considering what happened to Daren," Tessa mused before her gaze snapped over to me. "Do you know about him?"

"She doesn't," Noelle snapped.

"Ah, well." Tessa smoothed her hands in her lap while I wondered why everyone was so hush-hush about this Daren person. "Reaper just wants you to have a good man," she continued to Noelle. "Once you find someone worthy of you, I'm sure he'll approve."

"Again, acting like my father," the red-haired woman grumbled.

"He has to approve every union in the club," Tessa replied as if reminding her. "That's just our way."

"You ladies ready for steak?" called one of the men at the central fire pit.

"Took y'all long enough!" Noelle jumped to her feet. "Come on, Mari. Help me make a plate for Tessa."

"Better make it two," Tessa laughed, rubbing her belly.

Noelle and I grabbed paper plates and I nearly salivated when the thick, juicy hunk of meat dropped onto it. Saving the bigger one for Tessa, we made our rounds to the smaller grills where people roasted corn, potatoes, bell peppers, and other assortments of veggies and sides. If my circumstances of being here were different, I would have been thrilled to have been invited to this block party. It felt so wholesome, warm, and pre-Collapse. It made me nostalgic for the neighborhood cookouts of my childhood. I didn't know anyone still had a community like this, much less a biker gang.

"Having fun, *Marrriposa*?"

I looked up to see Jandro's flirtatious smile as he wielded a pair of metal tongs in one hand.

"I guess you could say that."

He laughed in response. "It's okay to admit you're having a good time. We know how to party." With his tongs he picked up an ear of corn from the grill, charred to perfection and slathered in butter.

"Would you like a long, hard, succulent corn to go with your thick, juicy meat?"

"Sure." I held out my plate, keeping my face neutral at his innuendo. "I'll take another one for Tessa."

"Mm, I love it when girls double up." He placed another on my second plate. "Makes everything so much more filling, doesn't it?"

"Thanks, Jandro," I grumbled, my face on fire despite my desperate attempt to be unaffected by him.

"Sure thing. Come back to me if you need more," he winked, thoroughly enjoying my discomfort.

I turned to head back to the couches, nearly crashing into a massive, dark form.

"Oh shit, I'm sorry!"

My neck craned up to meet the one dark eye staring back at me. Shadow. I didn't know how I missed seeing him with how big he was. He apparently lived up to his name.

The big man took a seat in a lounge chair next to Jandro's, bringing a large bottle to his lips and drinking deeply. My mouth fell open at the realization he was drinking straight tequila.

"Move it, girl. I'm starving," Noelle complained from behind me.

I hurried back next to Tessa, who licked her lips at the full plate I set down in front of her.

"You are a goddamn angel," she moaned as she began carving into her steak.

The three of us didn't talk much as we stuffed our faces. Tessa mumbled to Noelle between bites about her kids and pregnancy while I took the opportunity to people-watch.

Reaper and Gunner were nowhere to be seen, which surprised me. Scanning the area, I spotted Hades reclining next to a retaining wall, chewing on a bone while Horus perched on the wall above him.

The falcon gnawed at a piece of raw meat in his talon, tearing off chunks to swallow whole while Hades looked up hopefully as if waiting for a piece to drop. When the bird finished its meal without leaving a scrap behind, he let out a series of short screeches as if he were laughing. Hades responded with a toothy smile, yipping softly in return as he stretched out along the floor.

I blinked and returned to watching the humans on the patio. Watching animals act like they were communicating was a bit too trippy for me. But if they were here, their owners had to be nearby.

My attention returned to Jandro and Shadow, lounging by the grill as they drank and the handsome Latin man served up corn. While Jandro did most of the talking to his tall, dark friend, I did spot Shadow's lips moving as well.

So he's not completely silent, I thought as I chewed my steak. *He must just be highly selective as to who he talks to.*

Keeping this in mind, my eyes drifted over the pool just as a figure lifted himself out with a powerful push of his arms.

My chewed-up steak nearly fell out of my mouth at the sight of Reaper's lean, chiseled form rising out of the water. The grinning, horned skull of the Steel Demons emblem decorated his chest, accented by flames and smoke licking across from his collarbone to just below his pecs. His abs flexed as he stepped onto the pool deck, a tiny river of water running down between the ridges of muscle before he toweled himself off.

As if that sight wasn't enough, Gunner jumped out right behind him. The blonde, blue-eyed demon looked like a surfer, but coming out of the water, he could have been Poseiden himself. His long, golden locks slicked back, his physique was leaner than Reaper's. His muscles were just as prominent, but longer and with slightly less bulk. The V in his slender hips cut deep and defined, his swim trunks hanging dangerously low.

"Still think you're not Reaper's girl?" Tessa interrupted my ogling with a playful jab to my ribs. "Mr. President sure is easy on the eyes."

"Shit, two-thirds of the men here are," Noelle laughed. "That's the real torture, Mari. Being surrounded by all this eye candy."

My eyes bounced back and forth between Reaper and Gunner accepting drinks as they toweled off, a small crowd gathering around them, and Jandro and Shadow keeping quietly to themselves across the patio.

"Tell me something," I said to no one in particular. "I thought Jandro was Reaper's VP."

"He is," Tessa confirmed.

"So why are Reaper and Gunner always together, and Jandro's always with Shadow?"

My two companions exchanged glances and I wondered if, like the Daren business, this was something I wasn't supposed to know.

"All four of them are close. Best friends, basically," Noelle said, choosing her words carefully. "But Shadow is kind of a black sheep, as you can tell."

"He's not right in the head," Tessa added in a whisper.

"Well, something happened to him," Noelle explained. "I don't know exactly but whatever it was, Jandro knows best how to deal with him."

"He's like a service dog," Tessa nodded. "A service human, I guess."

"And Gunner is the club's arms dealer and captain of the guard," Noelle said. "He's basically the one in charge of bringing in all the goods to our community, so he always has Reaper's ear."

"I see." I bit off more steak and chewed it thoughtfully.

"Jandro's a good VP," Noelle mused. "He's one of those who considers all options, while my damn brother is more of a hot head. They balance each other well. It's just Jandro's usually stuck babysitting Shadow."

I hung onto every word she said, carefully filing the information away to use later.

For when I finally could escape without losing my life.

Chapter 11

REAPER

Gunner was only better than me at two things in life—negotiating weapons deals and holding his breath under water.

My lungs burning, I burst out of the water first. Again.

"Son of a bitch's tit," I muttered, pulling myself up out of the pool.

"Whooo!" the blonde asshole hollered, raising his fists as he flipped his hair back like a fucking mermaid. "I win again! I'll take my steak medium-rare, boss."

"You'll take my balls on your chin nicely, too," I shot back, snapping a towel at him with a grin. "Give me a second to dry off."

"Oh, I got all fuckin' night." He rubbed a towel over his head, making his hair stick out in all directions like a lion's mane, before grabbing a beer from an ice bucket and heading off to mingle.

After thoroughly drying my torso, I wrapped my towel around my waist and took a seat in a chair near the pool. I took a moment to soak it all in, the atmosphere and the energy. These were my people, and I was responsible for them.

Everyone seemed happy. The air felt upbeat and positive. We had a good run. Gunner negotiated a hell of a deal with General Tash and the exchange went smoothly, with both sides delivering exactly as promised. And most importantly, we didn't lose anyone.

I fished a beer out of the bucket next to me and cracked it open, taking long pulls as I people-watched. Dallas and Andrea kissed, staring at each other all googly-eyed while their kids chased each other around the fire pit. Big G played Marco Polo in the pool with his kids. Even Shadow was saying a few words, by the looks of it.

Something cold and wet nudged the edge of my palm, and I looked down to see Hades nuzzling me. I scratched his ears as he rested his head on my knee, looking up at me with those impossibly dark eyes.

"How long's it gonna last, boy?" I asked, moving the scratches down to his neck. "How long can I keep these people safe from what's out there?"

He licked my hand with a soft yip, then lifted his head from my leg to look behind him. Right at Mariposa, sitting between Noelle and Tessa.

The one place I refused to look.

With a sigh, I followed my dog's gaze. My eyes traveled up her legs, whose shape I could still make out in those loose harem pants, to the dipping curves of her waist. I was biting inside my cheek during that massage earlier, wrestling the urge to see just how well my hands would fit in those sweet curves.

As my eyes moved up, relishing in the swells of her tits and her long, graceful neck, her eyes jerked away from mine right before our gazes met. She suddenly appeared very interested in the conversation Noelle and Tessa were having.

I adjusted my dick and polished off my beer, then rose to grab a steak to throw on the grill for Gunner. As soon as the meat began sizzling, I grabbed another beer and meandered to where the women sat.

"Get enough to eat?"

Mariposa jumped at the sound of my voice. A whole lot of good that massage did, jumpy and tense as she was. Not that I would mind touching her again, preferably with less clothing on.

"Yes," she said carefully, watching me sit on the couch next to her. "And it was delicious, thank you."

"We've gone from threatening escape to thanking me," I noted. "Not bad progress for your first day here."

She bristled, her hands clenched in her lap. "I'll never be ungrateful for a good meal. No matter who it comes from."

"Splendid. You just may learn how to live in a post-Collapse society after all." I stood again to check Gunner's steak. The moment I turned my back, Hades stuck his face between her knees and turned up the puppy dog eyes.

"Why the hell does my dog like you so much?" The question had been on my mind since I watched him sit on his ass for a treat from her.

"I don't know." She massaged his face with her thumbs. "Dogs can sense things people can't. I had a veterinarian friend say they can smell your emotional state. Whether you're afraid, angry, or happy."

"Hades definitely smells fear." I flipped Gunner's steak. "But his normal reaction is to get his teeth in their face and turn that fear into terror, not ask for pets."

"Well, maybe he knows something else about me."

"Like what?"

"I'm not sure." Her eyes lifted to me again. "Maybe he knows all I try to do is help people."

"Huh," I scoffed. "Gunner! Come get your fucking steak!"

"Why, thank you, boss." His hair now fluffy like newborn chick feathers, he marched over to me with a shit-eating grin and his chest puffed out. "It better be medium-rare or you're gonna have to cook me another one."

"Don't push your luck, bimbo." I passed over the meat on a plate, noticing his eyebrows lift with curiosity at me sitting so close to Mariposa.

I ignored him and went back to sit down, her last sentence mulling around in my head.

"So if I or any of my men were badly injured," I mused, "you'd still try to save us?"

"Yes," she answered without hesitation. "It's my duty as a medic to protect life. I swore an oath upon completing nursing school."

"Huh," I scoffed again, almost choking on my beer. "Oaths are meaningless."

Her expression didn't change. "Not if you take them to heart. I've never gone against my oath to save lives."

"Really?" I leaned in closer to her. "You're telling me if Garold Richardson was lying at your feet right now, bleeding to death, you'd do everything in your power to save his life?"

Her eyes narrowed at the man's name, the eightieth and last President of the United States, and the dipshit who plunged the country headfirst into the Collapse. According to multiple radio announcements, he was one of the first to abandon this mess he created, taking off on his private jet to Morocco or who-the-fuck knows where.

"Yes," she replied with a bit more hesitation this time. "It doesn't matter who the person is. If a life is in danger, I'm sworn to save it."

"Hmm." I didn't entirely believe her. "You may be the only person in the world who takes your oath that seriously."

"It wouldn't matter if he died before, you know, all this," she continued softly. "At least I don't think so. The Collapse would have still happened whether he or some other bureaucratic shithead was in office."

"You're probably right," I mused, rubbing my jaw. "The Collapse was a long time coming."

"Seems you've done well for yourself." Her expression was somewhere between curious and challenging. My beer paused on its way to my mouth and I wasn't sure how to respond.

A smile twitched on my lips and I almost forgot about my regret of bringing an educated woman into my club. Not many people challenged me these days, and I forgot how much I liked it.

"Reaper?"

A shrill voice cut into my thoughts, quickly followed by a low warning growl from Hades.

"Heather," I returned begrudgingly to the woman making her way across the patio to me. Her bolted-on tits defied gravity in a way that I never cared for. Come to think of it, her fried, bleached blonde hair and caked-on makeup never did it for me either. Hindsight is 20/20 after all.

"You haven't come to see me since you got back," she pouted, crossing her arms under those ridiculous melons.

"I've been busy," I said dismissively. "So have you, apparently." I nodded to the two guys she'd been sucking face with all night, Bones and Python. They nodded back to me and lifted their drinks in respect.

"I'm never too busy for you, Mr. President," she cooed, running a manicured finger along my jawline. "Want to go back to your house? I missed you."

"I will eventually," I said, batting her hand away. "But not with you."

Her face fell. "Why not?"

"Because I don't want to fuck you." I shot her my best apologetic look. "It's nothing personal."

"But...why?" she asked with such a crestfallen look, as if it never occurred to her that a man could say no to sex.

"Because I'm fucking tired of questions like these," I snarled. "Almost as tired of thrusting my dick into you while you lie back and do nothing."

Python choked on his drink and a few conversations near us went quiet. I didn't set out to humiliate her, but the woman should've known to take no for an answer, especially from her president.

"Is there someone else?" Her lip wobbled. Fuck me, she would not quit.

"Of course there is." It wasn't true, not right at that moment. But I'd have some chick worshiping my cock soon enough for that statement to be true.

"Who?" Heather demanded, her eyes falling on Mariposa, who watched the whole exchange silently. "Who the hell are *you?* I've never seen you here before!"

"Bones, Python," I snapped before Mariposa could answer. "Come get your woman under control."

Both of them jumped to attention, practically shoving each other out of the way to reach her first.

"Sorry, Reaper," Bones mumbled, a blush creeping up his bald head. "We didn't know if you'd take her up on it."

"I won't be anymore, not after this bullshit. She's all yours, boys." I turned back to Heather, holding my index finger up in her face. "You don't make demands of me. You don't beg me for shit. If I give you an answer, you take it and move on. You're not in charge of anything here, especially not my cock. You understand me, woman?"

Hades growled louder and barked, snapping his teeth near her legs for added effect.

"Yes, Reaper," she whispered meekly, shrinking back to her two men, who looked at me expectantly.

"Punish her as you see fit," I sighed, reclining on the couch. "I'm done being involved."

"Yes, Reaper." They marched her away through the gate surrounding the pool.

I drained the last of my second beer, feeling Mariposa's eyes on me the whole time.

"What are they going to do to her?" she asked.

"Don't know, don't care." I rested a hand on my chest, partially on the SDMC skull inked there. "Not my problem anymore. They're not the brightest bunch, but they won't break any club laws."

"You said punish her." Mariposa's voice was more tense than a guitar string. "What does that entail?"

I shrugged. "Spanking. Whipping. Tying her to the bed for a full day. Not letting her orgasm for a month. Giving her an embarrassing tattoo. Walking her around on a dog leash. Whatever they see fit. Nothing that causes long-lasting harm."

Her shoulders relaxed just slightly, making me remember how they melted under my touch earlier today. The thought made my fingers on my chest twitch.

"That still seems harsh." She chewed her plump lower lip. "Heather clearly has feelings for you."

"Which are not reciprocated," I retorted. "She's so desperate to be someone's old lady, she'll let any man take a ride. She only had feelings for my position as president."

"Wow, a man talking disparagingly about someone he slept with to another woman," she sneered. "Color me *not* impressed."

I let out a dry chuckle. "Careful, Mariposa. You're in my kingdom now. I like your snark, but you don't want to see yourself on the receiving end of one of *my* punishments."

Chapter 12

MARIPOSA

Reaper's interaction with Heather stayed on my mind all next morning, while Noelle and I helped Tessa catch up on chores at her house.

"Doesn't Big G help you around the house at all?" Noelle asked as she moved a pile of laundry.

"He's too busy being the fun parent," Tessa said with an eye roll. "Right now he's on his patrol shift around the perimeter. When he gets home, the kids are going to be all over him and all this cleaning will be for nothing."

"I don't envy you," Noelle chuckled before tossing a stuffed dog at me. "What's on your mind over there, space case?"

"Heather," I admitted, folding a freshly dried bedsheet.

"Oh, don't worry about her," Tessa sank into a beanbag chair with a groan. "I know there's 'nothing'," she air-quoted, "between you and Reaper, but she's honestly no threat to that."

"Those two guys she was with," I said. "Is that common in MCs? For men to, uh, share a woman?"

Tessa and Noelle both laughed. "You really ain't from around here,"

Noelle teased me gently. "You never heard of those, what do you call 'em, the societies where the women are in charge?"

"Matriarchal?"

"Yeah, that's the one! There used to be a bunch of small ones in Arizona and Utah way before the Collapse, of course. They formed like thirty years ago as a response to the government turning to shit."

"Seriously?" I gaped at her. "I had no idea."

"No one did," Tessa chimed in. "They were very secretive about it."

"Only women and children were allowed into their communities without question. Some allowed men, but had very selective criteria," Noelle continued. "Ones that were honest, would be good protectors, help raise the children, and," she smirked, "I heard some of them were tested on their bedroom skills."

"I would've loved to be on the judge's panel for oral skills," Tessa sighed. "I love a man who knows how to use his tongue."

"A good tonguing is nice, but I'll take a thick cock on the hour, every hour," Noelle grinned. "Doesn't have to be an anaconda, just good and girthy."

"I used to feel the same way, until I ended up pregnant three times," Tessa lamented. "Being addicted to thick dick has grave consequences."

The two of them howled with laughter while I openly stared. Even in nursing school, while discussing and being surrounded by body parts all the time, I never heard anyone talk like this.

"You're gonna wake up the kids," Tessa squealed, wiping tears from her eyes.

"So the women in these societies," I said when they calmed down. "They had multiple male partners?"

"Oh, yeah. It sounds weird but it was one way they kept the power in their hands," Noelle said.

"How?"

"It was like," she thought for a moment. "Like it showed how sacred and necessary we are. How much power our bodies have. Creating life being just one of those things." She patted Tessa's belly affectionately.

"The whole movement of those societies was like a protest to society at large trying to take our power away. Powerful men always surround themselves with women, so why can't we do the same thing? Kind of like that."

"How do you know so much?" I asked her.

Her expression and body language stiffened, losing all the humor from moments before.

"My ma was in a matriarchal group." She busied herself with sorting more laundry.

I remembered when she mentioned having a different dad from Reaper and her other brother. It never occurred to me that her mom may have been with them all at the same time.

The air in the room shifted just after Noelle spoke. She busied her hands and made no eye contact. Tessa stared at her with a look of sympathy.

"I'm sorry," I said. "I didn't mean to bring up something painful for you."

"It's all right," Noelle shot me a smile. "Anyway, you were asking about Heather. I don't know her but it's possible she was born in one of those groups, too. But between us? She's just desperate for dick."

"Your brother's dick in particular," Tessa agreed.

"She just wants to prance around as the president's old lady," Noelle scoffed. "Snakey bitch acted like she wanted to be my friend just to get closer to him. I saw right through that shit."

"You gonna throw a punch at her at Fight Night?"

"Hell, maybe I will!"

"What's Fight Night?" I asked, a tremor of nervousness already creeping into my voice.

"Ohh shit, she doesn't know about that either!" Tessa squealed with delight. "You're in for a treat, Mari!"

"Basically the whole club gathers in front of our house to watch two people fight," Noelle explained. "We do it once a month just to let off some steam, settle any ongoing arguments between people. Gunner's men watch closely and call fights before it gets lethal."

"So it's like *Fight Club*?"

"You mean that movie from like a hundred years ago?" Tessa's eyes brightened. "Yes! Just like that. Only we're allowed to talk about it and girls can fight, too."

"Can I punch Reaper?" I asked, only half-jokingly.

"Nope," Noelle laughed. "Trust me, I want to hit him too sometimes. But at Fight Night, girls can only fight other girls. You can't have weapons on you, and that includes long nails. I think that's all the rules."

"You forgot the last one," Tessa piped up. "If you get challenged, you're not allowed to back down."

"That's right. And you're exempt 'cause of that kid inside you."

"Yeah. I kind of wish I could fight," Tessa sighed, running a hand along her abdomen. "I threw down on some bitches back in my day." She shot me a wink. "What do you say, Mari? Gonna get in the ring tonight?"

"No way," I shook my head. "I'm a healer, not a hitter."

I COULD FEEL THE AGGRESSION IN THE AIR THE MOMENT Noelle and I stepped outside. A crowd had already gathered in the cul-de-sac in front of Reaper's house. That dog barking its head off had to be Hades.

The night had cooled off considerably, a small bit of relief to the heat of bodies pressing close together. I hadn't seen Reaper all day, considering I spent it with the women but there he stood at the far end of the circle forming in the cul-de-sac. A king with no throne. Or rather, the only throne he sat in was his bike seat.

He wore faded black jeans, motorcycle boots, and no shirt under his leather cut. The SDMC skull on his chest peeked through, the PRESIDENT patch and reaper scythe on his left side the only non-black part of his getup.

Two men on motorcycles rode around in figure-eight patterns, revving up their engines and pumping their fists in the air. They drummed up the crowd, feeding their bloodlust with the roars of their machines.

Jandro was the first to step into the circle, peeling off his cut and tossing it to someone in the crowd. Forgetting myself, I stared thirstily as he swaggered back and forth in search of an opponent.

He was the shortest and stockiest of Reaper's men, but still a full head taller than me and built like a brick house. He flexed those thick arms and people cheered—mostly women. As he turned around, I spotted the SDMC skull tattooed on his ribs, along with a portrait of a woman on the other side. I didn't get a close look, but she had colorful face paint in the style of Day of the Dead skulls.

I was too busy staring at the muscles upon muscles of Jandro's back, his arms, and his chest, that I didn't notice him stopping right in front of me until he spoke.

"*Marrriposa*," he grinned, moving closer until he stood directly in front of me. "How about a *besito* for good luck?"

Jesus. Why did he smell so good?

"No."

His hazel eyes widened for the full puppy-dog effect as he pointed to his cheekbone.

"Not even just a little one?"

I didn't want to open that door of intimate contact, not even a crack. Reaper's massage had already been too much. I'd been craving his hands on me all day, even though I was barely sore anymore. I hated the feeling of wanting anything from these men.

But I also knew Jandro wouldn't go away until he got something.

So I leaned in, reaching on my tiptoes, and brushed a soft kiss against his cheek.

His arm locked around my waist the moment my lips touched him, pinning me to his bare chest with the strength of an ox.

And goddamnit, he felt so warm and his skin was surprisingly soft.

Then I felt his lips on my neck, the exposed side from my leaning in to kiss him, and the gentle suction followed by a flick of his tongue.

It was over before I realized what had happened. He released me, walking backward into the circle with that infuriating grin by the time my brain caught up to what he did.

My hand slapped to my neck, my pulse racing. *That motherfucker.* My skin was still wet from his tongue. *Oh, Christ. Did he give me a hickey?*

I felt hot enough to burst into flames. I could still feel the pressure of his arm braced against my lower back, the beating of his heart against mine.

My eyes remained glued to him as he looked over the crowd, his panty-melting smile now turned predatory.

Suddenly, I really wanted to see him fight.

"Do I have any volunteers?" His voice rose crisply into the night sky, hands spread out to his sides. "Whoever's wanted to land one on your vice president, now's your chance!"

Soft murmurs traveled through the crowd, but no one seemed eager to jump in the ring with him.

"Anyone?" he taunted, licking his lips. "I'll even let you take the first swing!" When no one stepped up, he shook his head as if disappointed. "All right, then I'm picking—"

"Me!"

Everyone turned to look at a guy in his early twenties with a similar height and build as Jandro, but not nearly as muscular. He didn't look terribly confident in himself, but seemed determined. Like the other club members, he too wore a cut, but his didn't have any patches.

"Prospect," Jandro purred delightedly, beckoning the young man forward. "Come here."

The guy swallowed and clenched his fists at his sides as he stepped into the circle.

"What makes you want to fight me tonight, Prospect?" Jandro asked innocently.

The guy swallowed again and took a deep breath. "For that thing you did in the shop."

"And that was?" Jandro pressed. "Let it out, kid. This is the night to get all that shit off your chest."

"When you...you..." He sucked in a deep breath and tried again. "When you shoved my head in that bucket of dirty oil."

The crowd burst into uproarious laughter. Even Reaper covered his mouth and chuckled. But I could only stare in open-mouthed shock.

"It's what you signed up for, Prospect," Jandro replied with a shrug. "But I get it. You're tired of being pushed around and you wanna hit back. So come on, boy." He beckoned him closer with his fingers. "Like I said, I'll let you take the first swing."

The young man stepped closer, sweat already forming on his brow. He shrugged off his cut, leaving it on the ground behind him. No one held onto it for him. He approached Jandro cautiously, their eyes glued to each other.

I could already tell there was no way this kid would win. The difference between his and Jandro's movements were like a sea lion approaching a bull. He'd be lucky to land anything on the vice president.

They circled each other for what felt like a full minute before the prospect took his swing. He aimed for Jandro's head, but was slow and unbalanced, leaning too much of his weight into the punch. The VP dodged it easily, his hands still relaxed at his sides. The return strike came almost too fast to be seen. The prospect's head snapped to the side and he stumbled, spitting blood on the pavement.

I wanted to cover my eyes but couldn't look away. The crowd cheered at the violence and bloodshed, but I could barely stand it. My job was to put people back together. Why would they hurt each other intentionally?

Jandro at least waited until the prospect was steady on his feet again. His next punch came to the man's belly, making him double over. Jandro then grabbed the back of his opponent's neck and drove a knee into his ribs. The prospect crumpled to the ground and raised one shaky hand.

"Stop...no more," he wheezed.

Cheers broke out and Jandro lifted his fists victoriously to the sky. He winked at me and bit his lip suggestively, but I was too stunned to respond.

In the next moment, he leaned over to say something into the defeated man's ear and patted his back encouragingly. To my utter shock, he held out a hand and lifted him to his feet. Together, the two men walked through the crowd of people to the sidewalk in front of Reaper's house, where Jandro sat him down and shoved a beer in his hand before returning to everyone else.

Knowing I couldn't just stand by and do nothing, I approached Jandro's defeated opponent once he was left alone.

"Hi," I said, kneeling in front of him. "I'm a medic. Will you allow me to look over your injuries?"

"Um." He looked up at me nervously, blood still dripping from his mouth. "I don't think Reaper will like—"

"Reaper doesn't control what I do," I cut him off. "I'm asking *you*. Would you like my help or not?"

"Um, okay."

I moved closer, inspecting his lip as closely as I could in the dim streetlight.

"I'm Mariposa. What's your name?"

"Stephan," he answered. "But just call me Prospect."

"Why? What does that mean?" The bleeding from his mouth had slowed, which meant he hadn't lost a tooth or part of his tongue. I moved on to ribs.

"It means I'm like an apprentice," he explained. "I'm not an official member of the club until I prove myself. So I don't have any patches on my cut and I do everyone's dirty work." He turned his head to the side and spit out a mouthful of blood before taking a long pull of beer.

"And what, you just have to put up with them abusing you?"

"It's hazing," he corrected me gently. "And yeah, it's just part of it, like Jandro said. He didn't even let me work in the shop with him until last month."

"So he gives you the privilege of a skilled job, then dunks your head in dirty oil?" I shook my head in disbelief. "How long have you been a prospect?"

"About six months. I hope to be patched in by a year." His eyes brightened. "Jandro told me I did good today. That stepping up for Fight Night earned me a lot of respect."

"I don't understand it," I sighed, pulling my hands back. "But he didn't injure you too badly, thankfully."

"Oh, I knew he wouldn't. It doesn't even hurt, really."

"That's the adrenaline talking," I chuckled. "You're going to be sore as hell tomorrow, though."

"Worth it." He gave a smile, which would have been cute if his teeth weren't smeared in blood. "Hey, can you do me a quick favor?"

"Sure."

"Can you grab my cut for me? I should be wearing it."

"All right." I rose to my feet, turning back to the circle of people getting hyped up for the next fight.

"And, uh, thanks," he called after me shyly. "For checking me over. Real nice of you."

"Just doing my job."

I slithered my way between bodies, already slick with sweat. Keeping my eyes on the ground in search of the patchless cut, I paid no mind to whoever stood in the circle. Not until I was called.

"Hey! New bitch on the block!"

I looked up, dread filling the pit of my stomach.

Heather stood in the middle of the circle, black combat boots on her feet, ripped black tights adorning her legs under a pair of black booty shorts. A white crop top showed off a stomach much leaner and flatter than mine.

Dark, smoky shadow surrounding her glaring eyes, and her bleached hair pulled back in a high ponytail completed her look.

"You looking for this?" She held up the blank leather cut with a cruel smile. "Fight me for it."

CHAPTER 13

MARIPOSA

"I'm not fighting you."

"Oh, yes you are." Heather's smile twisted into a hard grimace. "You came out here so I assume you know the rules. I challenged you, now you can't back out like a pussy."

"I'm not even part of this club!" I yelled back, panic rising within me as I searched the crowd for sympathetic faces. Someone, anyone, who'd be on my side in this.

"Neither is the prospect, not yet anyway." Heather smugly pointed out the flaw in my logic. "Nor am I. I'm just fucking two of them."

Any fleeting hope I had to escape this fight began to disappear. Reaper watched us both with passive curiosity, like this was some spectator sport on TV. Gunner, Jandro, and even Shadow looked on with bright eyes, eager for the action to start. Only Noelle had the decency to look worried, mouthing *sorry*, when her eyes caught mine.

Fuck, fuck, fuck. There was really no getting out of this for me, was there? I'd never even thrown a punch at someone before. I couldn't go toe-to-toe in a fight with an old man in a nursing home, let alone a scrappy mean bitch like this.

"Heather," Reaper barked, his voice cutting through the air.

All heads turned to him. Sitting on the ground in front of him, Hades' ears were pinned back but the dog was silent.

"Yes, baby?" Heather asked sweetly, twirling the end of her ponytail in her hand as she turned to face him.

"Got steel toes in those boots?"

"Nope." She tapped one toe on the ground and my stomach dropped. Fuck, I didn't even think about that. "Want to check 'em?"

"Nah. Carry on." Reaper returned to his original stance with arms crossed, waiting for the action to begin.

Someone pushed me forward and I went stumbling into the circle, not even six feet away from Heather. All I had on were a pair of Noelle's sandals, my freshly cleaned scrub pants, and another borrowed tank top. A fight was the last thing I was ready for, and Heather knew it.

All I could hope was for someone to stop it before I died. I still had to get the fuck out of this place.

Heather grinned maniacally as we made a slow circle around each other, just as Jandro and Prospect did. *You'll survive*, I told myself. *You'll survive.*

She lunged, heading straight for my middle to tackle me to the ground. My panic froze me and I did nothing but scream in pain as my back hit pavement. It spread all the way to my limbs, which I couldn't even bring up to defend myself. Fuck, a back injury could really screw me.

She grabbed a fistful of my hair and started with the punching. One, two, three, times across my face. My head bounced off the ground with each blow. *Yeah, a concussion wouldn't be so great, either.*

My ears rang and a mixture of blackness and stars dotted my vision. I heard distant yelling but couldn't make any of it out. I was so disassociated from what was happening, I forgot there was a crowd of people watching, probably urging this bitch to kill me.

Come on, Wilder. You know body parts. What does she have exposed? What's vulnerable?

I could barely see through my eyes now swelling shut. My face felt wet and I tasted a big mouthful of blood, but from the weight I felt, my adrenaline-stricken mind gathered she was straddling me. So I drove a knee up, just hoping to take her by surprise and buy an extra second, maybe two.

And it fucking worked.

My knee hit her somewhere in the back or the butt, I wasn't sure. But it made her fall forward. Through my bloody, blurred vision I knew she was close enough to my face to kiss me. So I grabbed her by the throat and squeezed.

Heather let out a gurgle of surprise then immediately started thrashing, clawing and twisting to get my hand off, but I held on like my life depended on it.

I used my free hand to punch her in the stomach, probably weak as hell but what else could I do?

At some point I couldn't hold any longer and she broke away, coughing and gasping for air. Somehow I got my feet underneath me, the ground rolling as if threatening to bring me down again. Heather was doubled over, coughing and trying to suck in big gulps of air. I stumbled over to her as she tried to get away, and just as I fell, I brought an elbow down right on top of her kidneys.

I couldn't tell if that ear-shattering scream was hers or mine, but I felt a hard kick to my ribs and the bite of the pavement on my face. There she was again, a face floating among the stars and blurred colors of my vision, so I swung my fist and hit something.

I felt wetness on my knuckles, and bones underneath soft skin, so I hit again and again, no longer certain where I was or what I hit.

At some point, my fist swung and hit nothing. Someone grabbed me from behind, so I twisted and tried to kick, but a voice came through the ringing.

"Stop, Mariposa. It's over."

"No! The fight's not over!"

"It should have ended minutes ago!" snarled whoever held me. "Get the fuck out of my way!"

Was that...*Reaper?*

The world spun and I thought was falling again, but no ground slammed up to hit me. As the voices and commotion drifted away, I realized somewhere in my foggy brain that I was being carried.

"What're you..." I squirmed in vain to get away from this person holding me under the knees and across my back in a bridal position.

"Stop it. I'm helping you."

That gruff voice was so close and clear now, I froze in disbelief. I almost felt Reaper's lips brush across my forehead as he spoke. This had to be a dream, or a hallucination. I definitely had a concussion. But then I heard his voice again.

"I want to show you something."

Oh, fuck. He's gonna feed me to his pack of dogs. That's why he kept me and fed me well at the barbecue last night. I'm dog food.

Wetness caressed the fingers of my hand hanging down. I thought it was blood so I tried to flick it away, only to feel a cold nose and a gentle tongue licking me again.

Hades. It felt like he was reassuring me that I was safe. I hoped he was right. Everything hurt and I couldn't fight anymore. And I was so fucking tired of trying to protect myself.

Succumbing to my exhaustion, I allowed my head to drop onto Reaper's shoulder. It was a good, solid shoulder.

I didn't know how long he carried me for, but his strength never faltered. At some point I heard a click and a door open, then bright lights stabbed me like knives in the eyeballs.

"Ahh!" I ended up burying my face more in Reaper's shoulder, practically nuzzling him.

"Sorry. When your eyes adjust, let me know what you think."

He sat me down on a cold, flat surface, then the support and heat of his body was gone. I brought my hands to my face, partially to check my injuries but also to shield my eyes, which now felt incredibly light-sensitive.

Some cursory poking and prodding of myself told me I didn't break any bones in my face. I probably looked like a bruised, half-rotten tomato, though. Blinking carefully, I slowly lowered my hands to gaze at what Reaper wanted to show me.

"What...is this?" I breathed in disbelief.

"The medic's office," he said, opening a drawer and pulling out a washcloth. He wet it under the sink and wrung it out before approaching me slowly. I sat frozen as he gently touched the cool, wet cloth to my cheek. Nothing ever felt so good in my life. He hesitated for only a moment before dabbing away at the blood on my face. I decided to distract myself from the swirling confusion at the gentle way he touched me, plus the fact he was caring for me at all, by looking around the room.

It looked exactly like a pre-Collapse doctor's office. Reaper sat me on the counter, but there was a bed complete with the sheet of paper covering it. The cabinets held tongue depressors, cotton balls, gloves, syringes with various sizes of needles, first aid supplies, surgical sutures and more. As my eyes moved along the lower cabinets, I also spied rows of pills. My vision was too fucked to make them out, but I could only imagine they were likely pain medications and antibiotics. Some of the hardest and most expensive drugs to come by.

"Where did you get all this?" I asked Reaper.

"Gunner," he answered simply, dropping the now blood-soaked washcloth into the metal trash can. He pulled open another drawer to reveal a box of sealed alcohol wipes. Grabbing a handful, he tore open one and began cleaning the cuts on my face.

"So Gunner's a skilled procurer of weapons *and* medical supplies?" I couldn't look at his eyes as he examined and touched me. It was too intense. He was so close. And like Jandro, he smelled really fucking good.

"No," he chuckled. "This was a nurse's office before we took over the community. It had already been raided by the time we showed up, of course. But an inventory list was taped to the wall. I told Gunner to get everything on it and then some. He's the best at what he does, so he made it happen."

"And why would you want a nurse, ah, medic's office?"

"Isn't it obvious?" He pulled away from me, those green eyes still every bit as intense. "Our way of life is dangerous. I trust my men with my life, but not everyone gets that privilege. Therefore, my men are not easily replaceable. I need to be able to keep them alive."

"So all you need's someone with the skills to do it," I concluded. "That's why you kidnapped me. And yet you let me get my ass beat."

"I can't interfere with Fight Nights. It's club law, which I am not above," he said. "Tell you what. I'll teach you a few things. So you can get her back next month and you'll be even."

"That's a shitty apology," I spat out. "And I'm sure you'll go back to fucking her anyway."

I had no idea where that last outburst came from. It sounded jealous and petty. My brain had been knocked around in my skull too many times, that had to be it. In any case, it was too late to take it back.

Reaper only grinned as he closed the distance between us again. He wedged open my thighs to stand between them, hands anchored on my hips and his chest just skimming contact with mine.

"How's this for an apology?" he whispered before cupping the back of my head and slanting his lips over mine.

My poor, rattled body exploded with new sensations. Shock, warmth, fear, and *what the fuck, he's a damn good kisser.*

As if by instinct, my mouth parted for his, letting his tongue slip through. When I realized I could still taste blood, I tried to pull away, but he held strong onto the back of my head and shoved his tongue in deeper, as if he *liked* the taste of my blood.

Every kiss rolled seamlessly into another, like he was savoring me. The blood rushing to my lips couldn't have been good for my open wounds, but his mouth was like a soothing balm over mine.

I didn't know how much I needed this, not until my sore, scraped hands reached up to wrap around his neck, my fingers threading through his rich, dark hair to deepen the kiss.

When my last touch was violent, I needed this to feel better. When my last kiss was in a drunken, sloppy haze over a year ago, I needed a skilled mouth like his to remind me of how good it could be.

The moment he pulled away for a breath, insecurities hit me like another punch to the face. After what just happened, how kissable did I really look? I sure as shit didn't even win that fight. Why wasn't he kissing and fucking Heather, who was surely riding high on beating me into the pavement?

His gaze had softened, eyes hooded with lust and taking off the edge of that intensity. He kissed my forehead and my swollen, bruised eyes. It almost seemed like he was reassuring me.

"You fought well," he murmured, lips grazing my cheekbone. "With some training, you can hold your own against anyone."

"I'm not a fighter," I protested, hyperaware of his hands returning to my waist. They felt so good massaging me, now his kisses seemed to be soothing my pains as well. What kind of witchcraft was this?

"Oh? You're a lover, then?"

I didn't miss the implication in his tone, nor the way his arms circled around me or how his lips found their way to my neck. Heather hadn't touched me there, only Jandro did.

A strange rush of heat filled me at the thought of two men kissing me in the same place less than an hour apart.

"I'm a healer," I answered. "And if I have to go along with your violent traditions, I won't be able to do my job."

"Let's make a deal then." Reaper paused to kiss my bare shoulder before lifting his face to mine again. "You'll be exempt from Fight Nights if you agree to be my club's medic."

I didn't know if I wanted to hit him or kiss him again.

"You know I can't refuse that," I seethed through my teeth. "Because of what I told you last night. Not much of a deal, is it?"

He lifted one broad shoulder in a lazy shrug. "I wanted to learn more about you before offering you anything. A medic that leaves my men to die isn't of much use to me."

I stared at him. "Were you waiting to see if I would help the people who fought tonight?"

He dipped his head in a small nod. "I value people who are true to their word. I wanted to see if you were true to yours."

"And Heather?"

"I've never seen her fight before. I didn't expect her to jump in, much less challenge you."

"And if she finds out about us...doing this?" He looked amused at my awkward gesturing between us. "You think she's going to wait until Fight Night to jump me again?"

"Yes," he insisted. "Fight Night is the only way she can take her feelings out on you and remain in the club. She won't try to subvert my authority."

"And your authority says what exactly?"

"That if she harms another club member, she'll be lucky to leave here with her life." He leaned in close again, his breath fanning over my aching lips. "Also that I'm not hers and I can kiss, touch, and fuck whomever I damn well please."

He rolled his hips between my thighs, just enough for me to feel his hardness pressing through his jeans. Sweet Jesus, the last time I felt a man inside me was before the Collapse. Nursing school kept me too busy for a relationship and I wasn't a casual sex kind of girl. And after school? Well, I didn't have the best opinion of men. Especially not this one pressing himself between my legs, no matter how well he kissed or likely fucked.

"Why are you protecting me?" I asked.

"Because you've proved yourself to be honest. And you're useful to me." His hands traveled up my sides. "And if you want something that's reasonable, just let me or Gunner know. I'm sure we can be useful to you, too."

A shiver went down my spine at all the things that word could mean. Useful for what? For feeling kisses like these? More massages? Or just...more?

"I don't understand." My brain felt like it was desperately trying to stay above water. "Why me? Why not anyone else from the service center?"

"You were the only medic, of course," Reaper chuckled. "And I still took a hell of a gamble. Few people are honest anymore. I had no idea if you were."

"But Gretchen, Tom, Liza," I choked out their names at the gruesome memories. "Why assault the teenage kitchen girl? Why kill the two owners? Why harm innocent people?"

Reaper pulled away from me like he touched a hot stove. His face twisted from lighthearted desire to something resembling shock and rage. And maybe even hurt.

I was even more stunned as he turned and left without another word, Hades' claws clicking on the ground after him.

Chapter 14

MARIPOSA

Three days passed without Reaper saying a word to me. I continued to stay at his house but barely saw him or Hades, for that matter. The two of them were so in sync, I wondered if the dog was pissed at me, too.

Thanks to Tessa making me her unofficial midwife, I was kept busy and could at least pretend Reaper's cold shoulder didn't bother me. I, along with Noelle, helped her declutter and clean for the baby's arrival. Without an ultrasound machine, I couldn't monitor her condition as accurately as I'd liked but made do with a stethoscope and old-fashioned feeling for the baby's movements. She was 31 weeks along by my estimations and the baby seemed to be healthy.

Despite Reaper's silent treatment at the back of my mind, I found myself happier while tending to Tessa than I had felt in years. Her sweetness and positivity were infectious. We often wore matching grins as we both felt the thumps and kicks from the baby's activity. I wanted to work in labor and delivery while in school, and those moments with her felt like I made it. My calling was answered. Until I remembered I had been taken to this biker gang compound against my will.

When not with Tessa and Noelle, I familiarized myself with the medic's office. After making note what everything was and where it was stored, I rearranged cabinets and drawers to give me quick access to what I'd need most in an emergency. Seconds or even fractions of seconds could mean the difference of life or death for someone. A former EMT told me that right before I left Texahoma.

I was so focused on my reorganizing, I didn't notice someone stepping into the office until I heard, "Oh hey, Mari."

My head snapped up to the open office door, where Gunner's tall, lean body filled up the doorframe. The light from outside illuminated the disheveled flyaways of his hair, giving him a golden haloed appearance. Once again, I wondered how such a bloodthirsty man could look so angelic.

"Hey," I replied, my task already forgotten. "Need something in here?"

"Yeah." He smiled sheepishly and held up an index finger covered in grease and blood with a deep gash across two of his knuckles. "Got a boo-boo. Can you kiss it better?"

A smile tugged at my lips. His face and the playful way he said that made it hard not to. But I steeled my features quickly enough to shoot him a scathing look.

"What did you do?" I turned on the water in the sink, ignoring his question about kissing it.

"I was just fucking around with some knives in the armory. Made a bad catch." He shrugged as if it were no more than a papercut.

"Well, come over here and wash it before you bleed all over the floor." I pointed to the antibacterial soap next to the running tap. "Use plenty of that and wash for at least five minutes. You don't want to give infection a chance to set in."

"Yes, ma'am," he grinned, walking up next to me to thrust his hands under the running water. "It's sexy when you tell me what to do."

I ignored that statement, too, choosing instead to rummage through some drawers while my insides fluttered.

"Depending how deep it is, you might need stitches," I said with my back turned.

"Whatever you say, Doc," he answered cheerfully, and even began whistling a tune as he scrubbed his hands.

"That doesn't look too bad," I remarked when I unflustered myself and turned back to look. "You might not need that sewn up after all. I thought I saw some adhesive here that'll work..."

"You've got everything you need here, then?" he asked, for once not teasing me.

"Oh, yeah." I remembered he was the one who restocked all the supplies. "It's everything a medic could need, short of a major surgery. Thank you."

"No problem," he seemed genuinely pleased. "Reaper always likes to think ahead. I don't know medical supplies that well, but I know some people who do. If there's anything else you need, just let me know." His grin turned lascivious. "And I do mean *anything*."

I heard his innuendo loud and clear, but the mention of Reaper's name turned my mood sour again. I missed him and that fucking annoyed me. I actually liked talking to him and the feeling seemed to be mutual. And after a dry spell of well over a year, I craved those skilled hands of his and the way his mouth claimed mine. It felt like my lips and my skin reawakened after a long dormancy and ached for real, human, non-medical contact.

I worked in tense silence as I cleaned Gunner's hand, the touch no longer clinical in my mind. With all his teasing and innuendo, my thoughts wandered to how *his* hands could make me feel. He had long, slender fingers on large palms. Small scars dotted across his knuckles, one stretching from the back of his palm to his wrist. Probably from many other mishaps with weapons, or incidents of violence that his angelic face would never give away.

"There's something between you and him, huh?" he mused, breaking the silence.

"Who?" I mumbled distractedly as I closed his wound with the surgical adhesive.

"You know who." I looked up to his playful blue eyes. "Reaper."

I huffed out a sigh as I released his hand and turned to the sink to wash my own. "Hard to have something between us when he pretends I don't exist."

My shoulders went up as I cringed hard at the words I couldn't take back. Could I sound any more like a stupid girl with a crush? I wasn't even supposed to *like* any of these guys.

"Oh shit," Gunner breathed. "So I guess you haven't heard the news, huh?"

"What news?" I shut off the water and looked up at him.

A smile overtook his mouth. "We're riding out tomorrow morning. And you're coming with us."

Chapter 15

GUNNER

"What?" Her mouth fell open and it looked pretty damn cute, I had to admit. "Riding out where? And why am *I* coming?"

"We're scoping out an outpost at the base of the Sandia Mountains, since we're no longer doing business with the service center near Old Phoenix," I said. "It'll be a couple days' ride. And you're coming because you're the club medic. We're potentially going through enemy territory and would like to survive."

"Wait, hold on." Mari's brow furrowed as she waved her hands in front of us. Damn, was there anything she did that wasn't adorable as hell? "Since when am I the club medic?"

I lifted an eyebrow and spread my hands out to the sides, the injured one throbbing just slightly.

"You're still here, aren't you?"

Mari huffed out a sigh that puffed her cheeks out and levitated a strand of dark brown hair in front of her face.

"I guess. When was this decided?"

"At Church this morning," I told her. "Reaper said for you to pack the essentials, but keep it light. It's going to be a long ride, even for us."

"Who's going?" She almost looked as though she feared the answer.

"Us four," I counted off my fingers. "Me, Reap, Jandro, and Shadow. Hades and Horus, of course. You, plus four of my guardsmen."

"So eleven of us, including the animals." She tapped her chin thoughtfully as her eyes drifted over the cabinets. I smiled, crossing my arms as I watched her think about what to pack. She was already one of us, even if she didn't know it yet.

"The animals are full-fledged club members, too," I chuckled. "Definitely can't forget about them."

"Reaper's gonna be thrilled about being stuck with me for days," she grumbled. "Especially if Hades still likes me."

So I was right—they *did* have something between them. I had my suspicions at the barbecue, and doubly so after he stepped in at Fight Night. Reaper practically spat through his teeth that we'd need to bring her on this ride. He didn't specify what happened, but I knew him half my life and never saw him get this worked up over a woman before. Mari barely found her footing with us and they were already fighting like an old married couple.

"Hey," I lifted her chin with a finger, bringing those pretty hazel eyes to meet mine. "I don't like seeing you down about Reap. Know what'll make him crazy?"

"What?"

"Ride with me," I winked at her. "Or Jandro. Hell, even Shadow. But if you touch the big guy, he might spontaneously combust. Women don't really go near him, and I'm not sure he'd know what to do."

She laughed softly at that, and I swore my fucked up finger throbbed even faster.

"Riding with one of you guys is probably my only option. I don't think he wants me anywhere near him."

Damn Reaper. I just might have to kick his ass for that. I wasn't the type to always sympathize with women like one of those pussywhipped white knights, but I legitimately felt for Mari. She was just doing her job and never wanted to be here in the first place. Then she was thrown into Fight Night and bore the brunt of Reaper's cold shoulder all in the same hour. That shit would be rough, even to a man in the same circumstances.

"Don't worry about Reap," I told her, unable to resist dragging my finger from her chin down her neck. "He does this shit sometimes. Stick with me and Jandro and we'll keep you smiling."

There it was again, the smile she tried to hide. She really didn't want to let us think she was happy here, but we'd show her in time how much she really belonged with us.

"I just have one rule," I said, reluctantly letting my hand fall away from the contact with her skin.

Her eyebrows lifted. "What's that?"

"No trying to escape," I grinned and winked as I turned to leave the office.

THE POOL DECK WAS QUIET THAT NIGHT. THE AIR HAD cooled down significantly, making steam rise off the surface of the heated water. Steam mixed with the smoke puffed from fat cigars, the cherried ends looking like red eyes in the dim outdoor light.

"Nice of you to join us," Reaper remarked when I sat down, his cigar already halfway to ash.

"Had to finish packing the shit. Our gifts are fragile and I'm trying to sleep in tomorrow." I grabbed a cigar from his lacquered wooden box and stuck it between my teeth, then struck a match and began puffing.

"What did we decide on for a gift?" Jandro asked. His cigar looked barely started. The man liked to savor the finer things, which I always respected about him.

"An array of weapons that benefits mountain dwellers," I said with my first exhale. "A few of the nicer bows. Arrows with ceramic tips, that's the fragile part. Throwing knives, double-headed axes. Primitive stuff, but the Sandia outposters should appreciate it."

"Am I missing something?" Jandro asked critically, dark eyes narrowed and smoke exhaling from his nostrils like a bull.

"Like what?" I asked calmly. I respected Jandro as VP and for his ability to think outside the box, but that didn't give him the right to question my expertise.

"What's with the cowboys and Indians shit?" he asked. "Why not sniper rifles and silencers? A lot more effective, and you know, keeping up with the twenty-second century."

"Because the Sandian outpost people are isolated," I explained after a deep drag. "They're holed up in the fucking mountains. They need weapons that can be reused over and over again, and that don't need ammo because who knows when they'll get another supply? Even if this works out, we can't supply them *and* General Tash's rebellion with modern weapons. It'll wipe us out. I can't get it from my supplier any faster."

"I'm just concerned about this deal going sour because we insult them with weapons from fucking three hundred years ago," Jandro said. "I mean, Tash wants fucking stealth drones now. And we're giving guys two hundred miles away bows and arrows?"

"I know what I'm doing," I assured him. "The mountain dwellers are old-timers who appreciate the skill that goes into old-school weapons. They wouldn't know what to do with drones. If they're interested in guns, too, we'll work that out. But we also don't want to spoil them with a gift that's too nice right away."

Jandro looked at Reaper, whose cigar became little more than a nub during our conversation. "What say you, boss?"

"I trust Gunner's judgment," Reaper answered, setting his spent cigar in the ashtray and picking up his whiskey. "He's never done us wrong before. But we'll proceed with caution. For all we know, Razor Wire may have gotten to them already."

"I doubt that," I remarked. "Sadistic bastards don't know how to play nice with anyone."

Jandro nodded his agreement before he carefully snuffed out his cigar and placed the remainder back inside Reaper's box.

"And with that, gentlemen, I'll say goodnight. Gotta make sure Shadow hasn't destroyed half the shit in my house again."

"The fuck?" I coughed up a cloud of smoke in surprise. "I thought he was drinking until he passed out every night?"

Jandro shook his head. "It's just making his tolerance go up higher and higher. Last night I woke up to him sleepwalking and his bedroom looked like a bomb hit. Just broken shit everywhere," he sighed, rising to his feet. "I feel bad for the guy. I know he can't help it but fuck. I'm getting tired of replacing broken shit, you know?"

"Maybe Mariposa has something he can take," I mused, thinking back to her cute smile and pretty blushing face. And the way she touched my hand while fixing up my cut. She didn't take me up on kissing it better, but I was satisfied with her blush and her smile.

"Mm, *Marrriposa,*" Jandro said just before polishing off his glass of whiskey. "Why do I get the feeling she's either going to cure us of everything, or be the downfall of us four?"

"'Cause you've been watching too many old chick shows," Reaper scoffed.

"Hey, *Supernatural* is high quality entertainment, asshole! Doesn't matter if that shit is nealy a hundred years old now, it's fucking timeless."

"If you say so, dude," I chuckled as I exhaled smoke.

"Anyway," Jandro sighed. "See you boys in the morning."

Reaper and I mumbled our goodnights as he walked off toward his house, then a companionable silence fell over us. Reaper wasn't much of a talker. He was too busy thinking about, well, everything. But it was that kind of quiet, stoic leadership that earned him the title of president.

"Mariposa knows she's coming," I reported after a few moments. For some reason, I didn't feel right calling her Mari in front of him. It felt too familiar.

"You told her." Reaper stated it like an observation rather than a question.

"Yes," I answered. "Since you are apparently avoiding her."

He coughed out a dry laugh. "I knew someone would tell her. I just wasn't sure if it would be you or Jandro."

I chose not to answer, helping myself to a couple fingers of whiskey instead while feeling his eyes on me the whole time. No matter how cool I played it, he always saw through me.

"I don't mind, you know," he said in response to my silence.

"Mind what?" I allowed the whiskey to burn a trail of warmth to my stomach.

"Sharing her." His eyes smoldered. He was completely serious.

"What," I choked, "the fuck?"

"Only with you and Jandro." Reaper's lip curled. "As long as you remember she was mine first."

"Reaper, dude." I scrubbed a hand down my face, trying to make sense of this. He grew up with one mom and three dads, so I knew he was used to the whole sharing one woman thing, but that culty feminist shit was too fucking weird for me.

"I was just messing with her, man, " I told him. "Making her blush and smile and shit. I'm sure Jandro was, too. She's new and pretty, so it's just fun. I'm not trying to—"

"She should have more than one man," he continued, not looking at me anymore. It seemed more like he was talking to himself. "Mom would say she has the *hechiza*. I realized it the other day."

He lost me for good there. I shook my head. "Man, I know y'all got something more than just bumpin' uglies. I don't know how you can be willing to share her but not Heather."

Reaper returned his gaze to me with a scowl. "It's not the same as just passing a service girl around. A woman has to be worth bonding with multiple men. It's...sacred." He shifted in his chair. "Heather grew up in the same environment as me, but she doesn't hold those same qualities. Not to me, anyway."

I poured one more glass and downed it. Our fearless leader liked to wax philosophical sometimes, and I couldn't begin to comprehend everything going on in his head. I was a simple guy. I liked weapons, women, and getting a great deal. Reaper and Jandro could sometimes talk for hours about what led to the Collapse and life's other great mysteries but that shit was way over my head. So was the whole sacred woman mumbo jumbo.

"Thanks for the cigars, Reap." I ashed mine carefully and stood up. "I'll see you in the morning."

Aside from a small nod and a grunt, he barely seemed to notice I was leaving.

The street was quiet as I walked down the block to my house. Word must have spread that we'd be leaving early, so everyone likely turned in around midnight. Even Reaper's house up the street was dark. Neither Mari nor his sister seemed to be waiting up for him.

Horus was asleep on his perch when I walked in. I wasn't sure how he knew, but he always liked to sleep a lot before flying with us on long rides.

Peeling off my clothes and crashing into bed with a groan, I already knew sleep wouldn't come easy. Getting on my beast of a bike always amped me up like a shot of adrenaline. I couldn't wait to feel the roar of my baby vibrating with power again.

And if I played my cards right, I'd have a sexy woman holding onto me, too.

CHAPTER 16

MARIPOSA

"You'll need chaps and a jacket." Noelle's bedroom looked like her closet vomited clothes everywhere. "And a helmet, not that the guys ever wear them. Mine should fit you."

"Jesus, Noelle," I huffed, sagging under the weight of all the riding gear she piled into my arms. "Aren't I going to melt under all this black leather?"

"Nah, you'd be surprised," she said, rifling through more items. "When you're going fast and the wind is whipping all around you, it won't feel hot even if you're covered. And you'll keep the sand and dirt off you. Ah, here!" She tossed me a round, black helmet with a mirrored visor. I barely moved in time to catch it.

"Thanks," I mumbled. "For letting me borrow all this stuff. I promise I won't use everything of yours forever. I'll get my own eventually."

"Oh yeah?" Her eyebrows lifted as she began shoving everything back in her closet. "Does that mean you plan on staying?"

I bit my lip, not knowing how to answer that. I just felt bad for constantly using her stuff and didn't give my own future here much thought. Reaper clearly didn't want me around. I was all but waiting for the day he kicked me out of his house. After what Gunner told me yesterday, though, maybe he was more likely to dump me off somewhere on this trip. Thankfully I packed enough water, first aid supplies and dried food to last me a few days in the desert.

Noelle playfully thumped me on the shoulder when I didn't answer her question.

"Don't think about it too hard," she teased. "But that is my best jacket, so make sure you bring it back."

"I will," I promised, knowing I'd pay a courier to return it to her if I did in fact get dumped off.

She wrapped me in a hug and I was surprised how nice and comforting I found it.

"Have a good ride," she said. "Keep those boys in line."

"Yeah, right," I muttered to her amusement.

After sliding on her borrowed chaps, buckling her boots, and shrugging on her jacket, I shouldered my new medic pack and grabbed the helmet as I walked outside to the rumbling of idling engines.

Gunner's men chatted and mingled, drinking coffee in the cul-de-sac next to their bikes. Shadow sat astride his beast of a bike a bit farther away from everyone else, arms crossed and looking forward as though waiting to take off.

Jandro knelt next to the bike I recognized as Reaper's, tightening something with a wrench as I walked out.

"Damn, Mariposa," he grinned when he looked up, drinking me in slowly from head to toe. "You look like you were born to ride."

"Thanks." I wasn't sure if he was being genuine or making fun of me. Gunner's men turned to look at me, too, and right then I did feel hot as hell under all my gear.

"Ho-ly shit."

I turned to see Gunner himself walking up to me, and wanted to melt into the pavement. His hair was thrown up in a loose bun, dark goggles resting just above his forehead. His black cut looked like a tactical vest, lined with pockets for ammo and a holster on each side—each with a gun, of course. Horus sat perched on his shoulder, looking around with sharp eyes. Gunner's own eyes reminded me of the pool late at night, the clearest blue and shining.

"You look like you've been in the club your whole life," he grinned at me appreciatively.

"I was just telling her that," Jandro slapped a grease-covered hand to Gunner's chest. His smile said he was joking but I swore a spark of warning lit up his gaze.

"Good shit," Gunner responded coolly. "So, you riding with me, Mari? Or did this grease monkey beat me to that, too?"

"Um..."

Jandro's jaw ticked. He didn't otherwise look annoyed, but it only occurred to me then what they might be secretly competing for.

"Sure, I'll ride with you," I mumbled, my eyes bouncing back and forth between them, unsure what was customary. Could I offer to ride back with Jandro? Or was that weird?

"Perfect," Gunner beamed, draping a long arm over my shoulders as he directed me toward his bike. "Sorry, J. Can't win 'em all."

Jandro snorted as he returned to working on Reaper's bike. "If he gives you any shit, Mari, you come straight to me."

Gunner just chuckled. Even Horus made some soft screeches and chirps as if he was laughing.

"Put that helmet on and hop up." Gunner pulled his goggles over his eyes and threw one long leg over his seat. He throttled the engine as my much shorter legs climbed up behind him.

"Let me see that." He turned around and helped adjust my helmet, pulling the strap tight under my chin.

"Your finger looks better," I observed as he gently touched my face.

"Thanks to you," he smiled.

No sooner had he turned back around, Hades raced past us like a black blur. With a thunderous roar, Reaper's bike shot after him.

"Hold on tight, baby girl!" Gunner yelled over the growling motorcycles as they followed their president.

I wrapped my arms around his midsection just as we lurched forward and rode like the wind through the open gates.

I NEVER REALIZED HOW BEAUTIFUL A DRY, DESERT landscape could be until I saw it from the back of a motorcycle. It felt like we moved through an old postcard, complete with the mountains in the distance and saguaro cactus standing tall in the edges of the frame. When I flipped up the visor on my helmet, the landscape seemed to explode with color. The sky was a brilliant blue and clouds looked like cotton candy. Desert flowers gave off pops of pink and white. I could see now why these men loving riding so much.

In one of Gunner's mirrors, I spotted Shadow riding behind us. He wore no helmet or eye protection, and his hair flew out loosely behind him.

I squinted at the tiny reflection of the large man's face, curious about his features that he always covered with his hair. He seemed to have a large scar going through one eye. And I couldn't be sure, but it looked like his eyes were two different colors.

I inspected him in the mirror until one of Gunner's guards fell in line directly behind us, blocking my view.

We rode for most of the day, only stopping for the occasional piss breaks. I wandered out from relieving myself behind a bush at one point to see Reaper relaxing next to his bike.

His legs stretched out on the ground in front of him, head propped up against his rear tire, with Hades hanging off of his lap.

Reaper stroked down the length of the dog's back as affectionately as he would his own child. Hades rolled over to look up at his master with an open, tongue-lolling smile. Reaper smiled back and even appeared to murmur something to him. It was an oddly wholesome thing to see, this ruthless man treat an animal with so much gentleness.

Then he looked up at me and the smile dissipated into a scowl.

"Let's roll," he hollered, patting Hades' flank as he rose to his feet.

The men zipped themselves up, ended their rests, and hopped back onto their steeds to continue our journey. And the Steel Demons' president once again ignored my existence.

While the first several hours of the ride were scenic and fun, I was over it by the time dusk fell. My thighs and back ached again, although not nearly as badly as the first time.

Reaper led everyone a few miles off the main road, eventually stopping in a flat area with three saguaro cacti standing like guards over twenty feet high.

"We're about an hour's ride out from Razor Wire territory, so we should be safe camping here for the night," he said once all the engines cut. "I still want guards on rotating shifts. Gunner?"

"Got it, boss."

Horus, who had been perched on his handlebars, flew to the nearest cactus while Gunner's guardsmen spread out to begin patrols. In the meantime, Hades helped to dig out a fire pit while everyone else set up tents and bedrolls.

I unpacked Gunner's stuff while he checked out the area with his men and gave orders for patrols.

"Mariposa," Jandro called. "Come have dinner with me by the fire."

I hesitated. "You're not going to trick me into kissing you again, are you?"

Two of Gunner's men snorted with laughter before quickly moving out of the vice president's way. Jandro cast them a momentary glare before returning a warm gaze back to me.

"I'll be on my best behavior," he promised with a palm to his chest. "Unless something happens in which I need another good luck kiss."

"Stephan had no chance against you in that fight," I said, making my way toward him.

"I didn't expect him to challenge me." Jandro unwrapped a cloth bundle from his saddlebag and held out a piece of jerky to me. "He did good, though. I went easy on the kid. He'll be a good soldier."

I accepted the dried meat strip and took a bite, chewing thoughtfully as I watched the rest of the men set up camp. Shadow set himself up alone far away from everyone else, as usual. He pulled a handle of liquor from his saddlebag and sat down on his bedroll. The jerky nearly fell out of my mouth as I watched him chug straight from the bottle.

"Holy shit, is he trying to kill himself?"

"No," Jandro sighed. His fingers skimmed across my lower back. "Have a seat, Mari."

I lowered myself onto a flat rock, still watching in disbelief as Shadow made quick work of the alcohol.

"He'll be dead in five years if he keeps that up."

"And he'll probably welcome it," Jandro muttered, setting up a cooking grate over the fire. "Shadow's been through shit none of us can even imagine."

He hesitated, glancing once more at his silent friend before continuing to set up. "He has nightmares where he wakes up screaming. The only way he and all of us can get a few hours of peaceful sleep is if he passes out from booze." His eyes lifted toward his silent friend. "And the big guy needs to put *a lot* of it away for that to happen."

"I have sleep aids," I said, reaching for my pack. "Side effects are minimal and he'll be—"

Jandro shook his head, looking at me with sorrow in his warm eyes. "No offense, Mari, but you're a woman. Shadow doesn't trust any women. The reasons why are complicated, but it's best you don't try to give him anything. At least for a little while."

His bottle now empty, the large man began swaying where he sat. He looked around the camp, but his one uncovered eye didn't seem to register what was around him. His lips began moving as if muttering to himself, which made Jandro spring into action.

"I'll be right back," he said, taking long strides to his friend.

No sooner had he knelt by Shadow's side, an arm fell over my shoulder and Gunner's smile beamed in front of my face.

"Aww, thanks for setting us up, baby girl! Keep doing that shit and I'll make you my old lady. Reaper will pitch a fit."

Said president and Hades were across the fire with Jandro and Shadow, talking softly among themselves while Shadow looked as though he struggled to stay awake.

But something the golden, smiling man said pulled my attention back to him.

"Set *us* up?" I blinked.

"Well, yeah. Where did you think you were gonna sleep? Not in the dirt by yourself."

"I, um..."

Gunner's smile faded as he slowly removed his arm from around my shoulders.

"Hey, you can relax. I remember how freaked out you were at the service center. I won't touch you like that again, not if it scares you." A lopsided grin returned. "I like weapons and dangerous shit, but I honestly don't want to scare anyone that doesn't deserve it. You've kinda been through a lot, so I get it."

I stared into the fire as I turned his words over in my head. "There's not a lot that scares me anymore, to be honest." Crackles and pops from the flames filled the silence. "But yeah, getting kidnapped and violated by a bunch of men on motorcycles is pretty high up there."

"We don't do that. Not the violating part, at least."

"You're the second man in this club who's told me that," I mused. "And with every day that passes, I want to believe you, but..." Gretchen's face haunted me every time I closed my eyes. How ashamedly she asked me for a morning-after pill.

Gunner scooted away from me with his eyes downcast, and I felt like I kicked a puppy.

"Well, you don't have to sleep near me if you don't want to. You can have my bedroll and I'll sleep on my leathers or something. I gotta be up for my patrol shift in a few hours, so—"

Goddamn it.

"Wait," I grabbed his arm, an apology stuck in my throat but it wouldn't come out. He almost *did* force himself on me back at the service center so why was I the one apologizing? One of these men *did* hurt Gretchen, but something at the back of my brain believed that it wasn't him.

"Maybe we can just sit next to each other first?" I suggested. "Just talk, and you know, get used to each other?"

That electrifying grin returned and my heart skipped a beat.

"You've been in my seat and holding onto me all day, baby girl. What's it gonna take for you to get used to me?"

"Tell me about you," I suggested. "I've been with you guys for almost a week and feel like I hardly know any of you. Where are you from? How'd you find Horus?"

"Now there's a story in both of those answers." He relaxed once again next to me. "I was Arizona born and bred, but my family's from California originally."

"Really? Before it sank into the ocean?"

"Yup, my grandparents were actors." He laced his hands behind his head. "They lived in Hollywood and did a few movies before that whole area went under. My parents were little when they headed east to evacuate."

"I heard you can swim out there and still see whole towns and neighborhoods underwater."

"I wouldn't," Gunner chuckled. "My folks said the pollution is so toxic, you'll get cancer just by letting the water touch you. I heard the coastline is pretty, though." He paused as he looked at me. "Maybe we can ride out there one day."

"Maybe," I mused.

"As for Horus," he continued. "I was bird-hunting, quite ironically. Not for falcons, though. For quail. Out of nowhere, this fluffy little fucker with big-ass talons starts clinging to my pantleg and screaming bloody murder. I knew he was some kind of raptor based on his feet, so I fed him some quail I shot. He's pretty much never left my side ever since." He nodded across the fire to Reaper. "Him and Hades have a similar story. Hades was an abandoned pup and they just seemed to find each other."

The dog rested calmly on the ground, his dark eyes blinking slowly with sleepiness while his owner continued talking with Jandro and Shadow.

"Does Horus do anything...unusual, like Hades?"

"Like what?"

"You know, like how Hades can just run alongside Reaper's bike for hours. No normal dog can do that."

"Hmm," Gunner pursed his lips as he thought. "I guess I never really thought about it. No, Horus seems like a pretty normal bird to me. Sometimes I have dreams like I'm flying, though, and it's like I'm seeing through his eyes. Hey," he tapped my arm with the back of his palm, looking excitedly at me like a little kid. "What's the freakiest dream you've ever had?"

"Oh, that's easy," I laughed. "In nursing school, I dreamed I delivered a two-headed baby."

"No shit! How did you react?“

“I just started talking to it and the baby talked back! But each head answered in a different language. I think one of them was Russian.”

Gunner howled with laughter. We talked until the fire burned down to embers, and I didn't think twice about following him to his tent and falling asleep next to him on his bedroll.

Chapter 17

MARIPOSA

I distinctly remembered how the temperature dropped during the night. So I was surprised to find myself in a cocoon of warmth when dawn approached.

Or rather, a sandwich of warmth.

My eyes fluttered open, expecting to see Gunner's fair, angelic features. Instead I found caramel skin and Jandro's full lips inches away from me.

With a gasp, I tried to push away but my back pressed against something solid. Looking over my shoulder, there was the angelic face I expected to see. And damn, did he look sweet in his sleep.

Gunner's lips were parted as he breathed softly, his hand resting on my thigh while Jandro's arm draped over my waist.

Turning back to the VP, his jaw was tight and his brow furrowed in his sleep. His fingers also periodically clenched around my shirt. Seeing how differently these two men slept was morbidly fascinating to me.

"Jandro?" I whispered, placing a tentative hand on his bicep.

"Huh!"

He jerked awake at my touch, sitting straight up immediately.

"Uh, hi," I said meekly.

He looked at me and only then did his expression relax. "Morning, Mariposa," he sighed while rubbing his temples.

"You all right?"

"Yeah, yeah." He shot me a sheepish grin. "I'm not an easy sleeper, that's all. Didn't mean to scare you."

"Can I ask what you're doing in Gunner's tent?"

The hand resting on my thigh wrapped around my waist in reply.

"I asked him to come," Gunner murmured sleepily at my back. "I didn't want to leave you alone during my patrol shift. But when I came back, the fucker wouldn't leave."

"You had your head on my chest. It was the sweetest thing," Jandro teased. "No way was I gonna move and disturb you."

"Wow." I drew my knees up to my chest. The cozy warmth of their bodies turning into a stifling heat all over me. "I must have been really out of it."

"Riding is exhausting if you're not used to it." Jandro's eyes brightened. "And you get to do it all over again today."

"Great," I grumbled, stretching my arms and legs out. I felt a little soreness in my limbs but nothing too bad.

"Aw, you'll be fine." Gunner sat up and kissed the back of my head before I could react. "We'll get some coffee and breakfast in you, then you'll be right as rain, baby girl."

He rose to his feet and exited the tent, leaving me to stare wide-eyed at Jandro.

"All you're missing's a kiss from Shadow now, huh?" He laughed as my eyes surely doubled in size. "Relax, you don't have to worry. He's not really the kissy type."

"So, uh..." Eager to focus on something else, I pulled a rubber band off my wrist and started tying my hair up. "How is he this morning?"

"Fine," Jandro shrugged. "Probably up early and packed before all of us. He doesn't get hangovers and never sleeps more than he has to."

"Really?"

"Yeah. I'm jealous, to be honest," he chuckled before going quiet. "You riding with golden boy again today?"

"I'm not sure," I admitted. "He hasn't asked me yet."

Jandro's eyes brightened. "Want to ride with me?"

"Um, sure."

"It's a comfortable ride, I promise," he winked. "My baby's made for long distance. And I know her down to every gear. No rattles, no bumps. Just smooth sailing."

"Sounds good." A smile came to my mouth and he returned it.

"Great. I'll see you at breakfast." He made a sudden movement toward me, then stopped, hesitated, then turned and left the tent.

I was alone. Just me and my racing heartbeat. I thought for a moment he was leaning in to hug or kiss me.

What would you have done?

Five days ago, I would have fought tooth and nail to get away from him. Now I slept between two of these men with no fear, and I wasn't so sure if I'd refuse him.

I PACKED UP GUNNER'S TENT AND BEDROLL, PUTTING everything away in his saddlebags when he brought me a tin mug of coffee and a bowl full of scrambled eggs, baked beans, and bacon bits.

"Jandro told me you're riding with him today, sly bastard. I gotta be faster next time."

"Just as long as you don't interrupt my beauty sleep to ask me to ride with you first," I joked.

"Wouldn't dream of it, baby girl," he said softly. Those bright blue eyes looked into mine long enough to make my stomach flutter. "Damn, Reaper has no idea what he's missing."

"What?" I blinked.

"Nothin'. Have a good ride." He reached out and stroked his thumb along my chin. "Wave at me if you want to switch off." Almost exactly like Jandro earlier, he paused as if considering something before walking away.

My stomach was doing almost too many flips to keep my breakfast down. What the hell was going on? Not just with them, but with me?

After finishing my food and washing out my dishes with sand, I spotted Hades as I approached Jandro's bike, which was conveniently parked next to Reaper's.

The dog waited patiently next to his master's front wheel, looking at me with a cute head tilt as I pulled on my riding gear.

"Hey, good boy," I whispered.

His ears pricked forward as his rear end lifted off the ground. Wagging his stub of a tail, Hades only made it a few steps toward me when a high-pitched whistle stopped him in his tracks.

We both looked to see Reaper and Jandro walking side by side in our direction. Like usual, the former wore his signature scowl, the latter his flirtatious smile. Reaper walked right past me without even a glance, even ignoring Hades' puppy eyes for affection as he mounted his steed.

"Ready, Mari?" Jandro's fingertips lightly grazed my back as he moved in front of me.

"Yeah," I smiled back but he seemed to sense my uneasiness.

"Don't worry about him," he nodded up ahead to his president. "It's not you. He's stressed about this deal working out. Nothing should go wrong, but we need to tread carefully."

"What should I do?" I placed my hands tentatively on his waist as he sat in front of me. Although just as solid, his body was broader than Gunner's so I couldn't reach around as far.

He answered me by lacing his fingers through one of my hands and throwing me a look over his shoulder.

"Just be you."

THE MOUNTAINS IN THE DISTANCE GREW LARGER AND larger until the highest peak blocked out the sun. At the head of the pack, Reaper gradually slowed as the road became narrow and winding.

"Are those..." I squinted at the sight up ahead, nearly resting my chin on Jandro's shoulder as I tried to get a closer look. "...palm trees?"

"Haven't seen those in a while, have you?" he chuckled.

"I don't think I've ever seen a real one before."

"It's tacky as hell to see 'em now in the fuckin' desert," he yelled over his engine. "But they used to be signs of an oasis, a place for rest and relaxation. Resorts planted them so you could see them from miles away."

"Is this place a resort?"

"Used to be."

The road took us between the two skinny tree trunks standing out like sore thumbs. We soon came to a building at least six stories high and dotted with many balconies and large windows. It made the Old Phoenix service center look like a rundown shack.

Reaper slowed to a halt and everyone else stopped behind him. Leaving his bike running, he dismounted and nodded to Jandro, who looked over his shoulder and nodded at Gunner.

"The three of us are going in first," he slid off his bike with a gentle pat to my leg. "Shadow's got our backs. Watch him if anything happens."

"Why, what's gonna happen?"

He smirked at me. "Hopefully we'll get some comfy rooms and a dip in the pool. But we've got to play our cards right. It won't be more than a few minutes."

He paused to look at me once more, eyes casting down to my lips before walking off to meet Reaper. Gunner followed him, carrying a large metal case. He winked one blue eye at me as he passed, and the three men went through the front door.

I looked behind me at Shadow, the furthest one in the back. He was still astride his bike but with his feet on the ground and a large assault rifle in his hands. Looming tall over everyone and dressed entirely in black, he really did take after a shadow.

Minutes crawled by. No one spoke. Some of Gunner's guardsmen drifted their hands to the weapons at their hips or backs.

A flash of movement caught my eye. Flipping up the visor on my helmet, I craned my neck to look up at the balconies on the tallest floor. I thought I saw a curtain move but upon looking more closely, it was armed men walking back and forth on the roof. Gunner's men noticed them, too, only they didn't look up as obviously as I did.

After what felt like hours, Reaper, Jandro, and Gunner, now empty-handed, emerged from the building. The whole club seemed to let out a sigh of relief.

"Weapons down. We're cleared to stay," Reaper announced. "No women here, though. Y'all are either fucking each other or your hands tonight."

A few of the men groaned in disappointment. Big G looked especially perturbed.

Ignoring them, Reaper gave Hades a quick pat before getting back on his bike. "They're setting up for us inside now. We'll park in the garage."

"How'd it go?" I asked Jandro as he resumed his seat.

"Worried about me?" he teased with a smile. "It went well. The owner was cautious, naturally, but pleased with our offering. The real test is how hospitable they'll be during our stay."

"How long are we staying?"

"Two days, maybe three. Reaper wants to ensure they won't backstab us if we continue working together in the future."

We pulled into the garage, which looked like a converted horse stable, then entered the lobby through a side door.

"Wow," I breathed.

It was much nicer than my old service station, and definitely kept cleaner. They went all out on the desert palace theme with sandstone columns, an open floor plan with high ceilings, and tiled floors in an elegant pattern of earth tones.

The furniture consisted of low couches and floor cushions, with coffee tables lined with exotic-looking fruit. Gunner's men didn't hesitate in sprawling out over the comfortable seating and helping themselves to food.

Two young women rushed out from behind a curtain carrying pitchers of water and ale. My pulse sped up as the men's eyes crawled over them perversely. *Fucking hell, not here, too.*

"Have a seat, Mari," Gunner patted the cushion next to him. Horus hopped off his shoulder and pecked curiously at some of the food on the table.

"It feels weird to be on this side of the table," I mused, easing into the seat next to him.

"Feels good, doesn't it?" He popped a grape into his mouth. "Riding all day long, then getting treated like royalty."

"Gun, get your bird off the table before it shits on the food."

We looked up together at who snarled the order. Reaper, of course. Acting like a crabby father after a long road trip.

Gunner let out a short whistle, and Horus immediately took off flying out the open door. "It's about time for him to hunt anyhow."

"Did you train him to do that?" I asked, helping myself to a few olives.

"No, more like he trained me on what sounds he would respond to."

We ate and relaxed for a few hours without incident. The bikers did little more than flirt and stare at the two kitchen girls, much to my relief. Once everyone was full of food and drink, Jandro left Reaper's side to sandwich me between him and Gunner again.

"They allotted us nine rooms based on our gifts for them," he glanced at Gunner. "That means you get your own room, Mari. If you want."

"Yes," I said, maybe a bit eagerly. I hardly had a moment to myself in days.

The guys exchanged a grin at that. "We'll still keep you between us, to be safe," Jandro said.

"And if you get lonely, just knock on a wall." Gunner squeezed my waist, his lips nuzzling near my ear. "Preferably mine."

My resulting squirm from the contact pressed me right up against

Jandro's shoulder. A giggle bubbled out of my chest before I could suppress it.

"You can knock on his wall if you like, but," the VP's fingertips grazed my lower back, "you know where to go for a nice spooning."

"Spooning?" I laughed, turning to look at him. "Is that what they're calling it now?"

Jandro shrugged, his expression innocent but the heat in his eyes anything but. "Cuddling. Canoodling. Cupcaking. Whatever you want to call it. I just want more of that sweetness from last night."

"Is that *all*?" I lifted my eyebrows. "I'm surprised."

"I'm full of surprises," he returned.

The two of them touched me with abandon now, and the flirty banter only escalated with each passing day. As time went on, my resistance to it only grew weaker. My insides felt like hundreds of fluttering butterfly wings.

This felt like a luxury I couldn't afford. These men were to be feared, not flirted with. They could hold me down and take what they wanted at any moment. So why bother with all this, the teasing and flirting? I wondered as everyone started getting up, dispersing down the walkways to their rooms. Jandro and Gunner led me between them, of course.

"Reaper gets the nicest suite, naturally," Jandro said. "Which means Gun and I get the second nicest." He looked at me and grinned. "Last chance to pick a room with your favorite."

"I'll be fine in my own room, really." I squeezed the straps of my pack on my shoulders, eager for some privacy. These guys were affecting my ability to think too much.

"Suit yourself," Gunner shrugged, opening a door. "Knock on your right wall," he added with a wink before going in.

"I'll be at the pool if you'd like to join me," Jandro offered from his door on the other side of me.

"Maybe later. I think I'm going down for a nap," I yawned.

Try as I might, I couldn't shut my brain off, no matter how exhausted my body was. The room was comfortable and spacious, but I couldn't bring myself to relax.

Frustrated, I decided to get up and take a walk. I didn't even make it to the end of the hallway when my heart jumped into my throat.

Through the doors at the end of the corridor, leaning over the balcony in a cloud of cigar smoke, stood Reaper.

I almost turned around and headed back to my room. His cold-shouldering since Fight Night hurt more than any of those punches I took. Why subject myself to that again?

Then again, why bring me all this way if he was just going to treat me like mud on his boot? I was fucking tired of waiting around for him to talk to me again. And as I forced my steps to proceed onward through those doors, it scared me how much I missed him.

Hades' ears perked up when I opened the door, but he remained sitting at his master's feet. Sometimes the two of them acted like independent beings, but right then they seemed to share the same mind.

Reaper's shoulders didn't even stiffen as I walked up next to him, leaning my forearms on the railing in the same posture.

"How long is this going to go on for?"

He took a long drag on the cigar and exhaled as if I hadn't said a word.

"I don't know what you mean," came his gruff, eventual reply.

"Are you kidding me?" I couldn't bring myself to be patient. I'd been patient for five fucking days already. "This. The silent treatment. Making me part of your club but acting like I don't exist. You can't keep this up forever."

"Watch me."

"Reaper, I-I don't get it." My voice cracked and I could barely bring myself to say the next part. "One minute you're...kissing me." It felt like so long ago, I began to question if it really happened. "The next, you're acting like I'm this huge inconvenience in your life. If you don't want me around, that's fine." It wasn't fine, not anymore. But he didn't need to know that. "One of the guys can drop me off in any podunk town between here and Sheol."

"That's not gonna happen." His teeth clenched on the cigar. "As much as I'd like to dump your ass in the middle of the desert, I need a medic."

Ow, fuck.

"Okay," I said cautiously. "So why—"

"Why do you fucking care?" he growled, turning to face me for the first time in days. " You see me as a murderer and a rapist. Aren't I doing you a favor by leaving you the hell alone?"

His words flung out at me from some deep, painful place. Too stunned to reply, I could only back away a few steps.

"Yeah, that's what I thought," he grumbled.

"I don't know, I—" My mind raced as I tried to reconcile the horrors he committed with the man who treated his animal companion so gently. "As I'm spending more time in the club, I'm starting to think, I dunno. Maybe you guys aren't all bad."

"Not all bad?" he laughed cruelly as he flicked the butt of his cigar, sending ashes raining down over the balcony. "Sugar, you haven't *seen* how bad we can be. We're the stuff nightmares are made of." He leaned in close to me. "The Collapse took all your rights away, but for men like me? We thrive in this world. A lawless land means *I* make the laws. And I'll dispense justice in any way I see fit."

His words swung heavily through the air as if made of battle axes, and my heart dropped in much the same way.

"So I was right about you," I said, nearly choking on my sadness. "My first impression, anyway." Nevermind if *he* never forced himself on anyone, or that his hands felt like magic or his kiss took my breath away. Reaper was the living embodiment of the Collapse itself. Cruelty, violence, and chaos wrapped in a sinfully beautiful package.

"Yeah," he scoffed, turning his bitter gaze back to the mountain view. "You were right about me."

With nothing else to say, I turned to leave. Hades' dark eyes followed me, wide and puppy-like as I reached for the door. I would've loved the company of a friendly, nonjudgmental animal since the surrounding humans proved to be just as awful as I thought. But I knew better than to touch Reaper's dog.

"None of us touched her, you know."

I froze a moment before slipping through the doorway, then whipped around to stare at his broad back.

"What?"

"The kitchen girl," he said, tossing the finished end of his cigar over the balcony. "Tom was the one who abused her while his cunt of a wife watched it happen without lifting a finger to help. He made no secret about wanting to do the same to you."

Chapter 18

REAPER

I shouldn't have told her. I should have let her keep on believing I was just another barbaric piece of shit senselessly killing whoever got in my way. At least then she'd feel better about not talking to me.

She was all I thought about as I rode out with Jandro the next morning, which really pissed me off because I needed to keep my head in the game. No woman ever succeeded in distracting me from my duties as much as her.

We were in foreign territory and I couldn't shake the feeling that something was fishy about this deal. It all went according to plan, but Hades' hackles had been permanently raised since we got here. His whole body was tense and he'd been growling more than usual. I swore he hadn't slept at all last night. Every time I woke up he was staring at the door, alert and on-guard.

"No sign of Razor Wire or any other club," Jandro said as we stopped at a ridge overlooking a canyon below. "Gun said Horus hasn't seen anything either. I dunno what to tell you, Reap."

"They're fucking us, somehow," I insisted, raising a canteen of water to my lips. "They wouldn't have gone along with the deal so easily if they weren't."

"Maybe our reputation does precede us," my VP smirked. "Word travels faster now that borders don't mean much. It's not just the Arizona-Utah territory that knows who we are."

"Nah," I shook my head. "There's always a bigger fish and Razor Wire used to be it."

"Til General Tash captured 'em," Jandro reminded me. "And Tash has always been honest with us."

"Yeah, but Razor's a slippery bastard. This area used to be loyal to him. I wouldn't be surprised if he had multiple failsafes in the event of his capture."

"Come on, Reap." Jandro leaned against his steed as he crossed his arms. "What's really got your asscheeks clenched? Mariposa?"

"You son of a horse fucker."

"Hey, don't get mad at me. You're the one being a moody bitch while she's doing the best she can in this situation."

I wanted to throw something over the edge of the cliff. I needed my water canteen for the ride back so I settled on a fist-sized rock on the ground and hurled it over the ridge.

"Feel better?" Jandro asked.

Who died and made you my fucking therapist?

"I told her the truth," I admitted. "About why we killed Tom and Liza."

"And?" he inquired. "Did y'all kiss and make up?"

"No."

The only sound that followed was the wind blowing through the canyon.

"But that's what you were hoping would happen," Jandro piped up after a few moments.

"Nah." I sealed up my water and returned it to my saddlebag. "I stopped hoping anything good would come my way years ago."

"Okay, so you didn't want her believing the rumors about you, which is almost the same thing," he concluded. "You want her to know the *real* you."

"You overestimate me, Jandro." I threw a leg over my seat and maneuvered my baby back to the road. "All I want is to ride and see another day long enough to smoke a cigar. Pussy's fine, too, but I don't give two shits what a woman thinks of me."

Jandro laughed, shaking his head at the sky as he followed me. "Oh, I know you much better than that, Reap."

THE SIGHT OF MARIPOSA LYING ON A DECK CHAIR NEXT TO the pool didn't help to prove my point at all.

"Fuck." I sucked my bottom lip between my teeth and felt all the blood rush to my dick.

She wore one of my sister's bikinis, which honestly fit Mari much better. I didn't know how the fuck women's clothing worked except that the red polka-dotted number accentuated, supported, and highlighted every delectable curve on her body. It was like magic. Or maybe it was just her body that was magical, or the fact that I hadn't fucked anyone in nearly three weeks.

Her lips curved into a smile as she watched Gunner do a flip off the diving board. Lips that I kissed, that tasted sweeter than the wild blackberries I picked as a child.

Jandro punched me in the shoulder, and the resulting grin he shot at me made me want to punch him in the face.

"Getting in?" He was already shrugging off his cut and pulling his T-shirt up. "I bet Hades will love it."

"Nah, later," I said. "I can't think straight around all you fucks."

"Or you're just thinking with the wrong head." His eyes slid appreciatively over Mariposa. "Not that I blame you."

I headed into the main building before he could give me any more shit, Hades loyally trotting at my side. Before I could talk myself out of it, I went up to the smoker's lounge and fished another cigar out of my cut pocket.

I didn't normally have more than one at the end of a long day, but this place seemed to wreak havoc on my nerves. Nothing looked suspicious, so why did I feel the need to look over my shoulder constantly?

Hades guarded the door like usual as I lit up. Daren would have pitched a fit if he knew I was smoking two cigars a day. His sire passed away in his early fifties from esophageal cancer. I was fourteen and Daren was twelve. As the youngest of us, he'd been sheltered from the pile of shit the world was becoming. His sire was the first of my fathers to go, and our lives only descended deeper into the shit pile since then.

"Would you really be so upset if we saw each other again soon?" I said to the empty room. "You're gone because I fucked up. A year later and I'm still willing to trade, if anyone's listening. It should've been me, Daren."

How ironic that I earned the name Reaper and couldn't even bargain for my little brother's death.

Hades' wet nose nudging my hand lifted me out of my guilt, if just for a moment.

"How do you always know, boy?" I scratched his ears as I looked into those deep, soulful eyes. "Whenever I think about him or talk like he's here, you just know."

"Excuse me, sir?"

I looked up, annoyed at the intrusion. In my rush to light up and be alone, I left the door to the lounge open. One of the kitchen girls poked her head through.

"Yes?" I snapped.

"Mr. Fischlin would like a word with you in his office. At your earliest convenience, sir."

"Regarding what?" I demanded. "The gift from yesterday?"

"I'm not privy to that knowledge, sir. But he requested that you come alone." Her eyes fell to Hades, who gave her a low, rumbling growl. "You may bring your animal companion if it suits you."

"It does suit me," I carefully ashed my cigar. "He goes everywhere with me. Tell Mr. Fischlin I'll be up shortly."

She left to deliver my message while I observed Hades' behavior. He was in full-fledged guard dog mode, which set my own alarm bells ringing. And wanting me alone? How obvious could Fischlin be?

I left the lounge and considered swinging by the pool to signal the guys something was up, but Fischlin's marksmen in the corridors made me think twice.

They looked casually posted enough but I felt their eyes raking over me like a woman's hands. A stolen glance told me a few of the higher-ranking ones already equipped the ceramic arrowheads we gave them yesterday. These fuckers didn't waste any time. If I tried to alert my men, they'd return our gifts right through our hearts. I wasn't about to take good men down with me, so I headed straight for Fischlin's office.

I kept my pace casual, my face neutral, while I tried to form a plan. Even Hades was able to relax his body language walking at my side. If only I knew what that brain of his sensed in the air.

It didn't help that Fischlin's office was at the far end of the building, away from all the rooms and public areas. Alerting anyone without some big commotion would be nigh on impossible.

My gaze turned skyward, looking through the columns lining the outdoor walkway for Horus. Gunner and his bird seemed to have a similar bond as Hades and me, although I wasn't entirely sure what that entailed. If the raptor was out there and saw me, I could only hope Gunner would know, or feel, something.

With no sight of the bird, I looked ahead to Fischlin's office door. My heart rate picked up and I fought the urge to quicken my pace. *Steady, steady.*

I never made it to his office.

Hades stopped in his tracks, bared his teeth and started barking wildly. His raised hackles gave him a humpbacked look.

"Easy, boy," I murmured to him, watching the marksmen nock their arrows in my peripheral vision. "Calm down. What is it?"

He kept fucking going. I never heard him bark so loudly before. It echoed off the columns and I had no doubt the others at the pool heard him.

"Hades!" I said with more force in my tone. "Quiet!"

He lunged at me in response, jaws open wide.

"What the—"

I was fucking stunned watching him come at me as if in slow motion. What the hell happened to my dog? He never attacked me. Even knowing full well how powerful those jaws were, I could never bring myself to hurt him. Not even to protect myself.

So I let him lunge at me. His teeth closed around my shirt and he twisted, pulling me to the ground with the strength of a two-hundred-pound man.

Not half a second later, the force of an explosion sent me rolling blindly across the desert ground. Heat singed the hairs on my skin as glass and rubble rained down on me.

Chapter 19

MARIPOSA

"Gunner, no!" I shrieked, flailing my arms and legs wildly. "Don't you dare!"

"Come on," he laughed devilishly. "The water feels amazing."

"I'll get in, just give me a second."

"No." His eyes flashed with the thrill of a predator on the hunt. "Now."

He lunged and I tried to dodge, but he was too fast for me. I only ran a few steps on the pool deck when his arm caught me around the waist. We spun around from the momentum until he leaned us over the edge, and we crashed into the crystal-blue water.

I remembered to hold my breath at the last possible second before the cold shock hit me. With how hot and dry it was, the water probably did feel good. I wouldn't know, not with the panic surging through my chest.

Rather than fighting Gunner in the cool, quiet underwater world, I clung to him like a raft. It must have been seconds, but felt like an hour before he kicked up to return us to the surface.

"See?" He flipped his hair back and grinned that pearly, boyish smile at me. "Feels great, doesn't it?"

"Yeah, about that." My legs wrapped like a vice around his waist, my arms clinging to his shoulders. "I can't swim."

"What?" His hands supported my lower back, a ghostly soft touch under the water. "How can you not swim?"

"I grew up in Middle of Nowhere, Texas, okay? Not a lot of swimmable bodies of water around."

He stared at me like I grew a third eye in the middle of my forehead.

"I don't think I've ever met anyone who couldn't swim. It's like second nature to me."

"Well, lucky you." I directed a small splash at him. "I hope giving CPR is second-nature to you, too, because I was about to need it."

"Sorry, Mari." His face fell. "I didn't know. I just figured everyone could."

"It's okay." I couldn't be mad at him for not knowing. Not with that adorable sad face he was giving me. "Just listen when a girl tells you *no* next time."

"Tell you what." His eyes brightened as he walked us to the shallow end. "I'll teach you how to swim if you teach me CPR." The devilish grin returned. "Especially if I get to practice mouth-to-mouth on you."

"Hmm, I'll have to think about it." I shot him a coy smile as I pulled myself out. "Show me how good of a swimmer you are while I dry off. I need to know if my teacher's qualified."

"Oh, you couldn't have picked anyone better." He began an elegant backstroke across the pool, eyes still locked on mine.

I settled into a deck lounger as he showed off, even doing flips off the diving board. My hair and skin were dry within minutes under the baking sun. The heat almost made me want to go back in the water just to cool off and cling to Gunner again.

Almost.

How long had it been since I just laid out in the sun, though?

Pushing away everything I learned in school about sun damage, I closed my eyes and basked in the heat. If I used my imagination a little, I could pretend I was on a beach vacation without a care in the world.

Murmuring voices pulled me out of the fantasy in my head, and I cracked my eyes open in curiosity.

Jandro and Reaper spoke in low voices as they walked between the columns of the elegant outdoor corridor, their heads bent toward each other as if discussing something important. Both had on their cuts as if they just returned from a ride.

My heart jumped at the sight of Reaper. Part of me wanted to hide, even underwater, while the other part wanted to march up to him and apologize.

What he told me on the balcony hit me like a baseball bat to the stomach. I thought wrongly about him based on, well, nothing. And while he did awful things for his own and his club's survival, he wasn't the monster I thought he was.

I laid awake thinking about it all night last night rather than sleeping. And the one thought that stuck to the forefront of my mind was what Tessa said that night at the barbecue.

What if he didn't actually kidnap me, but rescued *me?*

My throat turned drier than the desert surrounding me. I gripped the armrests of my lounge chair, trying to get up the nerve to talk to him.

"Mari, watch me!" Gunner called gleefully like a child.

I put on a grin as he moonwalked across the diving board then backflipped into the water. When I looked over to the two club leaders again, Jandro removed his cut and was in the process of taking his shirt off while Reaper turned and walked in the opposite direction.

My heart sank as I watched his form grow smaller until he disappeared from view. Of course he didn't want to be around me, not after what I'd falsely accused him of. But it still stung.

"Hey, Mari." Jandro approached me with his signature flirtatious grin, cut and shirt thrown over his bare shoulder. "Careful laying out for too long or you'll get burned."

"I'm working my way up to your shade of tan." I watched him sink into the deck chair next to me, not a single tan line on his caramel torso. For a moment I wondered if his skin tasted as sweet as he looked.

"You can thank my Guatemalan parents for this tan," he chuckled, leaning back and stretching his legs out in front of him. "Arizona and Texas were the Far North to them, and y'all still sunburn like lobsters up here," he teased.

"My dad was from Mexico," I told him. "So I can get as dark as you, I just might have to work harder at it."

"Mm-hm," he smiled before looking out at Gunner's antics in the pool. "Your old man still around?" he asked gently.

"No," I answered, bringing my gaze up to the palm trees overhead. "He was fighting in the Texas border wars and never came home one day. Then my mom went to look for him, and she never came back either."

"Sorry," Jandro murmured. "I barely even remember my folks. I was raised by my aunt and uncle in Old Tucson."

My chest tightened. What the Collapse did to families was so overwhelmingly sad, I preferred to talk about anything else.

"Where did Reaper go?"

"Went to be alone," Jandro humored my subject change. "He gets in moods like that sometimes."

"I guess he's never really alone with Hades."

"Yeah," Jandro breathed. "Sometimes that dog is the only company he ever wants or seems to need."

BOOM!

An invisible force sounded like thunder crashing next to my ears and nearly knocked me off my chair. The ground shook so hard, pool water splashed up onto the deck.

"What the hell?" Jandro jumped up and stood over me protectively, eyes narrowed and suspicious. "Gun, did you—"

"Oh my god!" I sprang to my feet at the sight of Gunner in the shallow end of the pool.

His head rested on the ledge, but his eyes had completely rolled back until only the whites were visible. He twitched slightly, his mouth going from open and slack to tightly clenched. And every small jerk of his head sent him closer to slipping underwater.

"Gunner!" I went to run to him but Jandro braced his forearm across my stomach and pulled me back. "He's having a seizure!" I yelled. "He could drown, let me go!"

"He's okay, Mari," he answered with unusual calm. "It's just something that happens, you'll see. Something else is going on, though. Fucking Reaper was right."

I didn't have a moment to think about what he said when a commotion on the roof brought our attention skyward.

One of the guards, armed with a bow and arrow, was desperately trying to fight off a bird. The animal hovered around him, too close for him to shoot with the bow, and darted down with its talons outstretched toward the man's face. His arms and hands were already bloodied and torn up as he raised them to shield his face.

"Is that...Horus?" I shielded my eyes as I watched.

"Get Mari out of here!"

Gunner, now looking perfectly fine, swam like a dolphin across the pool and hopped out right in front of us, his expression hard and jaw clenched. "We've been fucking set up. They're coming this way right now. We can't let them capture a woman, let alone our only medic."

"How many did you see?" Jandro demanded.

"At least twenty."

"Any sign of Reaper?"

"No."

"What the—!"

Jandro hoisted me over his shoulder without another word, carrying me to the sandstone brick wall that surrounded the pool area.

"Climb over, Mari," he instructed.

"No! What's going on?"

He lifted me up by the waist so I had no choice but to grab the top of the wall and hoist myself up.

"There's no time to explain," Gunner told me apologetically. "But you've got to hide and they can't find you under any circumstances, do you understand?"

"Stay out of sight of the men with bows and arrows," Jandro added, his hand lingering on my leg that dangled over. "Do *not* try to sneak back in, no matter what they do to us."

"What do you mean?" I demanded. Fucking hell, what was happening?

"When we break out, we'll come for you." Gunner, the taller of the two of them, reached up to stroke his thumb along my jaw. "We'll explain everything later. But in the meantime, you can't let them find you. No matter what. Promise us, Mari."

If I wasn't in danger of falling off this thin ledge, I would've leaned down to kiss him. Or hell, both of them.

"I promise." The words came out a shaky whisper.

"Good girl." Jandro flashed me a tight smile. "Now go."

I didn't know whose lives I feared for more, theirs or my own. At some point, I found myself caring for these men. I just didn't realize it until right then.

With a final look at their tense faces, I swung my bare leg over the wall and carefully lowered myself down the other side until they disappeared from view.

Now outside the grounds of the outpost, wild brush, sparse trees, cactus, and a rocky ravine greeted me. The best part? I was still in a bikini with worn out sandals as footwear.

"Don't move, Steel Demons," a voice followed by dozens of footsteps called out from the other side of the wall. Despite the speaker not seeing me, I hardly dared to breathe. "Where's the woman you came here with?"

"Who, your wife?" the snarky reply came from Gunner. "Still passed out in my bed where I gave her the dicking of her life."

"Search inside and outside the grounds!" The speaker was not amused. "Find the biker woman and bring her to me. Then," his voice took on a cold, calculating tone, "after I'm done with her, I'll bring her to Fischlin myself."

Fuck! I couldn't stay here. I had to move. But there was literally nowhere to hide except the ravine, looking like a steep, miniature canyon as I peeked over the edge.

Taking a deep breath, I lowered myself to the edge and slowly placed one foot on the rocky outcropping to begin my climb down.

Huge mistake.

The rock came loose and my foot slipped.

I could only grab desperate handfuls of dirt and sand as I tumbled down into painful darkness.

Chapter 20

MARIPOSA

"Ow...fuck."

Everything hurt except for my head, which was the first thing I thought of. The last thing I needed now was a concussion.

My palms, forearms, and legs, however, were a different story. I slid down some sharp rocks down into the ravine and fell about another six feet to the even rockier bottom. In a bikini, no less.

I tried to stay calm as I mentally checked myself over from head to toe, carefully wiggling fingers and other small joints before moving onto the big stuff. When it felt like nothing was broken, I let out a huge sigh of relief. The pain was intense but it all felt like bad scrapes and bruises.

"Find her! Search the ravine!"

I sprang into action, rolling to the wall of the small canyon I fell in and pressing myself against the rocks. The sky looked like a narrow tear at least ten feet above me. My heart crashed against my ribs like a drum as I waited for faces to poke into view.

Footsteps along the edge caused small showers of rocks and dust to fall on me. Fighting the urge to cough, I raised a bloodied hand to shield my eyes and mouth. The outpost guards kept walking back and forth, talking to each other in low voices.

"Fuck you, I'm not going down there!" someone cried out.

I looked around desperately, my eyes finally adjusting to the dim light. On the opposite wall was an outcropping of rocks just high enough off the ground for me to hide under. Looking up, I nearly bit a hole through my lips. If they looked while I ran to the other side, I was fucked.

"Don't be a pussy, just..."

I made a break for it, crossing to the other side in five big steps and curling into a ball under the rock shielding me from above.

"Did you hear that?"

"Just a fucking ground squirrel. Look, she can't hide forever. Me and Sen will patrol the ravine. The rest of you check the outpost perimeter. She can't have gone far..."

Their voices and footfalls eventually faded away. Still I waited, barely daring to breathe.

When my legs fell asleep from being tucked under me for so long, I dared to sit on the ground and stretch them out. After a few more minutes passed, I stole a peek at the thin sliver of sky up above me. No faces looked back at me.

Fucking now what?

They had to be at least walking along the edge of the gorge in both directions. I'd probably be safest if I stayed put. But what the hell was happening to the guys? Would they be killed? The explosion meant someone must have died or was badly injured.

Reaper!

A gasp of realization escaped me before I clapped my hand over my mouth. The SDMC president was alone. He was the most valuable person of the club, surely they wouldn't kill him. Maybe the explosion was a distraction?

A cold horror came over me, bringing goosebumps to my skin. I crossed my arms and rubbed them as I paced, trying to figure this all out.

The Steel Demons came here in good faith, I knew that for a fact.

They were trying to work out an honest arrangement like what they had in Old Phoenix. I didn't know all the details of their plans, just snippets that I overheard, but I never once heard any of them trying to double-cross anyone.

They weren't the bad ones here. The owner of this place had to be in someone else's pocket. Someone trying to bring the Steel Demons down.

I was so absorbed in making sense of this mess in my head, I didn't realize that I stopped pacing and started walking.

Stopping in my tracks, another shiver came over me. But not from fear this time.

Tiny trickles of ice-cold water flowed through my sandals. I knelt down and washed off a bit of the coagulated blood and dirt off my feet. Water down here was a good sign, especially if I had to hide out for several days.

I looked back to see how far I walked. About a hundred feet, give or take. The rational part of me knew staying in one place made the most sense. But once my feet started moving, something else in me didn't want to stop.

It felt like an invisible string from my chest pulled me to keep walking through the ravine. Every instinct in me screamed to follow it, to keep going. If the feeling had a voice, it would be saying, *Someone needs you.*

I remembered this feeling. This was exactly how I felt right before checking on Kitty that last night at the service center. I chalked it up to being concerned about her, knowing about her cyst, but now without the distractions of kitchen duties, I knew it was this exact tugging sensation in my chest.

I froze for a moment, torn. For all I knew, it could have been pulling me to one of the guards looking for me. One of them might have tumbled down and sprained an ankle. Jandro and Gunner were adamant that I couldn't get caught, no matter what. Even an injured guard would likely sell me out to his boss.

But that pull was so strong. And the thought of someone injured who needed my help only made it stronger. I nearly had to brace myself against the rocky wall to keep from moving forward.

Fuck it.

I followed the trickling water, the pull immediately lessening as I placed my feet in front of each other. With one hand on the wall I kept moving, kept following my instinct.

I'd been a medic for three years and never felt this instinctual pull before. But finding whoever needed me outweighed the weirdness of this new sensation. I'd deal with it later, after getting the hell out of here and finding the guys.

The trickle of water eventually widened into a small stream running through the center of the canyon. It was still gentle and shallow, but sprang hope for a larger source of water up ahead.

I stayed glued to the wall as I continued on, not wanting to splash or give anyone above a chance to spot me. The stream gradually spread out into multiple trickles nearly the entire width of the ravine when I spotted it.

Among all the sharp-edged rocks, it was impossible to miss the softer, human form that held onto what looked like a large, black garbage bag. As I grew closer, the bag squirmed and let out a high-pitched whine.

"Oh my God!"

I broke into a run, immediately recognizing Hades squirming in the arms of Reaper.

"Mariposa?" Reaper's voice was harsher and raspier than usual. "The fuck are you doing down here?"

"I could ask you the same thing." I knelt by where he sat, leaning against a boulder with the whimpering dog squirming in his lap. "What happened?"

"He saved my life."

Reaper's voice cracked. Whether from dryness or emotion, I couldn't tell. But hearing the stoic president as anything but stoic shocked me.

"He pulled me out of the path of the explosion right before it went off. The blast still sent us rolling down the hillside into this ravine. I tried to shield him, but he's hurt bad." Reaper's hand shot out, wrapping around my upper arm with an iron grip. His eyes glittered like two green gemstones in the darkness. "You have to help him. Please."

The coldness in him was gone. His hold on my arm was strong but had a tremor to it. And his other hand held the injured Doberman cradled like a baby against his chest. He had no overblown ego now, no pride. Whatever was between me and him didn't matter. He was just a man desperate to save his friend.

"Please, Mariposa," he repeated. "Please save him."

"Let me see him," I agreed with a nod.

Reaper released me and allowed me to come closer, loosening his hold on Hades so I could examine him.

"Shh, it's all right," he whispered, stroking the dog's muzzle. "You're gonna be okay, boy."

"He's bleeding pretty badly," I reported, my fingers moving gently over the dog's blood-soaked flank. When I applied pressure, Hades cried out in pain and kicked out to get away from me.

"Shh shh shh," Reaper wrapped his arms around his neck and closed a hand over his muzzle. "I know it hurts, boy, but you have to be quiet."

"He might have something stuck, like a piece of shrapnel," I said. "But if I try to remove it, there's a chance he could bleed out. I just can't fucking see down here."

"Let's move him into the light," Reaper nodded at the centermost trickling stream of water, directly under the sliver of sky above the canyon.

I hesitated. "But then there's a chance they'll see us."

"We've been down here for hours and no one's come searching. They must think I'm dead. Now help me move him."

"They know I'm missing," I protested. "They're looking all over for me—"

"No offense, Mari, but when it comes down to you and my dog, I'm picking my fucking dog every day of the week. Now, can you help him in better light or not?"

"Yes," I sighed, ignoring the sting of his words. "I got his legs. You hold his front half."

Taking care to move his position as little as possible, we gingerly lifted him up and side-stepped to the center. I almost forgot how muscular Hades was for a dog, and felt like I was lifting a pile of cinderblocks.

When we set him down again, the direct sunlight on his wound made a world of difference.

"Oh yeah," I confirmed. "He's got something in there."

"Can you remove it?"

"Be quiet for a second and let me check his pulse." Even right then, it felt good telling Reaper off for once. I was in my element.

"I can take it out," I decided after some careful prodding of the wound. "But I need your shirt to slow the bleeding."

Reaper set Hades' head gently on his thighs and peeled off his cut and shirt with zero argument. I jerked my eyes back down to the injured pup to concentrate.

"I can only do so much down here," I warned him. "The wound still needs to be sterilized and closed up. If we don't get out of here soon, he could bleed out or succumb to an infection."

"Do everything you can then," Reaper instructed. "And I'll worry about getting us out."

In the direct sunlight, I noticed blood trickling down his temple for the first time. It also seemed to be matted in his hair.

Without thinking, I reached for him. "You're bleeding, too—"

"Don't worry about me," he waved me off.

"Reaper, a head injury is serious—"

"I'm fine!" he snarled. "Just don't let my dog die." His voice echoed off the rocky walls and then his face softened. "Please," he added in a whisper.

I nodded, returning my attention to Hades. "It's going to hurt and he's going to struggle. I need you to hold him down."

Reaper placed his hands down on Hades' sides where I instructed, then leaned over to comfort his scared friend.

"I got you, boy," he murmured, placing kisses on the dog's forehead. Hades' tongue darted out to lick his master in response.

With my patient distracted, I reached into the open wound with my bare hand, grabbed the edge of shrapnel that I felt earlier, and pulled.

A stream of blood and Hades' panicked kicking and howling followed. I placed Reaper's shirt over the would and pressed down.

"Shh, shh," Reaper closed his muzzle again, resting his forehead on Hades. "I'm sorry, boy. I'm so sorry."

The bleeding thankfully slowed after a few minutes. I tore Reaper's shirt in half then wrapped it tightly over Hades' thigh and tied it off.

"He's stable for now," I sighed exhaustedly. "But he needs actual medical treatment within a few hours. The sooner the better."

"He's not crying anymore." Reaper almost seemed to forget I was there. His eyes were glued to his dog's face in his lap.

"He's in shock," I explained. "The body does that for pain management sometimes, but he might not respond to you."

When Reaper looked up, it felt like he was seeing me for the first time since we met in this ravine.

"Thank you."

"You're welcome." I began washing the blood off my hands in the water.

"I mean it." He gently slid Hades' head off his lap and joined me in the water. "Not everyone understands it but he's my best friend. If I lost him, I—"

My fingers drifted to the dried blood at his temple. "Will you let me check your head now?"

He smirked and splashed his face with water. "I suppose."

While checking his head and neck for any bumps or swelling, I ran my fingers through his rich brown hair more than I cared to admit. He washed his face and hands in the water and I felt like a pervert watching it stream down his naked chest and back.

"You're cold," he murmured, running a hand up my arm.

"Hmm?"

"You're covered in gooseflesh." He looked up. The sun was no longer directly over us and the sliver of bright light had all but faded. "The temperature's dropping fast."

He was right, and the freezing cold water didn't help. Except for where his hand still rested on the back of my arm, I was shivering. I wanted to lean into that touch, to lean into *him* like a cozy blanket.

"Your head seems okay," I mumbled distractedly. "Just a few bumps."

"Great," he scoffed. "So I have the same winning personality for you to deal with."

"W-why..." My teeth chattered as I hugged myself, shaking like a leaf. "Why is it suddenly so cold down here?"

"You're barely wearing any clothes, for one thing," his eyes flickered over my bikini. "And the sun never fully touches everything inside these little canyons like it does the surface. So when night falls and it cools down, it gets way colder down here."

"Is it night already?"

"Getting there. Probably close to dusk now." His hand slid from my arm down to my fingers. "Come here."

"What?"

"Just come here." One tug on my hand sent me careening into his chest. His *naked* chest. Pressing against my *nearly* naked chest.

My heart pounded like crazy and I hated that he most likely felt it. I felt his own heartbeat, calm and steady as he wrapped both arms around my back, rubbing warmth into me from his rough palms.

"I can't be having you save Hades and then let you go by freezing to death," he mumbled into my hair. "Just relax. We'll all make it out of here."

I relented, letting my head drop to his shoulder. He was a warm, solid wall as my body slumped against him. His arms felt like a blanket around me—not only warm but secure. Solid. As if nothing in the world could reach me in this protected space.

Hades whined near our feet and Reaper moved to sit next to him, pulling me down with him. Our bodies never lost contact, not even when he extended one hand to pet his dog. He even seemed to hold me tighter with the other.

I sat between his legs, my knees curled up to my chest. At some point both of Reaper's hands returned to me, moving in gentle exploration up and down my back, running through my hair.

Neither of us spoke for the longest time as the cave grew darker and colder, except to murmur some words of comfort to Hades.

Eventually, I couldn't keep it in anymore.

"I'm sorry."

Reaper's chin grazed across the top of my head. "You're sorry for what?"

"For thinking the worst of you with no proof." My lips skimmed across his chest as I spoke. "For assuming you did those things to Gretchen based on...the life you lead."

He didn't answer and his hands stopped moving. I was afraid to look up, and hardly dared to breathe. Did I say something to piss him off again?

"You made the assumption most people would have," he said softly. "But now I'm sure you know things aren't always what they seem from an outside view."

"Yes," I agreed, tentatively resting a hand on his bicep. "And I know you're not most people."

Chapter 21

SHADOW

My brothers were in trouble.

And my president captured, or worse, dead.

But before I could find out for sure, I had to hack my way through these guardsmen tearing through every room in the outpost.

I stayed back in my room while everyone else went to the pool. Sitting out in bright sun and removing my clothing were not among my favorite things to do. Reaper had confided his unease about the deal to me last night, so I told him I'd do what I did best.

Be forgotten. Blend into the shadows. Watch and wait.

When I felt the rumble of the explosion on the other side of the building, I readied myself.

Fischlin's men were loud, their footsteps amateurish as they stormed the hallways. I squeezed the handle of my dagger in annoyance. Archers were supposed to be quiet.

"Find the woman! I want every inch of this place searched until she's found!" bellowed their leader just on the other side of the wall.

Another thing I didn't understand. Why other men were so

obsessed with women. Yes, they were nice to look at and fucking them felt good, but I would be just as content to never see another one again.

My bedroom door burst open, concealing where I stood directly behind it. A man with a bow and quiver of arrows on his back began rummaging through my things, pulling back my sheets and kicking my saddlebags. He paused and looked inside my bags with interest at the clinking of my glass liquor bottles.

Oblivious to the movement behind him, he pulled one bottle out to examine. His next breath was a gurgled choke on his blood as I slit his throat.

I wiped my knife on my cut, sheathed it, took his quiver and bow for myself, then left the room as silently as a cat.

The hallway was clear both ways, so I headed toward the direction of the explosion. A cracked open door up ahead prompted me to nock an arrow. Another guardsman was tearing that room apart, by the sound of it. I pulled back on the bowstring and loosed the arrow through the crack.

A satisfied grunt escaped me when I went to check and retrieve my arrow. I got him right in the throat. Bows weren't my favorite weapons by far, but I was decent with them. Gunner and I had a successful bowhunting trip a few years ago where he taught me how to hone in my aim. I had been so resistant to trusting him, but Jandro practically forced me to go. And I was glad I did.

Running footfalls on the tiled hallway pulled me out of nostalgia and had me spinning back to the door.

"What the aughh—"

He caught my knife with his throat as my weapon sailed the short distance between us. He fell to his knees and died before he realized what had happened, let alone remembered to alert anyone else.

I continued moving silently through the hallway, picking off any guardsmen who stood in my way. The few who saw me before they died registered me with shock and surprise in their eyes. Of course, they had forgotten all about me.

I was a big fucker, but I was silent and trailed behind the pack.

Whenever I was with the group, people often ignored me. They preferred talking to Reaper or Jandro, and rightly so. I was not known for my stimulating conversation.

Only *she* attempted to speak with me, the woman all my brothers got themselves caught for. She didn't forget me and I couldn't begin to understand why. She said she liked it when I looked at her. I didn't understand that either.

It didn't matter. She would forget me eventually.

Eliminating the search party was child's play. When I reached a set of heavy, carved wooden doors guarded by four men, I knew it would be more of a challenge.

"Stop! Who are you?" their captain demanded as all four of them nocked arrows.

Saying nothing, I walked forward slowly with my hands raised and made a big show of dropping my bow to the floor.

"He's one of them!" one of the guards declared. "The Steel Demons! He has their patch."

"Smart of you to surrender to us," their leader sneered. "Tell us where your president is and you'll be a very smart man indeed."

I kept my mouth shut but mentality filed away that Reaper hadn't been captured after all. He had to be alive, in that case.

"No?" the archer captain's lip curled as he stared at me. "We'll get you talking soon enough. Search him."

His men shouldered their bows as they approached me—empty handed and too close for shooting range. Just how I wanted them.

The moment they came close enough, my hands snapped to my back where I had two more hidden daggers sheathed. In the blink of an eye, my arms extended out to my sides with the blades firmly embedded into their chests.

"Shoot him! He's armed!"

The captain had no one left to call out to as I withdrew my blades from his two men, spun and quickly slit the throat of his third trying to ambush me from behind.

How foolish of him to think he could sneak up on a shadow.

But turning my back and dealing with him gave the captain time to react. I felt the sudden pressure of something embedded into the back of my leg. An arrow.

I barely looked at him, but didn't need to. As he reloaded, I sent a knife flying at his chest.

He stared at it, frowning as if it puzzled him for a moment before falling to his knees and face-planting dead onto the ground.

I turned him over to retrieve my blade, wiped it down, and proceeded to the set of the doors they'd been guarding.

"Shadow! Holy fuck, am I glad to see you."

The declaration came from Jandro the moment I pulled the doors open. He stood in the center of the room in a barred cage, barely tall enough for him to stand at full height or turn around in. The other members of the crew were placed in similar cages spaced throughout the room as if they were a collection of pets. For bigger, taller men like Gunner and Big G, the cells looked especially uncomfortable.

"What took you so long, big guy?" Jandro grinned as I approached.

"I had to kill everyone in my way." I examined the lock holding his cell closed.

"Figures," Gunner muttered. "The captain of those guards should have keys—"

CLANG! CLANG! CLANG!

A few hits from the handle of my dagger had Jandro's lock broken in seconds.

"All right. Thanks, King Kong," the vice president laughed as he walked out. "You smash locks, I'll grab keys and look out for anyone else."

"They don't have Reaper," I said as I moved on to Big G's cage. "They're looking for him and the woman."

"She has a name, Shadow." Gunner called from across the room. "It's Mariposa."

I shrugged before getting to work on Big G's lock. It didn't matter to me if she had a name or not.

"Holy shit, dude! You're bleeding bad." Big G's brow narrowed in concern at the arrow in my leg, which I'd forgotten all about.

"It'll stop." I reached down and snapped the shaft in half before yanking it out, which only prompted more blood to dribble onto the floor.

"Jesus fuck," Big G's face paled. "I dunno how you can do that without flinching."

I tossed the broken arrow pieces, unsure how to respond. I didn't feel pain. I hadn't felt anything remotely painful in years.

"Listen up, Demons!" Jandro raised a fist in the air once everyone was freed. "We have two priorities now—one, finding Reaper and Mariposa. Two, finding Fischlin and questioning him. Do *not* kill him, that's an order." He looked pointedly at me. "We need to question him and find out whose pocket he's really in. Anyone else we run into, feel free to kill them."

The men let out a collective cry of victory while shooting their fists in the air.

"Let's head to the armory," Gunner practically skipped out the door. "They must have stashed all of our shit there, plus extra toys that'll be fun to play with."

My brothers followed his lead while I retreated to my usual station at the back. Jandro stayed with me, looking at me with an expression I couldn't read. Not that I knew how to read many expressions.

"You all right, man?" He practically stood on tiptoes to clap me on the shoulder.

"Yes. Reaching you was easy."

"Good. Just making sure." He clapped my shoulder two more times. "You seriously saved our asses, you know. We overheard them talking about publicly executing us. I'll make sure Reaper knows what you've done."

"I didn't do it for recognition or reward. Aiding my brothers is my duty."

"I know, big guy, but still," he began jogging ahead of me to catch up with the others, "you're valuable and you shouldn't forget that."

I knew exactly what my value was—covering the others' weak spots. Aside from that, no one had any use for me. I didn't feel one way or another about that. I fully accepted my role and felt no need for anything else.

The men excitedly emptied the armory, with Gunner complaining over and over how he should have hitched an extra compartment onto his bike to bring everything home.

"Grab everything you can carry!" he instructed, stacking cases of ammo outside the door. "This'll be a much sweeter payout than our first so-called deal."

"Will you hurry the fuck up? We need to be searching, not looting," Jandro growled. "Reaper can handle himself but if they caught Mari—"

"Someone's coming." I spotted the first flicker of a shadow at the end of the corridor and drew a knife.

Six other men pointed weapons toward the guard, his face pale and his empty hands raised as he approached us.

"Don't shoot, please! I surrender!" He fell to his knees. "I'll cooperate. I'll tell you anything you want, just let me live."

"You're full of shit," Gunner spat, shooting off one round that went wild. It hit a column and sent the man's arms wrapping around his head.

"I'm not, I swear!"

"Where's our president and our medic?" Jandro demanded.

"I don't know, we never found them! But Fischlin," he raised a hand, palm up. "He's in his office right now, gathering up valuables and documents. He's about to ride off with someone, I don't know who. But if you hurry, you might stop him!"

A beat of silence passed before Jandro sprang into action. "Big G, you stay with him. But don't kill him yet. Everyone else with me!"

He broke into a sprint, dashing down the corridor with the rest of us trailing after him. Night had fallen and the only lights were torches mounted to the columns, making it feel like were in some ancient dungeon. My chest tightened in a way that had nothing to do with my running. My scar felt hot and I could almost feel liquid dripping down the side of my face.

I knew more about dungeons than I cared to admit.

"Whoa, holy shit!"

Jandro skidded to a stop right in front of a pile of debris in our path. To our left, a massive hole in the wall looked like it wasn't supposed to be there. To the right, a dark smear on the tile floor trailed off into the wild brush of the landscape.

"This had to be the explosion!" Jandro cried. "You guys, follow that blood trail and find our fucking president. Gunner and Shadow, with me."

"Horus is helping you guys," Gunner nodded at his men. "He'll lead you to where they are."

Jandro once tried to drunkenly explain the type of bond Gunner and Reaper had with their animals, but I couldn't easily follow. Aside from what he and Reaper did for me, I never had any kind of bond with anyone.

The three of us ran up to Fischlin's office doors a few seconds later. Jandro and Gunner both slammed their shoulders into the doors and bounced off like tennis balls.

"Move," I said.

They got out of the way just in time for my foot to crash through the heavy wood.

Gunner shook his head. "Fuck, I forget about how freakishly strong you are sometimes."

The doors were barricaded on the other side, but a few more kicks made a hole big enough for my arm to fit through. I reached through and pushed away the chairs and tables set up against the door so we could get through.

In seconds, we did.

To an empty office.

"Fucking shit!" Jandro ran to the open window, Gunner and I right on his heels.

In the distance, a motorcycle sped away, carrying two riders. My two brothers lifted their guns and started firing without another word. Behind them and over their heads, I fired off arrows from my bow, but they were already out of shooting range. The riders leaned down low from the onslaught of bullets and the driver accelerated as hard as the bike would go.

The person in the bitch seat was definitely the owner, dressed in the same loose, light-colored garb as the others who worked this outpost. The driver wore a leather cut, but it was impossible to see the patch on his back with the owner clinging to him.

"Fuck!" Jandro punched the windowsill when the riders became a mere speck on the horizon.

"We'll get 'em, bro," Gunner shouldered his weapon, looking determinedly out the window. "Maybe that prick Big G is babysitting can tell us something."

"Jandro! Captain Gunner!" One of Gunner's men came running into the office.

A screech followed him, and he ducked just in time to avoid getting clawed by Horus swooping in to land on his master's shoulder.

"Please tell me something good," Jandro sighed.

Gunner's man beamed with pride. "We found all of them, sir. Reaper, the medic, and Hades. They're stuck in a ravine and we need a rope."

It didn't take much looking to find a thick, nautical rope to drop into the ravine. Looking over the edge, I saw the woman huddled up against Reaper, shivering and barely wearing anything. Hades laid next to them, a crude bloodsoaked bandage wrapped around his rear leg.

"Fuckin' pitch black down there," one of Gunner's men mumbled as he came over with a torch.

"I can see them," I said but he tossed the torch down anyway. It bounced with a hiss over the streams of trickling water running through the cave.

"Tryin' to get us killed down here?" Reaper bellowed from down below.

"No, President," I called back. "The others can't see you that well."

"Shadow! I've never been so happy to see your ugly mug. Pull her up first."

I felt a slight weight on my rope a few seconds later and started hauling it up. The woman was covered in dirt and dried blood. Her arms and legs wrapped tightly around the rope like her life depended on it.

"Mariposa!" Jandro called from behind me, his footsteps approaching quickly.

"Baby girl!" Gunner called. "Are you all right?"

When I finished pulling her up to solid ground, I expected her to run straight to them. Women always ran to the handsome men. But to my surprise and confusion, it was *my* neck she wrapped arms around. Her feet dangled above the ground as she clung to me tightly.

"Thank you for saving us," she whispered in my ear.

Chapter 22

MARIPOSA

Hades' large, dilated eyes followed me as I cleaned up my supplies. His tongue hung out the corner of his mouth, which further softened his intimidating appearance. A patch of shaved fur showed off the jagged incision on his flank held together by my sutures.

"That's my boy," Reaper laid on the floor next to him, just outside of the pile of pillows serving as a temporary dog bed. "High as a kite," he chuckled, stroking down Hades' side.

"He won't need another dose for about twelve hours," I rolled my gloves off and shoved them into my trash bag. "He might be lethargic from all the meds for a day or two."

"Oh, we won't be going anywhere right away," Reaper's eyes flashed as he sat up. "We're tearing this place apart for information and living like kings while we're at it."

"Have they interviewed that guard yet?"

"No, but he's being sat on twenty-four seven. I'll talk to him after he's had some time to sweat."

The Steel Demons' president watched me silently as I sterilized my tools and laid them out on a side table. "Why didn't you heal Shadow's arrow wound?" he asked.

"Because he walked away from me when I offered," I asked. "Which I took to mean he was refusing my help."

"Why didn't you do it anyway? I thought healing was the most important thing to you."

"It is," I breathed. "But I can't treat someone against their will. I need their consent. Especially now."

"Why's that?"

"Because in a world like this," I spread my hands around. "With no laws or rights to protect us, our bodies are the last thing we have control over. To treat someone when they've said no is violating that final piece of personal control, even if it's to their benefit."

Reaper's eyes rolled back to his dog laid out on the floor. "What about animals? Hades can't tell you yes or no. He probably didn't understand down in that ravine and thought you were hurting him."

"I just have to make my best guess," I shrugged. "He saved you, so I imagine he wanted to keep on living to protect you and stay by your side. And something tells me," I paused, "Hades is more intelligent than your average dog."

"What if," Reaper rose from the floor, coming toward me with a slow swagger, "I *ordered* you to treat my men, no matter what they said? If I had Jandro or Gunner strapped down because of some ailment and they were screaming at you to get away, would you treat them if I ordered it?"

I squared my shoulders toward him, refusing to be intimidated. He was using his president's voice and sharp gaze, but I had seen the softness in him. I heard in his voice how worried he was about losing Hades. He held me against that beating heart in his broad chest so I wouldn't freeze to death. Who knew if his men ever saw that side of him, but I'd never forget it.

"No one has that kind of power," I told him. "Not even you."

"Not even if I punish you?" A wicked smile came to his lips. "Humiliate you with a public lashing, maybe?"

"You can deal out whatever barbaric punishment suits you," I answered. "That doesn't change the fact that you ordered me to violate your men's rights to govern their own bodies. How much would they respect and obey you if you denied them this? If they survived this hypothetical ailment, they'd know you see them as nothing more than slaves."

"Some would say it's better off that way," he responded coolly, his eyes searching mine. "They're rounding up people like cattle in the Southern territories."

"That's not you," I said with a shake of my head. "You're better than that."

"How do you know?" he snapped.

"Because you treat your dog like a family member," I said. "The respect between you and your men is mutual. And you have..."

"What?" he demanded, leaning forward so his face was an inch from mine. His hands braced on the table on either side of me, caging me in. "What do I have that a slave owner doesn't?"

"You have a moral code." His lips and the dark stubble surrounding them consumed my vision. "You value honesty and trust. And you," my eyes lifted to his, "you don't hurt those weaker than you."

Reaper pulled back for a moment, turning his gaze to the window. "Fucking hell. I knew this shit would happen."

I blinked. "What?"

He turned back to me, and the next thing I felt was the heat of his mouth on mine.

My lips parted in shock and his tongue wasted no time in pressing between them, the weight of his hands now on my lower back and pulling me forward. Just like the first time, each kiss was effortless, seamless.

He'd been so calm and detached down in that cave with a steady heartbeat. Now it raced under my palm through the thin shirt he wore. I groped down his chest, feeling for the hem of his shirt to remove the barrier between his skin and mine. I *needed* that heat again, to feel the texture of his scars and the coarse hair dusting his chest and under his navel.

He pawed at my top with the same frenzy, his hands roaming further than they ever did in that ravine. When my flimsy bra came off, his mouth fell to my neck as his hands swept forward to my chest.

At the first sensation of his calloused hands on my breasts, my head dipped back with a shameless moan. My whole body responded with a shiver at his rough thumbpads pressing over my nipples.

"Sensitive here, huh?" he murmured at the base of my throat before his lips trailed down my skin to meet his hands.

"Yeah." The word came out a breathy whisper as I braced one hand on the table behind me. A dull ache pulsed between my legs, growing needier with every caress and swipe of Reaper's tongue.

I grabbed the sides of his face, returning his mouth to mine with a fierce hunger. An amused chuckle rumbled through him. I felt it from my lips all the way to my core, stretching on my tiptoes to kiss him harder, to taste him deeper.

His hands slid down to my ass, grabbing each side with a firm hold that bordered on painful. That small hint of roughness sent me climbing him like a tree, gluing my inner thighs to his hips until my feet left the ground and locked behind him. He helped me up, holding me securely by my ass as he lifted me off the table and turned toward the bedroom of his fancy suite.

Thump-thump-thump-thump!

A knock startled me mid-kiss and Reaper let out an annoyed growl.

"Not now!" he yelled at the door.

"Sir," it sounded like one of Gunner's men. "The VP and Captain Gunner want to meet with you about—"

"I fucking said *not now*! One more word gets you a black eye, kid!"

His next kiss was rougher—full of teeth, possessiveness, and growling groans. I grew lightheaded with desire at the sudden change, molding my body to his as I returned his kisses with equal passion. I wanted, no, *needed* to hear those moans from him again. When he laid me down on his unmade bed with surprising gentleness, I came to the stark realization I wasn't afraid of him anymore.

"What if that was important?" I asked, looking up at him.

"Even if it is, it can wait." His fingers slid into the waistband of my scrub pants, yanking them down my legs. "Nothing is as important as this right now," he smoothed a hand up my thigh, rough fingertips tracing over my hip bones.

"Oh, really?" I tried to make my tone flirty but I had to know something before *this* happened. "Does that mean you won't ignore me anymore after you get off?"

He didn't answer but laid on his side next to me. Silently, he traced small circles on my hips and lower belly.

His silence made me so insecure, I couldn't stop myself from rambling. "I'm not asking for this to be any more than sex. I'm fine with that, just, you know. Can we put everything else behind us?"

His hand slid across my ribcage, cupping my breast before his palm met the mattress on the other side of me. Then he was on top of me, green eyes practically glowing.

"You saved my dog, my best friend," he said. "I can't put into words how important that makes you."

His mouth descended on mine again with the same passion as before, but full of tenderness rather than rough bites. There were so many layers to this man and I had a feeling I'd barely scratched the surface.

As his thighs nudged mine apart, I slid my palm down the horned skull inked on his chest. After rows of hard abs, my hand met an equally hard bulge straining to be freed from his jeans.

His moan through his kiss was so loud and hot. I loved that I could feel him as well as hear him.

He helped me unbutton and unzip him with a hurried hand, allowing me to shove his pants down muscular thighs that clearly knew how to ride both a motorcycle and a woman.

His lower half, cock included, was just as tanned as the sunkissed olive glow of his upper body. A surge of heat and desire ran through me at the thought of this glorious naked man lying out in the sun. He graced me with another sexy moan, this time vibrating against my neck, as my hand wrapped around the base of his thick shaft.

"Yes," he hissed in a tight whisper as I stroked upward, following the curve of his luscious cock. "Just like that."

Cradling my head in one hand, his fist tightened in my hair as he pulled. Staring at the headboard, the column of my throat exposed, he alternated between rough and gentle kisses on the sensitive flesh of my neck. I felt his hips move, beginning to thrust into my hand as he nipped my throat.

His other hand made a slow, lazy descent down my body, stopping for detours at my breasts, my waist, and both hip bones before venturing between my legs. He let out a pleased hum at what he found here.

"I take it you're enjoying yourself?" he murmured, slicking his fingers in slow, teasing exploration of my sex.

"Mmm," was all I could reply, writhing wantonly against his hand.

I enjoyed what he was doing most of all, but words and sentences escaped me. From head to toe, I was nothing but a body filled with the most basic, primal need.

"Getting eager, are we?" Reaper smirked as my hips lifted off the mattress, one leg clinging to his side with my foot pressing into his calf.

"I didn't think you brought me to bed just so we could get to third base." I released his shaft and cupped his balls, tugging slightly as I watched his face.

"Fuck," he hissed and went rigid, pulling away for a moment to stare at the blank wall.

"Enjoying yourself, I take it?" I teased, raking my nails lightly down his thighs. "Maybe a little too much?"

He barked out a laugh, holding my jaw as he brushed his thumb across my lip.

"I should've known an educated woman came with a smart mouth," his lips hovered above mine. "I broke a personal commandment bringing you into my club, now I'm bringing you into my bed. What have you done to me, Mariposa?"

Rhetorical question or not, I had no chance to answer. He lowered himself down, aligned his silky, round head to my sex and pressed forward.

I cried out, more from surprise than pain, my moan quickly swallowed by a deep kiss as Reaper began moving.

Holy...fuck, was all I could think as he entered and left me. That upward curve hit all the right spots and then some. I held onto his wide, muscular back like I might come apart at any moment.

"Fuck," he groaned again, pausing his thrusts while fully sheathed inside me. His breaths came in ragged pants as he kissed and nipped every part of me that his mouth could reach.

"Something wrong?" I asked, my own pants matching his.

"No, sugar. Not at all." He tenderly brushed a piece of hair off my face. "I just want to feel you for a minute."

His cock pulsed inside me, filling up the aching emptiness that never felt so torturous until I met him and his men. *Wait...probably shouldn't be thinking about the other guys right now. Just focus on him. It's not like he isn't hot enough.*

I spent the pause in his movement doing just the same—feeling him. I ran my fingers through his dark brown hair that started growing longer. My fingertips traveled over his neck, his shoulders and biceps, pausing on the pale scars that dotted his olive skin. I traced the veins in his forearms, taking them in like winding blue rivers. When I moved to his chest, outlining the grinning, horned skull, he brought another kiss down on me. His hips rolled, abs flexing as he moved that dick inside me again.

I held onto him tighter, digging my nails into his back as my hips lifted. My clit tingled with increasing intensity as I matched him thrust for thrust.

"Don't stop this time," I whispered desperately in his ear.

The growling moan he answered with was the hottest sound I ever heard any man make.

He crashed into me faster, pressing me down into the bed with the impact of each thrust. My own moans became desperate whimpers as my orgasm peaked higher and higher, nearing its tipping point but always just out of reach.

"Mariposa," Reaper groaned into my neck, his fists tightening into my hair.

His cock swelled inside me just as my release convulsed around him. Hearing him moan my name was like the key that unlocked my pleasure. His warmth spilled inside me, shivers wracking his whole body as my pussy milked him.

We stayed locked together until we both came down from our highs. With post-orgasm clarity, I half expected him to roll over and fall asleep. Worst case, he'd shoo me off to my own room.

Instead he pulled me with him as he rolled onto his back, holding me against his chest with his arms around my waist. After a few moments, I heard his deep breathing with his lips on my hair.

Chapter 23

REAPER

Mariposa rolled away from me at some point while we slept. I also woke up to find Hades sleeping at the foot of the bed, but that wasn't entirely unexpected. He never left my side while in perfect health. His instincts didn't change even while drugged up and injured.

I rolled to my side, scooting closer to Mariposa's back. Not caring if I woke her, I nestled my palm into her waist and dragged my lips against the nape of her neck.

I loved how her curves fit against me, how responsive and sensitive she was. My cock twitched from where it pressed against her ass. If Hades wasn't in bed with us like a stage-5 clinger, I wouldn't have hesitated to go another round with her.

"Hmm."

Mariposa moaned sweetly as she stretched, her toes and fingers curling as she rolled over to face me.

"You're still here," she murmured sleepily, as if surprised by that.

I remembered her comment about this being nothing more than sex, which seemed to be in the same vein. She trusted me more than before, but still expected me to use and discard her. I wasn't sure how to tell her that wasn't where my head was.

"I don't want to go back to work yet." I traced her jaw, bringing her lips to mine for an open-mouthed kiss.

I wasn't normally such a kissy guy, but I couldn't get enough of how she tasted. Next time, I absolutely had to taste her pussy. She must have tasted divine.

"Hades," she giggled, noticing his big black form at the end of the bed. "You aren't supposed to be jumping on things, silly boy." She scratched his head with her toes, making him grunt and look at us upside down.

"Can't keep a good dog down," I mumbled against her cheek, dragging my mouth down to her collarbone. Fucking hell, her taste and smell were nothing short of intoxicating.

"So what's next?" she asked, her lips brushing my forehead.

I took my time kissing her collarbone before answering. "Next, we can fuck in the shower. Maybe by the pool. Somewhere the gimpy mutt won't follow us."

She laughed lightly, scooting down to rest her head on my shoulder. "So this is something you want to repeat?"

"Yes." I rested my hand on her waist again. "That sounds like a loaded question, though."

Her fingers began tracing the Steel Demons tattoo on my chest. "Will you be sleeping with others?"

My hand began mimicking hers, fingertips tracing on her skin. "I don't plan on it."

Her hand stopped.

"You don't plan on it," she repeated.

"If you want something from me, just come out and say it," I said. "I should warn you, though, I don’t do traditional relationships."

"I know," she whispered. "Noelle told me a little about how you grew up. In the matriarchal communities."

"Yeah? What'd she tell you?"

"That you had one mother and three fathers. That it was accepted for women to be with multiple men at the same time."

"Yeah, and look how well that turned out," I scoffed. "The Collapse put an end to those communities."

"What happened to your family?" she looked up at me. "How did you end up as an MC's president?"

"A long story for another day, sugar," I stroked my fingers through her hair. "Preferably after I find out who wants my club annihilated."

She was quiet for a moment. "Then can you tell me what happened to your brother?"

I almost said no. My own story was long and bloody, but it was mine. Ultimately I didn't care who knew it. But Daren's was different, partly because he was such a different person than me. He was bright-eyed and hopeful, nowhere near as jaded as me. I wanted to keep those memories of him close to my chest, a well-guarded secret. He deserved to be remembered as how he was, not how he died.

If it were any other woman next to me, I would have told her to mind her own fucking business. But somehow, I knew Mariposa would understand.

"Daren was nothing like me and Noelle," I said. "He was the youngest of us three, but acted like a fourth father sometimes." Mari's lips curved into a smile at that. "Noelle and I were the daredevils," I went on. "We had drinking and smoking contests in our teens. We stole a tattoo gun once and gave each other our first tattoos." I raised my arm to show her the faded blue squiggle near my wrist. "And it was never our parents scolding us, it was Daren. But as the world got shittier and the Collapse became imminent, he always believed things would get better."

"I used to think the same thing," Mari answered softly, her fingers resuming tracing the lines of ink on my chest.

"Right, well," I sighed. "Long story short, the club rode through this little shanty town near the old Utah border a bit over a year ago. Hardly anything was there, so we rode through without stopping. Not even a full day later, everyone is fucking sick. Like, deathly ill."

Mari's eyes widened. "A virus? Some kind of airborne bio-weapon?"

"That's what we think," I said. "Some asshole might've bombed the place in a border war. Anyway, we were all on death's doorstep and could barely sit on our fucking bikes. Somehow, we found a small clinic and just raided the fucking place. We shot ourselves up with every vaccine we could find. We holed up there for a week and most of us started to feel better."

My hand curled into a fist in her hair. I didn't even know if I could bring myself to say what happened next. I never talked about it. Everyone was there and saw it for themselves.

"Daren didn't get better." Mari said it for me.

"We were one short on the last vaccine. I don't even remember what it was," I said. Once I started talking, it all seemed to spill out of me. "I tried to make him take it but he refused. He said I needed to beat whatever this shit was, because I was president and the club needed me. '*The world needs you.* She *needs you,*' he said. He was already so weak, he was just babbling nonsense. I told him I'd take half the syringe if he took the other half. He finally agreed but when he stuck me, he emptied the whole syringe into my arm."

I rubbed my forehead as though trying to wipe that memory away. "God, I was so fucking pissed at him."

"I'm sorry," Mari whispered. "But if you had split the vaccine, probably both of you would have died."

"Good. Then he wouldn't have died alone."

"But then you wouldn't have Hades," she protested. "And your men would be lost without you."

And I wouldn't have you, naked and beautiful lying next to me.

While few and far between, I had my moments where I was grateful to be alive. Despite talking about something deeply uncomfortable to me, this was one of those moments. If I had to talk about it, I was glad it was with her. And not only because she felt like heaven wrapped around my dick hours earlier. She stayed calm and comforting without going into hysterics like some women did.

Even so, talking about Daren set a dark cloud over my mood. I needed to think about anything else.

"I should go interview this guard," I said, rolling upright. I gave Hades a few pats before looking around for my clothes. "You can stay here if you want," I told Mari. "Or walk the grounds, go down to eat. It should be safe to walk around anywhere now."

"Can I go with you?" she asked, biting her lip as if bashful.

"Probably not a good idea," I mused, tucking my junk into my pants before zipping up. "Depending on how cooperative he is, we might need to get creative extracting information out of him."

"You're going to torture him?" her eyes widened.

"I'm going to do what's necessary to find out who wants us dead." I leaned over the bed, holding her chin in my hands. "This is your life now, sugar. I'm not the worst of men, but I'm still not a good one."

She said nothing, but I saw the wheels turning in her head as she stared back at me defiantly. When I lowered my mouth to hers, she kissed me back, sending a jolt of pleasure straight to my cock when she bit my lower lip and tugged.

Hmm. Maybe my sweet medic had a little bad girl in her after all.

"On second thought," I groaned, my lips still pressed to hers, "you better be right here when I get back. Naked and wet for me."

"Hmm," she pursed her lips, a smirk tugging at one corner. "I'll think about it."

"You'll do it. If you want to come, that is."

She lifted one shoulder in a shrug. "Maybe I like a little delayed gratification."

"You don't want to test me, woman," I growled, cupping the side of her neck. "That is not a game you will win."

"You've never played with *me* before," she grinned before pressing lightly on my chest. "Go. Do your interrogation before I change my mind completely."

"You won't," I promised her, stealing one more kiss before turning to leave.

Just before reaching the door, I heard Hades grunt and whine, wishing to follow me. Then Mari's voice comforting him, no doubt giving him pets and telling him I'd be back.

It brought a smile to my face, a rare one of genuine joy. I got weirded the fuck out when he took to her so quickly. Now it almost seemed like it was meant to happen.

"That good, huh?"

Jandro stood right outside my door, arms crossed and eyes narrowed suspiciously. "I haven't seen you smile like that in a long-ass time."

"Fuck off," I snapped. "Who posted you at my door like my fucking keeper?"

"Just waiting for you to join us. But it's clear you're off doing," he licked his lips, "*much* better things."

"I do like to think I have my priorities in order. So, shall we?"

"How's the pooch?" he asked as we started walking.

"Better than expected," I admitted. "I almost thought I lost him. But Mari worked like hell to save him. He'll be on antibiotics and painkillers for a while, but right as rain in a few weeks."

"Mm-hmm. And I'm sure you thanked her properly," he said with a jab to my arm.

"I'd like to think so," I smirked. "I might a few more times just to make sure."

"Damn. Leave some for the rest of us, Reap," he laughed. The grin left his face the moment he saw my ponderous expression. "Wait, you're not actually thinking...?"

"I'm not thinking anything yet," I said dismissively. "It's too soon to tell. But she," I sucked in a breath, "she seems convinced I'll fuck anything that walks by. So if you and Gunner keep getting close to her and something happens, maybe she'll feel better about it."

"Did you actually *tell* her you don't work that way?"

"Not exactly," I sighed. "Like I said, it's too soon. For all I know, she just wants to use *me* as a fuck toy."

"You know it's not like that," Jandro shook his head. "At some point, you're gonna have to tell her sharing her with other men means she's special to you."

"I will if it gets to that," I snapped. "But she's still wrapping her mind around being in an MC. Let me fuck her a few more dozen times before we talk about getting serious."

We walked in silence down the corridor, our boots echoing off the stone tiles. The outpost was gloriously empty and it felt amazing not having some sneaky fuckers watching us at all times.

"She's not the only one who'll have to wrap her head around it," Jandro murmured. "You know Gunner's sweet on her, but he's the poster boy for pre-Collapse America. He doesn't get the whole matriarchal sharing thing."

"We'll cross that bridge when we come to it," I said through gritted teeth.

Jandro was a strategic and thorough thinker. His intelligence was a huge asset to me, but goddamn if his habit of thinking ten steps ahead didn't grate on me sometimes.

Gunner wore a grim expression at his post as we approached the room where our prisoner was guarded.

"President," he greeted me with a curt nod. He wasn't usually so formal with me. Was he sour because I fucked Mari?

"Is he talking?" I nodded at the set of doors behind him, choosing to ignore his sourpuss mood.

"Oh yeah. He didn't hold nothing back." Gunner's frown deepened.

"And?"

"It's worse than we thought."

"Quit playing hard to get, Gun. Fucking spill it."

"He said the man paying Fischlin to capture and kill us," his hands drifted to his weapons on his belt, "was none other than General Tash."

POWERLESS

STEEL DEMONS MC BOOK TWO

Prologue

JANDRO

THREE YEARS PRE-COLLAPSE

The coffee stopped kicking in six hours ago, but I choked down the bitter liquid anyway. It was the only thing that kept me going on this sixteen-hour shift. My fourth double-shift this week.

I winced at the sound of Sergeant Crodick's baton clanging on the inmates' metal doors. What an asshole. Guards, inmates, and even other supervisors hated that guy. Sure, this was the mental health building, where most inmates paced, rocked, scratched the walls, and talked to themselves at all hours of the night. But some of them were trying to sleep, too, goddamnit.

That smug asshole knocked his baton on every. Single. Cell door.

Whoever was awake became agitated, slamming their palms on the doors and yelling through the small plexiglass window. That alerted anyone who'd been sleeping, jolted awake by the initial clang and now disoriented by all the commotion.

Crodick chuckled as he returned back to the office. My grim expression apparently amused him even more.

"There ya go, rookie." He sat down in the chair and propped his feet up on the desk. "Get busy and settle the nut jobs down." With a lace of his fingers over his belly, he leaned his head back and closed his eyes. It didn't even take a minute for him to start snoring.

"Asshole," I grumbled, tossing my paper coffee cup into the trash can.

So much for a relaxing rest of the shift. I had a sinking feeling he'd call me for overtime again tomorrow. The supervisors always begged and pleaded and harassed the new guards to stay. Turnover was high at these government facilities while pay and benefits were laughably nonexistent. Only the old-timers could sit back and collect a decent check. Their wages had been negotiated back when labor unions still had power. Nowadays the newcomers did all the dirty work for basically slave wages.

We all knew the world was going to hell in a handbasket, it was just a matter of when. The twenty-year veterans who still had some value in their retirement accounts were just waiting for the right moment to cash out. They watched the slimy politicians pandering for votes and threw their support behind the most outlandish claims and emptiest promises —usually something to protect the dwindling assets they spent a lifetime building.

My generation? Oh, we were fucked. And no one gave a shit.

My footsteps were heavy as I walked out onto the floor, pulling my baton from the loop in my belt. Some inmates went quiet at just the sight of me holding it.

A sigh deflated my chest, the baton heavy in my hand. This wasn't me. I got no pleasure out of yelling at people in cages, many of whom didn't even know what was going on. All I wanted to do was fix motorcycles and bring a girl home once in a while. I didn't get paid enough to find any joy in scaring people.

Crodick was already asleep, so why did it matter if the inmates kept yelling and hitting the doors? If I got fired for insubordination, good fucking riddance.

I walked the floor like a zombie, then ascended the stairs to the upper tier. I looked straight in front of me, but my eyes didn't focus on anything. *Damn, my feet and back hurt like a bitch.* At twenty-one years old, this job already had me aching like an old man. Fuck, I just wanted to go home.

Just like on the floor, the inmates on the upper tier went quiet at the sight of me. No yelling or baton-banging necessary. Some of them were probably spooked by when I first got hired and did some baton-swinging to prove myself. Now a whole two months later, I was so fucking over it.

One cell at the end didn't quiet down like the rest. I paused in front of the door to the sound of incoherent mumbling, followed by guttural, tortured screaming.

"Hey," I knocked my baton on the door twice. "Calm down in there and go to sleep."

I heard a series of thumping sounds, like a body being thrown against the walls, then whimpering and more screams.

"Hey!" I knocked harder on the door. "I said calm the fuck down and go to sleep!"

"I can't!"

The answer startled me. Not that it was unusual for inmates to talk to us, but amid all the mumbling and screaming, those two words sounded strangely coherent.

I pulled my flashlight from my belt, clicked it on and shined it through the square window.

A pale, skinny kid shielded his eyes from where he sat against the wall. He wore the white inmate-issued pants but had taken his shirt off, as many of the male inmates did to sleep.

"Jesus fuck," I swore, lowering the light from his face to his torso.

He was covered in scar tissue. Burns, cuts, scrapes and everything imaginable crisscrossed over his thin, malnourished body. It hardly looked like he had any unmarked skin at all.

When he lowered his hands from his eyes, I saw more scarring on one side of his face. A wicked slash cut through one eye, the iris of which looked almost completely white. His other eye was dark brown, almost black like the hair buzzed close to his scalp.

"You don't have to sleep, just quit fucking screaming," I told him, making sure to add a hard edge to my voice.

"I'm trying!" His brow pinched tight with despair. I could now see the tear tracks on the kid's face, who looked no older than me.

I should have walked off right then but something pulled at me to stay with him. Most of our inmates went through some kind of trauma, whether before or after coming to our facility, but I never saw anyone so broken down as this kid. Even more unusual, he seemed sane now that he wasn't screaming his head off.

I sank to the floor, getting eye-level with the small foodport slot in his door and unlocked it. *Fuck. Maybe I'm the crazy one*, I thought as I slid it open.

"Hey, come here," I said through the slot. "Tell me what's going on with you."

"No! You're going to pepper-spray me again."

Shit. When was that, yesterday? Last week? All the long shifts had blurred together so much, I forgot Crodick and his asshole buddy had coaxed inmates to look through the foodport and sprayed them for fun.

"That wasn't me," I answered. "Look, I'm a new guy. I'm not even supposed to be talking to you. But you don't seem all that crazy and I'd rather level with you than yell at you. So what's wrong?"

He didn't come closer to the door, but his shaking voice floated from across the cell.

"I'm not crazy. I just get bad nightmares when I sleep. Sometimes they stay with me as I wake up. I don't *want* to wake up screaming but I can't help it. I've been trying to stay awake but when I nod off..."

"Okay. Have they given you meds?"

"All the nurses are female! I don't take anything from women. No, never again. No, no, no."

Hmm, maybe he was a little nuttier than I thought. But on a second glance at his scarred up body, maybe not. Either way, I couldn't blame him for being distrustful.

"Okay," I repeated. "Would you accept meds if they came from a man?"

He hesitated before answering. "If they work. And if no one hits me." A soft sob echoed against the concrete walls of his cell. "I just want it to stop."

I leaned my head and shoulder against the door with a sigh. I had no power to help him. Any requests to make inmates more comfortable would be met with suspicion and scrutiny. And I wouldn't put it past Crodick and his crew to double-down on harassing this kid just because I was trying to do something nice for him.

My head lifted off the door with a start, remembering something about Crodick that I could use. *No*, I thought. *You will get tossed out of this job so fast and maybe even arrested.*

The next thought came just as quickly, spurring my tired feet to get under me. *Fuck it. You're already done with this place.*

"I'll be right back," I told the kid, leaving the foodport open as I headed for the stairs.

This was stupid, bordering on dangerous. But the world was ending and I ran out of fucks to give.

Crodick remained in the same position I left him in—hands on his belly, head leaned back, mouth open and snoring.

I came up next to him as silently as I could, then held my breath as I slowly pulled open the file drawer just below his feet. He snorted once but didn't wake up. Only a few seconds of rummaging produced what I needed—his hidden flask of whiskey.

"When you win your first fight with an inmate, you can have a shot," he taunted me when I first got hired as he poured a generous amount into his coffee.

"Why would I fight one of them?" I had asked. "We're supposed to treat them humanely, right?"

He had doubled over laughing as if that was the funniest joke he ever heard. The memory followed me like a ghost as I left the office with the small bottle, taking it back to the door with the open foodport.

When I kneeled in front of the slot, one pale, scarred white eye and one brown eye peered at me through the opening.

"Here," I said, shoving the flask through. "It'll numb you and you might even be able to sleep a little. You're gonna feel rough tomorrow, though."

He took the flask and twisted the top open, holding it under his nose as he took a small whiff. Then he held it to his lips and upturned it to swallow every last drop.

"Well, that's one way to do it," I muttered. "You'll start feeling it soon."

The kid was so thin, he already began to sway where he sat. His lids half-closed and his brow finally relaxed.

"Hey, before you nod off," I said. "What's your name?"

His eyes snapped open, staring at me with their odd-colored gaze. For the first time, he looked confused. As if he didn't understand the question.

"I'm Alejandro de Leon," I offered. "But you can call me Jandro."

His expression relaxed again as he leaned heavily against the door.

"You can call me Shadow."

Chapter 1

MARIPOSA

PRESENT DAY

I flopped over in bed, my hand slapping down on someone's hard, muscular body. As my eyes cracked open, my waking brain registered that this body was covered in short, dense fur.

Sure enough, Hades grinned at me with his goofy Doberman smile before licking my face. "Ugh, dog breath," I groaned, rolling away for fresh air and to finish joining the waking world.

The palm trees cast long shadows over the desert landscape, which meant I slept for several hours. Reaper left to interrogate the outpost guard before I went down for a nap and still hadn't come back.

I sat up, rubbing my face in an attempt to let the events of the last twenty-four hours sink in and solidify in my mind.

There was an explosion, and not a minute later, the outpost guards descended on the Steel Demons MC, despite that we'd come peacefully as guests.

My heart skipped a beat at the notion that I included myself in that *we*, but was I part of them, really? I came as their medic, and I could still feel the ache of having Reaper between my legs earlier this morning.

My life flipped upside down in an instant, but several aspects remained the same. I still provided medical services, my latest patient being the massive Doberman in the bed next to me. I still traveled the Southwest, only I rode on the back of a roaring motorcycle instead of by foot or bus.

And just like before, I was surrounded by deadly men who killed with no hesitation. Only this time, I wasn't one of their targets. To make matters even more fun, I slept with the Steel Demons president. Making sense of my feelings for him or any of these men seemed as productive as unraveling a spider's web.

On the bright side, the Steel Demons were easy on the eyes and had no intention of killing me, since I was apparently useful.

I shook my head with a sigh and slid my feet down to the floor. These kinds of things shouldn't be thought about on an empty stomach and I was *starving*.

Hades lifted his head off the pillow, watching me as I got dressed.

"You stay here, boy," I told him. "I'll bring you something from the kitchen."

He was having none of that. As I headed for the door, he rolled over and jumped off the bed.

"No!"

I yelled too late, not that he would obey a command from me anyway. But I just put sixteen stitches in his flank to close up a shrapnel wound from the explosion.

"Hades, you can't go jumping," I scolded as he approached. "Your wound needs to heal."

I went to look at it and my heart nearly stopped.

"What the fuck?" I ran my hand over the shaved section of fur just above the incision. "How did you heal so fast?"

He wasn't fully healed, but the progress looked much further than just a few hours. Both sides of the incision had already sealed together, and shiny scar tissue was beginning to form.

I sat on the floor, stunned out of my damn mind. It should have been weeks before it looked like that. On top of his freakish ability to run alongside Reaper's bike without stopping, it became all too clear that nothing was ordinary about this dog.

"How long have I been asleep?" I asked his toothy grin. "Really now. Did I get put under some sleeping beauty spell and only your kiss could wake me up?"

He leaned forward and licked my face, assaulting me with slobber and dog breath again.

"Ugh, I knew it," I laughed, rolling backwards. "Your breath smells like the underworld itself, but you're the only prince around here."

He pranced around me playfully, eyes bright and alert. The drugs I gave him had worn off and he seemed like a brand-new pup.

"Well, if you're feeling better," I climbed to my feet. "I guess you can come with me on my quest for food."

He let out an excited yip and immediately went to the door. We left Reaper's suite together, Hades' back nearly brushing my hip as we made our way down the quiet halls.

I was honestly relieved to have him with me. The Steel Demons escaped the outpost guards and rescued me, Reaper, and a badly injured Hades from a ravine just outside the property. Reaper told me it was safe to walk around now, which I took as code to mean they killed everyone in retaliation for their capture.

Everyone except for that guard now being interrogated in their custody, and who knew what his fate would be in the hands of these men?

Despite the threat of danger gone, the eerie quietness of the place set me on high alert. My sandaled feet and Hades' claws were the only sounds echoing off the sandstone tiles and columns. The kitchen was just as quiet as I pushed open the swinging door.

I went immediately to the large refrigerator while Hades sniffed along the supply shelf on the opposite wall.

He's probably starving, too, I realized as I scanned the produce and prepped ingredients in sealed containers. Meat and dairy was scarce, but if I could find some rice or potatoes, he would probably make do with that for a little while.

I pulled open a drawer and almost shouted with excitement. Eggs! A good source of protein and calories for dogs and humans. Running my hands over the various shades of brown shells, I counted more than thirty in the carton. It had to be insanely difficult to get fresh eggs from a farmer this far up in the mountains. The more plausible answer was this place had its own chicken coop.

"Hades!" I whistled as I grabbed two eggs in each hand. "Want a yummy scramble for—"

A threatening growl and a whimper cut me off. I set the eggs down on the counter and darted in the direction of the sound. "Hades, what—"

Tucked back in a corner of the kitchen, a girl sat on the floor with her knees to her chest. Hades' teeth were bared as he snarled inches away from her face.

"Hades, back off!"

He ignored me, naturally, so I pushed him out of the way and kneeled between him and the girl.

"Hey, he won't hurt you. He's just protective. Are you okay?"

She lifted her head just a few inches and nodded, peering at me over her knees. I recognized her as one of the kitchen girls who served us when we first arrived.

"No one's going to hurt you." I placed a hand on her arm in an attempt to soothe her. "My name's Mariposa."

"They killed everyone," she said in a shaky whisper.

"It's...it's not what it seems." I sounded like I was making really lame excuses for the MC's carnage, and maybe I was. "The club was deceived by the owner of this place. They retaliated and won. But you weren't involved. They don't hurt innocents, I promise you."

Her head lifted another few inches. "They won't... take me?"

How was I supposed to answer that? They took me, albeit not in the way she was probably thinking. I was afraid of that too at first, but by the time Reaper slid inside me, I wanted him just as badly as he did me.

While my feelings were a jumbled mess, I knew I could trust the

Steel Demons president and his men to not hurt this girl. So I clasped my hand over hers and chose to reassure her.

"They won't touch you. I swear it."

"You better not fucking touch her!"

I turned my head slightly to see a gun barrel hovering in my peripheral vision.

"Step away!" the gun wielder demanded. "Back up slowly."

I did as instructed, finding out the gun's owner was the second kitchen worker as I backed up to the counter.

"Take it easy," I breathed, hands raised and eyes locked on the long, dark barrel pointed at my chest. "No one's hurting anyone."

Hades did not get the memo to calm down. He turned fearlessly to the girl with the gun, teeth bared and a low growl in his chest. It was enough for her eyes to cast a nervous flicker toward him, but she kept her focus on me.

"You're with them," she spat at me. "The road pirates who came here and killed everyone."

"Rightfully so because *your* boss was going to kill them first," I shot back. "Don't act like your side is so innocent in this."

"All we do is cook! We don't have much of a choice in what side we pick."

"Then put the gun down," I told her. "Because we're not your enemies. Shoot that thing at me or the bikers and you'll make enemies, though."

Her wide eyes darted with indecision as the barrel lowered just slightly. I couldn't blame the girl for feeling conflicted. Like me, she probably made it this far by not trusting anyone.

When she didn't lower it fast enough, Hades made an attempt to speed up the process.

By biting her hand.

"Ahh! Get it off!" she screamed as the gun clattered to the floor.

I held my breath as I watched the weapon fall and then kicked it away. Hades immediately released her hand and sat on his haunches like a good boy. He returned my bewildered stare with innocent, large eyes. The damn dog really was just making sure she'd drop the gun.

"I'm fucking bleeding!" the girl wailed, curling her hand to her chest. "Get the bandages!" she yelled to her friend, quiet as a statue still sitting on the floor.

"Let me see," I reached out for her arm and gave her an annoyed look when she pulled away. "You're lucky I'm a trained medic. If you want to handle a dog bite on your own, be my guest."

She stared me down with her best defiant look before relenting, holding her injured hand out to me.

"Let's wash it in the sink," I suggested, walking around the island counter. "If you have a first aid kit, you can grab that," I told the other girl.

"This doesn't mean we're going to service any of those men you came with," the injured woman hissed through gritted teeth as I washed the blood off.

"You're not expected to. Just do the same kitchen work you've been doing while we stay." I looked up and met her eyes. "Like I told your friend, they won't touch you."

Her eyes narrowed at me. "You shouldn't stay long, anyway. Our food stores are low."

"Really, now? When you're this far into the mountains?" I countered, scrubbing her puncture wounds with the soap bar. "You had an awful lot of eggs from what I saw."

She squirmed a little. "We have good relationships with farmers in the area. They make regular deliveries to us."

"In exchange for what?"

"Why are you so fucking nosy?" She pulled her hand from my grip. "I'm just saying your gang should leave if they don't want to starve. They're too big and have too many mouths to feed."

"It just doesn't make sense," I said coolly as I shut the water off. "A place this isolated would be a lot more likely to have its own food sources. You can't get *that* many fresh eggs without a chicken coop nearby."

"We don't have a chicken coop!" she insisted. "Those are to last us until the next delivery in a week. We just don't have enough for you, your dog, and all your men."

"And I think you're lying," I crossed my arms. "So how many chickens *do* you have? Any other livestock?"

"We don't have *any*—"

A clatter of metal on metal announced that her friend just returned with a first aid kit and dropped it on the counter. But it was the soft flapping sound that followed that drew mine and Hades' attention to the open window.

"Ahhh!" both girls screamed as Gunner's falcon, Horus, flew into the kitchen and skidded across the counter with his limp victim in his talons.

"What is that?" the first girl whimpered as Horus began plucking at his bloodied carcass on the kitchen counter like this was his roost all along.

Hades let out an excited bark, propping his front paws on the counter to sniff out his feathered friend's conquest. Horus had already made serious headway on tearing his prey open, but the downy feathers in the air, scaly feet, and short beak gave it away.

The falcon caught a chicken for dinner. And Hades gave him puppy eyes like he was asking him to share.

I turned slowly to the kitchen girl whose face paled as she watched the scene before us.

Maybe it was rude of me but I was completely unable to help the smugness in my voice.

"You were saying?"

Chapter 2

MARIPOSA

The kitchen girls, whose names I found out to be Marnie and Mimi, gave me no trouble after that. They showed me their small farm hidden at the bottom of a hill on the far side of the outpost—far away from all the guest rooms and accommodations.

In addition to about thirty adult chickens, they also had a small herd of goats, vegetable patches and fruit trees. Some supplies still required trading with other farmers but as I suspected, this place was largely self-sufficient.

When I asked Mimi, the girl who'd been bitten, if they could make chicken for the Steel Demons that evening, she was a lot more accommodating than before.

Horus gorged himself on his kill but left most of it on the counter, seeing as he wasn't a huge bird himself. The girls were thoroughly grossed out by the mess he made and refused to touch it. So I took to cooking up the leftovers with a mix of egg, rice, and a few vegetables for Hades.

"Why are you so cute?" I laughed as his stubby tail and whole rear end wiggled excitedly. "How do you know this is for you, huh?"

I put the food mixture in a clean, metal bowl and set it on the floor next to him, along with a bowl of water. As he scarfed down everything like he hadn't eaten in weeks, the healing scar on his flank caught my attention again. With him distracted by food, I ran a hand down his side as if touching him would reveal the trick my eyes were playing on me. But nothing changed. At this rate, he would be fully healed within two days.

Right then someone pushed forcefully through the kitchen door, making it bounce off the wall. The kitchen girls screamed.

"Thought I'd find you two together," Reaper's deep, gravelly voice traveled through the air and reached my ears like a caress. "Didn't think it'd be in here, though."

"I got hungry," I replied with a shrug, despite my pulse elevating with each step he took closer to me. "Hades decided to come with."

Reaper's bright green eyes dropped from my face to his dog, now licking his food bowl clean.

"He's walking already?" The Steel Demons president ran a hand down the dog's back, patting his ribs.

"More than that. Look," I pointed to the incision, "it's already closed up and scarring over. A week's worth of healing in hours."

Reaper looked pleased, but otherwise completely unsurprised. "You always were a fast healer, huh, boy?"

It was more than fast healing. I was pretty certain it was physically impossible. Just like running alongside a motorcycle going eighty miles per hour, for *hours*.

But before I could bring up any of this, Reaper pinned me with a stare that caught my breath in my throat.

"You weren't waiting for me in bed, like I told you to." He patted Hades out of the way to stand right in front of me with my back pinned to the kitchen counter.

"I told you, I got hungry."

"Mm." He rested his fingers gently on the edge of my jaw while his thumb stroked across my lower lip. "So did I."

"Lucky for you," I tilted my head just out of contact with his hand, "they have chickens here. We'll be eating well during our stay."

"That's not what I'm hungry for." A slow, devious smile formed on his lips. "You two," he addressed the kitchen girls for the first time. "Leave. Give us ten, no, five minutes."

Mimi's eyes darted back and forth just as they did when I told her to put the gun away. This time, she did as was asked much faster, scurrying out through the back doors with Marnie on her heels.

"What are you doi—"

My question was cut off by Reaper's mouth smothering mine just as he lifted me by the waist to sit on the counter. Flying to his shoulders for balance, my hands gripped the smooth, well-worn leather of his cut. His kiss was harsh, roughened by the dark stubble growing on his face. And still I held on and pulled him closer to deepen it.

"Hades, go." His mouth broke away to give the command and returned to conquer mine before I had a chance to take a breath.

"You want to do this *here*?" I panted when his lips dragged across my cheek to my earlobe, his fingers already hooking in the waistband of my pants.

"Sugar, I want you anywhere and everywhere," he chuckled with a nip to my ear. "But I'm about to hold church and only have a few minutes."

His mouth returned to mine as he stripped my lower half bare. The stainless steel counter was cold against my heated flesh and my mind still reeled with the question of what exactly Reaper wanted. A quickie? He stepped away when I reached for his belt buckle, bending at the waist to place a soft kiss on my thigh with a devilish smile.

Oh.

That was what he meant when he said he was hungry.

He pulled my hips forward with a grunt, making me lean back on my elbows and bringing my pussy right up to his face. Which seemed to be just where he wanted it.

He kissed me there with just as much need and passion as he kissed my mouth. My head fell back wantonly with a moan and he answered with a, "hmmm," of his own against my tender flesh. The vibration of his voice on my skin ignited every nerve in my body. I found myself raising my hips, pressing myself harder against his mouth in a silent plea for more.

Reaper's lips pulled back into a smile as a throaty chuckle escaped him. His eyes, hooded with desire, lifted to meet mine.

"Enjoying yourself?" He slid a hand down my thigh to press achingly slow circles around my clit.

"I can think of worse ways to spend my time," I panted, matching his cocky grin. God forbid this man's ego get any bigger. We'd all be crushed under the weight of it if that happened.

"I see," he mused with mock thoughtfulness as his hand moved lower, stroking through my wet folds until he found my entrance.

His eyes remained locked on mine as he pressed a finger inside me, then another. It was the most intense game of don't-blink-first as his fingers curled up to stroke my channel. He held me captive with that green gaze as he toyed with me, alternating between hard and fast, slow and gentle.

I was biting into my lip so hard, I was seconds away from tasting blood. When my lids fluttered closed and my head fell back again, I knew I'd lost. His soft laugh against my skin was cocky with his victory.

He pressed another kiss to my thigh right before dragging his lips to the small bundle of nerves that had been begging for attention since he first walked in. The moment his mouth sealed over my clit, I knew I was done for. He rendered me powerless with just his mouth and hands and it felt wholly unfair.

Rolling my hips shamelessly against his face, I raked my nails through the dark hair of his scalp, wishing I could touch more of him. Maybe then I'd have a shot at having him at my mercy for a change.

Reaper was a fair man, but I never pegged him as especially generous. So why he was pleasing me so selflessly, I couldn't be sure. Would he want something in return later?

My tongue wet my lips at the thought of taking his long, hard length into my mouth. I could see the shape of it now, practically punching a hole in his jeans. All men loved blowjobs, but could I reduce the almighty Reaper to a quivering mess like he was doing to me right now? Would he ever allow such a thing?

His skilled suction of my clit and rhythmic stroking of his fingers in and out of me took me right to the edge, but it was the thought of him at the mercy of my mouth that pushed me over.

Stars danced in my vision as my body convulsed with release. He let out another pleased hum against my clit as my pussy closed around his fingers. He pulled his hand out of me with a wet sucking sound and licked both his fingers.

"Delicious," he purred, standing to his full height.

I stared up at him, spread-eagle and exposed on the counter as I fought to catch my breath.

"I take it you want the favor returned?" My eyes fell to the bulge in his pants, my mouth already watering for it.

"Later," he said, kneeling to help me back into my pants. "I'm already late for church."

"Oh, right. You said that." I swore my orgasms before this never made me sound so dumb. All the blood rushing to my clit must have deprived my brain of oxygen.

I hopped down from the counter and smoothed my hands down my clothes, like I was going to fool anyone that Reaper and I had just been telling knock-knock jokes.

He grabbed my shirt in his fist and pulled me in for another kiss, with his lips and tongue still coated in my arousal and just as possessive as ever.

"I just had to taste you," he murmured with a light flick of his tongue against my lips before he pulled away. "You seriously better be waiting in my bed tonight. Or there'll be no more coming for you, sugar."

He grinned at my resulting frown, then playfully tapped me on the nose before turning to leave the kitchen.

"Hades!" he called, followed by a high-pitched whistle. Not a second later, I heard the trotting of four feet alongside his master.

Reaper left me so hot and bothered, I realized I completely forgot to ask about the man they'd been interrogating.

And possibly torturing.

Chapter 3

GUNNER

Fucking motherfucker of all fucking fucks. We were utterly and completely fucked, and not in the good way.

I barely took note of everyone filing into the conference room for church. My thoughts were too fucking loud. If what Fischlin's guard said was true, the entire wellbeing of the club was at risk.

No, not just the club. Sheol. Our home, the women and kids, everyone. And it all fell on my shoulders.

I trusted General Tash. Every deal we ever made had gone smoothly, no bumps or issues. He seemed like a fair guy, never asking for too much, nor trying to undercut us on our goods. The agreement we had seemed to be mutually beneficial. So why would he turn around and try to fuck us with a cactus? None of it made any sense.

A hand clapped down on my shoulder, jolting me out of my hamster wheel of thoughts.

"Not your fault, man," Jandro muttered as he sank into the chair next to me. Shadow slipped into the one on the other side of him without making a sound. "We'll figure it out."

"I need a fucking drink, bro," I sighed, dropping my forehead into my hands. "This is such bullshit."

"It's gonna be all right," he patted my back. "Plenty of other generals are looking for black market supplies. We have plenty to choose from."

"Tash was supposed to be one of the trustworthy ones," I groaned. "How many did we vet before going with him? A fuck-ton."

"Where the fuck is Reaper?" Jandro swiveled his chair to look around the room, only to be met with shrugs.

"Probably getting his dick examined by the medic," Big G snorted from across the table.

"She has to find it first," Dallas added, earning him chuckles from everyone except me, Jandro, and Shadow.

Then again, I didn't know if Shadow could laugh even if he was given step-by-step instructions.

"Motherfucker," Jandro slapped his palms down on the table and rose to his feet just as Reaper came through the doorway with Hades at his side.

"Sorry I'm late. Swung by the kitchen for a bite to eat."

The smirk he wore as he took his seat at the head of the table was more than telling. An exchanged glance with Jandro told me he was thinking the exact same thing.

"Close the doors. Church is in session." Reaper struck the gavel on the wooden table once before setting it down to rub his forehead. "We've got a lot to unpack here, boys. Let's start at the beginning. Jandro?"

"We arrived roughly two-and-a-half days ago," the vice president recounted. "Gunner, Reaper and I went in with an offering of ceramic-tipped arrows in exchange for three days' stay and the hopes of a future business relationship."

"How did Fischlin receive us, in your opinion?"

"As expected," Jandro shrugged. "He seemed surprised by our visit, and not pleasantly so. But he came around after seeing what we offered and the deal went smoothly."

"Gunner?" Reaper turned to face me. "Would you agree with that assessment?"

"I would, President. It wasn't until we stayed a full day that I noticed

Fischlin's guards keeping an especially close eye on us. And they were already utilizing the arrows we gave."

"I went up to the lounge to smoke after Jandro and I went for a ride that morning," Reaper continued. "One of the kitchen girls fetched me saying Fischlin wanted to discuss something right then. On my way over there, the explosion knocked Hades and me into the ravine."

"We heard it and sent Mariposa over the wall before they swarmed in on us," Jandro picked up where he left off. "At the pool we had no weapons, so we surrendered and allowed them to lock us up. We remained there until Shadow let us out."

"Shadow," Reaper addressed the large, silent man to Jandro's right. "Where were you while this was happening?"

The whole table fell silent. Shadow's jaw ticked as his dark eye slid over to Jandro, who gave him a nudge and an encouraging nod. The big guy didn't like to talk, especially at the church table, so we waited patiently for his piece.

"I was in my room when I heard the explosion," Shadow began. "I waited there while they captured the rest of you—"

"Yeah, thanks for the help," Big G interrupted to scoff at him. "Hiding out while they rounded up your brothers and took us prisoner."

"Hey," Jandro snapped. "Unless you've got something useful to say, keep your fuckin' mouth shut."

"Both of you shut the fuck up," Reaper pounded the table with his gavel before nodding at Shadow. "Go on."

"I had to catch them unaware to maximize the efficiency of an attack," Shadow stared directly at Big G. "Otherwise, I would have been captured like the rest of you and then *no one* would get you out."

"Big G's just being a big prick," Jandro glared across the table. "Everyone here knows how you operate. Keep going, man."

"A few hours after taking all of you, they began searching the rooms," Shadow continued. "They shouted loudly about finding the woman—"

"Mariposa," I muttered under my breath. For some reason it irked me how Shadow talked about her. I couldn't place my finger on it exactly, but he made her sound like an object. *The woman*, like she was some obstacle we had to deal with.

"Their shouting and carelessness made them easy targets," Shadow went on. "I knifed the man who got into my room, took his bow and quiver, then killed everyone in my way until I reached you all."

"Did you really sneak up on every single one of them?" Dallas asked in wide-eyed fascination.

"A few saw me right before they died," Shadow shrugged.

"Once Shadow got us out, we took weapons out of the armory," I decided to pick up the storytelling next. "One of the guards ran up to us in surrender, saying Fischlin was escaping with someone. We ran toward his office, saw where the explosion happened, but we were too late to catch him."

"He was on the back of someone's bike riding south," Jandro added. "They were too far away to see a patch on the cut."

"And our surrendered guard tells us General Tash has been here multiple times," Reaper drummed his fingers on the tabletop. "Pumping tons of resources into this place. Giving them solar panels, high-quality building materials, even chickens and goats for food. All to fuck us over. Why?"

"Another question," Jandro piped up. "How did he know we were coming?"

"Gunner," Reaper's gaze snapped to me. "When was your last contact with the general?"

"Same as everyone's, when we made our deal in Navajo almost two weeks ago. Right before we stopped in Old Phoenix for the last time." *And brought ourselves home a pretty little medic.*

"You're sure?" The question came from Big G. My head snapped over to him, the edges of my vision already tinged with red.

"Yeah, I'm fucking sure, G. You think I would keep secrets from the club? From *my brothers?*"

"I dunno, man. I'm just sayin'." The fucker leaned back in his seat as he backpedaled. "You're the one in charge of making the deals and shit. Maybe Tash wasn't too happy about something and—"

I was on my feet and my fists hit the table before I could stop myself.

"I'm your *captain*, you pussy son-of-a-bitch! You want to throw accusations at me? Get over here and back that shit up! Be a fucking man!"

The whole room broke out into a chorus of discernable yells, but I tuned it all out. I couldn't even hear myself. My only goal was to feel the satisfying crunch of my fist into Big G's skull. But someone grabbed me and held me back before I could reach the motherfucker.

"I said, ENOUGH!" Reaper bellowed with a raised hand.

Everyone quieted down, our ragged breaths the only sounds in the room as everyone looked to the president.

"Church is adjourned until everyone can fucking get ahold of themselves," Reaper snarled, his eyes scanning over all of us. "That goes for all of you. No digs at what anyone did or didn't do. No accusations without solid proof. Get the fuck out of my sight."

"Gun, you gonna be cool?" Jandro asked, indicating he was the one holding me back.

"Yeah," I didn't take my eyes off of Big G. "I'm good."

He released me and I straightened my clothes right before pointing at the loudmouthed piece of shit. "You're out of my guard. I'm giving your post to someone *loyal* when we get back."

"Gunner," Reaper cut in, stepping in front of him before he could respond. "A word?"

I blew out a long breath, pushing my hair back as I nodded. "Yeah. 'Course, president."

He clapped me on the back, leading me out of the room and toward an open balcony overlooking the pool. Reaching into his cut, he pulled out his cigarette case and offered me one. I accepted it and took a big drag the moment he lit the end for me.

"Anything you want to tell me, Gun?" The slim, black cigarette bobbed between Reaper's lips as he spoke.

I exhaled a plume of white smoke, leaning against one of the columns as the nicotine hit my brain.

"Nothing that'll help," I said before taking another drag. "I'm just worried, Reap. Our whole community depends on me for goods. Now I have to scramble to take care of our people." I hissed a breath through my teeth as a fresh surge of anger hit me. "I know what it looks like since I've had the most contact with Tash out of all of us, but fuck, man."

Reaper watched me silently, pale smoke swirling around him.

"You know I'm loyal, Reap," I said. "I've bled for this club. I'm a Steel Demon to my core. I would never, ever fuck us over."

"I believe you, Gun." Reaper turned and leaned his forearms over the balcony. "But someone within us *has* fucked us over." He glanced down at Hades guarding us faithfully before asking in a low voice, "Have you seen anything suspicious through Horus?"

"Nothing out of the ordinary since we got here," I answered with the same low tone. "I'll keep looking, though."

"Make sure you watch *everyone*," Reaper ordered under his breath. "Even Jandro, Mariposa. Hell, even me."

"Narcing on yourself, President?" I asked with a dry laugh.

"It's like how those old mysteries used to go," he chuckled as he tossed his cigarette butt over the balcony. "Everyone's a suspect. Especially the one who seems the most innocent."

CHAPTER 4

MARIPOSA

With the guys wrapped up in their business and now Hades abandoning me to be with his master, I ran out of things to do.

My belly was full of food and my latest patient had been treated for her dog bite. I could keep wandering the empty halls of this place, hide out in my room, or relax by the pool.

Or you could strip down and wait in Reaper's bed for him, like he wanted you to.

I huffed to myself as I dug out a clean swimsuit and stripped out of my normal clothes. Not that the idea wasn't tempting, especially after what he did in the kitchen. But I still didn't want to make myself *that* available to him.

A man like him got bored if women offered themselves too easily. His confrontation with Heather showed me that. He'd just jump to the next girl if I came to his every beck and call. I already figured he'd discard me for something new and shiny eventually. He all but promised me that with the whole, "I don't do traditional relationships" pitch.

But I had to admit I was enjoying my tryst with the Steel Demons president and wanted to make it last. And if I remained a career medic with the club, I had to accept the doggish behavior of its members. At least they didn't coerce women into bed with them and generally seemed trustworthy.

After getting into my suit, my pulse sped up as I walked out onto the pool deck. This was where everything happened. The explosion. Guards swarming in. Gunner looking like he was having a seizure.

I dragged a deck chair over to the sun and sank into it, keeping the doors in my peripheral vision. I had nothing to fear now but still felt the need to check my exits.

The hot, dry desert air parched my throat. I closed my eyes and imagined a margarita. Texas had several dry counties even before the Collapse, but the teetotalers wasted no time in coming out of the woodwork afterward. Nearly half of the former state of Texas forbade alcohol by the time I graduated school, which only created a black market for it. Beer was easy enough to make and no one cared much about how it tasted, but distilling liquor was more difficult. Especially on a large scale. Authentic tequila from Mexico cost a small fortune.

My dad had a bottle stashed away that we hoarded like gold. The last time I tasted tequila was when we took shots on my twenty-first birthday.

"There's three rules—lick, swallow, suck, but no one tells you the fourth one," Dad warned me.

"What's that?" I asked.

"Don't tell your mom," he laughed, pinching my cheek. "She'll kill me."

A splash pulled me out of my memories, prompting me to crack one eye open. I was greeted by the sight of Gunner cutting elegantly through the pool. He did several laps back and forth of a sleek butterfly stroke. It looked absolutely beautiful, but exhausting as hell.

His long arm swept through the water, every muscle flexed. He wore the Steel Demons horned skull tattoo on his upper back, the edges of the design stretching out to the backs of his arms. With the way he moved, it almost looked like demonic black wings spread across his back.

A demonic angel. How fitting.

Powerful kicks of his legs drove him up before crashing down. I lost count of how many laps he did, but he didn't stop until he looked ready to slip beneath the surface.

He held onto the edge of the pool with one hand, chest expanding with hard, ragged breaths. I startled when he punched the pool wall with his other hand, muttering curses to himself.

It wasn't until then that I realized the sunniest, most cheerful of the demons was seriously pissed off.

I lowered my feet to the ground and stood, walking tentatively toward the pool's edge. He flashed a smile as soon as he saw me, but I saw the grimace underneath.

"Hey, Mari," he greeted, shielding his eyes from the sun. "You are a sight to behold," he added, taking in my bikini.

I ignored his comment and sat on the edge, dipping my feet into the water next to him.

"Let me see your hand."

"Sweet of you to worry," he chuckled. "But it's nothing, baby girl. Church was just frustrating, that's all."

"I'm not leaving you alone until you let me see."

"Well, that's fine with me," he grinned, dipping his head back so his blond hair spread across the surface. "I like you right where you are."

"Come on, Gunner," I extended my hand to him. "I saw blood in the water. Give it."

"Hmm," he pretended to consider it for a moment. "Only because I'll never turn down a pretty girl holding my hand."

I couldn't think of a snappy comeback, so I distracted myself with examining his scraped knuckles while the flush creeped up my neck and into my cheeks.

"You'll be fine. Just don't make a habit out of punching solid walls."

I released his hand, but he kept it in my lap for a few seconds before letting it drop back into the pool. Water droplets trailed from my knees down my calves like fingertips.

"I won't." His voice carried an edge of seriousness. "I just had to pretend it was someone's face."

"Whose?"

"Doesn't matter. Hey!" His grin returned as he tickled along the bottoms of my feet. "Want your first swim lesson?"

"No!" I kicked toward his chest, hitting him with a good splash. "Not after that stunt you pulled."

This guy picked me up and dropped me in the pool *before* I had a chance to say I couldn't swim.

"I won't do that again, promise." He went serious again, grabbing my foot and giving it a gentle squeeze. "I'll just show you how to float on your back. Super simple."

I stopped kicking, enjoying his grip on my ankle more than I'd like to admit.

"You won't let me drown?"

"Cross my heart." He did the motion over his chest. "You trust me, Mari?"

I steeled myself, grabbing the edge just outside my knees. "Yeah, I do."

His smile lit up his eyes at that point, shining like two sapphires. "Okay. Hop in when you're ready."

We were at the shallow end, so I knew I'd hit the bottom safely. Still, I appreciated that he moved in front of me so I could hold onto his shoulders as I slid off the edge and into the water.

"I got you." Gunner placed a gentle hold on my waist until my feet hit the bottom.

"Okay," I breathed, looking up at him. "Now what?" The closeness of him was overwhelming, and yet the safest place to be.

"Turn this way." He guided me with a hand on the back of my arm until the side of my body faced his chest. "Now start leaning back like you're lying down in a bathtub."

"Uh..."

"Your feet are going to want to float up. Just let them. I've got your back." The weight of his hand pressed to my lower back. "I won't let you sink, Mari."

I nodded before grabbing his forearm with one hand and the pool ledge with the other. "Don't ask me to let go, 'cause I won't."

"That's all right," he smiled. "Hold onto me all you want."

I took a deep breath and started tilting my head back, the desert sky and tops of the palm trees entering my vision.

"Keep breathing. Just relax," Gunner instructed. "Your ears will go underwater but not your face. You'll be able to breath the whole time."

I nodded and allowed the back of my head to kiss the surface of the water. My toes stretched out along the bottom, curling to hold onto the sensation of solid ground. Gunner's hands on my back helped, but I was still scared to let go.

"Look straight up. Let your feet come up," he repeated gently. "I've got you."

When I leaned my head back just another inch, that was when my ears went below the surface and my feet lifted off the ground. I squeezed Gunner's forearm in a moment of panic. I couldn't hear him anymore!

But he leaned over me, looking down with a smile and mouthed, "Good job."

His voice was warbled and distorted but I could hear him after all, which was a huge relief.

"Am I doing it?" I asked, probably too loudly. "Am I floating?"

"You're doing it, baby girl."

He took one hand away from my back, which scared me into death-gripping his arm again, only until he pressed upward softly on my calves to float my legs higher.

"You're doing it on your own," he beamed down at me. "You don't need to hold onto anything."

"Don't let me go!"

"I won't." He leaned closer to me, the tips of his wet hair brushing my skin. "Promise I won't."

Goddamn, his eyes were gorgeous. And his smile. And...everything. He was such a beautiful specimen of a human being. I didn't notice how shamelessly I stared at him until he pulled back, looking at something in the distance.

"Ready to come up?"

I nodded and he returned both hands to my back, tilting me upward slowly until my feet found solid ground once again.

"That wasn't so bad, was it?" he grinned, lowering into the water until only his shoulders were exposed.

"I had a good set of training wheels," I laughed, wringing out my hair.

"You can totally do it on your own," he assured me. "I think your fear is worse than what you're actually afraid of. Like, what's that saying?" He ran his hands through his hair, creating drops and rivulets running down his neck. "The only thing to fear is fear itself. I think one of the early presidents said that."

"Can't decide if those are words of wisdom or total bullshit," I teased, aiming a splash at him.

He lifted a shoulder in a shrug. "There's a fine line between both, maybe."

A few moments of silence passed between us, with water lapping at the pool's edges as the only sound.

"Hey," I voiced softly. "Thanks, Gunner. I've never been able to do that before."

"Sure thing, baby girl." He looked toward the direction of the kitchen. "Think I'll head in for some grub. I heard chicken's on the menu. You coming?"

"I already ate, but thanks," I answered. "I got to watch Horus tear apart a whole chicken earlier."

"He's a savage," Gunner laughed. "That beak does not lend to careful eating. Sorry if that grossed you out."

"I have zero issue with blood and guts everywhere. But I think the kitchen staff were mildly traumatized."

"Ah. It's on them to get used to it then," he grinned, lifting himself out of the pool with one strong push of his long arms. "Have a good night, Mari. Keep practicing your float."

"You, too. Thanks again, Gun."

As he toweled himself off, he cast a downward smile that almost seemed shy. "I should thank you, too."

"For what?"

His eyes flickered up to meet mine. "For trusting me."

Chapter 5

REAPER

Never before had I ever seen my club so divided.

I was so careful to make the Steel Demons an army of *men*. A brotherhood that could trust each other, who could work seamlessly as a single unit. Now, someone I vetted and trusted was a backstabbing piece of shit. Someone in this dining room *knew* General Tash wanted to fuck us, and told that slimy shit bag we were coming.

And I had no idea who.

At dinner, people broke off to eat in pairs or by themselves, eyeballing everyone else with suspicion. No one received more stink-eyes than Gunner.

On the surface, he appeared to take it all in stride. He met the stares with defiance and never gave off a hint of guilt. But I knew it ate him up inside that his brotherhood, his chosen family, suspected him of betrayal so quickly.

He took up one of the low couches with his chicken burrito, pitcher of beer, and loyal falcon at his shoulder. His feet stretched out on the coffee table, crossed leisurely at the ankles. He was making it clear he belonged here and it was one of these other sneaky fuckers that didn't.

Only Shadow sat near him, devouring chicken tacos in between swigs of vodka. They didn't speak, but I knew without a doubt Shadow's presence close by was a silent move of solidarity. Those two weren't the closest in the club but the mutual respect between them was strong.

A plate clattered near my beer, followed by Jandro sliding into the seat next to me.

"You trust Gunner?" he asked before taking a large bite of his chicken taco.

"Yes," I answered without hesitation. "You trust Shadow?"

"Yes." He washed his food down with my untouched beer. "So it's safe to assume the weasel isn't one of us four?"

"I'm certain it isn't." I'd known Jandro nearly my whole life, and Gunner only a few years less. I knew Shadow the least of anyone, but if Jandro trusted him, that was all I needed.

"I asked Gun to have Horus keep a close eye on everyone," I said. "Including me."

"You?" Jandro scoffed. "Why?"

"I guaran-fuckin'-tee you someone thinks *I'm* the cause of this. If we're gonna have a witch hunt, no one can be exempt."

"Does that include Mariposa?"

I leaned back against a column, taking note of her absence in the dining room. Why wasn't she here? More specifically, why wasn't she lying back on this table, serving me up that sweet pussy for dessert?

"No one suspects it's her," I answered. "She has no power in the club and hasn't been with us long enough to know about our dealings."

"Is that what *you* think?" Jandro's gaze on me was heavy. "Has she really embraced being with us or is she still trying to find a way to escape us?"

I didn't have an immediate answer for him and he noticed.

"She's been with us a couple of weeks now," I sighed, rubbing my eyes. "And in that time, I haven't asked her what *she* wants."

Jandro tilted his head at me. "Whether or not it has anything to do with this, that might be worth finding out."

I FOUND MARIPOSA IN MY SUITE, WHICH DELIGHTED ME immensely. But rather than naked in my bed, she was dressed in a pair of shorts and a tank top, sitting in an armchair in the entry room.

Hades went to her immediately, forcing her to put her book down as he practically jumped into her lap.

"Hey, good boy! How are you?" she cooed, rubbing the sides of his face before placing a kiss on his snout.

"You're going to spoil him rotten," I groaned, kicking my boots off in the doorway.

"Good. He deserves it." She continued scratching him, making sure to get his ears and his belly as he twisted, contorted, and squeezed to get his big body snuggled up next to her.

He laid his head on her stomach and looked at me, smiling blissfully as if to say, *Oh yes. I deserve this.*

"And what does his master get, hmm?" I shrugged off my cut and draped it over the back of a chair.

"I don't know," Mari watched me with caution as I approached her. "His master doesn't strike me as a good boy."

"He better fucking not," I growled, curling my fist in the hair at her nape as I leaned over to steal a kiss from her.

She played a tough chick, acting like she could push my buttons and pretend like she didn't want me *that* badly. But I tasted it in the way her mouth melted against mine. Her skin flushed with heat. She may not have been in bed, but she'd been sitting here a while watching that door for me to come through.

I nudged Hades off of the chair so I could scoop her up. She smiled against my mouth as I lifted her in my arms, carrying her to the bedroom.

"How was church?" Her lips moved to my neck.

"Can't tell you that." I set her down on the bed and gave a swat to her ass. "Church is sacred. Top secret information privy only to those who attend."

She gave me a look over her shoulder. "Gunner seemed upset."

"Yeah," I sighed, pulling apart my belt. "Shit is just kind of tense right now, in light of recent events."

"The owner trying to kill you guys."

"Yeah, that." I slid a palm over her waist. "And trying to capture you. To sell or use you, no doubt."

She rolled over to face me, propping her elbow up. We were both lying on our sides with our legs dangling over the edge of the bed. At some point the mood shifted from expecting hot, sweaty sex to cuddling and pillow talk.

And I honestly didn't mind it.

"What did you do to the guard?" she asked.

"Nothing." I grabbed her thigh to pull her closer and she ended up swinging her leg over my hip. "He spilled everything like a waterfall. We were able to verify he was being honest, too. No creative extraction necessary."

"So I don't need to examine him?" She raised a quizzical eyebrow.

"Nah," I chuckled. "You can have the night off, Miss Medic."

"What *are* you going to do with him?" Her hand slid over mine resting on the side of her leg.

"Dunno yet," I admitted. "Probably drop him off somewhere far away when we're done here. He's no good to Fischlin's people now. They'll kill him if they find him."

Her fingers skimmed up my arm, drifting over my shoulder and then my chest. I secretly loved that she enjoyed touching me so much. Too many women were afraid to express their own desires nowadays.

"What if you kept him?" Her eyes lifted to mine as she posed the question. "Brought him into the club?"

"Fuck no," I scoffed. "He is *not* Steel Demon material."

"Why not? He's honest, right? I know how much you value that."

I sucked in a breath. She had no idea how ironic that statement was, considering my current dilemma at hand.

"If he rolled over and talked to us so quickly, there's no stopping him from ratting us out to someone else," I explained. "My guys would never crack under interrogation. I know that for a fact."

"What if this was an out he'd been looking for?" she pressed. "Slavery isn't just for women and free labor. A lot of guys have been forced to become soldiers."

"Don't play that card with me, sugar," I sighed. "I got what I needed from him. I'm in no position to adopt another stray, as Noelle puts it."

"You already know he's a capable scout and archer." Mari's eyebrows lifted. "Do you have someone with those sets of talents in your club?"

"I have Gunner, who can hit a sparrow with a slingshot from a hundred yards away." I chewed the inside of my cheek. What she didn't know was how busy Gun would be setting up new trade deals now that we no longer had Tash. The truth was, I *could* use another marksman.

"It still doesn't hurt to have a variety of talents, right?"

"God damn you, woman." I rolled onto my back, rubbing the heels of my palms into my eyes. "Why am I actually fucking considering this?"

"Because you know it's a good idea." She remained propped up on her elbow, her eyes traveling along the length of my torso stretched out on the bed. "You brought me on after all."

"I brought you on for your medical expertise, not for recruiting new members into my club." I rolled toward her, not stopping until I had her pinned beneath me. "But you have been beneficial in other ways."

She wriggled and shot me defiant looks but it was no true struggle. She was right where she wanted to be. The thought reminded me of what Jandro said in the dining room, and I halted the kiss I was about to plant on her.

"What do you want?"

She blinked up at me. "That's...an abrupt question."

"Do you actually *want* to be here? Or would you still run away at the first chance you got?"

Her gaze up at me was curious, trying to figure me out.

"Since when does what *I* want matter?" she asked. "You've never bothered to ask me this since tying me to you on your bike."

"I know. But I'm no slave owner, you told me that yourself. I truly don't want to keep you against your will, not if you'll take dangerous risks to escape." I was rambling now—my heart, mind, and mouth at war with how much I should say. "What you want *does* matter. To me, it does." I lowered my forehead to hers, our lips hovering less than an inch apart. "So tell me."

Her hands came up, wrapping around my shoulders.

"I want to heal those who've been hurt," she said, barely above a whisper. "I want to save lives and put fears to rest. I want to provide hope and a glimpse of humanity to those who see nothing but pain and loss." Her nails scratched across my scalp. "As long as I get to do that, I guess it doesn't really matter where I am, does it?"

My body hovered tense above her. She answered my question in every way but how I wanted to hear it—did she want to be *here,* as part of my club, with *me?*

"We'll provide no shortage of patients for you to treat," I said in a clipped tone. "I can promise you that."

“Oh, don’t get all grumpy on me.” She lifted her lips to press a long, languid kiss to my mouth. “I’m not afraid you’ll kill or torture me anymore, so no, I won’t run away. And I’ve resigned to enjoying the perks of being with the Steel Demons.” She shifted her legs underneath me until they straddled my waist, and my cock pressed against her core.

“*All* of the perks,” she added in a sultry whisper.

Chapter 6

MARIPOSA

I woke up with a heavy arm draped over my waist and a rhythmic, resting heartbeat against my naked back.

Reaper's breathing tickled the back of my neck. His other arm stretched out under my head, his bicep as my pillow. I didn't have to turn and look at him to know his hard, scowling expression was replaced with one of relaxation.

Careful not to disturb him, I pointed my toes and arched my back, letting out a soft groan in my stretch. The ache of last night's activities returned as my body roused, bringing a tiny smile to my face.

I'd never expect a man like Reaper to keep me but I chose to enjoy being his main course while it lasted. And now in the morning after, *enjoy* felt like quite the understatement.

He gave just as much as he took, which I should have realized after that surprise in the kitchen. Last night I lost track of the orgasms he gave me before chasing his own, and even after that, he held me against his rapid heartbeat, panting in my ear as his fingers found their way to my clit again.

A stallion in the sack, I expected. A healthy dose of tenderness with a near-obsession of getting me off? Quite unexpected.

I started rolling away, peeling my back from the heat of his chest only to feel his arm clamp down tighter around me.

"Where you goin'?" he murmured, voice gravelly with sleep.

"Clearly nowhere," I sighed under the weight of his arm. Come to think of it, he was being just as clingy as Hades.

"That's right." He brought the other arm to wrap in front of my shoulders, pulling my whole body back against his. "You're mine," he added with a smoldering kiss to my shoulder blade.

"Reaper..." Any protest I had came out shaky and weak, not due to the soreness in my body or lack of sleep. But because I *still* craved that stiff cock pressing against my ass, his mouth on my skin, and the way he moved against me.

"Reaper, I'm exhausted," I huffed, despite arching against him. "You barely let me sleep at all."

"I didn't hear you complaining last night," he teased, helping himself to a palmful of my ass.

"I think you broke me." I looked over my shoulder at him, unable to help the coy smile on my face.

"Then I have to fix you, don't I?" Green eyes, hooded with lust and sleep, met mine with a lazy grin. "I'm no medical professional, but I know what you need."

"I *need* a cup of coffee and a shower."

"Mm, you'll get that, too." He slid a hand down the back of my thigh as he spooned me from behind. The next thing I felt was something hot and solid pressing against my sex.

"Reaper, I'm still sore." The words came out with a moan, but not as a complaint. I still wanted him, he just needed to know what he was working with.

"So stay like this." He held my legs closed as we laid flush together on our sides. "Just lie with me."

Did I detect a hint of sweetness there? Maybe a tiny shred of vulnerability? Whatever it was disappeared the moment I looked over my shoulder, and he captured my mouth in a savage kiss.

He kissed with no less confidence and possessiveness than always, but they weren't nearly as bruising. Not even when his lips moved to my nape, merely teasing my skin with light suction even though he knew how much I liked his roughness. His hands came to my breasts, kneading them with far more gentleness than the manhandling of last night.

I reached him where I could, bringing one arm back to wrap around his neck, but I could do little else in this position besides press back and move with him. He let out a groan between my shoulder blades, only thrusting enough to rub his cock along my sex without penetrating me. My flesh slicked with wetness and my core hollowed out. Even after a satisfying, vigorous night, I needed every inch of him.

"Reaper..." His name was a plea now, not a protest. If I had to be honest, it was never a protest.

"Mariposa," he answered, burying his face in my neck as his arms wrapped around my chest.

Every slick of him *not* entering me was pure torture. My pulse thrummed in anticipation for that delicious fill of him that never came.

"Reaperrr..."

"I love how you say my name," he growled. "I could tease you all day just to hear you beg."

"You wouldn't."

"Watch me."

Every time I tried opening my legs to give him access to slide in, he held them closed.

"You're depriving yourself, too, you know," I huffed in frustration.

"Nah, sugar," he nuzzled my cheek. "I'm just making the ending that much sweeter."

I leaned my head back on his shoulder, giving in to his control and relishing in all the sensations running through my body. His hands moved where he pleased, exploring me as if this was our first time together.

He kept us that way for as long as he could stand it. When he finally slipped inside me he shuddered against my back, fingers digging into my waist.

"Keep your legs closed," he moaned. "You're so tight like this, my God..."

The angle of our bodies forced him to take shallow thrusts, which I was grateful for. I couldn't handle another session of deep pounding, but this right now was...*nice*.

I loved the full length of his body pressed against me, the way he grabbed me and how he kissed all of my sensitive spots. It was all the best things that lazy morning sex should be.

And my clit, still sensitive and overworked from the night before, tingled with the onset of yet another orgasm just from the pressure of my thighs glued together.

"Fuck, why are you getting even tighter?" he growled with a soft chuckle to my ear. "My poor cock can't take how good you feel."

"I'm gonna come soon," I panted, my fists curling in the sheets.

"Still got a little left in you, huh?" He nipped my shoulder. "Let me feel it, sugar."

His hand began a slow, sensual descent down my belly before I smacked it away.

"I'm almost there, just don't stop."

"Mm, I love when you tell me that." His hand returned to my breast, rolling my aching nipple between his fingers as he kept on with his steady thrusts. The stamina and control he had was mind-boggling to me. He never came until I did at least once.

The gentle build-up between my thighs ramped up as Reaper teased my nipples. I began quivering, tingling in all of my extremities as he sucked my earlobe and moaned against my neck.

"Fuck, that's so beautiful," he rasped. "Come for me."

I pressed back on his thrusts with soft whimpers, desperate and frenzied for a release that was inching along far too slowly. Reaper never tried to rush me there. He wrapped around me like he could spend the rest of the day just touching and teasing me.

"Fuck," I panted, squeezing my trembling thighs together like a vice. I was chasing a feeling that was always just out of reach.

"Relax, sugar. Just let it happen." He kissed my cheek in a way that was all too endearing for a man like him. "You feel incredible. I can *feel* how close you are."

"Ugh," I grunted in frustration. I was dehydrated, hungry, exhausted. No wonder I never used to care for morning sex.

"You sure you don't want me to touch you?"

"No, too sensitive."

"Here," he pressed on my back. "Roll over."

I rolled onto my stomach as the solid wall of his chest lifted away from my back. The next thing I felt was a playful smack on my ass.

"Keep them legs closed," he chuckled before pressing my hips down into the mattress.

When he started thrusting again, new sensations exploded within my body. Now the bed underneath me added indirect pressure to my clit, along with my thighs still squeezing together. His cock stroked inside me at a new, deeper angle. Instead of tiptoeing toward a release, I was now sprinting at full speed.

"Oh...God...fuck!" The moans and expletives left my mouth faster than my brain could catch up. I gripped the sheets in my fists and held on for dear life.

"That's my girl," Reaper groaned, his hips bouncing off my ass with each tireless thrust. "Come all over my cock."

"I'm gonna...God...Reaper..."

While teetering on the edge, I felt his body lean over to hover above mine. His lips skimmed over my nape as he whispered, "Mariposa..."

I hurtled over the edge and shattered into a million pieces. Reaper pressed one final, deep stroke inside me before he let out a shuddering moan against my back. The spasms and convulsions did all the work for us, drawing my orgasm out longer while milking his release deep within me.

By the time my orgasm subsided, I had no energy to even lift my head and rest it on Reaper's chest.

"That did it," I mumbled into the twisted, rumpled sheets. "You didn't just break me. I'm dead."

"Death by orgasms," he laughed breathlessly, running a hand down my spine. "What a way to go."

CHAPTER 7
MARIPOSA

I must have dozed off again, because Reaper's smack on my ass jolted me so hard I nearly hit the ceiling.

"Ugh, no. No more," I whined, covering myself with the sheet. "I need at least twelve hours before I can go again."

"Same here, sugar," he squeezed my shoulder as he kissed my neck. "It's coffee and breakfast time. For real, now."

I rolled over to find he was half-dressed and in the process of putting on a shirt. Giving him my sweetest, most alluring smile, I said, "Will you bring some up for me?"

"Hm," he pondered, stroking my cheek. "No."

"Ugh, what?"

The bastard had the nerve to laugh at my crestfallen face. "As much as I enjoy you," he pecked a kiss on my lips, "I'm not *that* pussy-whipped." He swatted my ass again before standing up. "Let's go."

I rolled out of bed and pulled on clothes while he and Hades waited by the door. The dog's ears perked up at the sight of me, his paws tapping excitedly on the floor as I approached.

"Hey, boy! Let me see your wound."

I shouldn't have been surprised but my pulse sped up at the sight anyway. The incision was completely closed and the scar tissue faded to a pale grey color.

"Looks like I can cut off those stitches, boy." Then to Reaper, "I can't get over how weird this is. This doesn't freak you out at all?"

"Why would it?" He pulled open the door and led us out into the hallway. "If it means my best friend can survive what's thrown at him and it keeps him around longer, why would I question that?"

"Because it's scientifically impossible," I said. "Tissue can take weeks to reconnect. Not to mention all the blood vessels and the nerve damage from a cut that deep—"

"You're talking to a guy who never finished high school, Miss Medic," Reaper looked at me coyly. "And I was stoned for most of the time I was there. I don't know any of that scientific stuff you learned with a fancy education. All I know is what the world has shown me."

"Oh," I said blankly, taken aback. "Sorry, I didn't know."

"You didn't ask." He threw an arm over my shoulder as we descended the stairs, then pressed a kiss to my temple. "It's all right, sugar. The onset of the Collapse prevented a lot of us from seeking higher education."

"How so?" I glanced at his hand hanging over my shoulder and wondered how weird it would be if I tried to hold it.

"Did you ever watch the news?" he teased. "The feds decimated school funding. Teachers' pay became a pittance. Nearly every public school in Arizona went on strike, which accomplished jack fucking shit. That was about five years pre big-C."

"I heard about the school protests all around the country then. But that was when the news channels in Texas started being cut off and we depended on random radio reports. We never knew what to believe."

"Which was exactly what they wanted," Reaper muttered.

"It just surprises me," I looked up at him, the stubble on his jaw getting longer in the past few days. "You lead a powerful MC, you ask so many questions, even about abstract ideas—"

"You saying I'm smarter than I look?" he grinned.

"I didn't mean it like that," I stammered. "You just don't *act* like you're uneducated."

"Something my father told me," his voice lowered after a few moments of silence, "was if someone claimed to have all the answers, they were full of shit. Question what they say, and see how their actions match their words." His arm lifted off my shoulders and I felt his fingers skim down my back. "Hades has always been loyal to me, so I'm less inclined to question every little thing that happens to him."

We made our way into the dining room as he spoke, his fellow Steel Demons milling about like regular hotel guests at a continental breakfast. Their eyes lifted to him as we passed, mumbling words of greeting to their president and none to me.

Of course not. Why would they? A sobering realization hit me out of nowhere. He might be sweet to me in the bedroom but out here, I was just Reaper's arm candy. His flavor of the week, or month if I was lucky. Aside from eye-fucking me at the Old Phoenix service center, his men barely acknowledged my existence.

It was painfully obvious as Reaper stopped to chat with two of Gunner's guardsmen. His hand drifted up to rub a gentle massage on the nape of my neck. I might as well have been carved from wood—nothing but a prop for him to touch and claim ownership of.

The longer I stood there, the more uncomfortable I became. Reaper must have noticed me stiffen because his fingers dug harder into my neck. I was moments away from slapping his hand off of me when I spotted Gunner striding down the long corridor ahead of us.

"Gunner!" I called to him with a wave and my heart lifted at his returned smile. Now there was a rare man who didn't see women as disposable sex dolls.

"Morning, Mari." Horus spread his wings and sailed off his shoulder to land on the breakfast bar next to us, much to the dismay of the guy Reaper was talking to.

Upon closer look, Gunner was dressed for riding. He has his tactical-style cut on, decked out with pockets and holders for weapons and ammo.

"Going for a ride?" I asked him.

His smile faded, lips pressing together into a thin line. "Yeah. I'd take you with, but I'm gonna be gone for a couple of weeks."

"What?" I cried.

“Fuckin’ *excuse me*?" Reaper whirled around on him at the same time. "Care to explain where the fuck *this* came from, Captain?"

"President," Gunner returned stiffly. "Can I have a word?"

"Can you have a word, just fuck me with a cactus already..."

Reaper stormed off grumbling. Gunner shot me an apologetic look before following his president to a private spot near the outside walkway. Now alone, I went straight for the food, not caring to stand around awkwardly by Reaper's men.

I piled a plate full of scrambled eggs with sides of potatoes and prickly pear fruit, then went on a hunt for coffee. Apparently I wasn't the only one.

Shadow towered over the drink counter, emptying a large French press into an even larger mug that was probably meant for beer. I came up next to him, grabbing the last coffee press that still had coffee in it.

"Good morning, Shadow," I greeted as I poured.

He responded with a flinch and a grunt, then slamming his empty coffee press down as he walked away quickly.

I watched him move swiftly through the dining room for a man his size. He sat next to Jandro, who was talking to another one of Gunner's men.

His behavior didn't offend me. I knew he wouldn't respond with typical behavior and was curious to see what that would be. At some point, I wanted to learn what it took to hear him say one word to me. I didn't even know what his voice sounded like.

Horus had apparently annoyed the two guys at the breakfast bar enough to make them move, so I set myself up a few feet away from the falcon.

"Hi, Horus. Can I sit with you?"

He looked at me, tilting his head a bit, then looked at my food before taking a few cautious steps forward on those menacing talons.

"Guess that's a yes." I slid into the stool, careful not to make any sudden movements.

Hades was one thing, but I wasn't foolish enough to think I could treat this bird like a dog. Horus seemed to tolerate my presence at least, eyeing me intently as I brought a forkful of eggs to my mouth.

Within a minute he seemed to grow bored of me, fluffing up his feathers to preen himself.

Every so often I glanced from the bird to Gunner and Reaper, who seemed to be having an intense conversation next to a column. Abruptly, Reaper turned away with his hands in the air as if exasperated. He marched to the drink table, apparently in search of coffee. Gunner came straight toward me, an uneasy smile on his face.

"You're really leaving?" was the first thing I asked.

"Yeah, baby girl," he sighed, reaching out to stroke Horus's chest feathers. "I don't want to, but important business has come up."

"Why's Reaper so upset?" My eyes slid over to the president cursing and gesticulating over the lack of coffee.

"I didn't exactly ask him for permission to leave," Gunner smirked. "He doesn't like that I undermined his authority, but he knows how important this business is."

"Top secret club business?" I lifted an eyebrow.

"Kinda, but more than that," he said softly. "It's for everything we've worked for. It's making sure everyone back at Sheol is safe and secure."

"Sounds serious." I took in how armed he was. A gun at each hip, knives on his belt, bandoliers of ammo across his torso. And that was just what I could *see*. "And dangerous."

"Both of those statements are true."

Without thinking, I leaned forward and grabbed the edge of his cut, drawing him a few steps closer to me.

"Be careful," I whispered, suddenly feeling too bashful to look him in the eye. So I gazed at his lips. "I won't be out there to fix you up."

"Trust me, baby girl," he lifted my gaze with a finger under my chin, "whoever gets in my way is the one that needs to be careful."

My thumb brushed over the 2A patch on his cut. The now-dissolved right to bear arms was a philosophy he embodied deeply. I'd never seen him in action with a weapon so he was probably right. Every time I looked at the beautiful golden-haired, blue-eyed man, it was hard to reconcile such an angelic face with bloodlust and violence. For all I knew, he probably used it to his advantage.

"Just make sure you get back," I laughed awkwardly. "You have to keep me from drowning."

"I will." His hand remained on my face. "Horus will stay here. Think of him as me in bird form."

"He's not going with you?"

"Not this time. We need him to keep an eye on things here."

"What do you mean?"

His eyes flicked up to Reaper, who appeared to have found some coffee after all and was coming toward us with his own plate of food.

"I should get going. Take care, Mari. I—" His eyes flickered down, the bashful one for once. "I'll be thinking of you."

He dropped a kiss to my forehead and was gone, booted feet stomping across the floor to the garage in the next moment.

"So." Reaper dropped his plate with a loud clatter next to mine, clearly still in a bad mood. "We're stuck with you now, are we?"

He was talking to Horus, who replied with a high-pitched screech and a beat of his wings.

"Great. Thanks for the fucking feather in my eggs, bird."

I hid my chuckle behind a sip of coffee. "What did Gunner mean, that Horus is going to keep an eye on things?"

He stabbed the feathered chunk of scrambled eggs and dropped it onto a napkin before answering. "Horus is a bird of prey. They have binocular vision and can see fine details from hundreds of yards away."

"Okay...?"

"And what he sees, Gunner sees."

"Come again?"

Reaper grinned deviously. "I thought you needed time off from me, sugar."

"Stop." I smacked his hand that began creeping up my thigh. "What do you mean, Gunner sees what Horus sees?"

"It's like a live video feed through those webcams. You remember those?" He swiped a tortilla from the warmer nearby and proceeded to fill it with scrambled egg and potatoes.

"You're fucking with me, right?" I stared blankly as he made a breakfast taco.

"No, I'm not." He dumped hot sauce into his taco and took a big bite.

"Reaper, this is like what I was saying earlier," I lowered my voice to a whisper, although I wasn't sure why. "That's not possible. It's completely and absolutely *im*-possible."

"Clearly not, miss fancy degree."

"Do you and Hades have that same kind of...thing?"

He chewed methodically before swallowing his food. "No. We have a bond, but I can't see through him like Gunner does with Horus."

"Reaper." My mind spun at a rate I couldn't keep up with. I felt like my head was going to implode on itself. "You realize this is *not* normal, right? Like, this is the most absurd shit I've ever heard of."

He laughed calmly as he made another breakfast taco. "Ain't nothing normal about the world we live in, sugar."

Chapter 8

JANDRO

I watched Mari and Reaper walk in late to the dining room with curiosity. She had that beautiful post-sex glow, and he swaggered in like a peacock.

And with good reason. He was the only Demon getting laid out here.

I never was a jealous guy. I knew my place well enough that I'd never undermine my president's and best friend's claim on a woman. If he was down to share her, I'd jump at the first chance. But it had to be his call.

Because of how Reaper was raised, bringing another man in was serious and meaningful. Which was the opposite of how most people saw group situations—as meaningless fun. The officials who raided the matriarchal communes claimed they were cleaning out dens of sin and unholiness. I preferred to think they were just jealous, frustrated virgins.

In any case, Reaper and I never shared a woman before because he never found anyone he cared enough about. He and I were close, but I didn't grow up in the communes. So I could see it both ways. I certainly had my fair share of casual group fun, but wouldn't mind doing it with a serious partner in the right setting.

Reaper was crazy about Mari, and it was plainly obvious to anyone who looked. He never stopped touching her, whether his arm was around her shoulders or on the small of her back. He'd broach the topic of sharing soon, if he hadn't already. And then it was still up to her to accept it. Not all of the matriarchal women accepted multiple partners.

But if she *did*, I wanted a shot at being her second man.

Just the thought of calling her mine sent a flutter of warmth through me. Maybe it was presumptive—we hadn't gotten to know each other *that* well yet. But I was drawn to her warm, caring nature like a moth to a flame. So many free women became tough and cutthroat after the Collapse. They had to be, to not be ruled under the thumb of men. But even with her sassy mouth and dirty scrubs, Mariposa had a soft, feminine nature in her that called to the traditional family man in me.

As Gunner walked down the corridor and came brazenly straight toward her, *that* was when the first spark of jealousy lit up within me.

We may have had a friendly, unspoken competition going, in regards to having her on our bikes, but he had no right to walk right up like she was *his* girl.

I knew it, and apparently Reaper knew it by the way he glared at the blue-eyed demon. To be fair, Gunner had no idea how relationships worked in the matriarchies. He grew up wealthy, the descendant of Hollywood actors who moved east as California began to sink into the ocean they poisoned. One rumor claimed his family had ties to the politicians who set the Collapse in motion, though he always vehemently denied it.

But what pissed me off the most was how Mari looked at him, smiling like the sun shined out of his ass. I had no one to blame but myself for staying out of the way, but what utter bullshit was that?

When Gunner and Reaper walked off to exchange heated words, I wanted to trade my scrambled eggs for a bowl of popcorn. What the hell was that about? Reaper said he trusted the guy.

Shadow sat down heavily next to me as I was pondering all this. He dug ruthlessly into his eggs as if the chicken had personally insulted him.

"She said *good morning* to me," he grumbled.

"Yeah, and?" I couldn't prevent my shoulders shaking from laughter. "Did you say anything back?"

"No! You know I don't talk to women."

"Bro," I rubbed my forehead with a sigh. "Just talking to them isn't gonna hurt you. You could afford to learn some social skills."

"I don't like being social."

"Neither do lots of people," I said. "But sometimes you run into situations where you have to do it anyway."

He wordlessly grunted as he dug into his breakfast. We had this conversation many times before.

"Tell me something," I said, watching Mari grab a seat at the breakfast bar next to Horus. "You've truly never said a word to the service girls I've sent you?"

"No," he answered after a swig of coffee. "They come to me, do what they're paid for, and they leave."

"Seriously, no cuddling afterward?" I asked. "No pillow talk?"

"I don't even know what those things are." He blinked at me, only his dark eye visible with the white one covered by his hair. "Why would a woman spend time with me beyond what she's paid for?"

"I mean, that's part of it sometimes, you know? Intimacy, closeness. At least the illusion of it. Everyone needs a little human connection."

He shook his head as if I were spouting nonsense. "I don't need anything from a woman. I keep telling you bartering with service girls for me is a waste of resources."

"You're telling me you can go without sex?" I demanded in disbelief. "For the rest of your life?"

"I can think back to my favorites and use my hand."

Anyone else would have been joking, but Shadow never joked.

"Unbelievable," I groaned. "Sometimes I wonder why I even try with you."

"You have stuck by me for years," he acquiesced. "And helped me in many ways. But I'm sure you knew when you first saw me that I would never be a 'normal' person."

"No one is normal, bro. I don't care what anyone says. Hey, tell me something," I turned to him. "How do you decide on a favorite?"

"You mean of women who've serviced me?"

"Yeah. You like blondes, brunettes? Thick and curvy or slim and petite? Maybe we can just find you more of whatever you like."

His gaze lifted across the dining hall, settling on the only woman in the room. Mariposa had her back to us, long brown hair cascading over her shoulders as she sat with Reaper at the breakfast bar.

"My favorites are the ones who are good at pretending they're not afraid of me," Shadow answered softly.

Chapter 9

MARIPOSA

No matter how much he tried to brush it off, I couldn't stop asking Reaper questions about what he called his *bond* with Hades.

The nurse in me wanted to examine it like an ailment. Or I guess it was more like an ability. Maybe even a super-power.

"Can you describe the bond with Hades?" I asked as we walked through the outpost after breakfast. "Have you felt it with any other animal?"

"Never." He lit a slim black cigarette and turned his head so the smoke wouldn't blow my way. "I've always been shitty with animals. I accidentally killed Noelle's pet fish when we were kids."

"Wow. She must have hated you." An unexpected pang hit me in the chest. I missed my friend, Reaper's sister, back at Sheol. I wasn't about to make friends with the kitchen girls and I felt a twinge of loneliness without another woman to talk to. If nothing else, she might be able to decipher her brother's behavior for me. I still felt so clueless about MC life and what roles women played.

"Oh yeah. She gave me a black eye and didn't talk to me for a week," he chuckled. "But Hades was different the moment I found him. Even before I found him, I had this...feeling. It sounds girly as shit, but I don't know how else to describe it."

"What kind of feeling?"

He gave me a sideways glance. "You're really not gonna let this go, are you?"

"I'm still astonished you haven't tried to pick this apart to understand it. I don't know how you just accept it as it is."

"Because it's always felt *right*," he answered after exhaling smoke. "Something nagged at me for a whole fucking day to check this pile of rubble. And when I did, and I found this tiny puppy who fit in the palm of my hand, I just *knew* I found what I'd been looking for."

He looked ahead to where Hades, now fully grown, trotted a few paces in front of us. He occasionally sniffed the ground, pissed on a bush, and looked back at us as if to make sure we were still following.

"I felt like I was *meant* to find Hades," Reaper continued softly. "Like we were always supposed to be together. I was meant to raise him and he was meant to look after me." He tossed his cigarette butt and added in an even softer voice, "And those closest to me."

"And you've done that for each other," I observed. "Since day one."

"If I had ignored that feeling back then," Reaper shook his head. "He wouldn't have lived. I'm sure of it. I saved his life and he's saved mine countless times in return. And it's only been a year."

"You two are closer than most humans are to each other. You're almost like brothers."

"Yeah." My pulse hammered as Reaper's hand bumped into mine and he grabbed it, lacing his fingers with mine. "I haven't really talked about this with anyone but Gunner, whose experience with Horus is similar but different. And Jandro and Noelle, who know everything about me. Most of the club thinks I'm just an expert dog trainer or some shit."

"See?" I dared to give his fingers a playful squeeze. "You do know this is unusual, otherwise you'd have no qualms talking about your...gift."

"Ain't 'cause of that, sugar," he chuckled. "I just know what it sounds like—feminine mumbo jumbo. Being sensitive to energies and shit. They wouldn't understand."

"I don't understand," I admitted, watching Hades stiffen and growl at a lizard. "But I'm trying to."

"I knew you would," he murmured.

"What made you pick the name Hades?" The dog in question grew bored with the lizard and moved on to sniffing in a lazy zig-zag. "Were you interested in Greek mythology?"

"I didn't pick it," Reaper said. "That was his name."

"Oh, you mean he had a collar on when you found him?"

"No, that was just *his* name. It came to me in my head but I didn't choose it, if that makes sense."

I stopped in my tracks, pulling him back by his hand when he tried to keep walking.

"That makes zero sense. You're actually fucking with me now, aren't you?"

"I swear I never heard the word Hades in my life before then," he insisted. "It was like," he paused to watch his dog chase after a bird, "like he *told* me his name."

"The more you tell me about this, the more fucking confused I get," I groaned, rubbing my temple.

"See? Better to not think about it so much," he teased, pulling me by the hand to keep walking.

The momentum sent me crashing into his side, which he used as an opportunity to drape his arm over my shoulders and kiss my temple. I slid an arm around his waist to coolly match his affection, but that didn't quell my insides shooting off like fireworks.

Fuck, fuck, fuck. I thought I could do casual sex but I really had to get my feelings in check. Chances were higher that he'd discard me than keep me, and I had to prepare myself for that. Which meant not reading into the hand-holding. Or the kissing. Or his flirting and playful banter. Nor his insistence on making me come no less than a dozen times in a night. That was probably just his kink.

"I don't know who or what exactly Hades is," he mused, oblivious to the turmoil of my inner thoughts. "But I'm glad he's on our side."

"Where did Gunner ride off to?" I asked, ready for a subject change.

"To take care of club business," he answered dismissively. "He goes off solo to secure deals sometimes."

"He made it sound like it was something big and out of the ordinary." I gave Reaper a jab in the ribs. "And that you were pissed because he didn't ask you first."

"Woman, you are too fucking observant and curious for your own good." He lowered his forehead to mine and dropped a kiss on my nose with a smile. "It's a good thing I trust you."

"So," I looked up, the sun and bleached desert landscape making his eyes shine like two emeralds, "what's going on?"

"We're dealing with something here," he sighed, "that requires all hands on deck. With him gone, it leaves me short-handed. And without going into specifics, him leaving with no warning looks bad to the club. But he is taking care of something of utmost importance so I had to let him go, as much as I don't like it."

We walked a few more paces. Hades rolled onto his back, twisting and squirming with his tongue hanging out the side of his mouth like a goofball.

"Anything I can do?" I asked after a few quiet moments.

"Aren't you sweet, sugar." He squeezed the nape of my neck. "Tensions are high, so the guys might take a few swings at each other. If they get seriously hurt, don't let them kill each other."

"That I can do," I smiled. "Anything else?"

His hand slid down to cup the small of my back.

"Scream my name when I'm inside you." His whisper was hot against my ear. "Come all over my cock like you'll never let it go. Sleep with your head on my chest and let me massage your worries away. Rub my balls—"

"Okay!" I laughed, shoving him away. "Jesus, I never know when you're going to be dirty or romantic."

"Gotta keep you on your toes." He pulled me into his side again with another devilish grin. "He likes you, you know."

"Who?"

"You know," he chided gently. "Gunner."

And I like him. Like hell I would say that out loud to Reaper of all people.

Of all these men, Gunner was the one I considered most like a friend. He was all smiles and lightheartedness, a pleasant distraction from his broody cohorts. His presence was like the sun's warmth, and not just because he was golden and gorgeous. If anyone else tried teaching me to not drown, I probably would not have been as calm. I was really sad to find out he'd be gone for several weeks. Not that I didn't enjoy being around Reaper or Jandro, but *friend* was not the first word that came to mind when I thought of them.

"He's a flirt," I said in response to Reaper's statement. "I'm sure he acts the way he does around all women, but I do consider him a friend."

"A friend," he repeated. "Nothing more?"

I looked up at him to find his gaze on Hades' antics once again. "Are you trying to insinuate something?"

"Not at all, just trying to gauge how you feel about him."

"He's a friend," I repeated. *That I'm really fucking attracted to*. "I trust him," I added.

"Jandro likes you, too," he chuckled with a squeeze of my waist.

"He's an even bigger flirt," I rolled my eyes. "But I don't know him as well. Gunner and I have actually talked a bit more."

"Ah. Well now with Gunner gone, you might have time to make *friends* with Jandro, too."

I stared at his side profile—the scruffy jawline, sharp cheekbones, and the straight bridge of his nose. But he kept looking at the path straight ahead of us.

"Why do I feel like you're implying something without coming out and saying it?" I asked. "Like you're trying to pass me off to your friends or something."

"I'm not." He stopped us, turning to face me with his arms locked around my waist. "It's not like that, sugar. I just—" He looked down, fingers gliding across my ribcage. If I had to guess, he looked nervous.

"I just want you to get to know my friends," he said. "As a way of getting to know me. They're like family to me."

"So," I tilted my head, still not buying it. "You want me to get closer to your family? By teasing me about your two most flirtatious men?"

"It came out wrong," he sighed, releasing his hold on me as he continued walking. "Forget I said anything."

"Reaper." I jogged after him to catch up. "I'm *trying* to understand you. All this is just a lot to take in—"

"I know, that's my bad." He shot me a sheepish smile. "One thing at a time. My crazy bond with my dog is enough for one day, don't you think?"

"Okay," I said, running a hand through my hair. "So what are you up to today?"

"Church for a second try," he grumbled, fishing for another cigarette. "Let's see if we can have a successful meeting without Gunner's hotheaded ass."

I had a hard time picturing my calm, reassuring swim coach as hotheaded. Something really had to be sowing discord within the club to get under his skin.

"Okay," I repeated, honestly grateful for some space from Reaper today. I needed alone time to digest everything he told me about the animal bonds, and his men. And to wrestle with my feelings for this man, growing like stubborn weeds through cracks in a sidewalk.

He slid both hands to my ass, drawing me flush against him and holding me there with his green gaze.

"See you tonight." It wasn't a request. "You know where to be."

He claimed my mouth in a bruising kiss while I held onto my sanity like a life raft, trying not to get swept away in the undertow.

But this demon was riding his way directly into my heart, and I was powerless to stop him.

Chapter 10

REAPER

"How's *Marrriposa?*"

Jandro and Shadow were the first two in the conference room. Already there when I arrived, the former had his boots up on the table. The latter sat strategically near the head of the table where he could see the whole room. Typical Shadow.

"She's great. Ruined," I smirked. "How are the bikes?"

"We'll be fine to head back, but they're gonna need some tuning once I get 'em back in the shop," Jandro shook his head. "The elevation and terrain aren't good up here, Reap. This is what I was saying before."

"We're no longer doing business with Tash now, so it's a moot point," I said, looking up at the rafters. "I wouldn't mind keeping this place for us, though. It's nice, well-supplied, and Fischlin's just abandoned it."

"He could come back with reinforcements," Shadow pointed out. "General Tash must know we haven't been captured or killed by now. He'll send well-armed reinforcements."

"Armed thanks to us," Jandro muttered.

"I did think of that, Shadow," I nodded. "This is a good outpost, although we're isolated here and not familiar with the terrain. When everyone gets here, I'm going to propose we ride back home tomorrow."

"Yes!" Jandro shot his fists in the air. "Can we take some chickens?"

"You gonna raise 'em in your backyard?" I scoffed.

"I dunno, maybe."

"I'm not dealing with any crowing at the ass-crack of dawn," I growled, taking my seat at the head of the table.

"Come on, Reap. You never know, maybe it's my calling to be a chicken rancher."

"I don't think that's what it's called," Shadow frowned.

"Gunner has a falcon. Maybe I was destined to have a chicken!"

"Enough already," I rubbed my forehead as everyone else started filing in.

My men took their seats, I hit the gavel and got right down to business.

"If you fuckers can act like adults this time," I glowered, "we'll begin the meeting."

"Hey, you all saw it was Gunner that came after me," Big G announced. "Not saying that's an admission of guilt, but—"

"Don't. Fucking. Start." Jandro pointed a finger at him in warning. "You provoked him. Any one of us would have acted the same way. I suggest you keep your mouth shut during this session, G."

The big fucker glared at his vice president but smartly held his tongue.

"General Tash, now a sworn enemy of ours," I began, "has likely heard by now that we've escaped capture and taken the outpost for ourselves. We have a well-stocked armory, but there are only seven of us. Plus two animals and one medic. It's fair to assume he'll return with a *much* bigger army to wipe us out for good. So I propose we ride back to Sheol in the morning, and figure out how to stick the two-timing shit bag from the safety of our own walls."

"Agreed," Jandro piped up right away. "All in favor?"

Every man at the table raised a hand.

"Good. It's settled." I struck the gavel on the table. "Start packing after dinner tonight and we'll ride at dawn. Next order of business." I set the gavel down and placed my palms on the table. "We have no need to kill Fischlin's snitch. So where do we drop him off?"

"Just leave him here," Big G scoffed. "Let Tash deal with him."

"Killing him will be the first thing they do," Brick pointed out.

"So? It ain't our problem."

"He's the reason we *know* Tash turned on us!"

Big G just shrugged and leaned back in his seat. A loyal guy and a good shot, he just didn't think very far ahead.

"President, if I may speak," Dallas piped up.

"Go ahead," I nodded.

He paused, tenting his fingers for a moment before speaking.

"I've probably spent more time with our prisoner than anyone else," he began. "He didn't turn on Fischlin because he's a little bitch. He *wants* to be a Steel Demon."

"Get the fuck outta here," Jandro cackled so hard, he nearly fell out of his chair.

"He has since we started building a reputation," Dallas went on. "Tash swept through his county like a wildfire just weeks after the Collapse. They massacred tons of innocents. His pregnant girlfriend died. He's wanted to take Tash down ever since."

"That's a nice sob story," I said. "Too bad everybody's got one. Losing everything to the Collapse sure as shit doesn't make you a Demon."

"He can ride," Dallas went on. "He used to build custom Harleys. Used to bow hunt for sport, so he's a good shot *and* can score us meat for the winter probably."

"I could use an extra hand in the shop," Jandro mused. "Especially after this trek home."

"*You're* getting on board with this?" I looked at my VP in disbelief. "You already have the fucking prospect!"

"I have to *teach* the prospect. I could use someone who actually knows what they're doing."

"Well, since you've gotten to be such good bosom buddies, tell me this," I crossed my arms, "is he loyal? Is he a man of his word? Will he ride with us to the center of Hell if I tell him to? Because *someone* who has sworn their loyalty, who I consider a brother, tried to get us all fucking killed!"

My fist slammed into the tabletop, creating a split in the flimsy wood. No one hardly dared to breathe as I shook my hand out.

"Who wants to keep the snitch in the club?" I growled through my teeth.

Jandro, Dallas, Brick, and Shadow raised their hands.

"You?" I looked at the large, silent man in surprise. "*You* trust the prisoner?"

"I'm not the best judge of people, but he seems genuine to me," Shadow answered. "If Jandro trusts him, then I do as well."

"All right, then." I looked at non-approving members. "We take him on as another prospect. He's not privy to church, patches, or any other privileges until Jandro and I both deem him worthy. Fair?"

A murmur of agreement rose from around the table. Satisfied, I struck the gavel.

"Any other club business to attend to?"

"Can we just come out and say it instead of dancing around the subject?" Big G asked.

I narrowed my eyes. "What are you referring to?"

"Did you not hear me about keeping your mouth shut?" Jandro leaned over the table like he wanted to cross over and strangle him.

"Gunner is the one who sold us out to Tash. Isn't it obvious to anyone else?" Big G looked around the table, apparently for rallying cries of support but was met with silence.

"Gunner is *our* brother. *Your* captain, until he rightfully kicked you out," Jandro seethed. "Why do you have such a hard-on for throwing him to the wolves?"

"Why can't *you* see what's right in front of you?" Big G shot back. "He's the only one in regular contact with Tash. He's got all these mysterious black market connections outside the club, and now he's just taken off to fuck knows where!"

"He's headed to the Colorado territory to work out new deals," I said. "Because Sheol depends on him and he's the only one who can make that happen."

"Sure, that's what he told *you*, Reaper."

"Do not take me for a fool," I warned him, my hands closing into fists. "I'm still your president, whether you agree with my decisions or not."

"You didn't answer my question," Jandro jumped to his feet, rounding the table toward the loudmouth. "Why are you so quick to be pointing fingers? You got something to hide?"

"Like what?" G brought his palms down on the table as he stood up. "I'm fucking loyal! I ain't hiding shit!"

"Everyone out," I barked, slamming the gavel down as I stood up. "Except you, G."

Jandro didn't move an inch, his shoulders squared and tense as a brick wall.

"You want to question your president's leadership and sow distrust, you're in the wrong fucking club." Even as he defended me, Jandro seemed to forget I was there, even when I brought a hand down on his shoulder.

"Easy, VP." I moved to stand at his side, arms crossed against my chest as we stared down Big G together. "You're not leaving this room until you tell us what your fucking agenda is."

"The fuck?" His mouth dropped open. "My only agenda is outing the son-of-a-bitch who sold us out!"

"It's not Gunner," Jandro hissed through his teeth. "We would know. So get that notion out of your head before we beat it out of you."

"Yeah?" G stepped closer into Jandro's face. "So your word is the law now, J? Even without any proof?"

"You don't have a shred of proof either, you dumb fuck!"

Big G pulled back his arm to swing. I stepped between him and Jandro but despite being right there, I still wasn't as fast as Shadow.

The silent assassin got behind Big G somehow, grabbing hold of his wrist to prevent him from slugging the vice president.

"Let go of me, freak!" G tried to wrench his arm away but Shadow was five steps ahead, holding strong while pulling him away from Jandro.

"I don't want to hurt you, Big G," Shadow said with an eerie calm. "But you're not thinking of the consequences if you lay a hand on Jandro."

Even without Shadow and Jandro being extra protective of each other, physical altercations were forbidden except during Fight Night. I had a feeling Jandro, Big G, and possibly Gunner would have some serious beef to settle at an upcoming fight.

"You're fucking lucky Shadow stopped you," I growled at Big G. "Attacking your vice president gets that patch ripped right off your cut in front of the whole club. Is *that* what you're trying to do here? Get yourself kicked out?"

"No." Big G deflated and Shadow cautiously released his arm, as he looked like he was finally coming to his senses. "Sorry, guys. I'm just trying to do the right thing. I hate that there's a snake among us, you know? It just feels so obvious that it's Gunner—"

"Even if it is," I interrupted. "This is not the right way to go about it. Talk to us like a man, don't throw tantrums like a child when you don't get your way."

"You're right, Reap. Of course." He forced out a dry laugh. "I got two kids with a third on the way. I should know better. Maybe the stress of a new kid is getting to me, I don't know."

"Well, get it together," Jandro snapped. "We don't need the club falling apart because of accusations and rumors. We *will* find who turned on us, and deal with him accordingly."

"In the meantime," I scratched the stubble on my jaw. "I think a slow cook will be a fitting punishment for you."

Big G opened his mouth to complain, then smartly closed it. "How long?" he asked in a small voice.

"The whole way home. You wanted to be a rabble rouser and bathe in the club's attention, now you'll get to."

Jandro stifled a chuckle as Big G hung his head.

"Thank you, President," came his humiliated reply.

"Think before you speak next time, chief." I slapped his shoulder and looked at my other two men. "We done here?"

We closed up the room and Big G hurried off toward the kitchen, likely to drink himself stupid in light of his punishment tomorrow.

"Go ahead and start getting packed," Jandro said to Shadow. "I'll meet you in the dining hall later."

With a curt nod, Shadow turned sharply down a corridor and disappeared without making a sound.

"So," Jandro said the moment we were alone. "You think it's G?"

I pulled out my cigarettes and handed one to him. "Nah." My inhale was sharp as I pulled my first drag. "He's not the sharpest tool in the shed, but he's loyal."

"Same." Jandro blew out a long exhale. "He's been wanting captain of the guard for a while now. Probably saw it as an opportunity for Gun's post and a chance for a little time in the spotlight."

"Please," I scoffed. "He is nowhere near qualified to take captain. I'd give it to Shadow before him."

"Dude wants to feel important," Jandro shrugged. "We're on the road so much, Tessa pretty much raises their kids and runs the home alone. She doesn't need him."

"You think she's caught on to him messing around?" I asked. "Maybe he's trying to overcompensate his usefulness."

"I dunno, man," Jandro raised both hands, "I'm not in their business much. I try to stay out of it. All I know is he's been trying to move up the ranks."

"Then he needs to fucking act like it." I tossed my cigarette butt over the balcony and headed for my suite.

CHAPTER 11

MARIPOSA

"Mari?"

"In here."

I was soaking in Reaper's bathtub when his loud, booted footsteps echoed through the suite. Hades ran to me, stubby tail wagging like he hadn't seen me in years.

"Hi, boy. Oh—okay!" I squeezed my eyes shut against the onslaught of licks to my face.

Reaper came into the bathroom a few seconds later, watching us with a lazy smirk.

"I was hoping to get some use out of that thing before we leave." He peeled off his shirt, discarding it on the floor before kicking off his boots.

"This tub's much nicer than the one in my room," I smiled back. "We leaving soon?"

"Tomorrow morning." He unzipped his pants and shoved them down his thighs, peeling them away until he was just standing there in his birthday suit.

My throat constricted just slightly, although I had no idea why. I'd seen him naked before, much closer than this, and touched just about every part of him that I could see.

"Quit drooling and move over, sugar." He came to the tub's edge and ran his fingers over the surface, splashing me with a grin.

"I was *not* drooling," I muttered, yanking my eyes away as I scooted to make room for him.

"Sure you weren't." He lowered himself into the steaming water with a sigh. "Now come here."

I moved back to the spot in front of him, where his arms opened. The water had a thin layer of pinkish foam from the bath bomb I used. So while the water was partially opaque, I still felt apprehensive and exposed. I'd had sex with this man half a dozen times at this point. Why did a bath feel so much more intimate?

The feeling intensified as he turned me around gently and pulled me toward him until my back touched his chest. I sat between his legs, which nearly extended the entire length of the luxurious porcelain tub. He let out a contented sigh when I relaxed against him, pressing a kiss to my ear as his fingers massaged into my arms and shoulders.

Jesus. It was like *he* couldn't relax until he was making *me* feel good.

That was a dangerous train of thought, and one I'd been trying to talk myself out of all day. I must have walked through every corridor of this outpost today while my mind went in circles about him. I could *not* afford to develop feelings for the Steel Demons president, and I was a damned fool to even entertain the thought he had feelings for me.

But from the way my insides fluttered as his touch drifted over my skin, I had a sinking feeling it was too late for me.

"How was church?" I asked, focusing on a random bubble on the water's surface.

"Marginally more productive than yesterday," he grunted. "We're taking Fischlin's guard home with us."

"Really?" I looked at him over my shoulder, genuinely surprised. "What made you change your mind?"

"Jandro and Dallas made pretty convincing arguments."

"Uh huh. And who put the idea in your head first?"

"Don't get cocky, woman," he laughed. "You're starting to sound like one of us."

"It was just a matter of time, I guess."

"Mm." He pressed a kiss to my cheek before slowly moving his lips down my neck. All the while, his thumbs pressed slow circles into my upper back.

"Why do you do this?" I groaned, letting my head fall back.

"Do what?" he chuckled, knowing full well what he was doing.

"Massage me. Get me off until my clit is completely numb before getting yours. It just seems like a lot of...effort."

"I like making you feel good." Another smoldering kiss dropped between my neck and shoulder. "I think you're worth the effort."

"Don't tell me things like that," I snapped, a knee-jerk reaction.

"Then don't ask questions like those." He nipped at my neck and it was frustrating how good that felt, too.

"Fine. Forget I said anything."

"Mm, can't put that genie back in the bottle now, sugar." He rested his chin on my shoulder as his arms circled around my waist. "Just imagine if there were two or three of me," he added in a sultry whisper.

"What?"

"Four hands massaging you." He began kneading my thighs under the water's surface. "Two mouths kissing all your little hot spots so we don't miss a single one. Roughness and sweetness at the same time. Would you like that?"

"Reaper," I lifted myself away and turned around to face him. "What are you talking about?"

"Pleasing you even more," his voice was thick with desire, "by bringing in another man."

"I don't want another man." The words came out before I could think, and I bit my tongue too late. It wasn't a true confession of anything, but still felt like it all the same.

Reaper cocked an eyebrow. "I don't know if that's entirely true." His fingers skimmed through the water, reaching for my hands. "It's okay, Mari. If you're into one or two of my men, I can work with that."

"What the hell?" I pulled further away, confusion twisting in my gut. "Do you do this with every woman?"

"No." Then softer, "I've *never* done this before." He sighed deeply and ran his fingers through his hair, making water droplets rain down on his face and shoulders. "And I'm doing a bang-up fucking job, it seems."

"You want to pass me around to your men like a pitcher of beer for what, exactly? So you can have free rein to fuck other women?"

"Fucking Christ, Mari. When have I *ever* said shit about other women? That's not what this is about."

"If you were done with me, you could have just said so." I dug myself into a hole and apparently insisted on digging even deeper. I was being ridiculous, pulling assumptions out of thin air most likely. But it dawned on me I could finally do what escaped me the last few days.

Protect my heart.

"You've got it all wrong, sugar. But fine, have it your way." He leaned back, propping one elbow on the edge of the tub as he looked out the window. "Leave."

I blinked, taken aback by the sudden change in attitude. "What?"

"You want us to be done? Fine. We're done. Get the hell out of my tub."

"I didn't say—"

"Get. Out." He looked at me with pure venom. "Before I do something I regret."

I stood up and stumbled so quickly out of the tub, it was a miracle I didn't slip and fall. Gathering up my clothes, I stole a glance at Hades with his head on his paws and ears back. He looked at me with such sadness with those big soulful eyes. I wanted to give him one last hug for comfort, but didn't dare.

I walked out of the bathroom, feeling crushed under Reaper's hurtful stare, with my clothes bundled against my chest. With shaking hands I got dressed in the bedroom as fast as I could. A high-pitched whine came from the bathroom.

"Hades, stay," Reaper commanded.

So this *was* the end. He wouldn't even allow me a goodbye with the dog. For some reason, that cut deeper than him telling me to leave.

I hurried out as quickly as my feet could carry me, not caring that my clothes were now wet and I dripped water everywhere. This room was going to suffocate me if I didn't get out.

"Mariposa."

I froze in my tracks. "What?"

"Leave the door open for the next girl," Reaper called out cruelly.

I placed my hand on the doorknob, gripping it so hard that my palm ached. A white-hot flash of anger brought a moment of clarity to the confusion swirling around in my head. *Fuck him if he thinks he can still tell me what to do.*

I opened the door and slammed it shut with all my might behind me.

The tears started before I made it to my own room. I hurriedly unlocked the door through blurry eyes and entered a room that felt like someone else's.

I did what I had to. He would've broken my heart so much worse if I hadn't. It was shitty, but I had to put self-preservation first. That was what post-Collapse life demanded. I provoked a response out of him to protect myself.

So why did my heart still feel broken into a million pieces?

Chapter 12

GUNNER

As much as I loved riding with my club, a solo ride had a certain kind of magic to it. There was nothing like exploring the world on the open road set out before me. I was the captain of my own ship, the president of Club Me, Myself, and I. The only thing that could beat this was if a beautiful woman hung onto me from behind.

And not just any woman.

Mariposa's face when I said I was leaving still tugged at my heart strings from two hundred miles away. If she tugged any harder, I might turn around and head right back to her.

Reaper better be good to you, baby girl, I thought, tightening my hold on my grips.

I had the utmost respect for my president and would defend his life in an instant. We were good friends, brothers, even. However, we had vastly different views on women.

While my parents worked, my grandparents watched me and taught me old-school values as I grew up. For instance, even if a woman had a good career, the man always paid for dates and treated her with small surprise gifts like jewelry or flowers. He opened doors and pulled out chairs for her. He gave her his jacket off his back if she got cold. Women were smaller, more fragile, and meant to be taken care of. A man's job was to provide her with security and protection.

It took me a while to wrap my head around Reaper's whole matriarchy upbringing, and I still didn't fully understand. To be honest, it sounded like a cult to me. In my world, some women you had fun with, others you married, but his culture threw that all out the window. Women with multiple husbands? How could anyone be okay with that?

My grandparents were together for over fifty years and were each other's worlds. How could a relationship feel special if it was crowded with a bunch of people? Why would a woman miss you if she had other guys to fill up her time?

So much I didn't understand. But if that was what Mari wanted, too, I'd wish her the best and keep my distance.

When I stopped for a piss break, I let my eyes close and my awareness sink into what I called my second-consciousness. It wasn't my subconscious but a place deep and instinctual, underneath the layers of my human awareness and tucked away in the depths of my lizard brain.

At least I thought so. I wasn't sure exactly how it worked. All I knew was that it was my connection to Horus, and it gave me the ability to see and feel everything he did like I was in his body.

"Gross, man," I muttered.

I checked in at a bad time, as Horus was currently ripping apart a rabbit carcass with his beak. But through the mess of blood, guts, and fur just under his talons, the Sandia Mountain outpost laid out before him.

It was quiet and without much movement, which didn't surprise me. The place was huge and sprawling with over a hundred guest rooms, each with mountain views, and we only took up nine of those rooms.

Well, eight if Mari was sharing a room with Reaper now.

As if he could hear my thought, Horus let out a disappointed squawk.

"Where is she?" I asked.

My raptor tore off another hunk of rabbit and swallowed it whole before turning his gaze to the southeast. He let out a soft chirp as if to say, *there*.

A small pen of animals was tucked between the kitchen and a steep hill. There was no clear outside path to it, only a single door on the building which I assumed to be the back door of the kitchen.

So that's where the chicken and eggs came from, I realized.

About twenty chickens milled about the pen—pecking, clucking, doing their chicken thing. Mari was scratching a goat behind the ears and smiling.

I finished pissing a whole few minutes ago, but didn't want to stop watching her. Still, I pulled my awareness away from Horus and back into my own body. With a sigh, I tucked myself back into my pants and zipped up. I had more of an already long ride ahead of me.

The terrain and atmosphere gradually changed the further north I rode. Dry, dusty desert grew rockier with cool, dark earth and more greenery alongside the road. The thick, hot air grew thinner and cooler as I climbed in elevation. Cactus and desert shrubs gave way to trees that grew steadily taller. When the early afternoon sun became dappled by the forest I rode through, I knew I reached the Colorado territory.

Or whatever it was named now. If I went looking, I could probably find the old "Welcome to Colorado" highway sign—covered in rust and filled with bullet holes, most likely.

A twinge of uneasiness hit me. I was technically in enemy territory. Well-armed, but alone. What most of the club didn't know was just how badly Tash's betrayal put us in a bind. Not that it was a secret, most of them just didn't understand the logistics of a carefully balanced economy. It was all gone to Hell now and only I could risk my neck to put it back together.

And shitheads like Big G wanted to throw baseless accusations and point fingers. Fuck him. He had no idea what I gave up to be a Steel Demon. If I wanted an easy life I could've easily had it, even after the world went to hell in a handbasket.

I cut ties with most people I knew before MC life. The majority of which I wouldn't hesitate to shoot if I saw them on the street. But I still had one big favor to cash in.

It was a long shot in the very best of circumstances. Reaper had smoke coming out of his ears when I told him at breakfast, but he knew it was our best chance. Even though I brought it up, I almost wished he ordered me *not* to ride out so I wouldn't have to face this person.

Because there was a slim chance I might not make it back.

If this did work, though, we'd have the club well-provided for and Tash taken care of in one fell swoop. And that was worth the risk.

In a week, maybe less, I hoped to ride home with good news.

Colorado looked practically untouched by the Collapse as I rode through. Charming ranch homes on large plots of land decorated with aspen, pine, and oak trees dotted the mountainous landscape. I loved a scenic drive as much as the next person, but the ominous dread in my stomach over what awaited at my destination kept me from fully enjoying the view.

The sensation only grew, like a black hole in my body, as I turned off the highway to a hidden winding road. Anyone else would've missed it if they didn't know what to look for, but I knew too well.

The road was freshly paved and smooth on my tires, unheard of in the last decade unless you had enough wealth and power to afford it. Trees shading the road gave way abruptly to hills covered in vineyards. Rows upon rows of grapes created a repeating pattern as far as the eye could see. It looked just like the pictures of the Napa Valley my grandparents showed me, a place in California once world-renowned for their wines.

Apparently still a booming business, especially with free labor, I thought bitterly.

The road took me for another mile before leading to a tall, wrought-iron gate. It looked similar to Sheol's gate, but a fancier version that could be opened with a push of a button. This one also had what looked like a family crest on it, crafted from a bronze-like metal to stand out against the black wrought-iron.

Wait a minute...

The armed guards tightened their grips on their weapons and walked to the center of the road, but it wasn't them I was leaning forward to see.

That crest looked familiar. I hadn't seen it in years but knew those crossed rifles, the extinct grizzly bear between the stocks, and the letters YB above the gun barrels.

It was *my* family crest.

That was not what I expected to see.

"State your name and business." The guards' leader approached my bike and peeked over his sunglasses to eyeball the patches on my cut. "And your MC and position."

"Gunner Youngblood, Steel Demons MC captain of the guard and arms dealer," I rattled off before nodding at the dude's gun. "Better clean that barrel, sergeant. It's looking pretty fucking filthy."

His jaw clenched, as did his grip on his gun. "What's your business with Governor Youngblood?"

I must have heard him wrong. There was no fucking way.

"Governor?" I repeated. "When did my uncle go from general to governor?"

The guard smirked at my ignorance. "You haven't been around in a while, I see. The governor's become quite ambitious."

"I can see that. A winery in Colorado, huh?"

"You're in the Province of Jerriton, son," the guard said smugly. "Get used to the name, 'cause it's gonna stick around for a *long* time."

"That's what they all say," I returned, still sitting astride my bike as I crossed my arms. "So you gonna let me in to chat with my uncle or what?"

"You haven't stated your business!"

"Family reunion," I said snidely. "The business I have with Uncle Jerry is with him alone. Just tell him his nephew Gunner is at the gate. He'll know what this is about."

The guy's jaw ticked again but he pulled out a radio and mumbled some string of code words into it as he walked back toward the gate. A response came through the scratchy speaker, then he said my name and waited for another reply.

I sighed as I took hold of my grips again. *Jerry, what have you done?* I wondered as I took in the neatly trimmed topiaries, the matching bear statues flanking each side of the gaudy, ornate entryway.

It was ridiculous. Who was he trying to impress with this shit? People just wanted to keep their families together and hold onto what little, meager belongings they still had.

Perhaps a better question was, how many people did he exploit to achieve this level of wealth? And what gave him the idea to flex like this?

The gate slowly began opening to one side with a metallic cranking sound, while the head guard nodded at me and waved me through.

I took my feet off the ground and drove forward, feeling oddly like going through that gate would seal my fate in a way. There would be no turning back from this.

Uncle Jerry and I shared a bloodline but we weren't family, not like I was with the Demons. I was nothing like him and never would be.

Hopefully he remembered that.

Chapter 13

JANDRO

I knocked twice on the door with my free hand, blowing out a deep exhale as I lowered my fist.

Reaper, why are you such a fucking idiot?

Mari cracked open the door a moment later, fully dressed but her face was puffy. She looked like she didn't get a wink of sleep.

"Hi, Jandro." Her voice was raspy and she cleared her throat as she opened the door.

"Morning, Mari." I held out the paper cup and bag. "Brought you coffee and a breakfast burrito. We're riding out in a half hour."

"Okay. Um, thanks." She tucked a strand of hair behind her ear, trying to look poised when all she wanted to do was go back to bed. "Did Reaper send you up?"

I didn't miss the touch of longing in her voice and treaded lightly on what I should say.

"He came down alone about an hour ago, extra grumpy and looking like he got just as much sleep as you. So I figured something was up."

"Oh." She swallowed. "We, uh—"

"It's okay," I raised a hand. "No need to rehash it while it's fresh. We'll get you home and then go from there."

She forced a tiny smile that made me want to shake Reaper by his dumbass butthurt shoulders.

"Thanks, Jandro. So I'm riding back with you, I guess?"

"If you want to," I told her earnestly. "Nothing says you have to."

"I will, if that's okay. The only other person would be Gunner and he—"

"Will join me in kicking Reaper's ass when he's back," I promised her. "I'm happy to have you ride with me, don't worry about a thing." I couldn't resist a smirk and adding, "I'll behave. Promise."

"I'll believe you *this time*," she replied, smiling like she was forcing herself to be cheerful. "Don't make me regret it."

"Oh, you'll never regret a single minute with me." *Shit, already too much. Pump your brakes, J. She's heartbroken.*

But Mariposa laughed lightly and I saw the hint of a genuine smile. "I'm almost all packed up, so I'll be down in a few minutes. Thanks again for bringing me food."

"Anytime, *Mariposita*. I'll see you down in a few."

Her door clicked softly closed while I muttered curses all the way to the bike garage.

"Where the hell have you been?" Reaper demanded the moment he saw me. "I need you to sign off on all this cargo strapped to the bikes."

"Yeah well, I'd tell you to sign off my foot up your ass but I don't need your permission for shit."

"...What?"

"I dunno, that was the first thing that popped into my head. But Mariposa is what."

He got within inches of my face right then, scowling hard. "What the fuck did you do?"

"Hm, I'm gonna plead the fifth, Mr. President," I taunted. "'Cause all signs point to, she's no longer yours. Therefore, what *we* do is none of your business."

"I swear to God, Jandro," he leaned in so close, I could've caught his spittle on my face. "If you really swooped in on her like a fucking vulture, I will—"

"Jesus, Reap," I shoved him back out of my face. "Your skin is paper-thin, lately. Of course I didn't do shit. I just brought her coffee and breakfast. Even if I wanted to swoop in, she's too fucking busy crying over you."

His eyes widened, then narrowed again like he wanted to slug me for fucking with him. A resigned sigh escaped him as he leaned against his bike, pinching the bridge of his nose.

"I fucked up, Jandro."

"I'll say."

"I didn't get a chance to tell her anything. Fuck, I don't even know where to begin with that shit."

"What, did you just suggest bringing other dudes into the bedroom?"

"Kind of, yeah."

"Ugh," I groaned, scrubbing my hands down my face. "You fuckers kill me. First I gotta tell Shadow why he should say good morning, now I gotta tell *you* how to not freak out a woman?"

"Fuck off. I've never done this shit before." He pulled out a cigarette, lit it and took a deep drag. "Heather used to beg me to share her. Others did, too."

"But that's like a one-night stand begging for old lady status," I said.

He nodded. "Now the one time I *want* it to happen, she goes off saying I'm just looking for a pass to fuck other women."

"Mari's from Texas," I explained. "She's probably never heard of the matriarchal groups."

"Noelle told her a little about ours but," he shook his head. "Clearly not enough." He sucked on the cigarette once more before tossing the butt away. "Women," he added with a scoff.

"Right," I crossed my arms. "This is all on you, buddy. Your ego got hurt and now let me guess, you're going to be too stubborn to man up and apologize."

"It's not that," he sighed. "I hurt her, J. When she left, I told her to leave the door open for the next girl."

"What?! Dude." I stared at him in disbelief. "You are the king of saying insensitive shit, but *really?*"

"I know. I know." He rubbed his forehead. "I dunno, man, maybe it's best that I just cut her loose."

"You mean cut her out of the club entirely? 'Cause that's the only way she's gonna get over your dumb ass."

"Can't do that," Reaper shook his head. "We need her. Especially if we go to war with Tash."

"Then it's time to put on your big boy pants and send her flowers or some shit, 'cause a girl's heart can only take so much. You have to show that you're sincere."

"How the fuck do you know so much?" he growled.

"Four older sisters, remember?"

"Ah yeah. I forgot."

"What can I say, being surrounded by hot-head Latin women taught me well." I smacked his arm. "It also taught me that women remember literally *everything* you've ever said or done."

"I don't grovel for anyone," Reaper snarled. "Not for a woman, not for a general with a gun at my head. *No one.*"

"If it were anyone else, I'd be right there with you," I said. "But look me in the eye and tell me you're willing to let this one go because of your fucking manly pride."

"Ugh..."

"I know, man." I clapped his shoulder. "But since the hurt is so fresh, you should give her some space first. Do your groveling when we get home."

"But I want to move past this and go back to how it was!"

"It's not about *you*, bro. That's what I'm trying to tell you. *She* needs to let the sting of you hurting her cool down a little. *She* needs to feel confident that you genuinely want this to work. See what I'm saying?"

"Damn it." He kicked at a pebble. "You're right."

"She's riding with me back home. Along with Chela, Perdita, and Letty."

"Who?"

"My chickens," I grinned. "A farm in my back yard don't sound so bad, after all."

"Jesus Christ, Jandro..."

"Hey, don't come knocking at my door for fresh eggs every morning if you're gonna bitch." I gave him a two-fingered salute as I walked off. "See you on the road, *presidente*."

"UH, JANDRO?"

"Si, Mariposita?"

"Why is Big G in his underwear?"

I looked up, then quickly ducked my head down to hide my laughter. While the rest of us were decked out in black riding leathers, Big G stood out like a sore thumb wearing nothing but a pair of boxers that showed *way* too much plumber crack. The pasty white boy's skin was already turning pink and had a thin sheen of sweat. Dude was going to be fucking miserable, but he would live.

"Don't worry about him. It's punishment for running his mouth."

"He's going to get a hell of a sunburn."

"Yeah, that's kind of the idea."

Mariposa turned toward my bike, winding her ponytail up into a bun to shove under her helmet. "Are your chickens going to be okay like that?"

She looked worriedly at the cages I attached with bungie cords to each side of my bike. One held two of my girls, Chela and Perdita, the other held Letty and a rooster I snagged last minute. I decided to call him Foghorn.

"They'll be okay for two days on the road," I assured her. "Once we're home, they'll have my whole back yard to roam."

After talking to Reaper, I decided to grab a male to breed the next generation of chickens. If we were smart about it, Sheol could have its own sustainable, healthy food source. But they had to be treated well and with respect, as much respect as one could give a chicken, anyhow.

My uncle used to work in a USDA-funded slaughterhouse. Conditions there were tough enough before the Collapse, but it turned into a straight-up horror movie after regulations and safety standards went right out the window. On top of already being surrounded by blood and death, overworked employees with worthless pay now had access to dangerous weapons and animals to take out their frustrations on.

And people wondered why I was so good with Shadow. I'd been soothing a grown man after his violent nightmares for years already.

"Are you going to build them a coop?" Mari asked with a smile. She stuck a finger through the cage and gently stroked Perdita's feathers.

"I guess I should, huh?" I scratched the back of my neck. "To keep coyotes from getting them."

"Don't ask me to play vet," she laughed. "I don't know anything about bird anatomy."

Together we looked up, finding the familiar sight of Horus perched on the roof just outside the kitchen. I didn't know much about birds either, but hoped the raptor had enough sense to leave my chickens alone.

"You miss Gun?" I caught Mari's wistful expression as she watched Horus take off from the roof.

"Yeah, I do," she admitted. "He took my mind off things and made me laugh last time."

She didn't have to specify. I hated that she got the blunt end of Reaper's silent treatment not once, but twice. She was too good of a woman for his butthurt reactions.

"He'll be back." I tucked a finger under her chin. "And he's going to be happy as hell to see you. In the meantime," I flashed her a grin. "I'll do my best."

"Thanks, Jandro." A soft blush heated her cheeks as her eyelashes fluttered. "You're already helping a lot."

"Anything to see that smile," I dropped my hand reluctantly, "and to see Reaper squirm."

She chuckled as she threw a leg over my bike, securing her helmet in place for the ride. I doubled-checked everything just as Shadow walked up.

"All the weapons and loot from the armory is secure," he reported. "They are heavy on the bikes, though," he added.

"It's tough having one less bike with Gunner gone," I said, rubbing my chin. "We'll keep a moderate pace to not burn fuel too fast. Thanks, man."

"Good morning, Shadow!" Mari piped up.

I knelt next to my front tire to hide my laugh, where I could see Shadow's hand clench into a fist. His eyes slid down to me with a scowl.

"Say it," I mouthed.

"Good morning," he grunted out before turning and high-tailing it back to his bike.

"Wow," I said, rising up to standing. "That's two more words than I've *ever* heard him say to a woman. The next two might be marry me."

"Shut up." Her eyes rolled under her visor. "Why doesn't he talk to women?"

"That's a long, horrendously sad story that isn't mine to tell." My gaze lifted to my big silent friend sitting astride his bike, waiting to go.

"How did you two meet?"

"Through my job before the Collapse." I needed to be on my bike, too, but I didn't want to stop looking at her or talking to her. "I don't mean to be vague but he's uncomfortable with people knowing about his past, so I try to respect that."

"You're a good friend." Her smile was hidden by the helmet but I saw it in the corners of her eyes anyway.

"Thanks, Mari." I threw a leg over my steed, knowing I'd be sitting out here forever if I didn't get moving. "Ready to ride?"

"I'm ready." Her hands slid around my abdomen with more confidence and assuredness than the first time she rode with me.

I almost sighed at her touch on me. And thought for the hundredth time that day how much of an idiot Reaper was.

The roar of his engine suddenly cut through the quiet desert morning. The Steel Demons answered with the growls and revs of our bikes, like a pack of wolves answering their alpha's call. Mari's fingers curled around the edges of my cut.

Hades let out a long, chilling howl before he darted out from the back of the pack. He looked thrilled to run again, jaws open in a wide smile with his tongue lolling out the side.

Reaper followed after him seconds later, his tires kicking up dirt and sand. Damn, I was going to be cleaning the chrome on these steeds until I was stooped over and grey.

We followed after him in our usual procession. Feeling my bike move underneath me was like returning home already. Sure, I had a home base, but the road was where I belonged.

As the Sandia Mountain outpost became a distant speck in my mirrors, I had to remember not to get too comfortable on the journey.

We still had a traitor among us. And it could be any one of these men riding alongside me.

Chapter 14

MARIPOSA

I forgot how comfortable it was to ride with Jandro.

Something about his tires or the design of his bike made it seem like a relaxing train ride rather than a bumpy desert highway. Even the chickens didn't seem distressed, despite being surrounded by rumbling engines.

Muffled by the padding inside Noelle's helmet, the noise quickly became a soft lull that was almost comforting. Combined with the ease I felt on the back of Jandro's bike, my lack of sleep started catching up with me.

My head wanted to rest on the back of his shoulder a few hours into the ride. My fingers started to slack on their grip around his waist. At one point he grabbed my hand and held it against his chest. I couldn't be sure if he was trying to prevent me from falling off or wanted to touch me for some other reason.

He didn't let go until we stopped for our first break, and it was a slow, gentle release finger by finger.

"Falling asleep on me back there?" he asked when he cut the engine and dismounted.

I pulled my helmet off and shook my hair out. "It feels like a princess carriage," I laughed. "I barely felt the road at all."

"Good. That means my shocks are holding up. I'm gonna have to replace these gaiters, though, the sun and sand are doing a number on 'em."

"English now," I teased. "Or I'll speak only in medical terms."

"Sorry." He shot me an adorably sheepish grin. "I geek out about bikes. And I'd *love* to hear you talk medic to me, baby."

"Well right now," I wiped sweat from my brow and shielded my eyes. "I'd say a *sphenopalatine ganglioneuralgia* is totally worth the risk in this heat."

"Okay, you just made that shit up," he laughed.

"I did not! *Sphenopalatine ganglioneuralgia* is a legitimate medical diagnosis."

"Sounds terrifying. What is it?"

"Brain freeze," I grinned. "From eating ice cream."

"Brain...freeze!" He doubled over his handlebars, laughing so hard he could barely get the words out.

A few heads turned to see what the commotion was. I didn't dare meet any of their eyes, for fear of looking right at Reaper.

"What the fuck! Oh God..." Jandro finally composed himself, even having to wipe tears from his eyes. "Yeah, I sure wouldn't mind a sphino-whatever-the-fuck if I got ice cream out of it."

We all took about a half-hour to stretch our legs and have bites to eat before Reaper gave the order to ride on. I climbed back on behind Jandro, remembering with sadness that I'd never ridden with Reaper. He'd been all pissed at me on the way to the Sandia outpost, too. We were together, maybe in not a super significant way, but more so than with anyone else. And yet I never rode on the back of his bike.

That time he took me from Old Phoenix didn't count—we'd been tied together by a rope so I wasn't exactly a willing passenger.

An ache filled me at the thought of never holding onto him as the world flew past us. I'd never rest my head on the back of his shoulder like now with Jandro. The vice president's hand caressed mine again, which felt nice but it wasn't Reaper's.

Hell, I didn't know if Reaper would even let me stay in the club after this. With Jandro and Gunner in my corner, I'd hopefully end up okay. But would I really be able to get over seeing Reaper all the time?

The landscape distracted me from my thoughts until dusk approached and we stopped for the night. I offered to set up Jandro's tent and bedroll, partially to be useful but mostly to keep myself busy.

"You're an angel. Thank you." Jandro kissed my temple so quickly, both of us froze and stared at each other as if to say, *did that just happen?*

"Sorry," he mumbled distractedly, jerking his gaze away. "I'm gonna get a fire started."

I set up his sleeping area, all the while still feeling the warmth and pressure of his lips on the side of my head. Reaper kissed me there a few times, but I came to realize I didn't mind that Jandro did it.

It was nothing like his sneaky neck kiss back at Fight Night. He was playing with me then, deliberately trying to get a rise out of me.

This was different. He seemed like a naturally affectionate person, but wasn't trying to play it up and be all smooth this time. He knew I'd be completely alone with Gunner gone and Reaper ignoring me again. As Reaper's right hand man, I had serious doubts he was being nice to me for his own gain.

I took a moment to stretch out on his sleeping bag, enjoying the quietness and solitude. The Demons' voices were a gentle murmur outside these canvas walls. Just like on his bike, Jandro's tent felt safe and comfortable enough that I could relax completely.

Rolling onto my side, I couldn't resist taking a small whiff. And then a bigger one. Goddamnit, even his sleeping bag smelled good.

"Hey, Mari."

"What!" I shot upright just as Jandro pulled back the flap.

He looked amused at my startled reaction. "Sorry, were you taking a nap?"

"No, no. I was just...resting. What's up?"

"Uh huh," he smirked but chose not to comment. "The fire's going.

Come out and make your dinner plate. Then you can rest on my sleeping bag all you want."

"Shut up," I muttered, climbing to my feet and following him out.

The club settled into their familiar evening routine--drinking, laughing, and swapping stories as the sun set below the horizon. Horus perched on a nearby boulder, preening his feathers next to the fire. It almost felt like Gunner was right there, but had just shifted into his bird friend.

"I miss you, Gun," I whispered.

Horus looked at me with a small head tilt, then made a few chirpy clicks in response.

Throughout the evening, Jandro kept me distracted from looking over at Reaper with stories from his childhood.

"My sister convinced me putting peanut butter in my hair would give me that badass spiky look." He shook his head sadly. "I was the youngest of five and the only boy. It was a nightmare."

"Aww, *pobrecito Alejandro*," I smiled. "That bad to be surrounded by women all the time, huh?"

"Awful. I'm scarred for life," he joked back. "Do you have any siblings?"

"No. Um," I paused and bit my lip nervously. "My parents weren't married when my mom got pregnant with me."

His eyebrows lifted with understanding. "Oh."

"Yeah, they were dating and falling in love anyway, but rushed into marriage to prevent my mom from being ostracized for loose morals." I threw back the rest of my lukewarm beer. "I think that whole experience put her off from having another kid, even though she was safe after getting married."

"They called it seductive witchcraft in Arizona," Jandro sneered. "After raiding the matriarchal communities, officials went on witch hunts for the most ridiculous shit. Women with tattoos, women who were *rumored* to have had children out of wedlock, widows who had remarried. You'd think this was the Salem witch trials after all that bullshit."

"Where are your sisters now?" I asked.

"Last I heard, hiding out in Oregon. I mean, excuse me, the Constitutional Monarchy of Cascadia," he added with an eye roll. "Supposedly one of the safest and most stable places after the Collapse."

"Have you heard from them?"

"I got a letter and a care package from the oldest one about three months ago." He was quiet for a moment, staring into the fire. "The second-youngest got pregnant by a man she's not married to, which worries me a little. But all four of them are super close, and from what I understand, they're all together and supporting her." He chuckled to himself. "And I guess I'm an uncle now."

"Well congratulations, *Tio Jandro.*" I knocked my empty cup against his. "I hope you'll see your sisters again and get to meet your niece or nephew."

"Thanks, *Mariposita.* Me, too."

The darkness of night grew deeper as the fire died down. Men started retiring to their tents, while the first ones on patrol loaded their weapons for their shift. I thought I should try to catch some sleep, too, but felt a stronger pull to keep talking to Jandro.

"So you knew about the matriarchal groups, but weren't a part of them?" I asked.

"Right," he answered. "They sold a bunch of their handmade goods at a weekly market near us. Our whole household would go, it was our weekly thing. My aunt loved the jewelry that Reaper's mom made, so that's how he and I met."

"Did your aunt know about...?"

"The multiple husband thing? I don't think it was ever *explicitly* said, but it was pretty clear. Reaper's dads would pop in and out of there, hauling supplies or bringing lunch or something. My aunt was Catholic and would pray for Reap's mom every Sunday, but I think it was more asking for protection than anything else. She knew why they formed their communities and was sympathetic to those reasons."

"Your aunt sounds like a kind woman."

"She was," he nodded. "A saint, really. She had to be to run that circus of a household."

He paused to turn to Shadow seated on the other side of him. The big man had been nursing his liquor bottle since we set up camp and seemed to have reached his limit.

"I'll let you tend to your duties, Mr. Vice President," I brushed my pants off as I stood up.

Jandro's head whipped back to face me. "Wait for me in my tent."

I nodded, gathering up our dishes as I headed that way. I kind of figured he wouldn't let me sleep alone, but it was still nice to get that confirmation.

In his tent by a dim flashlight, I unfolded several blankets and laid them out next to his sleeping bag. I wasn't presumptuous enough to assume I'd be sleeping all cuddled up *in* the bag with him. And anyway, I wasn't ready to do that with any other man besides Reaper.

God damn Reaper.

Lying alone in the silent tent with nothing to distract me, the pang of my heartache hit me hard. It was even worse than the night he kicked me out of his room.

I sucked in a shaky breath, willing myself not to cry. Jandro would be in here in a few minutes. He was already being so good to me, he didn't need to deal with this.

Reaper's final words to me seemed to cut physically through my brain matter and heart chambers. Did he really have someone else come to his room that night? Or did he say that just to hurt me? I still couldn't decide which was worse, not even when my thoughts circled like this that night, too.

When the first sob escaped, I slapped a hand over my mouth. *No, he's not worth it. He's across the camp right now, probably jerking himself off to thoughts of someone else. Don't give him another ounce of your power.* But once my body started its physical grieving practice, it was impossible to shut it off.

I curled up onto my side, turning away from the tent's entrance and brought the blanket up high over my shoulder. Hopefully Jandro would think I went straight to sleep and swiftly do the same.

My breath halted in my lungs as I heard him climb inside.

"You asleep, Mari?" he whispered.

I didn't answer, sealing my lips and breath inside myself.

I heard rustling as he took off his boots and settled into his sleeping bag. My heart nearly exploded when I felt his hand on my shoulder.

"You're holding your breath. What's wrong?"

All my air escaped in a shaking, sniffling wheeze. "H-how did you know?"

"Four sisters, remember? I shared a bedroom until I was fourteen. I know all the signs of a girl trying to cry silently." He scooted closer to my back, rubbing a hand up and down my arm. "Talk to me, Mari. I won't talk back if you don't want me to. I can just listen."

"It's nothing," I sniffed, wiping at my nose. "Sorry, don't worry about me."

"Too late for that. And it's not nothing." He scooted closer until I felt his chest brush against my back. Oh shit, he took his shirt off.

I struggled through my shaky breaths as he lay silently behind me, only his hand moving in a soothing motion up and down my arm.

"I'm just," I sniffed, "processing, I guess. Getting over him. I was starting to feel...too much. And I didn't want to get hurt. But I guess that happened anyway."

Jandro said nothing for a few moments, but his hand moved from my arm to make gentle strokes through my hair.

"You want to know a secret about Reaper? Something very few people know?"

"I dunno, Jandro."

"You can't breathe a word of it to anyone, not even him. But I think it's important for you to know."

"Um, okay."

"He's the most sensitive fucker I've ever met."

"What?" My laugh came out like a snort.

"He feels a lot for you, too, and I think that scared *him*. But what happens when he cares about someone is he takes shit *so* personally. Any perceived insult of his character will eat away at his soul. So he'll lash out in response to hurt the person who hurt him."

"Oh my God," I slapped a palm to my forehead. "That's exactly what I made him do. Both times."

"Don't beat yourself up, Mari. We've all taken the brunt of Reaper's temper before. He's been a lot more volatile ever since Daren died."

"I can't believe I never made that connection." A different ache formed in my heart, one of empathy. "He's been hurting the whole time I've known him. How could I miss that?"

"He shoves it down deep," Jandro answered. "Covers it up with that asshole exterior. But the happiest I've seen him in over a year is when he's with you. So you might be healing our president after all, Miss Medic."

I rolled over slowly, the darkness thankfully hiding my puffy face. "Can I be honest with you, Jandro?"

"Always." His hands pulled away from my hair to tuck behind his head.

"I don't know if I can go back to that. Having to watch what I say, dealing with him not talking to me for days if I say the wrong thing. I lov—he means a lot to me, but I can't live like that."

I swallowed the knot in my throat, the weight of what I *almost* said feeling like a brick in my stomach.

"The guy's not perfect, that's for damn sure," Jandro said. "And you're free to choose your own partner, or *partners*. But if anyone can remove Reap's head from his ass, I'm betting on you."

It was sweet of him to say, but my mind was made up even though my heart disagreed with every pump of blood through me. The heart was stupid, though. That was why it wasn't the brain.

After we got back to Sheol, I wasn't going to be anyone's girl. It didn't matter if they wanted arm candy, casual sex, or something more. I just wanted to be a medic and do what I loved most.

I'd have to move out of Reaper's place most likely, but I'd figure out the logistics of that when the time came. Maybe I could be Gunner or Jandro's roommate. Platonically, of course.

I smiled at the thought of seeing Tessa again. She'd be ready to pop soon and I couldn't wait to deliver and meet her baby. *That* was what I needed to focus on. My work, my calling in life. Not a guy, no matter how good in bed he was.

"Thanks for listening, Jandro." I reached out in the darkness, aiming blindly for a half-hug or maybe a pat on the shoulder. Instead my hand found a flat plane followed by ridges of hard muscle.

"Okay, this is really embarrassing as a medic but what am I touching?"

"You're like a half-inch away from tweaking my nipple. Which you are welcome to do, by the way."

I knew he'd expect me to pull my hand away, and so decided to play his own game and do just the opposite.

"Ow! I said you could *tweak* it, not give me a full-on titty twister!"

"It was too tempting," I laughed, sliding my hands under my head. "I'm learning how you play."

"I'm creating a monster," he chuckled before pulling his sleeping bag over him. "Goodnight, *Mariposita*."

I saw his dark outline lean over to me and I lifted my head without thinking.

The kiss he planted landed at the corner of my mouth.

CHAPTER 15

MARIPOSA

I knew before even fully waking that I ended up in Jandro's sleeping bag. After crying and spilling my guts out to him, I didn't even care.

My head snuggled into his chest, mostly smooth and hairless except for a small strip between his pecs. He was built broader than Reaper, with slightly thicker arms. His smell carried a hint of motor oil alongside clean earth. The same smell I leaned into on the back of his bike, and wrapped around myself in his blankets.

I let out a sigh and nuzzled my face deeper into him, not ready to leave this cocoon of warmth and safety I found. He responded by tightening his arm around me, pulling me flush against his torso.

"You awake?" he mumbled somewhere above my head.

"No."

"Me neither." He sighed contentedly, his chest expanding against my cheek. "You okay like this?"

"Mm hm." My hand drifted along his ribs. "I don't want to move," I confessed.

"Same here, *Mariposita*." He pulled back to look at me and I almost gasped at the sight of his hazel eyes up close. The shifting colors *almost* put Reaper's eyes to shame. "I don't want to make your feelings even more confused," he said.

"I'm not confused," I assured him. "Reaper and I are over."

He cocked an eyebrow, propping his head up with an elbow. "Is that so?"

I nodded. "It's still fresh. I mean, it'll take me a little while to move on. And he has so, *so* many great qualities, but—" I paused, letting it sink in that I was technically in bed with Reaper's best friend while gabbing about him.

"But he's Reaper and he's kind of exhausting," I finished.

Jandro looked at me curiously. "He never told you how relationships work with him, right?"

"All he said was he didn't do traditional relationships. I just figured that meant he liked to play the field." I ran a hand through my hair. "I thought I was okay with that but I guess not."

"I see," Jandro mused as if I had somehow answered wrong. "Well," he straightened his arm so his head flopped back down, "as much as I'd like to stay here all day, we gotta get moving."

"Ugh." I buried my face in his chest again, bracing my arm against his back to hold him in place.

He just chuckled as he dropped a kiss to the top of my head. "I'll bring you coffee." His hands stroked my hair and back as he made his offer.

"Fine," I grumbled, reluctantly letting go.

Jandro rolled away from me lazily, pulling on his jeans and boots but didn't bother with a shirt.

I watched him leave the tent, basking in the warmth of the spot he just left. He didn't make this weird, which he easily could have. I cried and lamented my heartache over his best friend all while basically spooning with him. Then I spent the night in his arms and in the morning, we talked about me and his best friend some more.

He made it all seem so...*normal*. Just being in his presence felt soothing and like a safe place to get things off my chest. It made me wonder how many people came to him with their problems. How many people who had no one, and like me, he took them under his proverbial wing.

I was still fully dressed except for my boots, so I pulled those on and pushed open the tent flap to see who was up.

Jandro was talking to Shadow, who was in a short-sleeved T-shirt for the first time that I saw. The texture on his forearms made me do a double-take.

Rows of scars crisscrossing and overlapping ran from his wrist and disappeared under his sleeve. They were pale and thin, clearly several years old, and looked like self-harm scars. Which wasn't that unusual but there were *so many.*

"*Un cafe para la Mariposita.*" Jandro pulled my attention away as he approached with two cups of coffee.

"Gracias." I accepted the steaming tin mug from him and cupped my palms around it. By the time my attention returned to Shadow, he pulled on his signature black long-sleeved shirt and was shrugging on his cut.

"Looks like Foghorn and the girls made it through the night." Jandro bent over the cages still affixed to his bike. All four birds appeared calm, either sitting or preening themselves. "Don't worry, you guys will be out before the end of the day."

"When do you expect to reach Sheol?" I asked.

"Before nightfall," he answered. "In plenty of time for a home-coming barbecue but I think everyone's gonna want to crash at home tonight. We'll throw a party tomorrow night." His eyes brightened as he looked at me. "Feeling homesick?"

"A little, yeah," I admitted.

His eyebrows lifted in surprise. "For Texas or Sheol?"

"Sheol," I clarified. "Texas changed so much in the last few years and I've been away for so long," I shook my head. "It's not my home anymore."

"Well, I'll be damned," he smirked. "Bet you never thought you'd consider a biker club home, huh?"

"I know," I laughed. "I miss Noelle and Tessa. I'm *dying* for pregnancy updates! I miss the little medic's office." My fingers drummed on my cup with a thought that popped into my head. "Do you know if the kids in the club are vaccinated?"

"They're not. A lot of the adults aren't either." Jandro sipped from his cup. "Even flu shots haven't been affordable for normal people in at least ten years."

"I'd like to start vaccinating everyone in the club then, if that's okay," I said. "I have a small stockpile of the essentials, but maybe Gunner can get me more. With the lack of medical care and rise of preventable diseases, I'd like to give the kids a chance at a higher quality of life."

"That's fine with me. I'll bring it up at the next church meeting." He grinned at me. "You are in *much* better spirits today, *Mariposita*."

"I feel better," I admitted. "And I owe a lot of it to you." My eyes fell to my coffee, a rush of shyness taking over. "Thanks for being there, Jandro. I needed someone just to lean on and listen, and there you were."

"Don't mention it," he said softly. "I'm always here for the ones that matter to me." A warm beat of silence passed between us before I pressed my mug back into his hand. "Thanks for the coffee. I'll get everything packed up. You do what you need to get this show on the road."

"Mmkay. Let me know if you need any help." He leaned over and kissed the edge of my cheekbone before walking off.

I watched him for a few paces, reaching up to touch where his lips made contact with my skin for a fraction of a second. He did it so casually, like it was the most normal thing to do.

And maybe it was. Cheek kisses were common displays of affection between platonic friends and even family members in Latin cultures. I wasn't sure when that barrier broke or whether it *was* completely platonic. But as I watched his broad shoulders swagger away, I realized it didn't matter. Kisses, coffee, a listening ear, or a gentle tease—all gestures that were Jandro's way of showing he cared.

I broke down his tent, watching as he paused to talk with Shadow, giving the big man a slap on the shoulder before moving on. Something else occurred to me then. Jandro wasn't just a caring guy, but the club's caretaker.

While Reaper barked orders and grumbled like a hungover bear, Jandro went around like the club dad and made sure everything got done. Shadow always stayed closest to him, like a son would hover near his father. The dynamic was so clear to me now, I couldn't believe I didn't notice earlier.

Reaper ignored me all morning, as expected. It still stung but not as badly as before. I'd probably have another good cry or two before it stopped hurting, but at least I wasn't completely alone anymore.

The whole club packed up and was on the road again within an hour. I leaned unabashedly against Jandro on his bike this time, even running my hands across his chest and abs. We played a game where I tried to tweak his nipple before he stopped me. He'd get me back by reaching behind to poke or tickle me.

On the last leg of the ride, the final stretch before reaching home, we stopped with the games. Everyone was exhausted and dying to sleep in their own beds. Jandro occasionally ran his hand down the side of my leg. When I massaged his chest, he brought my fingers to his lips and kissed them. After debating it for the last hundred miles, I placed a kiss on the back of his neck. His heart sped up under my hand.

I didn't know if this would lead anywhere but in the meantime, it was a fun distraction. Whatever the outcome, I knew Jandro wouldn't lash out at me like Reaper had.

The sky exploded into a brilliant sunset display—pinks, purples and oranges like it was on fire. I was enthralled by the view when Jandro squeezed my thigh to get my attention.

"Home sweet home!" he yelled over the engines, pointing straight ahead on the horizon.

I squinted and could just barely make out the tall, wrought-iron gate surrounding the community of Sheol. A tiny speck hovering in the distance, the black flag with the Steel Demons emblem flapped as if beckoning us home.

"SKREEEEEK! SKREEK! SKREEK!"

"Whoa, Horus!" I almost pulled Jandro and I off balance with how closely Gunner's falcon screeched in my ear.

He flew right alongside us, so close I could reach out and stroke his wing. And the screeching never stopped. He almost sounded panicked.

"What is it?" I asked the bird. Dread pooled in my stomach. Something wasn't right.

Horus cut away, angling like a fighter jet as he shot upward in a straight line, until he became a tiny dark speck in the sky.

"Jandro, I think something's—"

"Whoa, Hades!"

He braked as he turned sharply, drifting a few feet to miss Reaper's dog who ran straight in front of us. Hades sprinted to our left, while Horus had taken off to the right. What the fuck were the animals doing? The whole club slowed to a stop in the middle of the empty road.

"Reaper, what's gotten into Hades?" someone asked.

"He senses danger, but I have no clue." Reaper squinted in the direction his furry beast ran off to. "Someone get me a pair of binoculars."

I looked in the opposite direction and found the dark dot in the sky that was Horus. He hovered at a high altitude, almost directly above us from our perspective.

Then he divebombed.

The adorable little bird of prey turned into a missile, hurtling toward the earth almost too fast for my eyes to follow. I almost screamed. He was going to splat against the ground!

But in the last few seconds, his wings stretched out and his claws extended. Gunner's bird was hunting. And when he hit his target, I could see his prey was much bigger than him.

There were several of them and they were coming straight for us. I could barely make out shapes in the distance but they were definitely person-sized.

A low, constant rumble made me turn my head to the left. Hades' prey was much closer and approaching fast. Men on motorcycles formed one dark line on the horizon.

"J-Jandro," I whispered, clutching his shoulders.

"Steel Demons, draw your weapons!" Reaper bellowed, already wielding a handgun. "We're getting ambushed!"

CHAPTER 16

GUNNER

The guard detail beyond the gate led me down a long, winding driveway—freshly paved as the private road had been. I could still smell the asphalt.

In the distance, a massive house loomed up ahead. I couldn't even really call it a house, it looked like a fucking castle. We had pretty sweet digs back at Sheol, but this place even made Reaper's mansion look like a shack. It sprawled out to the sides and had tall spires that seemed to pierce the clouds.

Uncle Jerry, what have you done...

Some dude in a suit waited for me at the wide, arching front door. I drove around a huge ornate water fountain and pulled up to the bottom of the shallow steps where he stood.

"Mr. Youngblood," he said in a crisp accent. "Your uncle is pleasantly surprised at your visit. I'm his butler. You may call me Chandler."

A butler? What fucking year was it again?

"Call me Gunner." I dropped my feet to the ground but left my bike idling. "Wouldn't want you getting my uncle and I mixed up now."

He aimed a tense, patronizing smile at me. "I wouldn't dream of it. You may park your vehicle in the garage if you continue on this road.

Security will bring you inside to a sitting room, where you may wait until Governor Youngblood is ready to receive you."

"Thanks," I couldn't help but sneer the word out, "Chandler."

I was ready to eat my words when the garage door pulled up. "Holy shit," I breathed.

A car enthusiast's wet dream laid out before me. The cherry red Corvette caught my eye first—the thing had to be over a hundred years old and was still in pristine condition—but I also recognized BMWs, Mercedes, and even a Mach 1 Mustang that had to be from 1969. That thing wasn't just a car, but an *artifact.*

Whether in a luxury or sporty mood, Uncle Jerry had fine tastes.

I parked next to a BMW 8 series and went with the guard who kept mugging me from across the garage. He told me to wait in a room filled with stuffy furniture that was probably worth more than my bike and all the weapons I had on me combined. I was ready to put up a stink if any of these guards demanded I come in unarmed. But no one did, which meant security sucked at their job or Uncle Jerry had enough of his own firepower for it to not matter.

Chandler came to fetch me after about fifteen minutes, leading me through a long hallway with a tall, domed ceiling. Aside from him, the guards, and what looked like cleaning staff, not many other people seemed to be milling about the mansion. I couldn't decide if that was a good or bad thing.

Chandler knocked three times on a set of ornately-carved double doors—again with the Youngblood family crest. My insides churned at the sight of it. I purposely distanced myself from my blood relatives only to find myself right back in their shenanigans again.

The butler pulled the doors open right after knocking, revealing a comfortable study inside. It reminded me a little of Reaper's study at his house, only much bigger. Dark wooden accents, soft leather chairs, and warm yellow lamplight.

But here, a young blonde woman was straightening her clothes as she stood up from behind the desk in the center of the room. Pink lipstick was smeared on her chin. She was beautiful, but her green eyes looked cold and dead.

"Gunner!" my uncle cried out jovially, raising his arms out as if awaiting a hug. "It's been so long!"

He was sweating a little under his expensive smoking jacket and he panted slightly.

"Howdy, uncle," I returned flatly. "Didn't mean to interrupt anything."

"Not at all, Katya was just leaving." His eyes slid over to the blonde who took her cue to leave. "Can I get you anything?" His attention zapped back to me. "A drink? A cigar?"

"Sure, I'll take one of each."

"Excellent. Chandler!" He snapped his fingers. "Bring us a couple of Cubans and that bourbon I save for special visitors." He chuckled to himself. "You think we can still call it bourbon if Kentucky's not on the map anymore?"

"Why change a good thing, right?" I lowered myself into one of the chairs across from his desk. "So, seems you've done well for yourself, *governor*." I flexed my hands up to indicate the whole room. "Province of Jerriton, huh?"

"Oh, you know I've always been ambitious, Gunner," he grinned at me from across the desk. "All the men in our family are."

"Yeah, about that." I paused to accept the cigar from the silver tray held out by Chandler. "We're not family." I struck the match and lit the end, puffing on the dried, burning tobacco worth a small fortune. Once I got it going, I took the glass of bourbon on the silver tray. "I'm here because my *real* family did you a solid when they could have just as easily let you get killed. They didn't, so you owe a large part of your success to SDMC, *governor*." I exhaled slowly. "And I'm here to cash in on what you owe us."

"Still running around with that gang, are you?" my uncle remarked, lighting his own cigar. "You're almost thirty now, Gun. Don't you think it's time you settled down, started thinking about the future?"

"The future is fucked," I retorted. "It'll take decades to recover from the Collapse, if we ever do. Neither one of us will see a return to order in our lifetimes, so who gives a fuck? I ride hard and live like I'll die tomorrow because that's exactly what might happen. And you know what?" I turned sideways in his cushy chair, throwing my legs up over the armrest. "I've never been happier. Life is fucking good when you live it one day at a time."

"That's so typical of a young buck like you to say." Uncle Jerry leaned back, propping his feet up on his desk. "But planning for the future doesn't mean you have to sacrifice a fun life in the present." He spread his arms wide. "As you observed, I've done well for myself in a short amount of time."

"Yeah, how'd you manage that?" I didn't bother to hide the disdain creeping into my voice. "General to governor isn't exactly a straight climb up the corporate ladder."

"Are you lecturing *me* about survival tactics in a post-Collapse world, mister outlaw biker?" he chuckled patronizingly. "I haven't done anything you wouldn't approve of for yourself or one of your outlaw brothers."

"Right. Here's the difference between you and me, Uncle Jerry." I swung my feet back down to the floor, looking at him straight on. "A Steel Demon doesn't play politics. You couldn't pay me enough to stab one of my brothers in the back, no matter what the personal gain might be. And while we're the furthest thing from saints, we don't use people like machinery or sex toys. Whether we're buying weapons or women for the night, we pay fairly. All this shit," I gestured around the room, "and that dead-eyed, broken girl sucking your dick under your desk? I don't want any part of it. Hell, I'd drop the Youngblood name if I could."

He didn't say anything for a few moments that seemed to stretch on, but just watched me with a guarded expression as the cigar smoke swirled around him. The guy went from popular actor to decorated general because of his charm and charisma, but he was also manipulative and crafty as hell. I didn't trust him as far as I could blow smoke.

Under the former governor of the Colorado territory, Jerry kept the borders fairly consistent as when it was a US state and maintained independence from all the surrounding power grabs post-Collapse. Because of this, the state government held on much longer than most other former states. Colorado was known as a utopia of order, safety, and stability in the chaos that followed the Collapse. People flocked here by the thousands over the last five years. I was with Uncle Jerry in the broadcasting room when he announced over the radio that anyone was welcome in Colorado. The citizens, military, and governor at the time all trusted him.

Then he took that trust and brutally abused it.

Not long after thousands of new citizens got settled in, he recruited women for a "job fair." It turned out that job was servicing his soldiers and not being allowed to leave.

Frantic spouses, siblings, children, and parents all petitioned General Youngblood to find their missing loved ones, not knowing they were being held in cells right beneath their feet.

Until one woman escaped.

The public rioted when they found out what my uncle had done. His personal guard and the small military units with him were quickly overwhelmed. The Steel Demons were just passing through at the time of the riots and I had stopped by for a visit, as we were more cordial back then.

He threw himself down at my feet, begging for protection with tears in his eyes, just until the rest of the army came down from the capital. I told him he deserved a pitchfork up his ass for what he did to those women. I never should have listened to his hysterical whimpering about family and being there for each other. I should have kept walking. Everything would have played so differently if I had.

But had I done so, I wouldn't have him now in my back pocket for when General Tash fucked us. And as much as I hated to admit it, a governor would be a hell of a lot more useful than just another general.

"Fair enough, Gunner," my uncle finally said lightheartedly, although I knew for a fact he wouldn't let this go so easily. "What can I do for you and your adopted biker family?"

"We had a falling out with our biggest trade partner and need a replacement," I cut right to the chase. "We have a surplus of weapons right now, and I have good working relationships with firearm suppliers and manufacturers. Assuming you want to grow and expand the influence of your new province, you'll want to keep your position protected."

"What if I already have weapons deals?" he said smugly.

"That's fine, keep them. But as your province grows, you'll need more. Consider it an investment for the future," I used his own words right back at him.

"And in exchange, you want...?"

"Food, toiletries, clothing, motor oil and fuel, medical supplies, tools for home and vehicle maintenance," I counted on my fingers as I rattled off the basic necessities. "And building materials such as lumber and sheet metal on an as-needed basis."

"For how many people?"

"Around thirty. Mostly men, but some women and kids. A few pets."

"What are you running, a commune out there?" Jerry scoffed.

"Basically," I answered. "We have a permanent home with a thriving community. Taking care of our people is a priority."

"I see." His response was carefully measured. "This sounds like an exchange to me. A fair one, I might add, which still leaves me in your debt. How do you intend to cash in on your favor?"

"I'm so glad you asked." I took a hearty sip of bourbon. "Our former trade partner is a general who double-crossed us. He led us into a trap and tried to have us executed. We escaped with no casualties, but retribution must be paid for what he did."

My uncle swallowed. For the first time, he seemed nervous.

"Retribution as in?"

"Death. A nice, slow public execution. It's been a long time since my president's done one of those and he's probably itching for it. But we need manpower. This general has his own army, plus agreements with other MCs."

Jerry's face paled a little. "What's the general's name?"

"Renold Tash. He's holding power just south of here in the old New Mexico territory, which he's going to rename New Ireland, apparently. The territory has no governor as of yet. He's expected to take the seat himself or appoint someone."

"Gunner," Jerry shook his head with a grave expression. "I can't help you. Tash and I are in the middle of a ceasefire."

"So?" I retorted. "Break it."

"I can't."

"What, you don't like going back on your word when the other guys are pointing guns at you?" I mocked.

"Gunner, I have to be smart about this—"

"Oh, I understand. You only lie to those who are completely defenseless, got it."

"Gunner!" He coughed out my name with a thick cloud of cigar smoke. "If I play my cards right, there's a chance he'll sell me part of the New Mexico territory. My province could expand by twenty percent in one move and with no casualties. Think of all the goods I can trade with you then!"

I gave him a long hard look of bewilderment.

"Did you not hear a word I said? Everything was going fine, then he tried to have us executed! You don't think he'll do the same to you?"

"You've never been a general, so let me explain something to you, son," Jerry leaned across his desk. "We like hiring MCs because our hands stay clean while you all do the dirty work. And y'all are a dime a dozen, I'm afraid. When we no longer need your services, you're disposable."

"Not the Steel Demons," I hissed. "No other MC can touch us. Treat us like we're disposable and we'll return the gesture right back."

"Even so," Jerry tented his fingers. "General Tash and I have a mutual respect for each other. We both served our country, back when this place still *was* a country. And now we've carved out our own little empires. I'll always have a soft spot for you because you're my brother's kid, but I can't say I have the same respect for those thugs you ride with."

I threw my head back and laughed. Once I started, I just couldn't stop. My stomach ached but the laughter kept coming. I sucked in enough of a breath to say, "Should've thought of that before you begged us to protect you. Oh God..."

When my laughter finally ceased, I drained the rest of the bourbon, stood up, and ashed my cigar right on Jerry's desk.

"What are you doing?!" he demanded, gasping as the charred, circular mark permanently embedded into the expensive wood.

"Remember this, Uncle." I pointed at him with the cigar. "You and Tash may not ride, and you may not wear patches, but you're bigger thugs than we'll ever be."

I tossed the rest of the cigar carelessly and let it roll across his desk, but didn't wait to see where it ended up. I was already out the door.

Chapter 17

MARIPOSA

"Weapons out!"

"Tighten up, come in close!"

"Shoot their tires!"

Pure chaos surrounded me. The Steel Demons yelled back and forth, repositioned their bikes, ran to others' bikes to grab guns and ammo. And I just sat frozen and watched.

Reaper brought two fingers to his mouth and blew a long whistle.

"We're outnumbered, so do not group up like sitting ducks, Demons," he roared. "Ride your fucking bikes like you just came out of Hell! Make 'em chase you! No one fucks with us and our home!" He raised a pistol in the air, which I realized was a flare gun. "Let's spill some blood tonight!"

His men answered him with a roar of engines and clouds of dust. They peeled off the road one by one, heading off in different directions, but all going toward the enemy about to close in on us.

Reaper fired the flare into the sky before tossing the gun and brandishing one of the biggest handheld assault rifles I'd ever seen.

"Mari, come here." Jandro barked out the Reaper-esque command. "Sit in front and face me."

Only when I tried to move did I realize I was shaking like a leaf, so he grabbed and physically moved me to sit in front of him. I sat between his arms and the handlebars, straddling his thighs and looking directly at his rare, stern expression.

"Jandro, I'm scared," I confessed, my teeth chattering like I was freezing.

"I know, baby. Just do what I say and you'll be fine, I promise. Take this." He shoved a pistol in my hand.

"I don't know how to use it!"

"Point it at a bad guy and pull the trigger." In his other hand, he cocked an assault rifle of his own. "Tell me when you're out of ammo. And whatever you do, do not put your hands on my back. I'm shielding you, do you understand?"

"But that leaves you exposed!"

"Exactly. I'm going to draw them away from the gate so the others can pick them off." He cupped my face and kissed me too quickly for either of us to enjoy it. "We're going to make it through this, trust me."

"Jandro," my hands shook so hard, I was in serious danger of dropping my gun, "I can't—"

"You *can.* Hold on, we've gotta move."

Everyone else was gone. Only we were left between the two lines of hostile bikers converging in on us. Jandro weaved his bike in a wide, lazy figure-eight pattern.

"Keep your arms tucked in and hold tight onto my shirt," he instructed. "I'm gonna zig-zag like hell. Only point your gun when you have a clear shot. Got it?"

I nodded, despite feeling nowhere near like I had it.

"Jandro..."

"I know, I know. Trust me."

The roars of at least twenty bikes filled my ears. I could make out their faces now—hard, angry, and ready to kill.

I only hoped the Steel Demons were more ready.

Jandro looped the bike around back the way we came and accelerated hard. Our enemies picked up speed to give chase.

"Tuck in! Stay close!" Jandro yelled.

I curled into him just as his rifle hand pulled away to point behind him. Seconds later came the *rat-tat-tat-tat-tat* of his rapid firing.

The air grew thick with dust kicked up from all the bikes. My eyes burned and I thought I might fall at any moment with Jandro weaving back and forth at such high speed.

He kept looking back to shoot behind us while I clung to him with my tiny silver weapon in my hand.

"Watch out!" I screamed.

One of the riders broke off from his pack and was coming straight for us. We were going to collide head-on, but Jandro was dealing with the dozen or so chasers on our tail.

I shakily aimed my gun and waited. The biker smiled cruelly and let go of his handlebars to aim his shotgun with both hands.

Somehow, I fired first.

"Fuck!" He clutched at his side. I barely grazed him, but it was enough to surprise him and throw his balance to send him tumbling off of his bike. Jandro maneuvered us out of the way at the last second.

"Nice, Mari!" he praised.

Unseating one of their riders seemed to piss off our chasers even more. They returned Jandro's fire even more rapidly. Bullets whizzed by us and made *plink* sounds as they hit the frame of his bike.

"Ah!" Jandro's torso jolted forward, his face a grimace of pain and his knuckles white on the grips.

I touched his shoulder, my palm coming away red and sticky. "You're hit!" I cried.

"Keep your hands in front!" he bellowed.

"You're bleeding a lot!"

"Up ahead, WATCH OUT!"

I looked behind me, my arm already extended with the pistol. This time I hit the rider coming at us right in the torso. He slumped over his bike, which careened into a cluster of sharp boulders. Bodies and abandoned bikes already began piling up.

Bodies, fuck!

I tried to scan the faces of men strewn out among the landscape, but we were moving too fast. Some Demons must have gotten hurt, though. We were far too outnumbered and I had to save who I could. Jandro's bullet wound bloodied half of his shirt already but at least he was still riding.

"Jandro, I have to treat the wounded!"

"You're not getting off this bike," he growled, sweat beading on his forehead. "They'll steal you from us. You're too valuable."

"But your men could be dying!" *Oh God, Reaper!*

I hadn't seen him since he fired off that flare, which I could only assume was a distress signal to his men still inside Sheol. But with all the dust, the bikes, the noise and the chaos, I couldn't make out who was friend or foe.

"Reaper!" I yelled to Jandro. "We've got to find Reaper!"

If I was scared before, I was in a full-blown panicked meltdown now. The Steel Demons president *had* to be alive. He didn't even seem worried about going to battle—if anything, he seemed excited despite the odds not looking good. But if Jandro was taking shots, surely the others were, too.

"I know babe, but we gotta live through this first—gah!"

Another bullet grazed his arm, creating a surface wound that quickly pooled blood on his skin. It was his shooting arm, too, which I knew was becoming fatigued.

Still he raised it again, spraying gunfire behind us to mow down the three closest riders on our tails.

"Jandro, I need to slow your bleeding," I pleaded. "And we need to find Reaper, and anyone else who's hurt."

His gaze was sharp, but his breathing was ragged and he could barely hold himself up. Adrenaline pushed him to keep going but he was losing blood quickly. Just when it looked like he'd give in to my request, something caught his eye up ahead of us.

"Hold onto me. We're gonna roll."

"My pack!" I cried just before he pulled me against his torso and lurched us to one side.

For the briefest moment, I felt nothing but air. Then the hard ground knocked the wind out of me and the world spun as we went rolling. My vision kept spinning even as we came to a stop and Jandro pulled us behind a couple of crashed bikes for cover.

"What...what?" was all I could say.

"They dug potholes," he panted, wincing at the pain. "To catch our front tires and send us flipping over our handlebars." He forced a grin and held up his rifle, which had the strap of my medic pack barely hanging onto the end of the barrel. "Got you this, though."

"You probably just saved your own life then." I grabbed it from him and quickly pulled out my gauze and tape. "I'll have to look at it later but you won't bleed out now."

"Shit, shit, hide!"

Jandro shoved me against the makeshift wall of twisted metal, but it was too late. A rider pulled up, coming to a stop in front of us.

"What's this? A Steel Demon hiding like a little bitch?" the rider taunted, pointing his weapon at us. "And with a woman," he added, his voice going higher with interest.

"Take me as a hostage if you want but leave her alone." Jandro raised his arms.

I stared at him. "Jandro, no!"

"Fucking dumbass. Unless you're hiding a pussy, I have no reason to take you over her. Besides," he grinned evilly. "We have strict orders to eliminate your whole club, and take no prisoners. A woman, however—"

"I'm the vice president," Jandro pointed to his patch. "I'm a valuable bargaining chip. She's just a used-up piece of ass. You won't get anything out of her."

"All that's tellin' me is I should shoot you both."

He cocked his gun and raised it to aim. Jandro jumped in front of me.

"Wait, wait!" he protested.

"No..." I grabbed his shoulders and shut my eyes with my forehead against his back.

The shot rang out and his body jerked.

"No!" I cried, clutching him tighter.

But he was still standing on his own.

"Shadow, you motherfucker!" he yelled.

I peeked open one eye and peered over his shoulder. The biker's limp, lifeless body hung over his handlebars. Shadow approached from the left side and grabbed the man's body to haul it off the bike. When the man's head fell back, a dark, bloody hole decorated his forehead.

"Where the fuck is our backup?" Jandro growled before turning around and squeezing me tightly against him. "It's okay."

I couldn't reply. I was shaking again. How could he be so calm? He almost *died.*

"I don't know," Shadow answered his question distractedly while looting through the dead biker's pockets.

"Check his cut," Jandro instructed while rubbing my back. "Who are these shit heads?"

Shadow kicked the body over onto its back, then leaned over to inspect the patch.

"Razor Wire," he reported.

"Of course. In the pocket of General Tash, I'm assuming," Jandro grumbled. "How many of them are left? And how many of us?"

"I've taken down five, including this one," Shadow answered. "As for us, I don't know. It's impossible to see through this dust."

"Reaper!" I remembered now that my own life was safe. "You haven't seen him anywhere?"

Shadow's dark eye passed over me briefly, the pale one still hidden under his hair. "No," he answered.

"We've taken about six or seven down," Jandro said. "Mari shot two herself."

Shadow did not look impressed. "So that's twelve, out of roughly twenty-five total that I counted. To our eight."

"Ten," Jandro corrected. "You know Hades and Horus had to have gotten a couple of kills. They're in the fray just like we are."

"I haven't seen them either."

"Uh, guys?"

"Shit," Jandro cursed at the line of bikers, at least eight of them, coming straight for us on the other side of our cover. "Shadow, give me a full clip."

The large man opened his cut to reach into an inside pocket. It was hard to tell with him wearing all black, but his shirt was wet and sticky with blood.

"Shadow, did you get hit, too?"

He glanced up, surprise on his face before his eyes flicked over to Jandro.

"You definitely got shot, bro," Jandro confirmed.

"Must just be a graze," Shadow mumbled as he reloaded his weapon. "I didn't feel an entry point."

"Let me clean that up real quick," I reached into my pack.

"No," Shadow barked. "We've got incoming. There's no time."

"I'll be fast. It'll just slow your bleeding—"

"I said no!" he snarled at me.

My hands froze in shock. Not because he said no, but the *way* he said it. The way he looked at me when he said it. He glared at me like an injured animal backed into a corner, a mixture of intense fear and defensiveness.

"He'll be okay, Mari," Jandro said with a hand on my shoulder. "Duck behind the bikes and let us handle these fuckers first."

He physically shoved my head down so that I sat on the ground, then he and Shadow braced their assault rifles on top of the crashed bikes which served as our cover.

"Back away a bit, Mari. They're gonna return fire."

They started shooting right as I got moving, covering my head the moment I heard the *plink-plink-plink* of returned fire ricocheting off of metal.

"Just like shooting wooden ducks at the state fair!" Jandro laughed.

"They're still coming," Shadow said.

"Yeah, fuck! They're going around! Get 'em!" Jandro and Shadow slowly turned their rifles as the riders came around in a wide circle. Soon they'd be behind our cover and free to fill our bodies with bullet holes.

The engines grew louder, sounding slightly differently this time and...coming from a different direction?

I looked toward Sheol where the dust started to clear. It was only a few hundred yards away, and yet seemed impossibly far. Visibility was improving though and from inside the gate, I saw what looked like long ramps placed against the wrought-iron supports. And the strange engine sound seemed like it was coming from *inside* the Steel Demons compound.

"Jandro," my voice shook. "Do you hear that?"

"My ears are ringing, babe. I can't hear shit."

Shadow, however, cocked his head toward the direction of the sound.

"I think our backup's finally here."

The sound grew louder. I saw movement inside the gate and my mouth fell open at a sight I never expected to see.

Motorcycles flying through the air.

Chapter 18

MARIPOSA

One after another, riders on dirt bikes drove up the ramps and flew into the air to join us in battle. Their engines made higher-pitched grinding sounds, as opposed to the deep rumbles of the road bikes. The dirt bikes were also much smaller and lightweight. They hit the ground with a small bounce like a spring and rode on.

Some of the new riders carried guns, others wielded swords or machetes, but all were armed and ready Steel Demons.

"Fucking finally!" Jandro yelled.

Assuming all of our people were still alive, our numbers were now more evenly matched.

Reaper. I still had to find him. Or at least *see* him to know he was okay.

I hovered behind Jandro as he and Shadow kept shooting over our protective wall of crashed bikes. The returned fire gradually slowed down to nothing and then they stopped.

"Is it over?" I whispered.

"Don't know yet," Jandro muttered. "God, I wish we had Gunner's eyes right now."

One of the dirt bike riders emerged from a cloud of dust, a rifle slung across their back as they stopped in front of us.

"You got my boots and jacket all dirty, bitch!" a feminine voice snarled from inside the helmet.

"What?"

The dark visor flipped up to reveal familiar green eyes, the corners crinkled up from her cheeky grin.

"Noelle!" I screeched, on the verge of tears. "I didn't know you, uh—"

"Could ride and shoot? I'm the president's sister, dummy. Come here."

She lowered her kickstand and hopped off, arms open for my bone-crushing hug as I ran up to her.

"I'm so fucking happy to see you," I whispered against the side of her helmet.

"Same here, Mari. You look good dolled up in my shit." She pulled back from my hug, still smiling. "Speaking of my punk ass brother, where is he?"

"I don't know." The worry creeped back into my voice, taking over my relief. "These guys haven't seen him either."

"Is it clear out there, Noelle?" Jandro addressed her for the first time.

"No Razor Wire on wheels left. Some might be hiding or trapped under fallen bikes. I say we look for our people but proceed with caution."

"I thought *I* was VP?" Jandro teased, grinning at her.

"Tell 'em it was your idea. Y'all have been doing that for hundreds of years already," she joked back. "Mari, want to ride with me?"

"No, she stays with us. She's—"

"I can protect her, Jandro," Noelle rolled her eyes. "You guys got wheels?"

"Yeah, somewhere around here."

"Find 'em then meet us back inside the gate." Noelle threw a leg over her bike and looked at me. "I'm guessing you're going to have a few patients once we get everyone in."

I nodded, climbing on behind her and holding onto her waist. "If anyone has stretchers or long carts we can pull people in, we might need them for any leg wounds or head injuries."

"Got it." She kicked off the ground and off we went. "A couple guys have pickup trucks, we can put people in the truck beds. Anything else we should prepare for?"

"I'll just need extra hands," I said. "To apply pressure to wounds, to hand me tools if I need to do surgery. I won't know for sure until I see what injuries people have."

"You've got me, girl," Noelle patted my hand on her stomach. "I'll rally some other help, too. Don't you worry."

"Thank you," I sighed. "God, it's so good to see you."

"You mean you weren't in heaven surrounded by dick all day?" she laughed.

"That's not exactly what I would call it."

We passed by two other dirt bike riders and Noelle yelled at them to get pickup trucks.

The dust was now settling but night was falling. Noelle turned her headlight on as we maneuvered through bodies and debris.

"There's Big G!" I pointed and Noelle pulled straight up to him.

He got shot in the calf and would definitely need to be carried home, but thankfully he managed to get some clothes on at some point. I wrapped gauze around his wound, gave him a pill for pain and told him to sit tight. The trucks would be coming soon and he just had to wave them down.

"Poor Tessa," Noelle muttered as we drove away. "She's about to deal with four children instead of three."

"What do you mean?" I asked.

"Big G turns into a big toddler when he gets a cold. With a gunshot wound? Poor Tess is gonna be run ragged taking care of his ass."

"We'll help her," I affirmed with a squeeze around Noelle's waist. "I've been dying to see her and listen to her belly again."

"Oh, she'll be thrilled to see you."

We found a couple more Demons with fairly serious but not life-threatening injuries. I patched them up as well as I could, told them help was on the way, and moved on. But still no signs of Reaper.

When Noelle drove slowly past a big pile-up of motorcycles, I thought I saw movement inside.

"Wait!" I told her. "I think someone's trapped."

She parked her bike and cocked her gun, grabbing my arm as I hopped off. "Stay behind me. It could be one of the other guys."

I nodded, letting her approach the pile of metal with her gun drawn.

"Anyone in there?" she called.

"Help! I'm stuck!" a voice called out.

Noelle looked over her shoulder at me. "Who's that? I don't recognize the voice."

"I don't either."

“What MC are you with?” she yelled, raising her weapon again.

"Steel Demons! I was their prisoner. I, ah, gave them information..."

"Oh shit," I realized. "It's the guard from the outpost! We've got to get him out."

I ran toward the pile of metal. Noelle set her gun down and followed me.

"What's your name?" I asked the guard.

"Larkan," he answered, followed by a groan of pain.

"We're getting you out, Larkan. Can you tell me where you're pinned? Arms, legs, torso?"

"My shoulder feels fucked," he grimaced. "I kinda feel like I'm holding an entire bike on the back of my shoulders. If I move, it'll crush me completely."

"I can see you," Noelle said, peering through gaps in the pile-up. She looked at me. "How strong are you, Mari?"

"Uh, not strong enough to move a whole bike myself."

She stood up, stuck her fingers into her mouth to let out a sharp whistle, then waved at her fellow dirt bike riders in the distance. "Hey! We could use some muscle over here!"

A team of four came over, and with careful maneuvering and Larkan talking us through, they were able to lift the bike off of him.

"Don't move," I warned the facedown man with his forearms braced on the ground.

He wore no cut, and his shirt was bloody, covered in dirt and ripped to shreds. It looked like he went skidding with the bike when it went down.

"Your shoulder's dislocated," I observed. "Your other one looks fine, but I have to pop this one back into place. This is going to hurt, okay?"

"Okay," he panted.

"On three. One, two—"

"Ahhh, fuck!"

"Sorry," I told him. "It's better when you're not bracing yourself for it. You can move now, but slowly. Wiggle your toes, fingers, ankles, wrists. Tell me if anything hurts."

Larkan did as I said, checking every major joint gently for any breaks. "Everything hurts but I think I'm okay." He flipped over onto his back, making eye contact with Noelle and I for the first time, and I think we were both taken by surprise.

Even while covered in sand and blood, road rash all over his skin and his shirt hanging off of him in tatters, he was cute. Like, really cute.

His rich brown hair was a few shades lighter than Reaper's, with eyes almost as crystal-blue as Gunner's. His nose was a little crooked in an endearing way and his smile was pained, but heartfelt.

And it shone straight at Noelle.

"You two just saved my life," he panted.

"That was all her," Noelle waved her hand in my direction, but a nervous smile played at her lips.

I dug through my pack to let them have a small moment, smiling to myself before producing a pill bottle.

"Here, take one of these for the pain. We'll have to clean you up when we get everyone inside the compound. Can you walk?"

"I think so."

"Here," Noelle held an arm out. "Hold onto me."

I swore I saw literal sparks fly when he touched her arm, using it for leverage to pull himself to his feet.

"You're gonna make me lose my man card," he joked, seemingly unable to keep his eyes away from Noelle.

"Your dick still works, doesn't it?" Noelle's mouth dropped open and she slapped a hand over it as if someone else made her say that. "Oh my God, that's so inappropriate! I don't even know you! I'm sorry, the president's my brother and I just—"

"It's all right," Larkan seemed far more amused than offended. "And yes, it does still work. Guess I'll hold onto that man card after all."

Redder than her hair color, Noelle hid her face behind her hands when one of the dirt bike riders waved at us from a nearby crash site.

"Hey! Has anyone seen Reaper?" he called.

"No, why? What did you find?" I rushed over, Noelle's blossoming romance now the farthest thing from my mind.

"Here's his bike," he motioned. "And it's all fucked up."

No. Please, no.

Fucked up was an understatement. The bike looked like a giant tried to fold it in half. Reaper's personal items were strewn out all over the ground, including the gavel which marked his symbol as a leader.

I picked it up slowly, my fingers digging into the grooves of the wood.

"But his body isn't here?" I asked no one in particular.

"No. I think we got everybody except him. There are a bunch of un-ID'd bodies, though—"

"Find him," I demanded.

I didn't know who I was talking to. I wasn't even in a position to give anyone orders. But Reaper, dead or alive, *had* to be found. My body felt like it was going to burst from the inside out without knowing. But if he was one of those mangled, twisted bodies buried under a pile of metal, would I be able to handle *that* knowledge?

"Any sign of Hades?" I asked the dirt bike riders.

One of them pulled off his helmet and I recognized him as Bones, one of the men dating Heather, Reaper's ex.

"No sign of the pooch, either," he told me apologetically. "But if they're out there, we'll find both of them."

I nodded, at a loss for any more words when a hand squeezed my shoulder from behind.

"My brother's like a cockroach," Noelle told me. "Impossible to kill. He's on the wanted lists for at least five surrounding territories. Don't worry, Mari. He'll turn up."

"I hope you're right," I told her.

She gave my shoulder another affectionate squeeze before rubbing the top of my back. "Come on, medic. We've got a long night ahead of us."

She was right. I had to put aside my worries for the man I desperately didn't want to lose. I had to do my job, to focus on the ones who needed me right then and there.

Chapter 19

MARIPOSA

The chaos of the battle's aftermath continued inside the Steel Demons' gates but this time, I was in my element.

Everyone who needed immediate medical attention piled into the clubhouse conference room, where the lights were brightest and people could sit on the tables or chairs as they waited for me.

Those who had stayed home brought water and light snacks to those of us who'd been out in the field. I told Noelle to grab bandages, antibacterial soap, and rubbing alcohol, and clean up people with the minor injuries like road rash. Others helped by keeping pressure on more serious wounds. Meanwhile, I worked from most severe injuries to least. For those in the most pain, I stuck them with local anesthesia and moved on to do something else while waiting for it to kick in. Tessa waddled in just as Big G let out a loud whimper from my syringe.

"Tessie!" he cried out when he saw her. "Baby!"

"Hey, Tess," I gave her a tight smile as I wiped down the skin surrounding the bullet wound. "I'd hug you, but you know..."

She laughed at the sight of my scrubs, already covered with blood even though I quickly changed them from the road. "I'll stay out of your way. We'll reunite later, but I just wanted to see you." She rubbed her husband's back. "And you, I guess."

"Baby, stay with me?" he begged.

"You probably shouldn't stay in here," I warned her. "There are a lot of open wounds here and potential breeding grounds for infection. If you come in contact with anything, it could pose a risk to the baby."

"She's my wife!" Big G yelled. "She stays with me, medic."

"God, shut up," Tessa smacked him. "Don't yell at Mari. She knows more than you." Her eyes lifted to me with a protective hand on her belly. "I'll be in the kitchen, helping with food."

"Tell them lots of vegetables," I said to her. "Especially dark, leafy greens. And hearty soups with bone broth. This lot is going to be out of commission for a while and they'll need good food to recover."

"I'm so glad our boys are in your care," Tessa smiled as she turned to leave. "It's good to have you back, Mari."

I extracted the bullet from Big G's calf and stitched him up without much incident. He apparently didn't have much to say to me without someone else paying attention. I gave him his recovery instructions, then moved on to Jandro who I anesthetized earlier.

"How you holding up?" he asked, leaning over the conference table with his back to me so I could reach his shoulder.

"Better than all of you," I snapped on a pair of fresh gloves and carefully examined his wound.

"We'd be so fucked if it weren't for you," he murmured.

"I dunno. I have a feeling this isn't the first time you've all been in a gunfight."

"Far from it. See that scar on my other shoulder?"

I shined my light on it briefly. "Jesus. The surgeon carved you up."

"Yeah. We used to pile the injured into a truck, drive thirty minutes north to a clinic and pray it would still be open. Then had to threaten the medics at gunpoint to treat us."

"Jesus," I muttered again, not feeling particularly chatty as I worked.

"We paid them in food and basic supplies. But yeah, we've lost a few good Demons over the years. It's part of MC life, but Reaper's been determined to have our own medic. And holy fuck I'm glad we have you, *Mariposita*."

The sentiment was sweet but my work mindset refused to break. I had so much more to do. Flirting with him could wait, but the mention of Reaper's name brought a fresh ache in my chest.

"Has anyone seen him yet?"

"They're out searching right now." He reached over with his good arm to touch my knee. "Not just among the bodies. He might've chased one down that was trying to get away."

"But they found his bike in the rubble."

"He could've hopped on another one." Jandro gave my knee a gentle squeeze. "He'll come back, Mari."

I extracted the metal slug from his shoulder and got to work on his sutures in silence. Focusing on my task was the only thing that kept my hands steady and my heartbeat calm. Every minute that passed without Reaper's presence in his own domain just felt wrong. I saw the worry on everyone else's faces, too. We all wanted to believe he'd come swaggering back through that door, Hades trotting at his side, but what if he didn't? What was this club without its leader?

His gavel felt like a brick in my pocket. I probably wasn't supposed to have it, but it gave me an odd sense of comfort. Like he was still near me.

"How long you gonna be at it?" Jandro asked, pulling me out of my autopilot suturing.

"As long as it takes," I sighed. "Probably all night."

"I'll bring you coffee." His hand never left my knee and now slid up my thigh slightly.

"Thanks."

A twinge on my right side suddenly twisted and cramped. I'd felt some sensation there since getting back but it started getting more intense. My gut, or something within me, told me it had to do with Shadow.

"Has Shadow had his injury looked at?" I asked Jandro.

"He won't let anyone come near him," he sighed. "He gets like this sometimes, like a feral animal. I'll talk him into letting you see him, though."

"Thanks." I snipped the end of my thread after tying it off and wiped the surrounding skin clean one more time. "I don't think he had but a bad graze but it could get serious if left untreated."

"Leave it to me." He turned toward me, hand still on my thigh, then leaned in like he was going to kiss me.

The conference room door crashing open made me jerk away, partially relieved and disappointed at the interruption.

The search party had returned. Bones and Dallas walked in, grim expressions on their faces as they looked at Jandro.

"What is it?" he asked.

"No sign of Reaper among the bodies. Or Hades," Bones added with a glance toward me.

"So he's still out there," Jandro said confidently. "We'll search out farther in the morning."

Dallas glanced up nervously. "The thing is, some of the crash sites leaked oil and caught fire. When we put them out, the bodies were impossible to identify."

"Then go by the patch on the cut," Jandro snapped. "Did *any* of them have an SDMC patch?"

Bones shook his head. "There are three corpses so badly damaged, we can't ID them by anything. Their clothes literally burned away."

The whole room fell silent. As the information sank into everyone's mind, the worst part was that it told us absolutely nothing. Reaper could be one of those bodies, or he might not be.

"None of those are him," Jandro decided, raising his voice and turning around to look sternly at everyone. "If you didn't find a dog corpse nearby, none of those bodies are Reaper's. Hades never would've left his side."

Bones cleared his throat. "With all due respect," he said hesitantly, "while he's not here, club law says we're to look to you in the interim."

"He'll be here. It's only been a few hours. We don't need to catastrophize this yet."

"Jandro," I whispered.

He looked at me, then down at the gavel I held out in my hands.

"Where did you get that?" he asked.

"It was near his bike. It looked like a hard crash, all his personal stuff was out everywhere."

He closed my fingers over the small, wooden hammer, then gently pushed my hand back toward my body.

"When he shows up, you can give it to him," he smiled. "He'll love that. You two," he snapped to the two men who just walked in. "And everyone else who's not injured. Start cleaning up first thing in the morning. Haul the bikes to my shop. Pick up personal items and supplies and sort them out to their rightful places. We're *not* treating Reaper like he's dead until we have certifiable proof."

Everyone returned to their tasks with a low murmur, myself included. I peeled off my gloves and lathered up my hands with antibacterial soap as Jandro smacked a kiss on my cheek.

"Thanks, Doc," he nuzzled against my face for a moment. "Now, coffee."

I nodded and moved on to my next patient. What else could I do?

Noelle seemed to be cleaning up Larkan's road rash well enough, so I handed her cold packs for his shoulder and left them to continue making their googly eyes at each other.

The night wore on. Jandro brought me at least three cups of coffee while I wrapped sprained ankles, checked for head injuries, changed bandages, and so on. My brain was wired but my body wanted to drop from exhaustion. And that was with everyone stepping up to help. I'd have to express my gratitude one day, when I wasn't so tired.

Every so often I looked to the door. My heart jumped into my throat whenever someone came through, but it was never him.

"Mari," Noelle placed a gentle hand on my shoulder when I dropped into a chair, peeling off what felt like my hundredth pair of gloves. "You need to rest. I'm bringing Larkan back home to keep an eye on his injuries. You coming with us?"

I shook my head. "Jandro's still trying to talk Shadow into letting me see him. And if—*when* Reaper comes in, what if he needs attention right away? I should stay here."

"You're not superhuman, Mari. You're about to crash any second."

The moment she said that, I felt like all my systems were shutting down. "Maybe, but I need to stay here. I could take a nap or something."

"I'll clear off the couch and get you a blanket." She left my side, shooing people out of her way.

I paused for a moment to look around the room. The chaos had died down and most people left with their loved ones to return home. For the first time in hours, I didn't have anything immediately to do. And nothing to distract me from the fact that Reaper still wasn't here.

"Come here, girl," Noelle unfolded a large comforter and pointed to the couch. "Lay down."

I did as she commanded, dead on my feet as I stumbled over.

"Poor thing," Noelle mumbled as she brought the blanket over me. "We gotta take care of our little medic, now that she's caring for all of us."

"We are. At least *I* am." The voice sounded like Jandro but I couldn't be sure. My eyelids were too heavy. The blanket and couch too warm and comfortable.

And I fell into a restless sleep before I knew it. But even during sleep, the fear of never seeing Reaper again haunted me.

Chapter 20

MARIPOSA

"Reaper...Reaper!"

"He's not here, honey. I'm sorry."

My eyes snapped open to the familiar green eyes looking at me, but they were the wrong ones. Noelle's red bangs fell across her forehead, her brow pinched tight with concern.

"What do you mean?" I blinked, rubbing my eyes. "Where is he? How long have I been out?"

I swore he was here. I felt his hands on me—strong, possessive, and full of his want. I heard him calling me sugar into my ear. But none of it was real?

"You've been out a couple hours. It's almost dawn." Noelle squeezed my hand.

"And he hasn't come back?"

She shook her head slowly. "I'm getting worried, Mari."

That scared me more than anything. The unshakeable president's sister, who knew him better than anyone, was losing hope.

I sat up and pulled her into a hug. She curled up under the blanket next to me and rubbed my back. She didn't cry. Even now she was trying to be strong.

"Hey, girls."

Jandro came over, sounding exhausted. He picked something up from the couch cushion so he could sit next to me. I saw it was the gavel, which must have fallen out of my pocket as I slept.

"You should be holding that," Noelle said in a small voice.

"No." Jandro placed it back in my lap. "I meant what I said. He's still president until we have proof of otherwise."

"But you're—"

"I'm VP whether he's here or not. I'll act in his stead when he's not and carry out his word when he is. But until we have confirmation that the Steel Demons need a new president, I'm not the one meant to hold the gavel."

"Fuck no, you're not."

All three of our heads snapped to the door, where the man in question strode through with a cocky smirk like he owned the place.

"Reaper!" we all cried out.

"And Hades?" I asked, the panic refusing to subside.

The furry beast ran right up to me, attacking me with a strong, four-limbed hug and tons of puppy licks. I hugged him back, the laughter finally escaping me, but it was the sight of his master I couldn't believe.

"Reaper..." I ran to him, my medic's eye taking in the dried blood on his clothes, the tatters of his shirt from road rash.

"What happened?" The questions flew out of my mouth in rapid fire succession as my hands inspected him everywhere. "Where did you go? Did you hit your head? Is anything broken?"

"Mari, stop." He took hold of my wrists, pinning me with that green-eyed stare I saw moments ago in my dreams. "I'm okay. Most of this blood isn't mine." His road-rashed palm came to my face, his thumb stroking my cheek gently as his eyes burned with relief, and maybe a touch of regret.

"Forgive me, sugar?"

I pressed my hands against his on my face, not caring about blood or germs, just leaning into the need of his rough touch on me.

"Forgive me?" I whispered. "Again?"

The corner of his mouth ticked up. "Truce."

Like air out of a balloon, all of the fears and anxieties over the past day left me all at once. I went from feeling like my heart would explode with worry to feeling as light as air.

"Fuck." Reaper pulled me in close, one arm around my waist, the other wound in my hair. "I was so worried about you. I knew Jandro would keep you safe but still, if I lost you—"

He cut off his own thought with a hard kiss, rough and desperate like he needed my mouth to breathe. I grabbed the torn edges of his shirt to deepen it even more, pushing my tongue into his mouth. His moan was full of longing as his fist curled into the fabric at my waist.

"Well, seems like you two are on better terms since you left," Noelle laughed.

"We weren't talking again right before this," Reaper chuckled, still gripping my hair and staring at me.

"Jesus, Reap," Noelle rolled her eyes. "Mari is a saint to deal with you."

"She is," he sighed, resting his forehead on mine. "I'm not the easiest person to get along with. But I *want* this, sugar. I'll tell you right now, in front of my sister and the guy who is basically my brother," his eyes flicked up toward Jandro, "in front of my family. I want you to be my woman. Whatever that entails, we'll figure it out. But I swear to you, I'm not chasing tail. I'm not gonna have a wandering eye. I'm done with that. I want *you*, Mariposa."

For a man like Reaper, that was probably the biggest declaration of romance I would get. And coming from him, it was perfect. I believed every word. My first instinct was to jump for joy and confess how much I wanted him, too. How this dull ache in my chest spread throughout my bones every day we didn't speak. That I daydreamed about his pretty eyes, cocky grin, and the ways he pleased me in bed while riding on the back of Jandro's bike.

Speaking of Jandro, he was being extremely quiet during this whole reunion. I knew we passed the line of platonic friendship at some point, and we'd have to address that. I also wanted to ensure history didn't repeat itself again in my relationship with Reaper.

He squeezed my arms gently. "Please say something."

I looked up at him, releasing the edges of his shirt to caress his neck.

"I want you, too," I confessed. "But to make this work, I think we need to hash some things out. We need to make some ground rules on what's okay and not okay, then make sure we stick by them."

"I agree." His fingers curled around mine as he turned his head to kiss my palm. "There's a lot I haven't told you, and that's my fault. I forget that other people didn't grow up in the same culture as Noelle and me." He smiled as he gently lowered my hand. "But hopefully that can wait until Hades and I have a bit of time to recover?"

"I suppose," I sighed jokingly, kissing him one more time before stepping away. "If you're not hurt, you're definitely dehydrated."

"Yeah." Reaper eased himself down on the couch, wincing slightly. "We walked back, about thirteen miles by my estimate."

"From where?" Jandro asked, already filling a bowl of water for Hades. "And why on foot?"

"I crashed into a guy who was trying to knock Shadow off of his bike," Reaper accepted water from Noelle, gulping deeply. "We both got thrown off and went tumbling. Lost our weapons so came down to using fists."

"He's probably one of the un-ID'd bodies out there," Jandro muttered.

"Oh yeah. His lower jaw wasn't attached anymore when I was done."

Noelle jabbed me with her elbow at my open-mouthed stare. "Get used to it, girl."

"One of his buddies came at me shooting," Reaper continued after more gulps of water. "I ducked behind a crash site, saw one of their own bikes still ridable, so I got on and he gave chase. Next thing I know, Sheol is nowhere in sight."

"Hades was with you the whole time?" The pup had finished drinking his own water and now laid his head in my lap.

"Yeah, poor boy got run ragged. Didn't you?" Reaper stroked his head. "You've never ran like that, huh?" The SDMC leader looked up at us with pride. "He took down two riders himself but the guy on my tail, he was damn slippery."

"Mari took down a couple, too," Jandro cocked his head in my direction.

"Really now?" Reaper's eyes sparkled with glee. "I knew you weren't all sugar and sweetness."

"She needs to work on her aim," Jandro said, then laughed at my glare. "What? It's true! Your shots were a little wide."

"I'll be happy to never shoot a man again," I grumbled. "Yes, they attacked us, but I *killed* someone. That's a big deal to me."

"You'll get used to that, too," Noelle said. "'Cause it'll keep happening. And you'll need to know how to defend yourself."

"We'll teach you the basics," Reaper added. "Then Gunner can teach you fancy shit when he's back."

"He's already teaching me how to swim," I said. "I was able to float on my back at the pool."

"I know," Reaper said with a tone I couldn't place. "I saw you two together."

"I bet he's thrilled that Horus took down a Razor Wire, too," Jandro grinned. "He's probably celebrating right now."

"What?" I knitted my brow.

"The bond," Reaper reminded me. "With a kill that big, Gunner definitely would've felt his divebomb and seen the whole thing from the bird's-eye view."

"Anyway," Noelle waved her hand to catch the guys' attention. "How the hell did you end up walking here?"

"Oh, the gas tank was running on empty. I already figured I wouldn't be able to ride it back, so I decided to crash it."

"You what?" I demanded.

"I know my way around bikes, sugar," Reaper placated me. "I wasn't in danger but the dude chasing did not expect it, that's for sure. I let him crash into me, he flipped over his handlebars and cracked his skull open. I think Hades ate some of his brains."

I looked at the adorable, doe-eyed dog in my lap. "Hades, did you?"

He licked his lips and grinned at me. Everyone laughed at my horrified expression.

"Have I heard it all yet?" I groaned, lowering my forehead to my palm.

"Not even close." Reaper threw an arm around my shoulders and kissed my temple. "Welcome to life as an outlaw, sugar."

CHAPTER 21

MARIPOSA

Noelle and Jandro got Reaper and Hades well fed and hydrated. I cleaned Reaper's minor road rash, which turned out to be the most mild case of anyone I saw that day.

"How did everyone else fare?" he asked me as Hades snored by our feet.

"Some gunshot wounds, sprained ankles and dislocated shoulders, but nothing imminently life-threatening."

"Good," he sighed, visibly relieved as he leaned back on the couch. "And good thing you were here." He placed a hand on my thigh, looking at me affectionately. "You must be exhausted, sugar."

"I took a nap for a little bit. I sure as hell didn't go walking for miles all night."

"Yeah, a day with my feet up sounds great." A twinkle flashed in his eye as he smiled deviously at me. "I owe you a bath that's actually relaxing."

"That sounds amazing," I rested my chin on his shoulder. "I think I'll take you up on that."

"What are we waiting for?" His voice already grew husky, fingers kneading the flesh of my leg. Chances were we wouldn't be making it to the bathtub.

Jandro knocked on the conference room door and walked in just as we got to our feet.

"Shadow's on the patio by the pool," he said. "He kind of retreats to quiet places when there's a lot of commotion, but I think I convinced him you're not going to cut his dick off, or whatever he's afraid of."

"Oh, okay." I had forgotten about him for a moment after being so relieved that Reaper came back. I squeezed the president's hand and looked up at him. "I'll be quick."

"I'll get the bath started." He leaned down for a kiss, sensual and lingering. "Come to my room and meet me in the en suite." He squeezed my waist and whispered possessively, "You're not staying in the guest room anymore."

I smiled and gave him a gentle push to the door. "Go. Don't have too much fun without me."

"Never." He stole one last kiss before heading out into the hallway, Hades right on his heels.

Which left me and Jandro alone.

"I'm fucking glad he's back," he said with a sigh. "Honestly, I don't want the responsibility of being president. He's got his flaws but he's a damn good leader."

"I'm glad, too," I said softly, unsure what else to say. What happened now? Was it going to be awkward between us? Were we just going to pretend we never kissed and never spent a night together?

"I'm happy for you, Mari," he added with a tight smile. "I'm glad you two are going to work it out."

"Jandro—"

"Do you need anything? Shadow knows you're coming. If you're good, I have a bunch of wrecked bikes I need to comb through in the shop."

"Okay. Um, yeah." I returned the tight smile. "I won't keep you. Remember to get some rest. I'll look at your sutures later."

"All right. See you, Mari." He said it warmly but walked off like he couldn't wait to get out of there. And with no kiss or hug, or any contact.

I shook my head at myself as I gathered up some fresh gloves and supplies. *You just got back with Reaper. Jandro was a temporary distraction, but he's a friend.*

It took a moment for me to find Shadow on the patio. He sat on a couch tucked back in a dark corner, nursing a large bottle of liquor.

"Good morning, Shadow," I greeted as I approached him. The sun had just risen over the far end of the pool and looked spectacular.

He didn't return the greeting this time, just watched me warily as he took a swig from his bottle.

"I understand you're not comfortable with women or people in general," I said as I snapped on my gloves. "So I'll make this quick. Sound good?"

Again, no answer. His eyes slid away from me with a wordless grunt which I took to indicate consent.

I pulled a chair over to sit in front of him, while I laid my tools out on the couch next to him. His eyes widened and he hitched in a breath at the sight of my scalpels.

"I'm going to cut away your shirt," I explained, picking up my scissors. "I need you to not move so as to not agitate the wound, okay?"

Another non-reply followed by a swig of the bottle. I really wished he wouldn't. Alcohol thinned the blood and made bleeding worse, but I wasn't here to lecture him about his coping methods. I picked up the scissors and began cutting up the side of his shirt.

He or Jandro already applied pressure to the wound and soaked up a lot of the blood. The graze cut a long gash between his ribs and his hip. Thankfully, it wasn't very deep. The bleeding had slowed and begun to congeal.

I folded back the two sides of his now-cut shirt to access the wound easily. Rummaging through my stuff, my heart sank when I realized I ran out of rubbing alcohol. Fortunately, being a medic in a war zone taught me there were other methods of sterilizing.

"Can I borrow that?" I pointed to Shadow's liquor bottle, which he seemed very reluctant to part with. "I'm out of rubbing alcohol and I need to sterilize your wound."

He scowled at me but passed the bottle over. I hesitated as I held it over his wound. "This is going to hurt like a motherfucker." He looked off toward the pool, elbow propped on the arm of the couch and his chin in his hand, just waiting for this ordeal to be over with.

You and me both, buddy.

His expression didn't change when I poured the alcohol over his skin. Even the most stoic man would have hissed or grit his teeth or something, but Shadow gave no reaction. He only accepted his bottle back when I held it out to him.

"Stitching you up now," I said, preparing the sutures. "This might hurt, too. I'm sorry, I ran out of local anesthesia."

I got my usual response and got down to work. While the wound was shallow, it extended nearly eight inches long, wrapping around his waist from nearly his stomach to his back. It had to hurt like a bitch but he acted like he didn't even notice it. Frankly, he looked bored.

My hands were on autopilot pulling the surgical thread in and out of his skin, which allowed my eyes to wander slightly across his massive body. He had Jandro's beefcake muscles on a frame taller than Gunner. More pale, faded scars like the ones I saw on his arms crisscrossed up the exposed side of his body, disappearing under the remains of his shirt folded over his chest.

There was no way all of this could be self-harm, though they were clearly shallow cuts made by a sharp implement. Which likely explained why he looked nervous at the sight of my scalpel.

His broad chest rose and fell with deep, even breaths as I worked. The movement was calming, if even hypnotic. If he wasn't so damn intimidating, he'd probably make a great cuddler.

"Almost done here," I said with a handful of stitches left to go. "Then I'll be out of your hair."

Another grunt, another swig of liquor.

"And...done." I snipped the end of my thread. "Just let me put some ointment on this." I unscrewed a tube of Neosporin and dabbed it over the closed wound with a finger. "Come see me if this still looks really red in a couple of days, if you have any fever or weakness, or it's oozing stuff. It's been exposed for a while so your chances of infection are slightly higher than the other guys."

I'd bet my entire medical career he wouldn't willingly come see me, but I still found it important to perform my due diligence.

"I'll give Jandro some of this ointment for both of you to use. Just apply it a couple times a day until it's fully closed." I peeled off my gloves and began cleaning up. "Any questions?"

None, naturally, but it didn't hurt to ask.

"Okay." I stood from the chair and gathered up my supplies. "Let me know if you need anything else."

The absolute last thing I expected was his arm to shoot out and wrap around my waist.

“Whoa, Shadow! What?"

He pulled me across his lap, taking away my balance so I had no choice but to splay across his chest. I braced my hands on his shoulders, utterly bewildered as I stared at him.

"Shadow, what are you—”

My answer came as I heard his pants unbutton and unzip just behind my back. Before I could react, he yanked my scrub pants down, peeling them off my feet, and pulled my bare leg over to straddle him. Naked from the waist down, my bare skin touched his.

It happened so fast and out of nowhere, I could only gape at him. He didn't speak a word or look me directly in the eyes, not even as he reached behind my ass to stroke himself to full hardness. *What the fuck is happening?*

A million questions poured rapidly through my mind as Shadow touched himself almost like I wasn't even there. His hand left my waist, just limp at his side. He seemed so detached, even transactional about this.

I only snapped out of my stupor when I felt his hard cock flex against my ass. His hand returned to my waist only to lift me up so he could—

"Shadow, stop!" I pressed my hands to his biceps. "Wait."

He froze, looking at me directly for the first time. I couldn't read his expression, whether it was angry or confused. He just looked...blank. I said stop, so he did.

But what the ever-loving fuck? Where did this come from? And what would he do if I tried to get away?

His grip on my waist was tight, his strong fingers digging into my skin. Jandro trusted both of us enough to leave us alone—did he ever think this would be happening? He wouldn't let me come alone if he considered Shadow a risk to my safety, would he?

Because even though we were on the same team, Shadow was one big, intimidating motherfucker, and he only ever said two words to me in the weeks I'd been with the club. A memory flashed of him tying me up the first time the Steel Demons took me. He bound me tightly, doing as he was ordered by Reaper, but no one was ordering him now. What would he do to someone smaller and weaker than him with no one watching?

I didn't *want* to think the worst but here I was with my pants down, in the last situation I expected after Reaper and Gunner assured me their men didn't prey on women. The fact of the matter was I didn't know anything about Shadow, aside from his strong disdain of women and that he was an experienced, skilled killer.

In my panicked, utterly confused state of mind, it seemed the best course of action was to give him what he wanted.

So I raised my hips and reached behind me, feeling for the cock he was just about to shove into me with nothing leading up to it. No foreplay, no flirting, not even a word exchanged. And fuck me, it was huge.

My fingers nearly didn't touch as they wrapped around the shaft. Shadow's hand fell away from my waist, his eyelids softening at the contact of my hand on him. It seemed he wasn't bothered about putting in any effort once he saw that I was about to take the reins.

I can't believe I'm fucking doing this. Reaper is waiting for me in his fucking bathtub for fuck's sake! I screamed in my head.

Shadow's fists curled at his sides when I swept the crown of his dick against my entrance. Just that motion squashed any thoughts about running off. A single swing from one of those fists would send my brain matter all over the patio. The consequences of this would be grave but no one was coming to my rescue now, and I just had to get through it.

Lowering myself onto him was a slow, arduous process with his size and the complete lack of foreplay but I found myself wetter than I expected, given the circumstances. He was, after all, the first of the four sexiest Demons I really noticed. Reaper was the first one I *saw,* but it was Shadow who made me bump into his coffee table when I came over to serve him beer.

The tall, imposing frame, those tortured, soulful eyes, and all the scars he tried to keep hidden. He clearly had no idea how magnetizing that was to some women. To touch him was not only to flirt with danger, but to fall into it unabashedly. Even now, in this situation, my palm itched to touch the short beard covering his jaw, to push away the long hair he kept over his face so he'd look at me with both eyes.

But if I did, would I live to tell about it?

His head tilted back with a soft hiss as his length began disappearing inside me. I found myself doing the same as he stretched me out from the inside. The sensation was intense, but not painful. When I began a slow roll of my hips, my hands splayed out to brace myself for leverage. My fingers met the bare skin of his abdomen, his cut T-shirt now falling away to the side.

With my knees on the couch cushions on either side of his thighs, I found a somewhat steady rhythm as I rode him. He never touched me or made a sound. His eyes flicked up and down, from where our bodies connected, to where my hands rested on him, to my still fully-clothed torso hovering above him, but he never met my eye.

He was so...cold. Clinical and detached. Men who paid for whores showed more enthusiasm than this. That thought process only spiraled back to the pervasive question of *why* did he start this?

I tried to act the same way he did. Not making a sound, not looking at him, not doing anything but the bare minimum to get him off so I could end this and run to Reaper. But I could never treat sex that way, not even like this.

And I couldn't ignore the fact that he was a fucking specimen of a man. Beautiful in such a sad, dark way. Massive arms and chiseled shoulders I just wanted to run my hands across. The Steel Demons skull emblem sat inked on the left side of his chest, right over his heart. I wanted to trace it with my fingers like I did with Reaper's. Or maybe with my tongue.

I became so entranced with all the fine details of his body, I didn't notice the moan escaping my mouth until it was too late. For once, he looked up at my face, surprised. And my face burned red with shame at the realization that I was *enjoying* this.

He was hot as hell, with a huge dick that stretched me in ways I didn't know were possible. And yes, he was dangerous and a cold-blooded killer, but he wasn't forcing me to do anything. I probably had the advantage at this point to hop off and run for my life, but I didn't *want* to.

My hands skimmed up his abs to his chest, splaying open my fingers wide to *feel* the heat of his skin, the beat of his heart under that grinning skull. I rode him even more vigorously, taking the full length of him on every downstroke and moaning openly each time he filled me.

Still he didn't say a thing, or move his hands from his sides to touch me. I had so many questions, so many ways I wanted to test him with small gestures. How would he react to a kiss? Or if I just grabbed his hands and put them on me?

But as much as I enjoyed him, his complete lack of reaction also made me insecure. This could still end badly for me if I pushed things too far. I just didn't know him well enough to take that risk.

So I settled for caressing him, enjoying the view and feel of him as I rolled my hips back and forth. He let out a sigh as my hands reached his chest again, then his whole body stiffened with a groan.

A moment later I felt the swelling and spilling of warmth as he released inside me. He panted as I slowed my movements, and then I felt the first touch with the tiniest glimpse of intimacy—his fingers brushing against my knee.

And like that, I felt like a blindfold had been torn away from my eyes.

Fuck.

Fuck!

Oh fuck, what did I just do?

I pressed on his chest with my hands to swing my leg over, wobbling like a newborn giraffe as I grabbed my pants and made my best attempt to insert my legs.

Once dressed, I grabbed my supplies and walked away without a word or even a glance at the man behind me.

Chapter 22

REAPER

Holy mother of cunt balls, my whole body fucking hurt.

Motorcycle boots were not made for thirteen-mile long walks so not only were my feet killing me, my knees, hips, and back were feeling about eighty years old, too. But I didn't get any fresh bullet holes or road rash or cactus spines in my dick today, so at least there was an upside.

Hades and I limped home to find Fischlin's guard on one of my couches, wearing nothing but one of *my* pairs of sweatpants and a bag of frozen peas on his shoulder. To add insult to injury, his feet were also propped up on *my* mahogany coffee table I stole from a governor's vacation home.

"The fuck you doin' in my house?" I asked.

"He's with me."

The answer came from Noelle, who just emerged from the linen closet with a folded blanket and a pillow.

"Excuse me?" I asked.

"I said, he's with me." She dropped the blanket and pillow on the couch next to him, then faced me with her hands on her hips.

Oh hell. I hated when my sister got sassy.

"And what the fuck do you mean by that?"

"You bring home strays, I take care of them. Just the way it's always been."

"And you gave him *my* pants?"

"Well, he won't fit into mine!"

"Hey, hey, it's all right." The guy gave an uneasy smile as he stood up, hands raised in a de-escalating manner. "Reaper, uh, Mr. President, I appreciate you bringing me along with your club after everything that happened. I don't want to impose so if you'd rather not have me in your house, I can stay somewhere else."

"No, Larkan, it's fine," Noelle insisted. "Reaper's grumpy as hell on his best days, so he's bound to be a little moody after his trek through the desert."

"Noelle," I sighed, pinching the bridge of my nose. "Just...come here a minute."

I limped over to my study—Goddamn, I was dying to get off my feet—and closed the door after my sister followed me in.

"What the hell is going on?" I asked, folding my arms.

"What? Nothing." She matched my posture. "It's like I said. First Hades, then Mari, now Larkan. You bring home strays, I give them a home. Same as always."

"No," I shook my head. "This one's different."

"What do you mean?" Her voice went a little high on the last word.

"Are you just looking to get laid or is it something more?"

"Reaper!" she growled. "That's not what this is!"

"Yeah, right. He's a grown-ass man whose mechanic skills rival Jandro's and he's a sharpshooter. We're gonna integrate him as a prospect and see how he does. He doesn't *need* to be taken care of. But," I flashed her a taunting smile, "he does have a six-pack and pretty eyes, doesn't he?"

"Fuck you," she punched my arm. "Why would I set him up on the couch if I wanted to get laid?"

"Hence the other part of my question. Is it something more?"

"I literally just met the guy! You all kept him prisoner and never bothered to learn his name as you grilled him for information. Where else would he go? Maybe I'm just trying to be fucking nice? You know, like I was when you dragged Mari out here against her will!"

"Whatever. I'm too fucking tired to argue about this." I scrubbed a hand down my face with a sigh. "Just don't get involved with him, Noelle. That's an order from your president, not your older brother being protective."

"Hah!" she scoffed, raising both of her hands. "You are *way* jumping the gun, tiger."

"I mean it," I growled. "He's given us good intel, but we still don't know if he's loyal enough to be a Demon. And we—" I stopped myself, before choosing to go on with a sigh. "We've had a breach of trust among our own. I'll fill you in later, but this attack was orchestrated by General Tash. He has, for all intents and purposes, turned against us and declared war on us, based on information someone in the club has been feeding him."

"What?" Her mouth dropped open, for once speechless. "Who would do that?"

"I'm not sure," I admitted. "But whoever it is will fucking regret it."

A HOT BATH WAS JUST WHAT I NEEDED. SOAKING UP TO MY armpits, I puffed on a cigar next to the open window and sipped from a glass of my favorite whiskey. The only thing that would've made it better was my sweet little medic snuggled up against me. She was taking her sweet ass time but maybe Shadow's injuries were more extensive that she originally thought.

I puffed and exhaled, closing my eyes to lean my head back against the cool tile. I couldn't pussyfoot around it this time. She had to know not only my intentions, but the reasoning behind them. Best case scenario, she'd embrace it and be thrilled. Worst case, it would just be me and her.

And I was honestly fine with that. If she wanted me to be her only man, I'd do everything in my power to be everything she needed. It was all I thought about on my long trek back home.

Just my luck that the first woman I considered worthy of sharing balked at the first mention of it. Most women outside of my family's culture thought it was some culty brainwashing shit and I didn't give a fuck. I was fine to fuck them and ride off the next day anyway. They'd never get the irony of a one-night stand between two people, while completely dismissing the intimacy and trust between a woman and her harem.

But I desperately wanted Mariposa to understand. And if she didn't go for it, then I would try my best to understand where she was coming from.

That's what people did when they fell in love, right?

"Mari's here!" Noelle called from downstairs.

"Then get that sweet ass up here!" I returned.

"She's getting a robe out of my room!" Noelle reported.

"Fuck that, I want her naked!"

I chuckled to myself, puffing on my cigar, then cringed and coughed. I did not want to think about what Noelle was doing with that guy downstairs, nor did I want to give her any ideas.

Ah, whatever. My woman was here.

"There you are." I leaned back in the tub as Mari's bare feet padded over the tiled floor. "Almost thought the water would get cold before you got here."

"Sorry," she mumbled, slipping the robe off her shoulders and letting the fabric pool on the floor.

I didn't get a chance to enjoy the view. She looked away from me as she climbed in, settling between my legs with her bare back as stiff as a board. Aside from her hips brushing my thighs, she made no move to touch me. She stayed hunched over, knees drawn up and arms against her chest.

That was fucking weird.

I lifted my hand from the water with a small splash, moving her hair from her back to the front of her shoulder. Then I circled my thumb against her upper back, working the stiff muscles until she released a soft sigh. Taking hold of her shoulder, I pulled back gently and she followed until her back rested on my chest.

I moved the massage to her upper arms, letting the water trickle over her skin to aid in her relaxation. Dragging my lips along the back of her neck, I pressed a kiss to the soft spot behind her ear.

"What's wrong, sugar?"

Her heartbeat and her breathing accelerated. I waited, despite the urge of demanding the truth from her. It had been a long time since I comforted a woman who was more than just a casual fuck, but I did my best. My hands ran up and down her arms and I dropped more kisses on her neck and shoulder.

"I had sex with Shadow."

All my movements paused. The words tumbled out of her in a hurried confession, and her heart thumped erratically through her back.

"Okay." That was the last thing I expected to hear come out of her mouth. Shadow hadn't occurred to me as someone to share her with, mainly because he didn't seem interested in most normal things, least of all women.

"I didn't want to at first," she breathed in the same hurried, verging-on-panicked fashion. "I said stop and he did, but...I didn't know what he would do next, so I just...kept going until he finished."

"Wait." My own heart now crashed erratically as I grabbed her shoulder again and turned her so she faced me. "Are you saying *Shadow* forced himself on you?"

"It all happened so fast," her lip wobbled. "I finished cleaning his wound and then he's holding me in his lap and pulling my pants down. I stopped it before anything actually happened, but then I..."

Her eyes lifted to mine, wet with tears. "I didn't expect to feel like shit, but I—"

"Mari, was there *anything* you could have said that made Shadow think you wanted to? He won't even be in the same room as a woman if he can help it, let alone fuck one against her will."

"I don't know." Two fat tears tracked down her cheeks. "I don't even know why I'm so upset. I was scared at first but now I feel like...I cheated on you—"

“You didn’t cheat on me,” I scoffed. “What we have is not some outdated bullshit like that.” *Fuck.* I bit my tongue too late. So much for understanding where she was coming from.

“Right.” She wiped her tears away forcefully. “That’s right, Reaper. I know you don’t do traditional relationships.”

“Don’t put words in my mouth, Mari,” I warned. “I haven’t told you what that means so don’t make assumptions about me.” Then in my best attempt at a gentler voice I added, “This is how we end up fighting, remember?”

“I’m sorry. I just...I’m so confused.” Her eyes were gigantic and pained as they met mine. But *she* wasn’t pained, I realized. She thought she hurt *me*.

“Come here,” I pulled her toward my chest. “I’m not angry and I don’t blame you for this. I mean it, sugar. You haven’t done anything wrong by me.”

“How can you say that?” Her arms went around my neck. “I just slept with another man right after we agreed to work on us!”

“Mari, look at me.” I wrapped one arm around her back and held her chin in the other hand. “Do you still want to be with me?”

“Yes,” her breath fanned over my lips and I ached to kiss her. “Of course I do. But how can you—”

“That’s all that matters to me,” I told her. “You care enough to come straight here and tell me. You still want to be the woman at my side.” I dragged my thumb across the tear resting on her cheekbone. “You’re honest. You’re loyal. And you’re mine. There’s no reason for you to feel so guilty about this.”

"I do, anyway." She let out a shuddering sigh. "I can't believe I let it happen. I never want to be in that situation again."

"Come here." I pulled her in until her thighs wrapped around my waist and her arms encircled my shoulders.

My hands pressed up and down into her back in an effort to soothe her. I dropped kisses to her shoulder as she buried her face in my neck. All the while, I tried to rationally process what she told me. Why wasn't Jandro with her? Shadow only had sex with whores. What made him think she wanted it, when the aftermath clearly showed she didn't? And yet, it didn't sound like he raped her.

I pressed a kiss to her ear before asking, "Did he hurt you?"

"No. He didn't...*do* anything besides start it. It was all me. I guess that's why I feel like shit."

I waited a few moments before asking my next question.

"Did you enjoy it?"

She let out a soft gasp and jerked away from me like I hit her, her face crestfallen.

"I swear to God, Reaper. I don't know where I stand with you. First you're wiping my tears away, then you want to know sordid details like—"

"You want to know where you stand with me?" I pointed to the left side of my chest. "Right fucking here."

Her mouth snapped shut as she swallowed, starting at where my finger pressed directly to my heart.

"Now you're the medic, so correct me if I'm wrong," I continued, "but this organ is not the same thing as my dick."

She huffed out a soft laugh and a smile for the first time since entering the room. "No, you're right." Her eyes lifted up to mine and it looked like something clicked. "So what are you saying?"

"I'm saying sexual or even emotional monogamy is not a requirement for me in a partner. But," I lifted a finger to stop her from saying anything else, "in the culture I grew up in, only women were privy to this. I had one mom and three dads, remember?"

"You mean your dads were *only* with her and no one else?"

"Yeah. All three of them were completely devoted to her." I stared blankly at the water's surface as childhood memories filtered through my head.

"It never felt...I dunno, unfair?"

"Not at all. It was a beautiful, sacred thing cherished by everyone involved." My gaze returned to hers. "There were rules to it, though. Our society was a bit complex. Technically you broke a rule but that's okay." I directed a small splash at her to show I was joking. "You didn't know. And it's nowhere near as bad as cheating."

"So," she looked apprehensive, but not as crushed as a few minutes ago. "You want to have that kind of relationship with me?"

"Only if it's something you want, too." I grabbed her waist and pulled her back once again to straddle me. "I'll explain it later, lay it all out for you. Then you can think about it and decide if it's something you want to try. If not," I sucked in a breath, "I'll try my damndest to be good enough for you as your only man. I *don't* want other women, I'm not wired that way. But if you're only with me...sugar, I'm gonna piss you off. I'm probably gonna hurt your feelings again, even though I don't mean to."

Mari laughed lightly, running her fingers over my scalp as her forehead touched mine. "I have a feeling that's gonna happen regardless if it's just you or not."

"You're probably right." My hands molded to the curves in her back again. "Just hear me out before you write it off?"

"I can do that." She smiled against my lips before bringing a fist to her mouth to stifle her yawn. "Later, though?"

"Later," I promised, kissing her after she finished yawning. "Rest first. And I gotta hold church to bring everyone up to speed. I'm sure you'll have patients to check on."

"Yeah..." Her eyelids were already drooping as she leaned on me.

"And hey," I kissed her forehead.

"Hm?"

"I'll find out what happened," I told her. "And I'll make sure it doesn't happen again."

MARI AND I SLEPT FROM THE ASS-CRACK OF DAWN ALL DAY until the following afternoon. When we got up, she made her rounds checking on patients while I poured over some work in my study. Just to make her feel safer, I told Hades to go with her, which he seemed *very* happy about.

That evening, I found Jandro and some other guys drinking and playing cards around the fire pit next to the pool.

"One of you fuckers pour me something and deal me in. You," I pointed at Jandro, "I need a word. Alone."

His eyebrow popped up in surprise. "Sure thing, Reap."

He followed me into the clubhouse and through the hall until we reached the church conference room, neither of us saying a word until I locked the door behind us.

"What's going on?" Jandro's tone was cool, but brimmed with curiosity.

I huffed out a breath. "You need to find out from Shadow *exactly* what the hell happened after Mariposa treated him."

Jandro's eyes narrowed as he crossed his arms. "Wha—"

"She's saying he fucked her." The words came out with a growl, whether out of jealousy or protection, I couldn't be sure. "And she came to me right after, all upset."

"What, fucked her? You mean like actual...?" He made an O-shape with his hand and stuck his opposite index finger through to demonstrate.

"Yes, Jandro. That is generally what people mean by fucking."

"You can't be serious." He looked baffled. "This is *Shadow* we're talking about."

"I know. It makes no sense to me either." I scrubbed a hand down my face. "But Mari's not lying about this. She was all quiet, then she started crying—"

"You don't think—" Jandro cut himself off abruptly, jerking his eyes away for a moment before looking back at me. "Reap, no. Shadow wouldn't."

"That's why I'm telling you to find out what happened. He'll say more to you than anyone else."

"He's never hurt anyone in this club, you realize that?" my VP asked me intently. "He's never even showed up to a Fight Night. Reaper, she must've—"

"Don't say it," I warned him. "Don't you fucking say she wanted it to happen. She said it felt like *cheating* on me."

"Fuck me, man," he sighed heavily. "You still haven't told her?"

"I started to," I said. "She gets the basic idea but we haven't talked about it in depth yet." I cut my hand through the air. "Doesn't fucking matter, anyway. She did *not* want this to happen. And it will *not* be repeated, you hear me?"

"Yeah, man. I got it."

"So what the hell are you waiting for?" I snarled when he just kept fucking standing there.

"Shadow turned in early tonight. He's probably already asleep."

"Then wake his ass up."

"And get thrown across the room like a rag doll? No thanks," he huffed. "I'll talk to him in the morning."

"See that you do." I headed for the door. "I want two apologies—one to me, for having my woman without permission, and one directly to Mari—"

"Reap, dude," Jandro gave me a pleading look. "You know how he is—"

"—for upsetting the woman who saved all your lives." I opened the door. "That'll be all, Jandro."

I left him there, heading back to the patio where a card game, a drink, and a fat cigar waited for me. Sure, I knew exactly how Shadow was and tolerated it up until now. He was a loyal soldier and a damn good assassin. He didn't have to morph into a chatty Cathy but shit had to change from here on out. He needed to know Mariposa wasn't some whore to paw at. Hell, every Steel Demon needed to know it, but he especially needed it drummed through that thick skull.

She deserved to walk among us feeling safe and respected.

Because she was mine.

Chapter 23

JANDRO

"Chela, Perdita, Letty, Foghorn," I sighed, tugging on the string I just tied to make sure it was secure. "I swear you guys are the only ones *not* being a pain in my ass lately."

The girls just clucked as they pecked at the head of cabbage I strung up for them as a treat. Foghorn was chilling by the workout bench, nice and quiet after crowing at all ungodly hours of the night. That made my next-door neighbor, Big G and his family, less than thrilled. But I begrudgingly got them on board with my new pets after promising fresh eggs once the girls started laying.

Truthfully, though, with Reaper breathing down my neck about what Shadow did, Mariposa forgetting my existence since her man was back, piles of fucked up bikes in my shop, and *still* dealing with a betrayer in our club, hanging out with chickens seemed like a fine idea.

I watched them peck at the head of cabbage while enjoying my coffee in a deck chair. Foghorn decided to see what his ladies were fussing about and walked over with his dinosaur-like gait.

I sighed. If only sharing food was the biggest of my problems. I didn't expect it to nag at me so much that Mari and Reaper got back together so quickly. We all feared the worst for him, and I could only imagine how he felt leaving his woman in the midst of a battle.

My heart didn't hurt. It didn't even sting, really. I just missed her.

I felt like a fallback guy, the one she went to when things were rough with her main squeeze. When did that happen? Never before had I ever let a woman yank me around. I knew all the tricks in the book. Crocodile tears and pouty lips had no effect on me.

Who was I kidding? I knew Mari wasn't being manipulative and it was wrong trying to paint her that way. She was just doing her best to navigate her feelings in a world that was completely foreign to her.

And now this whole thing with Shadow threw me for one hell of a loop. I thought for sure Reaper was fucking with me, but the dude was fuming. Now I had to put on my dad-pants *again* and get everyone to make up. Just great.

I heard the sliding glass door whoosh open behind me, signaling that Shadow had risen and was coming outside for his workout.

"Mornin'," I greeted without looking at him.

I got a grunt in reply, then watched him grip the horizontal bar to begin his pull-ups.

The man worked out religiously every morning we were at home. He was shirtless and with his hair tied back. Only in this yard and in present company was he ever comfortable doing so. I'd bet my flock of chickens I was still the only person who saw his face unobstructed.

I lost count of his pull-ups around sixty. He did about twenty more before grabbing a 45-pound plate to hold between his ankles and began another set.

I could hardly believe I was looking at the same skinny, malnourished and timid kid curled up into a ball at my prison job so many years ago. With plenty of food and a set of heavy weights to lift, he turned into a beast.

Or rather, he was always a beast. Now he was just no longer caged.

"Your stitches look good, Frankenstein," I called out, noticing the clean, sutured wound just above his hip.

My shoulder was sore as hell from the gunshot wound, but I hadn't broken out in a fever this time. Mari must have done a good job of preventing infection from spreading.

Shadow didn't respond to my comment, but began his next set. Even with me, he chose not to say anything unless he had to. I was stalling and knew it was useless. Reaper would have my balls if I didn't get to the root of the matter *today*.

Time to rip the band-aid off.

"Can I talk to you for a minute, bro?"

"Yes," he grunted out between his hand-clap push-ups.

I drained the rest of my coffee and put it down beside me, knowing he'd want to finish his current set before talking.

He did fifteen more then rose up to standing, breathing with a bit of effort but otherwise not looking at all like he just completed a workout that would kill most men. And that was just his warm-up.

"What would you like to talk about?"

Even though we were friends and I trusted the guy with my life, he looked intimidating as hell walking across the yard toward me. The sun made him squint, adding more tension to his already permanently scowling face. The morning's brightness also turned his pupils to pinpricks, exaggerating the contrast between his brown eye and his white eye.

I blew out a breath. "Have a seat, man."

He cocked his head at me but relented, lowering himself down to sit on the deck next to my chair.

"What happened after Mariposa stitched you up the other night?"

"We fucked."

I groaned and raised a hand. "Okay, back it up a notch. *How* did that happen?"

"She offered and I accepted."

"What do you mean, she *offered?* What exactly did she say?"

"She said, 'let me know if you need anything else.' It *has* been over six months since you sent a woman to me, so—"

"Oh my God, Shadow," I groaned, slapping both palms to my face.

Fucking fuck sticks, this was my fault. "Dude, *this* is why I said you need to spend more time around people."

"I don't like people."

"I know, but ugh..." I rubbed my temples, trying to cool my shit. I should have fucking seen this coming but had so much other shit on my mind at the time, my own feelings for Mari included.

Shadow frowned, now apparently clued in to my reaction. "Did I do something wrong?"

"Yeah, man. You kinda did." I looked at him squarely, knowing that telling him straight was more effective than beating around the bush. "I sent her to you *just* to heal you. That is the service she provides, not sex. She's not a whore. She was offering you more medical attention if you needed it."

"Oh."

"Yeah, *oh*," I sighed. "She didn't expect or want to have sex with you. So she was pretty upset afterward—"

"Why?"

I groaned again, returning my hand to my forehead. Talking to him was like talking to a toddler sometimes.

"Because she barely knows you and had no warning it was coming. On top of that, she's Reaper's woman. At this point, he's the only man she's agreed to fuck. Make sense?"

"I guess so." He still looked puzzled.

"I'm not mad at you, dude. I'm just trying to help you understand," I said. "A lot of these things are implied and not explicitly said. If you spend more time in mixed company, men *and* women, you'll pick up on these things and avoid misunderstandings."

"I'm confused because," he scratched at his beard, "she didn't seem upset. She rode me herself. She was moaning and touching me here," he skimmed a hand across his chest. "No other woman has done that before. It made me come faster."

"Okay, I did *not* need to know that," I groaned. "But yeah, women who don't provide sex as a service treat it differently. Most of them only do it with people they care about. So there's more touching, kissing, little things like that. It creates intimacy."

"It felt good. I mean, it always does. But good in a different way." Shadow's hand rested on his chest tattoo, eyes unfocused as he seemed to recall the sensation.

"Well enjoy that memory because it's all you'll ever have," I said. "Reaper ordered me to tell you it's to never happen again. He also wants an apology from you for having his woman without permission."

Shadow's hand dropped from his chest, his eyes going from dreamy to stoic. "Okay. I can do that."

I sucked in a breath. "He also wants you to apologize to Mariposa."

His gaze snapped up to mine, wide-eyed and panicked. "I can't."

"You can and you will," I told him in my most stern dad voice. "You had your dick inside her. You can say you're sorry."

He shook his head. "I can't do it, Jandro."

"Dude, you're a three-hundred pound gorilla. She's *one* little woman. What's the worst she can do to you?"

He looked away without an answer but I saw the tremor in his hands.

I felt awful for the guy. He came such a long way since I found him but his trauma and his fears still ran deep. At least twice a week, all his progress seemed to reset due to his night terrors. Shadow was a beast feared almost more than the Steel Demons name itself. But no one else saw the man trembling in the center of a bedroom filled with furniture torn to splinters, wearing the face of a terrified kid I found in a prison cell.

"I keep telling you most women are *not* like your family," I said in a gentler tone, clapping my hand on his shoulder. "I can tell you until I'm blue in the face, but this is your chance to see it for yourself."

He still didn't answer and I knew he was off somewhere in his head.

"Hey," I snapped my fingers in front of his face. "Stay with me, dude. You're building this up in your head and it's really not that big a deal. You can do this."

"Do I have to?" Jesus, he really was like a child. "I'll apologize to Reaper and he can tell her—"

"No. He was very specific, Shadow. You need to tell her yourself." I sighed. "I know it's scary, man. I used to be terrified of talking to girls, too."

"You were?"

"Like twenty years ago, but yeah. It gets easier the more you do it, though. Trust me on that."

He sighed, resigned to his fate. "Will you help me with what I should say?"

"Sure thing, buddy." I slapped his back. "We'll work it out before church. Get on back to your workout."

He jumped up and returned to the weights like he couldn't wait to get away from this conversation. I, too, was glad to have it over with. Now if only I could get the image of Mari riding his dick out of my head.

A chuckle escaped me despite myself. Shadow had to be the only person in the world who found it easier to cut a man's throat than say a single word to a woman.

Chapter 24

MARIPOSA

"Ow! Fuck!"

I ignored Big G's complaints as I ripped the bandage off of his bullet wound.

"Ow, that was my fucking leg hair!"

"Oh my God, will you quit your bitching?" Tessa waddled over to the couch while I bit my lip to hold in the laughter.

"You've never been shot, woman!"

"And you've never pushed an eight-pound baby out of your body, so shut the hell up."

She lowered herself on the couch carefully, holding her belly. "Sorry about him, Mari. Don't let it deter you."

"It's all right," I applied more antibacterial ointment to the sutures. "I really do hope Gunner comes back soon so I can get some local anesthesia again."

I finished with her husband and sent him off limping and whimpering. The moment he was gone, I scooted closer to her with my stethoscope and a huge grin on my face.

"How's my favorite little man or lady doing?" I asked, holding the diaphragm end to her belly.

"I swear he's got a fucking motorcycle in there already," she sighed. "Running nonstop."

"Yeah? You thinking boy then?"

"I keep saying *he* but I don't really know." She looked at me longingly. "Can't believe they used to have those machines where you could *see* the baby and everything, all the little parts, too!"

"The teaching hospital at my nursing school had one," I told her. "The really advanced one where you could see everything in 3D. You could watch them suck their thumbs in there, kicking and flailing around, little boys playing with their willies."

"Sounds like my two boys," she laughed before turning serious. "Is it bad to want another boy, Mari?"

"Not at all. You know what to expect, right? Since you already have two."

"Yeah, it's not just that, though." She chewed her lip nervously.

I pulled the ear pieces out and let the stethoscope hang around my neck. "What's wrong?"

"I'm just scared to raise a girl in a world like this," she whispered.

"Oh, honey." I grabbed her hand and squeezed. "She'd have all these big scary men to protect her. Don't tell me the Steel Demons wouldn't kill for a little princess."

"They would," she gave a strained smile. "Dallas and Andrea's daughter is treasured by everyone here. But her options are so limited as she grows up, unlike for the men. She either stays within the gates of Sheol her whole life or goes out into the world. And what's out there for her? Nothing but a life of slavery."

"I hear you," I said with a nod. "I can't imagine having that kind of fear for my own child. But you know what I think?"

"Hm?"

"We need more women out in the world. To hide them away only creates a demand for them as commodities. We need women in positions of power, in educated jobs, in supportive and leadership roles. That's how we make the world a safer place for our kids."

Tessa gave me a nod and a gentle smile. "I agree with what you're saying. Really, I do. It's just that," she placed a hand on her belly, "it's going to take lots of time and sacrifice to get to that point. And what mother wants to send her children out to be sacrificial lambs?"

I didn't have an answer for her.

I FINISHED CHECKING ON MY PATIENTS A BIT LATER THAT night. The only house I didn't stop by was Jandro and Shadow's.

With Hades at my side, I probably would have been fine. I certainly wouldn't mind seeing Jandro, I even missed him. It was Shadow I was unsure about, so I thought it best to avoid it.

On the way back to Reaper's, we passed by what I assumed to be Gunner's dark, empty house. I let out a sigh at the thought of the sweet, angel-faced Demon. I missed him, too. Just another man in the carousel to send my head spinning.

Hades howled softly as we walked by, which was answered by a soft screech coming from the house's direction.

"Saying goodnight to your buddy?" I asked, scratching between his ears.

He licked my hand in response.

We walked into the house to the sound of Noelle and Larkan talking in the kitchen. The space was open and covered in marble and stainless steel, so their voices echoed despite talking at a normal volume. It sounded like they were trying to bake something.

Noelle suddenly shrieked which turned into uproarious laughter. Larkan chuckled softly and said something like, "I told you not to touch that."

Those two were nothing if not love at first sight. I smiled all the way to Reaper's study.

"What are you happy about?" he said the moment I stepped into the room.

He sat at the end of a long table similar to the one in the conference room. Papers were strewn out in front of him, a lamp emitting cozy yellow light throughout the room. The president wasn't wearing his cut, but the top three buttons of his henley shirt were undone. His green eyes looked predatory in the warm light and a glass of whiskey completed the ensemble.

"Noelle," I answered, making my way toward him. "She seems so happy."

"Ugh, don't remind me of *that*," he groaned as he stretched his arms above his head. "And here I thought you were happy to see me."

"I am." I leaned over to kiss him, which ended up being futile since he just pulled me into his lap and dominated my mouth. "And what's wrong with your sister being happy?" I asked when I broke away.

"She's going to get her fucking heart broken, that's what's wrong," he grumbled, taking a pull of whiskey. "Noelle is either all in or all out. She doesn't do anything in between. And that guy," he nodded his head toward the door, "I don't trust. Not until he proves himself loyal. And even then, it doesn't mean he's good for her."

"Why not just let her enjoy it?" I pushed his hair back with my fingers before lacing my hands around his neck. "And if it doesn't work out, at least he made her happy for a while."

"Noelle can't just have fun," he sighed. "When she gets her sights on someone, she falls hard and fast. When it ends, she completely breaks down and I have to pick up the pieces." He downed the rest of his whiskey. "She swears she'll never love another man again, then she gets lonely and the cycle repeats."

"She's never had, you know, like your mom and dads?" I'd been thinking of what he told me about his family for most of the day.

"A harem?" He shook his head. "Nah. Unfortunately, her trysts don't really last long enough for multiple relationships to be built, let alone one."

He set his glass down and wrapped both arms around my back, pulling me forward on his lap until his lips met my neck.

"Enough about my sister," he murmured before kissing the spot between my neck and shoulder. "How's my lover?"

I smiled against his ear, squirming a little from his stubble tickling my skin. "Good. No one's injuries got worse, which is a huge relief. I just didn't check Jandro and Shadow, though. I don't know if you..."

"I took care of it," he kissed me again. "Jandro talked to him and reported back to me. It sounds like it was a misunderstanding, which is kind of what I figured."

"A misunderstanding?"

"Yeah." Reaper leaned back, resting his hands on my thighs. "Shadow doesn't interact with people much, as I'm sure you've seen. Even less so with women. Pretty much the only female contact he's had is with service girls Jandro buys for him."

"Really? His whole life?"

Reaper nodded. "From birth until he met Jandro, he was kept very isolated. He didn't really learn social cues and appropriate behavior until after they met."

"He's covered in scars," I recalled the sight of his arms and torso. "Scars that look old."

Reaper nodded slowly. "The few interactions he had with people growing up were not positive, to say the least."

"Damn," I breathed. "Neurology is not my field, but I can only imagine what that does to someone's brain development."

"You're sexy when you talk medic nonsense," he teased, earning a swat on the chest from me. "Anyway, Shadow will make a full apology to you and me soon. I expect sometime before or after church tomorrow."

"You?" I asked. "What's he apologizing to you for?"

Reaper's hands slid up my thighs, reaching around to grab my ass with both hands. Heat and a dangerous possessiveness filled his eyes.

"Because he had what's mine."

Good lord, I didn't want to find that so hot but I did. It was the perfect opportunity to ask more about his whole sharing thing, but the blood rushing from my head to my sex made me stupid.

"Hm?" It was apparently so hot I zoned out on Reaper asking me a question.

His smirk made me even hotter. "I said, is that acceptable to you? An apology from him?"

"Yeah, I think so. It seems a bit," I thought for a moment, "a bit cruel, even. If talking to women in particular makes him so uncomfortable."

"A fitting punishment, then," Reaper said. "He's not afraid of anything else. And maybe he'll learn to socialize like a normal person."

"That's mean," I swatted his chest again. "He's not abnormal, just different."

"Mean is my middle name, sugar." He leaned in, grinning, catching my lower lip in his teeth.

"Oh yeah?" I giggled, pulling back. "Mine's Diaz. I took my dad's last name as my middle name and my mom's surname. A lot of women were doing it as a small protest at the time, giving kids their maiden names instead of their husband's names."

Reaper was silent as I blabbered, and I realized the moment got serious.

"I don't actually have a middle name," he confessed. "My family thought they were useless and outdated. But," he sucked in a breath, "my real name is Rory."

A huge grin threatened to split my face in half. "*Rory?*"

"I know, it's dumb."

"It's not!" I cupped the sides of his neck, the giggles spilling out of me. "It's *so* cute."

"Shut up, woman. You trying to take my man-card away?" But he was smiling and tickling my sides, making me laugh harder.

I leaned into him, holding his face and laughing as I kissed him.

It was a good day and I was happy. I saw my friend, did my job that I loved, then came home to a man who cared about me. In that moment, life felt so simple and pure. The words tumbled out of me before I could stop them.

"I love you, Rory."

Chapter 25

REAPER

"I love you, sugar."

The words came out a hushed murmur against her spine as I kissed her there, tracing her beautiful back with my mouth.

"I love you." I said it between her shoulder blades that time and would say it over every inch of her body if she let me.

I never said those words to anyone, except to my parents as a child. I didn't even say it to Daren before he died. I was too busy being pissed off at him for giving me all of the vaccine while he wasted away.

He died never knowing how much I appreciated his wisdom, despite being younger than me. He thought I was pissed about him lying to me when I was honestly scared to death about going on without him. I should have told him it was okay, that I had this shit in the bag. I should have been a big brother to him, not a pissed off president. Because I could never imagine how scared he must have been to feel himself slowly slipping away.

Telling Mariposa I loved her didn't make up for never telling Daren, but I didn't want to make the same mistake again—waiting until it was too late.

Now those three simple words sent my pulse racing every time they left my mouth. It was a better adrenaline hit than riding. And I could have it every time I looked at my woman.

"I love you," I said with a kiss to the nape of her neck.

Mari moaned softly in her sleep, rolling onto her stomach. Fuck me, how could anyone be so perfect?

Her skin and hair contrasted breathtakingly with my white sheets. She looked like an angel sleeping on clouds. How ironic for her to be in the bed of a Demon.

Not to mention falling in love with one.

When she told me that in my study last night, I didn't even care that she used my real name. I knew she meant it.

And I said it back to her. Again and again. It was the last thing on my lips when I fell asleep and the first thing when I woke up.

"Damn," I breathed, just staring at her. "I love you, Mariposa."

"I love you, too..." she mumbled face down in the pillow, "...*Rory*."

"Goddamn it, woman!"

I yanked the pillow out from under her head and smacked her with it.

"I'm still sleeping, asshole!" Her legs kicked out, narrowly missing my junk.

"Liar," I cackled, rolling her over and pinning her beneath me. "And I'd rather be Asshole than fucking Rory."

"I don't know why you hate it so much." She lifted her chin at me defiantly and it was fucking adorable.

"Because it's a stupid dipshit name."

"I think it's cute!"

"I," I grabbed her wrists and pressed them into the mattress on either side of her head, "am not *cute*."

Her smile was stunningly beautiful and devilish in a way that got me hard in an instant.

"Sorry to break the news, but you're actually pretty cute." Her head lifted to kiss my nose. "But I'll call you Reaper if it makes you feel like a badass."

"Woman," I sighed, lying my head down on her pillowy breasts.

"You're enjoying this, aren't you? Pushing my buttons knowing full well I won't do anything about it because I'm fucking crazy about you."

"Maybe a little." Her hands smoothed down my back. "Okay, more than a little. But it's payback for you being a dick before."

I lifted my head to look at her, my expression now serious. "I deserve it, then."

"Yeah, you do," she tapped her finger against my lips, the devilish spark still in her eyes, *"Rory."*

I groaned and rolled my eyes but otherwise didn't complain.

"You believe me, right?" I caught her hand and kissed her fingers. "That I'm going to be better for you. I've never been in love before but fuck, Mari, I want to do this right."

"Reaper." She whispered my *true* name, running her fingers through my hair. "I wouldn't be here if I didn't believe you."

I lowered my head back down to her chest with a sigh, still careful not to crush her under my weight. "I'm dreaming."

"Why do you say that?" she laughed, scratching lightly over my neck.

"I'm in love with a woman who loves me back. That kind of shit just doesn't happen to me."

"Should I call you Rory a few more times?" she joked.

"Call me that all you want. I'll just fuck you until you lose your voice." I kissed her collarbone. "Anyway, I still have all this club bullshit to bring me back to reality. Speaking of," I lifted my head up and gave her a long, languid kiss, "I gotta hold church, sugar."

"Okay, I'll be in the medic's office. Send anyone down who wants their injuries looked at."

"Will do." I kissed her again. God, why did she make it so hard to leave? "And thank you, beautiful, for looking after my people. I don't think I've told you that yet."

"Just doing my job, handsome," she smiled against my lips. "Oh! Before I forget," she grabbed my forearm, "I mentioned this to Jandro a while ago but I'd like to start vaccinating everyone. Kids especially. After the battle, I don't think having people donate blood would be a bad idea either. In case more serious injuries occur down the road. Can you bring those two ideas up to everyone?"

"You remember what I told you about my schooling, right?" I rolled to sit up at the edge of the bed.

"Don't act like you're not smart enough to relay a message." She nudged me with her foot. "I didn't even use any fancy medic words this time."

"No, but people might have questions I won't be able to answer."

"You can send them to me. I guess I should have office hours, huh?"

"You'll be repeating yourself a lot," I warned, sliding my pants up my legs before looking for a shirt.

"I already do that as part of my job."

"There's an easy solution to this, you know." The idea made me grin. It broke all the club rules but fuck if I cared.

She peered up at me curiously from the bed. "What's that?"

I leaned over and kissed her again, powerless to resist those lips.

"Come to church with me."

MARI FINALLY AGREED AFTER SOME CAJOLING, BUT STILL HAD to stop by her medic's office first. Something about heartburn medication for Tessa.

In any case, it worked out because I had a hunch a certain man wouldn't have the balls to apologize to me with a woman in the room.

The conference room was empty when I arrived, save for Shadow.

"President," he stood from the table immediately. "May I have a word with you in private?"

"Certainly." I locked the door behind me then came around to the chair next to his. "Sit down, Shadow. What can I do for you?"

The big man didn't appear visibly nervous, but I knew this was difficult for him. Being alone helped, along with the fact that he trusted me almost as much as Jandro. Still, speaking didn't come naturally to him.

"I want to apologize for my actions the other day," he said. "I meant no disrespect to you or your woman."

"You can call her Mariposa," I said.

"Mariposa," he repeated softly, his fingers twitching in his lap for a moment. "On top of misunderstanding what she asked me, I didn't know she was yours. But Jandro explained it to me, and I know better for the future." His odd-colored gaze met mine straight on. "I promise you it won't happen again. I'm sorry, Reaper."

"Apology accepted." I clapped him on the arm. "You're a good man, Shadow. I know you didn't mean anything by it and I'm glad you're able to learn from this."

He nodded, now looking visibly more nervous. "I still have to apologize to her—Mariposa—directly."

"You shouldn't have any issue with that." I got up to unlock and open the door. "I think you'll find her forgiving."

"Women are not forgiving in my experience," he muttered.

"To be fair, Shadow," I sighed, rounding the table to my seat again, "your experience is the exception, not the norm."

"That is what everyone tells me," he said. "But I have nothing else to compare it to."

"You will one day," I assured him. "Maybe even with Mari's help."

He looked at me with a puzzled expression. "How?"

"No idea," I shrugged. "But she's smart. And she's kind. She only ever wants to help people." *And be an adorable pain in my ass by calling me Rory.*

"Those are good qualities."

"They are," I agreed. "If there's a way to help your...condition, I'm sure she'll find it."

"She won't want to help me," Shadow grumbled.

"You might be surprised."

The club started filing into the room and for a moment I was proud to see a room full of Steel Demons again, instead of only the usual faces from the road. But the thought of someone in this room betraying us, putting us in danger, quickly soured my mood and made my blood boil.

I smacked the gavel on the table the moment the room filled up and the door closed. All murmurings died down to hushed silence.

"I'll get straight to the point," I said. "General Tash betrayed us and has tried to take us out twice now, thanks to insider information. And one of you is the general's little bitch."

I allowed a pause to let that sink in. Everyone kept their eyes straight on me, no side-eyes to the man next to him.

"One of you," I went on, letting my eyes linger on every single man in the room, "has desecrated the Steel Demons patch. Every time you put it on, you do so under false pretenses. You're not loyal and you're a dishonest piece of shit. I have no room for the likes of you in my club. And when I find out who you are," I couldn't resist the cruel smile spreading across my face. "I'll feed your balls to my dog. And I'll make you watch."

At my side, Hades barked and licked his lips. I never trained him to respond to anything I said. He just seemed to know how to add dramatic effect to my threats. Whoever the weasel was just had to be squirming now.

"To the rest of you, the *true* Steel Demons," I stroked Hades' head, "Jandro told me how quickly you all came to our aid on the dirt bikes, assisted Mariposa with the wounded, and cleaned up the wreckage outside. You did me and the patch proud."

"We deserve a party," Jandro cupped his hands around his mouth like a megaphone, earning laughs and murmurs of agreement from the others.

"Fine, handle it." I waved a hand at him. "I assume we have steaks and charcoal leftover from last time. Actually, that brings up another point of business."

The murmurs died down again for me to speak. "Our business with General Tash has obviously ended," I said. "As he was the biggest trade partner we had, Gunner is out securing new trade deals as we speak. We are well-stocked for the time being, but there may be a transition period where we'll have to ration goods."

"In addition," Jandro jumped in after a nod from me, "we have a surplus of firearms and other weapons from the Sandia outpost's armory which we fully intend to use. Once we eliminate Tash's bitch, we'll reach out to the MCs we're allied with and pool resources." He drummed his hands on the table. "We're going to war, fellas."

The whole room fell into stunned silence.

"Uh," Big G lazily raised a hand. "Which MCs are we allied with?"

"Iron Soldiers, Phantom Kings, and Dark Brotherhood, to name a few," I answered. "Gunner has his contacts, I have a few of my own."

A gentle knock came to the door.

"Ah, perfect timing." I stood from my seat and went for the door while everyone looked bewildered.

Hades trotted happily beside me, knowing exactly who it was. If we hadn't thrown anyone for a loop yet, a woman in church was certainly about to.

Chapter 26

MARIPOSA

Reaper opened the door with a sly grin, a sign he was up to something. I just couldn't be sure what.

"Hey, sugar," he greeted me, low and husky. "Come on in."

No less than fifteen pairs of eyes stared at me as I followed him to the head of the table. And none looked more terrified of my female presence than Shadow.

Jandro just smirked and winked at me. He had to be in on the same joke as Reaper.

"This is Mariposa, if you haven't met her already," Reaper's hand skimmed along my lower back, a clear sign of possessiveness. "She's the club medic and wanted to implement some new things for our health. Go ahead, Mari." He leaned against the back wall and folded his arms, giving me the proverbial spotlight.

"Uh hi, everyone," I said uneasily. "So the first thing I would like to introduce is regular vaccinations, especially for children. Many diseases have been on the rise since the Collapse, most of which are preventable with a vaccine. It'll be the best thing for your immune system if you go out and possibly encounter a disease while on a ride."

"How do you take a vaccine?" someone asked.

"With an injection," I answered. "Sometimes a series of injections over several months, depending on the type of vaccination."

"What if you're scared of needles?"

"You have twice as many tattoos as anyone, Python, shut the fuck up," Jandro yelled across the room. "Go on, Mari. Ignore them."

"The second thing I would like to introduce is blood donations," I said. "I would like to keep stock of the four main blood types in case someone is so badly injured that they'll need a transfusion." I raised a hand. "This is all on a volunteer basis, of course. If you don't want to get vaccinated or donate blood, no one will force you. But the vaccines will only help you, and giving blood can mean the difference between life and death for you or your fellow Demons."

I swallowed the dry lump in my throat. "Any questions?"

"Where do we sign up?" Jandro grinned up at me from the table.

I couldn't help but smile back. "Anyone interested can meet me in my office. I can get you on a vaccination schedule and determine blood types with a simple test. Once I have a catalog of volunteers' blood types, I'll start taking donations."

A bunch of blank stares met my eyes and I swallowed another dry lump of unease. Had I completely gone over everyone's heads? Or were they still stuck on the fact that a woman entered their sacred club meeting?

Reaper came up behind me and gave my shoulder a reassuring squeeze.

"I'll be the first to volunteer." To everyone else, "Mari worked tirelessly all night to patch us up from the attack. You can trust her, not only with your own lives but your children's."

"Any medical issues you come to me with will also be kept confidential," I added. "This is something I take very seriously, so please don't suffer in silence because you're ashamed or embarrassed. Trust me, I've seen every body part and organ you can imagine, and probably some that you can't."

That got a chuckle out of some people.

"So please," I reiterated, "come see me if you're having any medical issues or just have questions."

Jandro raised his hand next. "I also volunteer for vacs and blood donation." He shot me a grin. "As long as you don't hurt me too badly."

"I won't if you won't," I retorted without thinking.

Chuckling, his eyes dropped to the table.

Reaper's hand on my shoulder moved to the nape of my neck.

"Thanks, sugar." The pet name and the contact on my skin seemed to send a clear message without explicitly saying it.

I was his. And I liked that a lot more than I thought I would.

"Thanks, everyone." I gave a small wave as I headed for the door. "You know where to find me."

"YOU OKAY WITH THIS?" REAPER'S GREEN EYES SHONE LIKE bright jewels under my office lights.

"Of course. What matters is *you're* okay with it. You're the patient."

I glanced up at the dozen or so people crowded around my tiny office. Tessa was there, along with her two kids. So was Noelle, staring nervously at my blood-draw syringe despite the lengths of colorful tattoos decorating her arms.

"I want them to see that this isn't a big deal," Reaper said, lifting his eyes to our visitors. "That we don't have to be afraid of blood or needles or any of that shit. This can help us live longer, and therefore make the Steel Demons even stronger." He nodded at me. "Do what you gotta do, sugar."

"All right, I need your arm."

He extended his hand to me. I pushed his sleeve up past his elbow and placed the back of his forearm on the small pull-out table between us. Tying a strip of gauze around the widest part of his forearm, I began tapping the inside of his elbow in search of a vein.

"Why do you do that?" Tessa's older boy asked.

"This is to slow his blood-flow a little bit," I said, tugging on the gauze strip. "It helps me find a vein to draw blood from." Reaper's veins were already swelling inside his elbow. "Now," I said. "Here's a little poke."

I inserted the needle and opened the tube, then taped the needle down. A few people let out soft gasps as dark red blood flowed out of his arm and into the bag.

"That's all it is," I said, turning to everyone. "A pint of blood can potentially save three lives and it'll only take about ten minutes." I turned back to Reaper. "How bad was that?"

"Not bad at all," he grinned, staring at the needle in his arm. "Kind of a rush, actually."

"I want to go next!" Tessa's boy declared.

"Hey, little man," I rolled my stool over to him. "You're big and strong, but you need all your blood to grow even bigger right now. In a few years, though, you'll have some extra you can give if your mom says it's okay."

"Are there any, uh, side effects?" Noelle asked nervously.

"You might feel a bit weak and dizzy after donating. It's important that you don't exert yourself for several hours afterward. Drink plenty of fluids and eat well to help replenish what you donated. You might also feel sore and have a bit of bruising at the injection site but that will fade after a few days."

When that answer seemed to reassure her, I looked at everyone else. "Any other questions?"

Once Reaper finished up, the response was overwhelming. A line formed outside my office door of people wanting to donate blood, get vaccinated, talk to me about check-ups, or all of the above. I did my best to give everyone my undivided attention while also trying not to panic at the line growing longer.

But no one seemed to mind waiting. If anything, the hallway buzzed with excitement. And still, people kept a distance outside my office door to provide privacy to those I was seeing. It ended up being a long day, but one I'd been dreaming of for years. Seeing patients, putting fears to rest, and providing them with insight about their health and bodies. It was all I ever wanted to do with my life, and the Steel Demons MC made it happen for me.

When the last patient left, a tall, handsome man leaned into my doorway. He already had his arm bandaged so I jokingly made a shooing motion at him.

"Get out of here. I already saw you."

"No one told you I get extra benefits with the medic?" Reaper smirked, stalking toward me. "What did you think? Good turnout?"

"Yeah, really good. Amazing, even." I ran my hands through my hair and blew out a breath. "Now I'm dying to wind down with a drink and foot rub."

"I was hoping you'd say that." His arm hooked around my waist, drawing me against him for a deep kiss. "Let's go home, sugar."

Chapter 27

MARIPOSA

"What's this?" I gasped in shock. "You're bringing me a drink?"

"Don't get too excited," Reaper smiled in spite of his grumbling. "We're still in the honeymoon phase."

He handed me a glass of wine, then moved my legs so I could extend them across his lap.

"Then I'll enjoy it while it lasts," I sighed in utter bliss, swirling the wine while his thumbs pressed into the arch of my foot.

"I'll make sure you do." His voice rumbled like a purr as his hands worked magic into my sore feet. "Did Shadow apologize to you?"

"No, not yet." I smacked my lips lightly with a sip of wine.

Reaper grunted out a sound of displeasure while gently squeezing around my ankle. "He needs to get on that shit."

"He's uncomfortable around crowds, right? All the people in my office must have made him nervous." I took another delicate sip. "Getting an apology is not even a big deal to me. As long as it doesn't happen again and it truly *was* a misunderstanding—"

"It's a big deal to me," Reaper snarled. "The apology itself and the principal of the matter. He cannot set the precedent of treating club women like whores, nor can he disobey a direct order from me. If he doesn't come to you tomorrow, I'll have to expand on his punishment for disobedience." His gaze softened as it traveled up the length of my legs. "You don't seem too upset by what he did anymore."

"I think talking to you right after, and having some time after the initial shock wore off," I swallowed another sip of wine, "I realized there was nothing really traumatic or awful about it. He didn't hurt me or coerce me, really. I didn't ruin things with you. It's in the past now and I'm at peace with it."

"So you *did* enjoy it then," he teased. "Shadow got a nice, fat cock for ya?"

"Might I remind you that my feet are *very* close to your balls, Rory."

"And they'll be curling in ecstasy before you're done with that wine, sugar lips." His fingers trailed up my calves with a devilish grin.

"Something I wanted to ask you," I gave my liquid courage another swirl, "what rule did I break? You mentioned it in the bath that night."

Reaper's hands rested on my shins as his head leaned back on the couch with a soft sigh.

"Sharing partners is taken very seriously in the culture I grew up in," he explained. "It's almost on par with moving in together, or even engagement in broader society. Outsiders thought we were total hedonists, addicted to sex and fucking anyone we looked at. But that couldn't be further from the truth."

"It was a relationship," I said. "A serious one, just with more than two people."

"Exactly," he nodded. "Our tradition was that the man would suggest another person to bring into the love life and eventually, bedroom. Usually it was someone the couple already knew and trusted."

"A mutual friend," I realized.

"Yes. Doing this was a sign that he trusted and loved his woman so much, he felt she deserved the love of another person in addition to his. Another partner to support her emotionally when the first man had other obligations. Someone to please her sexually in ways the first could not, or just to double her pleasure in general." He smiled broadly at that.

"That is fascinating," I breathed. "Didn't the men get jealous?"

"Sure, at times. But here's where the rules come in." He lifted a finger to count off. "Each person in the primary couple had the right to veto other partners. So if a woman wasn't into her man's suggestions, she could reject them. Likewise if she started to like someone her man didn't approve of, he could forbid that person from entering the relationship."

"I see." My brain soaked up this information like a sponge. I had no idea societies like this even existed. "So because you didn't approve of Shadow..."

Reaper shrugged, placing his hands back on my legs. "I never considered him for you, honestly. If he made you happy, I don't think I'd mind. That doesn't seem to be the case, though." He turned his head to the side, looking at me with sexy, hooded eyes. "That's all this is really about. Showing that I trust you and I want you to be happy."

I had to take a moment just to sink into that, to sink into *everything* he said. Was I happy? At that moment, holy hell yes. My life felt meaningful. I had a community with friends, patients, and this man sitting across from me who drove me nuts but I couldn't help but love and crave with every fiber of my being.

Was being with Reaper enough for me? Again, yes. I'd had monogamous relationships before and lived in a culture that put monogamy on a pedestal all my life. I was confident I *could* be exclusively with him and him alone. But was I intrigued and even a little tempted by this offer he put on the table? Also yes. It felt like he set Pandora's box in my lap and cracked the lid open for the tiniest peek. I wanted to see more of what was inside.

"So you *have* considered other partners for me?" I said.

"Thought of, yes," he said coyly. "It's entirely up to you to approve them, though."

"Who?"

"I think you know," he teased, running a hand up to my thigh.

"Jandro," I breathed. "And maybe Gunner?"

"Mm, lucky guesses." He nudged my legs apart to massage my thighs. "Is it something you'd like to try?"

"How—" My breath hitched, distracted by the firmness of his hands on my flesh and moving higher up my legs. "How would you, or we, I guess, go about asking them?"

"One at a time," he said, fingers circling into my leg muscles. "I think we should ask Jandro first. He'd be more open to it. If anything, I think he's been waiting for me to ask him. Then we'll see how you feel. You might decide two is enough or that you want me all to yourself after all."

"Okay. We ask and then what?" I suddenly felt like a teenager asking for dating advice—from my own boyfriend, nonetheless. "All three of us spend time together? Or just me and him?"

"Whatever your comfort level is," Reaper assured me. "If you want me around, I'm sure he'll understand. But if things go well, you two should spend time alone to get to know each other."

I set my wine glass down on the end table and leaned forward to wrap an arm around his shoulders.

"And you'll really be okay with that? Me going off with him and..."

His hands slid up to my waist, pulling me closer into his lap.

"If you come home to me all smiles with a post-sex glow, a dreamy look in your eyes, and your legs all wobbly," he paused with a grin as I smacked his chest, "then I know my woman is happy and well taken care of. How could I be bothered by that?" His lips brushed my cheek until he reached my ear. "And if I feel you scream with my cock down your throat because another man is fucking you so good, you can't stop coming? Oh sugar, that'll be the *best*."

"Turns you on, does it?" I nudged my leg against the bulge in his jeans, growing thicker by the second. "Bringing other people in."

"*You* turn me on." He let out a lustful growl, running his hands up to cup my breasts. "Your body gets me hard as a rock. The sounds you make drive me insane. And I swear watching you come gets me so fucking high."

The last word barely left his mouth when I leaned in, dragging my lips across his in a needy plea.

He answered with a deep rumble of a moan in his chest, holding the back of my neck in place as our tongues lashed across each other as if fighting. His lips nipped and sucked at mine, making them so sensitive and pulsing. He moved my hand over his zipper, directing my strokes against his thick, solid length straining to be freed. After another deep, bruising kiss, he pulled away and gave me an order that made my core clench.

"Suck me."

A smile pulled at my lips. Sure, I'd do that. But my way. The Steel Demons president had no idea what was coming to him.

His breath hitched as I undid the button on his jeans and pulled down the zipper. Then my hand moved away, teasing the firm abdomen just above where he wanted me to focus. My fingers skimmed higher under his shirt, taking my time to trace the ridges of his stomach, ghosting over his nipples before flattening over the smooth planes of his chest.

His green eyes locked on me, he lifted his arms to peel the shirt off. Once it was gone, I feasted on his sexy tattooed skin with my eyes. This man was dangerous. Feared. Respected. And he was completely, utterly mine.

I began my descent back down his body—this time with my mouth.

He let out a delighted hum as I kissed the hollow of his throat, just between his collarbones, then dragged my lips lower to plant a kiss between his pecs. Never losing contact with his skin, I slowed way down when I reached his abs.

Now he let out a grunt of frustration, his hips shifting beneath me. I held back a smile, dragging my tongue over each defined muscle at a snail's pace.

"God, I love that tongue, sugar, but I need it on my dick." His voice was tight with restraint, his fingers curling in my hair to hold it away from my face.

"I know."

I sucked hard next to his hipbone, leaving him a nice little mark there. His cock was right under my face and I felt it twitch, begging for attention.

"Ugh, you are so bad," he groaned.

I kissed my way to his opposite hip, leaving a mark on that side, too, before peeling his jeans and boxers down to reveal him, fully engorged and absolutely mouthwatering.

"Ohhh fuck," he hissed when my tongue swirled the flared head.

I wrapped my hand around the base as my lips sealed over the crown of his dick. His curses grew louder and more drawn out as I steadily took more of him into my mouth.

But it seemed he had sneaky plans of his own.

He caressed my neck and back as I leaned across his lap. A shudder passed through me as he groped my ass, then his fingers moved lower to the back of my thighs. For a moment, he just teased the skin just under my cotton lounge shorts. When his fingers moved to rub teasing circles between my legs, I released a moan around his shaft.

"Yes, beautiful, tell me how much you like this," he rasped, stroking me through the thin fabric.

I sucked him harder, shuddering with each swipe of pressure he applied to my clit. He waited until I made a slobbery mess of his cock before pulling my panties and shorts aside to touch me directly.

"Mm, you're soaked." His hand pulled away for one tortuous second and I heard him suck his fingers before touching me again. "Wouldn't you like another cock to fill you up while you suck me so good like that?"

I moaned the loudest I had yet, not only because his words were so filthy and hot, but he chose then to dip two fingers inside me. The feeling mimicked another man penetrating me and I found myself bucking against his hand, pressing back to take more, deeper.

"Greedy girl. You really do want two cocks, don't you?" He added a third finger, stretching me to my limit. "You want a nice big one pounding you while you please me with that tongue?"

I already started convulsing around him, but his thumb on my clit did me in. I came hard, spasming around his fingers while I screamed around his cock.

I barely recovered when he pulled my head up, withdrew his fingers from me and pulled me roughly into a straddle position on his lap. He lifted me with an iron grip on my waist and pressed me down in one fluid motion onto his thick, rigid length already well lubricated in my saliva.

"So fucking good," he grunted out, arms around my waist as he drove up into me. "So fucking perfect," he added with a rough kiss to my neck.

I was on top but the control was all his. All I could do was hold onto his shoulders as his hips drove up like pistons, filling me up again and again until we both came undone with shudders and moans. He stayed seated inside me, fingers curled into my waist and face buried in my neck, until our rapid heartbeats slowed.

"At the party tomorrow night," he panted with a kiss to my forehead. "We'll ask Jandro then."

Chapter 28

SHADOW

"Where you been, man?"

I closed my eyes, counting Jandro's steps across the grass as he approached me. Twelve. I was right again.

"I've been here."

I couldn't see his expression but I knew how he was looking at me—with one eyebrow raised. He liked to do that a lot.

"You've already worked out today, dude. You're just avoiding the inevitable."

I opened my eyes and turned to him, dropping the barbell I was using to stretch.

"Come with me?" I asked. "I could talk to Reaper alone, but with her..."

"Mariposa."

"With Mariposa, I—what if *she* doesn't want to be alone with me and I'll just make it worse?"

"Ugh, fine," he sighed. "I only have floor-to-ceiling's worth of fucked up bikes to fix and part out, plus I gotta get the patio ready for the party tonight, but I *guess* I can hold your hand while you talk to a girl."

I stared at him, puzzled. "Why would you hold my hand?"

"I didn't mean literally, it's an expression. Anyway, you coming to the party?"

"No, I don't think so."

"Why not?" He tossed out a handful of grain to the chickens, who came running over to peck at the ground where it landed. "You had a good time at the last one, didn't you?"

"I did, but I have a drawing I want to finish."

"Oh, that's cool. A drawing of what?"

"Just something I saw in the desert while we were on the road."

Jandro nodded without saying any more. I knew other people would press for more information and I appreciated that he didn't. He often annoyed me with how much he pushed me to be social, but I knew he meant well by it. He at least respected what I preferred to keep private.

"Shall we go to the medic's office?" he extended an arm to our home's gate leading out to the street.

"I suppose," I grunted, pulling my shirt back on and loosening my hair from its tie.

"Man, you're gonna get this over with," Jandro said as he led us out, "then afterward, you're gonna wonder why you were so worried in the first place. She's easy to talk to, trust me."

"No one is easy for me to talk to," I muttered. "Except you."

"Because I'm basically your dad, even though we're the same age."

I didn't know how old I truly was. My birth was never documented or recorded. I had barely any sense of time growing up, except from what the others told me before they disappeared. When I was taken to Jandro's prison, I didn't have ID or even a name to give them. I stood silently in the corner during intake, a full foot taller than everyone, so they called me Shadow. The prison dentist looked at my teeth and estimated my age to be between twenty and twenty-three. Jandro was twenty-one when we met, so he said we could share the same age.

Back then, I never would have imagined I'd walk freely in the daylight next to someone I considered a friend—nor eat big, filling meals every day and learn to ride a motorcycle. Sometimes I still wondered if my life in the Steel Demons was a dream, and my nightmares were my real life.

My hands started to shake as we got closer to the clubhouse, where the medic's office was. I couldn't tell if it was because I needed a drink or my anxiety about this whole situation. Probably both.

"You good, dude?" Jandro asked.

"No. But you're not going to let me walk away from this."

"Damn straight," he said. "Least of all because it's an order from your president, who will have both of our balls if you don't follow through."

"And most of all?" I grumbled.

"Because it's the right thing to do." He pulled open a door and led me in. "Her office is this way."

My feet dragged over the floor like moving through concrete. I balled my hands into fists in an attempt to stop the shaking. A sign sticking out above the door ahead said MEDIC with a square red cross. And the door was already open, fuck.

"Hey, Mari." Jandro's voice took on a different tone, the one he most often adopted when talking to women, as he leaned against the doorway and smiled into the room.

"Hey, Jandro! What brings you here?" came the cheerful, feminine voice from inside.

"I'm just chaperoning," he smirked, looking at me before jerking his chin toward the inside of the small office.

Shit. I really had to do this now.

My feet dragged forward until I reached the opening of the doorway and turned to face the last person I wanted to see.

She sat on a stool with wheels on it, brown hair piled on her head in a bun with a few wisps falling out. Her face no longer wore the pinched tiredness from the night she was healing everyone. Instead, her eyes were bright and she smiled easily. Even when I blocked her view of Jandro.

"Hi, Shadow," Mariposa greeted me. "What can I do for you today?"

My mouth opened but words refused to work. It felt reminiscent of coming out of my longest isolation period, when I hadn't spoken to anyone for about six months.

"I, um..." I cleared my throat, my gaze darting around the room for something to remind me of what I was supposed to say. "I would like to donate blood."

Fuck. No, that was wrong. But it was the first thing that popped into my head because she mentioned it at church yesterday.

"Okay, sure." Her smile widened at me as she gestured to another stool like the one she was sitting on in front of a small, pull-out table. "You can have a seat right there, and I'll walk you through it."

I looked back at Jandro and he lifted up a shoulder. His face looked like he was trying not to laugh.

Mariposa prepared some things on the main counter where she sat, while I maneuvered to where she directed me. The stool was far too small and low to the ground for me, and the table felt like it would break in half if I leaned on it too hard. So I stayed upright, trying to balance like a cartoon elephant on a beach ball that I saw on a television once.

"I won't keep you too long, promise," Mariposa said as she wheeled over to sit across the table from me. "First, I'd like to determine your blood type. I just need a drop of blood from your finger, and my test kit will tell me in about three minutes. Then the donation process will take about ten minutes. Sound good?"

I nodded. Thirteen minutes. I would definitely live for the next thirteen minutes.

Jandro was right. This wasn't as terrible as I thought it would be. But I still hadn't said what I came to say.

"Okay. Can I take your hand, please?"

I extended one arm across the table toward her, where she took my palm and turned it face up. Her gloved hands were so small compared to mine.

A memory flashed of her bare palms splayed across my chest. They looked so small then, too, and moved over my skin like they didn't want to leave any part of my torso untouched. It felt so nice and different. I wanted to touch her in return but couldn't bring myself to. None of the women before responded well to my attempts.

She's not like them, I reminded myself. Jandro made that very clear. She was Reaper's and therefore off-limits. I made a mistake and she was too frightened to do anything but go along with what I started. Even now, as she pressed something down over my fingertip and pulled it away, she was probably filled with fear. Some women hid it better than others.

"All right, just a couple minutes for the antigen markers to show up." She placed something on the counter and grabbed a small wad of cotton to press over my fingertip.

Holding it there with one hand, she grabbed a band-aid with the other. When she pulled the cotton away, a small drop of blood was on it. She swiftly wrapped the band-aid around my finger and wheeled a few feet away to her testing kit on the counter.

I sucked in a deep breath. It was now or never.

"I'm actually here because I owe you an apology."

She looked up at me with an expression I couldn't read, so I made sure to continue on.

"I'm not around people very much and there are some things I still don't understand." The words tumbled out now. It was slightly easier with my eyes glued to the band-aid on my finger. "I misunderstood what you asked me the other night. If I had known, I wouldn't have...done that."

She didn't say anything so I dared to glance up. Her eyes, a shifting greenish brown color like Jandro's, met mine directly. There was no fear in them. Not even the most stoic of men could fake that.

"It was wrong of me and it won't happen again," I said. "I'm sorry for upsetting you and not knowing my place."

Mariposa's hands folded in her lap and a small smile returned to her face.

"I accept your apology, Shadow. There are a lot of things I don't understand either, especially about life in an MC." Her head tilted to one side as she lifted one shoulder in a shrug. "Who knows? Maybe we can be friends."

I blinked as a small jolt of panic hit me.

"I've never been friends with a woman before."

"Well, we're going to see each other around a lot," she answered. "It would be easiest if we got along, right?"

"I guess so."

Her smile grew. The more she did that, the more I realized how pleasing it was to look at.

"I won't be all up in your business, but don't be too surprised at me saying good morning or hello to you."

She wheeled back to the counter and picked up her test kit. "Huh, that's interesting. Your blood type is AB+. That's pretty rare."

"What does that mean?" I asked.

"Basically it means you can receive transfusions from any other blood type. However *your* blood can only be given to an AB+ person. So far, you're the only AB+ I've documented in the club."

"So my donation is not needed?"

"Donations are always needed. A matching blood type always works best in transfusion. If you'd still like to donate, you'd probably receive your own blood in the event that you needed it."

"Okay." I glanced up at the clock near her ceiling. It would keep me here longer than thirteen minutes. But now, I didn't mind that so much. "I'll still donate."

"Great! You can leave your arm right where it is." She wheeled a few feet away and pulled open a drawer to gather some things.

I looked over my shoulder once again, surprised that Jandro hadn't chimed in with his usual quips during our conversation.

Son of a bitch. He was gone.

I turned back just as Mari wheeled back over to me.

"I'm going to tie this here," her gloved fingertips skimmed over my forearm to loop a piece of fabric around it, "let me know if it's too tight."

She made no mention of my scars, nor did she pay them any particular attention. As she gently poked the inside of my elbow, I fought the nagging want to feel contact without the barrier of her gloves. I'd never feel anything remotely like her bare hands on me again, so I just had to accept it.

"You're going to feel a little poke," she murmured before piercing my skin with the needle. Of course, I felt nothing but the pressure of it and the sensation of my skin breaking.

My blood flowed through the tube and into the attached bag. The liquid was dark, almost black, and I watched it pool and slowly fill the bag. I'd seen my blood leave my body many times, but never like this. And never for a reason that would possibly help me in the future.

Mariposa and I sat there together in silence. She didn't seem at all bothered by being alone with me. Jandro probably left the moment I sat down.

"You don't feel pain, do you?" she said after a few moments. "Physical pain, that is."

I looked up at her, surprised. "That's correct. Not many people have noticed."

"I had a hunch the other night when I sterilized your wound with vodka, stitched you up without anesthesia, and got no reaction."

"Yes." I shrugged one shoulder the way Jandro did sometimes. "I suppose I'm fortunate. A lot of men were suffering that night."

"I'll give you that," she leaned one arm on the counter. "But pain is important, too. It's a signal to the brain that something is very wrong in your body. You can push yourself past your limit without that signal to stop you."

"You're the medic, so I'm sure you are correct," I answered. "But my inability to feel pain has only been an asset to the Steel Demons. It means nothing holds me back when performing my duties."

She smiled at me. I swore I received more smiles from a woman sitting here with her for the past ten minutes than I had in my whole life. Jandro was right. She was easy to talk to. And easy to look at.

"You're also correct," she said, checking my donation bag. "Neither of us have to be wrong, even if we see things differently. If you don't mind me asking," she paused, eyes flicking up to my face, "how long have you not been feeling pain, your whole life?"

"Since childhood." I paused to do a quick estimation in my head. "When I was around twelve, I think. I felt pain before then."

Her gaze dropped to the scars on my arms and anxiety tightened like a fist around my chest. I hoped she wouldn't ask. I didn't want to talk about it and I didn't want to scare her if she pressed. I didn't need that demon riding around on my shoulders today.

But all she said was, "Well, I don't blame you for being glad that you don't feel it anymore."

Her hands moved swiftly, like two small birds, as she closed off the tube and withdrew the needle from my vein. In the next moment, she pressed a small piece of gauze inside my elbow and wrapped a bandage around to hold it in place.

"Leave that on for a couple of hours and take it easy the rest of the day." She rose from her stool to clean up, and was still shorter than me sitting. "Make sure you eat enough and drink plenty of fluids, preferably not alcohol."

I watched her place my bag of blood in a small refrigerator then looked down at my arm. "That's it?"

"That's it, Shadow." She smiled at me again. "Easy, right?"

"Yes. That was not at all unpleasant."

She laughed lightly, a sweet sound I wouldn't mind hearing again. Nothing like the raucous sound out of some people's mouths that killed my ears.

"Stop by if you need anything," she gave a slight eye roll, "medically-related, as I'm sure you know."

"Yes, I know now."

She smiled in a way that made her eyes close slightly at the far corners as she gave me a small wave.

"See you around, Shadow."

"I'll see you, Mariposa."

Chapter 29

GUNNER

I bore down harder on the accelerator, pushing my bike to its limit.

The wind whipped past me so fast, it felt like fingers clawing at my face. And I still wasn't going fast enough.

Horus nagged at the back of my brain just as I was leaving Uncle Jerry's. My consciousness slipped into his body just in time to see his talons dig into the neck of someone I didn't know.

The rider screamed, clutching at his neck as blood spurted out while trying to bat at my falcon with the other hand. Horus flew away, the rider's jugular already severed, and gave me a bird's-eye view of the mayhem.

There was Sheol, our home. And a battle waging just outside our gate.

Tash, you piece of shit motherfucker. Wait, where's Mariposa?

Horus flew over the battlefield, soaring high but showing me every detail. Shadow stood in his seat, firing two guns at bikers coming straight toward him. Reaper was on someone else's bike, not his own, Hades running alongside.

My worry spiked as the one person I was looking for didn't appear.

All the bikes kicked up shit tons of dust and even with Horus's eyes, visibility was shit.

Come on, baby girl. Where are you?

There!

I didn't see her at first because Jandro sat her in front of him —smart man.

A shot hit him in the shoulder and he jerked forward. Mari went to put pressure on his wound and he yelled something at her, probably to keep her hands hidden.

That was two days ago. I'd been riding all day and night, stopping only for piss breaks and to refuel, but I was still too fucking far away.

I'd seen through Horus since then, and everyone seemed okay. But it was wrong for me to not be there. Especially after finding out where Uncle Jerry's true loyalties were—wherever he would benefit the most.

I thought I could play the family card on him, even though I didn't give a shit about it. He harped about it ever since I was a kid. *Take pride in your family name, Gunner. You're a Youngblood, one of the last truly powerful American families. No matter what happens, you'll always have your family.*

I always knew it was a crock of shit, but he harped on it so much I thought he actually believed it. But now I had to be the bearer of bad news to Reaper—my trump card got us a steaming pile of nothing.

The night grew darker and I switched on my headlight. Any minute now, I should be able to see the Steel Demons flag calling me home.

I wondered how much had changed in the time I'd been gone, if anything.

Who are you kidding, Gun? You're just wondering if Mari missed you. And if she still wants swim lessons.

My light picked up small bits of debris strewn in the sand, which I carefully swerved and maneuvered around. This must have been where the battle hit. The big pieces must have all been cleaned up, though, which probably meant plenty of work for Jandro.

The sky was turning deep purple and navy blue, allowing me to barely make out the black flag high above the gate. I felt more of a sense of comfort and longing for my home here among these "thugs" than I ever did at any of my family's mansions. This was my real home.

As I drove closer, I pulled out a rifle strapped to my back in preparation for the gate signal. But something caught my eye.

Around the side of the wall, I saw a figure with a motorcycle standing in the darkness alone.

Curious, I veered off in that direction. There was nothing around Sheol for miles, and no reason for anyone to be outside the gate by themselves. It was probably nothing, but my captain of the guard instincts kicked in and I followed the urge to investigate.

I drove up slowly. They'd hear my engine at any moment now, so it wasn't like I was sneaking up on anyone. As I got closer I saw another person, this one standing with their back to the wall, apparently talking to the person on the bike. It was too dark to make out faces, but my gut screamed at me that something was fishy.

"Oh shit," someone said.

The person against the wall took off running. The rider kicked off and started speeding away. I just chuckled at the sheer amateur bullshit of this.

Sure, it was dark. But I wasn't a weapons specialist for no goddamn reason.

I aimed at the rider first, lining my sight up with the center of his back. Dumbass didn't even have enough sense to zig-zag.

The first shot hit him and he went tumbling off the bike, which crashed right after he did. Another machine to part out for Jandro.

The rider was likely dead so I went for the runner next, aiming at his legs. It took two shots but I had him flat on the ground, moaning in pain in seconds. He wasn't going anywhere, so I checked on the rider first. Yep, dead as a doornail.

I didn't recognize his face. Kicking his body over onto its stomach, his back patch read Razor Wire MC. These fuckers again, the same club that attacked us outside our home. Their emblem was a Jesus figure with barbed wire around his forehead instead of a crown of thorns. Perhaps ironically, my bullet hole landed right between Christ's eyes.

Now to find out who the fuck was the sneaky weasel talking to him. I had a hunch I'd inadvertently found Tash's bitch. At least I'd have some good news to bring to Reaper if so.

Without the use of his legs, the guy tried crawling away on his forearms, but obviously didn't get very far.

"Aww, where you going?" I asked, delivering a kick to his ribs. "I just started having so much fun."

"Ah, God! Please..."

"Please what?"

"Please, don't tell them. I'll do anything..."

"Little late for that, bucko. Now let me see who's taking Razor Wire and Tash cock up the ass."

I grabbed his pant leg and dragged him back around toward the front gate.

"Yo, Dallas," I waved at the guard on duty. "Let me in."

"Captain Gunner! Good to see you and glad you made it back."

"Me, too, man. Me, too. Want to see who our traitor is?"

The sack of shit behind me moaned his protest as if his opinion mattered. "No, please! Just let me explain to Reaper..."

"Oh shit, is that what you're dragging?"

"Yeah, shine your light over here."

He clicked on a large flashlight and aimed where I stood just as I flipped the little bitch face up.

"You!" I cried in disbelief.

Chapter 30

MARIPOSA

The clubhouse patio was livelier than the first party I attended. Something about a battle just outside your walls and coming to a near brush with death made a person that much more appreciative about celebrating life.

People started drinking before the steaks even hit the grill. Children chased each other around and even Hades joined in on the playing, while their parents sucked face and toasted to another night together.

The whole time, my stomach fluttered at the thought of seeing Jandro, what Reaper would say, and how his VP would respond. And once I got a spiked lemonade in me, I even dared to wonder where the night would end up.

"Relax, sugar." Reaper slid an arm around me from behind, smacking a kiss on my cheek. "Don't be nervous. Enjoy the party."

"I'm trying." My fingers laced with his around my hip. "I just don't want to mess anything up."

"You could never. Just go with what feels right." He gave my ear a playful nip. "Worst case scenario, you come home with only me."

"Hm, I like the way you put that." I smiled up at him, leaning back into his chest as I started to sway to an upbeat song playing from somewhere. "Where's the music coming from?"

"Check this out." He took my hand and led me across the patio. "Dallas collects these things. Isn't this nuts?"

Noelle and Larkan sat on the loveseat next to a black rectangular thing on one of the coffee tables, where the music was coming from. Or rather, she was sitting more *on* him. Good thing, Reaper was in too good of a mood to complain.

"Look at these, Mari." Noelle handed me a stack of flat, square plastic cases. "Our mom and dads used to play these bands all time."

"Wait a minute, you mean that's a," I sorted through the cases, which sure enough had round discs inside, "a CD player? A real one?"

"It has a radio and a cassette player, too. Dallas said he has a record player in his house but it's too valuable to bring outside," Larkan added.

"Why did the old folks have to have the best music, huh?" Reaper asked, taking the loveseat across from them and pulling me into his lap. He nuzzled my ear, crooning the song currently playing. "With me it's gonna be a good story to tell. Cash, grass, and ass on the highway to Hell."

"Hey, guys."

I looked up, my heart jumping into my throat at the voice.

"Jandro, have a seat."

Reaper scooted over to give his VP room to sit while subtly shifting me over in his lap—putting me in the middle.

"Where's Shadow?" I asked, noticing the large man usually with him was absent.

"He wasn't in a partying mood, just wanted to chill at home tonight."

"Is he *ever* in a partying mood?" Noelle muttered, flipping through more CD cases.

"Hey, he came out last time and helped me grill corn! That's a lot for him."

"Sugar?" Reaper shot me an intense look that told me exactly what he was asking.

"He apologized in my office this morning," I answered. "All's said and done. It's behind us now."

He visibly relaxed. "Good." His eyes flashed with mischief now as he looked at me over his beer, and I knew easily what else was on his mind.

"So, uh," I turned to Jandro, my nerves eating away at me. "How are the chickens?"

He nearly choked on his drink. "You say that like you haven't heard Foghorn crowing at the ass-crack of dawn every morning."

"I actually haven't."

"She sleeps like the dead," Reaper shook his head at me. "I don't know how."

"I was a war medic and traveled by bus everywhere! I learned to take hard catnaps whenever I could."

"A little less catnap and a little more vampire," Reaper teased.

Noelle and Larkan chose right then to take a dip in the pool, and I knew the inevitable was coming.

Reaper's hand slid across my back and my heart felt like it was going to break out of my chest. I knew his touch was an attempt at being calming, but it only made me hyperaware of what was about to happen.

"Jandro," he began. "There's something Mari and I would like to ask you."

His VP's hazel eyes slid over to me, then back to him. "Yes?" he asked, his tone and expression cool.

"We're wondering if you'd like to join our relationship," Reaper's hand closed around mine. "As a second partner to her."

Jandro's eyebrows lifted but his expression remained otherwise unchanged as his gaze returned to me. "This is something *you* want?"

I took Reaper's beer for a drink of courage and swallowed it down along with the knot in my throat.

"I really appreciate you in my life, Jandro." My voice shook with nerves and I took a steadying breath. "You've been there for me in times when he hasn't."

Reaper nodded his agreement and I found the strength to keep going.

"You've protected me and listened to me. You were literally my shield when we got ambushed and I don't take that lightly at all. I'm so grateful for you, and I think we have...something worth exploring." My final breath released like air out of a balloon. "This is completely new to me and I have no idea what I'm doing. But I have to admit I'm intrigued by this dynamic that Reaper's told me about, and as long as you're all happy, I'm willing to give it a try."

"Like I said before, sugar," Reaper pulled my attention back to him, "this is all about your comfort level and making *you* happy. You have the power here."

"And if you're confused, talk it out with either one of us," Jandro added before looking across me to his best friend. "I gather you've learned a few things about listening and not flying off the handle, Reap."

"I'm a work in progress but I'm trying," he answered with an affectionate glance to me.

"I've already seen a lot of improvement in Rory," I agreed.

Saying his real name combined with the venomous look he gave me broke all of the tension of the conversation. Jandro slid off the loveseat and onto the ground in peals of laughter and I couldn't help the giggles myself.

"Oh my God," Jandro gasped while clutching his stomach, "I'll say yes just to see your fucking face when she calls you that."

"Is this what I have to look forward to?" Reaper grumbled, draining his beer. "You two stooges laughing at my expense?"

"Yes," Jandro and I answered in unison and burst out laughing again.

"I take it all back."

"No takesies-backsies!" I smacked Reaper's forearm, coaxing the reluctant smile on his face that proved he was joking.

Somehow in our giggle fest, I found myself leaning closer to Jandro as he got back on the loveseat.

"So, what do you say?" I asked when the laughter died down and my nerves came fluttering back with a vengeance.

Jandro shot me a charming grin, reminiscent of when I first met him.

"I think you should come closer and find out, *Mariposita.*"

My first instinct was to look back at Reaper, to make sure this was okay with him, but I kept my gaze forward. I already knew how he felt, now I just had to figure it out for myself.

I leaned in and Jandro met me halfway.

The kiss was soft, only a peck at first like the rushed one he gave me at the start of the ambush. He paused, his breath a light tingle on my lips before I closed the distance again and opened up to him.

He met me for every beat, never taking the lead like Reaper, but just matching me with gentle exploration. His lips were pillowy soft and his tongue swiped across mine playfully, but never forcefully pushing into my mouth. Just like any other time with him, kissing Jandro was light-hearted and with no pressure.

When we paused for a breath, I felt a hand caress my nape. Reaper's hand.

I turned to him, not knowing what to expect on his face but he only smiled at me before giving me one of his signature, domineering kisses. A sharp thrill ran up my spine at the contrast between his mouth and Jandro's, and maybe just from the sheer fact that I was kissing two men.

He released me for air and Jandro stroked my cheek, prompting me to turn to him where he awaited with a sly grin. This time, his tongue was more adventurous, his kisses deeper and more passionate but still with the same softness.

Reaper's hand kneaded my thigh as I kissed his vice president, his breath tickling my neck before leaving a bruising kiss on my shoulder.

Holy shit, this was intense.

My body didn't even feel solid anymore. I felt like I had to be melting down to the floor with how fired up these two men made me. And this was just kissing.

I broke away from Jandro, turning back to my green-eyed lover when a loud *pop* made me jump.

"Gunshot," Jandro said immediately, jumping to his feet.

"Where? Inside the gates?" Reaper growled, leaning over to reach underneath the couch.

"Guys, what's—"

Pop! Pop! Two more shots fired.

"Stay here, Mari." Reaper pulled two handguns out from under the couch and tossed one of them to Jandro.

"Better yet, go inside," Jandro told me. "Get all the women and kids inside."

The music stopped and the mood shifted from celebratory to tense in an instant. Men pulled weapons from all kinds of hidden places and ushered their women toward the clubhouse.

"Wait a minute," Reaper squinted toward the front gate entrance. "Is that Gunner?"

"Gunner?" I went to go see but Jandro blocked me with his arm.

"Hang on, let's figure out what's going on."

"Hah!" Reaper called out with a huge grin on his face and set his gun down. "Look what the birdman dragged in!"

Hades went running down the street toward the main gate with Horus flying right above him. Cheers erupted from the men now raising their weapons in the air as they crowded around to hug the man coming up to the clubhouse.

"A party in my honor? You shouldn't have," the blond demon laughed as he and Reaper clapped an arm around each other.

"Welcome home, brother," Reaper playfully messed up his hair. "What'd you bring me?"

"I brought you nothing but *this* was whispering to a Razor Wire right outside the gate when I pulled up."

I only then realized he'd been dragging a man behind him, who left a long trail of blood on the street all the way up to the clubhouse patio.

"Oh my God," I whispered, bringing my hands to my mouth. He'd been shot in each leg and would bleed out without medical attention soon.

"Python," Reaper spat the man's name with disdain. "What were you telling the Razor Wire, huh? Details from our church meeting?"

"Reap...please..."

"Where is the Razor Wire?" Jandro asked.

"Dead," Gunner reported. "Shot him in the back. Another bike for you to part out, bro."

"Great," Jandro mumbled. "More work."

Gunner's bright blue eyes focused on me for the first time and he shot me that dazzling smile I didn't realize I missed so much. "Hey, baby girl," he said softly.

"Hey, Gun," I returned.

"I asked you a question, you two-timing bag of shit!" Reaper grabbed the man's shirt and dragged him to the nearest fire pit. There he pushed Python's face next to the coals until he started screaming.

"The allies! I was telling him the other MCs we allied with and he was going to send it up to Tash. Reaper, I'm so sorry..."

"Well, even if Gunner wasn't the best shot on this side of the Mississippi," Reaper yanked him by the hair away from the fire. "You still would've been fucked, because I made those MC names up. I would've found you out sooner or later, you fucking bottom feeder. So congratulations, Python. You'll be the first to find out what happens to those who betray the Steel Demons."

"Reaper." I stepped forward, saying his name loudly to make sure I got his attention.

"Yes, Mari?" he gave me a curious look in return.

"Do you need him alive? For the next day or whenever you deal out his punishment?"

"Yes, maybe even for a week." The Steel Demons president lifted his chin at me. "Why?"

"He's losing a lot of blood and may die if he doesn't get a transfusion. I won't be nice but I'll heal him enough to keep him alive for your needs."

Reaper approached me slowly, a sinister smile growing on his face. Years ago, maybe even a week ago, I would have feared that smile. Only days ago, I feared what this man was capable of. What he may have done in the past and what he had yet to do in the future to protect his people.

But now his people included me, and I only burned with passion and love for the man cupping the nape of my neck, dragging his thumb across my cheekbone as his green eyes locked onto mine.

I was still a medic. I would always do my best to save lives and heal the broken. But I was no longer powerless in this broken down, collapsed society. I had people I loved, friends worth protecting, and nobody was going to hurt them without paying the consequences.

"That's my girl," Reaper said softly. "My Steel Demon girl."

Epilogue

REAPER

I watched the smoke from my cigarette drift into the night air and fade into nothing. The sky from my balcony was vast and speckled with stars.

One of the few times I paid attention in school was during an astronomy lesson. The teacher said every time we looked at stars, we were looking at thousands, maybe even millions of years into the past because light had to travel so far to reach our eyes.

Most of those stars had burnt out by now, or collapsed in on themselves to become black holes. I wondered if distant worlds faced rises and falls in their own societies like we had, and if they corrected their ways before their own suns died out.

Chaos and collapse wasn't uniquely human, I was sure. But right now it was peaceful. Tranquil, even.

Mari hooked Python up with fresh blood and stabilized him from Gunner's shots. She was worn out after that and wanted to come straight home. I let her, only after a long goodbye kiss from Jandro. Some people wanted to keep partying on the patio and they were free to. I thought about going back after Mari went to bed, but apparently I wanted to sit on the balcony and think about dying stars instead.

"Reaper."

I looked over my shoulder to see Noelle in her silk kimono, hugging her arms tightly around herself.

"What's up?"

My sister looked at me nervously. "I dreamed about him again."

I returned to facing forward with a sigh. "What do you want me to do about this, Noelle?"

"Stop acting like it doesn't mean anything, for one thing."

"It doesn't. It's just dreams. He was our brother and you miss him."

"Rory, you *know* they're not."

The cigarette paused on its way to my lips before I took a deep drag. Unlike my woman, Noelle did not call me by that name to tease me. I heard her slippered feet come up closer behind me.

"It's not just dreams," she repeated. "Daren is *talking* to me—"

"He's dead, Noelle."

"I know, but *something* about him isn't. You remember all that stuff he said—"

"A bunch of horse shit nonsense."

"That came true!"

She walked around to stand in front of me, blocking my view of dead stars.

"Tonight, he told me the love of your life would love four men, and that you would lose her forever if you chose to kill one of them."

"Yeah, that sounds like common fucking sense to me, not a prophetic vision."

"He said I would only love one man for the rest of my life," she continued, biting her lip. "I think he was talking about Larkan."

"Fucking Christ, sis, you just met the guy! And what happened to him just being a stray?"

"He said something else, too, and that's what's bugging me the most."

"What?"

"That when we're called upon," her voice took on a harrowed tone, "we must obey the order."

"Called upon by who?"

Her eyes shifted to the sleeping dog lying next to me.

"The gods."

FEARLESS

STEEL DEMONS MC BOOK THREE

Prologue

RORY

AGE SIXTEEN

"My mom is going to fucking kill me."

"At least you'll be put out of your misery," Jandro grumbled next to me. He shifted uncomfortably, straining at the handcuffs holding his wrists behind his back. "Tia Ana is gonna make damn sure I suffer if I get home. And if not her, my sisters will."

"Hey!" The sheriff's deputy in the passenger seat of the van slammed his baton against the partition separating us from him. "Shut the fuck up back there, fucking delinquents!"

"Fuck you, mall cop," I shot back, straining against the bite of metal on my own wrists.

"Watch your damn mouth, son. You want to spend some time in the hole?"

"You busted us for smoking weed and skateboarding in an empty pool. Don't try to fucking scare me!"

"Rory," Jandro hissed under his breath.

"What?"

"Ever think shutting your damn mouth might be a good idea?"

"We're minors, Dro. They can't do shit to us."

"Unless they want to try us as adults," he kept whispering. "In case you haven't noticed, we're close to the border and I'm kinda brown."

I bit the inside of my cheek. Fuck, I hadn't even thought of that. Jandro was like a brother to me. It hadn't occurred to me that he might have a completely different experience when it came to cops. As lame as these stupid deputies were, they still had guns, batons, and pepper spray. Assuming the news reports weren't faked, law enforcement had been targeting Latinos and other minorities for decades. Especially since that law passed that officers of the law couldn't be charged with murder. That was some bullshit.

"You speak perfect English though," was all I could think of to reassure Jandro. "No one's gonna mistake you for an illegal."

He gave me a scathing look. "Maybe not, *if* I get the chance to open my mouth before they pop a hundred caps in my ass." He sighed as his head tipped back to lean on the van wall. "And if they raid my aunt and uncle's place? What then?"

I swallowed dryly. His aunt and uncle were kind, albeit simple people. They spoke only broken English but welcomed me into their home like a son. I liked hanging out there because it was more low-key than my house with my mom and three dads hovering all the time. Plus, Jandro's sister Angelica was pretty, and I wanted to kiss her next time I went over.

I'd never see any of them again if the cops raided Jandro's house.

"Sorry, dude," I muttered. "I'll shut the fuck up."

"Why thank you," he declared sarcastically. "I swear to God, you'll be the death of me one day."

"Noelle tells me the same thing, especially after I lit that firework right next to her face," I snickered. "She's started calling me Reaper."

"Huh," Jandro snorted. "You could make that your road name. It actually fucking fits."

The deputies pulled up to the county jail and hauled us out of the back of the van by our arms.

"Hey, wait a minute." I struggled to catch my footing with how hard these assholes were shoving me. "We're sixteen. Why aren't we at the juvie hall?"

"It's packed full of other lowlifes like you. You dicks are overflow." A hard push slammed into the center of my back. "Move."

We got stripped of all of our belongings, then our fingerprints and mugshots taken before being shoved into an iron-barred cell not much bigger than a bathroom. At least the handcuffs came off then.

"Hey, don't we get a phone call or something?" I asked the deputy locking our cell door.

The fat, bald dipshit lifted one shoulder in a shrug before grinning snidely at me. "Maybe. If I feel like it on my next shift."

"You piece of shit! We have rights!" I called after him as he left the room.

"No, we don't." Jandro was already making himself comfortable on the cot along the cell wall. "Not really, anyway."

"Yeah we do, bro. They gotta give us lawyers and trials and shit."

"Have you listened to the radio lately? People are disappearing and jack shit's being done about it. They'll keep us here as long as they damn well please."

"Dude, we'll be fine. I mean fuck, we didn't even *do* anything!"

"Exactly my point." Jandro raised his pointer finger to the ceiling. "We're sitting in a jail cell for what? Stealing? Assault? Running a traffic light? No, Rory. They had no reason to arrest us and therefore, no reason to let us out. That's the way the world's going."

The door down the hall opened before I could retort. Expecting to see the deputy, I called out, "Yeah, thought you'd come back, dickwad!" much to Jandro's chagrin.

Instead, some kid, no older than us, came swaggering up to our cell wearing a smug, punchable smile. I hated him instantly.

He wore some kind of prep school uniform, shirt untucked and navy tie loosened around his neck. His blonde hair was cut close to his scalp, not a single strand out of place. Add in his perfectly aligned, white teeth and baby blue eyes, it was clear this kid lived worlds apart from me and Jandro.

"See something you like, punk bitch?" I challenged, pressing up against the bars.

"Stop it, Rory," Jandro groaned from the cot.

I ignored him, naturally.

"You want some of this?" I squeezed my dick through my pants, not taking my eyes off of the preppy dipshit. "If I squint real hard and pretend, I might even mistake you for a girl."

"I don't want to suck your dick," the kid said. "Just wanted to see what all the chatter was about upstairs," he nodded toward the hallway leading out. "Seems you all pissed off the deputies."

"What, and someone let *you* come down here and risk getting your hands dirty?" I mocked.

"My uncle's the sheriff," the kid grinned. "And trust me, my hands are way dirtier than he knows."

"Don't think you can impress us with your slum tourism," Jandro piped up.

"Aw, don't let the uniform fool you, *hombré*." The kid ran a hand through his blonde hair, a few strands coming loose. "I got connections you guys can't even fathom."

"Please," Jandro muttered, rubbing his forehead. "Just stop talking and don't ever call me *hombré* again."

"Fair enough. I'll prove it. You two want outta here?" That got our interest and the kid's eyes sparkled with glee. "I'll post your bail. You can walk out of here in an hour, tops."

"In exchange for what?" I crossed my arms.

The kid paused, shoving his hands deep in the pockets of his pressed slacks.

"Can one of y'all fix a vintage motorcycle?"

"For real?" I coughed out a laugh.

"It has sentimental value, okay?" He glowered at me. "It was my grandfather's before he passed. I've tried fixing it myself, watching videos and shit, but something's not clicking."

"Make, model and year?" Jandro asked, sitting up from the cot.

"Harley Road King, 2020."

Jandro let out a low whistle. "That was a damn good year. Hard to find parts nowadays, but I can probably scrounge 'em up."

"You can fix it?" The kid's blue eyes grew wide with hope.

"Depends on what's wrong, but yeah, most likely."

"That," I pointed over my shoulder at Jandro, "is the best damn bike mechanic you will ever fucking meet. We ride on weekends sometimes, and if you really can get us out of here," I leaned against the bars, "we might let you tag along once your granddad's steed is running again."

The kid smiled again, and it looked genuine this time rather than smug.

"I'll go talk to the bondsman," he said, walking backward away from our cell. "Back in a flash."

"Hey, hold up," I called after him. "What's your name?"

"Gunner," he answered. "Gunner Youngblood."

I stole a glance at Jandro. Maybe this preppy Gunner cat wasn’t so bad after all.

CHAPTER 1

MARIPOSA

PRESENT DAY

"Please..."

The man let out another pathetic wheeze like he was dying. Like he could fool me, the one keeping him alive in order to receive justice from the Steel Demons, from the brotherhood he betrayed. I ignored his plea, and proceeded to stick him with a fresh IV bag for his bare minimum of nutrients.

"You're a healer," he tried again, reaching for my hand. "You're a good woman with a kind heart. Please, if you just set me up with a bag of food, and let me out of here so I can get my bike—"

"I may be a good woman with a kind heart, Python, but I'm not an idiot."

He tried yet again, from a different angle. "I could take you with me. You're miserable here. I saw it from that first day Reaper dragged you in. You don't have to be scared. I can protect—"

"Python," I sighed. "Even if I wanted to run away with you, you've got gunshot wounds in each leg, are still recovering from blood loss, and you've been on a liquid diet for three days. You might make it from your bed to the floor, but not much further than that. You're certainly in no shape to ride through the desert."

I cleaned up my supplies, snapped my gloves off, then rubbed a generous amount of hand sanitizer into my palms.

"Because I have such a kind heart," I stood up, "I won't tell Reaper you offered to take away his woman. He'd surely dish out something extra on you for that."

Python's face paled. "He's sharing you?"

"Yes."

"With who?"

I hesitated for a moment, unsure of how open these multi-person relationships were to the rest of the club. Then again, I kissed Reaper and Jandro in front of everyone at the party. I didn't recall anyone reacting weirdly to it, although I was only really focusing on two people at the time.

"Just Jandro for now," I answered.

The prisoner scowled and looked off to the corner of his cell. It was a comfortable room, as far as jail cells went. It reminded me of a cheap motel room, with a bed, bathroom, desk, and seating area. Only it had no windows or entertainment.

Reaper told me the cells had been quarantine rooms. Rich people had them installed in their neighborhoods about a decade before the Collapse, to isolate people who displayed symptoms of contagious diseases that had been on the rise, such as measles, polio, and deadly strains of flu. All the more reason to get the entire club vaccinated.

"Same time tomorrow," I told Python before nodding at Dallas, who stood guard in the room.

Dallas let me out and proceeded to stand just outside the door after locking it, weapon brandished. I knew they changed shifts every few hours and Gunner would take his post eventually. The only one not in rotation for guarding Python's cell was Bones, with whom he had been close. Python and Bones shared the same woman—Reaper's ex, Heather.

"Thank you again, Dallas." I didn't know him well, but he always struck me as one of the warmest Steel Demons. He had a kind face for a biker, with bushy eyebrows atop smiling blue eyes, a shaved head, and a dark beard reaching down to the top of his chest. Unlike one of the other guardsmen, Big G, Dallas seemed completely devoted to his wife, Andrea, which earned him points in my book.

"No need to thank me, Mari," he chuckled politely. "Just doin' my job."

I smiled in return. "Do you know when your captain's coming on guard duty?"

"Another hour, I think." He tilted his head in the direction of the conference room down the hall, where the club usually held church, and gave me a playful wink. "He's in there with Reaper now. I'm sure they wouldn't mind if you interrupted," he teased.

"Or Reaper will blow a head gasket and not speak to me for the rest of the night," I returned, only half joking.

"That's always a risk," Dallas laughed. "But you have Jandro in case that happens."

Did I really? Have Jandro in the same way I had Reaper? Could I treat him like my man automatically? Did I have that right? Reaper encouraged us to spend time alone, to get to know each other. But the surly Steel Demons president was my safety net, and I didn't know how to navigate this thing with Jandro without Reaper there. In any case, I'd barely seen the charming VP since the party. He was buried in work at the shop with all the wrecked bikes from the Razor Wire ambush.

"Think I'll hang out with the guard dog to be safe." I tossed a small wave over my shoulder at Dallas, which he returned, before continuing down the hall.

Hades' big head lifted off of his paws, ears straight up in the air the moment he saw me turning the corner.

"How's my favorite boy?" I asked, quickening my pace toward him.

He let out a soft whine but didn't move a muscle from the closed door he guarded. I sat on the floor next to him and he immediately placed his head in my lap.

"Hades, I might love you more than your master," I said, massaging over his forehead and ears. "You are just the sweetest thing."

The affectionate, protective Doberman licked my hand and nuzzled into my pets, but his body remained alert and guarded. He took his job seriously, evidently, but who could resist pets? And Hades seemed especially partial to mine lately. Even Reaper started complaining that he liked me more.

The Steel Demons' president's low, murmuring voice floated to my ears through the door, though I couldn't make out the words. Gunner's voice answered him, whatever he said punctuated by an occasional chirp from Horus.

While I wasn't trying to eavesdrop, I still listened to their tones as I rested my head against the wall. They sounded tense. Not angry, but maybe a bit worried. Gunner just came back from a mission I still didn't know the full details of. All I knew was how pissed Reaper was about him going, but had allowed it anyway. And that it was some kind of last resort measure for the survival of the whole club. From how tense things were since Gun's return, the mission didn't appear to be a successful one.

He came upon Python, the imprisoned man I was just checking on, conspiring with a member of Razor Wire, the same club that ambushed us right on our doorstep. Finding the club traitor was the biggest Steel Demons victory, that and losing no one in the ambush.

But Python's punishment still had to be carried out. And I had a feeling the Steel Demons were wound up and tense because they felt like sitting ducks. Many of their bikes had been wrecked in the ambush.

Heavy footsteps approached the door and opened it before I could move. Hades lifted his head from my lap to look at his master with wide, innocent eyes.

"Some guard dog you are," Reaper huffed, reaching a hand down to pull me to my feet. He immediately braced a forearm against my lower back, anchoring my hip to his. "You didn't have to sit on the floor out here, sugar."

"I didn't mind." I scratched under Hades' chin. "And I didn't want to interrupt anything important."

"Nothing's too important for you," he murmured much lower and sexier than was necessary. "Just knock and I'll let you know what's up."

"Okay," I smiled, stroking a hand along his bicep.

He was being charming and sweet lately, all starry-eyed and smitten when he looked at me. This side of him was adorable, and I had to admit that I was surprised he kept it up for three days without totally putting his foot in his mouth. Not once did he take out club frustrations out on me. He snapped orders at his men, especially concerning the prisoner, then in the same breath, turned around and told me my ass looked nice in my scrubs.

Nothing but romance and poetry, being the president's old lady.

Even right then, his gaze softened from the pinched brow he wore coming out of his meeting with Gunner. He drew me close and kissed me full of depth and tongue, like we hadn't seen each other in days, much less a few hours ago.

"Done for the day?" he asked, dragging his lips to my cheek.

"Mm." I turned my head to catch sight of the tall, blonde captain of the guard, apparently trying to sneak out into the hall without saying anything. "Where you off to, Gunner?"

He whirled back around on the ball of his foot with a sheepish grin, the falcon on his shoulder fluttering his wings at the sudden change in direction.

"Grabbing something to eat before I relieve Dallas on guard duty." He reached up to stroke the feathers on Horus' chest. "This little guy needs to catch some food too, before it gets dark."

"You owe me more swimming lessons, remember?"

Thanks to his gentle guidance and positive reinforcement, I was able to float on my back in the pool at the Sandia outpost. If any of the other guys had attempted to teach me, I'd probably end up looking like a drowned rat, and trust none of them near a body of water again.

His grin widened with a shy glance downward. "I sure do, baby girl. We'll get around to it, okay? Once all this other bullshit is taken care of."

"Sure." I returned a forced smile through the pang of rejection in my chest. "See you, Gun."

Reaper pressed a kiss to my temple with a chuckle as I watched the back of Gunner's cut float further down the hallway. "He'll be yours one day, sugar. Just give him time to come around."

"It's not even that," I said, turning into him. "We used to be able to talk like friends. And now he keeps blowing me off every time I say hello."

"Because he wants you as more than friends. And in his mind, you're off limits now that you're mine and Jandro's." His hand slid down to my ass where he took a gratuitous squeeze. "Speaking of, want to pay your Latin lover a visit?"

"Can you really call him that if there's been no loving going on?"

The question came out more grumbly than I intended. Jandro was busy. All the Steel Demons were, but it was up to Jandro and the two prospects to fix up the dozen or so wrecked bikes from the ambush. You'd think these men were caged animals with the way they acted with no motorcycles between their legs.

"Greedy girl," Reaper teased me. "Trust me, Mari, he wants to see you but it's a two-way street." He gave me a playful tap on the nose. "He knows you're new to this and doesn't want to overwhelm you. Now that the three of us are official, hiding out in the shop is a convenient way for you to come see *him*. Your comfort zone is sticking with me and he's not going to be the one to pull you out of that. That's on you, sugar."

He was right. Reaper repeatedly reminded me that I was the one in control of this three-way relationship. I was setting the pace and so far, I'd taken the easy route of just spending all my free time with him. Because I didn't know any other way. He and Jandro directed the kisses at the party, but they couldn't take charge like that all the time. I was an equal, contributing part of this relationship and I couldn't treat this the way I always had before. Not when I had the hearts of two men to care for.

My decision made, I removed Reaper's hand from my ass and laced my fingers with his. "Let's go see him."

Chapter 2

GUNNER

"Do you have any good news to tell me?"

I wanted to drop my eyes to the table under the scrutinizing gaze of my president, but I wasn't a pussy. If I had to tell him I failed, I'd have the balls to look him in the eye as I did so.

"We have our snitch," I said. "Although that is some dumb fuckin' luck I rolled up at the exact moment I did, and nothing to do with my skills."

"I'm not even sure he's the only one," Reaper answered, rubbing his jaw. "If Bones and Heather knew about his scheming and didn't tell me, they have to answer for that too."

I nodded my agreement, drumming my fingers on the table while Horus adjusted the grip of his talons in my shoulder. Those sharp fuckers used to kill me. He dug in hard at first, and I had multiple scars on that one shoulder to prove it. Eventually, I got used to him always sitting there and he loosened his grip enough to hold on without piercing me.

"So you're holding him, then? Until you question the other two?"

"That's the plan. He's getting royal treatment for a prisoner, better than he fucking deserves, so he better not bitch." Reaper's lip curled. "If he does, I'm sure Mari will tell me about it."

Reaper's gaze softened as he uttered her name, and I fought the urge to snort derisively. He was utterly in love with our pretty medic and still passed her off to Jandro like some prized whore. I couldn't begin to understand it. If she were mine, any man that looked at her with desire would feel my knife at his throat. Women had to be cared for, protected. Especially in a world like this.

And fuck me, I did care for her. Maybe too much.

I could never bring myself to join the rotation of men who orbited her. I had to be content with my place on the outside. I was a guardian and provider for the Steel Demons. I'd guard her with my life and provide whatever supplies she needed for her medical practice. I knew what I was good at, and sharing a woman was not one of them.

"So your uncle really believes General Tash will sell part of his conquered land to him?" Reaper got back on topic, his expression hardening again. "He chose expanding his territory over paying a debt? Over his own family?"

"It was a long shot anyway," I sighed, propping my elbows on the table. "Tash has a way of making you feel like you're getting a good deal without being too generous. And he *will* honor his agreements, up to a point."

"Hindsight is 20/20, huh?" Reaper scoffed.

"Fucking tell me about it," I groaned. "I should have known a rising general wouldn't play ball with an MC forever. They all look down on us like scum."

"You couldn't have predicted this," Reaper said. "He didn't just cut us off, he worked to destroy us from the inside. Using another MC, no less."

"He probably pays Razor Wire a fraction of what he paid us," I realized. "We have standards and people to protect. They're just a bunch of dirty thugs on wheels."

"And he'll try to wipe them off the map too," Reaper added. "Once they've served their purpose for him. And good riddance to that, but," he tilted his head, "do you think he'll betray your uncle in the same way?"

I tented my fingers, idly tapping them together as I worked through all the likely scenarios in my head.

"Yes," I decided. "I don't believe for a second he's going to give part of the New Mexico territory to my uncle. Not after he obliterated the last governor's regime to take control of it. He's not a rebel anymore. He stormed the castle and now he's the new king. And he sure as shit wants to keep that crown on his head."

"That doesn't change a damn thing for us," Reaper growled. "He *will* be brought down. To keep using your metaphor, I want to throw his corpse over the castle walls wrapped in a Steel Demons flag."

"It'll be difficult," I warned him. "But easier with support, of course. The question is, are you willing to accept my uncle's help when he realizes the truth and crawls to us with his tail between his legs?"

"Hmm." Reaper lifted his gaze to stare at the wall, his jaw tense. "Maybe. Depends how badly he needs us. I regret not making him dance like a monkey last time he begged us for protection."

"We will be in a position to negotiate to our advantage," I pointed out. "How much depends on if Tash simply goes back on his promise of land or actually moves to invade Colora—I mean, Jerriton. If my uncle's back is pushed against a wall, it could work out very well for us."

In all honesty, I actually hoped General Tash moved his army into Uncle Jerry's territory and set the whole fucking thing on fire. The vineyards on rolling hills, our gaudy Youngblood family crest engraved onto every gate and set of doors. The manicured topiaries, marble statues, and high-arching ceilings of his mansion—all built on the backs of slaves. I couldn't get that girl out of my head, the skinny blonde who'd been servicing him under his desk when I arrived. The poor thing was already dead inside. She'd probably willingly jump into the flames if an invading army came.

Uncle Jerry just couldn't be satisfied with the title of General. Like most others in my wretched family, he sought power and prestige at any cost. In his eyes, he saw a lavish lifestyle just like that of his ancestors before they left Hollywood. The price tag? Free labor, now that he didn't have pesky laws and concepts such as human rights to keep him in check.

"And he'll keep his word?" Reaper lifted a skeptical eyebrow.

"Honestly, I dunno," I sighed, leaning back in my chair. Horus hopped off my shoulder and fluttered to my leg to avoid smashing his tail feathers into the chair back. "He rose to power by being a fucking backstabber, just like Tash. He's manipulated his citizens and kept them prisoner. But if he's desperate enough, he might be forced to keep his word."

"So we should use him, but not trust him."

"That's what I suggest." I massaged the back of Horus's head with my thumb and forefinger. "After that gigantic waste of time of a visit, I don't think I can even pull the family card with him anymore. He'll always do what's in his own best interest."

"You didn't completely waste your time." Reaper slid off the table and headed for the door, indicating our meeting was over. "We're slightly less in the dark and learned valuable information because of you. And we did catch a snitch."

"Aw, shucks. Thanks, Reap," I laughed, rising from my chair. Horus returned to my shoulder and nipped at a lock of my hair, his signal that he was hungry and needed to get outside to hunt.

"I'm just stating a fact, not complimenting you." Reaper rolled his eyes. "But really, good work, Gun."

"Thank you, President," I said in a more formal tone, but couldn't help the smirk that followed. "I do think Mariposa is softening you up, though."

"Get the fuck out of here before I take it back," he snarled. But the hidden smile as he opened the door said he didn't disagree.

Hades was in his spot just over the threshold, but rather than sitting guarded and alert, he laid on his belly with his head in Mariposa's lap. She looked up at us with a smile, and I resisted the impulse to grin back. She wasn't mine and never would be.

"Some guard dog you are." Reaper reached down to pull Mariposa to her feet, his hand immediately transferring to around her waist. "You didn't have to sit on the floor out here, sugar."

"I didn't mind." She looked at my president like the sun rose and set on him. "And I didn't want to interrupt anything important."

"Nothing's too important for you," he murmured, lowering his face to hers.

I tried to slip out behind him into the hall. Not that I was trying to avoid Mari, but just keep a respectful distance. I didn't want to give anyone the idea that I wanted to join their weird harem arrangement. Plus, it was just too fucking awkward to stand around while those two sucked face.

But of course, I wasn't fast enough.

"Where you off to, Gunner?"

Plastering a smile on my face, I whipped back around on my foot. Horus flapped at the sudden change in direction and puffed up with annoyance. He was hungry and hated flying indoors.

"Grabbing something to eat before I relieve Dallas on guard duty." I stroked the feathers on Horus's chest to calm him. "This little guy needs to catch some food too before it gets dark."

Mari gave me a challenging, playful look that made my heart skip a beat. "You owe me more swimming lessons, remember?"

Of course I did. It was all I could think about. The way she held onto me in that pool. The fear in her eyes, but her determination to overcome it. Not only was it sexy, I found it brave and admirable as hell. I'd be lying if I said I didn't consider making a move then. A wayward touch or a kiss would have been easy.

But she trusted me. And right after that shitty church session where Big G all but straight out accused *me* of being a traitor, I wasn't about to stomp all over that trust. Hell, it felt like she was the only person in the world in that moment who didn't look at me with suspicion and accusation. That swim lesson allowed me to calm the hell down.

She had no idea, but she'd already started talking me out of seeing red after making sure I didn't break my hand on the pool wall. It was just what I needed after feeling like I'd just been punched in the gut.

Once she started floating on her back all by herself, I felt like myself again. More than that—she made me feel like I was needed and valued.

Mariposa needed to learn how to swim. It was an important skill. But I couldn't be the one to teach her. Because the next time we were alone in a pool, I might not be able to stop myself.

There was no way I could tell her all that. So I grinned sheepishly down at the floor, unable to look her in the eye. "I sure do, baby girl. We'll get around to it, okay? Once all this other bullshit is taken care of."

"Sure. See you, Gun."

I tried to ignore how sad she sounded as my motorcycle boots stomped down the hall, putting as much distance between me and her as possible.

CHAPTER 3

MARIPOSA

"Have you seen the shop yet?" Reaper's hand remained clasped in mine as we walked through a quiet side street crossing the main road from the clubhouse.

"No. Was it already here or did you guys build it?" I asked.

It was fascinating to me how the Steel Demons and their families weren't only squatting in this once affluent gated community, they transformed it and made it into their home.

"It started out as one of the ugliest homes here," Reaper chuckled. "A two-story duplex, just this ugly-ass tall, rectangular building with no character. But the garages were spacious and really nice. They took up almost the entire first floor, so we opened up the ceiling, broke down the walls between the two duplexes, moved in some tools and equipment, and there you fuckin' have it."

He waved an arm as we turned a corner and there it was. The building was grey and stuck out like a sore thumb among the other nice houses on the block. But it had that masculine, old-school mechanic's charm with both garage doors open, tools and motorcycle guts strewn all over the place, and hip-hop music playing on an ancient looking CD-player.

"Jandrooooo," Reaper called as we walked up the driveway. "Where the fuck are ya?"

A man popped his head out from behind a wall. I recognized him as Larkan, the guard from the Sandia outpost who gave the Steel Demons information about the general who attacked them. And the guy Reaper's sister seemed to have an instant-connection with.

"Hi, Reaper. Mariposa," he greeted us with a friendly smile, wiping his hands on a rag.

"You can call me *president*, prospect," Reaper hissed. "I'm not Reaper to you until you've earned it."

I stifled a groan, but otherwise didn't comment. These men and their ridiculous pecking order.

"Sorry, president." Larkin's smile faded. "Jandro's inside. I'll let him know you're here."

While he left, I turned around slowly to observe the place some more. Motorcycles in various states of assembly were everywhere. Against one wall, piles of tires in various sizes were stacked up nearly floor-to-ceiling. A few posters of bikini-clad women leaning over bikes in suggestive poses decorated the walls.

"There's my baby." Reaper came up next to me, pointing to a bike next to a work-bench. "Looks like Jandro's been trying to realign her frame."

"It doesn't even look like the same bike," I mused. "Last I saw, it was pretty much folded in half."

"Mm. That's why Jandro's the best at what he does."

I playfully nudged him in the ribs. "You realize I've never ridden on the back of your bike? At least, not willingly anyway."

"That's true, huh?" A mischievous spark lit up the president's green eyes. "Wanna go for a ride tomorrow, sugar?"

"Tomorrow?" I repeated, surprised. "Jandro's gonna be done by then?"

"I have other bikes, you know." He pinched my waist until I squirmed and swatted him away. "What kind of MC president would I be if I didn't have at least three?"

"So maybe I can ride my own." I lifted my chin at him.

"Not a chance," he laughed. "Not until I feel you all snug and sexy on my back at least once."

"I guess that's fair," I said, but jokingly pouted anyway.

He ran his thumb down my plump bottom lip. "We'll start you on a little dirt bike like Noelle's. The fat boys like we ride are bigger and harder to control. Don't worry, sugar," he grinned at me. "We'll make a Steel Demon out of you yet."

"Que quieres, chingado?"

The voice made us both turn around to see Jandro wearing a white fitted tank top that made his arms and shoulders look even bigger than normal, and accentuated his warm, caramel skin tone. His hands were clean, but he missed a grease stain on his forehead, which did nothing to detract from his looks. If anything, it made him even cuter.

His hazel eyes widened the moment he saw me.

"Shit. Sorry, Mari. I didn't know you were here too."

"It's okay," I smiled. "It was this *chingado's* idea to stop by and see you."

Both guys snorted with laughter. Movement from behind Jandro in the house's kitchen, which looked like a converted break room, made me look past him.

"Stephan!" I called with a wave. "Hey! How are you?"

"Oh! Mariposa." His pale cheeks flushed a shade of pink. "Hi. Nice to see you."

I originally met Stephan at Fight Night, the monthly event where the Steel Demons settled conflicts between each other with their fists. As a prospect, Stephan was not an official SDMC member yet and wore no patches. He apprenticed for Jandro at the shop, and was subjected to his hazing. Fight Night gave him a chance to unleash his frustrations back onto Jandro.

Unfortunately for him, Jandro was a better fighter.

"Nice to see you too," I smiled. "That lip is looking much better."

"Yes, ma'am." He reached up to touch his bottom lip, which had nearly returned to normal size. "Thanks to you."

"So it looks like you," I turned my gaze to Jandro, "haven't been abusing him?"

"No, ma'am." Jandro mimicked Stephan. "Been too busy putting him to work, honestly."

"Speaking of." Reaper pulled his cigarettes from his pocket and stuck one in his mouth. "Let's take five, prospects. Out back."

Larkan and Stephan exchanged a nervous glance. Reaper just winked at me as he walked through the shop to the outside smoking area in the back. The prospects were quick to follow him, although clearly uneasy about having the president's undivided attention on them.

"That's one way to get us alone," Jandro chuckled, looking down as he arranged some tools in a metal box. He almost seemed nervous too.

"I just hope he's not a total dick to Larkan," I glanced toward the plumes of cigarette smoke already filling the air from the back patio.

"He won't be," Jandro grinned. "But I'll bet you every bike in here, he will use Fight Night as an excuse to beat his ass."

"Ugh. Is that coming up again?" I groaned.

"Next week," he confirmed with a nod.

"And are you going to use it as another excuse to humiliate Stephan?"

Jandro paused in his steadfast tool rearranging, pinning me with an intense look before answering. "Nah. I'm not fighting anyone this month. Honestly," he rubbed his jaw, glancing over his shoulder toward the others outside, "I'm really proud of Stephan. I'm gonna advocate for getting him patched in at our next church meeting."

"Wow," I breathed. "That's a big deal, isn't it?"

"He'll be a true Steel Demon." Jandro's eyes brightened. "He'll need a better road name than Stephan, that's for sure."

"How does that work? Do you guys give him a name or does he pick his own?"

"Depends. If something funny happens to him that warrants a nickname, we'll give him one. Or if all of his own ideas are dumb as hell."

"Why don't you have one?" I asked.

"'Cause there ain't no other Jandro," he grinned.

"You're right about that."

I slowly drifted closer to him as we talked. First my upper body swayed, leaning toward him as if carried by gentle breeze, and then my feet followed until I stood right next to him. He watched me with calm, measured interest, staying rooted to his spot.

"So how've you been?" My cheeks heated with the question. Reaper and I never really had the awkward small-talk phase in our relationship. But with Jandro, I wasn't sure how to act.

"Too fucking busy fixing all this shit," he grumbled, rubbing a hand down his face. "I've missed you."

My heart jumped into my throat at hearing that. When he reached across the short distance between us to rest his fingers on my waist, I had a momentary sensation of floating.

"I've missed you too," I answered, resting my hand on his bicep.

The touch barrier now crossed and miles behind us, he solidified his contact on me, pulling me closer as his other hand joined the first. The muscle under my hand flexed, his skin soothing and warm. This close, I picked up the scent of his soap, something citrusy mixed with a hint of motor oil.

"What have you been up to while I've been holed up in here?" His warm breath fanned across my lips. I could see my reflection in his green-brown shifting eye color.

"Babysitting Python. Monitoring Tessa's pregnancy. Some vaccine and check-up appointments." My hands drifted across his broad shoulders to rest around the back of his neck. "Nothing too exciting."

"Rory still being good?" He gave me a playfully stern look, lacing his hands at the small of my back.

"Yes," I giggled at his use of Reaper's real name. It became like an inside joke between us to tease the surly president. "He's been really good."

"Well, you know where to come if that changes." His voice grew lower, huskier as he pulled me closer still, widening his legs so I could stand between them.

"I won't just come to you for that." My torso now against his, I craned my neck to look up at him. "I've been wanting to see you. I just didn't want to bother you while you were working."

"Please come bother me." His forehead lowered to nearly brushing with mine as one hand slid up my back. "Your gorgeous face will be a welcome sight among all this fucking grease and metal and testosterone."

My lips pulled back into a smile. If this multi-partner thing worked out, I wondered if Jandro would keep the charm turned on or if he would stop eventually. It felt nice to be flattered by him, as much as I tried to resist it at first.

"Yeah, that's the smile I missed." One hand came up to cup my chin, his gaze flicking from my lips to my eyes in a silent ask for permission.

I answered by lifting onto my toes and pressing my mouth to his. He sucked in a sharp breath of surprise before crushing me to his chest. His lips parted, returning the pressure of mine with pillowy softness. The last time I kissed him was a whole three days ago at the party, and I almost forgot how much I loved it. His lips were thick and succulent, his kisses slow, drawn-out and sensual.

He turned me into a puddle with that mouth while somehow keeping me together with his broad, strong arms around my back. My fingers curled into the dark hair on his head, dragging my nails across his scalp as he elicited soft moans. Our tongues danced erotically, but he always met me in the middle—never dominating the kiss like a certain president.

I didn't even realize how much I needed to breathe until he broke away with slow reluctance.

"Thanks for coming to see me," he whispered, stroking his thumb along my jaw. "I'd love to keep you and do this all night, but..." His eyes drifted to our surroundings of unrideable bikes and their guts strewn everywhere.

"You have to keep working," I finished for him.

He nodded, but didn't release his hold on me. "It doesn't look like it, but the biggest repairs are done. In another couple of days, my workload should be back to normal again."

"How long will you be at it tonight?"

He shrugged. "'Til I can't keep my eyes open."

I pressed my palms to his cheeks and looked straight at him. "You need to sleep. And make sure you drink enough water. Medic's orders."

"Hmm, not sure I can remember all that," he teased. "I'm just a dumb gearhead."

"Shut up," I rolled my eyes. Like Reaper, I had a feeling he was far more intelligent than he let on. When it came to bikes, I was all but certain he was a genius.

"You should come see me again, Mariposita," he grinned. "To remind me of those orders."

"I will if I have to," I said in a playful warning tone.

"Hell, I'll let a fat boy fall on me if that's what it takes to get you out here."

"That won't be necessary." I re-wrapped my arms around his neck and hovered my lips a hair-breath away from his. "As long as you keep kissing me like that."

Chapter 4

SHADOW

Sunsets.

They were one of the few things I liked to take in and just appreciate. And from what Jandro and Reaper told me, the ones here in the Arizona territory were among the best in the world.

I liked to sit on the clubhouse rooftop balcony in the evenings and just watch the sky explode into colors. Some of which I didn't know existed until I was nearly ten years old. With a trusted bottle of liquor in my hand, it felt like I was swallowing the sun's fire from that sky. A death I would welcome, but whoever ruled the underworld these days didn't seem ready for me yet.

Soft laughter floated up from somewhere down below me, bringing my gaze from the sky to the streets.

Reaper and Mariposa walked together, looking like toy figures from my vantage point. Their hands clasped together, swinging between them. Hades walked a few feet in front of them, sniffing along the ground. They remained like that, their shadows long on the street until he wrapped an arm around her shoulders, drawing her into him as she laughed again.

I still wasn't all too familiar with what happiness looked like, or felt like, for that matter. But her smile at him appeared unrestrained. It reached her eyes, which remained glued to him. He looked and smiled at her in a similar way. Was that what happiness looked like? Or being in love? Did one automatically assume the other?

I took a pensive swig of my liquor bottle. Navigating the world in search of love or happiness seemed to be more trouble than it was worth. Especially for me, always trying to keep up with what was normal and accepted or not. Being brought into the club was the closest thing to happiness I would reach. It was better than anyone else born in my position could hope for. A connection with a woman, or anything beyond the brotherhood between my fellow Steel Demons and I, was simply out of the cards.

A door opened and shut behind me, but I didn't turn to look. The weight of the footfalls and the space between each step told me that Gunner had joined me on the balcony.

"Evening, Shadow," he mumbled as he fished a cigarette from his cut pocket and lit it.

I grunted out a wordless reply before taking another swig of liquid sunfire. Curiosity slid my gaze over in his direction. He didn't usually come up here during this time. The harsh exhale of smoke from his lungs indicated some proverbial weight sat on his chest. But I wasn't about to ask. We could drink and smoke, talk bikes, weapons, and hunting, but I couldn't offer deeper conversation than that.

I chalked it up to the ongoing conflict with General Tash, and how the club would be supplied with food and basic necessities now that our biggest trade partner was gone.

"Horus hunting?" I asked, noticing the absence of the bird usually perched on his shoulder.

Gunner nodded. "Yeah," he said with another harsh exhale. "He can't see that well once it starts getting dark, so thought I'd come up here so he can find me."

"Oh." I absently scratched at the scar cutting through my eyebrow and eyelid.

"He's a daytime hunter usually, but we've been meeting with Reap all day," Gunner continued, stretching his long arms above his head.

"Riding out tomorrow?"

"Yeah. Nowhere far, though. Just some local contacts for basic necessities." He looked at me with a smirk. Smiling came easily to him, whether he was with a woman or not. "I tell ya what, Shadow. I love riding as much as the next Demon, but I am not about to sit my ass on that thing for three straight days again. Gotta save some of my future children, you feel me?"

He cupped his crotch with a lewd chuckle. I understood what he meant, but couldn't relate to the feeling. So I just nodded and drank some more.

Returning my gaze to the sunset, a dark speck against the dark oranges and yellows of the sky slowly grew bigger. After a few seconds passed, I could make out wings stretched to the sides.

"There's my boy," Gunner muttered.

Horus approached us quickly. Gunner mentioned before that peregrine falcons were the fastest predators on earth. After seeing the crow-sized bird dive-bomb some Razor Wire members, I had to agree.

"What the—"

Surprising both of us, Horus's outstretched talons grabbed the balcony railing right in front of me, instead of his master. The falcon's beak and talons smeared with bits of fur and blood from his kill, he began to preen himself as if nothing was amiss.

"I guess he likes you," Gunner chuckled, lighting another cigarette.

I found that hard to believe, even for an animal. Nobody liked me, except maybe Jandro. And even then, I often felt like he tolerated me more than truly *liked* me.

Still, the close-up view of the curved beak and dark feathers on Horus's head pulled up a memory in my mind. My heart began to pound like a drum. Oddly enough, it was one of my last memories of being able to feel pain, but was one of the few positive, if even miraculous, occurrences in my life.

It had been years since I thought of that day, but I remembered it clearly. Drawing my blood had not been enough. The women were particularly ornery that day. When kept in darkness for most of my existence, bright light was an especially painful experience, and she had been eager to exploit that.

The cut over my eye still hadn't finished healing. She peeled back my shredded eyelid and shone a flashlight directly into my eye. It might as well have been a knife blade directly through my eye socket to my brain. My entire world was nothing but pain and darkness, and right then I had never experienced such pain in my life.

After she was done, there was more darkness and not the usual kind. I was almost certainly blinded. Whenever the mood struck her again, she'd surely do the same to my other eye. I'd never screamed like that before, and while I had a decent understanding of my bleak circumstances, I knew with absolute certainty then, that no one would help me. No one would ever stop them.

My sunset view back then was a mere crack in the wall of the prison I called home. I saw how the sky changed color throughout the transition from day to night. Sometimes I thought I saw slivers of clouds, but I could never be sure. The crack was only about an inch wide at the most.

The day after the light torture, I tried to look at the outside world with my one remaining good eye. But a fucking bird blocked my view.

Its dark eyes blessed with binocular vision taunted me. Small chunks of raw meat clung to its sharp beak, reminding me that I hadn't eaten anything in two days. I cursed out that bird and tore at the crack in the wall with my already weakened, bloody hands. I must have looked insane, scratching at a wall and yelling at a bird to get the fuck out of the way. But it was blocking the only view of the world I had from this cold, cruel prison.

I'd never forget the way that bird looked at me, with the wisdom of humanity and so much more, through an animal's eyes. Never would I forget what happened afterward.

My vision didn't just return to my blinded eye, but I saw what I never could before. While my occasional cell mates fumbled in the darkness, I could see everything as if it were broad daylight. When my torturers came down with flashlights and had to blink to adjust to the darkness, I saw every movement and expression.

That bird gave me the first, and one of the most precious, gifts I had ever received in my miserable life. I saw colors and details like I never imagined before. It was the first and only time I cried.

And that bird looked exactly like the one that rode around on Gunner's shoulder all day.

"Go ahead. He might peck at you as a warning if he doesn't like it, but he won't hurt you."

While lost in my memory, my hand reached out to touch Horus without realizing it. I knew Gunner and his falcon had some kind of otherworldly bond, just as Hades and Reaper did. But was it really the same bird that healed and enhanced my vision? I wondered ever since I first saw Horus with his talons curled into Gunner's shoulder. But it never felt right to ask. And the falcon had never flown so close to me before.

I stroked the back of my fingers against Horus's chest feathers a few times. When I put my hand down, the bird pecked at me.

"He doesn't want you to stop!" Gunner laughed. "Damn, look at you two all chummy."

"I feel like I've met this bird before." I looked at the blonde, smiling man with an uneasy glance, trying to gauge his reaction. Gunner was my brother by the Steel Demon code, but we weren't particularly close.

"Yeah, when?" His tone was curious, which came to me as a relief.

"Years ago," I confessed. "Way before I joined the club. When I was a kid."

"Not possible," Gunner shook his head. "Horus is just about two years old. I found him as a chick."

"Ah, okay."

He continued to look at me curiously. "What makes you think it was Horus?"

My heart rate sped up by half a beat. Despite knowing he could see through Horus at will, the gift of sight from my childhood felt deeply personal. I wanted to keep that knowledge under lock and key. Some of the guys figured out I could see well in the dark, but no one paid it any special attention. And I intended to keep it that way. No one could take anything away from me if they didn't know about it.

"I just knew the bird I met was different," I said.

A brush-off and he knew it, but he didn't bother prying.

"Interesting." Gunner flicked away his second cigarette. "Maybe there's more like him out there, who knows?"

Another question nagged at me. I almost couldn't bring myself to ask it, but not knowing the answer would torture me if I didn't.

"Does Horus ever...talk to you?"

Gunner's brow pinched. "What do you mean?"

"Like you can hear a voice in your head. But it's not your thoughts. It's like another person is talking to you, directly into your mind."

He took a long moment to answer.

"No, Horus doesn't talk to me like that."

"Oh. I was just curious."

The bird in question blinked his large, brown eyes at me before hopping a short flight across the railing to perch on his human's shoulder.

Chapter 5

REAPER

"You're wearing that?"

"What?" Mari stared down at her clothes before looking back up at me. "Should I change?"

She had on a long skirt with some bright tribal pattern, black ankle boots, and a simple black tank top. It was the skirt that concerned me. Not for riding, but for me. She'd have to hike that thing up, spread her legs open and press her bare thighs against me as we rode. Just the thought of it sent my cock twitching.

The fabric wasn't too form-fitting. She'd be comfortable, but the garment still outlined her hip and thigh in a way that drove me wild with wanting her. I had her every morning and night since after the party when Gunner returned, and it still wasn't enough. Oh, I *thought* I was sated after her sweet body drained my balls empty. But after a few hours of sleep, just a look, a wandering touch, or a kiss had me craving to get inside her again.

I've wanted women, but not like this. I never continued to want them once they were well and truly mine.

"Just be careful," I told her, hitting the button to open the garage door. “Don’t want you burning those legs on hot metal.” I grabbed one of Noelle’s helmets off the shelf and handed it to her.

“Where’s your helmet?” she asked, securing the strap under her chin.

“Inside my head,” I smirked at her. “It’s called my skull.”

“Rory,” she whined. “Don’t play like that. I’ve seen what head injuries can do, and it’s not pretty.”

“Relax, sugar.” I approached my vintage Triumph Bonneville and stuck the key in the ignition. It wasn’t my favorite bike, but it was one of the best for carrying passengers comfortably. “To keep you safe, I need to be in top shape. Trust me,” I turned the key and the engine roared to life, “I know what I’m doing.”

Her eyes narrowed at me through the helmet visor, but she didn’t argue. “Where are we going?”

“You’ll see.”

“Kidnapping me again?” she teased, grabbing the edges of my cut.

“I’m glad you see my daring rescue of you as such a lighthearted joke now.” I leaned in and kissed the bridge of her nose, the one part of her face I could reach through the helmet. It felt like an eternity since I rode off from the Old Phoenix service center with a bound, frightened medic in tow.

Mari’s eyes darkened at my mention of her kidnapping-slash-rescue. “I hope the other girls back there are okay,” she mused softly. “Especially Gretchen.”

“The ones exploiting them are dead,” I reminded her. “Those girls can take that building, those supplies, and turn it into whatever they want. We warned other MCs of Tom’s untrustworthiness, so no one will be coming around there any time soon.”

She nodded, still looking off in thought when I shut the visor down over her eyes. “Hop on, sugar. It’s about an hour’s ride.”

I sat astride the bike and felt her climb on behind me. Sure enough, bare legs pressed against the back of my thighs. My pants grew uncomfortably tight at the thought of no barrier between me and her spread open center, except for her panties. Only God knew if I'd be able to hold off from pulling over and fucking her right on this seat before we reached our destination. Her hands sliding under my cut, caressing over my abs and chest through the thin material of my shirt, did nothing to help my resolve.

And we hadn't even left the garage yet. Fuck.

I wet my lips with my tongue and let out a loud, high pitched whistle. Hades howled a reply and immediately ran from where he waited on the front porch out to the street, heading straight for the gate.

"Hold on," I yelled to Mari over the engine as I hit the throttle.

She tightened around me at every point of contact—legs, arms, and chest against my back. How Jandro and Gunner were able to concentrate with her holding onto them like this, I had no fucking clue.

We peeled out of the garage like a bat out of hell, following after my dog running on all fours. The guard at the gate waved as we passed through, leaving behind the safety of our home into a world constantly at its own throat.

My body remained rigid even as we hit the open road at a comfortable cruising speed. Only Mari's hands smoothing over my chest again relaxed me a little. I couldn't let myself kick back completely, because I wasn't just taking her to any place.

Today, I was showing the woman I loved what I'd never shown anyone.

My past.

"OH MY GOD, REAPER!" MARI HOPPED OFF MY BIKE AND fiddled with the helmet before I even came to a complete stop. Normally I would've chewed her ass out for being unsafe, but her enthusiasm was so fucking cute, I could only smile.

"Ever been here before?" I asked, shutting off the engine.

"Never! Is this really...?"

"The Grand Canyon," I finished for her. "This lookout used to be called Yavapai Point."

I'd seen it hundreds of times. The vastness of the canyon stretching out like it went on forever, the stripes of color on the jagged rock formations, the sheer size of everything making you feel like an ant on an edge of the world. And it never ceased to amaze me.

While Mari remained entranced with the view, I got to setting up our picnic. A tree offered shade from the sun, so I spread the blanket underneath it. From the other saddlebags, I grabbed our other essentials —aged cheese, olives, grapes, homemade crusty bread, and a bottle of wine.

She turned around just as I spread everything out on the blanket and lowered to the ground. "What is this?" Her eyes widened at the sight of the containers.

"It's food." I popped an olive into my mouth. "And me."

"You mean this is you being romantic." She lowered onto the blanket next to me and leaned over to plant a kiss on my lips. "Thank you, handsome. I love this."

That was partially true. I wanted to show her I wasn't just a brute who liked fucking and violence. Warmth filled my chest as I returned her kiss, holding the back of her head to keep her there for more. I was happy she was pleased. I always wanted to show her the canyon, but I had to give Noelle credit for the picnic idea.

The other part however, was that I wanted to ease her in to what I was about to show her. The view wasn't going to be nearly as nice as this. For me it might be downright unsettling, as difficult as it was to admit that.

"I love you," I murmured, finally releasing her so she could nibble and drink. "I would have brought glasses, but didn't want to risk broken glass in the saddlebags," I explained as she took a pull of wine straight from the bottle.

"Oh no. How will we ever survive?" she chuckled before passing the bottle to me. "This is perfect, and I love you too."

Her kiss landed on my cheekbone as I took small sips. I didn't like to drink a ton while riding, less so with a passenger I actually gave a fuck about, so I drank just enough to take the edge off.

"Something on your mind?" Mari asked, laying down with her head in my lap once she had her fill of food. "You seem a little distracted."

"Python," I answered, stroking her long, silky hair. On top of everything else, that certainly was one of the things occupying my mind.

"What about him?"

I took a few moments to think before answering. "I've executed and tortured men before. It's nothing to me at this point. But I always knew they were the enemy from the start. It just felt right to feel them die by my hands, like the natural order of things. With him...I know it must be done, but it doesn't feel right."

"Because you trusted him before?"

"Yeah." I stroked my fingers along her neck and shoulders. "He rode by my side. Proudly got the demon tattooed on him. He swore his life and loyalty to me and the club. Shit, I was happy he started fucking Heather 'cause then she left me alone."

Dappled sunlight through the tree made shifting patterns of light and shadow on Mari's face. Once again, I was awed at how naturally beautiful she was compared to the trash I'd woken up next to before.

"Are you worried you won't be able to do it?" She ran her hands up my forearms.

"No, I will. I'm just not sure how I'll be affected afterward." My fingers curled around hers, feeling the small, fragile bones in her hands compared to my heavy mitts. "I've never killed someone I considered a friend before."

She lifted her head from my lap, scooting over my legs to lean her head on my shoulder.

"And you have to do this? You can't just banish him?"

"Our code is very clearly spelled out. It was drafted by me, Jandro, and Gunner. If I go against something I helped make into law, that would put the whole club in turmoil. My leadership would be questioned, and rightly so." I cupped the back of her neck as my lips brushed across her forehead. "I might as well hand over the club to General Tash at that point. A club that's not unified and doesn't trust its president is already dust in the wind."

Her arms went around my neck with a deep sigh. "You carry so much on your shoulders for these people, and I don't think they even know half of it."

"It's better that way," I assured her. "They deserve a relatively secure life. Not everyone can handle this shit. I can."

"Trauma and heavy mental loads affect even the strongest of men," Mari said. "Just look at Shadow."

"Funny you say that," I chuckled. "He'd be able to end Python quickly, without a second thought. But every time you say good morning to him, he looks like he's gonna shit his pants."

"He's getting better." She drummed her fingers on my neck. "But he can't do this for you, huh?"

"No. It has to be me."

Her hands pressed to my cheeks, making me face her. "You know I'm here for you, right?"

I looked at my woman, wrapping tighter around her. I knew she was, and I'd never let her go. She had too much of what little remained of my heart for me to do that.

"You don't have to be the Steel Demons president with me," she whispered, thumb tracing my jaw. "You can just be Rory. And I'll be here no matter what."

She leaned in to press kisses to my neck, each pass of those soft lips a loving, sweet promise. But were they promises she could keep?

My eyes lifted to look over her shoulder at the dog watching us with more wisdom that any animal should have. How would Mari react if she knew I was just the instrument? I didn't choose who I killed, but followed the orders of someone else.

I didn't hear them often but when I did, it was unmistakable. I heard the same words when I learned Tom had been abusing Mari's friend in Old Phoenix, and when Gunner dragged Python's ass to me. I didn't know if my goofy, protective dog was saying them. Even that seemed far-fetched to me. But I never heard voices in my head until I found Hades. And it was always a variation of the same sentence.

His life is yours to take.

Their lives are yours. Reap what has been sown.

Chapter 6

MARIPOSA

"Come on, sugar." Reaper patted the side of my hip. "I want to show you something."

"More surprises?" I was content to stay snuggled up against him on the picnic blanket, but he was practically shoving me off his lap.

"Yes, but unfortunately the view isn't as nice."

He corked the wine and gathered up the food containers while I shook out the blanket and folded it up carefully. Once everything was packed away, he grabbed my hand and led me wordlessly toward a barely-marked trail I didn't notice before.

"Watch your step," he murmured, pausing to wait for me as the trail became steep, like we were hiking down into the canyon itself.

I kept a firm hold on his hand as I carefully maneuvered my feet over rocks and areas of loose sand. My mind buzzed with questions, but I kept quiet. He was showing me something for a reason, and his own quiet demeanor today told me that seeing with my own eyes would explain better than words ever could.

The ground finally leveled out again as we came to a small valley. All around us, the striped ridges of the canyon decorated the horizon. I spun around in a slow circle, still awed by the view. Texas had nothing like this, and I never ventured outside of my home state until after I began my adventures as a medic.

"Are we *in* the canyon?" I asked, my breath still stolen.

"Sort of," Reaper answered. "Not at the very bottom or anything. That's still another ten-mile trek."

When I finally tore my eyes away from the breathtaking cliffs, I realized we appeared to be in some kind of campground. Broken-down RVs, pop-up campers, and every kind of travel trailer imaginable laid out alongside a wider path in organized rows. Further back, I could see cabins and what looked like more permanent structures.

"What is this place?" I took a few steps forward, the silence and stillness of everything but us gave me an unnerved chill.

Reaper took a few moments to answer, his footsteps following me on the dirt path between the trailers. "This is where I grew up."

I turned to look at him, stunned. "You *lived* here?"

He nodded in a way that was almost defiant. "Me, Noelle, Daren, our mom, dads, and about twenty others."

I continued walking through at a snail's pace, taking in every detail of the now-abandoned miniature ghost town. So this was the matriarchal community where women were in charge and had multiple male partners.

I noticed one area had three trailers arranged in a semicircle, like each family member had their own space. Near the door of the biggest RV, a large bin still had toy buckets and shovels for building sandcastles. Their once-bright colors of pinks, purples, and greens were now bleached out and faded by years of sun exposure.

In the middle of the three RVs, a central fire pit still had grey ashes in the circle of stones. The rusted out frame of a folding chair had been knocked over and was halfway buried in the sand.

"What happened?" The question tore out of me painfully. I didn't know if I'd be prepared for the answer. Children and families once lived here and from the looks of it, they all vanished.

"I wish I knew." The ache in my voice was nothing compared to the pain in his.

"Reaper." I turned to him, my arms reaching, but he was already there.

Strong arms pulled me close, enveloping me in security. I stood to the side so we could keep walking through together as his head bent low to tell me.

"I first moved out when I was seventeen," he began. "For the usual shit, you know? I was tired of being around my parents and neighbors all the time. I took Daren with me and we got a shitty place together with Jandro, who was also sick of being around his family all the time."

"No Noelle?" I asked with a tiny smile.

"Nah, we were tired of being bossed around by women. That was the whole point. She was kind of being set up to become the new head of our family here, anyway."

"Really? At what, sixteen?"

"Fifteen. Other communities like ours had been raided by rogue cops and military, so no one really knew what the future held. Anyway, Jandro, Daren, and I worked odd jobs to pay rent and buy weed, then rode motorcycles every free chance we got. We wanted to play at being adults, but had no idea what that really meant."

My hands wrapped tighter around the back of his neck, rubbing into the tight knots there as his body tensed.

"My brother, Daren, he—" His voice cut off abruptly as he cleared his throat.

"Your brother that passed away?"

"Yeah, he...saw things, sometimes." Reaper's brow furrowed as he looked at me, as if gauging my reaction. "He had bad seizures as a kid, and had like, visions."

"Visions?" I repeated. "You mean, like he saw the future?"

"Yeah, but it was weird. He would have dreams of random, mundane shit. Like one day I blew out both tires in my bike and had to wait three hours for Jandro to pick me up in his uncle's truck. Before it happened, Daren told me I'd taste a clove cigarette for the first time that day. It was because Jandro's uncle had a pack of cloves in his glove box."

The explanation tumbled out of him, rushed and unfiltered. I could tell he hardly believed it himself, but was just explaining it as best as he knew how. He didn't understand his brother's ability any more than the fast healing and endurance of his dog. It was just a part of his life.

"Anyway," Reaper scrubbed a hand down his face. "Daren told me one day that I had to come back here and get Mom's stuff. That was all he told me. But he kept repeating it over and over, like it was really important, like I had to do *right then*. I kept trying to blow it off like, 'Okay, I'll go this weekend.' And he told me, 'No, now.'" I asked if they were moving or if anything was wrong, and he kept saying, 'I don't know, but you need to get her stuff right now.'"

His fingers curled into my waist, making a fist as he grabbed the fabric of my top. I pressed a hand to his chest and felt his heart racing underneath my palm.

"When I got here," he went on, "the place looked pretty much like this." He gestured to the scene before us. "Completely empty. Everyone was gone and left everything behind. I went home," he nodded up ahead to one of the cabins, "and found Mom's journal, her clothes, and a few pieces of jewelry she made but hadn't sold yet." The silence in his pause permeated deeply, wrapping around us like a cage. "A box of her things are all I have left of her."

Now my fingers curled into his cut, clinging to him as I willed myself not to cry.

"She could still be alive," I whispered. "Maybe they got word early that a raid was coming."

"No," he shook his head. "Everyone would have packed their belongings if they got word ahead of time. Trust me, sugar. I've considered all the possibilities."

"What about your dads?"

"One died when I was fourteen. Another was drafted to fight at the border. The other had to have been with her." He licked his lips and sighed. "I can't imagine him ever leaving her side."

“I’m sorry.” The words sounded so hollow but I didn’t know what else to say.

“What I think most likely happened was,” he went on, “they stormed the place, but didn’t kill anyone. From the looks of it, everyone went willingly, probably fearing for their lives. Once they rounded everyone up, people got sorted according to their skill. Men probably drafted into the military. Women sold to be used. Kids sent to camps to be further indoctrinated.”

“What about Noelle?”

Reaper smiled for the first time since stepping foot in his former home. “That crafty bitch,” he chuckled. “She hid. Mom had dug out a cellar in the floor of the cabin and Noelle stayed down there, dead quiet for two straight days. She didn’t even say a word when I came poking through until I went down there myself. Then she fought me, nearly scratched my fucking eyes out, ’til she realized who I was.”

“Oh my God.” I brought a hand to my mouth. “That must have been awful for her.”

“What she told me adds to my theory,” he said. “She heard voices threatening to shoot, but no actual gunshots or sounds of struggle. Then footsteps walking away, and then nothing.”

“It’s weird that no one would come back here and loot,” I observed.

“We were a bit hidden and tricky to get to, despite being so close to a tourist spot,” he nodded up the hill to the lookout point where we had our picnic. “But people also thought we were a witch’s coven, so that might have had something to do with it.”

“Witches?” I repeated. “Why, because this place was run by women?”

“Exactly,” Reaper nodded. “There could be no other explanation for women running an independent community, completely self-sufficient and off the grid.”

“I bet that was why they were attacked so often,” I mused sadly. “The people in charge are always afraid of what they can’t control.”

“Correct again.” He loosened his hold on me to resume walking through the central path. “Looking back, I’m honestly surprised they lasted as long as they did. I think ours was among those who hung on the longest. It was about five years before the Collapse."

"I'm so sorry," I repeated, hating that there was nothing else I could say or do. Healing was my specialty, but I couldn't do anything to alleviate the guilt he must have felt, the helplessness of not knowing what happened to his family.

"This was why I started the Steel Demons." Reaper kneeled to pick up something half-buried in the dirt. When he stood again, I saw it was a small toy motorcycle. "So the community I called home wouldn't be left undefended."

The toy was only a few inches long, cast from metal and encrusted with dirt. I touched it as he held it out for me to see, and the wheels still spun freely.

"Your mom would be proud of you, I'm sure."

"I looked at the cover of her journal every day for about a year." Reaper ran the tiny motorcycle across his palm before setting it back down on the ground. "But I could never bring myself to open it and read what was inside. I still can't."

I slid my arm through his, wrapping my hand around his bicep. "At least you kept it with you. Maybe one day you will."

He looked at me, green eyes dark. "You wanted to know about me, how I grew up. I've never brought anyone here. So," he tilted his head to indicate our surroundings, "what do you think?"

My head rested on his shoulder as I wrapped tighter around his upper arm. "I think your past made you the best MC president this world has ever seen. It made you strong enough to be ruthless when necessary, but you care enough to protect those that need it most." A smile pulled at my lips. "Thank you for showing me this. It even makes me love you a little more."

He mirrored my smile and leaned down to place a very un-Reaper-like soft kiss on my lips. "My parents would have adored you. They'd be trying to convince you to have a harem of ten guys."

"Yeah, right," I laughed. "Who knows?" I added, with a kiss to his shoulder. "I might still be able to meet them one day."

Reaper sighed and gave a slight shake of his head, but still humored me with a smile. “You might be right, sugar. In times like these, who knows what’ll happen.”

Chapter 7
MARIPOSA

We continued walking around the abandoned settlement for the rest of the afternoon. Reaper told me stories of his neighbors and childhood friends. However, we never went inside any of the homes, and kept a respectful distance away from the personal belongings that remained. Hades gave some things a curious sniff or two, but otherwise stayed near us and left things alone. It felt like we were visiting a cemetery, and had come to pay our respects.

I was moved that he brought me here, and felt like I got a glimpse into a part of him he kept locked away inside. The more I got to know Reaper, the more I saw how big his heart was. He just kept it protected, wrapped in steel.

The mood shifted throughout the day, from our flirty, sensual ride, to the lighthearted picnic, to the dark melancholy of uncovering his past. And he remained calm and even-tempered throughout it all. It made me realize the volatile temper was part of his armor to keep people out. Now that he had let me in, I found the calm within the storm.

We hiked back up to the picnic spot a few hours before dark. We'd have one hell of a sunset view on the ride home and I couldn't wait to take it all in, flying across the landscape while wrapped around my man.

"Hold on there, sugar." Reaper stopped me with a wily smirk before I could put my helmet on. "Hop in the driver's seat for me, but face backwards."

"What?" I stared at him.

"Just do it." His smile grew. "For me."

I straddled the bike, my back toward the handlebars. He climbed on facing me, and my pulse spiked when his fingers skimmed up my calf where my skirt hiked up.

"Scoot toward me." His voice took on a low, husky tone. "Come closer."

I did as he instructed, my eyes glued to his heated gaze as my legs went wider to drape over his thighs. My skirt crept up inch by inch as I moved toward him.

His touch ventured under the fabric, still lightly caressing me as his fingertips moved up my thighs.

"I swear you wore this to torture me," he said with a soft growl. "To see how long I would last without touching you like this."

My tongue darted out to wet my parched lips. All the moisture in my body seemed to surge to one place, mere inches away from his hands.

"I might have picked it with the idea that we might want to be...discreet."

He leaned forward, eyes already dilated and hooded with desire. "Is that so?" He sounded pleased as his forehead rested on mine. "My sweet little medic had some naughty ideas of what we'd be doing on our outing?"

"I didn't think it'd be happening on your bike," I admitted, leaning up for a taste of that mouth hovering over mine.

"Mmm." He kissed me in a rough claiming of teeth and tongue, his usual style that never failed to leave me breathless. "I've never been inside a woman on my bike before."

His hands continued to venture under my skirt, kneading my thighs in a possessive grip as they moved closer to my center. I dipped my head back, letting his kisses trail over my neck and jaw as my body continued scooting toward him in its eagerness. With my knees glued to the sides of his hips, he was moments away from finding out what else I'd been thinking when I picked the skirt.

When his touch reached my pelvis and felt bare flesh, he inhaled sharply and I physically saw his cock swell in his jeans.

"No panties?" His expression morphed as he stared at me. "You've been without panties all day?"

"They get in the way of things," I shrugged. "It would've been pointless to wear a skirt if I still wore something I had to take off."

"Oh, I'm sure I would've managed, but *fuck.*" His thumb stroked through my lips, eliciting a grin at my wetness as he circled that digit all around my sensitive, aching vulva. "You're fucking dirty, sugar, and I love it."

"Show me how much you love it," I moaned, reaching for the bulge in his pants.

He gave me another deep kiss as I unzipped him, supporting my back gently with one hand as I reclined on the bike. As I stroked him from root to tip, he shoved all the fabric of my skirt up to my waist, baring me to the world of only us.

"Look at you, getting my seat all wet," he groaned, returning his hand to my drenched core. "I'm never washing this bike again."

"Don't tell me that." I licked my hand and squeezed my palm around him again, rendering him speechless enough with wordless moans.

When he leaned down to kiss me again, both arms stretched above me. The next thing I heard was a deafening roar, and then felt the rumbling of the bike's engine beneath me.

"Reaper, what are you—"

"Did you like the ride over here?" he asked in my ear, nudging his cock against my thigh. "Feeling the whole bike vibrating under your bare pussy?"

"Yes," I breathed, sliding my hand under his shirt and up his taut chest hovering above me. "But I loved holding onto you more."

"You wanna know something?" He pulled back to look at me, and those green eyes shone with a new kind of mischief. "I've never ridden a bike and a woman at the same time."

My eyes widened and I immediately pulled my hands away. "Reaper, no."

"It'll be fine. I'll go slow." He reached up for one of the grips. "On the bike, not on you."

"What if I fall?"

"I won't let you. Just hold onto me with your legs. Please?" He looked like a child begging to do a flip off of a high diving board. "We can try it for this straight stretch of road. I promise I'll go super slow."

"I don't know—"

He kissed me sweetly, nuzzling my face. "I won't let anything happen to you. I just want to know what it feels like."

I sighed, leaning my head back to look at the sky above us both. "Why am I actually entertaining this crazy fucking idea?"

"Because you know it'll be fun." His hips rolled forward, the head of his cock caressing my clit as he kissed my neck. "Because you trust me."

I did trust him. Only weeks ago I questioned everything about him. I couldn't believe that a man like him was capable of caring for me, of loving me. It never occurred to me that wanting to share me was an expression of that care, but now it made total sense. Over the past few days, all those questions dissipated like evaporating puddles in the sun. I still didn't understand some things, but I found myself happier since admitting I was completely in love with the Steel Demons president.

"Slow," I contended. "Like a grandma using a walker slow."

"Mmm." His mouth moved to my chest, pulling my top and bra aside to reach my nipples with that devilish tongue. "We'll start without riding first. Then add it in. Slow."

"Very slow," I repeated, letting my eyelids fall closed at his hands and mouth doing what they did best.

"I love you," he moaned deliriously when his mouth found his way to mine again. "You let me be who I am. I love you so much for that."

"I love who you are—ohh!"

He slid into me in one deep stroke, swallowing my cry as his tongue dominated mine. His legs adjusted under mine, assumedly to set his feet on the footrests, and my legs wrapped tighter around his hips. We built into a steady rhythm, rocking into each other like our bodies were made for this connection.

"Comfortable, sugar?" He crashed into me solidly with each thrust, arms stretched out on either side of me on the grips.

My legs around his waist and my fingers curled into the worn leather of his cut, I was about as steady as I was going to be.

"I'm good," I breathed, trying not to squirm on the narrow seat as he fucked me.

"Here we go," he grunted, pausing while sheathed fully inside me to begin a gentle acceleration forward.

"That's good, that's good! No faster!" I pleaded, the sensation of forward movement already making me regret agreeing to this.

"No? How about harder?"

He resumed his thrusts, putting more force into his hips as his eyes kept looking straight forward at the road in front of us. His jaw tightened. He sucked his lower lip into his mouth. He wanted so badly to look at me.

And he looked so fucking hot, pounding into me while the muscles in his arms flexed and the landscape moved past us. I thought I'd be too scared and distracted to actually enjoy this, but holy hell, I did. The angle of him crashing into me sent my clit buzzing at each impact. He penetrated me deeply, knowing how much I loved to be filled by him and not skimping on any thrust.

His eyes still glued to the road, he brought one hand down to hold my hip. His palm added an anchor of stability to my position on the bike, while his thumb reached over to tease my clit.

"Put your hand back," I yelled over the engine.

"I'm good, sugar," he bellowed in return, grinning at me like a madman. "She's steady. You're steady. There's just one thing missing."

He pressed harder with his thumb, closing in on that bundle of nerves already sparking with tension like a live wire. Then he upped the ante by leaning down and sucking my nipple into his mouth.

"Stop that!" I cried. "Eyes on the road!"

He laughed wildly as he sat back up. "Goddamn, I'm in fucking heaven."

"How fast are we going?" I only then noticed how the landscape whipped past us, when earlier I was sure we were going slow enough to take in every detail.

"Don't worry about it," he smirked with a shift of his hips that lifted us both from the seat.

I whimpered and clutched desperately at him with the sudden change of movement, knowing the road running just a few feet below me would skin me alive.

"It's all right, I've got you." His eyes flicked down to me for a moment of warm reassurance. "I won't let you fall."

"How much longer do you want to do this?"

That grin filled with maniacal glee returned. "Until you come."

"That's not gonna happen! I'm too fucking scared."

"And I'm telling you not to be scared. You love riding. You love it when I'm inside you. So just combine the two of them in your mind."

"Easy for you to fucking say," I groaned, leaning my head back in defeat.

Looking straight up at the sky felt way too much like I was in freefall. And leaning my head to either side, watching the world zip by at speeds unknown freaked me out too much. So I looked at Reaper, calm and in control. The fucking daredevil would probably embrace death from a fiery crash, his dick still lodged inside of someone.

He was fascinating to watch, his hips rolling as he slid in and out of me. His left hand occasionally resting on me when it wasn't on the grip. The pressure of his palm on my hip intensified the vibrating of the motorcycle throughout my whole body. As minutes passed and we continued to be alive, I was able to feel less afraid and really feel the sensations coursing through me. From him. From the machine carrying us. And from the thrill of the ride.

"That's it, sugar," he rasped, sliding a free hand under my askew top to cup my breast. "I can feel you getting wetter. Just enjoy this for how good it feels."

The wind steadily grew colder, erecting goosebumps on my skin and turning my nipples into tight, aching buds. But his hands were so warm, soothing the bite of the cold, as they moved over me. I didn't even protest when he leaned down again to caress my other nipple with his tongue.

We took a few winding turns that required both his hands to steer, while he pressed into me with a new depth and fullness. A gasp stole my breath as my fingers dug into his muscular thighs. The force of gravity molded us into a single three-part unit—me, him, and the motorcycle.

"Reaper," I whimpered, each lean of the bike through the turns setting off a new mini-explosion within me. "I'm gonna..."

"God, yes, I can feel you," he growled back, jaw tight and his eyes staring straight ahead. "I always want to see your face when you come, but I'm not tryin' to run us off the road."

The crashing of him against me grew desperate, hurried. He barely left me at all before he filled me up again and again, until I overflowed with a crash of my own.

"Jesus, fuck!" The motorcycle wobbled for one tiny, heart-stopping second.

He quickly regained control, but barely. My orgasm closed hard around his thick shaft, pulling him in deeper and holding on almost as tightly as my hands and legs did. The shockwaves continued to roll over me, so much that I didn't realize the bike had slowed down until we nearly stopped.

"What are we..."

Reaper hauled me up, still fully sheathed inside me as he kissed me roughly. His arms clasped around my back, holding my chest to his as he swung a leg over the bike to dismount. As he stood, he shifted his grip to under my thighs and bounced me once on his cock. I moaned a whimper into his mouth as I wrapped my arms and shaky legs around him like a tree.

"Grab the blanket," he growled against my lips. "In the saddle bag."

"Mmph..." I leaned toward the bike, reaching with one arm and fumbled with the buckle for all of about five seconds.

"Nevermind. Fuck the blanket." He turned us away from the bike and looked over my shoulder. "There's some grass here. It looks soft enough."

In the next moment my back was laid gently onto solid ground, and the only movement came from the man hovering above me. Our bodies never disconnected once as he laid me down, then draped over me to kiss me deeply.

He shoved my top and bra up to my neck to maul the sensitive flesh of my breasts with both hands. I yanked his shirt up to the top of his chest because I was desperate to feel his skin on mine. The ride had been terrifying, exhilarating, and hot as hell, but it didn't give me a chance to touch him like I wanted to.

Our skin, cooled by the early evening air quickly heated up as our bodies seared together. He fucked me with his whole body, groaning like a beast mad with lust as he slid into me and against me.

Another orgasm began building deep within my core, still feeding off the thrill of the first one. From his ragged breathing, the wild, frenzied way he touched me, and how incredibly rigid he felt inside me, I knew he was close too.

"Come with me," I breathed against his ear. "Fill me up, you fucking daredevil."

His moan was animalistic, fingers curling into a fist at the base of my skull. The pull of hair on my scalp intensified the electric jolts shooting through my clit.

"Mariposa," he rasped, his voice tight as he swelled within me. "You fucking ruined me. I'm yours—"

His words choked off as his warmth spilled, flexing hard inside me as he took me over the edge with him. Our pleasure fed off of each other in an endless feedback loop, shooting off through the atmosphere before we returned on a gentle descent down to earth.

"Can I tell you something?" he murmured softly over our matched, thundering pulses.

“Always.” I slid my hands up his abs and chest to cup the sides of his neck.

“It’s weird, but,” he paused, turning his head to kiss my palm, “I think this was the best day of my life.”

I tried to think of some sarcastic remark about him almost killing us both on his bike, but no words broke through this heady, elated feeling. And I couldn’t bring him down with how blissed out, sexy, and sated he looked.

“I think it was mine, too.”

CHAPTER 8

JANDRO

"Fuck!" I spat, throwing the ill-fitting spark plugs on the concrete floor. *"Que chingon estes..."*

Naturally, all of the Razor Wire bikes we acquired after the ambush fit different-sized plugs than what the majority of our bikes had. And Gunner just told me the fantastic news that none of his current suppliers had the right ones. Just fucking great. I could tweak some things here and there, but it was just more work that I wasn't expecting to do.

In nearly the past whole week, I spent every waking hour in the shop. The last two nights I didn't even go home, opting to shower and crash here instead. We gutted most of the duplex to make room for all the bike shit, but kept the kitchen, a full bathroom, and one room that functioned as my office, or crash pad, depending on what I needed.

I slept on a futon against the wall. Other than that, the only pieces of furniture in there was a desk and a bookshelf filled with old manuals and random motorcycle books. Crashing here wasn't nearly as inviting as my house, but the lack of comforts didn't bother me. After spending so many nights on the road, sleeping under the stars and in all kinds of sketchy lodgings, crashing where I landed was second nature to me.

Besides, Shadow probably appreciated the alone time at home. Although, for being such a loner, he did seem to appreciate my company as a roommate. He was perfectly capable of living in his own place and had plenty of empty houses to choose from. But whenever I brought it up, he said he was fine to stay as long as I was okay with him being there. Sure, I might've picked living with a beautiful woman over a hulking giant of a man, but I was more than fine sharing a large house with someone else. He promised to feed my chickens, and while he'd never admit it, I had a feeling Shadow enjoyed having animals.

Right then, I would have happily been covered in chicken shit or dealt with another one of Shadow's nightmares than look at another fucking spark plug. Bikes were my passion, but after several days of little sleep or food, I was reaching my fucking limit.

"Piece of pig shit," I grumbled, rising to my feet.

My foot swung forward and kicked the tailpipe of the gutted Razor Wire bike. I was frustrated, exhausted, and not thinking straight. To add insult to injury, the metal dented cleanly where my foot connected. I barked out a defeated laugh. I wasn't even wearing steel toes! These bikes were so shitty and low quality, they weren't even worth parting out. Few things pissed me off more than a so-called MC that took no pride in their steeds and just bought the cheapest shit.

"What did that bike ever do to you?"

I turned in the direction of the playful, feminine voice. Mariposa looked like a mirage standing under the open garage door, an illusion of something too good to be true. Her dark hair was up in a loose bun and her lavender medic scrubs were on, indicating she'd just been working, or was heading that way.

"It existed," I answered her. "That's what it did to me. This piece of shit is a personal insult to any good mechanic."

A smile lit up her face as she adjusted the canvas bag on her shoulder. "Well I'm sure it's sorry after that kick."

A chuckle escaped me as I strode toward her. Not many women, or people in general for that matter, entertained my sense of humor. It felt like something unique and special between us and no one else.

Her eyes heated, lips parting just slightly when I stopped in front of her. A rush of need went straight to my dick and it was all I could do to not grab her and pull her into me.

Keeping my hands at my sides, knowing I was covered in filth and grime, I leaned down and smacked a peck to those pouty lips instead.

"You heading to work or leaving?" I asked her.

"Both." She laughed at my bewildered face. "I have a couple hours free before I check on Tess and Python this afternoon. Thought you might like some lunch." She patted the bag at her side. "Have you eaten today?"

It took me a few long seconds to answer. First, I had to come down from the high of realizing she came to see me, because she *wanted* to. She thought of me and brought me food because she was concerned about me.

It was such a simple gesture for a basic biological need, and yet I couldn't begin to express how much it meant to me. So many women thought they had to jump through hoops to impress a man—wearing tons of makeup, staying thin while having gigantic tits, sucking dick like a porn star, but *this* was all I ever wanted. Someone sweet and thoughtful enough to take care of me.

"That depends," I said skeptically. "Are you having lunch with me?"

"I will if I'm not getting in the way of your work."

"Oh, you are. And I'm so grateful for it, you have no idea." I kissed her again, longer this time, like she was the appetizer I was savoring before the main course. My fists curled at my sides, fighting the urge to touch more of her. "Come in. We can eat in the kitchen." Her lips were flushed and swollen as I reluctantly pulled away. "Give me a minute to wash up."

When I returned from the restroom with clean hands, Mari's simple lunch spread out on the table looked like a feast for a king to my half-starved body.

Rice, beans, salsa, grilled onions and bell peppers, and strips of well-done steak were arranged neatly in their own containers. The only things missing were tortillas, which Mari heated on the cast-iron griddle in the wood-pellet stove.

"Damn, we still got steaks, huh?" My mouth watered as I took a seat.

"We're down to the last pallet according to the clubhouse kitchen." Mari dropped a stack of freshly warmed tortillas on the table. "These were cooked a bit too long the other day at the party. So they said I could have the leftovers, and I sliced 'em thin, *carne asada* style. A bit tough but they're edible."

"I love a resourceful woman," I said, piling fajita fixings into a tortilla, then immediately bit my tongue.

It was way too soon to be throwing the L-word around. Mari was still figuring out how to be with two men, for shit's sake.

She took no apparent notice of the word I used and smiled sweetly, the apples of her cheeks flushing with color. "I just wanted to make sure you were eating enough. I know you've been putting long hours in here."

"And I feel every single one of them," I sighed, scrubbing a hand down my face. "But bikes are no good to a crew if they're unrideable."

"Not everyone has extras, I take it?" She took a delicate bite out of her own fajita.

"Nah. Reaper has a few. I got one spare and I think Gunner does too. But most of the guys only have the one ride. It's just hard to find good parts. Everything's been scrapped and scavenged."

"And you have an eye for quality, I assume?"

"I do," I said with a nod, appreciating that she seemed to take interest in my passion. At least enough to have a conversation about it. "Quality parts make all the difference, especially in the desert. With all the sand, wind, and changes in elevation, you need machinery you can rely on."

"I feel the same way about medical supplies." Mari paused in her eating, resting her chin on her hand. "Cheaply-made scalpels pose a higher risk of infection for the patient. Good quality materials help me do my job better."

"You'll hear no argument from me." I helped myself to a second tortilla. "So I saw you and Reap ride back in last night. Where did you two go off to?"

The pale pink in her cheeks immediately deepened to a bright red, the color spreading to her neck and the rest of her face.

"Um, we had a picnic at a lookout point at the Grand Canyon. Then he showed me where he grew up."

"That sounds nice. Well the picnic does, at least. I bet it was tough to see the ruins of his old home."

"It was. But it was good too, I think." She swallowed. "I think it was kind of like closure for him. And it seemed to mean a lot that he took me there and told me what happened."

"Yeah, that's huge. I don't think he's been back there since the last time, when Daren told him to get his mom's things." As I responded, Mari stared intently at the table, avoiding my eye. "What's wrong, *Mariposita?* You look uncomfortable all of a sudden."

"Is this weird?" She returned my gaze hesitantly. "Talking to you about what I did with him?"

"Why would it be weird?"

"Because I'm used to being with one guy at a time. A guy I'm seeing wouldn't normally be thrilled to hear about my date with someone else."

"Nothing about our situation is normal."

"I know, I just," she sighed, "I don't want to upset either of you. I care about you both and I don't want to like, rub in your face that I spent all day with him."

"Hey, you're not upsetting me." I leaned forward and grabbed her slender fingers. "And I asked the question, so of course I don't mind hearing the answer. Now, I'm not gonna ask about all the ways he fucked you yesterday because yeah, I might get a little jealous of that." Her eyes widened slightly and her neck flushed even redder. Damn, he must have turned her inside out.

"Only because I wasn't there to join in on the fun," I added with a smirk. "But don't forget, I care about Reaper too. He's the brother I never had. You're making him happy. And a happy president means less bullshit for the VP to deal with."

Her fingers curled around mine as she humored me with a giggle. "I suppose that's true."

"It is. And hey." I nudged my foot around the back of her chair leg to pull her closer. Lowering our clasped hands to her lap, I hovered my lips over her ear. "You have no idea what coming here with food means to me. Not saying you should be slaving in a kitchen all the time, but it's little things like this that make me feel cared for. So thank you, *Mariposita*. You're rocking this two-men thing."

I kissed the shell of her ear, dragging my lips down to the quickening pulse in her neck. Our hands untangled as if they had minds of their own. Mine nestled into the luscious curves of her waist while hers wrapped around my shoulders.

"You deserve it," she breathed, her voice warm against my cheek. "You take care of everyone here. Especially Shadow, Reaper, me... someone ought to take care of you too."

An involuntary groan of longing rose in my chest. She had no idea at all how perfect she was for me. This woman understood me, from my sense of humor and appreciation of fine machinery to the deepest, basic needs of a full belly and a cozy home—which was right here at this shitty table pulled from a dumpster. *She* was my home.

I did not fall in love easily. I could flirt and charm the panties off of any woman in my sleep, but that was a game. It was meaningless. This was real, and I was free falling into the Grand Canyon itself.

"Come home with me tonight." It was all I could do to not sound like I was begging. "I'll be done for the day in about four hours. Meet me back here after you see Tessa and everything else you gotta do."

"Jandro, I—"

"I'll make you dinner for bringing me lunch. We can just watch old TV shows, hang out with the chickens, and not do anything else. Shadow will be there, but he won't bother us. I'll walk you back to Reaper's if you're not up for spending the night. I don't care what we do, I just want to spend more time with you, Mari."

"Okay!" she laughed, planting a kiss on me like she was trying to shut me up. "I was about to tell you I'd love to, silly, if you'd let me get a word in."

"Oh." I grinned sheepishly, our smiles touching in a not-quite kiss. "I was expecting more resistance, but all right!"

"Yeah?" she challenged playfully. "I figured you knew exactly how irresistible you are."

"I do know, but a certain type of girl, called a Mariposa, has a knack for holding out on me."

She chuckled, but her smile was more cautious this time. "I guess I'll just have to let Reaper know where I'll be."

"You do that." I reluctantly pulled away from her, sliding my palms down her thighs. "And if he gives you shit for it, let him know I'm coming for him at Fight Night."

"Ugh, that again," she groaned, dropping her forehead into her palm. "I almost forgot."

"Yes, that again." I smacked a kiss on her cheek before standing to clear the table. "At the end of the day, we're just animals after all."

Chapter 9

MARIPOSA

My feet touched the ground, but it felt like I was floating on air after leaving Jandro's shop. I was really doing this—seeing two men. And feeling intense, vastly different things for both of them.

Even so, this floaty feeling, the smile I couldn't erase, and the fluttering in my stomach, it was all familiar. Every person felt this at some point in their lives, when someone stood out as special to them. My brain and body were processing all the chemical reactions of an intense crush.

And the crazy part was, I couldn't tell if it was over Reaper, or Jandro.

I still felt the physical, sweet ache of the green-eyed president on top of me, inside of me, and all over me. Yesterday consisted of the most thrilling, scariest sex I ever had, but the day was so much more than that. He took me to a painful place, trusting me, and himself, enough to open up and share a side of him that few others knew.

Everything seemed to change between us since then for the better, like we reached a new appreciation and understanding of each other. He couldn't keep his hands off me when we got home, and not for more sex. But from the door to the shower to the bed, those rough hands maintained some form of contact on me and he never stopped kissing me. Only this morning did we peel apart reluctantly to attend our separate duties.

Reaper was a deeply emotional man, but a man of actions more than words. On some level I knew every caress and kiss after that trip was a silent thank-you. A wordless whisper of appreciation for accepting him, loving him, despite what he perceived as flaws.

And every time I touched him and kissed him back, I hoped he understood that I didn't see his past as flawed. The fact that he missed his family, that he wasn't there in time to save them and it ate him up with guilt—it all just made him human. And seeing that side of him made me love him even more.

Jandro, on the other hand.

He talked endlessly compared to Reaper and still, I felt like I barely knew him. I couldn't always tell what was his flirty banter and what was the real him. Today, I was certain I got a glimpse of the real Jandro. But what would tonight at his house bring? A smooth-talking man trying to charm me into his bed or a deeper look at who he really was?

Rather than wrapping his heart in steel, he seemed to hide behind jokes, banter, and charm. The life of the party and a mind for mechanics. But the way he advised Reaper and helped Shadow was anything but attention-seeking. Helping others came so naturally to him, his most selfless actions seemed to slip by without notice.

Not to me, though.

I noticed. And I knew what it felt like, giving so much of yourself to help someone without a word of gratitude or appreciation. Jandro wouldn't be taken for granted, not by me.

My floating feet carried me to the clubhouse, stopping first at my medic office for some IV bags before heading down the hall to where Python was being kept. Dallas saw me coming from the far end.

"I take it you're having a good day," he teased me gently.

I laughed lightly, looking down at my feet. Not even tending to the prisoner could put me back into a work-mode mindset after the lunch I just had with Jandro. I was excited to see his house and spend more time with him.

"I am, Dallas. How's your day?"

"Oh, can't complain. Counting down the minutes until Drea's done schooling the kids so we can ride around on the mini-bikes I made them." He turned to unlock Python's cell door as he spoke.

"That sounds like fun."

"Sure is! My daughter's popping wheelies already. Scares me half to death, but I'm still proud as fuck."

I grinned at the mental image. Dallas seemed like such a sweet family man under the beard, the tattoos, and the leather cut. Andrea was lucky to have him. A passing thought of what kind of father Reaper or Jandro would be made my chest flutter.

Dallas opened the door to the quarantine room and stepped aside to let me through. I should have been more aware as I walked in, but I was looking down, fiddling with the IV bag when two hands grabbed my shoulders in a painful grip.

"Mariposa!" Python rasped, his rank breath in my face.

He startled me so badly, I dropped the bags and froze up. Thankfully, Dallas was right there.

"What the fuck d'you think you're doing?!" the gentle family man bellowed as he shoved Python away from me. "You don't put your hands on *anyone* coming in here, much less a woman!"

Still weak from his wounds and bare minimum care, the prisoner stumbled backward across the small room until he hit the frame of his bed. Dallas turned to me, concern and anger in his large blue eyes.

"You okay, Mari?"

"Yeah, thank you." I picked up the IV bag with a shaky hand. "I just wasn't expecting that."

He turned back to Python with a growl. "You have no right to be touching her and getting up in her face, shitbag. You bet your sorry ass the president is going to hear about this." He crossed his broad, tattooed forearms and widened his feet. "I'm not leaving you alone with him, Mari."

"Look, I'm sorry," Python groaned, moving to sit painstakingly back in his bed. "I didn't mean to scare you, just wanted to grab your attention before you stuck me and left."

"What for?" Dallas demanded. "You don't need to grab her attention for shit!"

"I have a...medical issue." Python's sunken eyes darted at me. "And I'd like to talk to the medic about it in private."

"Absolutely not!"

"He does have a right to privacy," I said, looking at Dallas. "Regarding medical information."

"Mari, I am not leaving this room. Least of all because Reaper would kill me if I left you in danger."

"I'll stay right here. I won't touch her again, Jesus fuck." Python laid back against his pillows, arms flopped defeatedly down to his sides. "I just have questions about...issues I'm having."

I placed a hand on Dallas's forearm and looked up at the big, protective man's frown. "Don't worry about me. Maybe keep the door cracked and just stay on the other side? If you hear anything except for normal conversation, come back in."

"This is not a good idea, Mari." His eyes shifted over to Python. "That sneaky fucker's up to something. He'll do whatever he can to escape Reaper's punishment."

"So watch us through the crack in the door, but I'll be talking quietly to keep the conversation private." I gave a gentle squeeze of his arm. "He might be scum, but he does have a right to medical knowledge about his own body. And that information is only his to share, if he so chooses."

Dallas sighed heavily, stroking his beard. "The door stays open. I'm not taking eyes off either of you, but I'll stay far enough to not hear the conversation. Deal?"

"That's fine. Thank you."

"If he so much as breathes at you in a way I don't like, I'm coming back in."

"Works for me."

Sucking in a deep breath to steady the shaking of my hands, I approached Python's bedside and set to switching out his IV bags.

"Okay, so what do you need?"

"Come closer," he whispered, leaning over to look at Dallas watching us from the doorway.

"No. He can't hear us, so just ask me what you need to know." Python flinched as I took his arm and and re-stuck the IV syringe where he had ripped it out. "Better start talking before I leave."

"Okay look. I just said that shit to make him go away." He covered his mouth as he spoke. "But I figured out a way to get out of here and take you with me. You'll have to steal a bike for me, though. Can you ride?"

"Are you fucking kidding me?" I raised my voice so Dallas would definitely hear.

"Shush!" Python hissed. "Look, you don't have to be my chick or nothing, but you're a prisoner here too. You can be free!"

"You're delusional." Finished with him, I stepped away and crossed my arms. Footsteps behind me indicated Dallas had re-entered the room, which helped me feel a little braver. "I was being nice the first time you tried talking me into escaping, when I said I wouldn't tell Reaper. Now? I'm all out of reasons to be nice. You have no one to blame but yourself for what happens."

"Please!" He was shamelessly begging now, tears rolling down his face. "You've got to get me out! He's going to feed my balls to his fucking dog!"

I turned to the door, Dallas following after me.

"I hope Hades finds them delicious."

The confrontation with Python had me so on edge, I blinked in confusion upon stepping back in my office to find Tessa waiting for me.

"Tess, honey. What are you doing here?"

She laughed darkly, running a hand over her 33-week-plus baby bump. "I had an appointment with you, silly. Did you forget?"

"Of course not! But I could've come to your house. You didn't have to walk all the way here."

"It's four blocks. I'm pregnant, not an invalid," she teased. Her smile began to fade as she looked down at her belly, still rubbing it protectively. "Besides, I wanted to get out of the house. I'm sick of being cooped up in there with endless messes to clean, and not just from my *little* boys."

"Well, you're welcome to come see me anytime." I grabbed my stethoscope off the wall and quickly cleaned it off with alcohol wipes. "And not just at work. We should have a girl's night with Noelle and Andrea soon."

"Good luck coordinating that with all we've got going on," she chuckled. "I've barely seen Noelle since she and Larkan have been all gaga for each other."

"She'll come around. It's just exciting being with a new man. Lean back a bit for me?"

We rolled up some blankets behind her so she could recline comfortably on the exam table. After sticking the eartips in, I lifted her shirt and placed the chestpiece next to her navel to begin listening to the baby's vitals.

"I'm sure you know that well," she teased, her voice distorted while I had the stethoscope on. "It's been so long, I can't even remember what the start of a new relationship feels like."

"Honestly, it's overrated." I moved the diaphragm over her belly. "Sure it's exciting, but you're also second-guessing yourself all the time. You don't want to be too eager or too aloof. It's hard to tell if your feelings are real or just infatuation that will fade. You over-analyze every little thing they do. It's exhausting really. I can't wait to get to where you are, knowing each other so well with years of memories together." I closed my lips, choosing not to voice the next thought floating through my brain, but Tessa went there anyway.

"It's not all it's cracked up to be," she whispered. "Years of being with the same person makes men bored. They start looking for what's newer, prettier, younger."

"Tessa!" I pulled the eartips out and let the stethoscope hang around my neck as I grabbed for her hand. "You are still young and *so* beautiful! No matter what Big G does, it doesn't reflect on who *you* are."

"I know what he does when they go on rides," she said flatly. "Everyone just looks the other way and doesn't say anything, but it's so obvious. His clothes smell like cheap hooker and he's a shitty liar."

"Tess..." I sat on the table next to her, squeezing her hands as if that would prevent her heart from breaking any further. "Honey, I'm so sorry. I wish I could do more, but I don't know what to say," I sighed. "I can heal cuts and fix broken bones, but there's no fixing men being idiots."

She huffed out a dry laugh. "It's all right, Mari. I knew what I signed up for, even though I hoped for better. Every other man in his family was the same way." She leaned her head back with a sigh. "If he wasn't so good with the kids, if they didn't idolize him as much as they do, there would be no question of what I'd do."

We sat together in silence for a minute, while I tried to figure out how to broach a solution for her.

"You can still let him be their father without being with him yourself," I said cautiously. "What if you moved out and agreed to split time with the kids?"

She shook her head. "He'd never allow that. For a woman to leave *him*? He's too prideful for that."

"What, is he going to physically prevent you from leaving? Keep you trapped in the house?"

"He might, I don't know."

"The other guys wouldn't allow that." I looked intently into her eyes. "Reaper wouldn't allow one of his men to mistreat his woman."

"We see it as mistreatment, they see it as keeping a family together," she whispered sadly. "That sums up why the Collapse happened in the first place, Mari. Men have never been able to see things from our perspective."

I opened my mouth to argue, but no sound came out. I never thought of it from that perspective before, but realized she was right.

Chapter 10

REAPER

What a fucking day.

I needed to find Heather and Bones, and find out if they were in on Python's scheme. But the two of them had mysteriously disappeared. They didn't leave Sheol, of course. Gunner with his people at every exit made sure of that. After wasting a day of trying to find them at their usual haunts, I sent a team of envoys to search for them more diligently.

They weren't guilty of anything. Yet. But hiding from me wasn't doing anything to help them. I didn't give a shit that Heather was a woman, or that I fucked her. If she was in on this, she deserved to be punished just as much as Python.

The day dragged on until I finally had enough, and broke out the cigars, whiskey and deck of cards by the pool. Some of the off-duty guys joined me, along with Hades, of course.

He laid at my feet like normal, facing the clubhouse door with his chin on his paws. He didn't start doing that until Mariposa came into our lives, like he was waiting for her.

Me too, boy, I thought, leaning down to scratch him. After the difficult, but amazing, time we had yesterday, I couldn't get enough of her.

Never in a million years would I have imagined going back to that place, nor taken a woman with me. But I was serious about this and I wanted her to know that.

Telling her I loved her was easy. Almost too easy. Easy enough that those words didn't seem very meaningful at all. I never was much of a poetic, wordsy guy anyway. I had to show her what she meant to me. And fuck me, it felt like she actually understood and felt the same way.

Halfway through the second card game, as dusk began swallowing the landscape in darkness, Hades lifted his head. His nose pointing stiffly at the door, I followed his gaze, waiting.

The door opened and he was off running, not even giving Mari a chance to poke her head through before jumping on her with excited whines and yips.

"Ha-*des*," I called, adding a high-pitched whistle. "Don't knock her over, you big oaf."

"Ohh, it's okay!" She laughed as she came toward us, walking my big mutt backward on his hind legs with her arms around him. "He's my favorite boy. Aren't you, Hades?"

He gave her a slobbery kiss, nuzzling and sniffing her as his stubby tail went nuts. Jesus, standing upright, he was almost as tall as she was.

"What am I, chopped liver?" I grunted around my cigar.

"That's what you get for having a dog, Pres," Benji, one of Gunner's younger guards, chuckled. "They seem like a chick magnet until you get the girl. Then you realize she loves the dog more than you."

"Unfortunately, I think you're right, kid," I sighed.

Gunner himself had been oddly silent at the table. Usually he talked the most shit during our card games as he tried to swindle us out of our chips. Now that Mari was here, he studied his hand like he wanted to disappear into the cards themselves.

"You know that's not true," Mari scolded, finally bringing Hades' front paws down to the ground.

I pulled the cigar from my mouth and leaned back in my chair. "Then get over here and show me how untrue it is."

She gave me a sultry look that made me so fucking hard before striding over. Sliding a hand along the back of my shoulders, she leaned down to kiss me. I knew she meant it to be a quick, sweet peck designed to be appropriate in the company of others right in front of us.

Naturally, I couldn't allow that.

I grabbed the back of her neck to prevent her escape before molding my mouth to hers. Soft and pliant, her lips opened for my invading tongue. My other hand grabbed the back of her thigh, pulling her around my leg so her sweet ass could take a seat in my lap.

She stopped resisting before ever sitting down, wrapping both hands around my neck to tongue-fuck my mouth with the same intense passion. This woman got me hotter than metal pipes in the sun and I didn't give a fuck who was in the front row audience. To be completely honest, I hoped Gunner got a sense of what he was missing now, and would think twice about blowing her off.

I smiled woozily as we came up for air. The booze, her lips, and the wild fucking realization that this woman loved me, hit me all at once in a heady rush.

"Now I hope to whatever fucking god that still listens that you don't kiss my dog like that," I teased, circling my arms around her waist.

"Only right before I'm about to see you," she dished back with a swat to my chest.

"That must be why you taste so good," I laughed.

"Hey." Her arms tightened around my neck as her lips brushed my ear. "I came to tell you something serious actually."

"Something wrong, sugar?" I cupped the side of her neck, pulling back to look at her.

"No, it's just," she bit her lip, visibly nervous, "Jandro asked me to come over tonight and I said yes."

"Really?" I squeezed around her tighter, a grin spreading on my face. "Finally getting some alone time, huh?"

"I guess." Her gorgeous eyes twinkled and a smile pulled at her lips. She was excited about this, which just made my heart fucking soar.

"You spending the night there?"

"I'm not sure, maybe. We'll see how it goes first."

"I won't wait up for you," I said with a kiss to her nose. "If you're in bed with me in the morning, great. If not, that's good too. It means you're in a safe place with someone I trust."

"You're sure?"

"Of course I'm sure, beautiful. Hell, you've already spent the night in a tent with him."

"Nothing happened back then."

"I know. Even if it did, I was being an ass and we all know it. You would've been entitled to a revenge-fuck."

"Reaper!"

"It's true. Anyway," I patted my fingers on her hip, "I'm glad you two are progressing, sugar. I know he'll make you happy, but in the event he fucks up, his ass is mine at Fight Night."

"He said the same thing about you," she groaned, rolling her eyes.

"See? You have good taste in men."

"Or the worst," she grumbled, but was unable to hide her smile as her fingers played with the hair on the back of my neck. "So I'll see you tomorrow?"

"You better." I closed my fist in her hair and pulled her mouth to mine again, sinking my teeth into her plump lip just enough to make her gasp. The territorial part of me wanted her to feel my bite when she kissed Jandro. "Have fun, sugar. I love you."

"Love you, *Rory,*" she snickered against my neck and bounced away before I could spank her for calling me that.

With a final head scratch and kiss for Hades, she left through the pool gate and headed down the street toward Jandro's shop.

"Man, I dunno how you can do that." Benji broke the silence that had fallen over the table. "Knowing my girl was spending the night with another man? I'd wanna punch through walls."

"That's 'cause you just grew hair on your balls last week and don't understand shit." I stuck the cigar back in my mouth and picked up my hand of cards, trying to remember what my strategy was while the blood drained from my dick and returned to my brain.

When my gaze slid over to Gunner, he was just as entranced with his five-card hand as the whole time Mari was here. I saw her stealing glances at him, but he stayed mum like a coward and didn't so much as look at her. She was only hoping for a hello from her friend, even my caveman ass could see that. And for him to ignore her was just rude as hell.

No one was a dick to my woman besides me, and that was only accidentally. Especially not my captain of the guard.

"You're awfully quiet there, Gun." I couldn't help but goad him. "Couldn't even say hello to our medic?"

"I'm not in the mood, Reap." He bit the phrase out with an edge of warning. The falcon on his shoulder turned its sharp gaze on me.

"Not in the mood?" I repeated. "For what, to not be a dick? You two were all buddy-buddy up until you got back from Colorado, now you're acting like she has the plague."

"Just stop. Can we play this fucking game or what?"

Nah, fuck that. He kept hurting my girl's feelings and I wasn't about to let him blow me off like he did her. I snatched the cards from his hands and tossed them over my shoulder, letting them flutter across the patio while he stared at me with an incredulous face.

"What the fuck, Reaper?"

"I asked you a question, captain," I growled. "I expect an answer."

Benji and the other kid mumbled excuses as they set their cards down and slunk away from the table. I wasn't entirely sure what was about to happen, but they were smart not to stick around.

"I didn't hear any question that warranted an answer." Gunner pushed his chair back noisily as he stood. "Just a bunch of chest-thumping bullshit from some asshole who doesn't know how to treat a woman."

"Ah, now we're fuckin' getting somewhere." I stood and blocked his path, Hades alert and ready at my side. "Was that not a happy woman at my side just now? What makes you think I'm not treating her right?"

"Reaper, come on," Gunner sighed. "I don't want to have beef with you. Just leave me out of it."

"Oh no. You're in it, golden boy, whether you like it or not." I stepped closer, my boots nearly touching his. He was a few inches taller than me, but skinnier. I didn't particularly want to come to blows either, but I could hold my own if it came to that. "You accuse me of mistreating my woman, you better give me a good fucking reason."

"What the fuck is wrong with you?" His laidback, sunny demeanor finally burst into flames. "You're pimping Mari out to Jandro, now you're trying to throw her at me too? She deserves better than that, you fucking pig!"

My hands shot out and shoved against his shoulders faster than I could think. He stumbled backward a few steps, eyes wide and mouth agape in surprise. I stepped in again, closing the distance quickly. Whether out of shock or restraint, he didn't try to hit me back, but I could see how much he wanted to.

"You don't understand the first fucking thing you're talking about," I hissed close to his face. "Remember how hurt she was when I didn't talk to her? Well, you're doing that right fucking now, and I'm calling you out on it *because* I love her. I'm putting my ego aside and trusting her with everything I am. I'm expanding her options for love and pleasure, and *I'm* the asshole?" I shook my head at him in disappointment. "You think you know what she deserves? Well, it's a hell of a lot better than you."

I stubbed out my cigar and walked off, Hades trotting at my side.

CHAPTER 11

MARIPOSA

I walked up the driveway to Jandro's shop just as he was pulling the garage door closed.

"Hey *Mariposita*," he grinned at me. "I was starting to wonder if you changed your mind."

"Why?" I asked. "I didn't keep you waiting, did I?"

"Nah, just, you know." He gave a sheepish shrug. "I know you've got options."

"Oh, stop that," I scolded. "I told you I'd come over, so that's what I'm doing."

"That might be common sense to you and me." He towered over me, grabbing both of my hands in his. "But it's not so common these days."

"That's a damn shame." I looked up at him, resisting the urge to kiss those pillowy lips of his. "And still, it's not just that. I've been *wanting* to see you outside the shop."

In the fading daylight I couldn't tell if he was blushing, but he looked adorably speechless all the same. A rarity for the quick-tongued vice president.

"Shall we?" He released one of my hands to walk me back down the driveway, lacing his fingers through mine in a tighter grip on the other hand.

I followed his lead down the quiet street, rubbing my thumb over the back of his palm. The only sounds I heard were excited voices of children and the rumbles of bikes a few blocks over. I imagined it was Dallas and his family playing around on their mini bikes.

"So you and Shadow live together?" I swung our hands between us like we were a pair of innocent kids ourselves.

"Yeah. At first it was out of necessity for him. He didn't know how to live on his own, and kind of just stuck by me so he could figure shit out. Now he's a lot more independent and also a great roommate, as it turns out. We leave each other be, for the most part, but even a loner like him doesn't like to be alone all the time."

More questions turned over in my head, but like usual, I sensed that Jandro purposely omitted details about Shadow's life out of respect for his privacy, and I couldn't violate that.

He led me up a wide, gently sloping driveway to a house with a similar floor plan as Reaper's, but a smaller version. It had the same central entryway with two wings on either side. I had a hunch that he and Shadow each had half of the house to themselves. When he pushed open the heavy wooden door and led me inside, I saw my instinct was right.

A central staircase greeted us upon entry, leading up to walkways branching off to the left and right at the second level. The first floor was clearly the common area, with a large TV surrounded by comfortable but mismatched furniture, and an open concept kitchen and dining area toward the back. I spotted Jandro's chickens pecking at the ground through the sliding glass door at the back of the house, and a large, dark figure leaning over a desk across from the living room.

"Shadow, don't be fuckin' rude," Jandro muttered under his breath after closing the front door behind us and leading me inside.

"Hi, Shadow," I chirpily greeted the large man hunched over the desk before he could say anything.

"Hi, Mariposa." A desk lamp pointed down at an open book in front of him, casting half his face in shadow as he glanced up at me. "How are you today?"

I felt elated that he said hi to me without any apparent distress. After greeting him at least once per day since he donated blood at my office, he seemed to become less abrasive to small, social interactions with me. Now that we had established that as a comfort zone, I couldn't resist pushing the envelope just a tiny bit further.

"I'm fine." He moved his forearm to rest on the page of what I now realized was a sketchbook. A pencil spun absently over his thumb and forefinger. "How are you?" he remembered to ask after a long pause.

I smiled wider at him, immensely proud at his progress. "I'm great, thank you."

Jandro cleared his throat, pulling me toward the kitchen as Shadow's attention returned to his sketchbook.

"You're brave," he murmured, brushing a kiss against my ear. "Want anything to drink?"

"For saying hi, how are you?" I asked in a low voice. Then louder, "What do you got?"

"I know you're trying to push him to be more social, and he doesn't usually react well to that." Jandro grabbed a lime from a small basket on the counter and tossed it in the air before catching it again. "I can make a mean margarita."

Forgetting about Shadow for the moment, my mouth dropped open. "You have tequila?"

"Do I have tequila," he scoffed, reaching under the counter to produce a large, unlabeled glass bottle. A pale amber liquid swirled in the lower third of the vessel.

"Is that an añejo?" Nostalgic memories of my father sneaking me shots of his "good stuff" as he called it, filled my brain. Tequila aged for at least one year was smoother than younger spirits and best for sipping.

"Ah, my girl knows her stuff." Jandro's eyes sparkled with glee while I tried to ignore my stomach flip-flopping at him calling me *his*. "It is an añejo. I've been savoring this since Gunner scored it about a year ago."

"It would be a shame to dilute it down in a margarita," I said. "I used to drink añejo with my dad with just salt and lime."

"Then that's what we'll do." He brought down two shot glasses and a salt shaker from a cabinet, then dug out a cutting board and a knife from a drawer. "You make those how you like 'em while I get the food started."

"What's for dinner?" I slid into a stool across the elegant, granite countertop and started cutting the limes.

"Breakfast," he grinned, opening a small, wooden crate to show me rows of eggs in various shades of brown to off-white. "Huevos rancheros, to be precise. My girls have been good to me."

I smiled back as I untwisted the cap of the añejo and began to pour. "That means they're happy with you."

"I like to think I know a few things about keeping ladies happy."

While the eggs fried and he prepped the sides, I poured the shots and dumped a few good shakes of salt onto the lime wedges.

"Bite the lime and then take a sip," I said, sliding his glass toward him across the counter. "Savor it in your mouth for a few seconds, like a good whiskey."

He took the filled shot glass and raised it carefully. "A toast first."

"To what?"

We pondered together in silence for a few moments. "To your dad," he said quietly. "For raising one hell of an amazing woman who knows her tequila."

That was so utterly sweet and unexpected of him to say. My throat closed up with emotion, but I gave a shaky, appreciative smile.

"To Javier Luis de los Angeles," I whispered, gently touching my glass to Jandro's.

"Salut," he murmured.

Our eyes remained locked on each other as we each bit the flesh of our lime wedges. Citrus and salt coated my tongue as I brought the drink to my lips. Jandro copied my movements like a mirror, sipping gently at the rim of his glass. The burn of the alcohol evaporated into a sweet, refreshing flavor as it mixed with the acid and salt on my tongue.

"Damn, that's good." Jandro turned away briefly to check on the eggs.

With the intensity of his gaze gone, I found it easier to talk again. "Do you need any help?"

"Absolutely not." He turned back toward me and flipped a knife in the air with a smirk before returning to chopping bell peppers. "Is your old man still around?" he asked in a softer voice as he worked.

"No. At least I'm pretty sure he's not." I took another small sip of añejo. "He was drafted for the border war between our county and Texahoma. Every two weeks or so, they gave him leave to come home for a weekend. Eventually, he just never came home again."

"Fuck. I'm sorry, Mari."

"Don't be," I told him. "The last few weekends he came, he was different. I was a year away from graduating school then, so I recognized the symptoms of PTSD, but it still hurt. Just violent outbursts out of nowhere, treating my mom and I like we were the enemy."

"How about her, she still around?"

"I certainly hope so," I sighed, taking another sip of tequila. "When he didn't come back for months, she decided to go out and find him."

"You're fucking kidding me," Jandro breathed. "She went out to find him and left you?"

"It wasn't like that. I was almost done with school and pretty independent. I was more worried that she was out there alone and unprotected. And even if she did find out what happened to him, who knew if she'd be able to handle the news."

"Did you ever hear back from her?"

"I got a 'congratulations on graduating' card from somewhere in Montana, but other than that?" I shook my head.

"I get that you were an adult and all, but it's still messed up." Jandro's hand clenched on the counter. "She left *you*, her daughter, a fellow woman alone in the middle of a war zone."

"I think she knew I'd be fine," I replied. "She figured I'd be valued with my medical skills, and that it was my dad that needed her most." I smile down at my tequila glass, circling a finger around the rim. "He was the love of her life. I can't say that I blame her."

"Well, I hope they're together," Jandro offered. "Wherever they are."

I took another nibble of my lime flesh. “How about you? Your folks still around?”

“Nah.” His voice softened. “I only really know them from the stories my sisters told me. The oldest two and my parents trekked up through Mexico from Guatemala to escape the dictatorship there. My mom found out she was pregnant again by the time she reached Arizona. She had me and the two youngest of my sisters, almost back-to-back, while we all stayed with my aunt and uncle. They were deported shortly after I was born, even though they were granted political asylum. Some glitch in the system that never got corrected.”

“I'm sorry,” I told him sincerely. “You never saw them again?”

“No. They sent letters with my sisters back and forth for a few years, but then the postal service got really unreliable and...” He lifted a shoulder in a shrug. “Kind of like with your dad. We just never heard from them again.”

“I had family on his side too that got deported despite having green cards and work visas,” I sighed. “Cousins, aunts, and uncles I've never met. It's so fucked up.”

“And look where we are now.” He huffed out a dry laugh. “Funny how no one wants to come here now that this place is a fucking free for all.”

“The people we trusted to protect us failed us,” I sighed. “Now we're on our own.”

“You know what this conversation needs?” Jandro spread his hands wide on the counter, lifting his eyebrows suggestively at me.

“A less depressing topic?” I asked.

“Yes. And also more tequila.” He leaned across the counter and placed a surprise peck on my lips. “Food's ready. I'll plate it up while you pour us another round.”

A HALF-HOUR LATER, I WAS SCOOPING UP THE LAST OF MY delicious egg-yolk and salsa mixture with a tortilla. If Jandro hadn't provided any, I would have licked my plate clean.

"Holy shit," I leaned back in my chair. "I don't think I've ever had huevos rancheros that good." Placing a hand on his shoulder, I leaned over to kiss his cheek. "Thank you. Breakfast-dinner was delicious."

"My pleasure, *Mariposita*." His hand slid along my back, resting with gentle pressure just above my ass as he leaned in to kiss me properly.

He tasted spicy, citrusy, hot and cool all at once. The tequila, now like liquid fire in my veins, burned away my shyness about exploring him through touch. My palm skimmed over his large, broad shoulder, fingertips trailing over his neck and collarbone as he turned in his chair to face me.

Grabbing one of my chair legs, he pulled me closer to secure both arms around me. I braced two hands on his chest to combat the falling sensation in the pit of my stomach. He stayed there the whole time, broad and solid. His kisses were the perfect dessert—smooth, buttery, and warm. Even as he kissed deeper, his hold on me growing tighter, nothing was rushed or rough.

Jandro was incredibly responsive in his affection, gauging my reactions with movements of his hands and soft flicks of his tongue. He took the lead, but never swept me away. I began to see taking full control wasn't his style—he gave just as much as he took. With every gentle pull back, he led me on a chase. And when I caught up, he matched me on every beat.

"This is the part where I either take you home, or you come upstairs with me." His voice grew lower, gravelly and sexy. "Because I can't keep my hands off you unless there are multiple walls and doors between us."

We both panted slightly, out of breath like we really did chase each other around. My whole body was a vessel of pulsing, liquid heat and there was no question of what I wanted to do. He was a decadent dessert, too delicious to be good for me, but I didn't care.

"What's it gonna be, Mari?" Impatience roughened his voice and I liked it.

"Take me upstairs," I breathed against his lips, eager for another taste.

He needed no further invitation. The moment our mouths clashed together, he released a deep, sensual moan. Large hand slid under my thighs to scoop me up and deposit me in his lap. I straddled his waist, my heartbeat spiking at the brush of a hard bulge against the inside of my thigh.

"Who knows if we'll make it to the stairs," he murmured, dragging that hot, luscious mouth over the pulse in my neck.

Just then I got hit with the memory of the first time he kissed me there—at the first Fight Night I witnessed where he split Stephan's lip open. He asked me for a good luck kiss and pointed to his cheek. I did, just to make him leave me alone, and got his lips on my neck in return.

"What're you giggling at?" he muttered, pulling my hair in a gentle tilt back so he could kiss my throat. "Am I tickling you?"

"I was just remembering the first time I saw you fight, and when you tricked me into kissing you."

"That feels like so long ago," he chuckled, grazing a kiss along my collarbone. "I was hoping to take you upstairs *that* night, after impressing you with my fighting skills. Before all that other shit went down."

"Hah, sorry that getting the shit beat out of me and being carried to the medic's office cockblocked you."

"I'm not. I mean—fuck." He leaned back, slapping a hand over his mouth. "That came out wrong."

"Uh-huh." I remained seated in his lap, but crossed my arms as I pulled away. "How was it supposed to come out?"

"Don't be mad at me, *Mariposita.* Come here." He wrestled one of my hands away from my cross-armed position and pressed a kiss to my palm. "I'm sorry you got hurt that night. Of course I'd never want that. What I meant was, I'm glad I didn't sleep with you then. Because if I had, we probably wouldn't be here right now." He laced his fingers with mine. "Like this."

Here it was. He pulled the curtain aside and gave me a glimpse at the real Jandro. But I wanted more than just a hint at what was underneath the charm and the swagger. I wanted him laid out bare for me.

"Why do you say that?"

"Because," his eyes closed for a moment with a sigh, "I didn't care about you then like I do now. I thought you were pretty and I wanted you on my dick. Nothing else mattered to me. I would've used you and discarded you. But *everything* matters now. When I don't see you, I miss you. I want us to laugh together until we make Reaper's head explode. I want to *always* feel like I did when you brought me lunch, and I want to keep showing you how much I appreciate that." His voice lowered to a near-whisper. "I want to be one of the reasons that you feel happy."

I was stunned. Speechless. I didn't just get him laid bare. I got a confession, atonement, and declarations of *always*. That free falling sensation came over me again—a rushing, thrilling mix of emotions, but with absolutely no fear. It was almost jarring how I *wasn't* afraid of diving headfirst into my feelings for two completely different men.

I wrapped both arms around Jandro's neck, bringing my lips down on his to kiss the tension away. He took a risk in showing his heart to me and I would treasure it.

Skimming my lips across his cheek to his ear, I whispered, "Try again for the stairs?"

He made a noise somewhere between a chuckle and a groan, then cupped my ass before lifting us effortlessly up from the chair.

Chapter 12

JANDRO

"Strong legs," Mari remarked with a soft giggle as I took the stairs two at a time. Her body bounced against mine, wrapped around me with her arms and legs.

"Nah, you're a light little thing." I set her down gently when we reached the second floor landing.

Her feet touched the floor but her hands remained solidly on my arms. "Oh, just take a compliment. You're strong as an ox."

"Nope, you're thinking of the guy down the hall." I wanted compliments and so much more from her. Reaper was the rough one, but I wanted to leave my own kind of mark on her. Right in that moment however, something else distracted me.

"My bedroom's the door at the very end." I turned her away from me and gave her a light swat on the ass. "Go on ahead. I've got to do something real quick."

She looked back at me, confusion furrowing her brow. "What do you have to do?"

"I'm just checking on something with Shadow. I'll be right in after you." I grabbed her arm and planted a quick kiss on her lips before letting her go. "Don't get naked yet. I want to do that to you myself."

The answer seemed to satisfy her and I waited until she disappeared behind the bedroom door. Honestly, she'd probably understand what I had to do if I explained to her. I just didn't want to right then. I wanted to get it over with and enjoy her for the rest of the night properly. Chances were, if she kept coming over, she'd see every facet of my and Shadow's living arrangement anyway.

I went to the opposite end of the landing, pausing just outside of his bedroom door. When Mari and I first went up the stairs, I noticed he wasn't drawing at his desk anymore. Usually he told me when he was going to bed, but this time was considerate enough to not interrupt our dinner and make out session.

"Maybe you really *are* getting better, man," I muttered to myself as I approached the heavy wooden door. The third one we had to install in as many years.

Eager to get back to the gorgeous woman in my bedroom at the other end of the hall, I moved quickly. First I slid all the deadbolts into place on the knob side of the door. Originally I installed three, then it became clear I needed more. I went from bottom to top, starting with the one at waist-height, then reaching the eighth one on my tiptoes near the top of the door. I wasn't a short guy by any means, Shadow was just *that* huge.

Once those were in place, I grabbed the handful of padlocks from the side table. Moving to the hinged side of the door, I closed the eight latches installed there before slapping the locks in place. It would take a group of men with a battering ram to knock this door down. Better than Shadow's shoulder or forehead.

I hated doing this, locking him in like he was some dangerous animal. But truthfully, he was. He couldn't control what happened in his sleep, but that didn't make me or our furniture any safer. I found some small comfort in knowing the extra locks were his idea. And so far, it was the only thing that worked.

Once everything was secure and I gave the door a few cursory pushes to check for any weak spots, I hurried down the hall in the opposite direction. Despite the necessity of it, locking him in always made me feel weird. Something was wrong about it. We did this nightly ritual for a month and a half now, and I had yet to get used to it.

It reminded me of my days as a prison guard, when I had to hide our friendship, cuff him, and lock him in his cell. When we left that hellhole together, I never wanted to lock another human being in a cage again.

So much for that.

Mari was standing next to the floor-to-ceiling panoramic window in my bedroom when I arrived. She looked over her shoulder at me with a sweet smile. "Everything okay?"

"It is now," I sighed, crossing the room toward her. My arms came around her from behind, hugging her back to my chest as I placed a kiss on her shoulder. "You like the window?"

"I do. The sunrise must be amazing. Did you make this yourself?"

"Yeah, I don't know construction like I do bikes, but I used to do some odd jobs."

She pressed her head back against my chest, looking straight up at me. "Is there anything you can't do?"

"Well, so far I haven't been able to get you in bed with me. Maybe you should prove me wrong."

"Smartass," she laughed, spinning in my arms before shoving me playfully back toward the bed. "You can do anything you put your mind to," she joked, sounding like an old teacher Reaper and I used to have.

"I like where this is going." I bit my lip, pulling her with me as I walked backward. "And you can do anything to my body that comes to mind. Is that what you're saying?" The mattress hit the backs of my knees and I sat down.

"No," she laughed again, climbing on to straddle me. "I have no idea what you're saying."

"I should probably stop talking, then."

"Yeah, maybe."

Our mouths crashed together. My palms slid under the hem of her shirt and found a slender waist and warm skin. Lifting higher, a bra blocked me from finding more of her. Her shirt went first, then mine, and then that pesky bra.

Her skin erupted in goosebumps as she became free from clothing, her nipples tight little buds that I wanted to soothe and soften with my tongue.

"You okay?" It came out a hoarse, lusty whisper.

She leaned against me, arms braced between my chest and hers while my hands did their best to warm up her long, curving back.

"Do you ever worry about someone seeing you?" She glanced behind her at the window.

Only the midnight blue of the sky dotted with billions of stars looked back at us. Underneath, the landscape was dark, murky and unknown.

"Nah," I told her. "This side of the house faces the desert outside Sheol. It's the main reason why I picked it." I brought my lips to her ear. "Only gods and stars can see us, but we can see everything."

I sucked her earlobe, eliciting a soft gasp and bringing her arms around my neck. She went wild every time I kissed this area of her body and I intended to fully take advantage of it. Her thighs squeezed around my hips as my mouth found the tender spot between her neck and shoulder. My hands came forward, running up her ribs to graze the undersides of her breasts, my thumbs sweeping over her nipples.

"Jandro..." She rolled her core over my dick, which was fighting like hell to get free of boxers and jeans. Her small hands went everywhere as if wanting to touch me all at once.

"Mari," I answered, my mouth now against her sternum as I lifted us and turned.

I held her by the waist, lowering her back to the bed while our lower bodies refused to separate. Her thighs remained glued to my hips, the friction of all our movement inching my jeans down too fucking slowly.

I pulled away from her just to get out of my damn pants, while she took the opportunity to do the same.

"Ha, I'm faster," she joked, flinging away her pants while mine were still around my calves.

"Fuck, I hope so," I said in a tight whisper, kicking them away as I lowered to hover above her again. "You got me feeling like I'm going to explode already."

"Well, we've got all night, don't we?" She curled one leg around my waist, running her foot down the back of my thigh. The same movement drew my cock to rub against her hot core. Fuck, her panties were already slick. I couldn't tell what was her wetness and what was my precome.

"That's certainly what I was hoping for." I palmed her breasts while I kissed the valley between them. "Is my bed comfortable?"

"Mm-hmm," she hummed, massaging down the back of my neck and shoulders. "I wouldn't mind a sleepover."

"Good." I dragged my tongue to a nipple, rolling over the tight little peak before grazing it ever so slightly with my teeth.

With a soft gasp, she dug harder into my back. Her fingers brushed over the still-healing scar she stitched up last week—the gunshot wound I took to protect her during the Razor Wire ambush. The tenderness of the wound made me flinch a little, bringing my eyes up to hers.

"I'm sorry," she pulled her hand back, "did I hurt you?"

Did she ask me a question? I couldn't say.

"Fucking Christ, you're beautiful."

All I wanted to do was look at her, and just marvel at the warmth, care, inner, and outer beauty of this woman. But I couldn't kiss and please her if I was too busy staring. Damn the choices a man had to make.

"You're not too bad yourself," she giggled sweetly. "And this has been a beautiful day with you—"

"Shh, it's not over yet." I moved lower, gliding the tip of my tongue just under her breasts now. "Not even close, *Mariposita*."

Her curves could make a grown man cry and I wanted to make sure she knew that. My hands ran up and down her sides, taking in every dip and swell from her perfect teardrop breasts to the edge of her panties at her luscious hips. All the while I kissed a trail down her belly, slow enough to torture myself as well as her.

She tried to wriggle and writhe underneath me but I kept her still.

And when I finally gripped the edges of that flimsy fabric and peeled them away, my mouth followed right after. Hot and delicious, her freshly uncovered skin was soon covered again by my lips and tongue, reaching lower until my kiss reached her clit.

Her legs sealed shut, she tried to buck against my mouth, but it was no use against me holding her down. I allowed her legs to stay closed only to slide those panties down and away, then opened her up again like a Christmas present.

"Jan—ah!"

Whatever she was going to say cut off as I sealed my whole mouth against her center, sucking on her lips and dragging my tongue up and down her slit. I wasn't even completely concerned with her pleasure at that moment, I just wanted to get drunk on her taste. She was absolutely delicious and I could not get enough.

I hummed and moaned against her sensitive skin as I lapped and sucked at her pussy, knowing the vibrations would drive her wild. Her nails dug into my scalp in a way that urged me on, tingling with a pleasure that bordered on pain. She was probably moaning but I couldn't be certain—her thighs made great earmuffs.

Bringing one hand in, I kneaded the inside of her thigh as I dragged my mouth away, kissing the crease between her leg and hip.

"Why are you stopping?" she panted.

"Because I need to breathe." I shot her a teasing grin. "I'm no good to you if I suffocate, am I?"

"But I'm so close."

"Fuck yeah, you are." I gazed in awe at her stretched out on my bed, quivering and breathing hard. My hand on her thigh pressed to her hot, drenched core. "You want to be filled, beautiful?"

"Yesss..." she dragged the word out into a sexy hiss as my finger pressed inside her. "I want you so bad, Jandro."

"Do you want *me* or just my dick?"

The question came somewhat out of nowhere. It rattled around in my brain sometimes as a random thought, often without any words attached to it. Just a worry. I knew how to bring women to bed, but wasn't the best at keeping them. Her, I desperately wanted to keep. But it was a two-way street, and my mouth ran before my brain.

"I want *you*, Jandro all of you." She sat up, pulling me toward her. My finger slipped out from between her legs, foreplay momentarily forgotten. "I want your smiles, your jokes, your cooking, your kisses." Her hands pressed to my cheeks and she kissed me languidly, apparently not caring that my lips and tongue were still coated in her sex. "I want your dick too, but that's far from the most important thing. I want everything that is *you*."

No one had said anything remotely like that to me before. Not even close. This adorable, sexy, kind, incredible woman reached a place deep inside me no one else had ever occupied. And I never wanted her to leave.

My next kiss pressed her back down into the pillows. My hands left her body only to take off my boxer briefs in a hurry. The next thing I felt were her slender fingers wrapped around my length. I sucked in a breath with a hiss. Just the contact of her gliding up and down my rigid shaft was enough to start unraveling my control.

"Damn it, Mariposa. I told you I was close to exploding already," I reminded her in a harsh whisper.

"And I told you we have all night." She released my cock, her hand traveling down to my balls. Her massaging and gentle tugging took me away from the edge just enough to think straight again.

I grabbed her thighs, kneading the sensitive flesh as I maneuvered between them. All the while, I made it a goal never to stop tasting her. From her lips, her earlobes, and her neck to her pert nipples and the sexy curves of her waist, my mouth needed to be on her at all times.

Her legs around my hips as they were meant to be, I pressed forward to sheath myself in the hot, slick center of her. She clutched my shoulders with a soft gasp upon entry. I covered her mouth with mine, and she opened up for my tongue just as she did my cock.

"You okay?" I murmured into her neck once fully seated inside.

"So, so much more than that..." Her arms and legs wound even tighter around me, nails scratching deliciously across my back. "Please, Jandro."

How could I say no to that? I could only pull back so much with the grip she had on me with those gorgeous thighs. Still, I made every movement count. I angled my thrusts to maximize her pleasure, listening to the shifts in her moans and breaths. Her clit felt harder with every impact from the base of my cock, which was the clearest sign she was getting close.

The soft whimpers and moans from her throat were the sexiest music to my ears, growing louder and uncontrolled as she neared release. Her thighs around me started to tremble and that was when I slowed down.

"Don't stop. Why'd you stop?" she panted.

"What's the fun in that?" I massaged her breasts in my hands. "We've got all night, don't we?" I pulled her nipples into my mouth, grazing them with just enough teeth to distract her. "God, I can't get over how beautiful you are."

"I'll look even better once you let me come."

She had the gall to wink and I burst out laughing. "Nah, I want you burned into my memory just like this. On the edge, flushed, and wrapped around me. Just putty in my hands."

"I can't imagine why," she teased. "Control freak."

"Because I never want this moment to end." I started moving in her again, but slowly, with her face cupped in my hands. "I'm sure we'll make love plenty more times, but we'll never have another first time. I want to savor exploring you, uncovering you, for as long as I can—mm! And thanks to you squeezing my dick like that, it won't be for much longer."

"Kegel exercises are important," she informed me with a devilish smile. "A nice side effect is they contribute to much stronger orgasms."

"And just like that," I sighed into her neck, "I'm done for."

Her walls contracted around me rhythmically as I picked up speed and intensity. Our sex was violent now, a relentless crashing of flesh on flesh—not to mention my headboard against the wall. My dick felt like iron as she became even tighter, wetter, and hotter. Mari bit her fist to hold back her screams, but I grabbed her wrist and pinned it down next to her head. I needed to hear how I was making her feel.

"Do you still want all of me?" I demanded, never missing a beat as I kept fucking her. "Do you want all of this and more?"

"Yes!" she cried out as her release closed around me like a vice, holding me inside her like she'd never let go. "I need you, Jandro..."

Her convulsions and her words were too much for me to handle. My release came just as violently with a final crash , her orgasm wringing me out and milking me for all I was worth. All the strength and rigidity in my body vanished, now turning me to putty in her hands.

Mari seemed to already be falling asleep as I withdrew from her, slid up next to her, and pulled the sheet over us. But she flipped over, curling into a little ball and nuzzling into the center of my chest. If the sex turned me to jello, I melted into straight-up liquid butter at that point.

I rested my chin on her head and slid an arm around her back as I listened to her deep breathing.

"You're stuck with me, little butterfly," I mumbled, sleep and relaxed bliss settling into my limbs. "You just had to go and make me fall in love with you."

CHAPTER 13

MARIPOSA

I awoke so slowly, I temporarily forgot where I was.

This bed didn't feel like Reaper's. The large bicep serving as my pillow wasn't his, nor was the arm draped over my waist. But a familiar weight pressed down on the foot of the bed like Hades was here, watching over us.

Hades? How...?

I had to be more asleep than awake. I remembered I was at Jandro's house, in his bed. There was no way Hades could be here. His presence was just what my subconscious craved as a familiar comfort while I slept.

And yet I swore if my toes stretched out just a few inches, they would touch whatever solid body weighed down the mattress at the end of the bed.

Maybe not Hades, but *someone* was in here with us.

I tried to force my eyes open but sleep still clung to me, pulling me back into unconsciousness like an anchor. I didn't know if my eyes were showing me or my brain was creating an illusion, but I saw someone sitting at the edge of the bed.

It looked roughly like a man facing the direction of Jandro's wall-sized window. No matter how badly I tried, I couldn't force myself to awaken, to see details of this person who snuck into the bedroom.

Looking at him, if I could even call it that, was like trying to stare into the bottom of a murky lake. Every time I almost made out some detail, like a nose, ear, or length of his hair, it would become obscured by some kind of fog or darkness. It seemed impossible to get a sense of his clothing or even how big he was. His weight on the bed felt solid, yet he seemed completely ethereal, like he could evaporate into thin air like a ghost. Was Jandro's place haunted?

I never believed in ghosts, and I didn't get a haunted vibe from this person. As I kept staring at him, I realized I never felt afraid for a moment. Whoever he was, he wasn't there to hurt me. He was just sitting, looking at the stars out the window.

"Hello, Mariposa."

It *was* a man. That voice was deep, rich and masculine. It was impossible for me to tell if I heard it with my ears or if it came from my own head. But I heard him say my name, unmistakably.

"I'm dreaming." That had to be the only explanation. I was in some kind of state between awake and asleep, and my mind was just playing out dreams that made them seem like hallucinations.

"Yes, you are." The voice sounded amused, but the figure remained completely still. "But that does not negate the fact that I'm here."

Again, I felt no fear. No sense of alarm of this strange man sitting on my lover's bed and talking to me in a voice just as dark and deep as the earth. I never knew my grandparents but he spoke in a way I imagined a grandfather would—full of wisdom and experience of time passed.

"Who are you?" I murmured groggily.

"I'm Hades."

I WOKE UP THE SECOND TIME WITH A START, NOW FULLY awake.

Rubbing my eyes, then blinking rapidly in the dim light, I stared at the empty air just above the foot of the bed. No one was there, not even a wrinkle in the sheets to indicate someone had been.

Crazy-ass dream, I thought, flipping over and snuggling into Jandro's warm chest.

"Mm," he groaned adorably in his sleep, wrapping around me tighter.

I tucked my head under his chin and let out a contented sigh, closing my eyes. If I was still asleep during that wild dream, what had startled me awake?

The answer came a few seconds later, when a loud thump made me gasp and freeze with fear. Next I heard voices coming from one of the rooms in Jandro's house. I couldn't make out the words, but then I heard a scream and another loud thump like someone was punching a door.

"Jandro," I whispered, shaking him desperately. "Jandro, wake up!"

"Hmm? You okay, Mari?" He rubbed at his eyes, his voice gravelly with sleep.

"Someone's broken in! I can hear them talking and banging on stuff in the house." Another yell and the loudest thump yet, like a body slamming into a wall, made me curl into him for protection.

But Jandro didn't seem fazed. He rubbed down my back and kissed my forehead with a sigh. "I was afraid this would happen tonight. Don't worry though, Mari. It'll be over soon."

I stared at him, bewildered. "What the fuck is going on?"

"It's just Shadow having his nightmares. It sounds worse than it is, but yeah. This is what I have to deal with a few times a week."

"Nightmares?" Another scream and unintelligible yelling made me flinch. "*Those* are nightmares?"

"Mm-hm." His fingers moved over my skin, caressing and soothing. "When I told you to wait here for me, I went to close up over a dozen locks on his door. He's not a violent guy when he's awake, unless he's doing his job. But when he sleeps, he's uncontrollable. He's destroyed so much shit in the house, dislocated my shoulder, given me black eyes. I fucking hate locking him in there, but we don't see any other options."

"Are so many locks necessary?"

"He's ripped the door off the hinges. Twice."

"Holy shit."

"Yeah." Jandro kissed my hair as he ran his fingers through the long strands. "He's my friend. I hate seeing him suffer, but he's strong as fuck and dangerous when he's like this. I just don't know what else to do."

Not a single brain cell was asleep in my head anymore. I mentally filed through everything I read about PTSD and the procession of trauma. God knew I researched the shit out of it, thanks to my dad.

"It isn't nightmares," I said after the thumping and yelling began to subside. "His brain is trying to process trauma from his past, probably from childhood. I'm only speculating, but from his screams...it sounds horribly abusive."

Jandro didn't speak for a long moment, his warm hands pausing their movements on my skin. "You're right," was all he said.

"Jandro." I slid out of his warm embrace, propping my head up on my arm to look at him in the dark room. "What happened to him? I don't specialize in this kind of thing but I might be able to help—"

"Mariposita," he sighed. "I know you mean well, and I love that you're so caring and patient with him. But you can't help. His trauma runs *deep*. It's not just from his childhood, it's all he's known since the day he was born. And," he hesitated, "your gender is an intrinsic part of that."

"So he was abused by women," I said matter-of-factly. "Since he was an infant?"

"Yes."

"Family members, I assume?"

"Look, even I don't know all the details," he said. "I'll tell you what I can, but please, Mari, you can't push him. He's come such a long way, but avoiding women is a safety thing for him. I know you have the best of intentions, but I can't let him regress."

"Trust me, I get it." I snuggled back closer to him, realizing he'd much rather sleep than talk, but I was dying to know more. Maybe I'd have to be creative around helping Shadow, but there had to be some kind of way. "So what happened?"

"I don't know specific methods of what they did to him, and don't really care to," Jandro murmured against my forehead. His fingers began a hypnotic, circular pattern on my back. "So, you saw where Reaper grew up, right?"

"Mm-hm." I rested my lips on his warm shoulder.

"Well, his was one of maybe a dozen female-run communities that said 'fuck the patriarchy' for a number of reasons and decided to live their own way. Most of them were based here in Arizona, some stretched up to Utah."

"Okay." His voice vibrated in his chest as he spoke. I curled into him as I listened.

"So, as with all types of people, you have normal folks in the middle of a spectrum, then you have people at extreme ends. Reaper's was considered pretty normal despite the polyandry thing, since they allowed men to live there too. Some communities didn't allow men at all. And others were just fucking psychotic."

I felt his heartbeat pick up speed, and I was certain mine did too.

"Psychotic in what way?"

"Like these women were fucking violent and deranged. I met Shadow when I worked in a prison, but those vile bitches should have been the ones locked up." His tone deepened to one of anger. "They hated men and everything to do with us. They ran their communes like cults out of a horror movie."

"So they would hurt men," I realized. "And abuse them."

"Even before I met Shadow, I heard rumors," Jandro went on. "That they seduced men, drugged them, and sacrificed them to their culty goddess. I heard that if a woman got pregnant and the baby was a boy, they'd kill it on the spot."

"Oh my god," I blinked away tears. "Poor Shadow."

"Local authorities said the same kind of shit about Reaper's community, so who knows what details are true and what's made up. But Shadow knew nothing but literal Hell his whole life until I brought him into the Demons. He's never said a peep about what the cult did but," he moved my hand up and over his shoulder, touching my fingers down on the gunshot wound I closed, "you can see the scars."

I didn't want to change the subject entirely, but the overwhelming sadness of Shadow's upbringing had me craving a happier topic to fixate on.

"Tell me how the Steel Demons formed." I scratched lightly over his scalp. "And how you brought Shadow into the fold."

"You mean Reap hasn't told you already?" he chuckled with a kiss to my temple.

"Maybe he has and I just want to see if your stories line up."

"You suck at lying and it's adorable," he teased, kissing my neck. "Well Reap and I knew each other since we were kids, you knew that already. We met Gunner when we were about sixteen, when he bailed us out of jail by flashing his family's money around."

"I can see him doing that," I giggled. "But why would he help you two?"

"He had a vintage motorcycle that was precious to him, a family heirloom of sorts. But he couldn't get it running. I promised I'd fix it for him and, surprise for us, the preppy little punk actually held up his end of the bargain and got us out. We got along remarkably well for being from such different backgrounds. He was always kind of an outcast among his rich, snobby family, and I think we gave him a sense of freedom he never had."

"So SDMC was just you three for a while?"

"Daren and Noelle were with us too. But yeah, the five of us were the OGs." He sat up halfway in bed, propping pillows against the headboard. Apparently he was fully awake now too, and getting into storytelling mode. His arm fell around my shoulders and I nestled into his side.

"I keep forgetting about Reaper's brother," I admitted. "He's only talked to me about him a few times."

"Daren was kind of like that," Jandro nodded. "Quiet kid, always kind of in his own head. My loudmouthed ass would forget he was around too, until he had something really important to say. Then he'd usually grab one of his siblings. But anyway," he rubbed his jaw, "the five of us lived in a tiny-ass apartment after Reaper's home got swept. He and I were twenty-one, the others a little younger. But you know, we partied, revved our engines loud in the streets, got into bar fights, went on longer rides together on weekends. That was SDMC in its infancy, just a bunch of dumbass hooligans."

Jandro's voice softened as he stared blankly at a random wrinkle in the sheet. "When Reap went back home for a visit and found everyone all gone, it was like a switch flipped. He left as Rory and came back home as Reaper, the SDMC president we know."

I recalled how Reaper told me the story, standing in the middle of empty homes and artifacts buried in the sand. I wondered if that was the most emotion he allowed himself to show regarding the loss of his family.

"He said everyone had been taken away, and we couldn't afford to fuck around anymore," Jandro continued. "We had to become a club, a real one with a hierarchy, rules, and a reputation. At first, it was to shape up so we could find his family. After some years passed without so much as a clue about them, it was so we could form and protect our own."

I drifted my fingertips over his chest and abs like how he was caressing me earlier. "How did Shadow get involved?"

"That was a whole other ordeal," he sighed. "I was working in a prison at the time, and he was in the mental health building, for reasons I'm sure you can guess."

"Nightmares, talking to himself, and erratic violence?"

"Yup. You wouldn't even recognize him, Mari. Same height but skinny as a rail. A shaved head, no facial hair. I don't think he ever got a proper meal in his life."

"Jesus. Poor Shadow."

"Yeah. I could tell he wasn't mentally impaired in any way, so I felt bad that he got placed in that unit. One night, I snuck him a flask of my boss's hidden stash of liquor. He slept like a baby, but now he's dependent on booze to sleep at all. And he's developed a hell of a tolerance over the years so he always needs more."

"I understand why you did that, but that kind of drinking is poisoning him. I'm amazed he's still alive and functioning as well as he is. How old is he?"

"No idea. There was no record of his birth, only a rough estimate of his age. He was never even given a name before coming to the prison. I told him we could share the same age and he could pick a birthday. But yeah, you seen that white eye of his? Sometimes I wonder if he's a mutant."

I drummed my fingers on Jandro's ribs. "So how'd he join the club?"

"The Collapse ensured that for us," he laughed dryly. "The prison shut down three years later. It was a federal facility so when the Fed went tits up, so did everything it funded. Retirement accounts and pensions became worthless in a matter of days. Nobody was getting a paycheck anymore, so everyone threw their middle fingers up and went, fuck it! At some point, someone unlocked all the cells. One of my coworkers who had finally snapped started shooting at inmates."

"Oh my God." My hand flew to my mouth. His words were a poignant reminder that the impoverished and disadvantaged suffered most from the Collapse.

"It's okay, though. No one got hurt because someone shot that motherfucker from a hundred yards away with a pistol. I'm talking clear across the building! Guess who that was?"

"You?"

"Nope. Shadow. He took another guard's pistol and honestly saved everyone. Anyway," his hand gesticulated wildly, engrossed in his storytelling, "obviously, he had nowhere to go after that happened. I couldn't just leave him, so I invited him back home with me and," his fist closed and pressed to his lips as he tried to stifle a laugh, "you think he's awkward now? You should have seen him standing in our dumpy-ass apartment living room, Reaper and Noelle staring at him like he's an alien and asking me what the hell this guy was doing here. So that was fun, especially with Noelle, because just being in the same room as a woman freaked him the hell out."

"As opposed to now, where he just looks mildly uncomfortable?"

"Yes, exactly. So it took some work convincing the siblings to bring him into the fold. He was a hell of a shot, but never rode on a motorcycle before. Eventually, I think it was Daren who convinced Reaper having him was a good idea. There were learning curves, but eventually it all worked out. Gunner taught him about different kinds of weapons. He understood Reaper was our leader. He and Noelle just avoided each other."

"And you were his friend," I concluded, pressing a kiss to his chest.

"And his father, mother, life coach, riding instructor, you name it."

"You're amazing for that, you know?" I reached up to wrap an arm around his neck. "He's so lucky to have found you."

Jandro fell silent, one of the rare moments he was speechless. Then his arm curled around me tighter as he dropped a kiss to my head. "Thanks, beautiful. He really is a good friend to have. I wouldn't have done so much for him if he hadn't saved my ass on numerous occasions."

I slid lower into the bed, satisfied with the conclusion of the story. "Well, then I'm grateful for him too. For keeping you around for me."

"Yeah?" His mouth nudged closer to my ear. "Show me how grateful."

"Come here." I pulled him down with me, wriggled my body into position underneath him.

He followed my lead with a salacious grin, nestling between my thighs so I could do just as he asked.

Chapter 14

REAPER

"Well, ain't this a peachy fuckin' turn of events."

Bones regarded me with a guilty look from my front stoop. He ran a hand over his shaved head, growing fuzzy from lack of upkeep.

"I wasn't hiding from you, Reaper. I just wanted to lay low for a bit. Until things calmed down, you know?"

"You can make your excuses inside." I turned and left the door open so he could follow.

His feet shuffled nervously over my marble tile floors, trailing after me to my study. Once I passed through the door, Hades looked up at me from his massive dog bed next to the fireplace.

"Have a seat." I waved a hand toward the chair across from my desk as I lowered into my own seat. "Was Heather *laying low* with you?"

"Um, yeah." He rubbed his hands together, leaning forward in the chair. "She'll be coming to talk to you later. She didn't want to, but I convinced her." He swallowed. "She's pretty upset about this whole thing."

"Tell that to someone who cares." I stuck a cigarette in my mouth and fished around for my lighter. "The only reason you're here is to tell me if you knew anything about Python's scheming."

"Absolutely not," he insisted. "He didn't breathe a word of it to me."

"Yeah?" I remarked, not buying it at all. "The three of you looked pretty tight to me."

"Maybe out in the open, among everyone else but," he shifted uncomfortably in his seat, "it wasn't really like that behind closed doors."

I narrowed my eyes. "What do you mean?"

"If I'm being completely honest, Reap," he sighed. "I was kinda their third wheel."

"How so?"

"Like, I've always had a thing for Heather. But she was with you, then Python, so I left it alone. But I got shitfaced one night and she came onto me pretty hard. We had a great time, in my opinion, and she talked up the whole sharing thing like it was so great. I was stoked 'cause it felt like this was finally my chance to be with her, you know? So I rolled with it."

"And?" I pressed.

"And it turned into her pretty much using me for threesomes. Which was fun, don't get me wrong, but I thought I'd have more time with her myself, you know? But she pretty much ignored me except for when she and Python wanted some extra fun in the bedroom. And of course, having two men on her arms at the parties."

"That fuckin' bitch," I groaned, leaning my head back.

It didn't surprise me at all that Heather would use a man so selfishly, but Bones's testimony just made me appreciate having Mari even more. She didn't have to let me know she was going to be with Jandro. It was her right to spend time with whoever she wanted. But she did anyway, because she cared. She wouldn't dream of manipulating a man's feelings to get what she wanted. That was why I shared her, and no other woman I met ever came close.

"So yeah," Bones concluded. "If Python was letting Heather in on it, I wasn't in that club. And if I was," he straightened his spine, "I swear I would've told you, Reaper."

"Would you?" I questioned. "Even if the woman you still clearly have feelings for begged you not to?"

He slapped a hand to his chest, where I knew the grinning, horned Steel Demon skull was embedded into his skin. "I might've been a doormat to her and that was my bad, president. But I live my life every day to do right by you and this club. I was a homeless nobody before you found me and I'll never forget that. The Steel Demons gave me a home and a life. I'm your man, Reaper. Yours, and no one else's."

"So why'd you hide?"

"Because I was afraid Python would throw me under the bus to save himself. I pussed out, but I should have come straight to you, Reaper."

His life is not yours to take.

My head snapped over to Hades, still in his dog bed. Those black eyes, filled with an unfathomable depth, bore straight through me. The voice felt like it echoed all over the room, but Bones made no indication that he heard it. No one but me ever did.

You will not reap. His life is not yours to take.

"Thank you, Bones," I mumbled distractedly, putting my cigarette out. "You can go now."

I NEARLY WORE A HOLE IN THE RUG OF MY STUDY, PACING back and forth as I waited for Heather. In reality, I was waiting for my dog, the god who possessed him, or whatever the fuck he was, to say anything else. But he just looked at me, curled up in his bed. I watched him lick his paws until the silence became too much.

"Why me?"

He paused in his licking, looked at me, but didn't answer.

"Why? *Me?*" I repeated, grinding out each word between my teeth.

"I'm some kind of…servant to you. I understand that much. You chose me when you, this dog, whatever, was born. But why?"

I got a head tilt and a lick of his lips.

"Can you even fucking hear me?" I demanded, my frustration rising. "Or is this a one-way line? Just you giving orders and I'm supposed to obey? To what end? Why do you decide who lives and who dies?"

He yawned and lowered his head back down to his paws.

"Just my fuckin' luck." I shook my head in defeat and headed back toward my desk.

I chose you, because you are the perfect instrument.

The voice nearly knocked me off my feet. My skin broke out in a cold sweat as I braced my hands on the desk. The whole room felt like it was tilting, sliding away from me.

You know loss. You know death as intimately as a lover, yet you do not fear it. Reap for me, and I will protect those you hold dear.

"Mariposa…" Her name left my mouth in a ragged, desperate gasp. I was going insane. I had to be. She was the thread tying me to reality.

"Reaper?"

All at once, everything stopped. The heaviness of that voice, the room sliding out from under my feet. Like a snap of someone's godly fingers, everything returned to as it was.

I looked up to see Heather standing in the doorway of my study, her eyes puffy and red. She wrung her hands nervously in front of her.

"Ah, Heather," I cleared my throat, composed myself quickly, and gestured to the chair across from my desk. "About time you finally showed up. Have a seat."

She moved stiffly toward the chair. Her gaze felt heavy on me, but I fiddled with my cigarette case rather than make eye contact with her. Hades lifted his head, ears pricked forward with a low growl already rumbling in his throat. He never was fond of her.

Anything you'd like to say, now would be a swell time, I thought, my eyes locked on the dog. When no words came, I released a deep breath to clear my head. I had to focus on the matter at hand.

"Were you aware of Python's schemings with Razor Wire?"

"Reaper," she sniffed. "Why are you treating me like this?"

"Because you associate with a proven traitor." I wasn't raising my voice. Not yet. But my knuckles were white on the armrests of my chair. What did I ever see in her? Even as just a casual fuck.

"He made a mistake."

"Excuse me?" I couldn't believe what I was hearing. Was this woman really that dense? "Meeting with an enemy club outside the gates in secret, plotting behind my back for weeks, if not months, does not happen by fucking *accident.*"

"Reaper, I know you're not heartless," she sniffed, trying to give me that sad doe-eyed look that worked on more desperate men. "You're a good man, even if the way you left me was cruel."

"I didn't leave you. We had nothing to begin with," I corrected her. "And you can stop trying to butter me up til I'm a soggy piece of toast. It ain't gonna work."

"I know, deep down, you don't want to do this to him," she went on like I hadn't said anything. That was another thing I hated. Even when I just tried to have a normal conversation with her, she never fucking listened. "He's one of your men."

"You're wasting your breath, Heather. My dog's morning shit means more to me than him."

"You don't mean that. Reaper, please." She leaned forward. If my desk wasn't between us, I knew she would've tried to reach out and touch me. "Please spare him."

"No. And I think you missed the whole point of you being here." I crossed my arms. "Python's fate is not up for negotiation. What I need to know is if he was operating alone or had allies in his little scheme."

"But he was the only man who would share me!" she whimpered, a large sob wracking her chest. Now that she saw her crocodile tears and doe eyes wouldn't work on me, she had no options left.

"Jesus Christ..." I set my elbow on the desk and rubbed my forehead.

"You've locked up the only man who cares about me, now you're interrogating *me* like I've done something wrong?"

"If you knew about what he was doing, you should have told me," I ground out. "So did you or not?"

She let out a dramatic sigh and carefully dabbed at the corners of her eyes with a tissue. "He bitched about you a lot. We both did, to be honest. He wants to run his own club one day. He'd be good at it, you know?"

"Absolutely none of that fucking matters to me," I said. "Did you know he was conspiring with an enemy to kill me and my men?"

"No," she finally said. "For all his complaining, he left that part out."

"If you're lying, I *will* find out," I warned her. "And I won't be merciful just because you're a woman."

Her life is not yours to take.

I nearly pulled a muscle whipping my head so fast. The voice was unmistakable, but Hades' demeanor hadn't changed. His ears were pulled back in annoyance at the sound of Heather's voice. His lips curled in the start of a growl, but she wasn't a threat, so he didn't react to her presence aggressively.

Do not reap. Her life is not yours to take.

She must have been telling the truth, then. It was the only conclusion I could reach.

Oblivious to my internal freaking out, Heather's lips wobbled as she continued trying to work me over. "Reaper, please let him go. Brand him, keep him imprisoned, do whatever you need to punish him, but he deserves—"

"He deserves what I *say* he deserves." I leaned back in my chair, itching for silence and a cigarette. "You can go now."

"But—"

"You're dismissed," I snarled. "Must I remind you how much I hate repeating myself?"

Heather stood from the chair, defeated. I fished out a cigarette as she made her way to the door, then glowered when she paused in the doorway.

"Is she really so much better than me?" she asked without turning to face me.

Despite myself, I huffed out a harsh laugh as I lit my cigarette, then sucked in the first drag and savored it before I exhaled. Hades said he would protect Mari, so I felt zero guilt at the words that left my mouth.

"In every way imaginable."

Chapter 15

MARIPOSA

This is a bad idea. You told Jandro you wouldn't get involved.

I ignored the dissenting voice in my head as I marched up to Jandro's house. I promised I wouldn't *push* Shadow, but I had to help in some way. If there were more baby steps between a cordial conversation in my office and this, I would take them. But some progress had to be made and I knew for certain Shadow would not step out of his comfort zone. Not without someone there to guide him.

I've slept with him and I have to talk myself up to having a conversation with him. How backward is that?

My throat closed up with nervousness. I hadn't talked about it again since that night with Reaper, and neither did the guys. No one treated it like an elephant in the room, but I thought about it more than I liked to admit. Shadow was attractive. Sexy even. Maybe not in a conventional way, but surely I couldn't be the only woman who thought that?

I didn't know if I was fixated on helping because of what happened between us, or just that I tried to fix everything in general. Shadow deserved healing more than anyone, not to mention a peaceful night of sleep. I couldn't help being female, but I could only hope that he was getting comfortable with me enough to not hold my gender against me.

I raised my fist and knocked softly at the front door. When no answer came after about thirty seconds, I turned the knob and pushed it open.

No one in Sheol locked their front doors, I noticed early on. It was the ultimate safe neighborhood.

"Hello?" I called, stepping inside cautiously.

Just then I realized Jandro didn't give me much of a house tour last night. We'd been so starry-eyed for each other and he pretty much led me straight into the kitchen.

In the daylight, I noticed all the smaller details and personal touches I missed last time. I didn't realize it last night, but Jandro and Shadow's sides of the house were like a night and day difference.

Jandro's side was brighter, both from the open windows letting light pour in and the metallic bike parts set out on his work table. He kept tools of every sort organized in a case nearby, several five-gallon buckets stacked within each other, and neatly folded rags next to degreasers and other cleaning products.

It was an organized clutter, one that showed care and respect for every piece and component of his work. Jandro was a man who brought work home with him, not out of obligation but because motorcycles were his passion.

Shadow's side on the other hand, was the complete opposite.

Blackout curtains over the windows didn't allow a crack of light to slip through. His area was dark and completely devoid of clutter. Compared to Jandro's side, the lack of any personal touch almost seemed sterile.

Only a desk lamp gave any touch of warmth to the dark living space. The bulb illuminated an open sketchbook on the desk. It must have been the same one he'd been drawing last night. Curiosity got the better of me, and I leaned over to take a look.

The page was open to a highly detailed pencil drawing of some kind of cactus flower. A circle of long, sharp spines grew out from behind the base of the slender, white petals and surrounded the flower like a crown. The actual cactus plant looked to be some kind of vine species, spreading out in long elegant tendrils across the page. I'd never seen anything like it. The squat, round cacti around here didn't even compare.

I skimmed my fingers over the page, convinced the flower would jump to life had it been colored in. Did Shadow really draw this?

Pulling myself away before I started flipping through pages, I headed toward the back of the quiet house. Jandro's chickens pecked at the ground just on the other side of the sliding glass door leading to the backyard. I paused to watch them with a smile, never realizing before what cute and funny birds they were. Movement at the corner of my eye caused me to turn, and I nearly had to pick my jaw up from the floor.

A shirtless Shadow was doing pull-ups on a horizontal bar. His back was to me and unsurprisingly, more scars covered the wide wall of muscle. Overlapping and reaching every corner of his body, whoever gave him those didn't want to leave any piece of skin without the touch of pain.

But his muscles moving underneath the skin were a sight to behold. He pulled himself up and lowered himself down with such control and precision, making it look effortless. It took me a moment to realize he held a large weight between his legs.

I knew he was big, muscular, and a skilled fighter. But it only hit me in that moment how utterly fucking *strong* he was.

Chill out, Mari. Be cool. You and Shadow are friendly now, like two peas in a pod. Okay, bad example. But seriously, be cool!

I pushed the sliding door open just as Shadow released the pull-up bar.

"Hey," I greeted when he glanced over his shoulder.

I'd never seen a man move so fast until just then. He pulled on his shirt in the same time it took for me to blink. In another fraction of a second, he loosened his hair which had been tied back. With his back still turned to me, he seemed to rake his hair forward to cover his face.

"Mariposa!" he barked, panting slightly when he finally whirled around to face me.

"Sorry, I didn't mean to interrupt your workout," I stammered out, my pulse elevating slightly at how he scowled at me.

But his gaze softened after I spoke. "It's okay. I just wasn't expecting anyone." He looked down and rubbed at the tape wrapped around his hands. "Jandro's not here. He's probably at the shop."

I swallowed. *Be cool.* "I actually stopped by to see you."

"Me?" His dark eye widened, brow lifting. "Why?"

I pulled the orange bottle from my pocket and held it at my side. "If you don't want this, just tell me and I won't bother you with it again."

"What is that?" he growled, eyes on the bottle of pills in my hands.

"They're sleep aids." I rattled the pills inside once. "I uh, heard you the other night, when I was with Jandro—"

"I'm sorry about the noise," he interjected sharply, "but there isn't much I can do about it. It doesn't happen every night and Jandro tells me it never lasts more than fifteen minutes. If you just ignore me, it won't affect you."

An ache gripped my chest and refused to let go. It killed me that he saw his nightmares as nothing more than a nuisance to other people. How long had they been happening for him to accept as completely normal?

"Well, it clearly affects *you.*" I held the pills out to him. "And these might help. You'll develop a tolerance over time if you keep taking them, but there are no major side effects." I lowered them to my side again. "But the choice is completely yours. If you don't want them, just let me know."

His gaze lingered thoughtfully on my hand before flicking back up to my face. "They'll stop the nightmares?"

"Maybe. I'd have to do a full sleep study on you to know more, but that's not my area of expertise. But I have seen cases of people having fewer trauma-related nightmares after taking these."

He took a few cautious steps toward me and I had to steel myself not to step back. Not that I was afraid of him really, just that his presence was so big and overwhelming.

"You said no side effects?" he repeated in a softer voice.

"Nothing major," I said. "Dry mouth is a possibility so make sure you stay hydrated. Heightened blood pressure is another. I can always check that for you if you're concerned. Other than that," I shrugged, "not much."

"And if they don't work?"

"Bring them back to me and we can discuss other options if you'd like. Or not. It's completely up to you, Shadow. I'd," I chewed my lip and swallowed, "I'd rather not see you suffer if it can be prevented."

He gave me a long look that I couldn't read. So many seconds ticked by without him saying a word, I was just about to say my goodbyes when he mumbled, "I'll try them."

I tried not to smile too wide, knowing what a milestone it was for him to trust me with something like this.

"Okay, great. I'll leave these inside and let you finish your workout."

"No! That's okay, I'll uh," he paused, looking off to the side as if trying to remember something. "I'll walk you to the door."

"Oh, sure. Thanks. Here you go, then."

I held the bottle out closer to him, watching the large man step closer toward me until he was within reach. When he took it from me, I noticed he took care not to touch my hand.

I turned to go back inside, his presence behind me like a solid wall against my back despite him keeping a respectful distance away. As we walked through the house, I had a small urge to stop suddenly, just to feel him a bit closer. Jandro once described him as feral, and it sure seemed that way. The tortured, haunted beast named Shadow was still skittish, but slowly trusting me more.

I had to remember not to push for too much too fast, or else risk sending him straight back into his shell. Stopping suddenly to force touch between us was definitely too far. That or he'd see it coming and dodge me with his assassin reflexes.

He gave me an inch, probably more than he'd allowed any woman into his life. And still I couldn't resist asking for a centimeter more.

"Did you draw that?" I asked, turning my head to nod at the sketchbook as we passed by his desk. "It's beautiful."

He leaned over and slammed the book shut with so much force, the desk and lamp shook under the weight of his hand.

"No," he growled. "It's nothing."

And like that, I learned one more centimeter was also too far.

Chapter 16

MARIPOSA

The bloodlust hung thick and cloying in the air, just like the sweat and motor oil permeating my senses. It turned my stomach. I'd been dreading this night since the first time I saw it.

Fight Night. Where friends and family settled their disputes with their fists. Just like last time, a crowd gathered in the cul-de-sac in front of Reaper's house. Two guys rode around in figure eight patterns, revving their engines loudly while everyone else drank, smoked and talked excitedly. Men began peeling off their cuts and then their T-shirts. They took off their silver rings, necklaces, and leather bracelets. Because fists were the only weapons allowed.

I leaned against a retaining wall off to the side of the action, a small first aid kit next to me. There was no sign of Heather, the skanky woman who slept with Reaper before me, and who turned out to be sleeping with Python, our prisoner. She challenged me last month and beat my face pretty badly, but it turned out to be for nothing. Reaper didn't want her back. He cleaned the blood off of my face and kissed me for the first time that night.

Now, I was happy to stand aside and clean up anyone else who would need it. Being the club medic gave me immunity to the violence that was about to break out in this otherwise caring community.

From my outside view, I spotted all the usual suspects. Like last time, Shadow was nowhere to be seen. I wondered if he ever attended the fights or just preferred not dealing with the crowd. I couldn't see him picking a fight with someone over some petty argument, nor could I imagine anyone having the balls to challenge him.

Jandro's cut and shirt remained on as he talked to people, indicating he wasn't planning on fighting anyone tonight. Whether or not someone else challenged him was another matter. I sucked my bottom lip between my teeth, thighs rubbing together as I remembered his sexy beefcake body sprawled out on the sheets.

In another small group of people, Reaper and Gunner had their heads bent low toward each other. Gunner was saying something into Reaper's ear, who nodded as he listened. Both of them were dressed too, but my relief was short-lived as Reaper slid off his cut, handed it to someone, and peeled off his shirt.

He was glorious to look at, as always. The contrast of his body to Jandro's couldn't be stronger, and yet they were both utterly sexy. But my pulse shot up, knowing what the removal of his shirt meant. I rose from the curb and cut through the crowd straight to him. Gunner pulled away from his ear and slid his tall, lean body away through the throng of people. At that moment though, his ignoring me was the last thing I cared about.

"There she is." Reaper grinned wickedly as I approached him. He took hold of my upper arm the moment I was in reach and pulled me into him. He dropped a crushing kiss to my mouth before I could speak, sending my head spinning.

"You'll have to tell me all about the fun you had," he growled against my mouth. "I want you home with me tonight." He stroked a knuckle against my cheekbone, green eyes alight with love for a moment instead of bloodlust. "I missed you."

"I missed you too. Of course I'll be with you tonight," I said in the rushed breath that filled my lungs. "Who are you fighting?"

"Don't worry, sugar." He cupped my chin and kissed me again. "I just have something to settle. He won't land a scratch on me."

"I'm more worried about what you'll do to *him*."

His laugh was throaty, dangerous, sexy, and accompanied by a gratuitous grab of my ass. "I'll just pop him a few times to teach him a lesson. Get my blood pumping for what I'm gonna do to you later."

My thighs clenched at his words, my core already hollowing from the inside out. Even after a passionate, sensual night with Jandro, I craved the rough touch of my president. And still, I wanted many, many more nights of talking, laughing, and lovemaking with the VP. The feelings didn't necessarily conflict with each other, I just wanted it all. Maybe I was finally getting the hang of this two-men thing.

With a final bruising kiss, and double-handed squeezes and slaps of my ass, Reaper slid past me into the open circle the crowd created. Engines lowered to a dull roar and people's conversations faded away until the crickets were the loudest noise. All eyes were on the shirtless Steel Demons president.

"My challenge is for Larkan," Reaper announced, turning around slowly until his eyes fell upon the blue-eyed newest prospect, who had his arm around Noelle.

Shit. Jandro was right.

Larkan said nothing and didn't look especially surprised as he slid off his patchless cut, but Noelle was wide-eyed and pale as a sheet. I watched her throat work as she swallowed her nerves, offering Larkan a tight, but encouraging smile as she took his cut and shirt. In a bold move, Larkan murmured something and kissed her before walking out to meet Reaper.

"On what grounds do you challenge me?" He pitched his voice so everyone could hear, lifting his chin bravely at Reaper.

"On the grounds that you have the fucking balls to put your mouth on my sister without my approval. The club is grateful for your information regarding General Tash, but this is a separate matter. As the president of this club and head of my family, your behavior with my sister is out of line."

"I disagree." Larkan's tone was remarkably calm and even. "I haven't done anything to disrespect you or Noelle. We are two consenting adults with a strong connection. I haven't forced or coerced her into anything. You care deeply about her wellbeing, which I admire. But I do too, president. You're challenging me out of overprotectiveness, and the need to control everything around you."

Reaper's fists clenched at his sides as he and Larkan walked a slow circle around each other like two predatory animals. I met Noelle's eyes across the crowd, but couldn't place what she was feeling or thinking. She knew better than me that there was no stopping this. Gunner's men would stop the fight before it got too bloody, but who knew what kind of damage would be done before then?

Noelle's hand moved at her side and my heart swelled when I saw that she was petting Hades. He probably knew she needed more comfort than me in that moment. The memory of my dream flashed briefly through my mind before I shoved it away. Maybe I'd tell Reaper about it tonight, but I had to focus. A bad injury could happen quickly, and I needed to be ready.

Like a flipped switch, Reaper suddenly relaxed. He smiled at Larkan, then swept his arms out to the sides with his hands open.

"Let's settle this, boy."

And then he moved like lightning.

I had never seen Reaper fight before. Even though it was happening right in front of me, I barely saw anything. I blinked and Larkan's head snapped to the side, spitting out blood. He recovered quickly, moving in to land a punch on Reaper, who dodged with fluid agility. It almost looked inhumanly fast.

Every one of Larkan's attempts did absolutely nothing, cutting through air. Reaper dodged and weaved while staying close enough to land strikes of his own. Larkan's ribs and stomach were bright red, mottled bruising already forming on his skin.

"You're good with bikes and a bow, man, but you can't hit for shit," Reaper taunted him.

Jesus, Reap. Just end it already, I pleaded silently.

I weaved through the crowd back to my first aid kit, unable to watch anymore. Just as I opened the case, a cheer went up with Reaper's name being chanted.

"Yay," I grumbled, pulling on my gloves and breaking two cold packs. Larkan didn't lose a lot of blood from what I saw, but the bruising would be intense and sore for a few weeks.

Someone had already thrown Larkan's arm around their shoulder and dragged him toward me, Noelle right on their heels.

"Sit him down. Noelle, support his head," I snapped in my bossiest nurse voice.

"Aye-aye, *Mariposita*," Jandro winked at me before removing Larkan's arm from around his shoulders.

Noelle sat next to me on the retaining wall, then Jandro gently lowered Larkan to sit on the ground against her legs. She cradled his head in her lap as she smoothed his hair out of his face.

"Make sure he stays conscious," I told her, handing her a cold pack. "Press this against any swelling you see."

"Reaper's gonna want you on his arm," Jandro said, his tone almost a warning. "Since he won the fight."

"Well, he's gonna have to wait." I wet a clean gauze pad with rubbing alcohol. "The only reason I'm here is to help those who need it."

I began wiping at the cut on Larkan's cheek. He hissed at the sting and tried to squirm away, but Noelle held him still.

"Shh, it's just Mari, baby. She's helping." Her red hair fell over both of their faces for a moment as she bent to kiss his forehead. "You fucking fool. I told you not to show up."

"He would've known," Larkan groaned. "And then he'd be able to call me a coward."

"Are you staying with Reaper tonight?" Jandro asked me.

"I guess. I told him I would." I didn't bother to hide the annoyance in my tone. He was pulling my focus away from my job. As I dabbed healing ointment onto a cut made by the first man I was sleeping with, while the second hovered over me for attention, I wasn't too thrilled with either of them in that moment.

"Don't be mad at Reaper for this," Jandro went on. "It's an expectation of him to smack around the new guy. The fact that he's with Noelle just makes it a more convenient reason."

"Okay, not really interested in club politics right now. I need to check his ribs."

Jandro finally seemed to get the hint, but he leaned in and snuck a kiss on my neck before walking away. I sighed the moment his presence left, feeling regret over lashing out at him.

"Fucking men, right?" Noelle grumbled. She held the cold pack tenderly to Larkan's jaw, all the while stroking his hair with the other hand.

I bit back a smile as I knelt next to her man. She could grumble all she liked. It was plain as day how much she cared about him.

"Can you take a deep breath for me, Lark?" I asked. He followed my instructions as I felt along both sides. "Nothing's broken," I reported. "You're going to be sore as hell for a couple of weeks, so just take it easy. Any pain reliever will do."

"Think I can manage that." He gazed straight up at Noelle like she was the only person that existed. "I got my pain relief right here."

"Oh my God, stop. He obviously didn't hit you hard enough to quit with the cheesy lines," Noelle laughed as she leaned over him again.

I gathered up my stuff to give them privacy just as the crowd's volume went up again. Another fight was about to start.

"Can you see who it is?" Noelle craned her neck.

"No, don't really care."

The sound of glass crashing made us both jump and silenced the spectators.

"Big G! Get your ass out here and fight me!" The words slurred and carried a dark animosity I'd never heard before.

"Oh God..."

The crowd thinned just enough for me to see Gunner, swaying drunkenly in the middle of the circle as he searched for his opponent.

Chapter 17

MARIPOSA

"That man is toasted." Noelle astutely noticed.

I looked at her. "They can't let him fight that drunk, can they? He can barely stand up!"

She shrugged and met my gaze with a sad shake of her head. "Nothing in the rules says you can't fight when shitfaced."

"He's gonna bleed all over the street with one hit."

"Then it's a good thing you're here." She gave me a playful nudge with her foot. "You're sweet on him too, aren't you? Why do you look so mortified about tending to him?"

I didn't want to get into the fact that he'd been ignoring me for days, nor did I want to admit how much his silent treatment hurt me. And why the hell did he get so drunk? His crystal blue eyes looked out over everyone, glazed and unfocused. They paused on me for several long seconds. Only a commotion from another part of the crowd pulled his attention away. Big G had emerged.

The size difference between them was staggering. Big G was, well, *big*. His cut and shirt came away to reveal a broad barrel chest and belly that started to hang over his pants. The guy clearly liked to eat and drink, but he was broad and looked strong. What made things worse for Gunner was that he also looked stone-cold sober.

Tall and lean, with long arms and slender muscles, Gunner would have owned this fight if he could keep control of his body. But he swayed unsteadily like a tree branch, while Big G was as solid as a rock. He would have to get lucky to land anything, while all his opponent had to do was flatten him.

"Jesus, Gunner. What are you doing?" I whispered.

"On what grounds do you challenge me, captain?" Big G asked with a casual cross of his tree trunk arms. He thought he had this in the bag. I prayed he stayed cocky like that and that it would cost him.

"On the grounds of you being a punk-ass bitch." Laughter and applause rose up from the crowd, but Gunner's face showed how seriously he took this. "You tried to pin me as a traitor to this club. But you can't even stay loyal to your own fucking wife."

A low murmur of, "Ohhhh" rose up from the crowd, making Gunner wheel around unsteadily to address them.

"Fuck all of you!" he yelled. "Most of you can't stay loyal to your women either! You pass them around and it's fucking shameful!"

Oh no... My heart dropped like a stone into my stomach. Jandro and Reaper exchanged wary glances but said nothing. *Please stop this fight*, I pleaded, but knew they wouldn't.

A cold, wet nose nudging my hand brought my attention down. Hades whined and licked my palm, deciding I was the one who needed comfort now. Stroking his ears and head with a shaky smile, I looked back up at the fight circle.

Big G didn't deny any of Gunner's claims. His smug, arm-crossed posture remained the same as he watched the captain of the guard sway on his feet. Finally, he held his hands out, beckoning Gunner toward him.

"Let's go then, captain." He sounded like he was mocking Gunner and I hated him for it.

Gunner brought his fists up in a defensive position, widening his feet. Despite his drunken unsteadiness, he was still light and agile, bouncing on the balls of his feet like a boxer moving in toward his opponent. A part of me hoped he was just faking being drunk to bring Big G's guard down, though that didn't seem likely. He wouldn't resort to being dirty and deceptive like that.

Big G held his fists up near his face, eyes locked on Gunner moving in. The crowd went completely silent, only the fighters' breathing and Gunner's shoes made any noise. They seemed to circle and watch each other for a full minute before the first strike landed.

Gunner aimed low, sinking a rapid pummeling of fists into Big G's gut. But the big guy barely moved. Because Gunner was so tall, hitting that low put his face in dangerously close proximity to Big G's fists, who took full advantage of his position.

I saw it in slow motion—large, hairy knuckles crashing against an angelic face. It only took one hit for Gunner's head to snap to the side, his hair flying out from the momentum before the rest of his body spun to follow his head.

"Ohhhh!" the crowd shouted like a single organism when Gunner fell to the ground.

My eyes went to Jandro and Reaper again, pleading for them to stop this now, but they remained motionless. Neither of them cheered with the crowd. They just watched, tight-lipped.

Gunner climbed shakily to his feet. Blood coated one side of his face, dripping down his neck and torso in long, dark lines. His abs flexed with effort as he drew in ragged breaths. I couldn't believe I found anything sexy about him bloodied, hurt, and intoxicated, but a small, primal part of me did.

Big G at least had the decency to wait until he stood up before coming at him again. He wasn't fast, but unfortunately slow was still faster than Gunner. His meaty fist swung into Gunner's gut so hard, it almost lifted him off his feet. I covered my mouth to hold back my scream as the beautiful, bloodied man doubled over with a breathless groan of pain, then received another blow to the face that sent a spray of blood through the air like a morbid fountain. He went down again, and this time I knew he wouldn't stand up.

"Enough!"

At least twenty pairs of eyes were now on me. I didn't realize I yelled or jumped to my feet, but instinct took over as I ran to the center of the circle. Big G stood over his crumpled form like he might kick him, so I made sure to cover his body with mine.

"Gunner? Gunner, can you hear me?"

"Mawwh..."

"Don't talk, I'm just making sure you're awake. I'm going to turn you over now. Can you hold your head up for me?"

"I dun..."

Two more figures stepped up and loomed over us as I pulled Gunner up to a sitting position. Blood was everywhere, dripping from his mouth and at least one cut on his cheekbone that I could see. One eye was already swelling shut. He turned his head and spit out another full mouthful of blood.

"You shouldn't have interfered, sugar. We would've called it," Reaper's voice said from somewhere above me.

"You might have been too late," I snapped back. "He wasn't getting up. Big G could've killed him with one kick to the head."

Jandro handed me a towel. "Why the fuck is he bleeding so much?"

"Because he's drunk, you idiot," I growled, using the towel to wipe at Gunner's chest. "Alcohol makes your blood thinner."

"All right, I didn't know that." I didn't miss the hurt in his voice, but couldn't be bothered to tend to his feelings now. Gunner needed a lot more than a first aid kit.

"Help me get him up," I instructed my two men who just continued to stand there. "I need to take him to my office."

They each kneeled and grabbed one of Gunner's arms to throw over their shoulders. "Don't let his head fall back," I instructed when they lifted him up and started walking. "I don't want him to choke on blood. He might've bitten his tongue."

I jogged ahead to get the room ready while the guys dragged Gunner between them. By the time all three of their big, sweaty bodies filled up my tiny office, I had propped up the exam table so Gunner wouldn't have to recline, set out my suture kit, clean towels, and antibacterial ointment, and just ripped open a fresh box of gloves.

"Put him there." I nodded at the exam table while scrubbing my hands vigorously with hot water and soap. "Thanks. I'll grab you two later to take him home."

Again, Reaper and Jandro hesitated, making the already-tiny space even more crowded.

"The fights are done for tonight," Reaper informed me. "No one else has anything they need to settle."

"Good. It'll be an early night for me then." I snapped on my gloves and wet one of the towels with warm water. They still hovered as I proceeded to wipe the blood from Gunner's chest and stomach.

"I'll see you at home then?" Reaper asked.

"Yeah, I might just go straight to bed though." I spared him a glance as I began to dab the towel carefully around Gunner's neck and jaw. "I'm feeling a little crowded."

"All right." He sounded defeated, exhausted, rather than angry, as he turned toward the door. "Tomorrow is Python's judgement day."

I paused, then set the bloodied towel in the sink. "Okay. I just need some peace and quiet after I'm done tonight."

He nodded before leaving the room, Jandro following on his heels. I turned back to Gunner with a sigh. Reaper was trying to say he needed me before a difficult day tomorrow, but I could only be stretched so thin. Gunner needed me more, and even still, I couldn't keep giving everything to these men and have nothing left for myself. I needed one quiet night to recharge, and hopefully he understood that.

"Mareh…" Gunner sat up painstakingly, turning to me. "Need to shpit…"

"Here, love. You can spit in this." I handed him a paper cup, my pulse skyrocketing at the pet name that slipped out. "Try not to talk. Since your blood is thin right now, it'll take longer to clot. Just relax for me."

He leaned back, silent except for the wheezing breaths he took. Every so often he spat a small amount of blood into the cup.

"Do you want some water?" Hell, *I* needed some. Cleaning the excess blood off his long, taut body stretched out in front of me had me hot and flustered. That was wrong of me and not fair to him. I never got turned on with a patient before. It wasn't professional.

I turned to the sink without waiting for an answer and poured two fresh cups. The water wouldn't get very cold, but it would have to do. When I turned back to him, he seemed more lucid than I'd seen him all that evening.

"Cheers," he joked, tapping his water cup against mine before drinking deeply.

I chose to soothe my own parched throat rather than chastise him for talking again.

"Why did you drink so much before fighting?" I ran my fingertips lightly over the bruise forming on his stomach, trying with all my might not to be indulgent with my touch. This was about his well-being, nothing else.

"I messed up, baby girl." His slurred speech was now due to the swelling in his mouth rather than his drunkenness. "Fuck, I *am* messed up."

"What makes you say that?" I moved my hands up to his face, dabbing around the cut on his cheekbone with an alcohol-soaked gauze pad. It would need a few stitches but not many. "I need to sew you up a little. This might hurt."

He appeared unfazed as I got my needle and thread ready. "I've always been able to get what I want. Whether for me or other people. I had money growing up, but I wasn't spoiled. I was a crafty little shit, so I was always able to get stuff one way or another."

"And why does that make you messed up?" I carefully pulled the thread through his skin, mindful to keep the needle away from his eye.

"Because for the first time in my life, I want something I can't have."

I closed the cut with only three small stitches. The silence felt heavy around us. I didn't know how to respond. What were the odds of us thinking of the same thing? Of this weird tension between us? The potential future he *thought* we couldn't have?

When I went to put antibacterial ointment on his cheek wound, he grabbed my hand and held it. Gunner stared at me with his one beautiful, not-swollen eye in a way that was both intimate and uncomfortable.

"Are you happy, baby girl?" he asked in a soft voice, barely above a whisper.

"I don't like seeing you hurt." I pulled my hand out of his, continuing with my task of putting the ointment on his cheek. "I'm not terribly happy about a brotherhood that comes close to killing each other once a month."

"You know what I mean," he chastised gently. "Are you happy with *them*?"

The silence after his question pressed in on us like an invisible, oppressive force. I didn't know what kind of answer he was looking for, but I had a feeling he only wanted to confirm what he already believed. He wouldn't listen to any other answer.

"Is my answer going to change anything?" I shot back. "Are you going to keep ignoring me if I tell you yes? Or will you try to swoop in and rescue me if you hear what you want to hear?"

He blew out a long breath, turning his face away from me. "So you really like having your variety, huh?"

"So what if I do?" I challenged. "You don't want to be my friend if that's the case? Am I too slutty now for you to hang out with?"

"Don't," he snarled, looking back at me with now a narrowed eye. "I didn't say any of that. Of course I like you, I just...don't like the situation. It feels like they're using you."

"That's not what it is. They care about me, Gunner," I said. "And I care about them. It's confusing and weird, but I'm figuring it out because both of them are worth it to me."

"What about *your* worth? I don't mean it like that." He raised a road rash covered hand in a defensive posture in response to my glare. "I'm just saying you could be one man's whole world, and you deserve that. Instead, you're taking on two men part-time. Don't you want someone who wants all of you?"

"What are we really talking about here?" I snapped off my gloves and crossed my arms. "Why does any of this even matter to you? I'm still the same person, no matter who, or how many guys I'm fucking. But *you've* changed, Gunner. Ever since you came back from Colorado, you haven't treated me the same. Why? Tell me, because," I drew in a shaky breath, "it fucking hurts."

His gaze dropped, looking defeatedly at his bloodstained hands in his lap. "Because I can't just be friends with you, baby girl. But I'll never share you, either. All I can do is distance myself and hope what I'm feeling goes away. I'm sorry."

I nodded like I understood, but that was far from the truth. I knew the meanings of the words he said, but I couldn't understand *why*. Ironic, considering that just days ago, I felt utterly clueless about being with two men.

And it wasn't like Jandro and Reaper weren't enough for me. They just weren't Gunner—the sweet, beautiful man who just dashed my hopes of anything between us, even a friendship.

"Can you get yourself home?" I asked as flatly as I could muster.

"Yeah—"

The word was barely out of his mouth before I turned and left the office.

Chapter 18

MARIPOSA

The smell of coffee nearly dragged me downstairs before I became fully conscious. I pulled on a robe haphazardly, just noticing as I went out the door that I woke up in an empty bed. Reaper's clove cigarette smoke reached my nostrils as I descended the stairs, mixing with the coffee aroma in an oddly pleasant way.

That smell was of him, I realized. The Steel Demons president, sitting at his massive kitchen table with his back turned to me. Steam and smoke circled around his head like an aura. My hands reached his shoulders and I bent to place a kiss on his cheek.

"Thanks for making coffee." He didn't respond right away, but those green eyes watched my every move as I poured myself a cup from the French press and took a seat next to him. "And for giving me space last night," I added.

His chin lowered in the slightest hint of a nod. "Are you upset about what I did to Larkan?"

I sighed and took a sip of my coffee while thinking of the right words to convey my thoughts. "I don't like it, but I can understand why you did it. You're protective of Noelle and want her man to show you respect. I was more frustrated at you and Jandro vying for my attention while I was with patients. When I'm working, I need to focus on those whose lives are in my hands. I can't be your arm candy and do my job at the same time."

"Hmm." A smirk pulled at his lips, eyes shining through the smoke as he dragged on the cigarette.

"What?"

"Nothing, sugar. I just love that you're so straight with me." He reached over to place a hand on my knee, making sure to touch my bare skin under my robe. "And that you care about what you do so much."

I covered the back of his hand with my palm, sliding my fingers through his. "We're lucky last night's injuries weren't any worse. But it could become a life or death situation in a matter of seconds. I need you to understand that."

"I get it, babe. I do. Thank you for telling me."

A smile tugged at my own lips that not even my coffee cup could hide. "I think we're getting better at avoiding this fighting thing."

He ashed his cigarette butt in his tray with a throaty laugh. "Can't say I wasn't tempted to go there." His eyebrow popped up at me. "I hate being ignored, and we have such good sex after we fight."

"I'm sure you can find a way to provoke me when the mood strikes you."

"Maybe." He leaned toward me, his hand creeping up my thigh. "Being a happy fucking bastard has its perks too, though."

"Yeah?" I molded my hand to the side of his neck, angling my head for the kiss. "You're happy with me?"

"As a fucking clam." His mouth met mine with equal roughness and sweetness, teeth dragging across my lips with his signature bite. Tasting him was such a treat after not kissing him for over a full day. It was over too soon. He pulled away with a sigh. "I'll be a lot fucking happier in general once this execution is over with."

I moved our clasped hands to his lap in a small gesture of support. "Can you make it happen quickly?"

He shook his head regretfully. "No, it needs to be just the opposite. I have to drag it out, make it a public spectacle. I need to use him as an example so that no one betrays the Steel Demons again."

Reaper's shoulders hunched forward as if carrying out this man's sentence was a true, physical burden on him. My hands circled his thick, corded forearm, drawing myself closer to place my chin on his shoulder.

How quickly times changed. Over a month ago, I wrote him off as a heartless murderer when I saw him slit a man's throat right in front of me. Now the lines etched in his face and the faraway look in his eye told me clearly—he did not take killing lightly.

Back then I also would have done anything to save a person's life, no matter who that person was or what their crimes were. But now, my sympathy laid with the man who held the reaper's scythe. If allowed to live, people who endangered others and abused the trust of their community would continue to do so. By taking Python's life, Reaper secured a safer future for his men who had been loyal, their wives, and their children.

And for us.

"Sugar," Reaper nudged his forehead against mine, "would you believe me if I told you I *knew* I was doing the right thing? Not because I *feel* it is, but something bigger than me has told me their lives had to end? And it had to be by my hand?"

"Bigger than you?" I repeated. "You mean like someone above you is giving orders on who to kill?"

"Kind of." His eyes shifted to where Hades snoozed on the floor by his feet. "Not another person, though. Something...bigger than humanity."

"Like what, some kind of spirit? A god?"

He huffed out a sigh, rubbing his eyes. "It sounds fucking nuts, I know. But I swear to you, every life I've ever taken has been for a good reason. Tom and Liza abused that girl you worked with. Razorwire attacked us. People have tried to kill me first, or hurt my sister. The only one that makes no sense to me is—"

"Daren," I finished for him, cupping his stubbled cheek. "You didn't kill your brother, my love."

"I let him die. That's close enough."

"There was nothing you could do." I stroked my thumb across his face. "Human life is fragile. Weapons and wars aren't what kill us most often, it's those tiny, single-celled organisms designed to destroy us from inside."

Reaper turned his head toward my hand to kiss my palm. "Do you believe me, though?"

"That something bigger is at play, instructing you on which lives to take?" I lifted one shoulder. "If I've learned one thing from being around you and this guy," I nudged Hades with my foot, "it's that anything is possible."

Chapter 19

REAPER

I left him at the kitchen table, the man Mari had been kissing, holding, reassuring. Only she could see that side of me—still wrought with guilt over my brother's death. Still coming to terms with being...*something*'s instrument of death. I wasn't sure if I could call it a god or something else. Noelle seemed convinced that was the case, if her supposed dreams from Daren had any merit.

But I left it all behind, downing the rest of my coffee and rising from the table as Death personified. A man awaited my justice and that was the last he would know of me—the instrument that took his life and sent his soul to whatever bleak underworld awaited him.

Hades woke instantly, his four paws tapping over the marble floor and then the sidewalk outside as if he'd been waiting for me to carry out this task.

Mari walked next to me on my other side. She didn't reach for my hand as she usually did. Perhaps she sensed the change within me.

We didn't have to go far. A platform made out of repurposed wooden pallets had been set up in the court outside my house. Python hadn't arrived yet, but a crowd of onlookers had already gathered. I made attendance for this execution mandatory. Every man, woman and child living in Sheol needed to witness the consequences of a betrayal.

Tessa sat on a retaining wall just off of my lawn with Noelle next to her. They each held the hand of Tess's rambunctious boys that wanted to run around and play. Tess talked nervously to Noelle, her free hand rubbing nonstop over her belly. She'd be ready to pop soon, a new life to replace the one I was about to take.

On the other side of the platform, Heather was already crying and wailing dramatically, sometimes into Bones's shoulder, other times to no one in particular. He rubbed her back, but otherwise looked like he had no desire to be there. Jandro and Gunner had been breathing down my neck about what we should do with them, and I honestly wasn't sure. My explicit instructions were to not take their lives, so I ruled out their guilt based on that alone. But I couldn't exactly tell anyone that.

After surveying my citizens coming out to bear witness, my gaze landed on Mari at my side. "Are you going to sit with Tessa?" I asked her.

"I will. But I'll stay with you until you need to go up there." She glanced up at me. "I should tell you something."

"Might have to wait, sugar." Down the street, Dallas and Big G escorted Python toward us, each of them holding one of his arms. "We're about to get this show on the road."

"It's about Python."

"What about him?"

"The last two times I checked his vitals, he tried to convince me to escape with him."

"Really." I couldn't bring myself to be surprised. That slimy bastard.

"The last time, he grabbed my shoulders. Dallas got him off me and never took his eyes off of him after that."

"Good to know." I watched Dallas and Big G tie the traitor to the sawed-off telephone pole erected in the middle of the platform. "You can sit with Tessa now, Mari."

She went without a word, leaving only me and Hades together.

What she just told me ensured that this execution would drag on even longer than I originally thought. But she gave me a gift.

She took away the burden of my guilt.

When my men secured him and stepped off the platform, everyone went silent as Hades and I approached. Python stared at me as I took slow, measured steps toward him. His skin was slick with sweat. He strained against his bonds with heavy, ragged breaths, but he looked too stricken with fear to struggle for his life. Maybe touching my woman and trying to rope her into his scheming was his last resort. Too bad it would only prolong his suffering.

I turned to face everyone who gathered, Hades mirroring my movement.

"The Steel Demons do not take prisoners," I began. "This man has already received more kindness than he deserves by being kept alive this long."

"Reaper..." Python choked weakly from behind me.

I didn't spare him a glance. By trying to beg now, he was only digging himself further into a hole of pain with no relief.

"This man was a brother of ours," I continued, ignoring him. "Sworn to uphold the SDMC laws and to follow my leadership without question. Instead, he took it upon himself to conspire with an enemy who tried to have us killed."

I paced across the platform, making sure to meet everyone's eyes as I spoke. This speech was for every individual person, even Jandro, Shadow, and Gunner, who stood solemnly at attention with their arms crossed. Because everyone watching me, I trusted. And I would not make the mistake of trusting the wrong person again.

"Lying to me will not be tolerated." I made sure to carry my voice to ensure it reached everyone. "Conspiring against the club will not be tolerated. Putting your hands on *my* woman," I turned to face the prisoner, his face white, "will absolutely not be tolerated."

My hand lifted to my belt, where I grabbed the small pocketknife and switched it open.

"Reaper, please! I didn't touch her like that! I didn't mean, oh no— "

I ignored him as I grabbed the front of his shirt and sliced up the middle with my knife. With a clean rip, his shirt hung open in the front. Each side flapped in the breeze until I pulled them back, tucking each side behind his shoulders so everyone could see him bare-chested. And most importantly, the grinning horned skull of the Steel Demons emblem tattooed across his torso.

Like me, he went big on the ink. The tips of the horns touched his collarbones while the base of them met the skull at his sternum. The full design ended just past his ribs at the top of his stomach.

"Shadow?" I called out.

The large, silent man was at the edge of the platform in an instant, holding up a blow torch to me. I accepted it, switched it on, and meandered back to a horrified Python as I adjusted the flame.

"Only a sworn, loyal patched-in member can wear the Steel Demon," I announced. Then to Python, "You are defacing that symbol by wearing it on your skin."

"Reaper, please..." he whimpered.

"Other clubs have a history of giving a choice to their former members of how the emblem will be removed." I held my knife's blade up to the flame until it glowed. "And I was prepared to give you that choice as a final act of kindness. That is until," I lowered the blow torch, examining my freshly heated knife in the air, "I found out you tried to lull Mariposa into your cowardly fucking escape plan."

He continued to whimper and plead with meaningless cries. A dark spot spread rapidly on the front of his jeans as the smell of urine assaulted me.

"Your choice has been taken from you, Python." I ignored his accident as I moved closer to him, standing to the side so everyone could see. "And no matter how much you beg, you'll never escape the the blade of the reaper."

I held the red-hot blade within an inch of inked skin as he continued to whimper and cry. He could feel the heat from it, but I didn't touch him. I just let it hover over him while he braced himself, waiting for the burn. But I wasn't about to give him anything he wanted.

I flipped my grip on the handle, pointing the blade away from me while I pulled out another knife. A dull, jagged-edged thing that I chose just for this occasion. I sank it into the right horn of the tattoo before he could see me coming, but he felt every jagged rip of flesh from my steel.

His scream pierced my ears but I worked diligently. The knife didn't go deep but I had to use sawing motions to cut through him. A bloodbath covered both of us in seconds. I heard some people shriek and cry, then my men yelling at them to watch. No one was permitted to look away.

I took my sweet, painstaking time to cut a diagonal line across Python's torso, dying half of the tattoo a dark red. Pocketing my jagged knife, I switched to the heated blade and dug the tip into the opposite tattooed horn. Yeah, he forgot about that little guy. I could see it through his pain-stricken face as I began a second diagonal line in the opposite direction.

I got halfway through cutting my X on his body when Python passed out. Shadow tossed me the smelling salts and we were back in business within a minute. Python woke up so hard, the back of his head bounced off the pole he was tied to.

"I'm sorry. Am I boring you?" I twirled the knife handle through my fingers. "I was just getting started."

"I'm sorry...I'm sorry...I won't...again..."

"Should've said that sooner." I picked up where I left off, continuing my diagonal line to create a huge, morbid X through his tattoo. "Not that it would've done you any good. The timing just would have been better."

My X was finished. But I still wasn't done.

As I picked up the blow torch and began re-heating the blade, my eyes lifted across the crowd. Expressions were grim. Some people looked green and covered their mouths. Good. They wouldn't forget this. When I looked for Mari's gaze, her eyes met mine with steadfast determination. She was the calm in this storm that raged just under the surface.

The urge was strong to make this execution quick, like she asked. I didn't enjoy humiliating a man, cutting into him like an animal for dinner. Every instinct in me wanted to pull my knife across Python's throat, or sink it into his chest to end his misery. But I had a responsibility in this execution, and that was to ensure no one fucked with the Steel Demons again.

I never said the words, but Mari and I both knew—I didn't know if I had the strength to do this, to make someone's death a horror show in order to send a message. Looking at her reminded me that I could. She stood strong and tall like a president's old lady should. And I, as her man and the club's president, had to hold up my end of the deal and do what I signed up for.

So I set down the blow torch and spun around with my freshly-heated blade. I pressed the flat of it against the word STEEL inked onto Python's stomach. His screams made my ears ring and burning flesh filled my nostrils. I pulled the blade away, leaving a grotesque red burn with no readable tattoo left. I flipped the blade and pressed it to his skin again, this time to the word DEMONS.

He passed out again, and we woke him up again. I made sure not a single readable letter was still on his body before tossing the burned blade away and retrieving my jagged one.

"I made a promise in church, Python," I said as I undid the top button of his pants and yanked his zipper down. "You were there. Do you remember what that was?"

He let out a pained, wheezing breath. I wasn't sure if he could hear me anymore and didn't entirely care. I just wanted him conscious. I wanted to own every bit of his pain.

As I cut away his soiled underwear and had him naked from the waist down, it seemed to jog his memory.

"No, no, no, no..."

"Unlike you, Python," I tapped my knife against his hip. "When I make promises, I keep them. It doesn't matter how small, I won't ever go back on my word to this club I would die to protect." My blade dragged inward toward the base of his dick. "What promise did I make?"

"My...balls...your dog..."

"Good enough. Hades?" I whistled over my shoulder and my furry beast's ears perked up as he trotted forward. Turning back to Python, I cupped his sack and tugged, stretching out the thin skin attaching his balls to his body.

"I hope you enjoy this and take a long, good look at me." I brought the edge of the blade right to the taut skin above my hand. "I'm the last person that'll ever touch you here." Then I drew the knife in one swift motion.

A river of blood followed and I tossed Python's family jewels over my shoulder. Hades jumped in the air to catch them like he was catching a frisbee.

The ringing in my ears hit a new pitch, and it wasn't because of Python screaming. Something, either externally or in my own head, was blocking out all sounds for the voice. *His* voice.

Even as Hades gobbled down on his meal, those dark eyes held me and gave me the command.

His life is yours to take. Reap him now.

"Gunner!" I yelled, disoriented like I was coming out of a daydream. The crowd was in chaos below me, stunned and horrified, but my captain of the guard pulled himself up to the platform, nearly slipping in blood coating the wood.

"What do you need?" he asked.

I pulled a handgun out of his holster, turned to Python, and shot him in the chest.

Chapter 20

MARIPOSA

Reaper retreated into the house moments after he put Python out of his misery. People worked quickly to break down the platform and move the body. With the show over, everyone started dispersing to their own homes and workplaces. They all wore the same shocked, harrowed expressions. This event would stay in people's memories for a long time afterward.

In that regard, hopefully Reaper accomplished what he intended.

Heather swam against the current of people leaving, crying and wailing, to get to Python's body.

"What will they do with his body?" I asked no one in particular.

"Wrap it in a sheet and dump it just outside of Razor Wire's turf." The answer came from Jandro, who I didn't realize had come to stand next to me. "They'll see what we did to their informant and send the message up to General Tash. Hopefully he'll think twice about fucking with us again."

"I need to lay down," Tessa announced suddenly, pushing herself to stand.

"I'll walk you home," Noelle muttered, taking her elbow.

"Need me for anything?" I asked.

"No. Thank you, Mari." She gave me a strained smile. "I'll see you for my next appointment, if not sooner."

I nodded, giving her a wave goodbye as she walked off, Noelle holding one arm and her oldest boy holding the other. Everyone had to be in a state of shock. We all acted like we gathered for some routine announcement and didn't know how to process what we just saw. I wasn't affected by the blood and gore itself, but still needed to come to terms with what I just witnessed.

That, and the fact that Reaper was the one who did it.

"You okay?" Concern etched through Jandro's features as his hand caressed over my lower back.

"Yeah, I think so." I leaned into him slightly as I looked up. "I'm a little worried about Reaper, though."

"Yeah, I wouldn't try to see him right away." He looked toward the house as he pulled me tighter against him in a protective embrace. "He needs some time too. Everyone does."

I rested my cheek on his chest, leaning into his solidness and warmth as he brushed a kiss along my forehead.

"You hungry?"

"Are you kidding me?" I barked out a harsh laugh.

"Yeah, me neither."

The platform had been broken down and disassembled as we watched. Python's blood that had run off into the street left behind dark puddles that started to congeal and stick to people's shoes.

"Is there any way to clean the blood off the street?"

"It's not worth wasting the water," Jandro replied with a shake of his head. "We never know when we'll see rain again, so we have to keep our water stores for us." His fingers created gentle, soothing pressure on my back. "It'll be gone in a few weeks. The wind, sand, and wildlife will make sure of that."

I knew he was right. The dark stains on the ground, the only evidence of what happened here, would break down and dissolve into nothing over time. Python's screams and the grotesque imagery of his mutilation would soon fade from our minds in much the same way. It just felt so permanent now. My ears rang and the dark blood soaked into the ground like a tattoo. But every second that passed moved us further away from this event.

Python, his pain, and his crimes would eventually be forgotten. Someone else would betray their community in a similar way. History had a tendency to repeat itself. What did that mean for the message Reaper wanted to send? Hell, what did it mean for post-Collapse life in general? Were we stuck in a hamster wheel, never making any strides toward progress?

I wasn't sure what got me on this train of thought. Python's death didn't exactly sadden me, but it got me thinking. Not long ago, an execution like this would be considered barbaric. But if the past was what put us on the hamster wheel, we had to do something different to stop it, right?

"I want to check on Reaper." Slowly, I pulled myself out of Jandro's embrace.

He allowed it, but closed a firm grip around my hands. "I'm coming with you," he insisted. "Just in case he's, I dunno, not really himself."

We took off our blood-soaked shoes before stepping into what felt like an empty house. Reaper had left his own bloody boots by the front door, but was otherwise nowhere to be seen.

"Reaper?" I called, my voice echoing against the high, vaulted ceiling. Then I tried, "Hades?"

A soft bark floated down from the second level. Jandro and I took the stairs together, following the sound toward Reaper's bedroom.

"Hey, boy." I kneeled to greet Hades, guarding outside the door like a loyal sentry. "How's our human, huh?"

His fur was wet when I pet him, but not with blood. Jandro leaned down over us and took a small sniff.

"I think Reap gave him a shower. He's as fresh as a daisy."

"I bet you're right." I stroked over the handsome Doberman's ears and scratched down his neck. "Can we check on your master? Huh?"

Hades licked my cheek and stretched his front legs out on the floor until he was lying on his belly. As if he understood my question, he tilted his head toward the door as if to say, *you may proceed*.

"That dog freaks me the hell out sometimes," Jandro muttered as he followed me through the door. "You ever seen how fast he runs next to the bikes too? It's unreal."

"Yeah." I stole a glance back at the dog, looking as proud and regal as a sphynx with his front paws crossed in front of him and his ears straight up in the air. I wondered how much Jandro knew about his special abilities, including how fast he healed from the shrapnel wound. "He's something special."

We found Reaper sitting on the edge of the bed, naked except for a towel wrapped around his waist. Water droplets still hung off the tips of his hair from his shower. His skin looked red and scratched on some parts of his arms and back, like he turned the water on to a scalding temperature and scrubbed vigorously to get the blood off.

Or to scrub away what he did to a man he once called a brother.

"Reaper?" I took a few steps toward him, but Jandro caught my wrist to hold me back.

"Reap," he called out. "It's Mari and Jandro."

His elbows on his knees, Reaper's head turned slowly to look at us. "I haven't gone deaf or blind in the last ten minutes, so I dunno why the fuck you're acting so squirrelly."

I wrenched my arm out of Jandro's grip and went to kneel on the floor in front of my first lover. "Let me see your eyes." I didn't wait for him to comply, but took his hands away from his jaw and pulled back his eyelids myself.

"Sugar, what are you doing?"

"Checking to see if you're in shock."

His pupils looked normal. Next I pressed two fingers to his pulse and flattened my palm against his chest. His pulse was elevated slightly, but at normal strength. And his skin was warm from the shower, not cold or clammy with sweat.

"Do you feel lightheaded?" I asked him. "Dizzy? Nauseous?"

"No to all of the above."

"Good." I lowered my hands to his towel-covered knees. "So you're fine."

He glanced up at Jandro, then covered my hands with his before looking back at me. "Honestly, I wasn't. Not until you two came up."

"Why?" Jandro remained standing at the far edge of the bed, arms crossed and brow furrowed with concern.

"I can't—" Reaper cut himself off, seeming to look past Jandro toward Hades on the other side of the door. "I can't do that again. I can kill a hundred men in a day if necessary, but...not like that."

"I don't think you'll have to," Jandro assured him. "No one's gonna forget that for a long time. You got the message across, now Gunner's men are handling the body."

I ran my fingers over his palms, trailing up over his wrists and to his forearms. "It's over now. You did what you set out to do, for the good of your club." My mouth lifted toward his. "And I'm proud of you, President."

"Sugar," he said in a strained whisper. "I found my strength in you out there. I've never been so glad to find a woman who doesn't faint at the sight of blood."

"I'll always support you." I rose to my feet, intending to sit next to him on the bed, but his hands closed around my upper arms and he pulled me straight into his chest.

"Don't stop touching me like that," he pleaded. "Only the way *you* look at me makes me feel like a man and not a monster."

"I don't give a fuck even if you are a monster." I placed my knees outside of his thighs on the mattress. "You're *my* monster."

"Really, Mari?" He stared at me as he breathed the question, as if he couldn't believe it. "Even after seeing what I just did, you're not afraid of me?"

"My love," I stroked the back of my fingers down his cheek. "You make me feel like I don't have to be afraid of anything. With you, I'm fearless."

"My God, woman." His voice grew thick and husky with desire. An erection already began tenting his towel as he pawed at me. "How are you so perfect for me? How are you always exactly what I need?" He searched for the answer in my throat with his tongue.

"Um." Jandro cleared his throat. "Should I leave?"

"No," Reaper and I protested in unison. We wore matching smiles as our foreheads nudged against each other. "Stay, Jandro."

Chapter 21

MARIPOSA

My heart crashed so hard in my chest, I was certain both of them could hear it. Jandro looked a little dumbfounded, like he didn't believe what he just heard.

"You're sure?" His eyes bounced from me to Reaper.

Reaper pulled my shirt over my head as he answered. "Shut the door all the way, or else Hades will think he's invited to this party."

While Jandro did that, my top and bra were discarded on the floor. I slid off Reaper's lap to stand while he pulled my jeans down. He was more attentive with my lower half, kneeling on the floor to pull the fabric down from my hips all the way to my ankles. I used his shoulders for balance as I stepped out of them. His spot on the floor put him right at eye level with my panties, and he took full advantage of it.

He placed a slow, smoldering kiss on the crest of my hip bone, hands inching up my ankles to my calves, where his fingers rolled into my flesh. Kneading the muscles with his skilled hands, his mouth ghosted a trail over my lower belly until his lips met my opposite hip. There, he used more teeth, sucking a hard kiss on the skin before soothing it with the flat of his tongue.

His breath through the fabric of my panties sent a shiver up my spine. My fingers curled into his hair with impatience. I wanted no barriers between that mouth and my skin. As his hands moved to the back of my thighs, Jandro approached us slowly.

"Where do you want me, *Mariposita*?" His voice was tight with restraint, like he had to hold back from just inviting himself in. Even though that was exactly what I wanted him to do.

"Right here." I held an arm out to him.

He grabbed my palm and kissed it sweetly before moving in close enough for me to really touch him. His eyes stayed locked on mine as my arm wrapped around those thick shoulders. Always wanting to read me, to watch me. But I didn't want him to pull back anymore, so I took his hand and placed it on my bare breast.

Jandro needed no further instruction. With a groan, his mouth fell to mine. I slid his cut off of his shoulders, then tugged up on the back of his shirt. We only separated at the mouth for him to take his shirt off, then he filled his palms with my breasts. He moved to stand behind me, rolling my nipples between the rough pads of his calloused fingers while moving his kisses to my neck. When I arched into him, he traced every curve, gliding his hands over me while the warm, soft pressure of his lips lit up every sensitive nerve like a match.

He had me so delirious and needy for his touch, I barely noticed Reaper had pulled my panties down my legs until I felt the rough stubble of his face on my inner thigh. When I looked down at him, he shot me a wry grin and smacked one side of my ass as if to say, *remember me down here?*

A jolt of panic hit me. Sure, I knew my way around a man's body, but two at the same time? Even when I started to get a handle on loving two men, pleasing them both in bed seemed like a monumental task when there was only one of me.

Jandro must have sensed how my body stiffened up, because he wrapped an arm around my waist and turned my head to one side so he could kiss me.

"We're here for *you*," he said as he molded the full length of his body against my back. "Don't worry about anything you *think* you have to do. Let *us* please you."

Reaper murmured his agreement as he nudged my legs apart, inching his burning kisses closer to my center. My knees were already weak, and I was all but certain my pussy would start dripping onto his face.

"Let me taste you," he moaned greedily, pulling me forward with his hands on my ass until I was practically sitting on his face. Right where he wanted me.

I gasped at the heat of his mouth on my sensitive flesh, rising on my tiptoes to ease the pressure a little, but he was having none of that. He devoured me like I was his last meal, holding me in place with his unforgiving grip. He sucked me into his mouth, alternating between teasing nibbles and deep strokes of his tongue inside me.

I found a rhythm, rolling over his mouth as Jandro supported my upper body. His arms wrapped around me, somehow helping to hold me up while also setting me on fire. He moved with me, his torso following my writhing as I rode Reaper's face. Jandro's erection rubbed against my ass, reminding me of his own need as a counterpoint to mine.

No matter what they told me, I couldn't bring myself to lay back and be selfish. To only take and not give. Part of my own pleasure was in giving, to hear those sexy masculine moans and watch them shudder as they lost control. And I wanted to ensure I gave to them just as much as they gave me.

With one hand still in Reaper's hair, I reached behind me to stroke Jandro's length through his pants. He hurried out of them quickly, all the while keeping one hand splayed on my belly to support me. When the hot, rigid flesh met the cleft of my ass, I wrapped a hand around the base and stroked upward. His pre-come already coated my palm, aiding in my gliding up and down to the rhythm of his tight breaths.

Reaper chose then to stop teasing me. Releasing my tender lips, his mouth dragged up to the tiny bundle of nerves that had been begging to be touched for ages. He stilled my squirming with a large hand on my hip, aided by Jandro's forearm against my lower belly. I was no match for all the sensory overload—not Jandro's mouth on my neck, his relentless torture of my nipples, nor Reaper's mouth sealing over my clit or his fingers pressing inside me to curl against my contracting walls. Those fingers beckoned me once, twice. On the third time, I shattered.

My feet left the floor and I was weightless, held up by four strong hands I knew would never drop me. My vision danced with stars and my pulse thumped like my whole body was a giant drum. I felt it throbbing between my legs and every point of contact my men had on me. Someone cradled my head. Another set of hands supported my ankles.

I found myself lying on my back in a familiar bed, looking up at Reaper's hooded green eyes instead of down.

"Welcome back, sugar," he purred, stroking a hand down my side. "I think you blacked out for a second."

"Show-off," Jandro muttered from somewhere else.

I lifted my head to look around for him, finding the Vice President looking fucking delicious seated between my thighs. His cock pointed straight at me, thick and stiff. When he ran his palms up my thighs, his length flexed, bouncing once. I could watch this gorgeous naked man all day if I didn't need him inside me so badly.

Pushing up to my elbows, I noticed Reaper had discarded his towel at some point. He leaned against the headboard, his own erection pointing straight up in the air. I watched him stroke it absently, heat pooling in my belly.

He shot me a cocky smirk, seeing the desire in my eyes. "You want it, beautiful?"

"Yes."

"Tell me where."

I turned on my side, scooting closer to him. Further down the bed, Jandro followed me. I figured I'd just show Reaper where I wanted him, wrapping my hand around the stiff base, but he cupped my chin just as I was about to taste him.

"Tell me where you want me, sugar," he repeated. "And tell Jandro where you want him."

Heat burned my face. I didn't want to talk, I just wanted to feel. I wanted to lose myself in how incredible both of these men made me feel. But one thing I loved about Reaper was his dominance. Sex with him was the perfect mixture of dirty and intimate. And he knew exactly how to toy with me before we even got started.

"I want you in my mouth," I whispered, receiving a pleased hum from him. When I looked back at Jandro, he leaned over me on all fours, the silky head of his cock trailing over my hip and outer thigh. "I want you in my pussy," I told him, shyness making my voice small.

He leaned forward with a grin, closing the distance between us with a deep kiss full of warmth and sensuality.

"I'll take you anywhere you'll have me." His kiss trailed to my neck, then my shoulder. Those incredibly soft lips never lost contact as they skimmed down my ribs and waist like gentle rain.

Turning back to Reaper, I kept my gaze on his lust-filled eyes until the final moment my lips slid over the crown of his dick. His moan was a deep rumbling above me as I felt Jandro lift my leg and open me wide. He placed my ankle on his shoulder and the bed moved underneath all of us as he got into position.

Reaper gathered up my hair and held it in his fist, allowing me to look back at his best friend stroking more pre-come up and down his shaft. The president's cock was halfway down my throat when Jandro's head kissed the opening between my thighs. He held my leg steady against his chest as he pressed forward, guiding himself in with the other hand.

The fullness in my mouth and my pussy at the same time was almost too much. Too good. Each man approached sex so differently, and having them together was simply everything. Reaper held my head still by my hair as he began to thrust into my mouth, curses and growls fluttering out under his breath as he fought to keep under control. Jandro's fingers dug into my thigh against his abs as he pressed into me in deep, fluid strokes.

"God damn." Reaper released me off his cock, giving me a moment to breathe. Too bad each of my breaths were stolen every time

Jandro filled me up, his free hand still caressing me everywhere he reached.

"You're fucking incredible." Reaper cupped my face and leaned down for a kiss.

Our current position would only allow for a quick peck, but I wanted more. I wanted my lover's tight clutch of teeth and tongue, his all-consuming kisses. My leg slid off Jandro's shoulder as I rolled to all fours, causing him to slip out of me. While Reaper's and my tongues made love, a sharp unexpected slap on my ass made me yelp.

"Damn right, she's incredible," Jandro panted with a grin, smoothing his palm over the flesh of my ass where he spanked me.

I looked apologetically over my shoulder. "Sorry, I didn't mean to make you stop."

"Don't be." He seemed mesmerized by me, hands running up and down my sides to fill his palms with my curves. His eyes remained glued to my pussy, lifted and on display for him. "I don't want to leave the party too early."

"I'd give you shit and call you a minute-man," Reaper teased, filling his own palms with my breasts, "but I know exactly where you're coming from."

"Puns in the bedroom. I can see why your girl spent the night with me," Jandro shot back, laughing.

"Shut it. She just likes your window up there."

Chuckling, Jandro slid a hand between my legs, cupping my whole core with delicious pressure that had me arching and writhing. Those strong fingers teased a circle around my clit, and then his tongue probed and kissed at my slit. Any witty comeback I could add to their pissing contest was lost as all conscious thought went out the window. I needed more of that tongue, more of both of them.

Reaper cupped my face in his hands, steadying my writhing, squirming neediness with his green gaze.

"Put that beautiful mouth back on my cock," he ordered.

I obeyed, sliding my lips over steel wrapped in velvety skin. He growled when I took him deeper, fingers curling into my hair. Taking him down my throat on all fours was much easier than while lying on my side.

When Jandro's mouth and hands pulled away from me, leaving me unsatisfied and empty, I moaned around Reaper's dick, arching my back higher with need. Over my sucking and slurping, I thought I heard an amused chuckle behind me. Then he slammed into me and I screamed at the sudden fullness, my mouth still stuffed.

"Oh yeah, fuck her like that. She loves it." Reaper brought a hand down to my breasts, pinching one nipple in place as Jandro rocked me back and forth with his thrusts.

He wasn't sweet and romantic anymore. He held my hips and fucked me hard, grunting like an animal with the occasional slap to my ass. He was nothing like this our first night together. I'd never seen this side of Jandro before and didn't know it existed. And Reaper was right. I fucking loved it.

Tingles turned to sparks inside me, climbing higher at a pace too fast for me to catch up. When Reaper stiffened and spilled his salty release in my mouth with a heavy groan, his pleasure sent me hurtling over my own peak.

Sparks roared into a blazing inferno, electricity and heat wringing through me in release so hard I could barely breathe. Jandro slammed into me with a final deep thrust, following my crash with his own.

When the world came slowly back into focus, I was sandwiched between two hard, spent bodies. All three of us were slick with sweat but no one seemed to care. I ended up on my side, my head nuzzled in the center of Jandro's chest. Reaper brushed a kiss along my back and spooned me from behind.

A smile grew on my face. These guys were the type to talk shit, tease and rib each other, compare dick sizes, all of that. And yet they snuggled and sighed contently in the same bed, the same cuddle pile. I just loved how normal and safe it felt.

CHAPTER 22

JANDRO

I brushed a piece of hair out of Mari's face, utterly helpless to stop myself from looking at her. She drifted off to sleep for a moment, but Reaper and I remained alert. We had to leave for church soon.

He propped himself up on his elbow on the other side of her, hand resting on Mari's side while I touched her hair.

"You can use my shower if you want," he grunted out. "I made sure all the blood washed off the tile."

I huffed out a soft laugh. "Thanks, bro. I appreciate you not kicking me straight out of your bed."

"Why would I?" His gaze flicked down to the sleeping woman between us. "Look at her. She'd be so fucking pissed if I kicked you out."

That was what I had to remember. The only reason I was in his bed at all was because of this gorgeous woman who somehow captured his heart and mine. Not only that, she cared enough not to crush those beating organs in her adorable little fists. This was all for her. Reaper and I were two completely different men and yet we found one person perfect for both of us.

Finding one partner to spend your life with was rare enough.

Adding in more people and having it just feel *right* between everyone? The odds had to be astronomical. Being involved with Reaper and Mari like this made me appreciate what I saw between Reap's parents when we were kids.

His mom was openly affectionate with all three of his fathers. It weirded me out a little back then, but nowhere near as much as my Catholic aunt. We'd be leaving the flea market after she bought jewelry from Reaper's mom, who we witnessed kissing three men one right after the other, and Tia Ana would pull out her rosary and start mumbling prayers. She thought the poor woman had been lured into sin by the devil, but little did she know that Reaper's mom had the lion's share of the power in the relationship.

Reaper explained more of it to me later as we got older, but nothing could've prepared me for experiencing this myself. It felt...oddly normal. We were just two guys who wanted to make one woman happy, because she made *us* happy.

"Fuck," I breathed, tracing a finger lightly over Mari's cheek.

"Hm?" Reaper grunted.

"This is just...nice, dude." I kept my voice low to avoid waking her.

Reaper made a sound like he was about to bust my balls for being sappy, but he stretched his arm out instead and let his head flop down to the pillow.

"I've never had anything like this with anyone," he muttered, running his fingers lightly over her waist. "Everything about her is just so damn good...I'm scared to death of something bad happening."

I looked at him, surprised. It was probably the first time I heard Reaper admit to being scared of anything.

"We won't let anything happen," I told him. "If you drop the ball, I pick it up and vice versa. That's how we've always been, Reap. Nothing will happen as long as she's got us. And," I looked back down at her with a sigh, "who knows how many more poor bastards she'll put under her spell. She could end up with a whole army to defend her."

"Two more," Reaper muttered. "Four total."

"Yeah? Not a bad guess."

He didn't respond to that. The next sound came from a pair of lips brushing against my chest.

"Please keep talking. I'm loving this conversation."

"You little shit." Reaper slapped Mari's ass hard, making her shriek. "How long have you been awake?"

"Ow! First off, you two aren't as quiet as you think you are. And secondly, you both keep touching me. It's not like you're whispering in another room."

"Sneaky, smart-mouthed little..." Reaper tickled her aggressively, gritting his teeth, but smiling. He tried to pin her down and kiss her, but her squirming and flailing escaped his grip.

"Save me, Jandro!" she yelped, burrowing into my chest.

I wrapped her in a bear hug and flipped us over to the sound of her laughter. "Sorry, *Mariposita.*" I began my own tickle attack across her ribs. "You're not safe anywhere."

"Nooo!" she howled dramatically until she was breathless from laughter.

"Now this is not something I had considered," Reaper mumbled behind me.

"What?"

"Having to stare at your ass instead of hers."

"Better get used to it, buddy." I wiggled my hips and backed up towards him. "You never know when we might end up spooning in the middle of the night."

"Get that nasty thing away from me. I'll shove my foot straight up there."

I planted a final kiss on a giggling Mari before I stretched and crawled off the bed. "I'll take that shower now. Thanks, Reap. I definitely *won't* rub my dick and balls all over your nice tile work."

His groan was the last thing I heard before I turned the water on.

When I got out, one of Reaper's towels wrapped snugly around my waist, he had already left and Mari was reclining alone in the still unmade bed.

"What do you have going on today?" I sat on the edge and leaned over, resisting the urge to ditch the towel and make the most of our precious alone time.

"Not much," she admitted, rolling onto her back to look at me upside down. "I'm getting low on medical supplies and already out of a lot of stuff, so I've been pushing back appointments with people."

"I'll make sure Gunner knows," I promised her, noticing how her face changed when I said his name. "What did he do?"

"Nothing."

"Mari," I warned. "It's obviously *not* nothing. What's going on?"

She chewed her lip, scooting across the bed until her head rested in my lap. "We talked a little after you guys dropped him off last night. I pretty much confronted him on how he's been acting."

"And what did he have to say?"

"Essentially that he's going to keep ignoring me because we can't be just friends. And he doesn't want to be a part of," she drew a circle in the air with her finger, "you know, this."

"That's his fucking loss then." I gripped her slender shoulder and started to rub. "If he can't see that this is good and working for us, it's his own damn fault."

"It just...sucks," she frowned. "I miss him. He was one of the first ones who made me feel welcome here, besides you. I understand if this isn't his thing, but to not even be friendly with me? I feel like I did something wrong."

A flash of anger hit me like a bolt of lightning. Fucking Gunner. "You didn't do anything wrong, *bonita*. You followed your heart and trusted us. Don't ever feel like being happy is wrong."

"I pretty much told him that. I just wish I could make him understand. But then again," she slid a hand up my abs toward my chest, "I didn't really understand it until this morning."

"Nothing like multiple orgasms from multiple dudes, huh?"

"Stop." She smacked me playfully, returning my smile. "I mean, that's kind of it, but it's more than that. It's hard to explain, other than it just feels right. I think you know what I mean."

"I do." I brought her palm to my lips and kissed it. "I was always fine with sharing in theory, but yeah. Like you, I didn't really understand it until today."

"Executions and threesomes," Mari sighed. "So much excitement already."

"You know the best part about this, though?" I leaned down to her, cradling her face.

She tilted her lips up to me. "Hmm?"

I kissed them and whispered, "rubbing my ass crack all over Reaper's shower."

"Oh my God, Jandro! You did not!"

"Seriously, I had to do handstands to get those hard-to-reach spots."

"You are...the absolute...worst!" she choked out in a fit of laughter.

"Not when I can get you to laugh like this." I kissed her again and released a sigh with my forehead on hers. "I have to get going, but I will tell Gunner to make your supplies a priority. And to stop being a fucking dipshit."

"You don't have to do that second part." She rolled up to sit. "I have a feeling Reaper gave him a piece of his mind, and that's why he was so drunk at the fight. If he doesn't want this, we shouldn't push him."

"I won't get on him about being with us, just about treating you with the same respect as any other member of this club." I pushed her hair behind her shoulder for one last look at those perfect tits. "Which you are, by the way. We're gonna need to tattoo you soon."

"Tattoo?" Her eyes widened. "You mean *that* tattoo?" She pointed at the horned skull running across my ribs.

"That's the one," I smirked. "It's in the rules, *bonita.* Everyone gets it as a symbol of commitment to the club."

"Does it have to be that big?" She tilted her head to peer at mine more closely. "And where would it go?"

"It should be big enough to see all the details. Mine's a little smaller than Reaper's, and Shadow's is probably the smallest of everyone's."

I paused for a moment to swallow. I'd forgotten that she'd seen Shadow's, because she fucked him. I was a little jealous before, but she was mine now. I had no reason to feel that way. Still, the recollection left me with a small, weird feeling. Like learning a detail of your lover's past that you didn't really care to know.

"As for placement," I went on, "that's up to you, as long as all the details can be visible. I'm partial to right here, personally." I dragged a finger from her collarbone down over the swells of her breasts, continuing down through the valley between them.

She smacked my hand away. "I'm not getting a giant skull on my chest as my first tattoo."

"There is also the classy, under-breast corset style." I touched her again, this time running my fingers over the sensitive underside of her flesh. "Lots of women like ink there. Tattooing over the ribs is painful, though."

Her lip curled in distaste. "What else?"

"Slightly less classy, you have the lower back area, affectionately known as the tramp stamp. Noelle had hers done there. Hers looks a little wonky because we had to go to an outside artist." I drummed my fingers on her thigh. "We'll probably have to do the same with you, unfortunately."

Mari's brow furrowed. "Why?"

"Because," I paused for a moment that stretched on too long. "Our resident tattoo artist is Shadow."

Chapter 23

GUNNER

My face fucking hurt. The swelling went down a little around my eye, but I could still barely see out of it. I knew what I should've done—swallowed my pride and marched down to the medic's office with an apology. But now, sober and with enough regret to last a lifetime, I wasn't ready to see her yet.

Horus and I weren't alone in the conference room long. Shadow came in a few minutes later, followed by Reaper and Hades. Our president greeted me with his cursory nod and grunt, like this was any other day. Like he didn't filet a man alive this morning. None of the men slowly filing in acted like they just witnessed a brutal execution. Big G had the balls to shoot me a smug look. Whatever. I purposely turned my chair to face away from him. I burned one bridge already. Why stop there?

Jandro was one of the last ones to arrive, slipping in quickly to take his seat next to Reaper. They bent their heads toward each other and started whispering, Jandro's face immediately taking on a huge grin. I rolled my one good eye and ignored them too. I didn't even want to speculate on what they were talking about.

"We all here?" Reaper asked the room when the last man shut the door behind him. "Good. Church is in session." He slammed the gavel down with a definitive blow, then folded his hands on the table. "Today I did something that I hope never to repeat."

A deafening silence filled the room. Hardly anyone dared to breathe.

"In fact," Reaper stroked his jaw, "I'll go ahead and say I will *never* repeat what happened today. Because no true Steel Demon is stupid enough to go behind my back. Do I make myself absolutely clear?"

"Yes, president," came the resounding chorus.

"Python was a trusted member among us, and that was my mistake," he went on. "I failed you as a president because I trusted a man who didn't deserve it. I will not make the same mistake twice." He paused, his gaze resting on a small chip in the wooden center of the table. "We're shocked at what we saw. Some of us are grieving, mourning a loss. But this had to happen. And now that it's over, we must move on. Remember, but don't dwell. I kept my word and I expect nothing less from the rest of you."

His eyes scanned the room. "Would anyone else like to bring up a matter of business to discuss?"

I cleared my throat.

"Yes, Gunner?"

I ignored the way his brow furrowed at me and addressed the room. "There's a traveling market setting up next weekend on the Navajo Flats, just an hour's ride from here. While I'm still trying to secure a long-term trade partner, the market's vendors should have enough goods to keep us well-stocked in the meantime. I suggest several of us ride out, to maximize our load."

Dallas raised a hand.

"Yeah?"

"The wife's been begging to spend some time outside of Sheol. You think this market will be safe for women?"

"I don't see why not," I shrugged. "Many of the vendors are women offering clothes, jewelry, crafty shit. If Andrea don't mind carrying her own stuff, she can make it a shopping trip."

"Great, now she's gonna tell my sister," Reaper grumbled.

"Will there be medical supplies?" Jandro asked. "Mari's running low on some things she needs."

"Might be a lot of those weird snake oil remedies, but there should be legit vendors there too."

"Who wants to ride to the market?" Reaper asked the room. Nearly every hand shot up and our surly president groaned. "Some of you fuckers need to stay here to defend this place."

"I'll stay, President," Shadow volunteered. "I have no need for anything at the market."

We all knew the big guy hated big crowds of people, but no one was about to point that out.

"Thank you, Shadow. I'll need a few more. You all can draw straws or whatever the fuck you do. Anyone else have business to bring up?"

Jandro raised a hand. "I want to propose patching in the prospect Stephan as a full member of the SDMC. He earned my respect when he stepped up to fight me last month, and he's had my back while I've been working overtime on everyone's bikes. I trust the kid. He'll go to war with us on a single word from Reaper. Of that I have no doubt."

"You think he's ready?" Dallas stroked his beard with a frown.

"He's young. He hasn't proven himself yet," Brick pointed out.

"Let's bring him on the market ride with us," Reaper suggested. "He'll bring up the rear, where Shadow usually is. If shit gets hairy, we'll see how well he does. If he impresses me, then we can patch him in."

Jandro nodded, accepting that solution.

All other church topics were mundane stuff—the status of our solar panels, water treatment systems, food rations, blah blah blah. I was itching to get out of my seat and go for a solo ride, maybe fly over some canyons while looking through Horus. Of course I wouldn't be allowed to leave that easily.

When Reaper banged his gavel, signaling the end of church, the next thing I heard was, "Hold up, Gunner."

Jandro, naturally. Reaper hadn't succeeded in bringing me into their weird, hippie love triangle, so now his tag-team partner was trying his shot.

"What's up?" I propped my elbow on the table as everyone else filed out of the room.

Jandro moved to a seat closer to me, mimicking my posture. "What's going on, Gun?"

I shrugged, regarding him with a bored expression. "Nothin'."

"Yeah?" He cocked his head. "Why did you get shitfaced right before fighting Big G?"

"Why the fuck does it matter?" I demanded. "And while we're at it, why is everyone grilling me about shit that's none of their fucking business?"

"Because it's not like you to set yourself up to lose." Jandro leaned back in his seat. "Come on, dude. I'm coming to you as your friend, not your VP. Everyone knows you can hold your own against Big G, but you put yourself out there intentionally to send a completely different message. Why?"

"It wasn't intentional. I meant to just have a couple to get warmed up. I drank too much. I fucked up, okay? You think I *wanted* to embarrass myself like that?"

"I think you wanted someone to see you in a different light." He gave me a hard look. "Someone who hasn't seen you fight before, who wouldn't know you well enough yet to see how out of character this is."

"Jesus Christ." I dropped my forehead to my hand.

"You didn't expect her to care," he went on. "You thought she'd just shake her head at the drunk captain acting like a fool. But instead, she got between you and Big G's kick that could've broken your jaw, or worse."

My spine shot up straight like a bolt of lightning struck me. "Did he hurt her?"

"No," Jandro said coolly. "And if he had, *we* would've taken care of it. You were in no shape to be outside your own goddamn front yard, let alone fighting or defending someone else."

"Huh. *We*, you say." I spat the word out. "Like you and Reaper are her knights in fucking shining armor. Give me a break."

"I don't give a fuck what you call it," Jandro shrugged. "Didn't expect that either, did you? That she chose this? That she actually *wants* to be with Reaper and me? Blows your little golden boy mind, doesn't it?"

"Your peacocking is not fucking impressing me," I shot back. "Don't act like your intentions with her are so noble and pure."

"And yours are?"

"Fuck off, Jandro." I stood abruptly, causing Horus's talons to dig into my shoulder. "Next time you or Reaper get in my face about this shit, I won't wait for Fight Night. You'll get my fist right in your fucking teeth."

"You're the only one that's hurting her here," he called after me. "And yourself. All because you won't get out of your own way."

I slammed the conference room door behind me and headed for my garage. I needed to ride. I needed to fly until none of these people could touch me.

Especially her.

Chapter 24

SHADOW

I sat on my bed, which was little more than a worn-out mattress and box spring. A crude table served as my nightstand. It had been broken and repaired more times than I could count. On top of it stood the small, orange container, now empty. Last week, the woman—Mariposa—gave me seven tablets to see if they would help me sleep better.

I almost didn't take any. I considered throwing them away. But my current regimen had been losing effectiveness for years. Alcohol numbed me to a certain point, which slipped further out of reach the more my tolerance grew. I didn't know of any other options for relief. Neither did Jandro. So after staying up half the night debating with myself, I took one pill.

I never slept so well in my life.

For seven nights in a row, always after I took a tablet right before bed, I woke up still *in* bed. Not sprawled out on the floor. No cold sweats drenching my body. No sore knuckles or pounding headache. Not even a single piece of furniture turned over.

I went to sleep. And then I woke up feeling...refreshed. At ease. It was hard to believe this was how normal people experienced sleep.

But now the container was empty.

She said I could just try them to see if they worked, then go see her for more. It sounded like an easy enough solution when she was right there, holding the pills out to me in my own home. Staring at the empty bottle now, no task ever seemed so daunting.

I would have to go to her office. Talk to her again. Think of the right words to say and not fuck it up like I did before.

The memory of her hands on me, her parted lips and the sounds she made, the silky heat and pressure of her gliding around my shaft, flashed through my mind faster than I could push it away.

"Fuck."

My cock throbbed and flexed on its own accord. I stood up and started pacing around my room, giving my dick a few tugs to ease the pressure it ached for.

She didn't want that. She didn't enjoy it. I was wrong to do what I did. She wasn't available to touch and never would be to me. I couldn't think of her like that. But it was difficult not to when that was the most pleasurable experience I ever had with a woman. And I couldn't just avoid her.

I saw her a few more times here at my house in the past week. Talking to her was getting easier, but only when she started it by saying hello or how are you. Thinking of a mundane question to ask her was like pulling teeth for me. Jandro and Reaper kept all of her attention anyway. She would smile and greet me, then forget I was there long before Jandro took her up to his bedroom.

I used to wish she would forget me like everyone else did. Her presence threw me off-balance and made me uneasy. She disrupted the almost-peaceful routine I had established in this club. Now, for some reason I couldn't place, I *wanted* her to see me. To remember I was here.

"Yo, Shadow!" Jandro called from his end of the hall, booted footsteps approaching quickly. "We're heading out. You got everything you need?" He paused in my open doorway, wearing mirrored sunglasses on his head and all his riding gear.

Thankfully, my semi-erection had subsided. "Yes, I'll be fine. See you when you get back."

"Cool. I'll get you a churro. See ya." He moved as if he was about to go downstairs, then swiftly backpedalled. His eyes fell on the pill bottle next to my bed.

"Where did you get that?" I couldn't place his tone. It didn't sound good, but there was no point in lying.

"From Mariposa. She gave me something to see if it would help me sleep."

He slid his hard gaze to me. "When did this happen?"

"Last week. The day after the first night she spent here. She came over while you were at the shop." I lifted my hands, anxiety clutching me like a fist in my chest. "I didn't do anything, Jandro. I swear to you, I didn't touch her. I know better now. She gave me a week's worth just to try because of my nightmares."

"Relax, bro." His palms lifted to mirror mine, taking a few steps into my room toward me. "I'm not mad, I know you wouldn't do anything. I'm just surprised, that's all. Neither one of you said anything to me."

"I didn't think to tell you. I'm sorry."

"No, don't worry. It's all right. Again, just surprised." He rubbed his chin, looking back at the bottle. "So they worked for you okay?"

"Yes." I ran a hand back through my hair. He was the only one who didn't flinch at seeing my face fully uncovered. "I've slept better than I had in...ever."

"And you were okay with, you know," he paused, "accepting medication from her?"

I knew what he was referring to. The mental health ward in the prison we met had primarily female nurses and orderlies. While in prison, the doctors diagnosed me with a whole slew of mental disorders and prescribed me handfuls of pills to take every day.

I tried to explain I didn't want any females near me or giving me anything. When that didn't work, Jandro tried to explain on my behalf.

That resulted in him being assigned to a new post far away from me. Without my only friend, and constantly having to be restrained so women could force pills and water down my throat, I snapped.

The next thing I remembered was waking up in the solitary holding unit, permanently restrained with cuffs around my wrists, ankles, and neck. Jandro told me what the report said—I had assaulted my whole nursing team. They suffered concussions and broken bones, and intended to press charges.

"Yes," I said, bringing my awareness back to the present. "Mariposa has always been kind to me. And she gave me the option of refusing if I didn't want to try them. It was nothing like before."

He rubbed the back of his neck, looking away from me. "I know you wouldn't hurt her, man. You gave them plenty of warning back then, and as far as I'm concerned, you acted in self-defense. I'm sorry I had to ask, but I just," he blew out a long breath. "I care about her. Fuck, what am I saying? I love her."

I nodded, like I understood anything about what that felt like.

"Hey, while we're on this topic. Um." He clapped his hands together. "Can I ask you to think about something?"

"Okay?"

"Mari needs her tattoo—"

"No," I cut him off with an abrupt shake of my head. "I can't, Jandro."

"Just think about it is all I'm asking. You've made tremendous progress since she's been here, dude. And she's the president's old lady, for fuck's sake. She deserves a damn good tattoo, not one from some junkie with a guitar string."

"Jandro." I rubbed my forehead, my throat already closing up. The thought of drawing the demon on her skin and making it permanent was both exhilarating and terrifying. "I would have to *touch* her."

He cocked his head, eyebrows lifting. "That ship's already sailed *way* off into the sunset, my friend."

"And it never should have happened. I know that. She's yours too, now. So I don't understand why you'd want me to—"

"Bro, I said think about it, not overthink it, okay?" He clapped a hand on my arm. "Just think of her as a blank canvas, like every other tattoo you've done. I trust you, dude. You don't have to make it all weird just because she's female."

"What?" I barked out in frustration. "Have we met before?"

He burst out laughing, practically falling into me. "Fuck me, man. You've got a sense of humor now too! She really is rubbing off on you."

Ten minutes later I was on the rooftop balcony of the clubhouse with a rifle across my lap. Motorcycles shot out of the gate with a roar, dark shadows racing across a pale, sun-bleached landscape.

Reaper rode up front, leading the pack as usual. Hades raced at his side, long legs stretching out and fearsome jaws open with a smile. And clinging to our president's cut, Mariposa sat behind him. Her hair flew out behind her like the tail of a dark comet. Our club followed them, off to the traveling market where they would spend most of the day. Me and a skeleton crew stayed behind to guard our home and valuables.

Gunner's men had dropped off Python's body at the front gate of Razor Wire's clubhouse four days ago. We heard no response and hopefully that was good news, but we could never be too careful.

Eventually the bikes disappeared into the horizon and the sound of roaring engines with them. The occasional screech of some bird of prey became the only sound cutting through the breeze. I lifted my face toward the sky, closing my eyes against the bright mid-morning sun.

Gunner's bird never did come close to me again since that one time we were both up here. Even if it was the same bird that gave me my sight, it didn't matter. I had no bond with any animal. Although I often wondered how I was able to hear that first bird speak, and why it chose to bestow me with the gift of my sight.

There were so many things I didn't understand, things I just never learned as I was growing up. One of the first men temporarily caged with me taught me how to read and write. He was surprised I knew how to talk. I'd heard people speak all my life. I just rarely had someone to talk to.

Another man who took the place of the first, taught me basic math and science principles. I must have been in my teens when I learned to add, subtract, and divide. I learned about the concepts of gravity and dividing time into seconds, minutes, hours, and days. He told me how the sun made plants grow, and that it nourished people too.

I became obsessed with sunlight and the sky after that. Feeling a sliver of sunlight on my face felt like a huge act of rebellion. The women would come in, cut me, and leave me bleeding, never noticing that I dared to soak up all the sunlight I could through the cracks in those dungeon walls.

The other men came and went while I was the only constant. They all taught me various things with one overarching concept becoming clearer as I got older—men were good and women were evil.

My time in prison was the start of me unlearning that idea. The male guards harassed and abused me. Jandro was the only male staff member that was kind to me. The female workers were afraid of me. That was the pattern I noticed after spending time out in the real world. I had feared women all my life and now I was the stuff of *their* nightmares.

Jandro kept telling me there was another side to them. Sometimes they smiled and laughed. They would talk softly and listen when I had something to say. If I was lucky, they'd sit in my lap and touch me. The mere idea used to send me into an anxiety attack, but Jandro assured me it was a good thing.

Regardless, none of those things ever happened to me. Even my sexual experiences happened with a sense of dread and fear hanging over me and the woman involved. I didn't know how to make them feel less afraid, so I just got it over with as quickly as possible for both our sakes.

Once I was with Mariposa, it was like everything Jandro told me had finally clicked. I liked seeing her smile and hearing her laugh, even when it wasn't directed at me. I realized being with a woman could be enjoyable beyond the fleeting pleasure of an orgasm. Sometimes it just took a while to find that person.

"No. Fuck."

I set the rifle down the moment I felt my dick begin to swell, and began pacing back and forth on the roof. "God damn it," I muttered to myself. "Stop this. Stop it. I need to stop."

There was no way I could tattoo her. Not if I couldn't stop thinking of that moment every time I heard her name or my mind drifted. I would fuck up somehow if I actually touched her. I always did. Maybe Jandro trusted me, but I sure as fuck didn't trust myself.

A sudden buzzing sound on the breeze had me cocking my head. It sounded like a bee colony looking for a new hive. I picked up the rifle again, scanning the horizon for the telltale swarm, but saw nothing but blue sky.

My grip tightened on the gun barrel as the buzzing grew increasingly louder. I blew a short, high-pitched whistle between my teeth, signaling to the other guards to stay alert.

A black spot hovering in front of the mountainside in the distance made me squint. It looked like a bird at first, casting a shadow on the ground below, but the shape was wrong. As it got closer I saw the flying, buzzing thing had four limbs connected to a single body in the middle, with the buzzing sound coming from a small propeller on each of the limbs.

The realization made me suck in a breath and bring the rifle butt against my shoulder. I waited until my shot was all but guaranteed before I fired.

My shot hit one of the limbs, sending it flipping over into a tailspin hurtling toward the ground. It crashed with a small plume of smoke just a few hundred feet outside of the gate.

"Someone go retrieve that and bring it to me!" I yelled to the men below. I wasn't a natural leader, but Reaper left me in charge. Next to him, Jandro and Gunner, I was the most senior SDMC member. The younger members would be smart to obey my orders without question.

The gate slowly opened and two dirt bikes zipped out, zooming across the desert to the crash site. I paced on the roof as I waited. The others wouldn't be back until tonight. What was I supposed to do in the meantime? I didn't make these decisions. Reaper did.

The guys retrieved the object and brought it back within minutes. I didn't want to leave my post in case I saw more, so I had them bring it up to me on the roof.

"Do you know what it is?" I asked Benji, who held the flying piece of machinery out to me. It looked vaguely like a small helicopter.

"I'm pretty sure it's a drone," he answered, turning it over in his hands. "You can use it to spy, drop off packages, stuff like that. See this?" He pointed at a small black circle on the central body. "That's a camera lens."

My blood turned to ice. I remembered a church meeting where Gunner brought up that General Tash had been looking to buy drones from us, before we found out he was working against us.

"So someone was controlling this remotely?" I asked.

"Yeah. Probably not too far away either. These things don't work over really long distances."

"Destroy it now," I barked. "The camera inside, the navigation system, whatever could send information back. I want every piece of this thing turned to dust."

Benji hesitated. "You sure? I'm not super techy, but someone here could probably get information off the chips and find out who it belongs to."

"Did I fucking stutter?" Reaper used that phrase when he got tired of repeating himself. "I already know who it belongs to."

Benji's wide eyes showed that I got the point across. "Yes, Shadow. Right away." He scampered off the roof with the drone under his arm.

Absently, I watched him and the other guys wrecking it in the street below. They took turns shooting at it, slamming it into the ground, and running over it with their bikes. I checked my rifle and returned my gaze to the sky, wondering how I would tell Reaper about this.

My hands squeezed around my weapon, ever vigilant. I silently hoped that whoever controlled the drone never got the information they were looking for.

Chapter 25

MARIPOSA

"Property of?" I glared at the jackets Noelle was holding up.

She rolled her eyes as she tossed one to me. "Don't get all high and mighty on me. It's an MC thing. If you're someone's old lady, you are considered property of that club. It means we protect you and it lets other clubs know you're off limits. Don't take it too literally, 'kay?"

I ran my fingers over the letters embroidered above the SDMC patch that all the guys wore on their cuts. An unexpected giddy feeling bubbled up in my chest. I was honestly excited to wear the demon on my back, even if I wasn't fond of the words "Property of" centered above it. Reaper and Jandro were the heart and soul of the SDMC and I was proud to display that I belonged to them. I just hoped my tattoo wouldn't require those words.

The leather jacket was already well-worn with lines and creases telling the story of its previous owners. It still fit like a glove when I slid it on, wrapping me in a new kind of armor. The type of armor that told onlookers I found safety in the arms of the most dangerous men in the Southwest.

"Why the fuck do you always look so good in my shit?" Noelle grumbled as I turned to look at the back of the jacket in her mirror.

"Don't worry," I laughed. "I'm done borrowing your stuff. I'm getting all my own clothes at the market today."

"Keep the jacket. It really does look good on you, and I don't need an extra," she told me with a wave of her hand. "What are you bringing to trade for goods?"

"Drugs, of course." I shot her a wry smile. "They're what got me here from East Texas. Pain pills, sedatives, amphetamines, you name it. If you want to feel something, there's a pill for it."

"Look at you, little dope slinger." She swatted my hip playfully. "Makes sense, considering you survived on your own this long. I don't think that's a market Gunner ever tapped into. He just doesn't have the knowledge you do."

Hearing his name brought on a twisting sensation in my stomach. He still hadn't said a word to me since after he fought, and Jandro never told me how their talk went. We could avoid each other easily enough, but nearly a week later, the pangs of missing him refused to go away.

I shook my head at Noelle, bringing my thoughts back to our conversation. "I only slung pills when I needed to pay for travel, or if real medical services weren't needed. My main priority is helping people, not profiting off of addictions."

"I know, babe. It's just interesting to know that about you." Noelle ran her tongue across her teeth. "You did dirty work to survive, but didn't backstab anyone in the process. You were a Steel Demon girl before my brother ever set eyes on you."

"Yeah, right." I blushed at the remark. "I wasn't nearly badass enough to fit in with all of you."

"Well, you're stuck with us now." She squeezed my shoulder through the worn leather jacket. "You might have noticed this already, but we're more than just a club. We're family."

"Even fighting like family members," I mumbled.

"Exactly. Now let's go shopping!" With an excited squeal, she pulled me down the stairs by the hand, practically skipping out the front door.

She wasn't the only one excited. Under the idle rumbling of engines outside, everyone was abuzz about this traveling market. Apparently it only came through the area sporadically, once a year at best since the Collapse. Because more people were nomadic these days, the market's vendors followed population density, which changed with the seasons. Most of the time, from what Reaper told me, it depended on whether a certain area was in a war zone or not.

Thanks to the Steel Demons keeping order and making agreements with local businesses, our section of the Arizona territory was considered relatively peaceful. It meant people felt safer living here, and made trading goods profitable.

The major border wars had shifted eastward, with conflict growing between the New Mexico and West Texas territories. When I passed through those areas on my journey west, the conflicts had been scattered and unorganized, run by small-time gangs with little resources or connections. General Tash, the central power in New Mexico, was highly organized and well-stocked with trained soldiers and heavy artillery, the latter of which was mostly supplied by the Steel Demons, before the general betrayed them.

Reaper and Jandro ranted at each other for half a night, fueled by whiskey and añejo tequila, about the many border conflicts surrounding us and their predictions on the generals' moves. I tried to follow and keep up, but with the booze making me drowsy and the orgasms they gave me earlier, I couldn't stay awake. But I still woke up cozy in bed and sandwiched between them, which was becoming our new routine.

"Mmm, I love that jacket on you," Jandro's honeyed voice murmured in my ear as a hug wrapped around me from behind. "When we get back, I want to get you completely naked except for the jacket."

Grinning, I looked over my shoulder for a kiss, covering his hands with mine at my waist. "If you promise to be a good boy."

"I'll be anything you want me to." His kisses moved to my neck, affectionate and sweet. "Who you riding with today?"

"Reaper on the way over." I kissed his pouting bottom lip. "You on the way back."

"Saving the best for last, I see," he smirked, then kissed me deeply before slowly untangling himself from me. "I'll see you there, *Mariposita.*"

I somehow made it over to Reaper and Hades on wobbly legs. Jandro never failed to have me swooning on my feet.

"Is that smile for me?" Reaper handed me a small mug of coffee, green eyes twinkling. Even he was in a great mood today.

"Always." I stood on tiptoes to reach his lips. "Jandro just put it there first this morning."

"That motherfucker," he growled in jest before his mouth descended on mine.

I had kissed both of them seconds apart for days now, and the contrast of Jandro's softness with Reaper's roughness never failed to send my nerves tingling. The thrill of it went straight down to my toes, concentrating in my core. Neither one was better than the other. My body craved each man for the unique pleasure he gave me.

We finished kissing and I drained the coffee before handing the mug back to him.

"Ready, sugar?" He screwed the mug back on the thermos cup and handed me my helmet.

"I still think you should wear one of these," I said, pulling it over my hair.

"I'll buy one today," he grinned.

Liar.

After an hour of riding through an uninhabited desert, colors and movement began to appear on the horizon. I popped up my visor and squinted over Reaper's shoulder. The colors expanded outward in both directions. I started to see tents and canopies, and what looked like metal shining in the sun.

By the time Reaper slowed, the club was pulling up to what resembled a bright and lively downtown district. This market was a whole lot more than just a few vendors selling things at tables. A pair of musicians played on a guitar and drums while children danced. One stall roasted a huge pig over a bonfire, turning it slowly on a spit. A repurposed taco truck advertised wood-fired pizza. The cute little cart next to it said, "Fresh-baked cookies!"

Every kind of food imaginable was here, and hundreds of other vendors on top of that. Just scanning from the bike I saw jewelry, clothes, furniture, books, teas, and candles. I began to see why everyone was so excited about coming here. It was a feast for the eyes. and one that made it easy to part with your goods to trade.

When Reaper pulled up to park at the crudely erected gate just outside the market, I only then noticed the other motorcycles parked in the area across from us.

"Reaper."

"I know, sugar. Other clubs are here to do business too, but they're nothing to worry about." He swung a leg off the bike, then picked me up by the waist to set me on the ground. "Just keep this jacket on at all times. Got it?"

"Yes, president," I teased.

"Fuck, you just had to call me that while wearing a *property* jacket." He stroked a thumb across my cheek. "You're so fuckin' hot, you know that?"

"Aww, thanks Rory." I grabbed his belt loops and pulled him closer. Somewhere behind me, Jandro cracked up laughing.

"And boner ruined," Reaper grumbled.

"There's pills for that, you know."

"Shut your damn mouth." Capturing my face between his palms, the kiss he gave me prevented me from doing just that. "Don't wander too far," he whispered against my lips. "Stay with Noelle, or anyone else in the club. And remember—"

"Keep the jacket on, I know."

"Good girl." A final kiss. "Love you." He sent me off with a swat on the ass to Noelle, who waited for me at the market entrance.

"He sent you away fast." She narrowed her eyes in suspicion at her brother as we started walking through a narrow path between colorful stalls. "I thought he'd want you glued to his side."

"What, you think he's up to something?" I looked back briefly. He was just digging into his saddle bags like the rest of the guys.

"You never know with him. Nothing bad, of course," she assured me at my wide-eyed expression. "You keep his dick locked in a cage as far as he's concerned. He's not going anywhere in that sense."

Now that she pointed it out, I was going to keep thinking about it if I didn't have a distraction.

"Let's find something for Tessa," I said. "Not for the baby, but a gift just for her."

Noelle grabbed my arm with an excited squeak. "That's a great idea! The poor thing probably hasn't gotten a nice non-baby related gift in years. Let's see, she loves anything to do with flowers..."

Noelle ended up picking out a hand-painted sunflower wall hanging and I got Tess a candle that smelled like roses. I couldn't read the foreign writing on the label, but the candle had a picture of a motorcycle on the tin, which seemed fitting.

We stuffed our faces with street food and meandered for hours. The market seemed to stretch on forever! I still hadn't found much clothing in my style, so while Noelle paused to look at garden statues, I moved on to a shop with lots of pretty fabrics billowing nearby.

The garments were lightweight and decorated in every color and pattern imaginable. A few mannequins showed their versatility—wrapped around the body to make a halter dress, a long skirt, or around the head for a scarf. It seemed like a great solution to keep the sand out of my hair while riding.

I flipped through the selections on the table when a tiny, elderly woman emerged from under her canopy and gave me a wide, toothless smile.

"Ohh, you!" She pointed at me. "So beautiful! You must try on, yes?

Please try!"

I smiled back, taking note of her broken English and heavy accent. "*Español?*" I was still rusty at the language, but Jandro had recently started teaching me more. Might as well practice it out in the wild.

"Oh no." The woman waved her hands and shook her head. "No, no, no. Is okay! Please just try!" She snatched the length of fabric I was holding with surprising strength and moved behind me, holding it out as if to put it around my shoulders.

"Oh, you don't have to do that." I turned around and held out my hand to take it back from her. "But thank you."

Undeterred, she waved the fabric at me. "You try on! So beautiful! I give you so cheap! Please!"

Deciding to humor her, I relented, turning around and lowering to her level so she could put the scarf on me. Rather than putting it over my shoulders like I thought she would, she proceeded to tug at my jacket collar.

"Take off. You must try on."

"Hey, hey, take it easy!" The jacket slid to my elbows with how insistently she tugged at it. I was already thoroughly turned off from buying anything from her, but didn't want to cause a scene in a crowded market. I'd try on the scarf, take it off, and politely tell her I wasn't interested.

I allowed her to peel the jacket from my arms, intending to hold it or tie it around my waist, but she suddenly turned and ran behind her stall with it.

"Hey, what the fuck!" I took off after her, mad as hell. "Give that back, you fucking thief!" I pushed fabrics out of the way, chasing her at full speed and crashed into a wall.

No, not a wall. Just a very solidly-built man. Tree-trunk sized arms came around me, crushing me against an unyielding chest.

"She the one?" A gruff voice above me asked.

Someone else lifted the back of my shirt, prompting me to kick and flail with all my strength, which wasn't much against the man restraining me.

"Don't touch me!" I shrieked. "Ugh, let me go!"

A bony hand grabbed my face and turned my head cruelly to look at one of my captors. His face was dark and lined with years of harsh sun exposure. I saw myself frozen with fear in his harsh, dark eyes. Who were these men? And what did they want with me?

"You got any club ink?" the face-grabber asked me. "Think carefully. I got no problem stripping you down and finding out myself."

I knew he wasn't lying. If he would just get out of my face so I could see one of my men...

"N-no," I answered. "But I had a property jacket. I'm with the Steel Demons and you assholes are *so* fucked!"

Both of them chuckled at my false bravado. "I don't see any jacket. Nor any of them pussy Demon fuckwads anywhere."

"They're here!" I insisted at the top of my lungs, though my voice barely carried over the hustle and bustle of the market. "And when they find out I'm missing, you're in for a world of hurt."

"How about you shut up and let that cunt do the talking?" He grabbed between my legs and I felt the first real jolt of terror wrack my body. These men were probably looking for unclaimed women at the market to sell. What did they give that old lady so she could take my jacket away?

Thankfully the chaps over my jeans provided an extra barrier between me and his groping hand. Still, my stomach roiled and tears sprang to my eyes. No, this couldn't be happening. After all this time wandering alone, then finding love and safety in the last place I expected it, and this was it? Meeting my end by getting tricked in a marketplace? Because I would rather die than endure what these men would put me through.

"Get her on the truck." The groper finally pulled his hand away from my crotch and wrapped it around my throat. "If you keep quiet, I won't hafta cut your tongue out. You understand?"

I gave a shaky nod with my head and allowed myself to be dragged away.

Chapter 26

GUNNER

Too many people. Too many weird smells. Too much bullshit.

This market was seriously lacking compared to the other ones I'd been to. Or maybe it was just my sour mood.

Nothing brought me out of my funk, no matter how much flying, riding, or swimming I did. Only seeing *her* lifted my spirits. Mari. She didn't need to kiss my wounds, just her voice and her soft touch was healing enough. Even I had to admit she seemed much happier in the past week than when we first brought her home. I always knew she belonged in the club, whether or not she was with me.

Then Jandro or Reaper would kiss her, sometimes they both did at the same time, and my mood took another fucking nosedive. If three was a crowd, four would be downright suffocating. I guess for them it made some sense. Jandro and Reaper were already best friends when I met them. They did everything together. I never saw it, but certainly wouldn't be surprised if they shared a woman before.

It wasn't just that they both had her, but how easily the three of them seemed to connect as a single unit. Mari and Jandro would share a joke at Reaper's expense, he'd grumble about it, then she turned around and was all cute and silly with him. They acted like this three-way relationship was completely normal, natural even.

But it wasn't. And after some time, they would see that. The whole thing would come crashing down and I refused to be caught in the middle when that happened. I refused to be a reason Mari got hurt.

You're hurting her right now, douchebag. You saw those fucking tears in her eyes when she left you in her office.

I shook my head as if to clear away the dissenting thoughts and threw back another beer. I found the brewer's stall right away and had been parked here for a good hour, but I was nowhere near as fucked up as the night I fought Big G. That was a mistake. An even bigger mistake was letting Jandro see right through me. I didn't know how he caught onto that, but that fucker was nothing if not perceptive.

Shutting my eyes, I let my consciousness slip in Horus's. He was sitting on a cactus just behind the market, watching for rabbits and ground squirrels. A sound rattled through his mind and my own, pulling me back into my own body with confusion. It was hard to make out over all the noise in the market, but I cocked my head and listened again.

"Gunn...!"

I swore I heard my name being shouted but something wasn't...

"...rus! Gunner! Help me!"

"Fuck, Mari!"

I ejected off of the barstool and started running, slipping into Horus again to use his eyesight. There she was, being dragged off by two slimy-looking fuckers toward a box truck.

"Stop them, Horus!" I pumped my arms and legs as fast as they would carry me, but no animal on earth was faster than a peregrine falcon diving for an attack.

He came down like a bullet just as I turned a corner and saw them with my own eyes. The big guy carrying her got a neck full of talon from my loyal bird, forcing him to release Mari with a bloodcurdling scream.

"Gunner!"

"Come here, baby girl! I got you!" I held my arm out to her while drawing one of my guns with the other. She curled into me, trembling as she clutched at my cut. I wrapped a protective arm around her back while scoping out what I was up against with a sinking feeling of dread.

The other guy had a gun on me, standing over his big friend, who was still bleeding profusely from the neck. Horus was nowhere to be seen, but he'd done his job. The big fucker was growing pale and would be dead within an hour. But more of their crew started coming out of the woodwork—from behind the truck and hiding places between crowded stalls. All of them armed.

Fucking sex traffickers. They must have been scouting this place for fresh merchandise. I had no idea how they managed to touch Mari and get her jacket off, but it was too late to dwell on that now. My only hope for her safety was to convince these shitbags she was already my property.

Literally.

"Sorry for what I'm about to say," I mumbled into her hair before raising my head to address the men closing in on me. "This woman belongs to me!" I declared, keeping my shooting arm outstretched. "None of you had a right to touch her."

"She's not tatted, Demon," the scrawny guy with a gun on me snarled. "Where's your proof?"

"She's a new purchase, so I haven't inked her yet, but I have a receipt. It's on my bike."

"What, and let your club gut us? No, thanks."

Damn it. Mari must have told them we were all here. They weren't buying it and my hope started to dwindle. Thankfully, she caught on and made a convincing actress.

"It's true!" She peeked back fearfully at the trafficker as she molded her body to mine. I clenched my teeth against the sensations of her hips and and hands on me. This was the wrong time to enjoy it. "This is my master. My body is his."

"Prove it," the dipshit said again while a dozen guns cocked. Mari flinched at the sound and glanced up at me with terror in her eyes.

"I'm sorry," she whispered, bringing a trembling finger to my jaw. "I know you don't want this, but—"

Her lips tilted up to mine with the softest ghost of contact. How I wanted to savor the warmth of her breath on my mouth, to taste her slowly and explore her kiss properly. To do so with no one else around us, just me and her learning about each other this way. But our very lives were on the line, and I had to play the part of a callous slave owner.

So I grabbed the back of her head and claimed her mouth roughly, choking off her gasp with my tongue. She went along with it, wrapping her arms around my neck and digging her fingers into my ponytail. Her leg lifted to wrap around my hip, drawing me tighter into her body. I couldn't figure out whether to be sorry or glad this wasn't real. I never would've kissed her for the first time like this. But I may also never get a chance to kiss her again.

"Quit fuckin' around!" the small guy with a gun roared. "This bullshit proves fuck-all."

"Well, what do you want?" I demanded. "I told you my receipt is on my bike!"

His mouth twisted into a cruel smile.

"Describe her pussy *in detail.* I'm talking size, shape, color, and any marks she's got down there. Then we'll check to make sure you're right."

Fuck.

"Her tits too," one of his homeboys added.

"She's not yours to inspect," I growled. "You're not touching my property and lowering her value."

"Think of it as verification," he said smugly. "Which you conveniently can't seem to do."

Shit, shit, shit. My eyes darted around, looking for any possible way out. We'd be shot before I could squeeze my trigger. Reaper and Jandro had gone off to a completely different side of the market and no one else was around. I purposely went off by myself because I was tired of getting the third degree from everyone.

And it was a good thing I did. Otherwise Mari would've been

captured and completely alone. I stayed away from her enough in the past two weeks. I wasn't about to leave her now.

My arm tightened around her shoulders as my gun hand lowered slowly. "I don't give a fuck who you all are. She's mine and I'm not letting her go."

"Suit yourself," the scrawny guy shrugged. "You're almost pretty enough to pass for a bitch." He jerked his head toward the box truck. "Get in."

His gang moved in, took my gun, and patted me down for the rest of my weapons. When they succeeded in fully disarming me, they ushered us into the back of the truck. The big guy bleeding from the neck was shoved, then dragged, out of the way. He was completely motionless and must have died minutes ago.

Just before they pulled the door down to seal us in darkness, I saw my falcon diving across the sky.

Chapter 27

JANDRO

"Nah, nah, nah, man," I waved my hand at the auto parts vendor. "Your prices and your parts are bullshit. Don't be trying to hawk this cheap shit at me. I know you got Harley branded clutches. Where they at?"

The guy switched to Spanish to pretend like he didn't understand me, then looked like a damn fool when I told him off in a rapid string of insults that would've earned me one hell of a beatdown from my aunt.

He finally quit trying to swindle me and I got an alright deal on the parts I needed. This whole bartering system wore me out. I didn't have Gunner's patience for getting the best deal I could. Maybe one day we'd have a national currency and fixed prices again, but I wasn't holding my breath.

I made my way over to Reaper and Hades emerging from one of the metalsmith stalls. Hades' nose immediately went to my pants pocket, sniffing aggressively at the brown paper bag I had stashed in there.

"Okay, pooch." I held up an index finger. "*One* doughnut hole. That's all you get, all right?"

He licked his lips and stared up at me expectantly. I pulled the snack from my pocket and tossed it in the air so he could catch it in his mouth. Reaper shook his head disapprovingly.

"You're gonna fatten him up like a Christmas ham."

"Nah, he'll run those calories off on the way back." I nodded at the small drawstring bag in his hand. "You get what you need?"

"Yeah. Will you tell me what you think of this?" He glanced up at me as he opened the bag, and I dare say he looked nervous.

Inside the bag was a velvet ring box. He popped it open and carefully lifted the ring from the cushion to show me.

"Damn, dude." I accepted it carefully, turning it over to see the light catch the stone. "You did good."

Polished to a high shine, the stone in the center shifted from pink to green depending on which way the light hit it. Ridges and formations within the stone made it look like a tiny landscape full of depth. A microscopic world of canyons, valleys, and meadows.

The setting was a simple silver bezel, sitting on top of a band that twined around like a length of rope. The letter R was stamped on one side of the band, and the letter M on the other.

"You think she'll like it?" Reaper asked with more than a hint of eagerness.

"She'll love it, bro. She's gonna flip." I grinned as I handed the ring back to him. "What kind of rock is that?"

"Watermelon tourmaline," he said softly, examining it one last time before returning it to the box. "It was one of my mom's stones. The setting was hers too. I just needed to find a smith that could put it together."

"Awww, look at you, Reap!" I gave him a good-natured punch to the shoulder. "Make sure you tell her that. Girls love that sentimental shit. When are you giving it to her?"

"I dunno, not today." He wrapped the drawstring bag around the ring box and slid it into the inner pocket of his cut. "When it feels right."

I rubbed the back of my neck. "I uh, might've gotten her something too. Not all sentimental like yours, but something I thought she'd like."

"Yeah?" His eyebrows lifted. "Let's see it, Romeo."

I dug through my pack, reaching for the pocket I carefully sectioned off from my tools and bike parts, and produced the slender, shallow box.

Reaper took it from me and carefully pulled off the lid, looking up at me with wide eyes and a grin when he saw the necklace laying on the tissue paper.

"Jandro, are you fucking serious?"

"Please don't tell me it's lame," I begged. "I traded a set of perfectly good spark plugs for it."

"No, dude. This is really nice." He lifted the pendant, a monarch butterfly, and carefully ran his thumb over the surface. "What is this, iron and stained glass?"

"Yeah. She said the wings were made from windows in a cathedral. Probably a bunch of bullshit, but it made me think of Mari when I saw it, so—"

"She'll love it." He replaced the box lid and handed it back to me just as a low growl emitted from Hades' throat.

"Oh, you don't think so, pooch?" I slipped the necklace back into my pack. "Should I give Mari the rest of your doughnut holes instead?"

"Something's wrong," Reaper muttered, his fingertips drifting over Hades' raised hackles. "Where *is* Mari?"

"She went off with Noelle last I saw." I pointed in the general direction, but Hades was already taking off in a completely different direction. He cut straight through the center of the market, heading for the back side.

Reaper and I followed him without a moment's hesitation, dodging shoppers and vendors alike. When the dog broke into a full-on sprint, my hand drifted to the gun in my holster. Reaper did the same, handgun already drawn as we hurried to keep Hades in our sight. He started barking his head off, which helped to get people out of our way.

We reached the last row of stalls and pushed through, with only the barren desert to greet us. It wasn't too windy but a fair amount of dust had kicked up and stung the hell out of my eyes.

"Look!" I grabbed Reaper's shoulder and pointed to someone laying motionless in the dirt.

It wasn't Mari, but a big dude who had bled out from a serious injury from the looks of it. We turned him over and found that his neck had been shredded, like someone started decapitating him with a rusty saw and abruptly stopped.

"What the fuck?" Reaper whispered in disbelief.

"Your guess is as good as mine." I began searching his pockets, lifting up his shirt for any tattoos or signs of who this guy might be. "He hasn't been dead long, that's for sure."

"Look," Reaper pointed. "Tire tracks."

My heart nearly collapsed in on itself like a black hole. "Those are big tires. Some kind of truck."

"Oh God..." Reaper tipped his head back, grabbing a chunk of hair in his fist. I knew we were both thinking the worst—human traffickers.

"No time to worry. Let's round up the Demons," I slapped his shoulder hard to make him focus. "And follow those fuckin' tracks. Where's Gunner?"

Our answer came in the form of a screech and a fast-moving shadow above our heads. Hades stood on his hind legs, barking at the falcon who clutched something in his talons.

"Shit." The color drained from Reaper's face. "They got Gunner too?"

Horus screeched again and released what he was holding--a scrap of the property patch from Mari's jacket.

I couldn't tell how he knew, but Reaper somehow understood what this animal communicated to him. His expression contorted into one of pure hatred. Not even when we caught Python did he look this pissed.

"Horus can see the truck from over a mile away," he said with an eerie calm. "They couldn't have gotten far. Hell, they're probably not even a mile away right now."

"We can be on 'em in minutes, then," I said, my blood simmering. Python got it easy compared to what these scumbags were in for. Snatching women from a public market was bad enough, but to rip *our* patch off of our woman and not think there would be retribution for it? The entire Arizona territory would hear about this. Fuck, the entire

Southwest would. I hoped our revenge would reach General Tash's ears and make him shiver just a little.

"Hades, follow those tracks. We'll catch up." The dog took off, following Reaper's orders. Horus soared high, following Hades from above. If I wasn't so messed up with worry about Mari, it would've weirded me out how humanlike the animals' responses were. Not that it was that different from how they usually acted, but this time was particularly obvious.

Reaper then turned to me, his face hard and determined. "Round up the Demons. We're getting our girl back."

Chapter 28

MARIPOSA

Gunner never let go of me. The walls he set up between us over the past two weeks collapsed into nothing the moment he saw I was in trouble. From that moment at the market to our dark, musty prison in the back of the truck, he held me as tightly as either of my men would.

"They're coming to get us, baby girl," he assured me, lips against my forehead. "Reaper and Jandro already found the body. Horus is right above us and Hades isn't far behind. Our people will be on these fuckers like flies on shit."

Somewhere in the back of my mind I remembered Reaper telling me of Gunner's otherworldly ability to see through his falcon's eyes, but his words didn't register. I was in some state of shock. Either by pure, dumb luck or something else altogether, I had never gotten this close to being truly kidnapped. The Steel Demons taking me out of Old Phoenix didn't count, as they technically rescued me from people who would have pimped me out. I just didn't know it at the time.

My hands groped in the darkness, feeling for Gunner's hands, his face, his hair. Anything to paint a full picture of him in my mind and confirm he was really here.

"I'm so sorry you ended up here with me—"

"Stop." His thumb caressed over my lips, halting the guilt bubbling out of me. "Don't apologize. You think I'd let you get taken on your own? Not a chance. You're safer with me."

I tucked my head under his chin, seeking comfort in the space next to his neck. He smoothed out my hair in a gentle, repetitive motion. Being near him was always calming in a hypnotic way, just like when he taught me to float on my back.

"What are they gonna do?" I asked, my lips pressed to his throat.

"Strip us down. Appraise us like cattle to determine how much value we have," he said matter-of-factly. "They won't hurt us. We're merchandise to them and our value will decrease if we're injured. The club will reach us before they find buyers. We just have to sit tight, baby girl."

He sounded so sure, so confident. Not a single tremor in his voice or his hands soothing me. I wished I could soak up his fearlessness and wrap it around me like a shield. The Steel Demons had a reputation for power and no mercy to their enemies, but what if these people were their match? This world was filled with predators, each bigger and hungrier than the last. Even Reaper had to know he wouldn't stay at the top of the food chain forever. There was always someone bigger.

I had no sense of time in the darkness of that truck. We could have driven for twenty minutes or two hours, for all I knew. Once we stopped, a fresh burst of fear spread throughout my chest. I heard the truck cab's doors opening and slamming shut, then the quick footsteps of the scrawny guy walking around to the back.

Light flooded in as the door rolled up. I shielded my eyes with Gunner's chest while his arms tightened around me.

"Get up." Cruel, bony fingers grabbed my arm and pulled me roughly to my feet. Scrawny guy was surprisingly strong for his size.

"Hey, take it easy!" Gunner glared as he sprang up from the floor. "She's still mine, despite this bullshit charade. Don't leave bruises on my property."

I didn't know why he was still keeping up the act. It was clear they didn't care.

Three more guys walked up the ramp to grab him, their holstered weapons clearly on display. Even with an unarmed Steel Demon, they weren't taking any chances. Together, they walked us out of the truck.

With a few quick blinks I realized we weren't out in the desert in direct sun, but somewhere shaded. Large rock formations loomed all around us. The ground felt cool for a change, and had quite a bit more grass and vegetation growing due to the lack of harsh sun.

As we walked through, I saw that the rock formations contained dozens of caves and small alcoves within them. Supplies and personal items sat within the grooves of several walls like shelves. If I wasn't so terrified, it would have been fascinating to see how these people turned this natural formation into a permanent home. It made sense—this place provided strong shelter that didn't succumb to harsh wind or rain, and the caves gave a sense of privacy.

Our captors led us through a short tunnel that opened to a large, open room. I couldn't call it a cave because it had no ceiling. The sun illuminated a flat area in the center like a spotlight. We were shoved directly to that spotlight, where dark iron chains and manacles had been hammered into the rocky ground.

I wondered, through the numb fear in my mind, how many people had stood here before. One manacle clapped around my ankle, the other around Gunner's. How many frightened women, children, and even men had been bound here in such a dehumanizing way?

Without another word our captors retreated into the tunnels, leaving us alone. The chains didn't give us much movement, only about three feet or so around the spike anchoring it to the ground. But we were still close enough to hold each other. Just like in the truck, we sat together on the floor, me wrapped up in him.

Gunner gave a few tugs to his spike with no result. Next, he tried sliding one of the chain links under the head to use leverage to pull it up. No dice. After giving up on his own chain, he tried to do the same with mine.

"Stop." I took his hands away from the iron and brought them clasped between us. "I'm sure they'll punish you for trying to escape."

"Good. It'll distract them from paying attention to you." But he didn't go back to testing the chains. Instead he brought my hands to his lips and pressed soothing kisses to my knuckles.

"You picked a hell of a time to start being sweet to me." Despite the dire situation, my insides fluttered at the warmth of his lips.

He raised those gorgeous blue eyes to me, sadness and regret pooling in them. "I'm sorry, Mari. I'm just trying to make you feel safer. I'm not thinking about before or what'll happen once we're back. Maybe it's selfish, but I'm taking this one second at a time, and I'm all you got right now. So I'm going to be what you need."

We were already so close, it was impossible to tell who leaned in first. In the next moment, we were simply kissing. It was nothing like the rough, possessive grab in the market. Gunner was warm and sweet, but still kissed me with a sense of urgency, like we would be ripped away from each other at any second.

I wound my fingers through his hair, gliding my tongue across his to deepen the kiss. I didn't want this to be the last time, but the first of many more to come. This didn't have to be just because I was afraid and didn't have anyone else to lean on. I desperately wanted him to see that, to know I'd been wanting this for weeks, if not the past month. My feelings for him were real, they always had been. And being in love with two other men didn't diminish them in the least.

"Gunner."

"Shh." He sipped another sweet kiss from me, cradling my face in his hands. "Don't say anything, baby girl. Don't remind me that you're not really mine."

"Gunner..." His name came out in a choked plea that time, my throat already closing up with heartache.

What was the point of all this if he was just going to return me back to my men and ignore me all over again? My heart couldn't take this yanking around from him. I'd rather deal with Reaper's cold shoulder over this.

A series of footsteps echoed throughout our stone prison before I could say any more. The guys who captured us returned, solemnly leading another person through the tunnels toward us. As they fanned out to the sides of our open room, I was shocked to see a woman walking straight toward the flat area where we were shackled.

She was attractive in a cold, bitchy way. I estimated her to be in her late thirties or early forties. Pale blonde hair was pulled back in a French braid, the length of it falling over the front of her shoulder. Icy blue eyes peered at us shrewdly. She was dressed like a soldier, in a camo jumpsuit with black laced-up boots. Just by the way she walked, I could tell the uniform wasn't just for show. By the men's stiff spines and sharp eyes at attention, all signs pointed to this woman running the operation.

"I had to see for myself to believe it," she mused, her footsteps halting just out of reach of our chains. "A Steel Demon, and one who came willingly." She all but ignored me, her eyes resting on Gunner appreciatively. Turning to her men, she asked, "Did someone search him for a tattoo to be sure?"

Silence answered her. A few of them swallowed nervously.

"THEN WHAT THE FUCK ARE YOU WAITING FOR!"

Her shout came so loud and suddenly, even Gunner flinched. The sound echoed off the stone walls, repeating her wrath down to the men who rushed at us to fulfill her order.

Three of her minions wrenched Gunner away from me, two of them holding him still while the others stripped off his cut and then his T-shirt. Both clothing items discarded in the dirt, they victoriously turned him around to show the proud, grinning demon inked onto his upper back.

"So it is true," the woman purred. "And what role do you play in your little biker gang, handsome?"

He turned back around to face her, wrenching his arms out of the grips of the men who held him.

"My title is the arms dealer," he answered flatly. "But I oversee all the major exchanges of goods into the club."

"I see." The woman began a slow walk around us, eyes feasting on

Gunner like he was the main course of a five-star meal. He ignored her and drew me back into his chest. Despite trying to hide in his embrace, the woman seemed to notice me for the first time. "And who is this?"

"My woman. I purchased her." He threw a glare at the men surrounding us. "Your goons were trying to steal her, then ignored me when I offered to show them my receipt! Once I'm outta here, I'll make damn sure no one buys skin from you, lady! What kind of business are you running here, trying to poach what's already owned?"

"Firstly, my name is Corinne. Remember it. You'll be moaning my name tonight." She paused in her appraisal of his body to give a cruel smirk. "And secondly, I know for a fact that you're lying. It's common knowledge that the Steel Demons don't deal in flesh. Fortunately for us, that makes the trade far less competitive. And keeps you out of the loop."

Gunner's hands on me stiffened, pulling me into him ever so slightly with protective determination. Corinne continued walking her circle around us, sizing him up as she probably fantasized all the ways she wanted him.

"Now that we've established the girl is not owned by you, I frankly don't care who or what she is." Her gaze leveled on me, heavy with loathing and disdain. "Females are always in demand, so she'll go with the rest of them. As long as you have functioning holes for cocks, sweetie, you'll have purpose here."

I never saw a smile so evil in my life. What happened to this woman, what twisted her mind up in such a way that she treated fellow women, let alone any human beings, in such a way?

"As for you." Her voice took on a more wistful tone as she returned to looking at Gunner. "You put me in a predicament, Demon. Your body is an exquisite specimen to be sure, but male flesh is a harder sell."

"A hole's a hole," Gunner shrugged. "Throw me to your buyers, not her. If the only requirement is a hole to stick cocks in, why does male or female matter?"

"Gunner!" I hissed in a whisper. It was bad enough that he got dragged along with me at all. I was *not* going to let him be sold off in my place.

"Just further proof you know nothing about the subtleties of this industry," Corinne said. "Ultimately it comes down to a hole, yes, but what I'm selling are fantasies. A buyer comes to me with an image of a perfect bedroom companion already in his mind. My job is to match that description with an actual body. Rarely are my buyers women. And they're even pickier in their fantasies than the men."

She motioned at one of her men, who pulled me away from Gunner. "Stop! What are you doing?" I demanded but there was no use fighting. He dragged me back until the iron cuff bit into my ankle. I could only watch in horror and rage as Corinne approached Gunner and ran a finger just above the waistline of his pants.

He shoved her hand away with a snarl. "Don't fucking touch me."

"Elric?" she chirped.

The scrawny man who snatched me at the market walked up with a satisfied smirk. He flipped his gun around to hold it backwards, then slammed the stock into Gunner's stomach.

"No!" I tried to run to him, but my feet wheeled in midair. My guard held me back like I was weightless as I watched helplessly.

Gunner doubled over, choking on ragged, pained breaths. Corinne grabbed his shoulders to make him stand upright again, then ran a hand sensually over his chest and abs. This time, he didn't push her hand away.

"You are exactly what my female clientele is looking for," she drawled with huskiness in her voice. "Good skin. Nice muscles. A handsome face." Her hand slid into his pants, groping unabashedly as he winced and squirmed, but her guards held him in place. "Nicely-sized dick too. Although there's still the question of whether you know how to use it." She looked over her shoulder at me, utterly nonplussed at my horrified face. "What do you think, sweetheart? You want to take a test drive to see if he provides a satisfying experience?" Her hand slid back up his body all the way to his neck, where she grabbed his jaw with a rough hand. “If he knows how to make a woman come, I just might have to keep him for myself.”

“Why are you doing this?” I demanded, tears springing to my eyes. Watching her grope and grab him was too fucking much. His eyes had gone vacant, his mind off somewhere else while she made her dehumanizing assessment of him.

Corinne turned back to face me, her carefully drawn eyebrows raised in smug indignation. “I do this because no one says I can’t.” A manicured hand went to her hip. “Because it’s what I’m good at. Because we all had to resort to extremes in order to survive the Collapse. And because if I didn’t,” she lifted her chin at me, “it could’ve been me chained up for sale and you lording over me, touching a man I love.”

I shook my head, the tears falling freely now and making dark spots on the ground at my feet. “I’d never subject another woman to this. I’d never treat *anyone* like this.”

She tilted her head at me with a pitying, patronizing look. “That’s why you’re chained to a rock and I run an empire, sweetheart.”

Chapter 29

REAPER

My tires flew over the sand like I barely touched the earth at all. Hades sprinted about twenty feet ahead of me, his paws also barely on the ground. At my back, my club rode in a tight formation with Jandro just over my right shoulder and Dallas on my left. Usually an easygoing smiling pair, each of them wore solemn grimaces as we rode hard.

Dallas wasn't in love with Mari, but they had grown close and he considered her family. Every man behind me did. We were going to war for her.

I never got eyes on the truck that had taken Mari and Gunner, and judging by Hades' running pace, that was intentional. Seeing them meant they could see us, or worse, hear us. We could've caught up quickly, but since we were going in blind to our enemies, it was better to keep them unaware.

Hades veered us toward a large outcropping of sedimentary rock. He didn't use words, never unless he told me who to kill, but I understood his meaning all the same, and signaled to my men.

We pulled up the shady side and parked the bikes, cutting off the engines quickly. I swung a leg off just before coming to a complete stop.

"Where is she?" I demanded the dog who had run up to my side. "Where's our girl, Hades?"

He looked at the rock towering over us, placed his front paws against it, and whined. I looked up the steep rock face, as tall as a three-story building, and saw nothing but...rock. I scratched his ears, looking into those deep, dark eyes.

"I don't understand. Is she up there?"

His head fell back in a long howl that morphed into a bark. The next thing I felt was my ear getting pierced.

"Ow, fuck!"

Horus nipped at my ear again with that crazy sharp beak. Making soft chirps, he released the chunk of rock wall and set those talons into my shoulder.

"Jesus fucking Christ! How does Gunner walk around with you like this all the fucking time?"

"They want you to climb to the top, Reap," Jandro observed, craning his neck. "I don't think anything's up there, but maybe you can see where they're keeping her."

"Are you fucking kidding me?" I stared up at the sheer rock face in front of me going straight up to the sky. "Maybe you two missed the memo," I said to the animals, "but I don't have wings, or claws, or four fucking legs."

"There's footholds and edges to grab." Jandro wedged his foot into a little nook in the rock, then pulled himself up a few feet, arms and legs out to the side like a gecko.

"You coming with me then?"

"Better if only one of us fell and broke our neck than two, don'tcha think?"

"Fuck, we don't have time for this." I went to my saddlebags and pulled out a set of riding gloves with the fingers cut off. After pulling them over my wrists, I stretched my fingers out and got to climbing.

The first twenty feet or so wasn't so bad. I made it about halfway up before my dumbass decided to look down.

"Jesus." I never had an issue with heights, but I now knew why some people did. It was a long, rocky way back down to the bottom. I didn't even think about how I'd get back down.

The wind up here also felt much stronger than on the ground. I felt it pushing me around like a leaf on a tree branch, only my fingers were far less likely to stay connected.

I pushed on, with Horus occasionally hovering around me and chirping like a small, feathered cheerleader. The gloves were a good idea, but the soft leather was quickly getting shredded by the sharp rocks. The rock wall started biting into my palms, and not even my thick calluses could protect me. I ignored the trickle of blood running down my forearm. I was too close to stop now.

"Ah, fuck!"

One of my footholds tumbled loose and I found myself scrambling for a hold. My knees crashed into the rock face as my hands cramped painfully to bear my entire weight. A small shower of pebbles rained down, quickly going silent as they hurtled toward the earth. I never wanted to be a tiny rock so badly before now. If I fell I'd bounce and be unharmed, rather than raw meat splattered all over the place.

I took a breath. And then another. And one more.

I was still here, clinging to this cliff face for fuck knows what reason.

A harsh laugh escaped my lungs at the sheer absurdity of it all. I followed my dog and a bird to this wall, and was only climbing it because they indicated I should. If Mari was here, she'd be trying to make me see how impossible and unscientific this was.

But she's not here. The whole reason you're doing this is because she's not here.

Hades had been silent in my head ever since Python's execution, but I swore my bond to him only grew stronger since Mariposa came into our lives. That first night she spent with Jandro, he wasn't sleeping at the foot of my bed like usual. When I got up to take a piss in the middle of the night, I didn't see him anywhere. Stumbling around my house half-asleep, I finally found him sitting at a window, looking toward Jandro's house.

When he growled in the market right before he started running, I felt *his* fear and rage separate from my own. It was like I could feel him in some compartmentalized part of myself that I never knew was there. I couldn't even place if I felt him in my body or somewhere in my mind. All I knew was we felt the same thing, in the same space, but separately.

Whatever he was—dog, god, or something else—I trusted him. He cared about Mari and sought to protect her. And I knew that without him, my girl would be long gone.

Looking up, the top of the rock wall was only a few feet above me. Two more pulls and I'd be there. My hands were a bloody mess, but I couldn't let that stop me. I gritted my teeth against the pain of my torn-open palms as I secured new handholds. *One, two, three, pull up—*

"No!"

The rock I grabbed came loose and my arms were windmilling. My hands held nothing. Everything slowed down as I teetered backwards, the rock wall getting further and further away as I tried desperately to grab for it. Only my heel remained connected as sorrow filled me and the open, endless sky filled my vision.

I love you, Mari. I'm so sorry...

Pain sliced through the top of my back. I didn't expect to hit the ground so fast. Eyes closed, I waited for pain to wrack the rest of my mangled body and for death to take me.

Except it never came.

"Screeeeech!"

Horus cried out right next to my ear, but why...

I cracked one eye open, then the other to find myself staring at the rock face with my foot still connected.

And something holding onto the back of my cut.

"Horus?" I twisted my neck around trying to figure out how I was hovering with all but one foot in midair.

Another piercing screech filled my head, then the sound of cloth ripping as I dropped a few inches. I scrambled for the wall, leaning my weight forward. Only when I was secure did Horus's talons unhook from the back of my shirt.

"No fucking way..."

The falcon, no bigger than a raven, flew to perch at the very top of the rock only a few inches away from my hands. He looked at me, tilting his head in a way that was eerily human. I never heard Horus speak like Hades, but if he was saying anything, it had to be something like, *Yeah, I weigh two pounds and I just saved your ass, motherfucker. Now you gonna finish what you started, or what?*

My hands reached the edge. All the pain was gone, either from the adrenaline or the sheer disbelief at being alive. I hauled myself up, placed one boot on solid ground, and then the other. I could've kissed the ground beneath my feet, but I wasn't done yet.

"All right. I'm up here," I said to the bird. "Now what?"

He turned and walked on those wickedly curved talons toward the far edge of the rock. It wasn't completely flat up here, so I carefully side-stepped boulders and ridges to follow him. The moment I saw what was on the horizon, I dropped down out of sight, peering around a boulder.

Not five hundred feet from here was another huge rock formation, at least ten times the size of this one. Formed by millions of years of erosion from wind and rain, dozens of tunnels and caves had been carved into the stone. And parked outside one of the caves, surrounded by armed guards, was a box truck.

"Bingo," I whispered, all the pieces clicking into place.

Had we rode up any closer, they would have been alerted to the sounds of our motorcycles. But from what I could see, the guards were at ease, if even bored.

I turned to Horus. "You know exactly where they are, huh?"

A screech and a few head bobs were my answer.

"And if Hades doesn't already know, I bet he can smell them." A plan began forming in my head.

I stayed up there at least ten more minutes, trying to memorize the layout of the rock formation and the guards' movement. By then, the bleeding of my palms had slowed considerably. I shrugged off my cut and pulled my T-shirt over my head, tearing open the jagged holes Horus's talons had made. When my shirt was nothing but strips, I wrapped them around my hands and tied them securely.

Mari would be fretting about infection and nerve damage probably, but they would have to do for now. Despite the new hand protection, my white T-shirt bandages were stained dark red by the time I made it back to the bottom.

"So?" Jandro wasted no time when my feet touched down. "What'd you see?"

"I can see where they've got them." I pressed my thumbs into each of my aching palms. "We've got to go on foot, a small team of us. Everyone else wait here for a signal."

"And the animals?"

I grinned, stretching my fingers out. "They're going in first."

Chapter 30

MARIPOSA

I winced as the needle jabbed cruelly in Gunner's arm and quickly filled the attached tube with blood.

"What are you doing with that?" I demanded through gritted teeth.

It was beyond infuriating what Corinne was doing to him. Touching him, poking, prodding, and now taking his blood without permission. She hadn't done anything extreme yet, considering the world we lived in, but she was still taking away his agency. Not giving him the option to consent or refuse. She was violating him and I never hated anyone so much.

"Running tests," she answered snippily. "For diseases."

"Hope you find a whole cocktail of 'em," Gunner hissed at her. "Everything under the sun, 'cause God knows I've been everywhere."

"I doubt that very much, Demon," she purred. "Any idiot can see how you touch and look at this woman." Her head snapped over to me. "You treat her like no other woman exists, but my men tell me you haven't slept with her. You're holding out for some reason, waiting for her."

His jaw tensed, Adam's apple bobbing as he swallowed. The clever-tongued Demon was speechless for once.

"It's a fascinating love story, I'm sure," Corinne sighed. "But I have no time for it, as I have profits to make. Still," she ran a finger along his jaw, her men restraining him against leaning away from her, "I'm not above petty victories. Maybe I'll let the little female watch when I tie you to my bed tonight."

"Fuck you," he spat. "You'll never have this."

"I already do," she chuckled. "Once your blood tests come back clear, you are mine to do with as I please. There is another test I must conduct however, and you'll see I'm not completely heartless."

She turned to me, smirking gleefully.

"You can have him first. It's the one and only time you'll get with him, so make it count."

I stared at her in complete disbelief. "What?"

"You two are going to fuck. Right here. Right now." She waved away her men holding us and stepped off the flat slab of rock we were chained to. Someone brought out a metal folding chair and she took a seat less than ten feet away from us.

Without anyone to hold us apart, Gunner and I found each other again. He pulled me into his chest and my finger immediately went to apply pressure to the puncture wound in his elbow from the needle.

"What's taking them so long?" I whispered, hiding my face in his hair.

He squeezed my nape, lowering his forehead to mine. "I don't know, baby girl. Maybe something happened."

"Get on with it already," Corinne demanded from the sidelines. "I don't have all day."

I glared at her, somehow feeling safer behind the barrier of Gunner's arm. "Why do you want us to...?"

"Like I said before," she rolled her eyes at me, "A nice body and big dick mean nothing if he doesn't know how to use them. I want to see how well he pleases you before taking him for myself."

"Fucking hell." Gunner sucked in a breath, his arms sliding protectively around me.

I kept my eyes trained on her, my hand wrapped around his bicep with my forehead on his shoulder. "You can't force us to do anything."

She gave the tiniest jerk of her head and the scrawny guy, Elric, quickly shouldered his weapon. He fired one shot toward our feet, making us both jump back with a cry as sparks flew from the round's impact.

"Actually, I can," Corinne retorted. "I'm well-practiced in forcing my merchandise to do anything and everything I want. So I suggest you get started before I use more...*serious* methods."

My hold on him now trembled, my body otherwise frozen in fear. This bitch wasn't just on some power trip, fulfilling a mission to topple everyone who got in her way. No, she was certifiably insane.

"Mari..." Gunner's lips tickled my ear, his hands sliding up to caress my neck. While fear froze me, threatening to make me shatter, the beautiful golden man held strong like a fortress wrapped around me.

The kiss he pressed to the edge of my jaw was tantalizingly slow, his lips open as the tip of his tongue danced along my skin.

"Gunner, no," I whispered, the tears threatening to return. "Not like this."

"I didn't want it like this either, baby girl, but what choice do we have?" He held my face with one hand, pulling my hip forward with the other. "I won't let them hurt you."

"But what about you?" My breaths came out ragged and choked. "She's going to—"

"Don't worry about me. I'll only give her what she wants as long as she guarantees no harm will come to you."

"Reaper and the others," I argued desperately. "The club. They wouldn't leave us. They have to be coming."

He released a sad sigh. "I don't hear any motorcycles. Do you?"

"It can't be—"

"Shh." His kiss was achingly sweet, full of sadness and apology. "Remember what I said when I first touched you?"

How could I forget? He was the first one of them who touched me with real desire. His body pressed to mine in the kitchen at Old Phoenix. I was so scared he would assault me back then, but now I knew that was the last thing he would ever do.

"You said you'd make it good for me."

His eyes bore into mine like two glittering swimming pools—full of depth, regret, and unabashed want.

"I meant it back then," he whispered. "And I still mean it now."

This time, when his mouth swept across mine, I let him in.

His tongue flicked over mine in a soft, but insistent caress. When his hands fell to my waist and pulled me flush to him, I let him. No more complaints and threats came from our audience, so I figured we were doing well enough. My eyes closed as my fingers dove through his blonde hair, filling my senses up with him as I shut out the rest of the world surrounding us.

He skimmed those long fingers under the hem of my shirt, then molded his palms to the curves of my sides. His thumbs grazed the edges of my breasts but didn't move higher, nor did he attempt to take my top off.

"I don't want them to see you," he murmured into my ear. "They don't get to enjoy you like I do."

"Gunner..." My head leaned back as his mouth moved down my neck. There was so much I wanted to tell him, so much I wanted to say. If this was truly our last moment together, it should have come pouring out of me. But every word was stuck. Blocked by the tight fist of despair in my chest.

And this gorgeous, infuriating man kept shushing me whenever I said his name, like he didn't want to hear any of it. Maybe it was better that way. Better to not know what was never able to happen.

He took my hand from his shoulder, kissing my palm once before bringing it down his body to press against the front of his jeans. My throat tightened up, choking off all of my air. He was hard, forming such a sexy outline of his length through his clothes.

But I couldn't bring myself to touch him. None of this was right. It was so wrong, my stomach contorted into knots. This should only be happening with his full consent, because he *wanted* to be with me, alongside Reaper and Jandro. Not because we had guns pointed at us.

"Gunner, I can't—"

"It's okay, Mari. Please." His voice held a tinge of desperation. "I want this. I want *you*. Fuck the circumstances. I've always wanted you." His palm cupped the back of my neck, holding me in place for another deep kiss full of longing. "If this is the only way I can have you, so fucking be it."

"Elric. Make them hurry it up."

Corinne's voice snapped me out of it like ice injected into my spine. A gun cocked, the barrel pointed at Gunner's legs. "Pants off. Now." Gunner obeyed without hesitation, unzipping and shoving the worn denim down his thighs while leaving his boxer briefs in place. "And you," the barrel swung to point in my direction. "Top off. Let's see those pretty tits."

"No," Gunner bit out, moving to stand in front of me. He glared directly at Corinne. "You want to see how good I am? She doesn't need to be naked for that. And you're not gonna find out anything by rushing us. As a woman, you should know it takes time to get warmed up."

"There's a difference between warming up and stalling," she retorted. "And I don't appreciate you wasting my time. In any case, I think I've seen enough. Unchain him, Elric, and bring him to my personal slave pen."

"No!" Now it was me fighting to get in front of Gunner, trying as hard as I could in vain to prevent them from taking him.

But his body went impossibly stiff, rigid like a block of stone.

"Gunner?" I looked up to see his eyes had rolled back so only the whites were visible. His brow and eyelids twitched, his mouth slack and open.

"What's going on with him?" Corinne demanded. "Is he fucking epileptic? Oh, that won't do at all..."

I used to think the same thing, but when my eyes caught sight of the bird circling above us, my heart dared to soar with hope where there had been none before.

"Horus!"

It had to be. And Gunner must have been seeing through his falcon's eyes right at that moment. He was right about no motorcycles being nearby, but the club *had* to be here if Gunner's falcon was.

The bird circled so high, it became a barely visible speck. Gunner seemed unsteady on his feet, so I wrapped my arms around his waist to support him.

"Shoot him," Corinne ordered with disdain in her voice, seemingly oblivious to her impending peril. "The last thing I need is a twitching, drooling idiot in my bed or on the market."

"No!"

I covered as much of Gunner's body as I could with mine just as Elric took aim. He squeezed his trigger with an evil smirk, and I shut my eyes as the shot rang out.

"Aghhh, fuck!"

Something hit me, but it wasn't a bullet. It was wet and warm. Blood.

I cracked my eyes open to see Elric clutching at his neck, blood spurting between his fingers with each beat of his heart. He fell to his knees, on death's doorstep already.

"Elric—what?" For the first time, Corinne showed emotion besides smug superiority. Her eyes widened in fear as she watched the life drain from her favorite henchman.

Above and behind her, dark feathers clung to a chunk of rock wall. It was clear from her and everyone else's reaction that no one saw Horus shred Elric's neck open.

"Madam, we seem to be under attack—"

"NO FUCKING SHIT, WE'RE UNDER ATTACK!" she roared at her guard. "Secure the perimeter! Find out who—ahhh!"

A dark blur moved like lightning throughout the room, going so fast it seemed to defy the laws of physics. An image flashed in my mind's eye--the rough shape of a man whose face I couldn't see. The man from my dream who claimed to be Hades. A voice rang out so loud, it should've echoed off the stone walls. But it seemed to come from within my head.

Their lives are ours to take. We will reap what has been sown.

Gunner had come to at some point and wrapped me in a protective embrace as we observed the carnage around us.

Corinne and all her men were on the ground, wailing, screaming, crawling. Blood dripped from their ankles as though a major tendon had been severed. And Hades, muscles sleek and rippling, walked between the bodies with his lips pulled back and teeth stained red.

His dark predatory eyes met mine and once again, I got a flash of the faceless man who sat at the end of Jandro's bed.

"Mari! Are you hurt?"

Hands covered in bloody bandages grabbed my shoulders and spun me around. I choked out a sob at the sight of the familiar handsome face and green eyes.

"Reaper!" I didn't even hear him run up to us. "I'm fine. What happened to your hands?"

"I'll tell you later, sugar. We're getting you home." He kissed me deeply, full of relief and longing. "These fuckers have keys, right?"

"Too bad Shadow's not here. He'd smash those locks in two seconds."

"Jandro!"

"Oh, baby." He yanked me out of Reaper's arms and crushed me to his chest. "Don't you ever scare me like that again."

"Not planning on it," I murmured, wanting to burrow in the scent and safety of him.

Reaper pulled the keys from Elric's lifeless body and unlocked both of us. The moment we were free, he whistled and Hades came running to him.

"Now, boy." He gave the dog an affectionate ear stroke. "Call the Demons here."

Hades trotted to the center of the flat stone where Gunner and I had been chained, then threw his head back and let out the most haunting howl I ever heard.

"Don't worry, sugar." Reaper caressed the nape of my neck. "They're going to pay for this. All of them."

Chapter 31

MARIPOSA

"My poor baby." Jandro lifted my foot and brushed a kiss against the red line where I'd been chained. "I'm never letting you out of my sight again."

"That's fine, but stop kissing me there." I wiggled my toes at his face. "I don't want more germs on your lips."

Expecting a silly comeback, Jandro's solemn face stunned me as he moved up my body. He'd been so doting when we got home, parking me permanently on his couch with blankets and pillows, forbidding me from getting up except for bathroom breaks. Surrounded with warmth and softness, the guilt on his face still cut me deeply.

"What's wrong?" I held the sides of his face. "Don't tell me you blame yourself for this."

"No, it's just, when I realized you were actually gone, I—" his voice cracked. "I never got to tell you."

"Tell me what?"

His mouth slid over mine, stealing my breath. "*Te amo, mi mariposita*. I love you so fucking much. *Tu eres mi corazon*."

"*Te amo tambien*," I murmured in my clumsy Spanish in between breathless, needy, all-consuming kisses. "I love you too, Alejandro."

He broke away mid-kiss, reaching into his saddlebag next to the couch. "I got you something at the market."

My eyes widened. "Jandro, you didn't have to—"

"I know. I wanted to, though." He handed me a slender, clamshell style box. "Don't tell me if you don't like it. Save my pride and fake it for me."

"Don't say stuff like that," I chided as I lifted the lid.

There was no possible way I could fake my reaction to the butterfly pendant resting on white tissue paper. "Oh my God, Jandro. This is..."

I had no words because it was absolutely perfect.

The pendant felt heavy when I slid my fingers behind it to lift it out of the box. Light shone through the yellow-orange wings, a delicate contrast to the gray metal frame they were embedded in. The metal created the shape of the wings and the signature dark stripes of the monarch butterfly, while the colored glass accentuated the beauty and fragility of such an insect.

"Do you like it?" Jandro prodded gently.

"Are you kidding me? I *love* it!" The metal chain spilled over my fingers as I lifted the whole necklace from the box. I couldn't stop staring at it, nor sliding my fingers over the smooth glass. "I don't think anyone's ever gotten me a more perfect gift. Help me put it on?"

"Don't speak too soon," he chuckled, taking the clasps from me as I moved my hair. "Someone else might've gotten you something special too."

"Oh?" I looked at him over my shoulder, touching the pendant now sitting just below my throat. "Are you going to tell me any more than that?"

"Nope." He kissed the crook of my neck, wrapping me in a delicious hug. "I'm glad you like the necklace."

"I love it so much." I leaned back against him and kissed his temple. "Thank you. I'm never taking it off."

"Mm, that's what I like to hear." He rained more kisses down on my neck and shoulder before slowly unwrapping from me. "I'm going to check on the food. Don't go anywhere."

I snorted. "Like I could if I tried."

He went to the kitchen, humming to himself as he stirred the tortilla soup. Traditionally the recipe called for chicken, but he couldn't bring himself to kill any of his girls. He was tempted with Foghorn, but needed him for future generations. So we were having a vegetarian version tonight.

I sank into the pillows, reminiscing on this crazy fucking day. Once the rest of the Steel Demons rode up to the caves, they thoroughly searched the entire place. No other slaves were to be seen, but they did find plenty more chains and shackles.

On Reaper's orders, they shackled one ankle of every trafficker still alive, even Corinne, and attached the other end to their bikes. We rode home, dragging them behind us until their bodies were unrecognizable.

Halfway to Sheol, we stopped to unhitch the dead weight. Reaper and Jandro heated up two brands with a blow torch and stamped the bodies with the Steel Demon emblem. If anyone found them before the vultures picked them clean, they'd know exactly who these people crossed.

Jandro's front door opened as I was lost in my macabre thoughts. I looked up to see Shadow's large form crossing the living room toward me.

"Hi, Shadow," I smiled at him.

"Hi, Mariposa." He stopped several feet away from the couch, hands clasped behind his back like a soldier standing at attention. "I'm glad to see you're unharmed after what happened today."

My smile grew wider. The statement sounded rehearsed, like he practiced saying it several times. But it didn't take away from the sentiment. I actually found it endearing. He was trying, and getting so much better with every baby step.

"Thank you. That's really sweet of you."

"Yo, big dude!" Jandro called from the kitchen. "Reaper let everyone go?"

"Yes, he'll be over soon. He's helping unload supplies." Shadow's eyes darted from me to the kitchen. "I have something to fill you in on later."

"Cool. We'll talk after Mari goes to bed."

Reaper called an emergency church meeting right when we got home to let everyone who stayed back know what happened. Only Jandro stayed glued to my side to look after me. From the way Shadow was acting, my guess was they saw their own share of action here while we were gone.

"Is Gunner helping with supplies too?" I asked Shadow, wondering how much more conversation I could drag out of him before he retreated.

"No. He went home as far as I'm aware."

"Oh."

And just like that, my mood spiraled. After everything, he still went back to avoiding me. Did he not mean everything he said while we were chained up together? Did he touch me, kiss me, protect me all that time, just out of a sense of duty to his club and president?

It took a few moments of racing thoughts for me to realize Shadow was still there. And to my complete shock, he came closer until he took a cautious seat on the arm of the couch. We were still a good six feet away from each other, but his presence was so large and overwhelming, he might as well have been sitting on top of me.

"Is everything okay, Shadow?" I noticed his distressed expression.

His odd-colored eyes flicked up to mine and I felt that familiar heat rush through me whenever he looked at me.

"Reaper gave me orders to tattoo you as soon as you feel up to it." He swallowed thickly, looking massively uncomfortable. "To prevent something like this from happening again."

"Oh. Okay." I folded my hands on top of the blanket covering my legs. "And would you be comfortable doing that?"

He raised a hand as if to run it through his hair, then seemingly changed his mind and dropped it back to his lap. "I've never tattooed a woman before but...I think I'm willing to try."

I offered him my biggest smile yet, beaming with pride. "I'm sure we'll both get through it when the time comes. From what I've seen, you do great work."

His lips twitched in what could've been the start of a smile. "Thank you." He jerked his gaze away from me abruptly and returned to standing. "I'll let you rest now. Just let me know when you're ready."

I nodded, watching as he retreated to his area of the house. "I will. Goodnight, Shadow."

"Goodnight, Mariposa."

IT TOOK NEARLY A HALF HOUR OF CONVINCING JANDRO TO let me stop by Gunner's house. I ate my weight in tortilla soup, demonstrated that I could walk just fine, and reminded him that double guards were posted around the perimeter that night. He begrudgingly accepted after I promised him I'd have just a quick chat with Gunner and come right back. I probably could have talked to him the next day, but my damned heart wouldn't let me wait that long.

And yet I found myself at his front door, just staring at the painted wood for minutes. My heartbeat wouldn't slow the hell down and one deep breath didn't feel like enough. Neither did five or ten.

Come on, Wilder. Time to be fearless. I raised my fist and knocked before the next thought could talk me out of it.

Of course, Gunner had to answer the door looking so damn delicious in sweatpants and an unzipped hoodie with no shirt on underneath. His hair was freshly washed--still wet in some parts, fluffy and soft in others.

"Hey, Gun." Everything I wanted to say evaporated from my brain like a puddle on the street.

He pushed his sleeves up to his elbows, regarding me with a curious look. "Hey."

Not *hey, Mari*. Not *hey, baby girl.* Just hey.

"I, um." I fiddled with the sleeves of Jandro's sweater I borrowed. "Just wanted to see how you were doing."

"Probably about as well as you." He crossed his forearms, leaning against the door-jam like waiting for the real reason I came over.

I didn't miss the fact that he didn't invite me in. The fortress that had shut me out, that laid down its defenses when I got captured and kept me safe, was slowly closing itself off to me again.

And I'd had enough.

I'd scale those walls he was trying to put back in place. I'd take a battering ram to the doors that guarded his heart, whatever I needed to do. I got through to one man who hated being vulnerable, I could do it again. There was no undoing what had already been done.

As the silence dragged on between us, Gunner sighed and returned a hand to the doorknob.

"Well, thanks for checking on me—"

"We're not doing this again, Gunner Youngblood."

He froze, staring at me bewildered. "Doing wha—"

"This. You, shutting me out. Ignoring me. Ignoring everything we did and what was said today. I've tried to be patient with you, but I'm not playing this game anymore. If you want this to happen, just *try*." I sucked in a breath, realizing I hardly breathed at all as the words finally poured out of me. "Don't kill this before it has a chance to start."

His eyes were glued to the floor as I went on my tirade. When he looked up, I saw nothing but aching sincerity.

"You're right. About everything," he said almost too softly for me to hear. "I got the stupid idea to distance myself from you to save us both from pain. Even when Reaper and Jandro tried to talk sense into me, I was too fucking stubborn to change my behavior. I'm sorry, baby girl. I'm an idiot and I never wanted to hurt you."

Silence wrapped around us again. I was honestly floored by the sincerity of his apology. But the hurt he spoke of was still fresh.

"Okay. Well, that's a start," I mused.

He gripped the edges of his door frame as if stopping himself from reaching out to touch me.

"For what it's worth, I meant every word I said to you in that cave. To this very second, everything I said remains true. It's just..." He ran a hand through his hair, fluffing up the golden locks as he trailed off.

"The sharing aspect," I filled in for him.

"Yeah," he sighed. "That."

My mind raced with assurances to tell him, although nothing felt quite right enough to reach my mouth. They all sounded like excuses, really. Sneaky methods to coerce him into this situation he wasn't thrilled about. And the last thing I wanted to do was drag him into an arrangement if he really didn't want to be there. The truth of the matter was, what Reaper, Jandro, and I had wasn't for everyone. And it was entirely possible and fair that such a relationship was just not right for Gunner.

No matter how badly I wanted it to be.

"Can I just," his hand flopped out of his hair, "have some time to think about it? Get used to the idea first, maybe ease myself into it? I'm not saying no, I just...don't want to make any promises I can't keep."

"Y-yes!" I stammered in disbelief. "Of course!" Then more coolly, "And if you're worried about anything, or just have questions, you can ask me anything. This only works as long as I'm an open book with everybody. But you can ask Reaper and Jandro too."

Finally a heart-melting smile cracked the solemn facade. "I'm sure I'll have them. It's a starting point, I guess." He sighed. "If I'm going to do this, I have to go in with the right mindset. And I know I already got started on the wrong foot. Now I have to backtrack and start all over." His hands scrubbed down his face with a laugh. "My brain is so fucking fried, I don't even know what I'm saying anymore."

"We'll take it one day at a time," I assured him. "So, I'll see you tomorrow?"

"'Course you will." He finally released the door-jam and reached for me. "Come here."

Warm skin pressed against me as he held me tightly. A kiss dropped to my forehead like gentle rain. For some reason, that kiss unwound everything I'd been holding back and a shuddering sigh escaped me.

"Thank you," I whispered shakily into his throat. "For being there today. For giving this a chance. For being you. For *everything*."

Another kiss, this time at the corner of my eye to catch the tear that threatened to fall.

"I'll always be here, baby girl."

Epilogue

MARIPOSA

After leaving Gunner's house, I caught up with Reaper and Hades just as they were leaving the clubhouse.

"What're you doing out here, sugar?" He tucked me into his side with Hades falling into a walk beside me on my other side. "I thought Jandro wasn't going to let you out of his sight."

"I talked him into letting me see Gunner for a minute. Alone."

Reaper gave me a knowing look. "Things happened while you two were locked up there, huh?"

I swallowed, giving myself the conscious reminder that it didn't bother him. He didn't see it as cheating. I had nothing to be ashamed of, nor did I do anything wrong. I knew it well now, but sometimes old thinking patterns cropped up.

"We kissed...kind of a lot. Most of the time, he was just holding me or shielding me. But they almost forced us to—"

"Mari, you don't need to confess every little detail to me." He chuckled as he stroked a thumb along the back of my neck. "In fact, I'd probably prefer you didn't. But is he going to join the fold or not? There's no in-between. He either has you and us, or he doesn't have you at all. That's the deal."

"He's...going to think about it."

Reaper made a disapproving sound as he stuck a cigarette in his mouth.

"Don't," I warned him. "This is weird to him. Hell, it was weird to me. The whole reason you didn't tell me right away was because you thought I wouldn't want to be shared, right?"

"But then I explained it to you," he retorted. "Gunner knows the deal. I've known him half my life. He's seen how my family worked. He should know how he feels about you. In my humble fuckin' opinion, he needs to shit or get off the pot."

"Just give him a little time." Feeling impulsive, I snatched the cigarette from his hand and took a long drag before returning it back to him. "To get used to the idea."

"Mm," Reaper chuckled amusedly, running his tongue along the filter. "I'm never throwing this one away, knowing your lips were on it."

"Gross, Rory."

"I'll give him time, only because you said to." He ignored my use of his real name. "But I don't have infinite amounts of patience. And as you know," he squeezed the back of my neck with light pressure, "I have zero tolerance for anyone who hurts you."

Hades suddenly stopped.

And like a pair of hands sprung up from the sidewalk to hold me in place, my feet stopped too.

Both of us halted with no warning at all, Reaper continued walking a few steps before noticing.

"What's gotten into you two?"

Hades stared directly down the intersection we just passed. The next block up would be Jandro's house. Down that intersection was his shop.

I had to go there.

The same force that stopped me from walking pulled me toward Jandro's shop like a rope around my waist. I couldn't explain it as anything other than a *need*. I had to go there. And I had to hurry.

"Mari?" Reaper called after me as I started down the street, Hades at my side.

"I don't know what's going on," I called back to him. "I just...need to see something."

The feeling grew stronger, more urgent, the closer I got. I bypassed the front of the duplex and went around the side. A wooden fence with a gate blocked my path to the backyard.

No, no, no. I stood on my tiptoes to reach over the fence with the latch, but wasn't tall enough. I was this close to climbing the damned thing to get to where I needed. Hades scratched at the wood and whined.

"Reaper, help me!"

Thankfully, he could see how serious I was and didn't dally.

"Mari, what do you need back there?" He reached over me and unlatched the gate with ease.

"I don't know, I just have to go there."

I ran through, following nothing but the feeling in my gut. It led to me to a large pile of debris. Ducts, hoses, chunks of drywall, concrete, and old motorcycle scraps piled nearly as tall as the fence itself. Some of it had to be from when Jandro tore down the walls between the duplex garages.

The feeling tugged me straight to that pile in a way that was almost painful. Oh no. I thought it was bad, but it was getting worse.

"Mari, what is it?" Reaper followed me, concern filling his voice.

"We have to hurry!" A desperate sense of urgency clenched my heart like a fist. I moved rocks and debris as fast as my hands could move, paying no attention to the cuts and scrapes on my hands.

This was life or death.

I could feel her life, fragile as a newborn baby, hanging in a delicate balance. I didn't know how I knew this presence was a her, but for some reason my instinct was to give her a female gender.

"Help me, Hades!" I begged as he came up next to me to sniff the rubble pile.

He barked once and immediately began digging. His front paws pulled away more dirt and sand than I ever hoped to with my bare hands. I helped him move the heavier stuff—slabs of rock, concrete, and piping.

"Wait a minute, boy. Stop," I told him.

I turned my head and leaned my ear down close to the pile when he paused. I thought I heard something but maybe...

"Meowww! Meowww! Meowww!"

"She's alive!" I cried. "Keep digging! We have to save her!"

At that point, Reaper snapped into action. He came up next to me without a word and picked up the heaviest pieces to toss over his shoulders. Hades dug out a small burrow just big enough for his head and front paws to fit through. He paused to stick his face in all the way, snorted out a nose full of dirt and kept digging.

"Please, please, please..."

I couldn't begin to understand this at all. Yes, a kitten was stuck under there, which was awful. But the idea of losing her wasn't normal sadness, it was devastatingly painful. Like I'd be losing a part of myself.

"This whole fucking thing is gonna collapse if you're not careful," Reaper warned.

"No, we can't let that happen!"

My vision grew blurry with tears. When I blinked them away, Hades reached into his burrow again, ears folded back carefully in the cramped space. When he scooted back out and turned to look at me, he held something in his jaws.

"You got her!" I gasped in relief, holding my hands out. "Is she..."

As gently as I'd ever seen him be, he placed a tiny, black saliva-soaked kitten into my awaiting palms. Her eyes still had that bluish color in very young kittens, and she barely weighed anything at all.

"Meowww!" she yelled at top of her tiny kitten lungs, squirming in my fists. "Meowww!"

She looked and acted just like a kitten, as far as I could tell with my bodily senses. But there was something else I couldn't quite place. The feeling that pulled me to this scrap pile, the desperation and the need to dig her out had calmed, but the presence of it remained within me. It felt like something separate from me, and yet a part of me all at once.

Reaper looked at me knowingly as I held the tiny kitten to my chest.

"You were meant to find her," he breathed softly. "And nothing else in the world mattered until you did."

"Yes," I nodded. "That's exactly right."

"She chose you," Reaper added. "Like Hades chose me."

The dog sniffed the tiny, squirming ball of fur and gave her an affectionate lick. I didn't know what was happening, what this was. But right then I only saw Reaper's loyal companion. The strange, faceless man who shared the same name did not make an appearance in my head.

Reaper reached out one finger to stroke the top of the kitten's head. "Has she already told you her name?"

I nodded again, rubbing warmth into the tiny, helpless animal that I already knew was so much more.

"Her name is Freyja."

Thank you so much for reading! The adventure continues in Steel Demons MC Volume 2! Books 4-6 are available now!

Start reading:
http://books2read.com/SDMCV2

Read on for exclusive bonus content!

In appreciation of all the amazing Steel Demons fans, Reaper allowed me to publish a few excerpts from his mother's journal. I hope you enjoy this peek into the past, and seeing how our surly president learned to share. ;)

Bonus content

Excerpts from the journal of Reaper's mother

Alisa's journal

March 08, 2071

I'm not going to cry. I'm not going to cry. My name is Alisa Daley and goddamnit, I'm not going to start crying now.

Not that anyone would blame me if I did. My husband, who I've been married to all of two weeks, just left on his first deployment. He's supposed to be gone for six months. This morning I took a pregnancy test and it gave me a Big Fat Positive, as the ladies in my Air Force Wives group would say.

And yet here I am, scribbling in a notebook because my mind keeps racing and it feels like I have no one to talk to. My best friend and love of my life is halfway around the world. I'm already dreading to have to tell him the news in a letter. I won't be able to see the smile light up his face when he finds out. I hate that I'll already be huge like a whale when I see him again, and that's the best case scenario. For all we know, his deployment could be extended and he'll have to miss the birth completely.

Finn and these blank pages are the only ones I can be

honest with. The military wives would balk at my true feelings but I have to get them out somewhere.

The truth is, I'm not sure if I want to keep this baby. How horrible does that sound?

With the way the world is going, I'm terrified of a daughter growing up to be treated like a piece of meat. Just the other day, the Supreme Court found the members of a sex-trafficking ring not guilty, despite overwhelming evidence! So many people pointed out how unbalanced it is that we haven't had a woman on the bench in twenty years, but of course, the government doesn't care.

It's because of shit like this that men are becoming so brazen and shameless lately. When my mom was younger, she said men were called out on disgusting behaviors. Bosses lost their jobs over sexual harassment. People went to jail for it. Now there's no consequences. Cases are dismissed left and right because no one takes a woman's word seriously. I don't want a daughter to be a victim of that, or a son to think that behavior is okay.

It's just my luck that the only decent man I find has to be away from me during the scariest part of my life. Finn wants a large family, and I thought I did too. He'll be overjoyed at the news, and thus disappointed when he hears about my doubts. But he'll leave the decision to me. I know he will. He's always made the point that we're partners in this marriage, and I'm not his property. Of course, I joke with him that he's my property. With a husband as sexy as him, a girl's got to be a little territorial!

Fuck, I miss him. If he were here now, he'd know exactly what to say to reassure me. I'm going to be watching the mailbox like a hawk for his letters. I'll keep them here in this journal, tucked between the pages. This whole little book just might turn out to be quite the unfiltered autobiography during this uneasy time. If the world does go to Hades in a handbasket, maybe my children will keep this as a document to remember how things got to such a point.

Okay, maybe I am leaning toward keeping the baby, but I'm still scared as hell! Finn still has some good benefits from the military, but I don't know how affordable doctor's visits will be. And maybe it's childish of me, but I just don't want to deal with everything without him here. The military wives are nice and I can talk about surface-level stuff with them, but I still feel completely alone out here.

ALISA'S JOURNAL

MARCH 15, 2071

I went to the doctor today. Everything went well and a lot of my fears were put to rest. I didn't tell them everything, but still, it was nice to vent to a living person.

I also wrote a letter to Finn, telling him pretty much everything I wrote in my last entry. That made me feel better too, and like I'm less alone. I didn't want to stress him out though, on top of everything else he has to worry about.

My metalsmithing class is going well! I'm getting better at saw piercings, and collecting pretty gemstones is such an addiction. It's pure luck that we moved to Tucson, home of the most amazing gem show in the world. I'm still hoarding stones from last year like some kind of dragon. I want to get better at smithing before I place them into jewelry settings.

I can't wait to go to the gem show again this year, but sad that Finn won't be there with me. He made fun of me for oohing and ahhing over pretty rocks last year, but it still won't be the same without him. Maybe I could go with some people from my class, if I get over being so damn shy.

Oh, I ran into Finn's friend Carter on my way out of the pharmacy the other day. And holy shit, he got so much hotter! I hadn't seen him in like two years, and he was kind of dorky and shy back then. But he's all buff and covered with tattoos now. I tried not to stare too much, but he was just as sweet as ever. He must have women hanging off of him all the time now. In fact, I hope he does! Last time I saw him, he was sad about the girl he dated leaving him for someone else. If she saw him now, I'm sure she's kicking herself for that! I really wish the best for him. In fact, it would be nice to see him around again. We talked outside the pharmacy for at least ten minutes catching up! I don't really have other friends in this town, and he's known Finn since they were kids.

I kind of wish I got his number, though that probably wouldn't be appropriate. It would be just as friends of course, but I don't want to give Finn anything to worry about.

More journal excerpts and letters are available in Volume 2 of the Steel Demons MC omnibuses!

Start reading here:
https://books2read.com/SDMCV2

Also by Crystal Ash

Harem of Freaks: The Complete Series

Say Your Prayers

Steel Demons MC

Lawless

Powerless

Fearless

Painless

Helpless

Heartless

Senseless

Ruthless

Merciless

Endless

Shifted Mates Trilogy

Unholy Trinity: The Complete Series

For a complete list of books by Crystal Ash, visit her Amazon page.

About the Author

Crystal Ash is a USA Today Bestselling Author from California. She loves writing steamy, heart-wrenching romance with tortured heroes, especially if they're in a reverse harem. Crystal's other loves include animals, mythology, and well-crafted alcohol, most of which can also be found in her stories.

When she's not writing, she's probably drinking craft beer with her husband or trying to coax her feral cat into accepting affection.

crystalashbooks.com

facebook.com/Crystal.Ash.Romance
instagram.com/crystalashbooks
amazon.com/author/crystalash
bookbub.com/profile/crystal-ash

www.ingramcontent.com/pod-product-compliance
Lightning Source LLC
Chambersburg PA
CBHW020719310726
48979CB00004B/979

9781959714156